SIGNS OF FATE

SECOND IN THE ISLAND SERIES

BY

KRISTEN HARTMAN

Fort Myers, FL

This is a work of fiction. Names, characters, places and events are either the product of the author's imagination or are used fictitiously. The author has represented and warranted full ownership and /or legal right to publish all materials in this book.

SIGNS OF FATE

All Rights Reserved
Copyright 2012 Kristen Hartman

v2.0

Cover Illustration by Fanqi Zeng
Cover Illustration © 2012 Beach Reader Books All Rights Reserved.

Author Photo by Joan Burke

This Book may not be reproduced, transmitted, or stored in whole or part by any means, including graphic, electronic, or mechanical without the express written consent of the publisher except in the case of brief quotations embodied in critical articles and reviews.

Beach Reader Books
http://www.beachreaderbooks.com

ISBN: 978-0-615-75485-7

PRINTED IN THE UNITED STATES OF AMERICA

Also by Kristen Hartman

THE THREE SUNRISES

Dedications and Acknowledgments

I'd like to dedicate this book to two very special people- First, to my father-in-law Jim Hartman who we sadly lost November 1, 2011. He told me to keep writing and that's just what I intend to do! Thanks Jim for being a wonderful father-in-law and a great 'Pops'. You are thought of and profoundly missed every single day.

And second, to my grandmother Evelyn Noone who died peacefully in April of 2012 at the age of 99 just shy of her hundredth birthday; an amazing, inspirational, and accomplished woman who I miss greatly.

My heartfelt thanks first go to my husband Mike for all his love, support and devotion. As always you are the inspiration for every alpha male I create and the absolute reason I believe in "signs of fate". Everything happens for a reason, sometimes we figure it out sometimes we don't but for all our bumps in the road, tragic or trivial, we've always come out stronger because we have each other! I love you more with each passing day. Here's to making yet another dream come true!

And as always a heartfelt thanks to my father's unyielding support that will never go unappreciated! I love you Dad, thanks for everything you do! (Including delivering heavy cases of books, to jumping in the car and driving 24 hours when we need you!)

And of course I want to thank my two children who are my whole world! Thanks for being patient when sometimes I may half listen and type at the same time. Just know I always hear you, I'll always love you, and I'll always support you!

To my mother and sister: your unconditional love and support is greatly felt! Thanks for being two of my biggest cheerleaders and promoters! I love you both!

And lastly to all the people who read **The Three Sunrises** and enjoyed it. It's all I wanted, to have someone pick it up and get invested in the characters like I did. It is such a huge compliment and hearing and reading the positive feedback is incredible and I thank you all for that. I hope you enjoy **Signs of Fate** just as much!

CHAPTER ONE

The sharp tip of the needle punctured her delicate skin but she didn't flinch. She had expected to feel sharp pain upon the needle's first impression, but instead its continual penetration felt more like a vibrating scratch. Like someone was persistently scratching her with the tip of a safety pin, back and forth, back and forth. This isn't so bad, she thought to herself, surprised; it's actually kind of relaxing in a weird, pleasurable, painful sort of way.

"How you doin', hon?"

"I'm good." Jenna smiled and laughed. "I'm actually kind of enjoying this." She was staring up at the ceiling. There were numerous pictures taped up there just like at her gynecologist's office, only these pictures were all of tattooed bodies. She imagined they were there for the same reason, so the patient—or customer, in this case—could focus on something else besides discomfort. It worked here, she thought. But Jenna didn't care how many palm trees and tropical beach pictures her doctor taped to the ceiling; when that cold hard metal went between her legs and invaded her body, focusing on anything else was laughable.

Stacy grinned knowingly. Seventy-five percent of her clients were repeat customers. "I hear that a lot and I'm obviously not immune."

"Yeah, I noticed. Your tattoos are really cool." Jenna looked away from the ceiling and down at the tattoo artist's full sleeves. She really did think it looked cool but she couldn't imagine her own arms completely covered in ink.

"Thank you." Stacy smiled, uninterrupted.

Jenna continued to stare at the ceiling while she was being tattooed. Directly above her was a really cool black-and-white picture of a gorgeous man and equally gorgeous woman naked and intertwined, very suggestive. They shared an intricate tattoo that started on his upper right arm and blended onto her left side under her breast and snaked down to her hip. It was extremely sexy. Jenna thought about Jake in the waiting room and wondered what he'd decided to get for a tat.

"Is that your boyfriend out there waiting?" Stacy asked.

Jenna laughed at the notion, settling her eyes on a colorful Asian-inspired tattoo. "No, he's just a really good friend. He's leaving for New York in a couple of days so we wanted to do this together before he goes." She smiled. "He's going there to become an actor."

"Wow, really? Well, he certainly has the looks for it." Stacy grinned. She'd caught a glimpse of the guy in the waiting room.

"I know," Jenna agreed. "He looks like a walking Abercrombie ad."

"So what's the problem?" Stacy laughed in agreement while tracing over the small stencil with her needle.

Jenna laughed, too, at her implication. "What's always the problem with guys who look like that?" she exaggerated. "He's gay."

"Oh! What a shame!" Stacy shook her head. "Well, for womankind anyway." She wiped the tattoo clean then rolled her chair back.

"Trust me," Jenna chuckled, looking at her, "knowing him as well as I do, I'd rather be his best friend!"

Jenna definitely anticipated a tearful goodbye with Jake. He had been one of her roommates for the past four years and had also become one of her best friends. He was moving back home to New York City to pursue a career in acting and modeling, and Jenna had no doubt he'd be a success; he was unbelievably handsome and talented.

Jake had been the last roommate to arrive at the old Victorian rental house on Bellevue four years ago. Jenna and her three female roommates had openly gawked the day he'd arrived. He'd pulled up in front of the house in his red Mustang, stepping to the curb and stretching his long muscular limbs while they'd looked on from behind the curtains. Jake pushed just past six feet, was lean and muscular all over, had dark hair, flawless olive skin, and piercing green eyes that were of course framed by long, thick lashes.

Sue, who'd lived at the house the longest, had called dibs as he'd approached the front door and they had all laughed, knowing Sue's boyfriend of four years probably wouldn't have approved. But all their fantasies had quickly been snuffed anyway when they'd welcomed Jake inside the house and he had introduced himself. He must have seen the hungry, predatory looks in their eyes because his introduction was expelled on a nervous laugh. "Hi, I'm Jake Larson, your new roommate, and. . ." he'd hesitated, "I'm gay." The women had collectively groaned in disappointment, causing Jake and then the roommates to laugh out loud. They all still got a good laugh about it 'til this day.

Jenna had grown especially close with Jake because he had taken the last bedroom on the third floor of the old house across from her own and they had shared a small TV room between the two bedrooms. They had spent many a late night getting to know each other well and Jenna treasured his friendship dearly. She would miss him terribly, but she knew that it was just a matter of time before he was discovered by *GQ* magazine or by some famous movie director. He was that good-looking and had an outstanding personality to match. Jenna wished him all the success in the world. She would miss the old house, too, she thought.

The house was an old Victorian mansion once belonging to some shipping magnet back in the day. It had changed hands many times over in the past decade and finally ended up as a rental house when the last owner could no longer afford the up-keep and expenses of a house its size. It had been convenient to campus and it was close to town, two features Jenna appreciated. The outside still held its old charm and grandeur and with only a modicum of renovations to accommodate the four rental units, the inside did as well. The interior boasted high ceilings, a grand staircase, and ornate wood carved moldings, a mark of the fine craftsmanship reminiscent of old Newport. However, the original plumbing did leave a lot to be desired.

Jenna had enjoyed her time living there and was going to miss it. She was leaving herself the day after Jake for an extended vacation to her grandmother's house on Captiva Island in southwest Florida. She was taking a couple of weeks to herself before her family arrived for her sister's best friend's wedding. When Jenna returned from Captiva, the plan was to move her belongings back to South Boston and into her sister Nicki's apartment. Nicki would be moving into her fiancé Matt's newly renovated home in the 'burbs and Jenna would have the Southie apartment all to herself.

Less than thirty minutes after the needle first touched her skin, Jenna was bandaged and given care instructions for her tattoo, and she now waited patiently in the reception area for Stacy to tattoo Jake. It was another thirty minutes later when he finally reappeared wearing a disgruntled expression. Jenna laughed and mouthed "pussy" as she stood to join him at the counter. She continued to laugh even harder when he gave her the finger and then made a disgruntled face of her own when Jake wouldn't show her his tattoo yet. They paid Gwen the receptionist for their tattoos and then left the shop to walk the short distance to their favorite waterfront restaurant. Jenna's cousin Paige was already waiting at a table with their regular order of salads and drinks.

"Okay let's see them," Paige demanded after they'd all eaten.

Jenna discreetly showed hers, getting compliments from Paige and a crude comment from Jake, which she promptly smacked his arm for, and then Jake stood up and not so discreetly showed his tattoo. Paige and Jenna both burst out laughing at the large star he'd had tattooed high on his right butt cheek.

"It's perfect!" Jenna laughed. "When I came out and said go get your ass tattooed, though, I was kidding!"

"I thought you were making a suggestion." Jake winked and laughed, too, sitting down with a grimace.

Paige shook her head, still laughing. "Did a woman or a guy do it?"

"A woman." Jake frowned. "I didn't see any guys in there, did you?" He turned to Jenna.

"No." Jenna shook her head. "But Stacy was cool, I'd go back there."

"I've been thinking of adding to mine," Paige told them. "Maybe I'll walk over tomorrow. Which tattoo shop is it?"

"The B—"

"No! Don't tell her!" Jenna laughed, covering Jake's mouth with her hand. Both he and Paige looked at her like she was nuts. "She'll know when she sees it." Jenna gave her cousin a wily look then shot Jake a disgusted one as she felt his tongue slime her palm. She quickly took her hand away from his mouth and grabbed her napkin, rolling her eyes and suppressing her laughter. He could be so gross.

"And how am I supposed to guess which shop?" Paige smirked. There were a bunch of tattoo shops in Newport and all in close proximity to one another too. Jenna and Jake could have been in any one of them.

"You'll see." Jenna grinned, still wiping Jake's cooties off her palm. As gross and annoying as he could be sometimes, she'd miss his brotherly antics. "And we'll meet you there so we can do lunch again. I want to spend as much time with you guys before we all go our separate ways for the summer."

"Uh-uh, I'll be packing," Jake told Jenna apologetically. "But make sure you both come by after and show me."

"Of course we will." Paige was going to miss Jake too.

Jenna grinned at her cousin. "Don't worry, you'll know which shop it is right away. It's what Nan would call, an 'obvious sign.'" She raised her brows to Paige and laughed, shaking her head at the same time. It was a friggin' weird coincidence was what it was, Jenna thought.

* * * * *

The following day Jenna made sure to arrive at the tattoo shop before Paige to see her reaction. The cluster of bells hanging from the shop's plate glass door clanged loudly again not long after Jenna's own noisy arrival, and she stood and smiled, seeing Paige enter. The steady drone of a needle working nearby replaced the noise of the settling bells once Paige had stepped inside. She saw Jenna right away standing in the waiting area and her cousin smiled a knowing grin at her.

"Oh my God, how weird is this?" Paige asked.

"Told you." Jenna nodded at her cousin. Paige looked radiantly beautiful as ever. Jenna's cousin was naturally gorgeous without having to do a thing and completely comfortable in her own skin as well. Paige was tall and blonde and "stacked," as Jenna and her sister Nicki liked to tease her. She had the prettiest blue eyes and they were shining even brighter than usual with the light tan Paige had going already.

"You look great as usual." Jenna smiled. Paige also kept herself in great shape, running and working out at the gym with her older brothers, whom Jenna trained with too. Her cousin Ryan Thompson, the younger of Paige's two brothers, was a promising cage fighter, and had taught his sister Paige and Jenna lots of great self-defense moves. Paige and Ryan's older brother, John, was Ryan's trainer and had worked with the girls just as much.

"Look who's talking, island girl." Paige always teased Jenna that she belonged in a grass skirt on a tropical island. Jenna had dark, exotic features, tanned olive skin, large almond-shaped brown eyes, and a sheet of straight dark hair that hung well past her shoulders. Paige and Jenna's dads were brothers but Jenna took after her mom. No one would ever guess Paige and Jenna to be cousins.

Paige was four years older than Nicki, Jenna's sister, and five older than Jenna. And even though Paige had grown up in Rhode Island and her cousins in Boston, it hadn't made a difference; they all got along like sisters and were the best of friends. Paige had been thrilled four years ago when Jenna had chosen to go to college in Newport.

"So I have to admit, I'm kind of creeped out right now." Paige laughed, looking around the shop.

Paige had walked past Captain Jack's, the bar where she would be starting work the next night, and had continued up the sidewalk trying to guess which tattoo shop she was heading to. She'd spotted the sign soon after and had slowed with a gasp. She'd somehow never noticed the shop before. It was called *The Blue Wave*. Paige's thoughts had immediately gone to the picture she had taken and given her grandmother years ago. It hung in the living room of Nan's house on Captiva, The Three Sunrises.

Paige had taken the picture the day after Hurricane Charlie. She'd flown in to Ft. Meyers with her dad and her brothers and when they were finally allowed onto Sanibel, they'd discovered so much damage had been done there. They'd worried about the possible damage to Nan's house during the drive to Captiva but had discovered with much relief that The Three Sunrises had been spared. Paige had later walked across to the beach with her camera to see the damage done there and not surprisingly had found the otherwise docile gulf churned up like storm waters more prevalent around the New England coastline. The normally inviting turquoise hues of the water had deepened and clouded menacingly and had closely resembled the Atlantic.

Paige had taken a rare shot of a young man surfing the Captiva beach that day. She had kept snapping away with her camera until the white cap of the near perfect wave had finally broken and the surfer's ride had petered out close to shore. Since large waves along the island beaches were rarer than a coveted Junonia shell, Paige's photo had prompted Nan to send a copy of it to the local *Beach News*. It had made the front page in the very next publication, thrilling Paige to death. They had asked her to name the photo before they published it and she had called it "The Blue Wave."

"Gives you the chills, doesn't it?" Jenna asked.

Paige laughed but she couldn't help the tingling sensation she felt all over, thinking it was indeed what Nan would consider an "obvious sign." "You know what Nan would say?" She voiced her thought.

Jenna laughed too and ended on a sigh. "Yeah, I do, and if I could only read signs like Nan, I wouldn't be the ex-girlfriend of a lying cheating asshole."

Paige was momentarily taken aback by her cousin's sudden and angry turn in conversation. She shook her head in admonishment. "*Jenna...*"

Jenna turned away with a shrug, avoiding the sympathy she knew she would find in Paige's eyes if she met them. Instead, she focused on the square boards attached to the walls and the variety of tattoos each displayed. They hung in page-like formation and Jenna had just started over to the first illustrated board when Gwen the receptionist appeared, saving Jenna from having to explain her untimely, angry outburst to Paige. Jenna turned and put on a smile again to say hello, ignoring the pang of hurt that had surfaced from mentioning her recent humiliation.

The receptionist said hello to Jenna, remembering her from the day before, and turned to address Paige. "Hi, can I help you?"

Paige shot Jenna a "to be continued" look then took the receptionist in. She was probably Jenna's age with full sleeves tattooed on both arms. Paige thought it looked pretty cool and wished she could be so ballsy. She presently had only a small tattoo below her hip and she'd thought that had been the coolest thing when she'd done it.

Paige told her why she was there and what she wanted done and the receptionist handed her some paperwork.

"Okay, sure. Justin is actually available now and can take you right away. I'll just need you to sign the waiver and get a copy of your driver's license."

"No problem." Paige reached for her wallet and dug out her license. Justin? She'd assumed she'd be getting Jenna's chick.

"Is Stacy here today?" Jenna asked, reading Paige's thoughts.

"She is but she's only about an hour in on a three-hour sitting."

Oh well, Paige thought, thinking of where this guy Justin would be tattooing her. Who cares? He's probably seen it all and much more. When Paige finished signing the waiver and had her license back she went to sit down and wait. Jenna went back to the boards.

"I'll tell Justin you're here," the receptionist said to Paige, then left the room.

"What should I get for my second one?" Jenna asked her cousin as Paige took a seat in the small sitting area.

"A skull and crossbones." Paige smiled teasingly.

"I'm trying to entice a man, not scare him away!" Jenna joked.

Paige laughed and treaded lightly. "I thought you were through with guys for a while." Jenna was obviously still hurting based on her blatant statement moments ago.

"I'm only through with relationships. I've decided I'm too young for all that drama. I need to have fun and enjoy life again!"

Paige was glad to hear Jenna say that. "Well, even though I'll miss you, it'll be good for you to get away from here for a while."

"I know and I'll miss you too." Jenna flipped the boards, thinking about it. Nan had suggested Jenna take the vacation before everyone got there for the wedding. Jenna was not only heeding her grandmother's advice but going down a week earlier than planned so she could have nearly three whole weeks to herself. She had just finished school and a one-year relationship with her boyfriend—her lying, cheating bastard of a boyfriend. Her whole family seemed to think going to Captiva alone would be good for her. They knew if Jenna went to their family getaway she would forget about *him*. The idea of chilling out on the beach and reading a ton of books was heaven and even better because she could do it without running into her ex on any of the Newport beaches, where she'd normally be this time of year.

"Maybe you'll meet someone and fall in love." Paige smiled, joking with Jenna as she flipped through a magazine full of tattoos. She did hope her cousin met someone great that would take her mind off the little punk she had dated for the last year. Paige knew it was still bothering Jenna, finding out the hard way what a complete jerk he truly was. No one in the family had liked him. He was a DJ in one of the waterfront clubs she and Jenna often frequented on the weekends and he was a total player. Jenna had met him dancing; she loved to dance. She and her sister Nicki had been dancing for as long as Paige could remember. Jenna had started dating the punk after just one night of him playing all of her favorite songs, keeping her glued to the dance floor and flirting with her relentlessly. Jenna had been taken in.

"You think I'll come back engaged like Nicki and Ali?" Jenna joked as well.

Paige laughed. "You never know!" Nicki and Nicki's best friend Ali had both spent the previous summer at Nan's house on Captiva, and had both ended up engaged before they returned home. The running joke in the family was "don't drink the water at Nan's."

Armed with the information that Nicki had been in love with Ali's brother Matt for years and years, Nan had taken matters into her own hands and had orchestrated a reunion of sorts for Matt and Nicki at The Three Sunrises last summer. And Nan's plan had worked like a charm.

Nicki's best friend Ali had fallen in love with Rafe McDonough, who had been staying at the beach house across from Nan's. He had been living there undercover on the island investigating a prominent local businessman involved in drug trafficking. Ali, unfortunately, had been attacked by a couple of thugs who had been involved in the investigation. She had been grazed by a bullet and nearly raped, but had walked away just fine, thankfully, and was now set to marry Rafe, the undercover FBI agent.

The last news Paige had heard from her cousin Nicki was that Nicki and Ali were knee-deep in wedding plans. Paige couldn't wait to attend both, especially Ali and Rafe's, because it would be on Captiva in just a couple of weeks. Nicki and Matt would have a traditional wedding at the end of the summer, courtesy of Nan, and of course it would be held in Boston. Paige knew that with Nan behind the wheel her cousin's wedding would be an extravagant, elegant affair. Nan had promised both her sons—Paige's dad and Nicki and Jenna's dad—decades earlier that she would pay for and throw each of her granddaughters their own fairy-tale weddings, but Paige, being the oldest at twenty-nine, had stopped imagining a fairy-tale wedding long ago.

Paige had been in a boring, loveless relationship for three years and had finally ended it the summer before. Rather than sulk or brood about it, she had decided to take her life back. She'd started a photography course, taken a few odd jobs as a photographer, and saved enough money to rent her apartment in Newport for two months. Her plan was to save the tips she made working at Captain Jack's this summer to support her budding photography career.

"Just don't get mixed up in any FBI investigations," Paige added dryly.

Jenna turned from the boards of tattoo samples and rolled her eyes with an "as if" look at Paige. "That was probably the most exciting thing that's happened on that island in decades," she returned drolly. "The worst that could happen to me is to get pulled over for speeding on SanCap."

Paige laughed. "Well maybe the cop will be ho. . ." Before Paige could finish her sentence a man appeared behind the front desk with Gwen. Paige's breath caught in her throat.

Gwen sat back down behind the desk and smiled over at Paige. "Okay, Justin can take you now."

Paige stood automatically, intending to move forward and greet the man, but instead she found herself rooted to the floor, staring, and dammit, blushing from head to toe. Her first comprehensive thought was that he was just staring at her, too, and hadn't bothered to introduce himself or to greet her. Her second thought was that he was so ridiculously good-looking she didn't care about her first thought.

She heard Jenna clear her throat, and Paige shot her cousin a sidelong glance as she forced her feet to move.

Jenna's jaw was all but gaping as she turned from Justin to Paige. "Hmmm, a day late and a dollar short," she murmured so only Paige could hear her. "I guess I'll just wait out here for you then." Jenna couldn't believe Paige's luck; the guy that was going to tattoo her was un-freaking-believably gorgeous! He was covered in ink in all the right places, had short dark hair, scruffy with the haven't shaved in three days badass look they both loved, visibly fit and muscular, on the tall side, and just stupid, stupid good-looking! And he was about to see Paige's undies! If Jenna wasn't so jealous, she would be cracking up right about now, knowing what was going through Paige's mind. Totally not fair! Where the hell had this guy been yesterday?

CHAPTER TWO

Paige knew what Jenna was thinking and quickly turned away from her cousin so Justin couldn't witness a silent exchange that would no doubt be embarrassing. Holy crap! He was something. Paige gave Jenna a mumbled, "Okay," then made her way to the front desk.

"So let's see what you've got." Justin had been immediately struck dumb at the sight of his next client and hoped it didn't show. He'd tattooed lots of pretty girls before but this girl wasn't merely pretty, she was... stunning. Her smoky blue eyes were looking right into him and he found it hard to look away. She studied him intently as he waited for her to show him her ink. *Jesus.*

Paige watched his eyes and narrowed her own. Hmph, he was all business and got right to the point. He had yet to even offer up a friendly smile. With his strong tattooed arms crossed over his equally strong chest, Paige got the quick impression that this guy thought he had her pegged, that she was just getting tattooed because it was the new hip thing to do. He probably had plenty of customers like that, she thought, and he was not impressed in the least. So maybe she wasn't a tattoo junkie like his receptionist or him for that matter, but for Paige, getting a tattoo today was important. It would commemorate a new beginning; she was finally single and happy again and starting a new career. Adding to her existing tattoo was just the kind of liberating thing she wanted to do to kick off her summer.

She looked back at Jenna, who was now openly grinning at her with raised brows, and then at the receptionist, who seemed rather bored as she leafed through a cooking magazine. Finally Paige's eyes settled back on *Justin*, the tattoo artist, who seemed rather bored as well.

"Uh, do you want me to show you right out here?" She wasn't too keen on unzipping her pants in the reception area.

Justin saw the almost haughty look on her face and inwardly smiled. Okay, so she wasn't the usual type of girl who came to see him. How refreshing that she actually seemed modest and wasn't there on some agenda like some of the young women that frequented the shop.

"Why don't we can go right into my studio?" He kept his tone neutral but the instant attraction he felt for her burned beneath his skin. She was freaking hot. He was never anything but professional at work but he couldn't help thinking that she was going to be the highlight of his day.

He led Paige through a doorway on the left behind the reception desk, where they passed through a small office to get to a much larger room Paige assumed was his studio. He shut the door behind them once they were inside.

Paige, all too aware of the sound of that door shutting, felt a twinge of anticipation in her belly as she took in the large open room and the massage-type table that stood in the center of it. She presumed that's where she'd be getting tattooed and felt her pulse quicken.

Justin went over to his metal desk, feeling a little off balance now that they were alone in the closed room, and sat down in his rolling chair before turning to face her. "Okay, now let's see what you've got."

Paige gave him a small nervous smile and hesitated. Okay, so she was about to unzip her pants in front of this ridiculously gorgeous guy. It was no different than being at the doctor's office, right? He did this every day; he'd seen it all. This would be nothing to him. Looking in his eyes again, Paige actually confirmed it—the guy couldn't appear to be more stoic; in fact, he still looked downright bored! Well, hell! If he was going to be unaffected, she could be too!

"Well, okay," passed her lips for lack of something better to say. Paige unfastened the button on her jeans then proceeded to unzip them. She kept her eyes averted from his until she slipped the jeans low past her hips along with the right side of her panties. Only then did she dare to look up. Jeez! He was still completely stone-faced. She'd even waxed for the occasion! Can't I get a whoop whoop? she thought, searching his eyes—nothing! He couldn't care less about the skin she'd just bared.

She supposed because she hadn't actually taken her pants down for anybody in the last year, she had imagined the sound of a full brass band filling the air at the occasion, but that just wasn't happening. She didn't even get a complimentary smile from him; he was all business! God, she was being such an idiot! She should be happy that he was being professional, not be disappointed that he wasn't checking her out. It was quite possible that he was happily married or had a girlfriend as gorgeous as him or was even sleeping with the young, hip, tattooed receptionist, but whatever the case, he was clearly uninterested in Paige and her overly depraved body.

Justin watched her take her jeans and panties down with widened eyes as she revealed her small tattoo. He quickly got it in check and had to force himself to think about how he'd have to pick up the puppy's shit later when he got home from work before he could mow the lawn—anything besides thinking about what he was actually seeing before him and his body's natural reaction toward it. This woman was fucking sexy as all hell.

"So what do you want to add?" He ran a hand over the scruff on his chin as he watched her, depicting his best impression of a man composed when inside his blood ran like molten lava and his body tightened uncomfortably.

Paige's thumb hooked around the waistband of her jeans and underwear, holding the one side down and open for his viewing. "More butterflies, only smaller and with different colors." She used the fingers of her left hand to trace her skin, showing him where she wanted the butterflies. "I was thinking above here"—she touched the side above her hip bone—"and below here." She pushed the side of her underwear down a bit further to show him the smooth area below her hip.

Justin followed her fingers intently with his eyes as they pushed that bit of soft-looking lace even further down. Ohhoo, man. He managed to swallow past the sudden dryness in his throat.

"That's not a problem," he managed to say hoarsely. "Let me just trace what you have, then I'll draw some more around it and you can take a look." *Jee-zus!* God was testing him today.

"Okay." Paige held still while he turned for a piece of paper and a pen. He then turned back to put the see-through paper against her hip area and used a thin marker to trace her existing tattoo. Paige tried to remain as unaffected as he seemed to be but found it impossible. He was so damn good-looking and the large fingers that held the flimsy paper in place and the tattooed knuckles that lightly brushed the skin around her hip were undeniably turning her on. She couldn't help but stare.

Justin traced her small tat quickly because to trace it with a deliberate lack of speed, and keep his hands on her like he wanted to, would be obvious. He had to remain professional as he held the tracing paper against her and moved his pen over her lightly tanned skin. Her lower stomach was toned and hard and he could see she was quite fit. He imagined palming that smooth hard skin and felt his body temperature rise rapidly.

"Have a seat," he said, finishing. "I'll just be a minute." Justin turned back to his desk and started to sketch her design. He felt a film of perspiration break over his forehead and he quickly swiped it away. He could do this. He'd tattooed plenty of girls in that area before, so why did he suddenly feel like a lit fuse around this one? He turned on the radio over his desk, hoping the music would redirect his thoughts.

Paige zipped her pants back up, feeling awkward as the rock music filled the room. Why couldn't the tattoo artist be some ugly dude, or a woman, like Jenna and Jake had yesterday? She thought about Jenna waiting upstairs and smiled to herself knowing Jenna was completely envious thinking of Paige down here with this ridiculously hot guy.

Paige studied Justin's back from where she sat. He had broad shoulders that tapered down to a trim waist and his jean-clad legs were spread apart appearing firm and muscular beneath the material. She noticed he had been a good six or seven inches taller than her when she had stood in front of him upstairs and he looked rather imposing now sitting in the small rolling desk chair. His fitted T-shirt revealed two toned arms completely covered in ink. Paige couldn't believe her good fortune; the guy was so damn hot and he was about to tattoo her, right close to her girl parts! Thank God she had waxed and worn new underwear, she thought, and couldn't wait to giggle with Jenna about this over lunch.

Paige studied him some more while she sat and waited. His hair was dark and cut short, and he had just enough stubble on his face to make him look badass and unkempt. She loved it. As if he could feel her eyes on him, he looked over his shoulder to face her.

"I'm almost done."

Justin gave her a smile and Paige stilled as his whole face transformed. *Whoa!* An actual smile! Now that was more like it! His smile was as sexy as the rest of him, and it made him appear much less serious and so much more approachable. Paige felt a jolt right away. "Take your time," she said and smiled back, wishing she could have every inch of her body tattooed now. His dark eyes were intense and Paige felt them look right through her; she actually had to look away first. This guy could probably read right into her soul with those eyes if she let him. They were a deep chocolate brown framed by long, black, thick lashes and when he smiled he revealed a perfect row of white teeth and full kissable lips that Paige momentarily envisioned pressed right against her own. This was so not good; she was already picturing herself kissing him. She should do a little fishing around first before her thoughts got too carried away.

"Do you do this every day?" Paige asked him. Her voice sounded foreign to her and she cleared her throat.

Justin turned around in his chair slowly to look at her. Her slate-blue eyes met his. Damn. "Every day but Sunday." She smiled at him again and his heart quickened. There was definitely something in her pretty blue eyes that danced when she looked at him; she wasn't timid by any means. She had a playful, outgoing look about her. Justin slowly took in the rest of her. Her long golden brown hair hung straight past her shoulders and framed her oval face perfectly. She had lush pink lips devoid of make-up and that he imagined tasted just as sweet as they looked. He noticed she nibbled at her bottom lip while he took her in and the sight sent a fast zing below the waist and sent vivid pictures to his imagination. Her breasts were quite generous and pressed against the simple T-shirt she wore and Justin knew his eyes had probably lingered there a little too long. He quickly moved them back up to her face.

Paige watched, feeling her face warm, pleasantly surprised and amused as Justin perused her. She knew she should probably look away but she couldn't; there was definitely a current of energy flowing between them now. *Nah*, not energy—good ol'-fashioned chemistry was what it was. She took a lot of pleasure in knowing that her hot tattoo artist wasn't so unaffected after all. This might be interesting, she thought with a little excitement.

"Only one day off, huh? That must be hard on your family." So, so obvious but she kept her eyes locked on his and matched his bemused grin.

Justin bit back a grin and liked her right away. He especially liked that she was flirting with him. "Nah, my mom and dad are happy to see me just once a week on my day off." He gave her a sly little smile and leaned back in his chair.

He was teasing her by not taking the bait and revealing his status. Paige gave him her own little smirk, letting him know that she knew it.

Justin gave a little chuckle at the silent exchange and rolled over in his chair toward her. Wow, this was unexpected, and so was the slow burn that hadn't left his body since he set eyes on her. "Okay, come here; let's see how this is going to look."

Paige rose and stood in front of him again. She was feeling a bit braver and excited now that there seemed to be a mutual attraction. She unzipped her jeans yet again but this time dared to look at him while she did it. She was definitely flirting and she was rewarded when they made eye contact and he gave her a crooked grin. Oh boy!

Justin shook his head, grinning. This girl was fresh and he wouldn't mind putting her over his knee for teasing him. He placed the stencil against her skin instead and held it there firmly while his other hand rubbed it on with a damp cloth. Her waist was small and his large hand spanned nearly half of it as she held her shirt up with one hand and her jeans pulled back with the other. He just tried to breathe normally. All he could picture were his lips kissing her exposed skin and traveling even lower. Ah, shit. The sudden swelling behind his zipper reminded him to get a grip.

Paige felt the weight of Justin's hand on her waist, his long fingers resting on her lower belly, and she inwardly quivered, savoring the touch for the brief moment. There was something completely intimate about the whole thing and she had all she could do to take a deep breath.

"Okay, take a look in the mirror and tell me if you like it." Justin rolled his chair back and faced his desk to prepare the needle and inks. If he got through this without embarrassing himself it would be a goddamn miracle. "Any particular colors?"

"Yes, blues and greens, the brightest you have," Paige answered, going over to the full-length mirror on the wall and admiring how the stencil looked on her skin. "I love this! It's just what I envisioned. You're really good." The butterflies were small and delicate. She was impressed with how quickly he'd drawn it up and how pretty it was.

"I'm glad you like it." He met her eyes in the mirror. "Come on over and lay down on the table here." He actually felt his cheeks warm as he said the words; she was definitely having an effect on him.

Paige approached the massage like table and sat, swinging her legs up and settling back to rest her head on a paper-sheathed pillow, trying not to think of him leaning in to kiss her or better yet cover her whole body with his own. Jesus, her imagination was getting the best of her. To distract herself, she looked up to the ceiling and rested her eyes on a picture of a gorgeous tattooed naked couple, entwined rather suggestively. Oh great.

Justin came around to the side of the table and adjusted the swing-arm light so it shone on the stencil he'd just placed on her. "I just need you to scoot those jeans down a bit more, okay?" Christ, everything he said sounded sexual and he felt like she could read his thoughts. He was starting to sweat again.

Paige felt her tummy tighten with anticipation and placed her hands on her waistband to wiggle her jeans down a little bit more. If she flipped over the tops of her buttocks would be showing, for God's sake. "Is that good?" She didn't dare meet his eyes, just kept them on the naked couple above her, which wasn't helping any. She tried for the pirate ship off to the left but her eyes went right back to all that muscle and skin and Jesus, a nipple. This was getting way too hot for her; what had she started? And my God, did he do the tattoo on the couple in the picture above her? She did not want to think about that.

Justin was trying with all his might to keep his composure but holy God, the sight of her lowering her white lace panties partly down was not helping at all. The area of skin she revealed was bare and smooth and he was so fucking thankful that her angle of him was from the waist up. "That's perfect, just keep your arm above your head for me. Are you ready?"

He cleared his throat as he looked up at her but damn it, even his voice sounded strained. She was staring straight up at the naked picture. It was a great distraction for most of his clients, who were mostly male. The female in the picture was hot and completely naked. The side of her breast showed an aroused nipple and her leg was wrapped tightly around the man's. Their eyes and faces depicted two people intimately joined and Justin supposed it was a turn-on for anyone looking at it. He naturally pictured this girl pressed against him like that then mentally slapped himself.

Paige followed Justin's hands with her eyes and watched as he expertly used the needle to scratch into her skin, leaving behind a trail of ink which he quickly wiped away with the damp cloth in his free hand.

Justin looked up for her reaction. "You good?" He felt better now that he'd placed the needle to her. He was working, and he could focus.

Paige simply nodded with a smile. Oh yeah, I'm real good!

He smiled back, glad she didn't seem as uncomfortable as he was. He'd never had a throbbing erection at work before and he was pissed at himself because of it. What was he, fifteen, for Christ's sake? No woman had ever gotten to him like this. "Just let me know at any time when you need a break."

Aw, he was great looking and thoughtful. "I will," Paige answered.

"So what's your name?" He realized with embarrassment that he didn't even know.

Paige laughed. "I thought you'd never ask—*Justin*." She emphasized his name, teasing him.

He laughed, too, feeling like an idiot. "Yeah, sorry, sometimes I forget my manners." Or was it because since seeing her in the waiting room he'd been rendered brainless?

"That's quite all right, I forgive you, and it's Paige Thompson." Their eyes met and she melted right into the table. Oh no.

"Nice to meet you, Paige Thompson." Damn, he had to stop looking directly into her eyes; they held his and he could almost see the fissures crackling between them. What an unexpected surprise she was. He refocused on her skin and moved the needle over it, tracing the outline of a small butterfly.

"How long have you been doing this?" Paige asked.

"About fourteen years, I guess, right out of high school I started."

"Wow, that's a long time," Paige commented. So he was about thirty-two, she surmised, only a few years older than her. "It seems like a really cool job. You probably meet lots of interesting people."

"I love my job and I do meet lots of interesting people." He smiled up at her, the needle paused in his hands, its steady hum stilled. She was no longer looking up at the ceiling, but at him. "You never know who's going to come walking through the door." Okay, so he could focus and flirt a little too.

Paige smiled back at the innuendo, even though his attention had just as quickly returned to her hip area. She hoped it took him a good long time to tattoo her. "You probably have a ton of stories to tell." She grinned.

Justin stole a quick look at her. Man, she had a nice smile. "I've got a few." He grinned back. "So what's your story?"

Paige laughed. "Boring, I'm sure, in comparison." God, she liked the feel of his free hand on her skin aiding his working hand.

"Try me." He loved the sound of her voice. It was sexy, soft, and kind of smoky. It suited her.

Paige winced as the needle hit her bone, thinking *she'd love* to try him. Jesus, she'd gone way too long without sex.

"Doing okay?" He'd felt her flinch.

"Yeah, I'm fine." He was on top of her hip bone now, *carving*, it felt like, and holy shit it hurt! Paige wasn't about to admit to it though. "I just took an apartment here for the summer and I've got a job bartending down the street."

"Oh yeah, where?"

"Captain Jack's."

"I go in there sometimes after work; I'll have to watch out for you." Justin had been friends with Jack, the owner, since he'd opened the shop.

Paige smiled in response. Yay! She would possibly get to see him again. "I'm looking forward to working there."

"You'll make a fortune in there." He traced another butterfly above her hip and thought about where his hand would be resting when he ventured lower. He looked up at her and smiled.

Paige returned his smile, enjoying the compliment. "I sure hope so, and I hope I get to see you in there." Okay, so that wasn't so subtle but screw it, why not be a little bold?

"How could I keep away now?" Justin smiled but he didn't look up when he said it or he might be tempted to stop what he was doing and kiss her. He just kept maneuvering the needle over her skin, but he could feel her eyes on him. He couldn't believe he was flirting with her, and blatantly so. She was a customer, for God's sake, but he couldn't help it, she was fucking hot and she was definitely flirting with him so why not? Not to mention it had been awhile.

Paige looked down to eye his progress and loved what she saw. Justin had managed to make the butterflies swarming inside of her belly emerge right through her skin, and Paige was glad she had decided to add to her existing tattoo. She thought about where else she could get one. There was something about tattoos that was addicting, and besides, if it meant she could have Justin working on her again she'd get them all over her body. Well, maybe just the stencils; that could be just as much fun.

"Who did all of your tattoos?" Paige admired all the work up and down his arms and hands. She imagined he had even more and wondered where they might be.

"All different people, some artists I didn't know but mostly friends who own their own shops."

"I like them." God! Like he cared whether she liked them or not. She was embarrassed as soon as she said it.

Justin looked up at her again and grinned. "Thanks." He knew one thing for sure; he knew where he'd be stopping in for a drink the following night.

"How you doing, okay?"

Paige nodded and smiled, still feeling like an idiot. "Are you booked the whole rest of the day?" she asked, resorting to small talk.

"Yes, straight through." Then he would go home, mow his small yard, and work into the night stripping walls. He thought about what he'd rather be stripping.

"It must be cool, though, never doing the same thing twice." Paige could only imagine the tattoos people ventured in wanting.

"You're right, it is different every time." Justin dared a glance over her exposed skin. It was tanned and taut except for the small area above where her underwear rested. The line of skin revealed was paler, hairless, and smooth, and thinking about how far that might go did not help his aroused state.

"I know one thing. I'm finding this pretty cool." He cocked a brow and chuckled when she smiled and blushed. "So where are you from, Paige?"

Oh my God! Oh my God! Paige was definitely flustered. "Middletown," she managed to say.

"And you moved here for the summer?" Justin laughed. Newport was right next door to Middletown.

Paige heard the confusion in his amused voice. "I know, not very far, but I've been living with my parents for the past year, and before that I was in Jamestown for three years with my ex-boyfriend." She made sure she put the ex in there.

"So Newport just for the summer?" he asked. Nice to know there wasn't a boyfriend anymore.

"Yeah, while I figure out what I'm going to do with the rest of my life." Paige laughed.

"Are you in school?" She looked fairly young to him, but he couldn't tell for sure.

"Not anymore, I graduated five years ago."

She wasn't much younger than him then. "What did you study?" Justin continued to bring the butterflies to life on her skin.

"Everything." Paige laughed. "I was all over the place, kept changing my mind. It wasn't until last summer when I took a photography course that I finally found something I loved."

"So you want to be a photographer?" Justin looked up briefly. She should be in pictures, he thought, not taking them.

"I do." Paige had only said it to Jenna and it felt pretty good telling him. "I've been taking pictures since I took the course and I've even done a few small jobs."

"What do you take pictures of?" he asked, interested.

Paige thought of "The Blue Wave" hanging in her grandmother's vacation house but decided against mentioning it; why would he care? "People mostly." Paige smiled. "But I especially love to photograph old houses."

Justin's head came up again and he held the needle paused above her skin. "Really?" He was intrigued and a little taken aback.

"I love driving around and finding beautiful old homes. It's one of the reasons I wanted to live here for the summer, there's so much history and beautiful architecture. I take pictures of houses and dream about what they look like inside. I especially love the homes with the big, deep front porches." Paige smiled. "They don't build them like that anymore. They build these tiny farmer's porches you can barely get a swing on."

Justin stopped what he was doing and just looked at her. He wondered how life worked sometimes. It was freaking him out the way she was talking and he had to wonder what brought her in here or more likely, *who*.

When he'd come out to the front desk he'd found her attractive, no doubt about it, and that was without even speaking with her, but now he was even more so. He wondered if his sister had anything to do with her being here; it seemed a little too coincidental. He thought about telling Paige about his new home, but something held him back. "Old houses are pretty cool," he said instead and continued on with her tattoo.

Paige watched Justin carefully; he had seemed surprised when she had told him about her love for old houses. Maybe he thought it was boring. She probably shouldn't have revealed something so personal, and now she was feeling embarrassed again. What was it about this guy? There was definitely an attraction between them—she wasn't stupid—but she couldn't help but feeling it was a little bit more than that and that thought made her feel even sillier considering she had just met him less than an hour ago. Paige thought about the sign outside again and what her grandmother would say, and she smiled.

Neither of them spoke for several minutes and Paige stared again at the naked picture above her, listening to the drone of the needle. Save for the sharp point continuously embedding her skin, it was actually relaxing. She was disappointed, however, that their chatting had ceased. He probably did think her life was pretty boring compared to all the cool people that probably came in to see him. Oh well, he was still hot and she would enjoy telling Jenna about the experience.

"Do you know a girl named Sara Reid?" Justin broke the silence.

Paige looked down at him, perplexed at the random question. "No. Why?"

Justin kept working, somehow not relieved. If his sister hadn't set this up then he didn't know what to think.

"Who's Sara Reid?" Paige asked with curiosity.

"She's my sister." Justin couldn't shake the weird feeling that fate had just punched him in the gut. "I'm almost done." He rolled away to his desk to add more color to his needle, then rolled back to complete the last of her butterflies.

"Great," Paige answered, not meaning it. She didn't want to leave quite yet. "Should I know your sister?" She thought it strange that he'd asked her that. Sara Reid. Justin Reid. *Paige Reid.* Hmmm.

"No, I just didn't know if she had sent you in here. Sometimes she sends friends in."

"Oh." Paige wondered about that. "Actually, my cousin Jenna was in here yesterday with her friend Jake. They recommended I come in." Should she mention the sign? Was *he* the reason she was supposed to come in here? The thought sent a thrill up her spine.

"Oh yeah? Stacy was here she does good work." Whatever or whoever had brought Paige here, Justin was glad for it.

"Yes, they were real happy with her. I was expecting to get her myself."

Justin smiled as he worked. "Sorry, you got stuck with me."

Paige sure wasn't sorry! "I just meant I didn't realize you worked here too," she laughed. "They didn't tell me about you." Paige paused. "I'm glad it wasn't Stacy." Damn, her face felt hot again!

"Me too." Justin met her eyes and chuckled when he saw her blush again. He loved that. "I didn't come in until late afternoon yesterday; the shop is mine so I'm in and out at weird hours sometimes."

"Wow, how long have you had it?" Paige asked, impressed, trying to cover her embarrassment. She'd basically just told him how she felt.

"Five years now." He was definitely asking this girl out, just not here at the shop.

"I like the name of it and I love the sign." Paige was dying to know if he had named the shop himself.

"Thanks." For some reason it made him extremely happy that she liked his sign. He had designed it for the shop himself out of old shipboard. The wave shape was designed with a surfer riding its crest and had been a bitch to cut, but had come out pretty well. It reminded him of his childhood summers and he'd designed it that way for just that reason. Justin loved summer and had surfed as a kid whenever he got the chance. It had been a long time since he'd ridden the waves, but he hoped to get back out there one of these days.

He'd opened The Blue Wave Tattoo five years ago after working several years in other people's shops. The shop had become quite successful and it kept him extremely busy. The tourists made summer his busiest time of year and he hoped this year would prove even better than the last. But between the tattoo shop and working on the new house, he didn't have high expectations for catching any waves in the near future.

"I enjoy it," he said, continuing to work on filling in the tiny wings of a butterfly with color. He was now working below her hip and the heel of his hand hovered over the open zipper of her jeans right on top of her crotch. He had to work the lower portion of her tattoo, and her jeans and underwear were in the way. In the subtlest of movements he hooked the thumb of his free hand inside the denim and lace at her hip and pushed slightly down with his fingers. He saw her stomach contract and could see her holding her breath while his fingers held back her clothing. He kept tattooing her and said, "Breathe, Paige."

She tried, watching his hands closely. *Oh—my—God.*

"So you're working tomorrow night?" He ignored where the fingers of his free hand were. Ignored that they held her panties pushed down low enough so that he could see that yes she was still bare to that point and he could only assume that the rest of her was the same. Having settled that mystery in his mind he now had the mother of all hard-ons going but it couldn't be helped. He simply ignored that too.

"Yes, I'm working five to close. Luckily I don't live too far away, I can walk." But I can't breathe like you asked, your fingers are mere inches from my...

"That's good. I live in walking distance from here too. Do you have to do the whole bar training thing?"

Paige laughed and thought it sounded a little too high-pitched. If he moved his fingers just two inches to the left there'd be contact. "No training period. I actually bartended all through college so I know what I'm doing."

Justin grinned. "Good, because I'm thinking I might come in after I get out of here tomorrow night." Might? Ha, he was definitely going in there.

Paige felt the fluttering in her stomach and a tingling, torturous heat in another place. "It will be nice to see you again." She smiled and drank in the sexy smile he returned. It would be oh so nice!

Justin wiped away the excess ink and dots of blood on her skin with a cloth and removed his fingers from her clothing reluctantly. "That's it, kid, you're done." He rolled his chair back to his desk.

Paige sat up and swung her legs around to the edge of the table. She hopped off to stand and her jeans fell a little bit lower. She quickly grabbed the edges and glanced at Justin, who had turned away politely and was now busy cleaning up at his desk. Paige walked over to the mirror and admired his work.

"It's so beautiful, you did such a great job." Paige turned to the side; her skin was red and slightly swollen around the tattoo but the butterflies really looked like they were taking flight over her skin. "I love it. Thank you so much," Paige told him.

"You're welcome. I'm glad you like it," Justin answered, genuinely glad that she did; her compliment meant more than she knew. He turned around to face her and their eyes met once again. Jesus, she was something. "Come here so I can bandage you up."

Paige found herself warming at the husky tone of his voice and the intent look in his eyes. She was sure he hadn't meant to sound so intimate, so personal, but he had and she went to him willingly. She stood before him, her jeans still parted, and she held her undies below the fresh ink like he had moments ago. She watched as he wiped the tattoo again with an antiseptic that thankfully didn't sting; then he put some ointment on his finger and carefully went all over the tattoo with it. Paige held her breath as Justin touched her but he didn't meet her eyes, thank God, because she immediately felt the heat pool right between her legs at the feel of his touch. His touch felt as intimate as his voice had sounded and if he had looked in her eyes just then he would have seen just what she was thinking. Paige had to get the hell out of there before she jumped him like a savage woman.

Justin placed a sterile bandage over Paige's tattoo just as gently as he'd placed the salve and then he did finally look up at her. They stared at each other as he taped down the edges and oh God, Paige let out the breath she'd been holding as he smoothed the tape down with his hand. Her body responded instantly to the eye contact and to the still light touch of his fingers on her and she prayed he didn't notice the sudden rise of goose bumps on her flesh or the heated blush that burned her cheeks.

"You can take this off in a couple of hours; put some bacitracin on it for about a week and when it looks dry." Justin kept his eyes on her as he spoke softly, getting lost in her gaze, wanting desperately to pull her against him and kiss her blind. But then her hands distracted him and he looked downward to watch as she fumbled with the zipper and button of her jeans. Damn, she's just as affected. Bringing his eyes back up he cleared his throat and said, "It was really nice to meet you, Paige." He wanted to ask her out right then and there but he refrained. He wouldn't hesitate tomorrow night though.

Paige smiled, feeling shy all of a sudden and not wanting to leave. What if he didn't come into the bar tomorrow night? She definitely had to come back for another tattoo. "It was really nice meeting you too, Justin. I'm already thinking I want to come back."

"Really?" She did? Great! Wow!

"Yeah, I just have to think about what else I want to get and where to put it." Paige smiled, wishing she could think of something more to say to extend her time with him.

"Oh yeah, anytime." Justin looked at his desk, feeling like an idiot. God, of course that's what she meant, to come back for another tattoo; she had him all fucked up. "You know where to find me now."

"Yes, I do," Paige answered in a purposely soft voice, causing him to look back up at her, which was what she intended. She gave him a daring little grin and bent to pick her pocketbook up off the floor. "Maybe I'll see you again tomorrow night?"

Justin felt the soft tone of her voice and the suggestive little grin she gave him zing straight to his cock and he stood up purposefully to walk her to the door and open it for her. "You can count on it, Paige." He gave her a telling grin of his own and watched her leave the room. Ho-ly shit! He let out a long low whistle as he went back to his desk, wishing it was already the following night.

CHAPTER THREE

Mike found the key exactly where his friend Rafe said it would be, under the welcome mat at the front door. He'd definitely have to suggest a better hiding spot. He'd also have to rib Special Agent Rafe McDonough, now working out of the Boston field office, about what kind of FBI agent let his friends keep the key to their house under the welcome mat. Rafe's friends obviously weren't much on security. Mike picked up the key, shaking his head, and used it to get in. He missed his good friend Rafe; they had worked well together.

The last time Mike had been to this house he'd been delivering a bit of bad news on Rafe's behalf. His only wish upon opening the front door now was that the hot piece of ass he had delivered the news to was here, so he could make it up to her. But that was never going to happen. Nicki Thompson was not an option, especially since Mike had been informed by Rafe that Mike would be invited to Nicki's wedding in the fall. Oh well, timing was everything and Mike actually really liked the dude she planned to marry. He was Rafe's soon-to-be brother in-law and was a pretty cool shit.

Mike walked inside the beach house and looked around, flipping lights on as he did. He put some of the bags he carried down on the kitchen counter and held onto his duffel. Technically the house wasn't on the beach but being directly across from it and having the bay right in your backyard damn sure qualified as a beach house in his opinion. He had only made it as far as the kitchen the last time he was here but now he continued past it and followed the spacious hall to the right. He checked out the two bedrooms, each with its own generous bath, and went to do the same on the other side of the house. Yeah, he liked the west side better. He chose the largest bedroom of the two, with the sliders going out to the pool, and placed his duffel on the queen-size bed. The crisp white walls and the plantation shutters gave the room a resort-like feel and he was starting to warm up to the idea of staying there. It had been Rafe's idea, and Daniels, the special agent in charge of their investigation, had gone for it. Rafe had guessed Mike wouldn't want to be holed up at Tween Waters again with his team. Last time had been a little too much like sharing a college dorm and had cramped his style. Agent Reynolds was a great guy, but left a lot to be desired in the neatness area.

Rafe had cleared it with Grace Thompson, the beach house's owner, and had offered it to Mike, knowing it was only for a week and that Mike would have just as easy a time, if not easier, with surveillance from this house as he would from Tween Waters. Prior to Rafe's offering, Mike had asked the SAC for the cool beach house that Rafe had occupied for nearly all of the previous summer, but Daniels had laughed at him. As it turned out, the federal judge that owned it was occupying it himself anyway and as Mike left the bedroom through the slider doors and looked out at the bay, he realized this place was going to suit him just fine.

Special Agent Mike Caplan and his fellow agents were on the sunny island of Captiva awaiting the arrival of Jay Scintillo, Jr. He was due to dock at the Tween Waters marina in the next day or two and the FBI had good reason to believe his father, Jay Scintillo, Sr. , a known drug trafficker and fugitive, would be on board with him.

Junior was currently aboard his recently purchased fifty-foot Four Winns fishing yacht he had arrogantly named *Liquid*. The vessel had been spotted the night before just outside the channel in the intracoastal, tied off to an eighty-eight-foot sleek Ferretti yacht. The Ferretti was registered to one Miguel Soto out of Cabo San Lucas. Soto was a major player in the luxury resort industry. His wealth of properties included a string of resorts along "The Corridor," the twenty-mile stretch of beach between the famed tourist destinations of Cabo San Lucas and San Jose del Cabo, and several properties throughout the Caribbean as well, but his most recent business was taking place in Miami. He'd obtained several properties along Miami's famed South Beach purported to be worth billions. At forty-nine years of age Soto was a renowned businessman, considered a captain of his industry by his peers and a man to be feared by anyone who crossed him.

Soto was also a very close friend of Jay Scintillo Sr. and was suspected of harboring the fugitive for the past year in one of his luxurious Mexican resorts. Coincidentally, since Scintillo Sr.'s disappearance, Soto had become a regular in Scintillo's gentleman's club on Miami's South Beach. Whenever Soto was in Miami, he spent all of his free nights in the upstairs lounge of Scintillo's gentleman's club paying for sex, which according to the FBI's inside man, Scintillo Jr. had, in his father's absence, taken to a whole new level. The FBI suspected, in light of Scintillo Sr.'s absence, that a new business relationship had developed between Jay Jr. and his father's good friend Miguel Soto.

Mike stared out at the bay. He knew Jay Jr.'s arrival from Miami Beach was imminent and the hope was that he was arriving with more than just an overnight bag. With last night's rendezvous the FBI believed Jay Sr. had just arrived back on US soil, or waterways as it were, and they hoped Junior would deliver pops right to them. His father was a wanted man, and the charges ran deep; drug smuggling, prostitution, and racketeering were among the many. Thanks to the FBI's newest technology with cell phone and Internet surveillance, they had intercepted messages to Scintillo Sr. from his daughter Maria and had overheard her invitation to her father. She had invited daddy dearest and several other family members to her beach house on Captiva to celebrate the upcoming birth of her first child, Scintillo's first grandchild. Scintillo had promised he would try to make it to the multimillion dollar beach house overlooking the gulf, which had been his gift to his pregnant daughter before he went into exile. She resided there with her husband, Manuel Santiago.

Mike and his colleagues had been waiting patiently to bust Scintillo Sr. for a year now. They had taken down his partner, Xavier Constantine D'nafrio, the previous summer for drug smuggling and murder, but Scintillo had fled the country soon after D'nafrio's arrest. Scintillo himself had been under investigation for suspected drug trafficking long before D'nafrio, but had managed to keep the FBI at arm's length. Scintillo was believed to be filtering hundreds of kilos of cocaine as well as an abundance of the club drug Ecstasy out of his Miami nightclubs, onto the city streets, and into clubs all up and down the East Coast but it wasn't until his pairing with D'nafrio and D'nafrio's subsequent arrest that the FBI was finally able to get concrete evidence of Scintillo's crimes.

Scintillo had manufactured the club drug Ecstasy in his Cuban tobacco plant that he'd owned with D'nafrio before it had mysteriously burned to the ground, but D'nafrio had sworn he'd never known Scintillo's source for the cocaine. D'nafrio had given his partner up easily under interrogation and the FBI had placed an immediate warrant for Scintillo's arrest. However, Scintillo had disappeared, dropped off the radar, and his source for the cocaine remained a mystery to the FBI. It wasn't until recently, when Miguel Soto and Scintillo Jr. had started getting chummy, that the FBI started putting two and two together. Business at his father's South Beach gentleman's club had recently been making Junior a very rich young man, and with Soto's yacht being identified alongside Junior's boat out in the Gulf, the puzzle was starting to fit together nicely, Mike thought.

He opened a beer and looked out at the bay, taking a long draw from the cold bottle. There were quite a few boats out there, some puttering along, some anchored with lines cast, and others moving in the channel with a destination in mind. It would be nice to close this case, Mike thought. He'd be on vacation next week and it would sure be nice to have Scintillo filed away by then. He only wished he had his good friend Rafe by his side when it happened. It would make the bust that much sweeter, but Cap's days of working with Rafe were over. With Rafe in the Boston field office it was unlikely they'd work together again anytime soon. Maybe Mike could get him down here before the wedding for a weekend and do some fishing. He'd have to put the bug in his ear, he thought.

CHAPTER FOUR

Jenna woke up to the sound of a text message coming in on her phone. She opened a heavy-lidded eye, reached for the intrusive instrument, and read the screen.

U kno I fkg hate g-byes
I luv u and I'll miss u to death
last nt was a fkg blast
u and P were so funny dancing
I'm so fkg hungover but i would have
felt worse saying g-bye to u
coward i kno- luv u J

Jenna felt the tears stinging her eyes as she got up and looked across the hall. Jake's room was empty, all signs of him gone. The pounding in her head that occurred upon getting out of bed was made worse by the valiant effort not to outright sob. She'd known he would do something like this; that's why she had hugged him fiercely the night before when they'd returned home from the bar. Jake's friendship meant so much to her and she would make sure he stayed a part of her life. She went back to her bed and picked up her phone, moving her fingers over the keypad.

coward-yes but I still love u
i had a blast last nt too
i luv fighting over the same guys lol
don't even kno how much i'll miss u
hope u r on the unlimited text plan bitch!
safe drive- call when u get there- luv u J

Jenna lay back down in bed and pulled the covers up to her chin, closing her eyes. When she awoke again sometime later, she stretched lazily across her queen-size bed and reached for her phone to check the time. Holy crap! Five o'clock! How was that even possible? She set her feet on the floor and checked her messages on the way into the bathroom. She turned the shower on and brushed her teeth while she waited for the water to heat up. The sound of her stomach growling competed with the sound of the old pipes coming to life, reminding her that she hadn't eaten since sometime the previous night.

After a lukewarm shower, she dressed for the night in a new summer top and a pair of jeans and wedged flip-flops. She blew her hair dry, primped a little more in the bathroom, then sat down at her laptop to check her e-mail, which was mostly junk. She sent a short e-mail to both Nan and to her sister Nicki. Satisfied with what she'd written she shut her laptop and went down to the kitchen for a quick sandwich. She was out the door fifteen minutes later.

It was still quite early in the evening as Jenna headed to Captain Jack's to see Paige. She took in all the people out and about as she walked down Memorial Boulevard toward the bustling waterfront, and she smiled. She absolutely loved the start of summer in Newport. She loved seeing the crowds emerge again and watching them drinking and dining on the outside patios of all the waterfront restaurants and bars. There was a buzz in the air that was infectious. You never knew who you would see or what house party or club you would end up at; it was always so exciting.

She especially relished the summer weather. She was all about the beach and being active outdoors; she loved breaking out the shorts and tanks and being able to ride bikes to the kite park, or jog up and down Bellevue. Summer in Newport was just the best. People had a much better attitude and always seemed happier when the weather was beautiful, and looking around tonight as she walked, there was no doubt that the depression of the previous New England winter and rainy spring was becoming a distant memory.

Jenna soaked in everything as she walked. She walked everywhere in Newport in the summer and never took for granted the beautiful architecture of the old homes and the history that surrounded them. She loved admiring the older houses and the window boxes that adorned them, especially by midsummer, when they would be full to overflowing with impatiens and pansies in every color. The leaded windows and the white painted porches always made her long to step inside and see if life on the inside was as beautiful and simple as it seemed on the out. She liked to think it was. She was a sucker for romance, as was her cousin, and Paige was convinced they got that way from Nan.

Nan's brownstone in the Beacon Hill section of Boston was historic and right out of the pages of *Town & Country*. The three-story brick-fronted building had its original leaded windows that were capped with ornate plaster moldings and adorned with their own fancy window boxes forged from black wrought iron, also always bountiful with flowers for any given season.

The decorative black wrought iron fence encompassing the brownstone complemented the old windows and completed the overall look. Both Jenna and Paige especially loved seeing Nan's house at Christmas time, when she would hang tiny white lights from the fence finials and hang beautifully decorated pine wreaths on the windows and door. The window boxes were usually filled with fragrant, jumbo-sized pine cones and great big silver and red balls and if it snowed, forget it, it was picture perfect. In fact, Paige had taken some great shots of Nan's home last winter that she planned to have made into Christmas cards for Nan's birthday present. Jenna had thought it was a great idea and would make a wonderful gift.

Once she reached Thames, Jenna continued her leisurely pace and window-shopped as she walked. She eventually made it the few more blocks to Captain Jack's and the oversized, heavy wooden door stood ajar to the warm night air. The bar was relatively full but Jenna spotted two empty stools at the end of it, which was perfect for people watching. She caught Paige's eye behind the bar as she made her way to sit down.

"Hey, cuz!" Paige yelled over the music to Jenna, smiling happily.

Jenna smiled and waved, ignoring the several pairs of eyes that followed her to her stool. She reminded herself that she was only in the bar for Paige's benefit. She would ignore the three handsome young men that Paige was pouring drafts for. She settled at the stool and waited for Paige to come over.

"How are you feeling today?" Paige shook her head and laughed when Jenna rolled her eyes.

"Like hell but I'll rally." The emotion of Jake leaving had left her exhausted, but she was excited to be leaving on her vacation for Captiva the next day.

Paige laughed. "Good girl, right back on the horse. I'll get you one, be right back."

"Nothing yet?" Jenna called after her.

Paige turned around to shake her head no. She wondered herself if indeed he would show up. She looked at the neon lights of the Guinness clock hanging over the bar and saw it was only eight thirty. The business card she'd taken said The Blue Wave closed at eight so maybe she would see him soon. She finished pouring Jenna's drink and made one for herself before bringing it over.

"Cheers." She clinked Jenna's glass before taking a sip. They both grinned as their favorite Nickleback song came on.

"Cheers! Here's to the summer—may yours be filled with lots of tips and hot, tattoo guy sex, and mine. . . ." Jenna raised her brows, leaving her wish hanging.

"Lots of hot, island guy sex!" Paige finished for her, grinning.

Jenna laughed sarcastically. "Yeah, I'll have my choice of all the married dudes on vacation."

Paige laughed. "So hook up with a couple, make it a threesome!" Paige laughed, teasing her cousin.

If they hadn't already, they now had the rapt attention of the three guys sitting nearby. Jenna glanced their way, then back to Paige, shooting her daggers.

"What?" Paige asked over the music, pretending what she suggested was completely normal. She winked at Jenna as she walked away and chuckled at the three guys who were now looking at Jenna again with interest.

"You suck!" Jenna called out, knowing full well what Paige was trying to do. She took out her phone and pretended to check her messages until the three guys lost interest and went back to their conversation. Jenna watched as Paige waited on some customers and laughed when her cousin threw her a "gotcha" look.

A three-way! As if! She was just hoping for a two-way since lately it had just been a singular experience and that was getting pretty old, especially without any recent inspiration. If Jason Statham didn't make any new movies soon she was S. O. L.

Jenna put her phone away and looked up to find that Paige was no longer behind the bar, replaced by an older bearded gentleman chatting it up with some of the customers. Jenna wondered if he was Jack, the infamous Captain. Her attention quickly turned to the front entrance when she heard the unmistakable sound of a pack of motorcycle engines revving their way by on the busy street outside. With the bar door open and all of the windows too, the noise from the motorcycles competed with the music inside. Jenna watched as an utterly gorgeous man entered the bar through the din.

She recognized him right away and her heart leapt for Paige. There was no mistaking the dark, brooding features and Jenna felt her pulse quicken just looking at him. Her eyes went right to his muscular arms, which were completely covered in ink, and she grinned with happiness for Paige. Jenna looked around the bar room, quickly noticing every woman in there checking him out too. Justin the tattoo artist had made an entrance. But where the hell was Paige? Jenna sat up straight and kept her eye on him, wondering what he would do. She did another quick scan of the bar and realized the only other empty stool was right beside hers and as luck would have it he realized it too. He was heading her way. Jenna pulled her phone from her bag again and tried to appear busy; seconds later she felt tattoo guy's presence over her shoulder.

"Excuse me, is anyone sitting here?"

Jenna swallowed and turned to face him. "No, go right ahead." She gave him a small smile and turned back to her phone.

"Is Jack the only bartender on tonight?"

He was obviously wondering about Paige. This was good, Jenna thought, except where *was* Paige?

Jenna turned and smiled again. "Actually no, my cousin Paige is on tonight, too, only she seems to have disappeared."

"Paige is your cousin?" Justin asked, taking in the petite, attractive girl beside him. He thought he recognized her; she had been with Paige at the shop.

Jenna smiled, studying him from top to bottom where he sat. "Yes, and you're her tattoo artist."

Justin returned the smile, amused at the once-over. He realized it wasn't in a flirtatious way but more of an assessment. He hoped he passed muster. "That's me; you were with her yesterday right?" He had to speak loud to be heard over the music.

Jenna nodded and was immediately taken in by his smile and perfect row of white teeth. His intense dark chocolate brown eyes had her tingling too. Oh boy! Lucky Paige!

"I'm Justin." He held his hand out to her in greeting.

"Hi,"Jenna said, taking his hand and noticing the tattoo across his knuckles. "I'm Jenna." She too spoke up over the loud rock music playing in the bar.

"Nice to meet you, Jenna. Stacy did your ink the other day, right?"

Jenna nodded, taking a sip of her drink. "Nice to meet you too and yes, Stacy was really nice." She saw his eyes quickly dart away from her and she followed with her own as Paige reappeared behind the bar.

Jenna grinned from ear to ear the moment she saw Paige notice Justin sitting next to her. Paige's whole face lit up and Jenna looked quickly at Justin to see his own big smile. Jeez, Jenna thought, she could see the sparks flying between them immediately as Paige approached. Okay, I'm out of here soon! She picked up her phone and shot a quick text to Jake.

omg! sitting at bar next to P's hot tat guy

he came in and sat rt beside me!

they just noticed each other and i feel like

a total third wheel. I think everyone

in the bar does now lol

i'm so out in ten-

gotta make sure he's worthy first-lol

ttys

Jenna pressed send and kept fooling with her phone.

"Hi!" Paige said loud enough to Justin as she came up to lean against the inside of the bar.

"Hi!" Justin answered with a smile, taking in the white fitted T-shirt tucked into a pair of low-slung, form-fitting jeans. The Captain Jack's logo stretched across the upper part of her right breast. He felt an immediate tug in his gut seeing her. Her dark blonde hair hung straight past her shoulders and was tucked back behind one ear and her bright blue eyes sparkled while she looked at him. She wore large silver hoop earrings that grazed her cheek when her head moved and she looked sexy as hell just like he remembered.

Jenna kept her head down, pretending to be busy reading her e-mail and trying to shrink into the wall.

"I wondered if I'd see you tonight," Paige told him, feeling giddy all of a sudden. She'd hoped and prayed he'd come in actually.

"I told you I'd be in, didn't I?" Justin grinned. Man, she looked amazing.

Paige's heart danced in her chest. She did a quick scan of him, taking in the tattoos and the T-shirt and the scruff. Damn, she still had five more agonizing hours of work and wished she could be on the other side of the bar sitting with him. "Well, I didn't know if you were just trying to be polite." She laughed.

Justin rested his elbows on the bar his tattooed knuckles touching. "Nah, remember I have bad manners."

"Oh, that's right, I'm lucky to even know your name." Paige shot him a grin.

Okay, private joke obviously, Jenna thought. This was getting more and more uncomfortable. She snuck a glance at Paige, who was all but glowing. Jeez!

"How's the tat?" he asked.

"Good, thanks, a little sore when it rubs against my jeans, but nothing I can't handle." Paige grinned. "I really love it, by the way."

Justin smiled; he loved it too and hoped to hell he got to see it again real soon. "I'm glad."

"Justin, this is my cousin Jenna."

Justin smiled at Paige and then to Jenna. "We just met."

"Oh good." Paige tried not to meet Jenna's eyes directly, knowing her cousin would make her laugh with the awkwardness of the moment. "I'll get you a drink."

Jenna watched her walk away and watched Justin watch her too. It was obvious he thought Paige was hot.

"Her tattoo came out really nice." Jenna's teasing smile let him know she'd obviously seen the whole thing and heard about the entire experience.

Justin looked at Jenna and read the mischievous look on Paige's cousin's face. "Thanks; it was one of my easier pieces to do." He grinned back.

"I'll bet." Jenna smirked at his knowing grin, causing him to softly chuckle. She laughed a little herself, liking him instantly, and watched Paige pour him a beer from the tap. She came back and set it on the bar in front of him.

"Thanks," Justin said. "Have you been busy tonight?" He took a grateful sip and smiled as he put the mug back on the bar-top.

"Yes, actually, it's been great!" Paige dared a look at Jenna, who grinned and widened her eyes in silent communication, causing Paige to flush. "I'll be right back," Paige said apologetically as she looked over her shoulder. "Some people just sat down." She smiled at Justin before quickly turning away again.

"So are you in Newport working for the summer like Paige?" Justin asked, turning to Jenna.

"No actually, I just finished school here and I'm leaving for Captiva Island tomorrow for a few weeks."

"Oh really? Where is that? It sounds familiar." Justin took a sip of his beer, keeping one eye on Paige as she mixed drinks and noticing the defined shape of her legs and ass in the fitted jeans she wore. The bar had become more crowded and she was hoppin' back there.

"South Florida, just past Ft. Meyers, on the gulf side. Our grandmother owns a house there."

"Oh yeah, that's next to Sanibel, right?" He remembered his parents had visited Sanibel Island a long time ago.

Jenna nodded as she sipped her own drink, not surprised that he knew of it.

"My sister's best friend is getting married there in about three weeks and the whole family is going. I'm going a couple of weeks earlier to chill out by myself."

"Cool," Justin commented and continued to watch Paige mix drinks and pour beer. "So do you and Paige hang out a lot?" Justin watched as Paige started talking to two guys who had just come in and he felt an instant pang of jealousy which took him by surprise. What was it about this girl?

Jenna followed Justin's narrowed eyes and she grinned. Already a little jealous? How 'bout that? "We're best friends as well as cousins, so yeah, we hang out a lot. I'm going to miss her until she gets to the island. She's so much fun to hang out with, and just as funny and smart as she is beautiful too."

Justin grinned, thinking Paige's cousin was a funny little thing. She was totally trying to sell him on Paige; little did she know he didn't need any encouragement. "She's extremely beautiful and I don't doubt for a second she's just as smart and funny."

"I'm so glad you think so." Jenna said with approval and a grin of her own.

Justin shifted on his stool. "So what will you do on the island until your family gets there?"

Jenna smiled just thinking about it. "The usual, beach, pool, work out, read, swim, shop, hang out at Tweenies', everything and nothing." She described Tween Waters when he asked and gave him a little history about Nan's house, The Three Sunrises, and how beautiful Captiva is.

"Sounds nice," Justin told Jenna, meaning it, and smiled as Paige approached again. "You are busy, huh?" he asked her, speaking over the music.

"Yes, I'm sorry I haven't been able to talk," Paige answered loudly and looked from him to Jenna trying to gauge the tone of their conversation.

"Don't even think about it. I just wanted to come in, have a beer and say hi, wish you luck your first night." Justin smiled. "It looks like you're doing just fine."

Oh no! Paige didn't want him to leave and she sensed he was going to. "It'll probably slow down soon; can I get you something to eat while you're here?" Maybe she could get him to hang out a bit longer.

Justin really wanted to stay but knew he would have to get home soon. "Maybe I'll have some wings, I haven't eaten yet. Do you want anything?" he turned to Jenna, asking politely.

Jenna smiled, impressed that he'd asked, and gave Paige an approving look. "I'm set, thank you, I ate earlier." Jenna became momentarily distracted by a set of waving hands trying to get her attention from across the bar. "Oh, some friends from school are here," she said to Paige and Justin. "I'll go have a drink with them before I go home to pack." It was the perfect excuse to leave them alone.

"Okay, I'll be here." Paige watched as Jenna got up, taking her drink from the bar with her.

"Justin, it was great to meet you, I would have liked to get to know you better. You seem like a great guy. Maybe I'll hear more about you from Paige." Jenna gave him a conspiring look and a wink, causing him to grin and for Paige to look away utterly embarrassed.

"It was great to meet you too, Jenna." Justin chuckled. "And I'm going to try my best to make sure you hear more about me from Paige."

Paige whipped her head around to look at him and saw Jenna give him a fist bump like they were already old friends.

"I like you, Justin," Jenna said decisively as she walked away.

Justin laughed, watching her go, and turned back to Paige, who stood staring at him with a look of surprise. He was well aware that she'd heard what he said and he could see the blush on her cheeks. "Your cousin's really nice and pretty funny too, huh?"

Paige felt the heat that had risen to her cheeks at Justin's declaration to Jenna and averted her eyes. She used the cloth hanging from her apron to wipe the counter in front of him and answered, "Yeah, for a tiny little thing she doesn't hold much back." And Paige was going to throttle her cousin's little neck for embarrassing her. But thanks to Jenna, Paige now knew Justin wanted to get to know her better. Maybe he had felt something more than just a physical attraction between them yesterday too.

Justin laughed again and then said seriously, "I meant what I said to her. I hope we can get to know each other better."

Paige nodded slowly, daring to meet his dreamy eyes, "I'd like that a lot." She smiled at him then laughed a little to ease the awkwardness. "So how about one more beer and some wings?" Oh please say yes, please stay!

"Sounds great, then I have to go home and take care of my pup." He smiled.

Paige gaped. "You have a puppy?"

Justin laughed. "Yup, a little black lab, the terror of my life."

"Awww, I love labs, I had one growing up. Boy or girl?"

Justin laughed, loving how she lit up at the mention of the puppy. "Boy. His name is Sam."

"Aw," she crooned again with a smile and out of the corner of her eye she saw that she was needed. "I'll go get your beer and put your order in. I just have to wait on those guys, and then I'll be back." God, she never thought she'd be wishing her first night wasn't so busy.

Justin smiled as well. "Go do your thing. I'll be right here."

Paige left him, feeling her blood warm. She was so happy he'd come in to see her.

Justin finished his first beer and placed a mercy call to his sister Sara. Hopefully she would run over and take care of Sam and then he could take his time here at the bar with Paige. When he heard her voicemail come on he swore silently and didn't bother leaving a message. Sam had been alone in the crate since five o'clock when Justin had run home to feed him and he probably had about a half an hour before an accident occurred. Justin felt bad; he didn't want to leave Paige but it looked like he would have to. He waited until she came back with his second beer.

"I put the wings in, they should only be about ten minutes," Paige told Justin, placing another beer in front of him with a warm smile.

Man, this sucked. "I'm afraid I'm going to have to take them to go. I tried calling my sister to take care of Sam for me, but she didn't answer and I haven't been home since five o'clock. I'm crate training him, so I really don't want to make him wait too much longer." Justin could see the disappointment cross her face and it actually made him happy. She didn't want him to leave, how about that?

Paige tried to cover her disappointment quickly with a smile. She couldn't exactly ask to see him again without looking eager so she tried to be nonchalant. "Oh, I understand completely," she said, smiling. "You can't let the poor thing wait it out." She laughed. "I'm really glad you came in though, I appreciate it. It was really nice to see you again." Ugh, I appreciate it? Did she just say that? Feeling like an idiot she turned to walk away. "I'll go tell them the wings are to go."

"Paige," Justin called out. "Wait!"

Paige turned back around, her heart pounding.

"Can I come back and walk you home?" Justin's heart was beating like a friggin' teenager asking a girl out for the first time. Jesus, this girl had him all tied up, especially when her face lit up at his question. He breathed a sigh of relief at her reaction and returned her beaming smile. "I'll bring Sam."

Paige was on cloud nine and trying to remain cool. "I was going to say yes before you mentioned Sam," she said, grinning, "But now you have to come back because I'm excited to meet that puppy. I'll be thinking about it until my shift is over."

Justin grinned as well. "So if I hadn't mentioned Sam, what would you be thinking about?" He was teasing her now and he saw her blush again. God, he loved that.

"Oh, I don't know." Paige looked down at the bar and then boldly back up at him. "Maybe how I wish my shift would end a lot sooner." She stared him dead in the eye and gave him a crooked smile, pleased with herself that she had the courage to say it.

Man, Justin actually felt the heat rise to his own cheeks and he chuckled, nodding, giving her a sly grin of his own. "Well, what time should I come back?"

"Is two a. m. too late for you?" Paige cringed, knowing it was real late, but he had offered.

"Nope, Sam and I will be waiting for you." He looked at her intently; her blue eyes hadn't wavered from his. Man.

"I can't wait," Paige said seriously and then teased, "To see Sam, that is."

Justin smirked. "Then I guess it'll be my own fault if you fall for him instead."

Paige's eye brows rose. Fall for him *instead?* Wow. Excitement and adrenaline surged through her. Paige just laughed in response but a full conga line was dancing around her stomach. "Finish your beer. I'll pack up your wings and come back."

Justin smiled, doing as he was told, happy that he had come in to see her.

Not that there had ever been a consideration not to, but it had worked out even better than he'd anticipated. What had ignited between them yesterday was still smoldering there in full force.

Paige wrapped Justin's food in a to-go bag and cashed him out at the register, paying for his bill herself. She wished desperately that it were already closing time and she hoped the rest of the night flew by. She served two more customers and cashed one out before returning to Justin at the end of the bar.

"Here you are." She handed him a bag with his container of food. "Go take care of that puppy." She smiled, watching him stand. God, he was handsome and his tattoos were such a total turn-on. She couldn't keep her eyes off him; the way his arm flexed as he reached into his back pocket, the way his T-shirt stretched across a broad chest and shoulders, his hands…oh God, she needed a cold splash of water.

"Hey," Justin said to her, amused and turned on by the ocular scan.

Paige looked up, embarrassed to be caught checking him out. "Yeah?" She swallowed at the dark, intent look in his eyes. Oh boy, this was going to be some walk home.

"I'll see you in a few hours." Justin couldn't help but react to the way she was looking at him and the thought of seeing her later on that night.

Paige nodded, still somewhat flustered.

Justin took his wallet from his back pocket and pulled out his cash. "How much do I owe you?"

Paige waved his money away. "It's on me." She was embarrassed again and hoped he didn't think it was weird that she'd paid.

"Well, thank you," he smiled appreciatively. "Now you have to let me reciprocate sometime."

"It was my pleasure," Paige said, meaning it. "You don't have to do a thing." What the hell was she saying? "Unless you want to," she quickly added.

Justin laughed, throwing a twenty on the bar and looking right into her eyes as he leaned in. "I want to."

Paige bit down on her lower lip as her pulse pounded. "Okay." And then she looked at the twenty. "What's that? Take that back."

"Your tip." Justin gave the bar a slap and Paige one last wide smile before walking away.

"Hey, that's too much!" Paige called after him, smiling from ear to ear as well. She wanted to jump right over the bar and throw herself at him but she pocketed the money and did a little happy dance in her head instead. She went back to her customers and watched as Justin made his way toward the door. She saw him wave and stop to say goodbye to Jenna again and she laughed, shaking her head, when Jenna stood up and gave him a big friendly hug. Paige could only imagine what Jenna was saying to him and when she sat back down, Paige shot her a reprimanding look, garnering a devilish smile from Jenna.

Paige rolled her eyes happily and turned to cash somebody out at the register. She could see the reflection in the Harpoon mirror that Justin was now at the front door speaking with Jack, her boss, who had been mingling around the bar room. They were laughing about something and then they shook hands before Justin glanced in Paige's direction once more. He met her eyes in the mirror with a smile and then he walked out the front door. She turned and met Jenna's eyes again and gave her a wide victorious grin.

Jenna was at the bar scoring an empty stool seconds later. "Oh my God! Are you psyched or what?"

Paige looked around and leaned forward to make sure she couldn't be overheard. "He's coming back to walk me home!" she said excitedly.

Jenna smiled. "That's awesome! He's so into you, you should have seen him watching you while you worked."

"Really?" Paige looked around the bar then back to Jenna. "He's so damn hot! It's driving me crazy." She shuddered, just thinking about him again.

"Yeah! The ink is a total turn-on. I'm completely jealous, and I'm completely wiped so I'm going to leave with Amy and Sarah."

Paige laughed. "All right, text me in the morning and let me know what time to pick you up."

"I'm thinking ten will be good. My flight's at quarter of one, so that should be plenty of time."

"No problem, I'll be there." Paige told her and said goodnight.

CHAPTER FIVE

Jack had shouted out last call while Paige was wiping off the sticky bar top, singing and moving her hips to the loud music still pounding through the speakers as she cleaned. She jumped when he came up behind her.

"Hey, Paige, why don't you clock out?" he suggested. "You did great your first night. I'm glad to have you on. You worked your ass off, I'm impressed." Jack cocked his head toward the now closed front door then slapped her on the arm playfully with a dish rag. "I got it from here. I'll see you again on Sunday."

"Really? Are you sure? I don't mind staying." Otherwise she would have to wait a while for Justin; he had no way of knowing she was getting cut early.

"I mean it, go."

Jack's tone indicated he didn't want her arguing, so she smiled gratefully and went out back to get her pocketbook and the hoodie she brought in case the walk home was cool. She used the restroom to freshen up and took as much time as she could. It was still only one thirty when she came out and she figured waiting a half hour outside wouldn't be too bad. She said goodbye to Jack and when she pulled open the big front door, she was immediately greeted by a shiny black nose sniffing her shoes and pants.

"Hey!" Paige said happily, bending down upon seeing the puppy and stroking his ears. She looked up to see a smiling Justin looking down at her.

"Hi."

"Hi! What are you doing here now?" Paige asked, happily surprised. "I got cut early." Paige petted the adorable pup and laughed at his energy while she waited for Justin to answer.

Justin laughed, watching her pet Sam, "Jack told me he was going to cut you a little early, so here I am."

Paige looked up, surprised. "He did? You guys are friendly, huh?"

"Yeah, I've known him for as long as I've had the shop."

Paige shook her head, laughing and feeling grateful toward Jack. "Well, thanks for coming." She continued to pat Sam and love him up. She noticed others walking by admiring him too. "He is the cutest thing I've ever seen."

"See, I knew it!" Justin sighed. "I shouldn't have brought him." He winked at her.

Paige laughed and corrected herself. "The cutest *puppy* I've ever seen."

"Thanks for the clarification, I feel a little better."

Paige grinned but didn't look at him. "As if you need clarification. You probably have girls fawning all over you wherever you go, just like Sam here. Isn't that right, Sam?" Maybe it was the late hour, or just the warm night air, but Paige jumped right into the flirting and fishing around.

Justin smiled at the compliment and remembered the similar conversation the day before when she had inquired about whether he had a family at home. It sounded to him like she wanted some confirmation before their night continued. "Believe me; nobody's scratching me behind the ears these days." And hadn't been for a while, he thought.

Paige looked up from where she still crouched on the sidewalk and shot him a skeptic but teasing grin. "I find that hard to believe." There was no way he wasn't getting laid on a regular basis. The man was irresistible. He was lean and muscular with rugged good looks and bedroom eyes that would have any woman trying to get him into that very room. Never mind the tattoos that covered him, lending to his bad-boy looks. He was a genuine heartthrob with a capital THROB!

Rather than trying to convince her at the moment of his very single status, Justin bent down and picked Sam up instead, holding his wriggling body out to Paige.

Paige laughed as she stood and took the puppy in her arms. She kissed the top of his soft head. "Hey, baby, you know how cute you are, don't you? I'm glad you're daddy brought you along to meet me. But you want to get down, dontcha?" Paige set the squirming puppy back down gently, holding the leash for Justin. "Can I walk him?"

"Sure!" Justin held his hands up in surrender. "Please. Maybe he'll do better for you."

Paige bent and adjusted Sam's collar and gave him a little slack on the leash, giving him the right commands as they walked. She led them toward Thames and was glad it was relatively quiet out on the streets.

"So did you have a good night?" Justin asked. He was taking her in as they walked. She was quite a few inches shorter than him and he liked that. After tattooing her yesterday, he had envisioned all types of things and having her pressed up against him was one of them. She looked like she would fit against him just right. He also kept picturing the smooth skin of her lower stomach—the way the bone of her slim hip had jutted out and the delicate lace panties she had worn had made for a fitful night of sleep.

"I made some great tips for my first night." Paige hadn't counted exactly how much yet, but she guessed she'd made a couple hundred dollars at least.

"That's great! I'm happy for you," Justin told her. He imagined all types of dudes tipping her generously and just as quickly pushed the thought away; not what he wanted to think about.

"Thank you, by the way," Paige looked up at him. "That was a generous tip."

Justin smiled. "Are you kidding? I had a good time, it was worth it, and I would have stayed much longer if I could have."

"I was so glad you came in." Paige looked straight ahead, feeling shy now that they weren't very far from her apartment and she was anticipating their arrival. She desperately wanted to invite him up but didn't know if she should. What would he think?

"I'm glad I came in tonight too." And he really was. He'd been looking forward to it since she'd left the shop the day before. And right now he wanted badly to reach for her hand; it felt like the natural thing to do but he didn't for fear she would think it strange. They knew next to nothing about each another, yet Justin felt like he'd known Paige his whole life.

Sam was now doing the little pre-dance Justin had become so familiar with so he slowed when they neared the park. "Would you mind if we stopped here for a sec? I think he has to go."

"Of course not." Paige took a seat on an empty bench and handed the leash over to Justin. He unclipped the pup and let him loose to sniff his way around the grass. "How old is Sam?" Paige kept her focus on the puppy and averted her eyes from Justin, trying to ignore the excitement coursing through her that she was actually with him.

"Twelve weeks. I've only had him for a month." Justin was standing beside the bench watching Sam too and was grateful when the pup just lifted his leg then came running back to them. Justin clipped the leash back on the pup, tied it off to the bench, and sat down beside Paige, looking down toward the waterfront.

Paige instinctively inhaled when Justin sat beside her. Her senses were on overload. He was all male and she could smell the clean scent of his soap and freshly laundered clothes. She wished she smelled as good. She was embarrassed knowing her own clothes smelled of beer, wine, and booze. But there was nothing she could do at the moment and he at least didn't seem to mind. He was sitting pretty close and making no moves to distance himself, so she figured she was okay.

He was close enough that she couldn't help but stare down at the tattoos on his arms. It was hard to make out most of them in the darkness, but the dim light from the street lamp overhead gave off just enough light that his left forearm was visible. Paige reached out and placed her fingers on it, causing Justin's head to whip around and his eyes to seek her own. She immediately drew her hand back. "Oh, I'm sorry. I was just looking." Paige curled her fingers into her palm; they were tingling from the warmth of his skin and she realized she shouldn't have touched him. The heated way he was looking at her now was dangerous.

"Don't apologize," Justin said quietly. Jesus, her touch had sent a jolt right through him and more than anything he wanted to kiss her. "Go right ahead check 'em out."

Paige gave him a small smile and diverted her eyes back to his arm. She touched upon the tattoos with her fingertips and turned his arm over to look at the underside as well. "They are so cool; they kind of tell a little story about you, don't they?" She traced the tattoo that was the same as the sign for his shop and felt a weird sense of déjà vu. The blue of the wave stood out on the underside of his forearm, and when she felt his muscle tense under her touch, she looked up at him. What would he think if she told him about her picture?

The light touch of her fingers tracing his skin and the firmer touch of her other hand holding his arm in place was about all he could take. "Hey." He spoke softly, his heart beating loudly in his ears.

Paige looked up and saw it in his hooded eyes, heard it in his husky voice. She knew what he was going to do and she wanted him to, but for some reason she was ridiculously nervous. She looked back down to his arm when she answered him, but her lips curved up in a knowing smile. "Yeah?" She spoke softly too.

She felt Justin's hand against her cheek and her whole body became electrified. It was a strong hand, rough and masculine, and it guided her chin up so she could look him in the eyes. His eyes were so full of the same desire she was feeling that a small mewl escaped her as he caressed her cheek. Paige tingled all over with anticipation and her heart beat furiously in her chest as Justin leaned in, and just before he pressed his lips to hers a low moan escaped him as well. The seductive sound vibrated against her lips and Paige melted on the spot, knowing how much he'd wanted to kiss her too.

His kiss was slow and exploratory at first until Paige instinctively moved closer to him, wrapping her arms around his strong neck, and then Justin's kiss became more thorough and deliberate. And if kissing were an Olympic sport he surely would capture the gold. He was an unbelievable kisser and wasted no time parting her lips with his tongue, maneuvering it with such skill that she felt the heat pool right between her legs. Paige kissed him back with equal fervor and heard and felt another pleasured moan come from him. *Oh God.* The sound caused her whole body to tingle right down to her toes. She felt Justin's arm around the small of her back guiding her even closer to him while his other hand was on the back of her head, gently massaging through her hair.

Paige was putty in his hands. Her hands dropped right to the tops of his jean-clad thighs and held on for dear life. He was kissing so intently and she was giving back as good as he gave. She could feel the muscles in his legs tighten under her grip on them and it was hotter than hot. She wished to God they were in her apartment right now and not on a public park bench.

She felt his hand slowly making its way up her back and when his fingers lightly grazed the side of her breast the mere touch sent another instantaneous jolt traveling deliciously through her body that settled achingly between her legs. And that's when she pulled back. *Oh boy*. Just the slightest touch to her breast and he had her nearly writhing where she sat. She tried to catch her breath but when she looked into his eyes, the hunger she saw there made her stomach flip. "Uh, maybe you should take me home."

Justin wanted nothing more than to take her home, but he wasn't sure if she meant that he could stay for a while or just deliver her there. "Probably a good idea." Her face was flushed under the street lamp and she looked so beautiful. He had messed up her hair when he was kissing her and he reached over to smooth the wayward strands. "You're so beautiful, Paige."

Paige smiled at him, her heart beating wildly, his light touch once again sending tingles up and down her spine. She just wanted to kiss him again; she had never been kissed liked that. "Thank you," she said quietly. "And you're a really good kisser," she told him boldly.

Justin searched her eyes and laughed softly. "Ah, so are you. I dreamt all day of doing that."

Paige was happily surprised. "You did?"

He raised his brows. "Hell, yeah, I did, and honestly? I wanted to do it yesterday too while I had you on my table."

Paige sat up straight, grinning. "*Really?*"

Justin laughed. "Yes, really, you can't be surprised." He thought it had been obvious.

"Well, at first you seemed so, so. . ." Paige paused with a small grin. "… unaffected."

Justin laughed out loud, causing Sam to jump up on his lap with nervous energy, which made Paige laugh too.

"What?" she asked, still laughing and petting Sam.

"You have no idea how affected I was! *Am*," he corrected with a smirk. "Are you kidding me? Look at you. I came into the waiting room to get you, saw you standing there, and was blown away. Then when you showed me where you wanted the tat"—he closed his eyes and shook his head—"forget it, you were driving me crazy!" Justin laughed, looking at her again. "When you pushed those jeans down and I saw that bit of white lace. . ." He grinned at her. "That was it. I had to really concentrate to be professional. And it didn't help that you were flirting with me just a little, c'mon, admit it." Justin raised a brow, teasing her.

Paige's mouth was open in surprise at his admission, and she was just a little embarrassed at the mention of her underwear, but then she laughed. "Wow, when I first got there I was thinking that you had no interest and rather than be grateful that you were being totally professional, I was actually disappointed." She laughed again. "I probably shouldn't be admitting *that!* And yes, I was flirting, but so were you eventually, by the way!"

"Damn right I was." Justin laughed. "I probably shouldn't have told you what I was thinking either but I think that kiss just made it okay." He took her hand in his and grinned. "So you were disappointed I remained professional, huh?"

Paige laughed. "I was a little." She shrugged, feeling playful. "But I could tell you weren't the kind of person who would do something like that."

"Do something like *what* exactly?" He laughed again as he placed Sam back on the ground and stood up, pulling Paige with him off the bench. He was having fun with her now and he was surprised at how comfortable he was with her. He liked this girl a lot. That kiss still had him reeling, though, and he was anxious to do it again.

"That's probably better left to the imagination, don't you think?" Paige gave him a crooked smile.

"I'll tell you one thing; I wish I had it to do over again," he teased as they walked.

Paige laughed softly, just imagining what he would have done instead, and wondering if he would take his chance tonight. She raised her eyes to find him watching her and he gave her palm a squeeze. Paige just smiled, enjoying how her hand felt in his, and kept moving forward. She couldn't help but feel the flush that came over her whenever he looked at her, and she didn't know what to make of things moving at lightning speed between them. She was completely comfortable walking hand in hand with him and joking around but she was afraid to think too optimistically because it almost seemed too good to be true.

When they finally turned onto Paige's street, the puppy had slowed to their pace and was panting.

"I think he's pretty thirsty," Paige laughed, approaching the two-story home where her apartment was.

"Looks that way." Justin picked the pup up and ruffled Sam's head. "This you?"

"This is me." Paige nodded nervously. And this is it, she thought. "Do you want to come up and get some water for Sam?" She held her breath, waiting. Jeez, she was being so forward but he was so damn hot!

"Yup." Justin smiled and ruffled Sam's head again. "I'm glad I brought him along after all."

Paige chuckled, giving Justin a knowing little grin, and led him by the hand up the stairs to her apartment. She dug her key out and tried to keep a steady hand as she opened the door. Then she led him and the dog inside. Letting go of Justin's hand, she went right to the kitchen and put some water in a bowl for Sam. The sound of the bowl touching the floor had the pup scampering into the small kitchen to lap it up greedily. Paige and Justin laughed watching him and found themselves standing next to each other in the small kitchen opening.

"It's kind of tiny, but it's just for the summer." Paige was filled with nervous energy and she hoped she'd done the right thing inviting him up. It certainly felt right.

"It's perfect for what you need it for, right? Eat, sleep, and shower?" He moved a little closer to her.

And incredible sex with a hot guy hopefully! Paige laughed softly. "Exactly."

"Can I have the tour?"

His tone was deep and the huskiness in his voice had Paige shivering slightly with excitement. "Sure, if you have about thirty seconds." What was she *doing?* She just met this guy!

Justin laughed and turned to the puppy that was now splayed out on the kitchen floor ready for a nap. "Sam seems to be settling in; I guess I have a little time."

Paige placed her hands on Justin's shoulders playfully and turned him around. "There's the living room." She turned him again. "There's the bathroom. We're obviously in the kitchen." She waved a hand around them. "And down there is my bedroom." She pointed down the short narrow hallway and to another open door.

"Very nice, but how come I don't see any of your pictures on the walls?"

Paige looked at him, impressed that he remembered she took photographs. "I didn't bring a hammer and nails, so until I make it to the hardware, they are leaning up against the wall over there." She pointed to the corner and Justin walked over to them.

"I can bring over what you need and can help you hang them if you want. Can I take a look?"

Wow, he wanted to see her again? That was good! "Sure to both," she answered. That was an offer she'd gladly accept and what the hell, it would be good to get someone else's opinion of her pictures other than Jenna's. Jenna loved everything Paige shot but Paige knew she was biased. "Can I get you something to drink? I have water, Sprite, and vodka." She laughed.

"All the essentials, huh?" Justin joked and smiled over his shoulder. "I'm all set, thanks anyway."

Paige watched from the kitchen doorway as he flipped through her framed prints.

"These are really great, Paige." Justin was really impressed. She seemed to really capture the personality of each old home she shot. There were some photos of people, too, and he wondered who they were. The expressions that she captured on their faces drew him right in. He couldn't help but wonder who each person was and what their story was. She really had a talent. He was thinking to himself that he would love to have her photograph his own home when he came upon the largest of her framed prints. He had been squatting down to view the photos but he immediately stood at the sight of the framed shot he now held in his hands. He turned to her, a feeling of confusion and something else he didn't quite recognize coursing through him.

Paige was smiling when Justin turned to face her but it disappeared when she saw the look on his face. "Is something wrong?"

Justin looked at her and felt the same punch to his gut as he had yesterday when she'd started speaking of old homes. "What's this?" He held the picture out to her.

Paige looked at him, a little confused and nervous at his tone. Why wasn't he smiling at her anymore? His intense eyes were staring right into hers questioningly almost accusatorily.

"It's… my house," she told him. "My favorite house," she clarified as she saw his brows rise. *Why does he look kind of angry?* Does he know the house? Does he not like it for some reason?

Her house? "When did you take this?" Justin asked, his heart hammering in his chest.

"About a month ago, I guess." What was the matter with him? Paige wondered. It was just a picture. "I was out driving around and taking pictures and I just came upon it. It was for sale. The porch was so spectacular and I wanted it. I couldn't have it, of course." She laughed softly. "So I took a picture instead. That one is going in my bedroom. I want a house just like that someday. Maybe it won't be as big, but I would love to duplicate that porch." She crossed the small room to stand beside him, forgetting his confused and somewhat angry look and tone. She became animated talking about her favorite house. "Look how it wraps around like that, isn't it beautiful? And look at all the old arched windows."

She pointed to the porch in the picture and looked up at him and Justin felt his heart climb right up his throat. Look at her, he thought. She's lit up again like when he mentioned he had a puppy. What the hell was going on here? He'd come up here wanting to be with her and now he couldn't even think straight.

He put the picture down gently on the coffee table and turned to face her; he brought her right in against his chest and kissed her, hard; kissed that beautiful excited look right off her. She fit perfectly against him just as he suspected she would and dammit he groaned when he felt her relax in his arms. He continued to kiss her and taste her feverishly and felt her body respond and mold against him. Her nipples were hard pebbles against his chest, her heart beat as wild as his, and her skin was warm to the touch. Justin wanted her so badly, more than he'd wanted any woman, yet he had to think about what he'd just seen. If he thought meeting her had fucked him up yesterday, then now he was totally whacked. He heard her moan softly beneath his lips and knew it was time to go. He needed to figure this out before he took things too far.

Paige moved her hands down to Justin's lower back just as he pulled away from her. She looked up at him expectantly.

"I should go." Justin gave her a tight apologetic smile and backed out of her arms. "Sam!" he called a bit too loudly.

Paige's arms fell away. She was shocked and speechless. What the hell had just happened? Holy shit; he apparently wasn't into her like she thought. How had she read that wrong? Oh my God! Was it because she stank like the bar? She immediately flushed in embarrassment. His kiss in the park and his kiss just now had been so intense, what the hell? Did he not like the way she kissed? *Oh God!* She was mortified. She'd thought she given as good as she got. She tried to compose herself and to respond with as much indifference as she could.

"Oh yeah, sure, I should be going to bed anyway. I have to shower, and get to bed, and I have to drive my cousin to the airport tomorrow morning." God, she was rambling and repeating herself. Maybe she had just read way too much into those kisses since it had been so long since she'd kissed anyone. She felt like such a fucking idiot and felt the sting of hurt, mortified tears behind her eyes. Oh no! She looked away abruptly and took a deep breath to ward them off; thankfully it worked.

Justin now held an uncooperative Sam against his chest. The dog had seemed completely at home sleeping in Paige's kitchen but now struggled and squirmed uncomfortably in Justin's arms. "Thanks for tonight," he said, knowing he was being a complete dick and shamefully doing nothing to correct it. He headed to the door and tried not to look back at Paige, but she stopped him with her voice.

"Justin..." Paige walked to the door, falling in behind him and still trying to process what had just happened.

Justin turned and waited, astounded by the small genuine smile on her beautiful face. He felt like a complete asshole but what was he going to say? Paige, I think the universe has decidedly thrown us together for some reason and it's fucked me all up, I have to go home and think about it what it all means. Nah, she wouldn't think he was too much of a fucking pussy.

Paige felt a strange sadness wash over her but she hid it well. She'd just met him. It shouldn't be such a big deal to let him go, but it somehow was. She took a deep breath and held her smile. "I'm sorry." She shook her head. "I'm all grungy from work, it's late and it's been a good while since I…" Oh hell, now that she thought about it she refused to apologize for her kissing! She'd never had any complaints before!

She sighed. "Listen, I had a good time tonight, no worries, okay? Sometimes people just don't click, but I like you, you do really great work and I hope I can come in for another tattoo again soon. I don't want it to be weird between us. We can forget about tonight, okay? Probably for the best anyway. I need a shower, I'm tired, you're probably tired. It's just late, you know?" She wanted to let him know this had been just as spontaneous a night for her. She didn't make a habit of bringing men home and certainly if circumstances had been different she'd be showered and smelling beautiful, not like stale beer and liquor, and she'd be wearing something far better than a beer-stained T-shirt and jeans. God, she wished she had declined his offer to walk her home. Maybe he would have asked her out for another time when she wasn't working. She'd just been so damn anxious to see him again. She'd had the feeling he felt the same way. But obviously something had changed his mind.

Paige forced a smile and held out her hand in a friendly gesture. "I'm good if you're good." But the squeezing feeling around her heart was almost unbearable.

CHAPTER SIX

Justin couldn't believe it; he looked down at Paige's outstretched hand. *Forget about tonight?* Oh shit, she thought he wasn't into her and she was handling it with so much grace and dignity instead of being pissed off like she should absolutely be right now. It bowled him over. How could she not think he was a complete jerk for kissing her the way he had and then shutting her down like a tool? How could he even be thinking of walking out on this girl? What the fuck was there to figure out? The universe or something put a woman he could only dream about at his literal doorstep and he was trying to run in the other direction? What was he, crazy? Fuck that! He put Sam back down and the pup scampered away happily right back to the cold tiles of Paige's kitchen floor. Then Justin completely ignored Paige's outstretched hand, took her right back into his arms, and kissed the hell out of her.

"Whoa!" Paige said after a foggy minute, pushing back from Justin's tight embrace, her hands on his chest, looking at him, utterly confused.

"That's *my* house."

Justin moved her purposefully back into the room, lowering his hands to her hips as he kissed her again, backing both of them up and away from the door.

"Wh. . . what?" Paige asked, dumbfounded, pulling back. Justin's kisses were aggressive and full of passion and it wasn't lost on Paige as she found herself being backed up into the room, but she still didn't know what the hell had just happened. Her traitorous body had no problem jumping right back into the swing of things though.

"Your house? Your favorite picture?" Justin stressed. "That's *my* house. I just bought it a month ago and seeing it here, in your apartment, just fucking freaked me out." He saw realization and shock slowly dawn in Paige's eyes and he smiled convincingly. His brows raised and he watched as hers did too in surprise. He nodded knowingly.

"Are you kid—"

Justin covered her lips with his own, preventing her from finishing her sentence, and backed her right onto the couch. He fell on top of her and nudged her legs open with a knee to accommodate his own between them. His hands thrust into her long hair and cradled her head as he kissed her.

"And by the way, you smell like heaven and kiss like a fucking dream." His tongue was right back inside her waiting mouth.

Paige chuckled against his lips. She knew she was a long way from smelling like heaven unless Justin's idea of heaven's scent was *eau de Irish bar*. But hey, to each his own! She wrapped her arms around his back and threw herself into his kiss again, her mind and body reeling. The man could seriously kiss and she didn't want him to ever stop. She was so thankful it hadn't been her kissing that had scared him off; she wanted to laugh at herself for the silly notion. She was a great kisser, dammit! She should never have doubted herself! She was just so glad he wasn't leaving! She'd gone from being completely crushed to exhilaratingly happy in just minutes.

Her hands found the edge of his T-shirt and she moved them up underneath to smooth over his naked back. The feel of his taut, smooth skin over all those corded muscles? Now *that* was heaven, and she felt them contract beneath her hands as he held himself above her. She was so hot and ready for him, and yet she wanted to take it all in slowly so the moment would last forever. How could the picture of her house be his house? She couldn't believe it; first the name of his shop and now this? What did it mean? She couldn't even put it into a coherent thought at the moment; she just knew by the goose bumps all over her body that it meant something.

Justin wanted all their clothes off now. The feel of Paige's soft hands all over his back was making him harder than steel. They were so soft and gentle that he ached to feel them all over. His swollen cock ached to near painful in his jeans and he ground himself between her hips for a little relief, evoking a moan of pleasure from her that had him repeating the motion again and again. Her hips rose up to meet his and that was it; he was all but fucking her right through her pants.

She felt so good under him but Justin wanted more, he wanted the real thing. But he couldn't stop kissing her, and grinding her felt so good too. They were like two horny teenagers on their parents' couch. He lifted his head away for a minute and looked down at her. God, she was gorgeous with her lips all swollen from his kisses and her face flushed from the heat between them. "Paige," he breathed, "this is going somewhere fast if I don't stop and get off you."

Paige grinned and pulled him back toward her. "I kind of hoped so."

Oh yeah! Justin kissed her again and slid his hands up under her shirt, finding the clasp to her bra and unhooking it. When it was loose he pushed it aside and felt two full mounds of exquisite flesh spill into his hands. "Oh God, I want to see these." He sat up straddling her legs and used his hands to pull her toward him so he could lift the shirt over her head. Paige slid the bra from her shoulders, helping him, and then sat before him topless and beautiful, her hair mussed and hanging partly over one breast. Justin lifted his hand and slowly caressed the strands of hair away, revealing the covered breast. He looked at Paige admiringly. "This body should not be hidden under clothing."

She laughed softly. "Thank you."

Justin reached out again and then held a breast in each hand, squeezing and caressing them until Paige found herself lying back down and raising her hips to meet his once more. The sight of his tattooed knuckles on her was doing her in and she was more than ready for him and wanted him to know it. "Justin," she breathed in ecstasy, "you're torturing me, between your kisses, your touch, and oh my God, all your tattoos, I'm going crazy here."

Justin laughed softly. "The tattoos?"

"You have no idea." She closed her eyes and pressed herself into him, moving her hips just so.

"Wow, I guess that's a bonus for me, huh?" His tattoos had been a part of him for so long he hadn't really thought about the impact they'd have on Paige; if anything he would have thought she might not like how many he actually had. He was pleasantly surprised that they turned her on.

"I was looking at them as more of a bonus for me, but whatever." Paige kissed him hungrily and took his hand, unable to wait any longer. She placed it inside of her waistband and moved it down between her legs. He didn't need any more direction, so she unbuttoned her pants, giving him more access. When his hand touched her moist underwear Paige gasped.

Holy shit she was wet. "Oh yeah, baby," Justin groaned as he felt her.

"I told you," she whispered against his lips as he softly stroked her through the silky material of her underwear. She moaned in pleasure when he moved them aside. Holy God, she wanted him inside her, needed him inside of her! She pressed into his fingers.

"I want you." Justin couldn't get enough of the slick wet heat that surrounded his fingers. He looked down as he moved aside the silken material that covered her and was met again with more soft smooth skin. Jesus, he'd noticed she was waxed when he'd tattooed her and he'd wondered just how far it went. Now he knew. "Oh, baby, that feels and looks real nice." Justin stroked the slight mound of her sex lightly and heard her whimper. He looked up to see her eyes closed and he watched her face as he pleasured her. Her back arched in pleasure when he slipped a couple of fingers inside of her and he was surrounded by slick wet heat. She was ready for him.

Justin slipped another finger inside and worked her at a steady pace, feeling Paige's inner muscles tightening around him as he listened to her moan his name softly. Watching her and feeling her was sending him right over the edge. Her heavy-lidded eyes and her flushed cheeks, her lips slightly parted, oh man, she was something. He used his thumb and rubbed small circles around her clit at the same time he fingered her and he felt her release almost immediately. He withdrew his hand slowly from inside her pants and kissed her lips, swallowing her cries of pleasure and squeezing her heaving breasts. He had to get inside of her.

Paige was taking deep breaths; he had just made her orgasm! She was shocked and a little embarrassed but also so damn turned on she wanted to rip all his clothes off. She couldn't remember wanting someone more. Her hands found the hem of his T-shirt and lifted. He helped her lift it over his head and dropped it to the floor. Paige then moved to his waistband. She needed to feel him. "Oh God, I want you too, Justin. This is insane!" She didn't make a habit of falling into bed with men she just met; in fact ,she hadn't been with anyone but her ex and that was a year ago, probably why she was having a hard time exhibiting any control now, she thought.

Justin leaned down, putting their faces inches, apart and pressed his bare chest to hers, relishing the sensual pleasure of her soft skin against his flesh. "Can we move this to your bedroom?"

Paige nodded and kissed him softly. She wasn't nervous or scared like she thought she would be after so much time without sex. Something felt so right about being with Justin. It had felt that way in his shop yesterday and again when he had kissed the hell out of her in the park. She'd been so confused, and actually sad when she thought he was leaving because his first and then second kiss had said the complete opposite of leaving. Now she knew there was more at work here than just chemistry or sex.

Something else was happening between them; this was more than just a hookup. Her favorite house in Newport was *his* house for, goodness' sake! And the name of his shop was the same name she'd given Nan's picture on Captiva! That was too freaking weird! It was too much of a coincidence. And she hadn't even told him about that! But gauging from his reaction to the house picture she just might keep the whole sign thing to herself for now.

Paige's eyes followed as Justin stood and held a hand out to her. She reached for it and let him pull her up off the couch to stand beside him. Now that his shirt was off and he was standing, she could see clearly the tattoos across his chest and along his side. "Oh wow, turn around." She sighed in pleasure.

Justin smiled and slowly turned while her hands traced over the tribal design on the backs of his shoulders. He turned back around and laughed softly. "Wow, you really like the ink, huh?"

"It helps that it's on this body." Paige grinned, now smoothing her hands over his taut, defined chest. He was looking at her intently with those chocolate brown eyes again and melting her insides. She held his gaze and traveled her hand down over a flat, ripped stomach, to just above his waistband. She felt his breath hitch and his skin flinch at her touch and she smiled, liking the fact that she affected him.

"Follow me," she said softly.

They passed the kitchen and both checked on Sam, who was out cold on the floor. "He's going to get a big treat for his cooperation after tonight." Justin laughed.

Paige laughed, too, leading Justin into her small bedroom. She had a queen-size bed that took up nearly the whole room and Justin went right to it, playfully pushing her back on it.

"I want you naked," he growled and started lowering her pants. He took them by the sides and pulled them down, slowly revealing black lace and satin panties that were just as enticing as the white pair she'd worn the day before. "Oh God, your body is amazing."

Paige loved that he thought so.

Justin stood above her just admiring her body; she was slim and toned with nice long legs and womanly curves in all the right places. Her naked breasts were generously full and round with perfect pink nipples that beckoned to be sucked. He felt his cock straining to get out of his pants but he wanted to savor her with his eyes first. Her skin was lightly tanned and the colorful butterflies he'd put there showed up nicely against it. The tattoo was still raised and red around the edges where the needle had traced and he felt a weird sense of possession looking at the design, as if she were his because he'd marked her. He smiled inwardly at the thought and saw Paige smile as he traced a finger lightly over it.

"I like that you put that there." Paige's whole body was humming with excitement. This was not normal, the way they were connecting so fast, and part of her couldn't help wondering if maybe it was because there had been no real chemistry in her last relationship. Maybe this thing with Justin was just insane lust, not some universal kismet thing. Maybe they were just going to have over-the-top sex and nothing more and when Paige thought about it, she couldn't find anything wrong with the idea.

"I like that I put that there too." Justin voiced what he'd just been thinking.

Paige sat up on her knees and reached for his waistband, quickly unzipping his jeans and reaching inside his fitted boxers to wrap her hand around the girth of him.

Oh fuck. He enjoyed that for a minute before kicking off his sneakers, shoving his jeans and boxers down and stepping out of them in two swift movements.

Paige lay back on the bed watching as Justin bent to get a condom from his pants pocket. She smiled, pleased that he had been thinking this might happen too.

Justin put the foil package on her nightstand and brought himself down on top of her. Paige's body immediately conformed to his and he pressed himself against her heat. The feel of her voluptuous naked body beneath his was enough to detonate him. Her arms were snaked around his back and one long, trim leg entwined with his, pulling him closer to her. He kissed her hard and placed his hands right into her silken hair again, holding her head while his tongue showed her mouth what his body would soon do to her. He could feel her moans vibrate against his lips and he slipped a hand down to knead her breasts, pulling on her nipples until they were hard peaks and bringing her to grind her bare mound against his engorged cock. He couldn't wait much longer but he wanted to pleasure her some more.

His hand traveled deftly between their bodies and he shifted himself to the side so he could plunge his fingers inside of her again, feeling all of her. The inside of her was so warm and wet and she pulsed around him, coaxing him to delve deeper. He moved his fingers faster, in and out, hooking them up inside her, feeling the moist, ridged walls contract around them. He couldn't wait to get his cock inside of her, and as her hand stroked him torturously he slipped another finger inside, feeling again how tight she was, and he groaned out loud.

His thumb found her clit again and he played with it like he had before, causing her hips to buck under his touch. He watched in awe as her eyes closed and her head went back. Her hands gripped the blanket that covered the bed and her hips rose, encouraging him to play more until he felt her whole body suddenly tighten and tremble and she let out a fierce little cry that had him grinning from ear to ear in satisfaction. Oh yeah! Oh man! Her juices covered his fingers and he slowly pulled them out to stroke over his cock; slickening it. He was throbbing now in his own hand as he reached for the rubber with the other. "Paige," he told her commandingly, "I'm going to fuck you so hard." He covered himself with the protection and came down on top of her again.

Paige groaned in anticipation, her body like a live wire ready to whip around the room with his blatant declaration. "Yes!" she hissed. She reached for him and kept her arms tight around his back as he entered her in one quick thrust. She cried out as he filled her so completely, it felt as though he were filling her right up into her chest. "Oh my God, Justin!"

"I know, I know, it's so damn good in there." He kissed her hard as he thrust into her, feeling her legs wrap tightly around his back, her heels digging into his ass and pushing him in deeper. Holy shit, she was wet and slick all around him and he wished he didn't have a fucking rubber on so he could feel that slick heat directly on his skin. He pounded into her, loving her cries and her strength as she hugged him fiercely to her chest. His head was against the side of hers and he whispered in her ear, "Baby, you are so beautiful and you feel so incredible."

Paige couldn't believe it. His warm breath in her ear and his term of endearment sent shivers down her spine despite the sweat that slicked both of their bodies. "Justin," she heard herself whisper, but no more words came out. She was overwhelmed with passion for this man she'd known for mere hours. She felt each powerful thrust, felt his want for her each time he slammed his hips against hers. Her legs were wound tightly around his back, giving him all she could of herself and taking all of him in. She moaned shamelessly each and every time he entered her and heard Justin's own expressive grunts of pleasure which pleased her to no end. When he slowed his pace Paige looked up at him expectantly.

"I want more of you," he whispered in a husky tone. He withdrew from her and pushed her legs up so that the front of her thighs bent and rested against her belly and chest. She was completely open to him. And he took his eyeful.

Oh God! Paige braced herself, he was going to take her so deep and she didn't know if she could handle it.

Justin saw her face and smiled assuredly. "Just relax, let me have you, Paige." He fisted himself and found her entrance again, slowly pushing the head of his cock inside, feeling her envelope him, sheathing him and drawing him in. "Oh, you are so tight around me it's fucking heaven." And it was. He was taken in by this woman on every level and it was unnerving.

When he was buried to the hilt inside of her, he tested the waters by increasing his momentum. He quickened his pace and thrust as deep as he could and she took him all the way. Justin could see and feel she was okay with it, and he smiled. She was more than okay with it; from her compromised position she was doing her best to thrust herself back up against him. Justin was on his knees now, leaning over her, his hands pressing her thighs into her chest as he moved. Paige cried out as he became more aggressive, her fingernails digging into his chest and arms as he pounded away at her faster and faster. Justin couldn't remember wanting someone more, wanting to take someone so hard and fast and just claim her, make her his own. She felt so good in his hands and he sank back to grab the flesh of ass and pull her against him possessively; he wasn't going to last another minute.

Paige was in another dimension. She gripped Justin's thighs and knew she was leaving marks on his skin but the sex was so intense she couldn't help it; he had taken over her body. She was sure she was being too loud but every time he entered her he hit upon a spot that had her exploding all around him. His cock seemed enormous inside of her, filling her and stretching her, claiming her until it felt as if his body were one with hers. She opened her eyes when she heard his sudden intake of breath. She watched as his slammed shut and she felt his whole body stiffen. His arms were flexed and glistening with sweat as he rocked into her. His hands moved from her bottom to the backs of her thighs again where he gripped them possessively and slammed into her with two final thrusts, grunting loudly as he did so. Paige felt Justin's whole body spasm as he came inside of her and her own trembled with aftershocks. She now knew what people meant by "mind-blowing sex."

Justin massaged Paige's legs as he caught his breath and gently lowered them back down to rest on the bed. He rested his weight on his elbows and forearms as he hovered over her. "Oh, Paige," he breathed and bent to kiss her lips. "That was incredible." He looked at her to gauge how she was feeling and smiled at what he saw.

"So when can you move in?" Paige joked, breathing hard.

Justin laughed appreciatively. "I hope I didn't get too carried away on you." Man, she'd brought out the animal in him.

It was Paige's turn to laugh. "You can get carried away on me anytime you want."

He laughed again softly and kissed her. "I'm glad you said that because I was thinking of doing that again tomorrow."

"It is tomorrow." Paige moved a hand across his cheek and smiled when he turned to kiss it.

"Then tonight, can we do this again tonight?" He was still inside of her and he felt her tighten around him. Justin groaned at the motion. "Are you trying to kill me? I need at least ten minutes," he joked.

Paige grinned. "Yes to the first, and I like the way you feel inside me."

Justin met her eyes. "Me too, but unfortunately not a good idea to overstay my welcome."

"I'm protected too." Paige held his eyes.

He gave her a little nod and a quick kiss. "Good to know." Justin withdrew from her reluctantly and left the bed to clean up quickly. He came back seconds later with a towel and sat down on the edge of the bed beside her and stared. "Look at you," he said softly, taking her hand. "You're beautiful, Paige, your body is glistening, your cheeks are all flushed, and your eyes are the brightest blue I've ever seen." Justin shook his head with a small laugh. Jesus, he hadn't expected to feel so damn…hell if he knew what he felt right now.

Wow. Paige looked at him and could see he felt embarrassed for speaking that way. She reached out to touch his arm affectionately and said, "Thank you." And her heart just swelled.

Justin laughed again, suddenly overcome with affection for her. What the fuck?

"I think I need a shower." Paige smiled, sitting up and taking the towel from him and wrapping it around herself, feeling shy, too, all of a sudden.

"I'll run it for you." Justin got off the bed, grateful for a chance to be doing something other than contemplating what had just happened between them. Paige wasn't someone he wanted to just kiss on the cheek, thank, and say goodbye to.

In the bathroom, he got the shower going while trying to sort his thoughts and turned when he sensed her in the doorway, the towel covering the body he had just physically ravished. He looked at her hungrily again and moved to stand in front of her. "I told you this body should not be covered up." Justin took the towel away from her and felt his own body responding once again.

Paige stood before him naked and drank him in. "I have to say the same to you." His broad shoulders tapered down to a trim waist and narrow hips and his impressive erection was blissfully evident between them. She reached for him. "I don't think sleeping is going to be an option today."

She moved around him to lean against the small vanity sink and gave him a crooked smile. He responded in turn with a guttural groan and Paige gasped as Justin took her fast. She had always fantasized about a bad boy and here he was giving it to her good against her bathroom sink, bringing her sordid fantasies to life.

Paige felt the liquid warmth of Justin's climax fill her moments later. His head was buried between her breasts as he tried to catch his breath and his arms were wrapped around her tight. Paige fought to control her emotions as she hugged him back. Even though she was protected the primal act of what he'd just done brought an onslaught of feelings to the surface she hadn't expected.

"Wow," she breathed. The steam from the shower completely enveloped them and she laughed, contentedly perched on the edge of the sink vanity.

Justin lifted his head to look at her. "You're killing me." He kissed her lips and withdrew from her slowly, letting her feet hit the floor before he embraced her again. "Paige. . ." He didn't know what to say. They'd just met the day before and he was feeling like his whole world had changed. He couldn't even think straight, he felt. . . shit, he didn't even know what he felt. He didn't even know but ten things about her.

Paige looked into Justin's eyes and felt them look right down into her soul. She looked away first and laughed nervously. Oh boy. "Maybe we should get in the shower." He nodded and Paige took his hand as he stepped over the tub and pulled her in with him. He shut the curtain, enclosing them, and took her in his arms again. She loved the feel of his strong body against hers and she savored the moment, running her hands up and down his back, then cupping his nice rounded behind. She gave it a playful squeeze and heard him laugh against her ear.

"Sam is now getting two huge bones." Justin grinned against the top of her head.

"One from me and one from you." Paige laughed and thought this might be the best night, or morning as it may be, of her life.

An hour later, freshly washed and dressed, they were walking Sam back toward the park as the sun came up. The morning air was cool but the day promised to be warm as the temperature slowly began to rise with the sun. Once at the park they sat on the same bench they had sat on only hours before and let Sam play in the grass. An early morning fog was breaking up over Newport Harbor and only a handful of cars traveled along Thames Street. Starbucks had just opened and their early-morning customers were the only people Paige and Justin could see from where they sat.

"What time do you have to drive your cousin to the airport?" Justin kept Paige close to him on the bench, his arm draped around her shoulders.

"She wants to leave at ten, so I can probably sleep for a couple of hours." Although Paige didn't think she could sleep a wink now.

"Sorry I kept you up so late." He nudged her playfully and grinned.

"I'm not." Paige met his eyes, answering seriously.

"I'm not either." Justin kissed the top of her head. "Can I see you again tonight?"

Hell yes! "I'd like that very much." She didn't know what was happening between them but she was more than open to exploring it.

"Will you have dinner with me?" They might be working backwards but so what? he thought.

Paige grinned from ear to ear. "I'd love too. Should I call you this afternoon when I get back?"

"Will you be home around six?"

She nodded. "Yes, I'll probably do a little shopping for the apartment on the way back from the airport but that's it. I'll be home all afternoon."

"I'll pick you up at six then, okay?" Sam ran back to them at Justin's short whistle and Justin put him back on the leash.

"Sounds good. How should I dress?" Paige wondered where he would take her.

"Casual, I'm going to pick you up on my bike."

Paige opened her mouth wide in surprise. "You have a motorcycle?"

"Is that okay?" He laughed at her look.

She laughed. "Oh yes! You're completing my bad boy fantasy."

Justin laughed and leaned toward her. "Well, back in your apartment, you completed my hot, naked, Sports Illustrated swimsuit model fantasy." He sat back and sighed, just picturing her naked body again.

Paige guffawed. "Yeah, right!"

He leaned back over to kiss her. "Paige, you have no idea, do you? You're absolutely gorgeous and I had an unbelievable time with you. An unforgettable time," Justin added. He really liked this girl. A lot.

Paige kissed him back, a long, slow, meaningful kiss, trying to convey just what she thought of him. "Thank you," she said when their lips parted.

Justin felt that punch in his gut again and swallowed. "You're welcome and I mean it." Sam jumped up on the bench and onto Paige's lap, where he stood on hind legs and put his front paws on her chest to lick her chin. "He really likes you." Justin looked at her, smiling. "And I do too." It felt good to tell her.

Paige laughed and felt herself blush. "Well, I like him." She smiled, kissing the top of Sam's furry head and meeting Justin's eyes. "And I like you, too." *So much!*

Justin held her gaze, wondering just what would happen between them. He could see their relationship being much more than out-of-the-ballpark sex. There was something special about Paige that drew him. He ran the back of his hand across her cheek, thoughtful. Her eyes were the color of the ocean today. "You know, I really don't want to leave you just yet. Would you let me take you to breakfast, Paige?"

Paige lit up, feeling the exact same way. "Sure, that sounds great!" Her heart swelled and she took the hand that he offered, standing up and following happily beside him.

CHAPTER SEVEN

Jenna drove over the Sanibel causeway in her rented car and felt the instant calm wash over her. The bridge to the islands never failed to immediately put her in a better mood. The cool blue waters of the bay held a slight chop and Jenna smiled at the jet skiers jumping the small swells below her. She loved how people enjoyed the beaches along the causeway; they always looked like they were having fun. Someone always had a grill going, kids were running around or swimming, parents were fishing or soaking up the sun, the daring were sailboarding and windsurfing, and the rest were boating or jet skiing. It made Jenna instantly happy just to see it all. Not that she wasn't happy already; she had stepped on the plane deliriously happy for Paige, who had reportedly had a sex-filled, early morning with Justin.

Jenna couldn't be happier for her cousin. It was about time Paige had some down and dirty fun with a guy and Jenna was thrilled it was Justin. Besides being a stunner, he was genuinely nice and Jenna hoped something started up between them. They already had a dinner date planned for tonight so that was a good sign. Jenna couldn't wait to hear about it, never mind the friggin' whole weirdness of Justin owning Paige's favorite house or his shop being named The Blue Wave. Jenna predicted Paige would get her wish and she would be living in that same house very soon, only with Justin. Paige had laughed her off, but Jenna was like their grandmother—she took shit like that seriously. It was just plain spooky. Nan would say it was a big fat slap from fate if you asked her.

Nan was a big believer in signs of fate and Jenna romanticized about it, too, only she'd yet to see any signs in her own life. Nan said fate could bring people together but it was up to those people to know what to do with it once it happened. Jenna had told Paige on the way to the airport that if Paige didn't recognize that she had two neon signs the size of friggin' billboards with Justin then she was blind as a bat.

Jenna came to the four-way at the end of the causeway and took a right onto Periwinkle. It was not the dense green, jungle-like covered canopy that it used to be a few years ago, but all the new plantings along the road were pretty and plentiful and she was actually glad to now be able to see the colorfully painted buildings along the way.

Halfway down the shop and restaurant-laden street, she pulled into Jerry's supermarket and parked the car. The rental was small but it was all she could afford. She kept meaning to have Nicki or Matt teach her how to drive a stick so she could just use the old Jeep at Nan's house, but she'd never gotten around to it.

She passed G. W. as she walked through the prettily landscaped shopping area and ascended the short steps that led to the market. She exchanged repeated hellos and wondered just how old the tropical bird taunting her actually was. Once inside she loaded up a cart with fresh fruits and vegetables, and then as a splurge went back to the bakery for some freshly made key lime pie. Hell, she could work it off, she thought with a twinge of guilt, besides, when was the last time she had eaten it? Okay, it was at lunch with Paige a week ago, she remembered, but so what, Jerry's was better.

After placing a few more essentials in her cart, she cashed out and walked back down to the car, resisting the urge to go into the little shops surrounding the market. She had plenty of time to come back.

Jenna got in the rental car and drove around to the pick-up area, waiting patiently under the pavilion until her groceries came rolling down the conveyer. She thanked the young boy who worked there for helping her load the car and drove off, munching on the grapes she had purposefully set aside on the passenger seat. She was starving, having not eaten since breakfast, and the plump green grapes that snapped refreshingly in her mouth were delicious.

Her phone rang halfway down SanCap Road. "Hi, Nicki."

"You send me an *e-mail* to tell me you're leaving a week early?"

"Oh, good, you got it." Jenna grinned, popping another grape in her mouth.

"Uh, yeah, I got it. Why would you do that? We were going to have a big dinner at Nan's tomorrow."

Jenna could hear the disappointment in her sister's voice and she did feel bad, but there was no way she could have sat through another family dinner listening to talk of Nicki and Matt's upcoming wedding. She was happy for Nicki but it was just a reminder of Jenna's own failed attempt at love; she had totally gotten played and it was humiliating.

Nicki knew her little sister better than anyone. "Dinner would have been about you, Jen; we just want to make sure you're okay."

Jenna sighed. "I know, Nick, I just needed to do it this way, and I couldn't hang around anymore."

"I understand, but you could have at least said goodbye to Mom and Dad in person."

Jenna sighed again, her stress-free drive becoming sucky. "I called and talked to them this morning, they were fine, I just saw them Wednesday night and besides they're leaving for Vegas tonight and wouldn't even be at dinner tomorrow."

"Well, they would have at least liked to have seen you again before they left," Nicki countered, laying on the guilt.

"Nick. . ." Jenna droned, "I'm on SanCap and you're totally bringing me down."

"All right, all right, but you better call Nan, she'll want to know."

"I e-mailed her yesterday too," Jenna said, hoping to avoid calling her grandmother just yet. "If you talk to her before me, just explain."

"Chicken shit." Nicki laughed, lightening the mood.

Jenna laughed too. "I am. I don't want her to be pissed at me."

"Are you okay?"

Jenna could hear the concern in her sister's voice. "I am now that I'm here. I'm going to relax and get my head on straight. I'll be good by the wedding, I promise."

"That's the spirit. Make sure you call me if you need anything, okay?"

"I will, thanks." Jenna said goodbye to her sister and pressed end. She hoped Nan wouldn't be upset but she didn't want to think of that right now. She just couldn't wait to sit by the pool with a drink in her hand.

Minutes later she was pulling into The Three Sunrises and loving the sound of the shells crunching under her tires. Home sweet home, at least for the next few weeks, she thought. She carried the grocery bags to the front door and set them on the ground while she reached in her pocket for the key. She unlocked the door and brought the bags into the house. She wasn't surprised to find it already cool; she figured Nan had the AC set on a timer. She was surprised, however, that the house didn't seem as clean as it usually was whenever she'd arrived in the past. There was some sand on the tiles and the counters held some clutter where she set the bags down. She'd have to mention to Nan that the cleaning service hadn't done a very good job. Nan didn't rent the house out and Jenna had to wonder who the last family member was to stay.

She glanced over her shoulder at the living room couch as she made her way back out the front door. There were some pillows out of place too and Jenna smirked as she went outside—weird. She took her luggage from the trunk and wheeled it awkwardly over the shelled driveway until she reached the slate path of the walkway. Inside once again, she brought her bags to her favorite bedroom, which was the same one Nicki always chose too. When they were there together Nicki would inevitably force Jenna to take the room across the hall, but not this time, Jenna thought with a grin, she had the whole house to herself. She unpacked her bikini, excited for the pool, and stripped out of her jeans and shirt to put it on. She put her hair up in a ponytail then went back down the hall to the kitchen to put her groceries away.

When she opened the refrigerator she stood with the door open in surprise. *What the hell?* It was fully stocked. Jenna was really confused now and reached for her phone; she was going to have to call Nan. This was what she deserved for not telling Nan she was arriving a week early. Shit, she thought as light dawned, Nan probably had friends staying here. Jenna knew it wasn't anyone in her family, nor was it any of the Fullers.

Ali Fuller was Nicki's best friend who was getting married in a few weeks, and Ali's brother Matt was Nicki's fiancé. Both Ali and Matt's parents were also best friends with her own parents and friends with Nan too, but Jenna knew none of them were due to be here until the wedding, unless Jason, Matt and Ali's older brother, had decided to take Nicki up on her standing offer. No, Nicki would have obviously mentioned that.

Jenna dialed Nan as she slowly made her way past the living room and down the short hall to the other end of the house to check out the bedrooms. Shit, the bedroom facing the pool definitely had an occupant. The bed was unmade and clothes were spilling out of a big black duffel on the floor. Jenna backed out quickly and listened as Nan's voice mail came on. Jenna left a message to call her and ran to her room to unpack her laptop. She signed on and waited to connect to get her e-mail, but there was no response from Nan.

Jenna sat on the edge of the bed to think. There hadn't been a car in the driveway so whoever was here had to be out and about. Well, it's not like she could go anywhere now, and it was her grandmother's house. She would just stay out of their way until they left, whoever they were. Maybe they were friends of Nans she'd sent down for a golf vacation. Nan was a member at the Sanctuary so maybe that's where they were right now. It was no big deal, Jenna supposed. Not what she had planned for but the house was big enough for one more person.

Jenna decidedly went back to the kitchen and made herself a frozen drink in the blender. She opened the big sliders to the pool and welcomed the hot air that hit her when she stepped outside. She grabbed a beach towel from the towel bin against the house and draped it over a lounge chair facing the pool and the tranquil bay beyond. Then she made herself comfortable. Might as well enjoy her alone time while she could, she thought. She breathed a sigh of contentment as she lay back and relaxed her body into the lounge. It wasn't long before her peaceful thoughts had her drifting off under the heat of the sunshine.

CHAPTER EIGHT

Mike let the oars hang from their rungs as he leaned back in the kayak. The surrounding bay was quite still in the late afternoon save for a few ladyfish breaking the placid surface close by him. He was glad to have had the day off. Not much was happening on the Scintillo front and he knew the team up at Tween Waters would give him a shout if any surprise guests were to arrive.

He looked at his watch; it was just about five thirty and he felt the first pangs of hunger rumble in his stomach. He'd cook the steak he bought this morning at the market. He was thankful he had the privacy of his own house. Just being up at Tween Waters again and seeing the other agents hanging around the pool area had depressed the shit out of him. It should have made him envious; he should want to be out there with them. But for some reason today he didn't want to be hanging out by the pool drinking and looking to get laid, and that just wasn't like him. Maybe it was the phone call from Rafe this morning. He and Ali were coming to the island in a little over two weeks to be married and Rafe had called reminding Mike to have his tuxedo fitted.

When Rafe had asked him to be his best man, Mike had accepted readily, and now that the wedding was upon them Mike couldn't help but feel a little envious and that wasn't like him either. He had been single for so long that he forgot what it was like to have a girlfriend for more than a weekend at a time. He worked hard and he played hard; he didn't have room in his life for anything long term. He'd been at the Miami field office for five years and that could soon change at any time. He'd just finished a ball-busting two weeks of training at Quantico for the HRT (Hostage Rescue Team), which Daniels had suggested and then recommended him for. Mike had gone without telling anyone. When asked by fellow agents, Daniels had just said Mike was taking some tactical training classes. The two weeks had been intense but Mike had loved it and now he just waited to hear whether he'd been chosen. If selected he'd undergo another four months of rigorous training and then be part of an elite group of men, the best of the best from the FBI and military, working 24/7 to keep the country safe. He got pumped up just thinking about it but with the HRT he could be deployed at any given time, for any length of time, and that didn't make for good boyfriend material, let alone good husband material, and that's what he kept reminding himself of when he grew envious of Rafe and Ali.

Mike had never been in love and he knew getting married just wasn't in the cards for him and up until today he'd always thought he'd be fine with that, but something had stirred in him while talking with Rafe and hearing how happy he was. Mike didn't know if it was his age, loneliness, anxiety about HRT, or what, but he was starting to second-guess himself and that pissed the fuck out of him. He felt like his balance was off. What he needed was to be up at Tween Waters eyeballin' babes in bikinis. He should be heading right up there after he ate. But all he really wanted to do was have a cold beer by the pool and watch the boats go by in the bay, maybe drop a line off the dock. The thought of a prospective meaningless night of sex depressed the hell out of him. What the fuck was wrong with him? He hoped after this week when he got back to Miami he'd have some definitive answers about the HRT that he could set his sights on and he could focus all his attention on that.

Mike grabbed the paddles and rowed the short distance back to the house. He tied the kayak off and used the wooden slats hammered against the dock to climb back onto it. It had been a great workout. He had kayaked all through Tarpon Bay and back and now he was hot as shit. He pulled his sweat-soaked T-shirt over his head and slung it around his neck as he took the walkway up to the pool. He dropped his shirt on the deck, kicked his sneakers off, and dove right in, the cold water refreshing him immediately.

* * * * *

Jenna woke up, instantly startled from her sun-induced nap when she heard the splash. She was disoriented at first and waited until the little white spots behind her eyes cleared before she could focus on the pool. When her vision improved she quickly sat up, using her hand as a visor, and watched in shock as a man emerged from the water. He walked out of the low end of the pool and just one persona came to mind—GI freaking Joe.

Holy crap! Was *this* Nan's houseguest? His short, cropped, pale blond hair was longer on the top than the rest of his head and spiked a little after he ran two large tanned hands over it to remove the excess water. His shoulders looked at least three feet wide and his biceps were as big as mountains. Jenna noticed the large tattoos on his tanned back and down one shoulder and watched his leg muscles flex as he took the three short steps out of the pool. When he turned toward her she saw a defined six-pack—make that eight-pack—of abdominal muscles on a very large man with a nicely tanned body that obviously was no stranger to the sun. Jenna couldn't take her eyes off him and she instinctively lowered her gaze. He wore navy blue board shorts with a white flower print adorning them that covered two long muscular legs and clung to him just right, causing Jenna to avert her eyes quickly. She continued her curious gaze back up to his face and gasped at two of the bluest eyes she'd ever seen staring intently back at her.

Jenna jumped from her chair, suddenly nervous and feeling the need to explain her presence. "Hi, I'm Jenna; this is my grandmother's house. I didn't know anyone was here. I'm a week early. I sent Nan an e-mail but I don't think she's read it yet, she prefers the phone so that's why. . ." She was rambling as she moved her hand gesturing between the two of them. "I'm here and. . ." She paused, letting her explanation die. He was staring so intently at her and damn he was soooo hot!

It dawned on Jenna that maybe he wasn't there by himself. How could a guy who looked like him be by himself? She realized the tattoo on his back and right shoulder came down and connected with the one across the right side of his chest and she felt beads of sweat break out over her forehead. "I didn't see a car in the driveway, is there anyone else here with you?" she asked finally, taking a deep breath all the while staring back at him.

He was without a doubt the most magnificent man she had ever seen. He was a little older than her, she could see that—probably thirty-something if she had to guess—and she found herself instantly attracted to him. He wasn't handsome in a traditional Ralph Lauren model type of way; he was rugged and tough looking, like the cage fighters she loved to watch on TV, and the ones who trained alongside her cousin Ryan in the gym, minus the gross ears. This guy was loaded with muscles but not puffed up like she hated. He was cut and well defined, long and lean. He was definitely over six feet tall and his muscular body was proportionate to his height. Jenna waited uncomfortably for him to speak, feeling naked under his penetrating stare, and she supposed she basically was, standing there in just her bikini.

"I'm Mike Caplan, a friend of Rafe's; I just arrived yesterday by myself. My Jeep's in the garage next to your grandmother's. I was told nobody would be here." Mike knew he should smile and be more polite but she had surprised the hell out of him, not only by being there but by standing in front of him like that, dressed in three pieces of the skimpiest material he was more used to seeing on the women on South Beach. She looked a lot younger than him but she was smokin' hot, from her long raven hair to her sexy bare feet. She was also a tiny little thing compared to him, not much over five feet if he had to guess, but she had long toned legs that made her appear taller. She was trim in the waist with a flat-toned stomach and her breasts weren't large but sure were in proportion to her sexy little body. She was very athletic looking, an absolute knockout.

Her dark hair was long and held back in a ponytail, giving Mike a good look at her pretty oval-shaped face. She had high defined cheekbones that held a hint of the sun she had obviously been lying in and deep dark brown eyes that were almond shaped and wide set, giving her an exotic look that he found over-the-top sexy. Her lips were full too and a warm shade of pink that had him thinking of things he shouldn't be. Fuck! Of all the fucking things he didn't need to deal with right now this was one of them. He had to call Rafe ASAP. What the fuck!

"Hi, Mike, it's nice to meet you." Jenna stepped forward smiling shyly and held out her hand.

Oh oh, Mike recognized that look in her eye and purposefully ignored her hand. "Nice to meet you too, Jenna, and no worries, I'll be out of here by tonight." There was no friggin' way he was staying in the same house with *her!*

Jenna pulled her hand back in reproach, his rudeness surprising her. She blushed with embarrassment. "Oh, you're leaving so soon?" She couldn't help but feel disappointed.

Mike saw the look of surprise at his rudeness *and* the disappointment on her face and found himself feeling bad. Any other time and he'd have already been flirting and trying to impress her. "I'm here for the week but I can easily get a room at Tween Waters."

"You're a friend of Rafe's you said?" Jenna looked him over again, taking in his size and his cropped hair and the ripped body. She would have definitely pegged him as a fighter or a military man, but light suddenly dawned. If he was Rafe's friend then.... "You're an FBI agent, aren't you? Oh my God, what's happening now?"

Aw *shiiiit!* Mike shook his head; he should have expected she'd guess. "I'm just here on vacation." He gave her a look that he usually reserved for perps and saw her visibly shrink back. He felt bad, but he couldn't have this girl running around the island telling everyone who he was. He definitely had to put a call in to Rafe to head her off and he definitely had to get the hell out of there. "And you say this is your grandmother's house?" He watched as she reached for her towel, wrapping it around herself in full defense mode—that was a shame. He knew he had scared her but it was probably for the best.

"I'm Jenna Thompson, and yes this is my grandmother's house." Jenna knew she sounded indignant but she didn't care. For someone wearing a flowered bathing suit, the guy was clearly not very friendly and she didn't care how good he looked, he was completely rude and just a wee bit scary!

Shit, she must be Nicki's little sister; Mike should have realized it. He could see it now. Jenna's features were darker but earlier when she had smiled he thought it familiar. He knew Nicki and Ali were younger than he and Rafe by a lot of years and this girl looked even younger than them; shit she might even be jail bait! He had to go pack. "I'll be out of your way in less than an hour."

Jenna watched him head into the house, and she felt like she had just been scolded for some reason. What the hell did she do? She only asked a simple question, and the look he had given her would have had grown men shaking in their boots let alone her. Jeez, good riddance! Jenna went back into the house, picking up her cell phone on the kitchen counter along the way, and went to her room. She texted Jake right away.

Ha! arrived at Nan's to find GI fkg Joe has infiltrated the place

Had no idea there'd be someone here,

rude and unsmiling

he's leaving now, supposed to stay the week

but i apparently scared him off

he's Rafe's friend so i think FBI

he got all pissy when I asked

anyway how's the restaurant?

bro give u any good shifts?

Jenna sent the text then lay back on her bed with a sigh and waited to hear the front door open and close.

* * * * *

Mike got out his phone and paced the bedroom while he waited for Rafe to pick up. Four rings later he heard his voice.

"Dude, what the fuck?"

"Nice to hear your voice again too, Cap, what's up?"

"What's up? How about all of a sudden I've got a Victoria's Secret model as a roommate. Did you forget to tell me something?"

"Nice! Which one?" Rafe laughed, wondering what Mike was talking about.

"Does it matter?" Mike sat on the edge of the bed. "Does the name Jenna ring a bell?" He exhaled, exasperated. The last thing he wanted to do was have to bunk in with Reynolds again.

"Nicki's sister is there? Now? She's not due in until next week. Shit."

"She was kind of hard to miss in a hardly there bikini when I came out of the pool." Mike ran a hand over his head. "There's no way I can stay here now."

For several reasons, he thought.

"Let me make a phone call and see about the mix-up, and just relax, she's harmless. She's Nicki's sister, for Christ sake." Rafe could understand Mike's concern, but it wasn't that big of a deal. Jenna was cool and would stay out of his way.

"She's, she's. . ." Mike found himself stuttering, "and young!"

Rafe swore under his breath and laughed, getting it. "Relax, she's twenty-four and yeah," he chuckled, "she's pretty hot."

"That's what I'm trying to say. I can't be here! She's fucking twenty-four with the tight little body of a twenty-four-year-old. This is not cool, Rafe." Mike got up and paced again.

"Relax; you can go stay with Reynolds if you can't handle it. Are you telling me you can't handle it?" Rafe asked, incredulous. Jesus, normally Mike would be in his glory.

"Listen, you were alone in that beach house on this island too and what happened to you when you encountered a sweet little twenty-something?" Mike had no room in his life for anything like that.

"That's different." Rafe found himself smirking. "Okay, not that different," he admitted after a beat, "but Jenna just broke up with her boyfriend, she won't even be interested," Rafe tried to reason.

"Too late, she gave me the eyes, man; I had to give her my asshole face."

"Not the one you give to perps?"

"Yeah, that one, what was I supposed to do?"

"Jesus, she's probably locked in her room petrified. Let me call you back."

Rafe sounded aggravated when it was Mike who should be. "Dude, I'm just going to leave. I appreciate what you did, setting me up here, but I think I should just go. I'm sure Jenna would appreciate it too."

"Daniels is going to tell you to stay put, you know it and I know it. That house is in perfect proximity to keep your cover and to do what you are there to do. It's only a week. I'll have Ali call Nicki and Nicki will explain to Jenna that she needs to keep quiet about who you are. Did you tell her?"

"Basically, she put two and two together, she asked and I didn't deny it, I just said I was a friend of yours on vacation."

Rafe grinned. "She's a great girl, Mike, she just graduated from college. She's a dancer." He laughed. "And not what you're thinking, she's been an instructor since before college, you know, little girls and adults too. She's a lot of fun to be around, you'll like her."

"That's great," Mike said, dripping sarcasm and rolling his eyes. Now he knew where the tight little body came from.

"Why don't you go and make sure she hasn't called nine-one-one on your ass and buy her some dinner," Rafe suggested. "Call a truce; it's only for a week."

Mike thought about it. If he stayed on his end of the house and she on hers then it probably wouldn't be so bad; they would have to work out some kind of schedule for the kitchen so they weren't in each other's way, but that was about it. He'd be gone a good part of his days on surveillance so it might just be okay. It would really suck if he had to leave. "All right I'll stay, but please have Nicki call her and give this girl the heads-up."

"I'll do it right now." Rafe said goodbye and hung up, laughing his ass off.

"He's fucked."

Ali came up to the counter and put her arms around Rafe. "Who?"

"That was Mike. He's staying at Nan's on Captiva. Apparently Jenna showed up there a week early." Rafe was still chuckling picturing it.

"Oh no!" Ali let out a little laugh, picturing the scene as well. "What the hell is Mike doing there?" Ali narrowed her eyes. "I suppose you want me to go call Nicki?" Ali watched him nod, giving her a sheepish grin. "You have a lot of explaining to do!" Ali called out as she hurried away to call and warn Nicki, leaving Rafe chuckling in the kitchen.

CHAPTER NINE

Mike sat on the edge of his bed. He had to think. He could do this; just because she was gorgeous didn't mean he couldn't just be cordial without getting a hard-on. Wasn't it just a little while ago that he was thinking he wasn't feeling it this week? He wanted to just relax with a beer, maybe do some fishing, and concentrate on Scintillo. Okay except that was before someone placed a ridiculously hot bikini-clad woman five feet in front of him.

He got up, threw a clean T-shirt on, and headed toward her room. He could hear her on the phone as he approached and he politely waited outside her door in the hall until she finished, *and* so he could overhear what she was saying. He was FBI, after all.

"Nicki, what the hell? Matt knew and didn't tell you?" Jenna was still wrapped in her towel and had yet to hear the front door open and shut. "And Ali didn't even know? No, of course not, because she would have told you." Jenna answered her own question then listened to Nicki talk. "What? He's staying?" She let out a deep breath. "Have you seen him? He looks like GI Joe, for God's sake!"

Mike frowned and crossed his arms. *GI Joe*? He guessed that wasn't that bad of a comparison.

Nicki put down the paintbrush she'd been holding and sat on her stepstool. "Jenna, he's really nice, and he's just there for a week to do a quick job. Rafe says it's no big deal and to just pretend he's not there. He's good-looking and he's funny, he'll make you laugh."

Jenna frowned, feeling a little jealous that her sister had met him and thought he was funny. If he had laid eyes on Nicki then he wouldn't think anything of Jenna; not that she should care, but for some reason she did. Nicki was only older by eighteen months but she was gorgeous and had always had plenty of male attention. Their looks couldn't be more different. Nicki had paler skin and auburn hair taking after their father and Jenna had olive skin and dark hair like their mother. They had the same smile, though, and that's the only way people knew they were sisters, that and they each had their mom's nice long legs—thank God, Jenna thought.

"Besides," Nicki teased, "you always loved GI Joe, even better than Ken.

Remember when I caught you making Barbie have sex with him?"

"Yeah, I know I loved GI Joe better than Ken," Jenna huffed, not wanting to laugh at Nicki's childhood memory; she was too aggravated. "And I did not *make* Barbie have sex with him! She wanted to!"

Out in the hall, Mike had to shove his fist in his mouth to keep in the burst of laughter that threatened to escape.

Nicki laughed out loud. "You loved his blond hair and said that's what you wanted your husband to look like."

"Oh my God, will you be serious?" Jenna smirked, biting back her own laughter. "This is a problem; you should have seen how he looked at me. I should be scared right now!" Why did Nicki so not think this was a big deal? "I'm hanging up. If they find my body in the bay, you'll know who did it." Jenna stood up from the bed.

Mike winced at that, feeling bad for the impression he must have given her.

Nicki tried to convince Jenna what a great guy Mike was and told her how he was the one who had driven her to the hospital when Ali had been attacked.

"Yeah, he probably drove you to the hospital because he wanted to score points and get in your pants!" Jenna could just imagine.

Mike shrugged; maybe there had been a little of that going through his mind when he first met Nicki, but not after he knew she was in love and he'd met her man. He liked Matt, and he wasn't in the habit of poaching other men's women.

Jenna held the phone away while Nicki yelled at her and continued to sing Mike's praises.

"I'm sure he has a great smile, Nicki, but that might be on his alter ego. The face I saw would scare the fur off a cat."

Mike flinched at that one too; no one had ever described him quite that way before. He had to redeem himself fast.

"I'm going to go lock my door, goodbye, Nicki." Jenna listened to Nicki's last words. "Yes, I realize it's my own fault, I should never have come early without telling anyone, I know," she droned. "But I'm here and I'm staying too, so he's just going to have to deal. Tell Ali to tell Rafe that I won't interfere in his secret spy work, I'll be at the beach every day anyway."

"He's a great guy, Jenna, try to get to know him, trust me, okay?" Nicki pleaded.

"We'll see. I'll call you later." Jenna hung up, pissed. This was not how she wanted to start her vacation, but she knew it was her own fault. If she had just called Nan instead of e-mailing her, this whole thing could have been avoided. Why had he been such a jerk to her? Nicki couldn't tell her enough about how nice he was and how funny he was, making him sound like a real charmer.

Huh! Where was *that* guy?

Jenna took her towel off and rifled through her bag for a sundress to throw over herself before she headed back out to the kitchen to make another drink, which she desperately needed. She hadn't even put a dent in her first one before she had drifted off and by now it would be a melted hot mess. She had her dress just over her head when she heard a cough.

"Excuse me." Mike couldn't believe his timing. Jesus, she was trying to get dressed and he stood there gaping at her in her bikini again. "I'm sorry; I'll be out in the living room."

Jenna was taken aback again by his ridiculous good looks and forgot that she temporarily hated him. She let the skimpy dress fall over her body, which inadvertently had become covered in goose bumps *which* she told herself were from the AC. She rubbed her arms distractedly and followed him out of the bedroom. This ought to be interesting, she thought. "I hear you're staying." She started talking before he could speak.

Mike turned to face her and could still see her bikini right through the little cover-up she wore. He tried to look away but her two erect nipples pressed against the thin material of the dress and he couldn't help but stare. Shit. He forced himself to look up and found her staring at him with a scowl. She was even cute when she was mad. What the hell was wrong with him?

"It'll just be the week, possibly less," he said, his voice surprisingly hoarse. "I'll be gone mostly in the day and promise to stay on my end of the house. I'm sorry things worked out like this, but I had no idea you would be here too."

Jenna rolled her eyes. "God, I didn't think arriving a week early would have so many people up in arms! I just needed to get the hell away, okay!" She was feeling like a jerk and wishing she had the money for a hotel. She never imagined she'd have to share the house with a stranger.

Mike looked at her and could see she was upset and figured it was the whole breakup with her boyfriend deal. She probably still loved the guy. "Well, I get up pretty early so I won't be in your way for breakfast. Lunch is usually on the fly and I'll try to be quick in the kitchen at dinner."

Jenna took him in again. He still wore his bathing suit, only now with a white T-shirt, which enhanced his build and made him look even bigger if that were possible. He had a great tan and his eyes were as blue as the bay when she drove over the causeway. She studied his face and even that looked strong and muscular. It was a well-defined face with a little bump on the bridge of his nose, as if it had once been broken, giving him an extra edge of toughness. Like he needed it, she smirked.

"My sister speaks highly of you." She waited for the inevitable onslaught of compliments for Nicki but none came. The man still hadn't even cracked a smile, he was all business.

"Your sister is a great kid." Mike had watched her size him up and caught the smirk that had crossed her face. He wondered what she'd been thinking. No, he knew what she was thinking, that he was a hard ass and probably a jerk. Every instinct told him to let her go on thinking that way, but the little cock-shaped devil that sat on his right shoulder had him thinking of ways to turn that opinion right around.

That's it? She's a great kid? If he thought of Nicki as a kid, what must he think of her? "She's hardly a kid." Jenna knew she sounded bitchy—but tough!

"Well, compared to me, I guess she is. I'm thirty-two." Jesus, what the hell made him tell her that? *Idiot.*

Thirty-two, huh? Pretty much what she figured but why did he feel the need to tell her? "Big deal, that's not old." She didn't dare tell him *her* age, and why were they even talking about age? She was supposed to be mad at him and ironing out their temporary living arrangements.

Okay, so she didn't think thirty-two was old. That was a plus but he had to get a fucking grip here. "Okay, so one last thing. Nicki explained to you that you can't tell anyone who I am, right?"

"So you're admitting that you're FBI?" Jenna asked, crossing her arms and wearing a smug expression.

Mike took his hand and rubbed it over his chin, trying to decide whether to laugh or put her over his knee and spank her. "I am FBI, yes, and would appreciate your cooperation in keeping that quiet."

"Fine, I have no problem doing that, you don't have to worry about me." Jenna walked into the kitchen in a huff. "I'm going to make myself a drink and then the kitchen is all yours." She mixed the ingredients and turned on the blender, stealing glances at him from inside the kitchen while the ice churned. Each time she looked up he was looking straight at her, his arms crossed against his wide chest. God, he was like a statue, no expression other than that "don't fuck with me" look he had down pat. Oh yeah Nicki, he's a barrel of laughs.

Jenna couldn't wait to tell Paige about this guy. She turned off the blender and poured the slushy consistency into another tall plastic hurricane glass then picked it up and started back down the hall. "I have one last thing, too." She stopped halfway and turned to look at him.

Mike's eyes had been on the sway of her hips and he diverted them back to her almond-shaped eyes.

"Do you ever smile, Agent Mike Caplan?"

Mike was momentarily taken aback by the simple question and by how she had addressed him. He remained completely stone-faced when he answered. "Yes, as a matter of fact, I smile all the time, and it's *Special* Agent."

Special Agent, huh? Jenna shook her head. Was he kidding? He was like a freaking robot. She stared at him a bit longer then felt a smile creep along the sides of her mouth when she spotted the twinkle in his eyes. He was totally screwing with her! Her laughter escaped almost in relief, she couldn't help it, and was thankful when he laughed too and oh-my-God! She almost spilled her drink as his brilliant smile took over his face. Jenna immediately felt a flip and a twist deep inside her belly. If she had thought he was gorgeous before, now he was just ridiculously so! Her laugh abruptly stopped as surprise took over. He was, he was. . . a totally different man when he smiled. She could see what Nicki apparently saw, that he *was* nice and he had a sense of humor, she could see it in his eyes. Without a hint of laughter in her own voice, she slowly backed down the hall as she spoke. "You should do that more often, *Special* Agent." Jenna turned and escaped the short distance to her room then shut the door behind her, leaning against it and taking a deep breath. Ho-ly shit!

Yeah, baby, score one for Mikey! The smile got her, he could tell, but why did he care so much? He was at least glad she no longer seemed afraid of him. He walked into the kitchen and pulled his steak out of the refrigerator, noticing the additional groceries she must have bought…hmmm, she had bought steak too, and eggs, and jeez, basically everything he had bought. He also noticed there was still some frozen drink left in the blender and he poured a little into a small glass, tasting it. It was sweet and he frowned, thinking she was in her room drinking alone. He wondered if she had eaten, and guessed probably not. He could hear Rafe's voice telling him to buy her dinner. Well, he could do the next best thing. He pulled a bottle of beer out from the fridge and went out to the pool deck to start the grill. The sliders to her room were shut and the blinds drawn, so he knocked.

Jenna had just left a voice mail for Paige, remembering too late that she would already be on her dinner date with Justin. She was itching to talk with her but it would obviously have to wait. She still hadn't heard back from Jake either and she was starting to feel sorry for herself. She should have just arrived at the house when she was supposed to. She took a sip of her drink and sat down on her bed. She'd no sooner sat when she heard a knock on her sliders, startling her, and she hopped off the bed. She did a quick check in the mirror before sliding them open. G. I. Joe stood there smiling again. *Oh boy.*

"Yeah?" It probably would have been more polite to say "hi" but they were already past that so it seemed redundant.

"I just wondered if you've eaten, I'm grilling up a steak and there's plenty if you want some." God, he felt like an ass, why was he so nervous? He never had any qualms asking a woman anything!

Jenna was still having trouble getting past the smile. "Uh no, I mean no I haven't eaten," she clarified quickly. "So, sure, steak will be great. I bought stuff for salad if you want." Now they were going to be friendly? She hoped so, but she was still cautious.

"Great, sounds good." Mike was grinning like an idiot but he was just happy she seemed to be coming around to him. He had started them off on such a bad foot.

Jenna took her drink from the nightstand and joined Mike outside. She stood next to him and watched as he cleaned the grill, preparing it for the steak, and felt a little bad that they'd had such a sucky beginning. "Hey, I'm sorry about earlier; I guess we were both just surprised."

Mike turned to face her. "I was going to apologize to you. I didn't mean to give you the wrong impression, or maybe I did." He grinned. "But I shouldn't have."

Jenna raised a brow. Oh man, the smile made him gorgeous but that crooked grin made him sexy as all hell. "Why did you then?"

Mike turned back to the grill, still brushing the rack. How to answer that honestly? "I guess because I came here to do a job and wasn't expecting any distractions."

Jenna felt a slight glimmer of satisfaction and decided to test him a bit. "You assumed I'd be a distraction?" she asked him in a flirtatious way and smiled up at him, taking a healthy sip of her drink. Her eyes suddenly went wide. Oh shit! Brain freeze! So much for the seductive look. She rubbed the heel of her hand over her forehead.

Mike looked at her, about to answer honestly, but laughed instead when he saw her face and guessed what had happened. "Smaller sips and that won't happen." Saved by a frozen drink, he chuckled and walked past her, thinking she was pretty cute, and went back into the kitchen for the steak. When he came back out she was sitting at the patio table, long bare legs crossed at the ankles; she was pretty damn sexy too.

Jenna couldn't help laughing at herself, feeling silly. Okay, so she was no seductress, she'd just made that abundantly clear, so she'd just shoot for friendly for now. "Where are you from, Mike?"

"Miami, born and raised." He eyed her.

"Wow, that's pretty cool." Jenna was immediately jealous. When he wasn't working he was probably on South Beach partying with beautiful women from all over the world, models probably. "So how long have you been with the FBI?" She had to admit his job was pretty cool.

"Eight years." Mike downed the last of his beer.

"In Miami the whole time?"

"No, actually when I first joined I was up in your neck of the woods. I started out in the Boston field office."

"Really?" Jenna knew Rafe had just recently transferred there for Ali. "So can you just go wherever you want?"

Mike laughed. "No, you go where you're needed, but basically you stay where you're assigned, unless you specifically put in for a transfer like my pal Rafe. Do you know him well?"

"Well, I've gotten to know him well just by him being around the family. He's awesome; I can't wait for their wedding. It'll be fun having it here on the island."

"Yeah, it will. I'm the best man, you know," he said, trying to impress her.

"That's right!" Jenna leaned forward, smiling. She hadn't even put two and two together at first. She had to say she liked this Mike a whole lot better than the first Mike she'd met. His smile was contagious and she found herself growing more and more attracted. "So I guess we will be seeing each other again after this."

"Now that's encouraging." Mike smiled at her.

Jenna blushed. Wow, actual flirting, who would have thought? There was hope for him yet. She wondered if he had a girlfriend in Miami and figured Nicki probably would have said so when she was teasing her about GI Joe and Barbie.

Mike turned the burners down on the grill and walked over to the table where Jenna sat. "I'm going to grab another beer; can I make you another drink?"

Jenna stood up facing him; they were just inches apart. He was so much taller than her and she had to look way up to see into his eyes. "I'll come in and make it; I should make the salad anyway."

Mike backed up to let her by and loved how petite she was next to him. He followed her inside and again found himself looking at her tight little ass and how it moved beneath the see-through dress. She seemed like a nice kid and he was glad they were getting along now. He was starting to feel comfortable with her and hoped she was feeling the same. She had definitely flirted with him a little and he had to admit he liked it. She was young, and thankfully more than legal, which had him thinking thoughts that would only lead to trouble, trouble he had no business getting into.

Once inside he grabbed another beer then sat at the counter stool watching her make her drink and then start on the salad. "So how long has your grandmother had this house?" He could see she was perfectly at home here.

"Oh, about five or six years I think." Jenna grabbed a large bowl out of a cabinet and reached in the refrigerator for the salad ingredients then brought them to the counter in front of Mike where she started to prepare it. "It's a lot of fun when the whole family is here, but I'm looking forward to being by myself." She looked up quickly. "You know what I mean."

Mike laughed. "Yeah, as soon as I'm out of here."

Jenna laughed too. "I'm starting to realize you're not so bad. You had me worried for a while there though. I thought Nicki was nuts. The bad guys must want to curl up in a corner and die after you give them that mean look of yours."

Mike winced. "I'm really sorry about that, you just surprised me. The last thing I expected was to see a practically nude, gorgeous woman lying by the pool."

Jenna's eyes shot to his again in surprise and she felt her face reddening.

"Well shit," he laughed, "just calling it like I see it, even though you're way too young," he added and waited for her reaction.

Jenna had been about to thank him for his obvious compliment but felt her back stiffen instead. "Way too young? Too young for *what* exactly?" She hadn't expected that to come out of his mouth, especially since they had just flirted a little. Humph!

And there it was, he thought with amusement, that fire in her eyes again. "For me." He gave her his best grin and watched her face get red with anger. Oh oh. He had to admit he liked her mad; her dark eyes blazed and her chest heaved.

"Of all the gall, what the hell makes you think I would even be interested?" Jenna sliced cucumbers with a vengeance. Ha! He was conceited; she knew there had to be something about him.

"I'm just saying, I think you're extremely beautiful but you're way too young for me. I usually date women my age or older." If you could call a weekend here and there dating, he laughed to himself. He really shouldn't be goading her but he couldn't help himself. She was too cute and he supposed he wanted to see what she thought about their age difference. Why it bothered him he didn't know. He shouldn't care one way or the other.

Wow, he thought she was extremely beautiful? Jenna shook the thought away quickly, realizing she was supposed to be mad, and looked at him with her knife poised over the vegetables. "Who said anything about dating? As if I'd be interested!" she huffed. "Besides I'm done dating men of any age for a long time!" God, he had her so flustered and feeling like a damn child. She continued to toss the salad, all the while fuming, and watched as a grape tomato flew out of the bowl and landed across the room on the floor.

Okay, he'd definitely asked for that but Mike couldn't help but grin as he watched the tomato fly and then as she bent over to pick it up. "Take it easy, I didn't mean to insult you." Her dark brown eyes became two little black orbs as she straightened to find him staring and she glared at him. She was a knockout. If she only knew he'd ask her out for a date in two seconds if he wasn't who he was. "I'm just kidding around with you."

"Oh, so what, you *would* date someone as young and inexperienced as little ol' me?" She put her hands on her hips.

Mike frowned, about to take a pull on his beer, feigning concern. "Are you inexperienced?"

"Ugh!" Jenna exhaled, exasperated with him. "You'll never know, now will you?" She grinned in satisfaction. "You should probably go check on the steak."

Mike laughed loudly, liking that she gave it right back to him. He took his beer and went back out to the grill still chuckling. At the very least for his own good, he got her thinking there was no chance between them. He would treat her like a friend's little sister; after all, that was what she was. If he continued to think of her the way he was thinking of her, he'd be fucked this week in more ways than one and wouldn't be able to concentrate on the job at hand, which was to nail Scintillo. After that was done, well, he wouldn't be back until the wedding and then, who knew?

Jenna couldn't believe it; what a self-centered jerk! And she had actually pictured herself hooking up with him! She would coexist with him for a week and their relationship would strictly be on a friendly basis. She could tolerate his conceit; after all, Jake wasn't much different, she thought with amusement, but this guy would surely drive her nuts if she let him.

CHAPTER TEN

Justin finished getting ready and put a disgruntled Sam in his crate. "Sorry, pal, no more playing until later, but I'll bring you home a surprise." At least he hoped he would. He hoped Paige would return home with him after dinner to see the house and he hoped she wasn't feeling any regrets about their previous night together. He wanted to be with her again. They had definitely jumped right into things but Justin was glad; he had wanted Paige from the moment he'd seen her. He'd known sex would be off-the-charts great with her and it had been. Now he looked forward to getting to know her much better.

Justin had never been one to believe in love at first sight or fate or any of that weird shit his sister and mother believed in, but he couldn't help but be rattled when Paige had come in for her tattoo the previous day and started talking about her love for old houses. And then when he had ever seen the picture of *his* house in *her* apartment that Paige had taken, Justin had to wonder if there was something to all that shit. It was just weird and he knew damn well what his sister and mother would say if he told them about Paige and her picture.

Justin gave the place one last look around before he left. There was nothing he could do with the unfinished rooms. He'd started to remodel as soon as he'd bought the house and at least had the kitchen and downstairs bath completed, not to mention his own master bedroom and private bath. The rest of the house, though, he was taking one room at a time and he hoped Paige loved it as much as he did. He had a feeling, given the enthusiasm she expressed just showing him her picture, that she would love it and he found himself really excited to bring her back.

He locked the large front door behind him and walked the few steps down the deep front porch and over to the detached carriage house. He opened the large barn door and straddled his motorcycle. He started it up, backed out, and hopped off to shut the door again before donning his helmet and heading toward Paige's apartment. It was another beautiful early summer night and he planned to take her to eat at one of his favorite spots on Ocean Drive. It was a perfect night for the bike and he knew she would appreciate their destination.

* * * * *

Paige stared at the picture of Justin's house while she waited for him. She had fallen in love with it the first moment she saw it and still found it difficult to believe that Justin was the new owner. What were the odds of that? Jenna had said it was simply meant to be and Paige had to admit it kind of felt that way but she knew life wasn't that simple. There had no doubt been an instant attraction between her and Justin, but for Paige's part she just assumed it was due to her yearlong celibate lifestyle and the fact that her jeans had been wide open in front of a really hot guy. She smiled, recalling their subtle flirting while he'd tattooed her, and smiled even wider remembering their bodies pressed together just that morning.

Her thoughts were soon interrupted by the sound of a motorcycle engine outside. She put the picture down, checked her appearance one last time, and left the apartment. She was on the front porch before he could take his helmet off. Damn, he looked hot!

"Hi!" she said, nearly breathless.

"Hi! You look amazing. Are you all set?" Justin smiled as he got off the bike and walked over to her. He kissed her in greeting and felt the brief contact zip right to his groin. Jesus, he couldn't remember ever feeling all these little twinges of excitement with any other woman. Maybe as a teenager and with the first girl he'd ever kissed but that was about it. And Paige looked like a teenager, he thought. Her hair was pulled back in a ponytail and the features of her face were more pronounced, giving her a fresh, clean look. She was dressed casual like he told her, wearing a sleeveless top, shorts, and sandals that had him staring at her nicely toned legs. "Did I already say you look amazing?"

Paige laughed. "Yes, and thank you. I just put my hair up so it doesn't fly all around on the ride. I'll take it down when we get to the restaurant." Paige smoothed a hand over her ponytail self-consciously, hoping she didn't look too casual. He was only wearing jeans and a T-shirt but he looked like he just stepped off the cover of *GQ*.

"I like your hair like that, lets me see your beautiful face." Justin smiled and tugged on her ponytail.

Paige felt her face get hot. "You look pretty amazing yourself. I love the motorcycle."

Justin cocked a brow, smiling. "You like the bike, huh?"

Paige grinned. "It's pretty sexy, yeah." He looked so damn sexy on it. She thought briefly of asking him if he wanted to skip dinner and just go inside then quickly banished the wicked thought. She wanted a date with him more, well, just as much.

"So where are we going?" Paige admired the big black Harley at the curb. It really suited Justin perfectly.

Justin grinned, loving that she thought the bike was cool. "We're going to one of my favorite restaurants, not so much for the food as for the view. But don't worry, the food's good too." He helped her with his helmet then got on the bike first. "It's okay, hop on." He laughed at the skeptical look she held.

"I'm not going to throw you off balance?" Paige had never been on a motorcycle before not even her brother John's, whose bike was very similar. She was a little frightened suddenly.

"No way, just hold onto me and lean with me." Justin thought she looked damn sexy and he couldn't wait to have her up against him on the bike.

Paige lifted her right leg and straddled the motorcycle, sliding right up against him when she was on. She definitely wasn't going to mind this part. She brought her arms around his waist and leaned her chest against his back. "Okay, I guess I'm ready." Paige jumped on reflex when Justin started the motorcycle and felt him laugh. She laughed too and spoke into his ear. "Go easy on me, it's my first ride." He turned around and gave her the sexiest grin, prompting her to give him a playful slap on the thigh.

Justin laughed and pulled away from the curb, heading toward Bellevue. Paige's arms were clasped tightly around his waist, her hands splayed across his stomach, and he could feel her full breasts against his back, pressing into him every time they hit a bump. He wanted her again, real bad. They were on Bellevue when he felt her breath in his ear.

"That's where Jenna lives." Paige pointed to the old Victorian and immediately placed her arm back around his waist.

Justin looked to where she pointed and nodded. "Cool house," he called back.

"You should see it inside," she said loud enough for him to hear. There was a little bit of traffic so they were going slow enough to hear each other without screaming.

Justin looked down; Paige's legs squeezed against his and he reached a hand down to run over one smooth leg. Man, she was driving him wild, he thought as he felt her lean in just a little closer. As they hit Ocean Drive, he had both hands back on the handlebars and was able to open the bike up a little more. It was dinner time so people were heading into town, not away from it, and the road was wide open. The view along the ocean always amazed him and he was glad he could enjoy it with Paige.

Paige had the shivers but not from the temperature, it was the adrenaline pumping through her from the ride and holding Justin this close. She officially loved motorcycles and the view was gorgeous. The homes along Ocean Drive were impressive beyond compare. They were built right into the landscape, their stone and shingled facades hovering over grassy hills and ledges that faced the Atlantic Ocean. The newer mansions with large paned windows and deep wraparound decks had more chimneys than most average homes had bedrooms. There were older homes too, large rambling beach cottages, like the one overlooking the ocean that her brother John had recently purchased, which she pointed out to Justin when they passed it. Her brother's house and others like it nearby oozed old New England charm, which Paige loved best. The architecture and landscape of Newport felt like home to her every summer.

What a life! Paige felt pretty lucky at the moment and wondered where they were going as they passed Brenton Point. The parking lot along the outskirts of the park was still filled with cars and RVs in the early evening and people were grilling and picnicking while others watched the variety of colorful kites overhead or flew their own. Paige looked up as they drove slowly past to see a kaleidoscope of colors dotting the sky. It was a perfect kite flying day with probably a good two hours left of flying time before night set in. She and Jenna would often ride their bikes to the park just to watch all the different shapes and colors of kites flying and sometimes they would eat lunch across the street overlooking the waves crashing on the rocks below. It was one of Paige's favorite spots in Newport.

They continued traveling west on Ocean Drive and just moments later were taking the winding drive up to Castle Hill. Paige smiled happily; she loved the old inn and was pleasantly surprised that Justin did too. When they reached the top Justin parked in the lot overlooking the ocean and turned off the bike's engine.

Paige took off his helmet and smoothed back her hair. They were still straddling the bike and Paige sat there staring at the view. "I just love it here."

"I thought you would." Justin got of the bike and smiled, glad that she was pleased. "I came here for the first time last year, believe it or not, and thought it was great. I had a few beers at a table on the lawn out there and thought it would be nice to come back here again." He reached for her hand to help her off the bike.

Paige got off the bike awkwardly and was grateful for the help. "Were you on a date then too?" she asked, standing upright with a little smile.

Justin smiled and winked at her. "Actually I was here with two women."

Paige chuckled, wishing she hadn't asked.

"I was with my mother and my sister," he laughed, securing the helmet to the bike.

Paige grinned. "Oh good, because here I was thinking I'm going to need a stiff drink before I hear about any other women in your life."

Justin laughed again and took her hand leading them to the front entrance of the inn. "A drink sounds good, and trust me there won't be much to tell."

"Ha! I don't believe that for a second." Paige savored the touch of his hand but averted her eyes. She actually felt a pang of jealousy just thinking of any other women he'd been with. What had she been thinking coming out and asking that question?

Justin shook his head in denial but decided against continuing the topic until they were settled at a table. The hostess led them to the outside lawn where tables and chairs were set up for outdoor dining. They chose one with an umbrella due to the sun that was still going strong in the early evening hour.

"A server will be right with you."

"Thank you," they said in unison to the hostess as they sat. Justin moved his seat beside Paige's so they could both look down toward the ocean, and he casually draped an arm around the back of her chair. There were some children tumbling playfully on the rolling green lawn in front of them and both Paige and Justin watched the scene for a minute. The children's parents were sipping cold drinks and watching the kids from Adirondack chairs casually placed along the grass covered hill. There was a light chop in the ocean below the cliff and several sailboats glided by at full mast.

"This view is beautiful." Paige took it all in, hearing Justin agree. She wished she'd thought to bring her camera.

A waiter came over promptly to greet them and took their drink orders. He recited the dinner specials and left them both with menus to peruse. When he was gone, Justin turned to Paige.

"So..." Justin started.

Paige looked at him with amusement. "So..." she countered, immediately in tune with him. She was so comfortable with him already. "Kind of backwards I guess, huh?"

"All first dates should start out the way ours did in my opinion." He smiled, teasing her.

Paige laughed. "Maybe we're on to something, huh? Start a new trend—sex as the ice breaker?"

Justin laughed out loud, loving that she had a sense of humor and that she wasn't uncomfortable with what had happened between them so quickly. "Think of all the time that could be saved. I mean if the sex sucked then the couple wouldn't have to waste all that time getting to know each other, they could move right along to the next person." He grinned, knowing how awful it sounded.

Paige laughed, playing along, "I'm so glad the sex didn't suck." She reached back and pulled the elastic from her hair, letting it spill around her shoulders.

Justin felt that inexplicable pull toward her as he watched her hair fall and he leaned in and kissed her, lightly running his hand through the now loosened strands. "Me too."

Paige blushed and nearly purred at the feel of his fingers in her hair. She couldn't help it, Justin gave her goose bumps and made her think about things she hadn't really paid much attention to in the past year, like how she wore her hair or if her undies and bra matched or not. She was actually wearing a new set that she had purchased just that afternoon at Victoria's Secret. She smiled at him and was grateful when the waiter came back with their drinks.

"Are you ready to order?"

Justin looked at Paige and she shook her head. "Actually," Justin told him, "we haven't even picked up the menus yet, we'll need another minute."

"No problem, sir, I'll come back when you're ready."

Justin picked up his beer bottle and clinked it to Paige's glass. "Here's to a great summer."

Paige gave him a sly smile. "I'm enjoying it so far."

Justin laughed at the innuendo. "How's the tat today?"

Paige lifted the hem of her shirt and looked down. "Still a little red but not as sore. Has anyone ever come back with a complaint?"

He laughed. "Thankfully no. That would suck, it's not like you can take it back." He resisted the urge to reach out and touch the skin she'd bared.

Paige laughed, agreeing. "No, I guess not." She looked at his arms and really studied the artwork on them. She wondered if any of the tattoos had anything to do with past girlfriends and he seemed to read her thoughts.

"Go ahead and ask."

"What?" she laughed, a little embarrassed and pretending she didn't know what he meant.

"Okay, I'll ask first then. Did you get that little butterfly that I added to for you ex?"

Paige laughed out loud. "Hell no! I got that with Jenna. We were down at my grandmother's one weekend and drove over to Ft. Myers Beach so I could get it. He hated it." She smiled.

Justin gave her a crooked smile. "Good, for some reason that makes me happy."

Paige smirked. "My odds aren't very good though," she said, looking at his covered arms and playfully lifting up his T-shirt. The sight of his stomach looking well-muscled even as he sat in a relaxed way did things to her insides that caused her to shift in her chair.

"Not one has any significance to anybody I've ever dated," Justin told her proudly, enjoying their banter and her hands on him.

"Really? That's pretty amazing, I'd expect an initial or a little heart or something," she said playfully and lowered his shirt back in place.

"Nope, my dad told me a long time ago that if I was going to cover myself with ink then not to put anything stupid on myself. He promised me I would regret putting anything to do with a woman on my body unless I planned to marry her and spend the rest of my life with her."

Paige laughed. "Good advice. I like your dad already."

"He'd like you too." Justin took a sip of his beer and watched as a large sailing yacht cruised by, its colorful spinnaker bulging in the wind. He pointed to it and Paige commented on its vibrant colors and how she wished she had her camera. When Justin offered next time, Paige smiled and felt her heart flutter at the very thought.

She asked him about his family and loved that he seemed to be close to them. It sounded as if he had grown up in a happy, loving environment much as she had. She spoke of her own family, filling him in on the latest family news, which was her cousin Nicki's wedding, and telling him all about Nicki's previous summer on Captiva and all that it had entailed. She also told him about Nicki's best friend Ali and her upcoming wedding.

"So, your cousin and her best friend got engaged at the same time?"

"Within a month I would say. We all warned Jenna not to drink the water while she's there."

Justin laughed, taking a sip of his beer. "Yeah, sounds dangerous on that island in more ways than one."

Paige laughed too. "Well, the whole drug trafficking thing was crazy; that kind of thing just doesn't happen there. It's a beautiful place to vacation, family friendly, you know? I don't want to give you a bad impression of the island."

"Maybe you'll have to take me there so I'll believe you," he teased her.

"Anytime," Paige said seriously. How about in three weeks? she thought to herself. She would love to take him to Ali and Rafe's wedding and spend a few days with Justin there.

Their eyes met and Justin leaned over to kiss her again. He was inexplicably drawn to this girl and the realization was kind of nice. His hand was on the back of her head as he continued to kiss her more intently, warming to his own thoughts. He could already picture his family welcoming her with open arms.

His thoughts were interrupted by the sound of the waiter clearing his throat and Justin broke the kiss reluctantly. After getting the go-ahead from Paige he ordered dinner for both of them; lobsters and steamers and another round of drinks. When the waiter left he reached for her hand and they sat looking out at the ocean in silence, enjoying the warm breeze and each other's company.

Paige was feeling perilously close to falling for this guy. He was too good; he was nice and attentive and saying all the right things. They were so comfortable with one another and seemed to be a great match; she could picture her family embracing him, even her brothers, and that wasn't something she could say about anybody she'd ever dated. John and Ryan had been her toughest critics of boyfriends growing up and still were. In college they'd started their own Internet search engine and much to Paige's dismay would use it to "thoroughly research," as they'd put it, anyone she'd ever dated. They'd since sold their little company for millions and thankfully stopped prying into her love life.

Her brothers had barely tolerated her ex, but Justin, Paige knew, they would like. He was just like them, street smart and well grounded, and he had a sense of humor she knew she had yet to see the extent of. She could just picture him hanging out drinking with John and Ryan and having a lot of laughs. Her brothers were two of the biggest jokers she knew.

"Can I ask you something personal?" Paige leaned back in her chair.

Justin turned and smiled. "I think you reserve the right." He'd tell her anything and everything.

Paige smiled at the implication. "How long were you with your ex and why did you break up?"

Without hesitation Justin told her. "We were together for two years. We broke up six months ago because she was pregnant."

Paige swallowed the sip of her drink, nearly choking in the process, and was suddenly sorry she'd asked. She definitely hadn't seen that coming. "Oh," she sputtered.

Justin gave her a reassuring smile. "It wasn't mine." He took a long pull on his beer finishing it.

"*Oh.*" She didn't see that coming either, but the sinking feeling in her stomach instantly buoyed. "I'm sorry." Paige felt her heart break for him; she could see it was still painful.

"Don't be, I thank God it wasn't mine." Justin laughed. "We had been having problems for the last year. She didn't like that I worked so much, and she started going out more with her friends. She came to me six months ago and told me she was three months pregnant."

"Did you think it was yours at first?" She couldn't help but notice that he seemed awfully glad not to have been the father. Paige wondered if he even liked kids.

"No, I pretty much knew it wasn't mine. She wasn't on the pill but I made sure we used protection every time we were together. She didn't try to make me think it was my kid either." He laughed. "Told me straight out who the father was."

Paige watched Justin's face and her heart sank again. "Oh no."

"Heard this one before, have you?" Justin grinned and stopped their conversation as the waiter placed their new drinks and a basket of bread on the table. "Thank you." Justin took a sip from his fresh beer and looked at Paige. "Yup, my childhood best friend."

"Oh, Justin," Paige groaned, placing a comforting hand on his arm. "I'm so sorry." She felt sick for him.

"They were married two months ago. I actually went to the wedding."

Paige's mouth fell open. "*You did?*"

"When I realized that they were really in love, I kind of forgave them both. I wasn't around, and I guess deep down I knew we weren't good together but I didn't have the balls to break it off, it just got too comfortable, you know?"

She did know. Her relationship had gone stale way before they had actually broken it off. She nodded, sipping her own drink. "That's quite a story; mine's rather dull in comparison."

Justin smiled. "I'm actually glad to hear that. I wouldn't want to think anybody had hurt you in any way."

Paige smiled at that and felt her blood warm with the idea of him caring about her feelings. Despite his bad boy looks he was truly a nice guy. "No, it was a mutual breakup. We both had different ideas about the future. He wanted a country club wife who booked his golf times and planned his meals every evening and we both knew I was not that person." She laughed and said almost apologetically to him, "I don't cook and I'd make a lousy secretary."

Justin chuckled. "Well then you're in luck because I am a genius in the kitchen and I learned how to run my own life a long time ago."

Paige laughed. "Really, you cook?" She raised a brow, impressed.

"I do, my dad taught me. My mom doesn't cook either," he laughed. "She bakes though."

Paige gave him a wide grin. "Both your parents sound fantastic! Your father gives sound tattoo advice and cooks and your mom *doesn't* cook, but bakes just like me! When can I meet them?" she kidded.

"How about tomorrow night?" Justin knew his parents would absolutely love her. And he really wanted them to meet her.

Paige nearly choked again on the sip she had just taken. "What?"

"I have dinner with them every Sunday night, come with me."

Wow, he was totally serious. "I have to work until six," Paige answered him hesitantly. She was taken aback—meet his parents? Paige looked at him and then saw the crooked grin come across his face. She exhaled in relief. "I'm going to kill you! I thought you were serious!" She laughed and loved his sense of humor, not that she wouldn't have gone in a heartbeat, she thought to herself. If he only knew what had been running through her mind!

Justin took another sip of beer. "I'm not joking. I'm just grinning at the look of shock on your face." He supposed meeting the parents was more of a second or third month in kind of thing but Paige was different and he knew it. She was special.

"Oh." Paige stopped laughing and looked at Justin, seeing that he was indeed not joking. "Well, I would love to but I do have to work until six." Oh my God, he was serious! Meet his parents? Already? Did he take all his dates to meet his parents or was she different? She was flattered and... well, she was surprised, but pleasantly so.

"So we'll go for dessert." Justin was watching her reaction and he was glad she seemed to be considering it.

Paige smiled at him as she thought about it. Okay, it's just dessert, he's not proposing, for God's sake, stop arranging guests at their tables. "Okay then," she answered happily. "That would be nice." *Wow.*

"Good," Justin said, changing the subject. "Now we've both been avoiding it so let's just get it out there." He placed both hands on the table to commence the conversation.

Paige laughed, taking another sip of her drink and feeling really good suddenly, for several reasons. "You start, it's *your* house." She was totally in tune with him.

"Well, last night you called it *your* house," he teased.

"That was before I knew it was actually *your* house." Paige loved that they were teasing each other. She felt like she had made a new friend, in addition to the obvious intimacy they'd shared, she felt closer to him on a whole new level. There was still so much to learn about each other but she felt as if they were off to a good start. "Tell me everything about it."

"I'd rather show you, can I bring you there after dinner?"

"Are you serious?" Paige asked excitedly, coming forward in her chair. "Of course you can! I hoped you would ask. I can't wait! Jenna says she thinks..." In her excitement Paige nearly blurted out Jenna's prediction that Paige would be living there soon. She meant to say it as a joke but realized how it might sound to him before it escaped her mouth.

"What?" Justin asked, curious and squinting an eye. "Tell me what you were going to say."

Paige gave a little laugh. "She just said she thinks," she paused, "well, that it was kind of odd that you bought my favorite house, you know seeing that we just met and you know..."

Justin leaned into her and gave her a crooked grin. "You told Jenna about us?"

Paige was immediately embarrassed. "I'm sorry, I did, she asked and I told her on our drive to the airport."

"That makes me happy." Justin smiled. She had talked about him, and he really liked that.

"It does?" Oh, thank God he wasn't offended!

"Hell yeah," he laughed and kissed her.

"Oh." Paige laughed too and reached for the bread. "Well good, because she got an earful," she added and popped a piece of bread in her mouth, grinning playfully.

Justin chuckled, imagining the conversation, and took his own piece of bread to eat. They sat back drinking and joking until their meals came then they feasted on the steamers. Justin helped Paige crack her lobster and laughed when she cleaned all the gooey white stuff off thoroughly before eating the meat. They each had one more drink and shared an oversized strawberry shortcake before he paid for dinner and they were walking back to the bike.

"I'm going to have to run five miles before work tomorrow after that meal." Paige patted her tummy.

"You're crazy, your body is smokin'."

"Well thanks, and might I say, right back atcha." Paige poked him in his hard stomach playfully. She was on top of the world being with Justin and couldn't believe how well things were going.

Justin laughed. "You're buzzed, you lightweight."

"That's true, I am." Paige nodded, smiling, and then frowned. "Are you? Can you drive us to our house without crashing? Because I really want to see the inside before I die."

Justin laughed and put his helmet back on her. "I'm great, no worries. I'll get you to *our* house in one piece." He had to admit he liked saying it as much as he'd liked hearing it. He kissed her before lowering the shield on the helmet then helped her onto the bike. "Are you cold?"

"Nope," Paige answered happily, her lips tingling from his kiss. "And if I were?" She had her arms crossed as she stood there grinning at him.

He chuckled; she was cute in his helmet and when she was buzzed. "I'd offer you the sweatshirt I put under the seat."

Paige shook her head no and waited until Justin got on the bike. When she was settled in behind him she put her arms around his waist again and snuggled up close speaking close to his ear. "You'll keep me warm."

Justin rubbed the goose bumps on both her thighs with his hands and turned around. "You bet your beautiful ass I will." He turned back to give her a searing look before starting the bike. He couldn't get home fast enough.

CHAPTER ELEVEN

Paige held on tight as they drove back on Ocean Drive. The night was gorgeous and the stars were shining bright over the ocean. When they hit Bellevue she glanced over at Jenna's house wistfully as they passed and wished her cousin were home so she could stop there with Justin. She would love for Jenna to get to know him too and Paige couldn't wait to call her cousin and fill her in.

They continued traveling slowly through the crowded waterfront and some minutes later pulled into Justin's driveway. Paige was so excited to see the house that she was handing him her helmet and was off the bike before Justin could turn back to help her.

"Damn, girl, wait for me, will you?" he laughed as she ran from the driveway. He secured the helmet on the bike and followed her up onto the wraparound front porch. Paige was walking the length of it and running her hand over the thick paint-encrusted railings. "It needs a good scraping and repainting but otherwise it's in good shape. The previous owners had it shored up last fall I guess. Some of the balusters were duplicated and replaced and the steps are new."

"It's gorgeous and so is the front door! I wish it was daylight to see it all better." It was like stepping back in time, Paige thought as she admired the depth of the grand porch.

If things went as planned she would see it in the daylight. Justin smiled at her and took out his key to open the large front door. There was a large square piece of glass cut into the top half of it that he needed to re-glaze but otherwise the door just needed a fresh coat of paint or maybe a stain; he hadn't decided.

"I can't tell you how excited I am to get inside." Paige was bouncing on the balls of her feet behind him waiting for him to unlock the door.

"I can see that," Justin laughed. He was psyched that she loved the house and couldn't wait for her to see the inside as well. "Hear that?"

Paige fell silent, listening. "Oh, poor guy, is he in his crate?" The puppy's whimpers were pathetic.

"Oh yeah, believe me, he is nowhere near ready to be trusted on his own." Justin unlocked the door and stepped inside with Paige right behind him. He flipped on the foyer light and turned to watch her reaction.

Paige gasped as she stepped inside to a huge open foyer the size of her whole apartment. The ceilings had to be twelve feet high at least and the hardwood floors were the widest planks she had ever seen in a house. Straight ahead to the left was a large empty room and in front of that were a set of grand stairs that had to be six feet wide at least with thick turned spindles and a wide balustrade ending in a large ornate newel post. The stairs turned halfway up, stopped at a generous open landing, and continued up to the second floor. Paige could just make out the landing and the large stained glass window on the outside wall above it. She could already picture a cozy window seat beneath it.

Her wide eyes came back down and took in the chunky moldings outlining the door frames and papered walls. To the right of the stairs was a generously wide hallway with two openings; one door was closed and the other was open to what appeared to be another large room. To Paige's immediate right was a double wide opening with French doors that stood open to what could be a large sitting room. There wasn't a stitch of furniture, but instead, saw horses and all kinds of construction materials were strewn about the room. She stole a look at Justin, who watched her with a big smile.

"I'm so utterly jealous of you right now, you have no idea." It was her dream house and he owned it. Not that she could have ever afforded to buy it herself, but she'd dreamt of it so many times. "Show me everything, please."

"Absolutely, let me just let Sam out back, wait here, don't start without me, I want you to see it the same way I did." Justin went down the hall and through the empty dining room and on into the kitchen. He let Sam out of his crate and opened the back door to let him into the small enclosed yard. When he came back to Paige she was in the front room, or sitting room as it was called, where he had been stripping wallpaper. "This is the current project."

"I can see that. What are you using to get the paper off?"

"I rented a steamer; it sucks though. I'm making divots in the plaster."

Paige shook her head. "Return it. Fabric softener. You just spray it on and the paper will come off easily. How many layers do you think?"

Justin watched her run a hand over the wall. "Appears to be just two. Really? Fabric softener?" She would make his whole year if it worked. He was losing his mind with how long it was taking to scrape the walls, and nearly every room was papered.

"Yup, and I'll help you do it if you want," Paige offered, hoping he'd say yes.

"Uh, hell yeah! Are you serious?" He would love the help and he would love to spend more time with her.

"I'm totally serious." Paige turned to him. "I love this kind of stuff."

"You're crazy; I thought I did too, until I got to this room. My room was much easier."

"You finished your bedroom?" She was impressed; she knew he'd just bought the house a month ago.

"Yeah, you'll see." Justin gave her his crooked grin, eliciting one from her. "The kitchen and downstairs bath are finished too." Justin gestured down the hall.

Paige felt the adrenaline flow through her just from his look and she shivered in excitement remembering the previous night.

"The windows are incredible, aren't they?" They ran from about a foot off the floor to about six feet above it. They were arched in a transom style at the top with real wooden grids adorning them. The wide casings around the windows were fluted and capped off with a complementary piece of arched crown that had to be six inches thick or more and as Paige took in the rest of the room she could see the same chunky crown over the doorways as well. The baseboard came up almost to the windows and she could just picture all of the original trim painted a fresh coat of white and the room fully decorated. "Can you imagine what it would cost to build a new house with these moldings?"

"No kidding." Justin nodded in agreement. "Sick money." He beckoned her forward.

Paige followed him through the sitting room and down a small step that ran the width of the room into what was obviously a sunroom. The outside walls were made up mostly of large, glass-paned windows that faced the side yard and two sets of double- wide, lighted French doors. One set led to the backyard where Paige could see the shadow of Sam's little form running about, and the other set led out onto the deep front porch. The ceiling in the room was vaulted and Paige craned her neck to look up at the old-fashioned paddle fan hanging there.

"You've got to be kidding me, this is incredible."

"Yeah, this room is going to be something." Justin nodded, looking around. "It might be years before I'm done with the place, but someday it will be nice."

"This is the first room I'd finish, I can already picture it." Paige walked over to the windows. "I'd put the biggest Christmas tree right here, so everyone driving by could see it through the windows. When it snows, the lights reflecting on the windows will look amazing!" Paige was lost in thought picturing the tree, and was surprised when Justin took her arm and led her back through the sitting room. She half laughed. "I'm sorry, I'm busy daydreaming. I'm completely jealous of you right now."

Justin laughed too. "It's a lot to take in." Problem was he could just picture her decorating the tree out there and that was freaking him out.

"Oh my God! How did I not notice the fireplace in here?" Paige was on the other side of the sitting room now staring at a fireplace that was probably eight feet wide and four feet deep. "I didn't notice the chimney on the front of the house," she said, perplexed.

"It's actually part of the porch; the porch is just so deep you don't notice the bricks."

"I could almost fit in there!" Paige walked over to the hearth and stepped inside. "Oh my God!" she said in disbelief, her palms up. "I do fit in here. I'm *in* the fireplace!"

"I can see that." Justin laughed. "Now come here, there's a lot more to see." He laughed as he grabbed her hand because he had actually done the same thing when he had first seen the fireplace. She was funny and he loved her reactions. He took her through what would eventually be the dining room and on into the finished, large eat-in kitchen beyond which was bright and open with loads of cherry cabinets and stone counters. He was excited to see her reaction to the kitchen.

"It's huge!" Paige exclaimed, running her hand over the gleaming stone top of the large center island. "Did you do all of this yourself?" The house was overwhelming and she was so excited to be seeing it. She had longed to get inside when she saw the for-sale sign. Justin was doing a phenomenal job renovating. She was impressed.

"Not all of it. My dad and some builder buddies of mine helped." It felt nice having Paige here and appreciating his hard work, Justin thought.

Paige took note of the new stainless appliances and the bright red microwave oven. "Nice microwave." She laughed, pointing to it.

"What? I like red, and it goes," he said defensively, but smiling.

"I'm not saying it doesn't, I just said it was nice." Paige grinned. "I can see the appeal."

Justin laughed. "All right, I know it stands out but I really liked it."

"And that's all that counts, it's your house." Paige smiled. "Oh my God, is that another staircase?" Paige headed toward it, coming around the large center island and noticing another fireplace in front of the island as she moved. This fireplace was of a more normal size, but still plenty large. She shook her head, marveling at all the details throughout and wondering how Justin had come to be interested in such a house.

"Can I go up?" Paige stood at the bottom of the stairway.

"Of course, lead the way." Justin followed close behind her and stopped at the open landing where Paige did.

Paige gasped. "Oh Justin. it's gorgeous!" She was standing in the entry to what was obviously the master bedroom. The ceiling height was just the same as the downstairs and the room itself was enormous with yet another large impressive fireplace. There was a large masculine four-poster bed neatly made with a comforter and shams in shades of navy and grey, complementing the soft slate color on the walls. Paige looked at Justin appraisingly.

Justin shrugged. "My mom and sister bought me all that stuff as a housewarming gift."

Paige smiled. "It's perfect." There were three doors in the room and she could see the open one clearly went out to a hallway. The two others were shut.

"Step in, let me show you the rest." Justin opened one door, explaining the other was the closet, and showed her the newly renovated bath with his and hers sinks and a large walk-in, glass-enclosed shower. There was a separate enclosed toilet area and another small doorway in the bathroom that led into the enormous walk-in closet that Justin could barely fill with just his clothes.

"You did an unbelievable job." Paige was thoroughly impressed. The soft earth tones of the tiles and paint color mixed beautifully with the smoked glass and nickel fixtures in the bathroom. She envied the closet space which was actually a good-sized room and made a disgruntled face at him as they entered it and she looked around. "Now this is just not right."

"My mother and sister hate me too." He shrugged in apology.

Paige just shook her head in feigned disgust.

Justin laughed and took her through the rest of the upstairs rooms that were unfinished. There were five additional bedrooms in need of paper stripping and floor re-sanding just down the hall from the master that were all accessible from a large landing at the top of the main staircase. The landing area alone was big enough to be considered its own room. Paige could picture large leather chairs casually placed around a huge area rug in the center and overstuffed bookcases along the walls. She unconsciously let out a sigh.

At the end of the hall, toward the front of the house, there was yet another set of narrow stairs that Justin told her led to a walk-up attic that he would show another time. He told her there weren't any working lights yet and there could very well be bats up there. Paige was happy to wait. Justin finished the tour and they arrived back to the large open landing by the main grand staircase.

"I'm dying to walk down these stairs." Paige turned and noticed that the stained glass window she'd seen from the front entry rose up higher than the top of the stairs and she could imagine the pretty design it made on the wood floor of the vast second floor landing when the morning sun shone in.

"Head on down, careful of the railing though, that needs some tightening," Justin warned.

Paige went down slowly, appreciating each wide expanse of step and the feel of the wide wood stained rail beneath her hand. She stopped at the large open landing where the steps ended before starting down again and she looked up at the window. The design held her gaze, and she gasped yet again. It wasn't exactly clear in the dim moonlight but she could just make it out. "Is that the harbor? Oh my gosh! Look at the sail boats!" It was a whole historic scene of the Newport waterfront. "It's beautiful. I'd love to see this in the sunlight."

"Sleep over tonight and see it in the morning," Justin offered, feeling his heart pound inexplicably. "It's beautiful when the sun shines through." Justin stood at the top of the stairs watching her; *she* was beautiful. He found himself holding his breath while he waited for her answer.

Paige turned to look up at him, surprised. He was serious and the way he was looking at her had her heart thumping. "I don't have any clothes or a toothbrush or. . ."

Justin walked down the few steps to the landing and brought her into his arms. "I have a brand new toothbrush and you can sleep in one of my T-shirts. I'll take you home in the morning to change whenever you want."

Paige looked up into Justin's eyes and felt her whole body relax against him. "Yeah?"

"Yeah." It felt right having her there. He'd be crushed if she wanted to leave.

"Okay." Paige smiled, not taking more than a minute to think about it. She was ridiculously happy that he'd asked. "This will be fun. Are there any ghosts?" Her eyes twinkled.

Justin laughed out loud. "I haven't heard or seen any yet, but you never know!" He bent to kiss her and put his arms around her waist. He couldn't wait to spend the night with her. She felt so good against him and he wanted her. "Want to go to bed now?"

Paige laughed. "You have to let Sam in and pay him some attention first. Let's go get him; I want to check out the downstairs again."

"All right." Justin sighed, cursed Sam, and followed Paige down the stairs, wondering again why he chose to get a puppy.

CHAPTER TWELVE

Jenna left the kitchen with the prepared salad, her drink, and everything else they would need for dinner on a tray. She stepped out onto the pool deck and brought it all over to the table. Mike was just turning the grill off and placing the cooked meat on a plate. Her stomach began to flip like a fish out of water just being near him. Great, she thought, I'm attracted to an arrogant, conceited jerk. Why does this sound familiar?

"I hope you're hungry." Mike cut the meat and put half on her plate, giving her another smile.

"Thanks, but I'll never eat all of that so please take some back." Jenna absorbed his brilliant smile grudgingly and looked up at him. She was trying not to like him and finding it very difficult. His arrogant attitude earlier in the kitchen just did not match up with his polite mannerisms or the nice things Nicki had said about him.

"Suit yourself." Mike shrugged, cut her piece in half again, and took back the rest. "That better?"

"Much, thank you." Jenna sat down and handed him a bowl and a fork.

"Thanks." Mike took the bowl and filled it with the salad she had made then filled her bowl as well. He got the sense she was a little ticked off under all the pleasantries and he felt bad knowing he was the cause.

"Thanks," Jenna said again. God, now they were just being sickeningly polite to each other. She reached for the steak knife just as Mike started to hand it to her, handle first. "Thank you." She rolled her eyes and sighed. "This is silly."

Mike took a bite of his salad, trying to suppress his amused grin. "What is?" he asked obtusely around a mouthful.

"Us being so cordial. Can we just get past that neither one of us wants the other here and just deal with it?"

"You don't want me here?" Mike asked still chewing, still goading. Why did he keep doing that? He could see she was getting aggravated and he wanted to laugh but he kind of felt bad too; under different circumstances he'd already be trying to get her into bed.

Jenna smirked. If he would stop acting like a jerk she would enjoy every moment of him staying there. She would love to look at him all week long and maybe even have a little fun flirting with him too, but he obviously didn't look at her as anything other than a nuisance.

"I'm just saying." She leaned forward, her elbows resting on the table. "You have a job to do and didn't expect me here and I'm trying to have a relaxing little vacation and I certainly didn't expect I'd be sharing the house with an FBI agent."

Mike swallowed and put down his fork, replacing it with his beer. "Listen, kid, I can deal if you can. I'm not going to get in the way of your vacation. Do all the things you would normally do. Read a book, go kayaking, go to the beach, hell, go skinny-dipping in the pool for all I care." He gave her a little grin before taking a big bite of his steak.

Jenna smirked again. *Kid?* She'd change his tune about *that*. "Thanks, I think I know what to do with my vacation time, and by the way I happen to thoroughly enjoy skinny-dipping." She watched his smug look turn slack and watched as his eyes traveled away from her face to peruse her body. Ha! Score one for Jenna!

Mike got the steak down his throat and swore to himself. He was toast if he came out to the pool and saw her naked; it was going to be bad enough to see her swimming in that bikini. He would have to swim at the beach if he needed to cool off; he decided he would spend as little time at the house as possible. Rather than comment on *her* comment he continued to eat and just stared at her.

Jenna stared back challengingly; she wasn't going to let this larger than life man intimidate her. His stupid good looks weren't helping but she was determined to let him know how tough she could be too and that she was no kid! She cocked an eyebrow up at him and took a bite of steak. It tasted really good considering she hadn't eaten since the grapes in the car.

"This is good," she relented after she swallowed. "Thank you."

"You're welcome; the salad is good too, thank *you*." Mike took another long pull on his beer and sat back in his chair. Maybe they could be friends. He didn't want it to be uncomfortable for either of them all week; after all, it was her grandmother's house and Rafe had pulled a big favor for him to be there. Mike supposed he should start being a little more gracious. It wasn't like he planned on making the moves on her or anything.

"So where would you be right now if you weren't here?" He opted for small talk; small talk was safe. Thinking of her skinny-dipping was not. But his damn thoughts were stuck there still.

Jenna put down her fork and took a sip of her drink. "Home in Boston or Newport, which is where I went to school and spend most of my summers, but

I needed a change of scenery this summer."

Mike nodded. "Newport, huh?" He'd never been. "What's it like there?"

"It's beautiful. I have family nearby. My cousin Paige is living there for the summer and her family live in the next town. We spend a lot of time together." Jenna couldn't wait to talk to Paige and find out what happened at dinner with Justin tonight. She sure hoped it was more exciting than her own.

"Rafe and Ali's wedding isn't for three weeks so why did you come so early?" Mike knew he was prying, but he was interested in her response.

Jenna studied him, wondering if she should open up to him. He seemed genuinely interested so she went for it. "I just broke up with my boyfriend. I was with him for a year, and caught him with another chic." She picked up her drink and waited for his reaction.

"Were you in love with him?" Mike asked pointedly.

Jenna looked at him, surprised at the blatant question. He was looking at her so seriously that she found herself thinking hard about the answer. "No, I don't suppose I was." Humph, what do you know? One penetrating look from a stranger and the truth comes out. "I guess it was more of a bruised ego type of deal." And the fact that I regrettably gave myself to him, she thought.

"I can understand that." Mike nodded slowly. "You put your trust in someone, and it hurts when they betray you, plain and simple."

Jeez, it didn't feel plain and simple at the time but he was right. "Yeah, in hindsight I should have seen it coming. That's what gets me the most, I knew deep down from the beginning he wasn't worthy. I guess I got caught up in his minor celebrity and the fun we were having hitting all the clubs. He's a DJ, a pretty popular one around town you know?"

Mike smirked, feeling a stab of jealousy that he immediately shook off. What the fuck? She was a mere girl. "Sounds like a player." He could just picture the punk.

Jenna grinned back. "I suppose it takes one to know one." She could only imagine the women Mike had at his disposal.

Mike shot her a reprimanding look. "Do I look like a player to you?"

"Whoa! Do you ever!" Jenna laughed. "Have you looked in the mirror lately? You're ridiculous!"

Mike frowned, affronted, leaning forward with his beer. "*Ridiculous?*" He'd never been called that!

Jenna laughed, a little embarrassed, but screw it, she could be honest; he wasn't interested anyway. "Ridiculously *good-looking!*"

Mike's frown quickly turned upside down. He beamed and gave her a genuine smile then sat back again giving his chair a little spin back and forth. "Well, thank you, sweetheart, that's awfully nice of you to say." And he had to admit he liked hearing it from her.

Jenna rolled her eyes. "As if you aren't aware."

"Hey, I'm no wall flower I'll admit." Mike held up his palms, grinning. "But hearing you give me a compliment is pretty nice considering I think you're pretty ridiculously good-looking yourself." Damn hot was what she was.

Ignoring how *that* made her feel, Jenna smirked and pointed out, "But still too young for you, remember?" Now wait a minute, he just said he thought she was pretty *again*, that's twice now, *ridiculously good-looking* was what he said—if she were going to quote him.

"Yup." Mike picked up his beer and finished it. Shit, she was really stuck on that age comment.

"Well anyway, I'm sure nobody is out there cheating on you!" Jenna stood up to clear the table.

"Hey."

Jenna stopped what she was doing, surprised at the serious tone of his voice, the skin-tingling huskiness of it. She looked over at him and felt her heart trip when she met his eyes.

"That dude was an ass to cheat on someone like you; it definitely wasn't because he found someone more beautiful or likable. It was just because he's obviously an asshole. Don't make the mistake of thinking it had anything to do with you." Mike swiveled in his chair and looked out toward the bay. He would have treated Jenna like gold given the chance.

Jenna just stared at Mike's profile. *Wow*, someone like her? Beautiful and likable? "Thanks for saying that," she said somewhat shyly and gathered up what she could from the table. She walked into the house, feeling really confused about Mike. He certainly had his moments where she could totally see herself going for him, but he was also making it clear that he wasn't interested.

Mike stood after a moment, shaking some distracting thoughts from his head, and cleared what was left on the table then followed Jenna into the kitchen. He came up behind her petite form at the sink and reached around her to put the last plate in.

Jenna turned, startled that Mike was so close, and found herself inches away from his solid mass of chest. She looked up and found he was looking down at her intently. Their eyes met and held and Jenna felt the air between them crackle with tension, the good kind—the really, really good kind. She turned away first and muttered a thank-you. Holy shit, what was that about? He looked like he was going to…kiss her! Oh boy!

Mike closed his eyes. *Oh fuck*. "I'm going to bed. Good night, Jenna." He left the kitchen quickly before she could say anything and shut the door behind him when he got to his room. For some reason he wanted to call Rafe and give him hell but it really wasn't Rafe's fault that Jenna was there a week early. Mike was just screwed.

Jenna turned again to see Mike's back disappearing behind his door. Well, that was abrupt, she thought. Jeez, he was weird! She loaded the dishwasher and rinsed the blender. It was eight thirty, for God's sake! Going to bed? What was he, a monk? She walked back to her room, ignoring her body that had heated rapidly despite the coolness of the house, and picked up the phone, smiling at the string of texts from Jake.

G I Joe? didn't u make all

your Barbies have sex with him?

Oh my god! She should never have admitted that, she was never going to live it down. Jenna read his next text.

No, u will nvr lve it dn!

She laughed out loud. God she missed him.

He's sounds great, y leaving?

keep him there honey

you can be Barbie!

Jenna laughed again.

Yes all good shifts, wking my fine ass off

Sting came in for dnnr last nt.

had hm wrapped around my fngr!

wt happnd w/ Paigy and hot tat guy?

call me! xoxoxox J

Jenna dialed Jake's cell and grabbed a beach towel from the bathroom. She was bored and was dying for a swim. She walked through the sliders and back out to the pool, glancing in the direction of Mike's room. She could see the blue light from his TV shadowing the blinds to his room and was glad he wouldn't hear her out there because she in fact did like to go skinny-dipping and fully intended to right after she talked to Jake, only he wasn't answering. Damn it!

She left him a voice mail and placed her phone on the lounge with her towel. With another glance toward Mike's room she daringly slipped off her cover-up and bathing suit and quietly entered the pool by the steps. The water was chilly and she did a few quick laps to warm up. As her body adjusted to the water temperature, she relaxed and thought about what an unexpected first day she'd had. Mike had certainly been a surprise. She had been expecting a little old couple coming back from a round of golf and instead got a life-size action figure pushing all her buttons. She hadn't quite figured him out yet though. The way Nicki described him he was the greatest guy on earth, but he seemed to be going out of his way to make Jenna think he was a jerk. She just didn't get it.

She floated on her back and looked up at the stars. Twilight loomed over the island and there were so many stars brightening the sky. She spotted a shooting star and closed her eyes and smiled as she made a wish. She wished for an exciting vacation and at the same time got a brilliant idea. She thought of who could give her the real deal on Mike and she quietly exited the pool to get her phone.

She dialed the number and waited; on the third ring Ali picked up. "Hey Al, it's me." Jenna went back and sat on the first step of the pool, still naked. She kept an eye on Mike's sliders and was satisfied she could still see the light from the TV. What would she do if he came out and saw her? She grinned just picturing his reaction and felt a thrill race through her body.

Ali smiled and leaned up against the kitchen counter. "Hey, Jenna, what's up?"

"I was wondering if I could talk to Rafe for a minute."

"Sure, let me get him, hold on," Ali shook her head, only imagining what Mike might have done or said to Jenna for Jenna to be calling Rafe. Ali called out to him and held her cell out when he emerged from their bedroom.

He was holding his own cell and whispered to her, "Who is it?"

"*Jenna*," Ali whispered back, grinning.

Rafe shook his head, smirking, and spoke into the phone, "Mike, talk to Ali for a sec."

Ali put a hand over her mouth in disbelief, trying not to laugh as she and Rafe swapped phones. "Hey, Mike!"

"Hey, sexy!"

Ali grinned at Mike's greeting and waved at Rafe as he walked back down the hall to talk to Jenna.

"Hey, Jenna," Rafe greeted. "Ali said you wanted to talk to me?"

Jenna cleared her throat, suddenly nervous; she liked Rafe and hoped he didn't think it was weird that she would call him like this. "I just wanted to ask you a couple of questions about your friend Mike. I know that probably sounds weird but I'm just a bit confused."

Oh brother, here we go. Rafe grinned. "Sure, ask away." Rafe tried to contain his amusement.

"Well," Jenna began, "Nicki couldn't say enough good things about him and don't get me wrong, he's been polite and everything, but he's also a bit standoffish so I was just wondering…" She let her question hang. Now that she was actually about to voice her question out loud, Jenna felt utterly stupid. She realized she'd sound completely conceited if she asked Rafe why Mike didn't seem to like her. Oh God, she was such an idiot!

"Jenna?"

"Yeah, I'm here, just realizing how idiotic this phone call is." She laughed, embarrassed. Rafe was laughing too.

"Jenna, Mike is a great guy, he's everything Nicki said. If he's acting standoffish it's because he's there to do a job and honestly?" Rafe hesitated, then decided, fuck it, he'd have a little fun. Mike could curse him out later. "Mike thinks you're incredibly hot and he's afraid to be in the same house with you. He's says you're a distraction." Rafe laughed again, remembering what Mike had said about her; of course Rafe made sure to give Jenna the G-rated version.

Jenna stood up from the pool step, shocked. "*What?*" she hissed in disbelief. "He told me I was too young for him!"

Rafe chuckled. "Yeah, he acknowledged that you're younger than him, but don't let Cap fool you." Rafe leaned against a door frame. He couldn't believe he was about to play matchmaker, but he would love it if Mike hooked up with Jenna. Mike needed a steady woman in his life and Jenna was perfect for him; they both had the same wise-ass sense of humor. "So, why are you asking anyway, are you interested, Jenna?"

"Umm, *no*. I mean I don't know," she quickly corrected. "I've known him for ten minutes." Jenna hadn't expected Rafe to ask her *that*. "He's incredibly hot, I won't deny it," she said ruefully, "I just didn't think *he* was interested." Until she felt the fireworks going off between them in the kitchen, which kind of led her to this phone call. Now she didn't know what to think.

"Well, trust me when I tell you Mike's a great guy, he'd give you the shirt off his back. I'd trust him with my life." Rafe laughed. "In fact, I have."

Jenna smiled. "Well, I'm glad I called then." Then she worried. "Are you going to tell him I asked about him?" She walked back to the chaise lounge, water dripping from her as she reached for her towel, keeping a close eye on Mike's closed slider doors.

Rafe laughed. "No way! Are you kidding, I'm going to sit back here and wait to hear how this plays out."

Jenna laughed softly and shook her head. "What makes you think something is going to *play out* as you say?"

Rafe laughed again. "Remember, I was on that island too, and look what happened to me."

Jenna smirked. "Rafe, I just met the guy like three hours ago, and he's only here for a week, what could possibly happen?"

"I'm going to let Ali answer that one," Rafe said, grinning as he walked back toward Ali in the kitchen. "Have fun, okay, and I'll see you in a couple of weeks. If you have any more questions about Mike just give me a call, anything you want to know I'll tell you."

Rafe was grinning like a fool as Ali shook her head and mouthed, "You're terrible." She said goodbye to Mike and handed Rafe's cell back to him as he said goodbye to Jenna and handed Ali her phone.

"Hi, Jenna."

"Hi Al, sorry, I hope I didn't interrupt your night."

"Don't be crazy, you know you can call whenever you want."

"Thanks, I appreciate that." Jenna couldn't help but smile, now armed with Rafe's information. "How are the wedding plans, by the way? Do you need me to check on anything while I'm here? And how is the store coming along?"

Ali smiled. Jenna was being polite in asking and Ali appreciated it but she knew Jenna really had other things on her mind, Ali remembered all too well what it was like arriving to Captiva and encountering Rafe for the first time.

"Everything's all set, thanks, just a few last-minute things Rafe and I can handle, and I hope to open the shop when we come back from the honeymoon," Ali answered then added, "Jenna, I know Mike's there to do a job, but I'm sure he'll have a lot of down time too. You should get to know him better, it could be fun at the wedding when you see him again."

"Yeah, I guess it would be. Hey, Ali?" Jenna was feeling giddy all of a sudden and figured if she couldn't share with her own best friend, her sister's would do.

"Yeah?"

"Why the hell didn't you and Nicki tell me how freaking good-looking this guy was when you came home last summer? I mean, oh my God! And have you seen him smile?" Jenna got goose bumps thinking about him just beyond the glass, his big hard body probably lying in bed.

Ali couldn't stop laughing. She *knew* Mike had gotten to Jenna already! "I guess it never came up, we had our own hotties to drool over." Ali gave Rafe the once-over and stifled her laughter when he gave her his own heated look and parted his suit jacket, giving her a glimpse of his holstered gun. Ali cleared her throat. "He is a great-looking guy, that's for sure, I'm sure it won't be too much of a burden sharing Nan's house with him all week." Ali silenced her gasp as Rafe pulled her in flush against him.

Jenna laughed knowingly. "You're right. I think I'll manage just fine." She was already formulating a plan. "Thank Rafe again for the insight. I'll talk to you guys soon."

"Okay, keep us posted." Ali hung up and grinned knowingly at Rafe, who had just hung up with Mike too.

"They're screwed!" The soon to be married couple laughed together.

* * * * *

Jenna nodded her head, grinning satisfactorily. So, Mike was afraid she'd be a distraction, huh? He'd actually admitted that to her earlier but when he had added that she was too young for him Jenna's ego balloon had instantly deflated. But now she knew he was lying to keep her at arm's length. She put her phone down and wrapped her towel tighter around herself. She picked her bikini off the lounge and carefully draped it over the railing leading into the deep end of the pool, if he came out in the morning he would surely see it there and maybe, just maybe, picture her in or out of it! Jenna smiled a Cheshire grin and went back through her sliders, shutting and locking them before heading to the bathroom for a warm shower.

* * * * *

Mike sat up in bed leaning against the headboard, watching TV with the sound down low. Rafe had been no help on the phone at all; he actually found the whole thing humorous and Ali had played at matchmaker trying to tell him how great Jenna was. Mike didn't want to know how great Jenna was; his life was all mapped out. But damn it, he couldn't stop thinking about the sweet, strong-willed, sexy little pint-sized woman on the other side of the house.

He got out of bed feeling restless and opened his sliders. He stepped out on the pool deck and could see instantly that it was wet around the edge of the pool. Mike shot a glance toward Jenna's sliders and realized he must have just missed her swimming. How had he not heard her? He would have been out there like a shot had he known, it's a damn good thing he did. . . . not. His thought fell off as he noticed the pool ladder. Ah, man. Mike walked over to the deep end and picked up three little pieces of material draped over the ladder rail—the bikini Jenna had been wearing all night. It was dry, which meant she hadn't been wearing it swimming. *Oh fuck me.* He looked again toward her door and slowly, instinctively, brought the bottom half up to his face. Oh man. He inhaled and grew instantly hard. This was so not fair, someone was testing his resolve here. *Jenna* was testing his resolve, the little shit.

Mike stood there holding her bikini, reluctant to put it back down, picturing her naked. What would be so wrong if they did hook up? It's not like he couldn't walk and chew gum at the same time; he could do his job and still have a little fun, couldn't he? But all night he'd made her think he wasn't interested. He ran a hand over his chin; he'd have to think about this. Thinking he had a plan, he put her bikini back on the rail and dove into the chilly water, making a loud splash.

He came up for air and hoped she'd heard him. Maybe she'll come back out for a swim, he thought, still *naked.* Ha, wishful thinking. Mike could see her shadow move on the other side of the blinds. Maybe she had heard him. He did a few laps and splashed as loud as he could, keeping an eye out every time he surfaced for air, but his lame plan didn't seem to be working; she wasn't coming out. He stilled in the water when he thought he heard a beeping noise. It was coming from one of the lounge chairs. Mike looked over and saw it was coming from a cell phone, Jenna's obviously, and he grinned.

He stepped out of the pool and took a towel from the bin near Jenna's slider doors and dried his hands. He walked over to the phone and could see she had received a text. He picked up the phone without hesitation to read it.

Message from: Jake

Srry Barbie mssd ur call

busy 2 nt

hows GI Joe, u 2 gttng it on yet?

be hm tmorrow a. m.

Mike laughed. He wondered who Jake was, a friend? a relative? Whoever he was it meant Jenna had mentioned Mike to somebody else besides Nicki—interesting. Mike slicked the water off his hair and dried his face with a towel then walked back into his room with her phone. He set it down and quickly changed out of his wet bathing suit into a pair of cargo shorts. Wearing nothing else he made his way down the hall past the living room and toward her bedroom. When he was outside the door he took a deep breath and knocked softly.

Jenna was running a comb through her hair when she heard him knock. She quickly looked down at what she was wearing. She was bra-less and her thin white tank was completely see-through, especially the parts that were wet from her dripping hair. She wore thin pink pajama short shorts and bare feet and smirked in satisfaction as she went to the door like she was about to make a brilliant chess move.

Mike was about to knock again when the door opened beneath his hand and Jenna stood there before him. Okay, she was definitely testing him here. He laughed in defeat; he couldn't help it. "I give up." He stood taking her in. "Here's your phone. It was out by the pool." He knew he had just addressed the nipples he could so clearly see through her wet shirt but really, what else could he do?

Jenna looked up at him, confused at first by his short laugh and the words that followed but then she noticed where his eyes rested. Admittedly it had been her goal to turn him on, to *distract him,* but she didn't expect *him* to be shirtless and looking like some Roman God. Her eyes traced the tattoo that covered one muscular shoulder and part of his defined chest and she felt herself grow instantly hot. She looked up at his face and his eyes were still averted, this time a little further down, and Jenna became fidgety, wishing she had put on a robe before answering the door. She suddenly felt as though she were dangling a piece of raw meat in front of a hungry lion. Her eyes roamed as his did and rested on his low-slung shorts but just as quickly she darted her gaze back to his face. Ho boy!

"Thanks," Jenna managed to squeak out taking her phone from him and feeling a dazzling jolt of electricity as their fingers touched with the hand-off.

Mike's next move was definitely not thought out but instinctive. He stepped into the room, looking down at Jenna hungrily. She stumbled back a few steps automatically but when he moved slowly toward her again she stayed put. "You aren't making this easy," he growled softly. He took a deep breath and reached his hand around to the back of her head, bringing her close enough to him so that he could bend his head to press his lips to hers. She didn't resist at all, which prompted him to part her willing lips with his tongue and taste her. Oh man, her lips were nice. Mike kissed her briefly and pulled back to see her reaction. Her eyes were closed, lips slightly parted, and she held just the slightest grin, causing him to smile. The little shit had been expecting this to happen! He chuckled softly and closed the distance between them again. He kissed her a little more aggressively this time and groaned when her tongue mated with his.

Jenna was reeling inside. Special Agent Mike was *such* a great kisser! Oh my God, he's done this a few thousand times before! She brought her arms up around his neck and had to stand on her tip toes to do it, he was so much taller than her. She felt his large arms encompass her waist and next thing she knew her feet were dangling off the floor and he was holding her effortlessly against his body while he kissed her. She felt light as a feather in his arms.

Mike held Jenna pressed against him close, just where he'd wanted her as soon as he'd set eyes on her. He felt her soft breasts and hardened nipples on his bare chest through the thin material she wore and he brought his hands down to rest on her sweet little ass. He felt her long legs come up and wrap around his waist and *oh yeah*, he was hard as granite. He found himself walking them slowly toward her bed. Jenna's arms were still around his neck and Mike heard the thud of her phone as it dropped from her hand and hit the floor. Jesus, he hadn't intended for this to happen but when she'd opened the door and was barely dressed with her hair all wet and dripping down her shirt, he couldn't resist her another minute.

He continued to hold her bottom with one hand as he maneuvered the other around to caress her breasts; they were utter perfection and he wanted more, needed more. He pulled back from their smoldering kiss and looked her in the eye. He could see the desire there and knew his own eyes were searing with it. "You're gorgeous, Jenna." She was so petite in his arms too, and he just wanted to keep her there.

Jenna looked into Mike's brilliant blue eyes and saw the fire there that she had been deliberately playing with. Now she wasn't quite sure she could handle a man as virile and imposing as him and she began to feel just a little bit nervous.

Mike saw it flash quickly in her eyes. It only lasted a second but the uncertainty he saw had him taking a deep breath and gently setting Jenna down on the bed.

Jenna looked up at him. Oh God, her body was taut and her breasts burned beneath her tank top from his touch. She wanted him fiercely but he was such a big guy! It was intimidating and she was nervous all of a sudden. She'd only ever had sex with her ex-boyfriend and if she had to guess, Mike was definitely going to out-do him in the size department.

Mike kissed her on top of her head. "I'm sorry, kid, when I saw you standing there I just had to kiss you."

Jenna laughed nervously, "I kissed you back, you know, there's no need to apologize." She was disappointed and relieved at the same time. She wasn't ready for him. He was a force to be reckoned with and she probably deserved to be called a kid.

Mike couldn't hide his obvious desire for her and now that she was sitting down in front of him it was basically in her face, so he sat down next to her on the bed. "Well, I guess I'm not really sorry." He laughed softly and stroked her cheek with the back of his hand. "I just don't want you to think I was taking advantage of the situation."

"What situation is that?" He clearly wasn't getting that she was into him too, and that she was just a chicken.

"You know, that we're both under the same roof, I'm a guy... and you"—he paused and smiled—"look like you do." A goddess—a mirage that any stranded man would conjure up a thousand times on a deserted island.

Jenna laughed softly and tried to sound as seductive as she could. "How do you know *I* wasn't taking advantage of the situation?"

Mike looked at her intently, weighing that question for all of two seconds. "Because this night would be ending a whole lot differently." She may have teased him into this room but that timid look in her eye let him know who was really in charge here.

Jenna swallowed the frog in her throat, meeting his serious eyes. "Oh." What had she been thinking trying to seduce him?

Mike studied her, wanting desperately to kiss her again. She had definitely returned his kiss but when it started to heat up he had felt her withdraw. She'd been nervous, like... like she was... oh damn! "Jenna, did you and your boyfriend..." He paused. "I mean, was he your first?"

Oh great! He was totally on to her! Color quickly shaded her face.

"That's none of your business!" she said defensively, leaping off the bed. "Just because I'm not going to jump right into bed with you doesn't mean I'm inexperienced, okay? We just met, for God's sake!" Oh God, how mortifying!

Mike stood up, too, at her defensive words. "Okay, okay," he said softly, holding up his hands. Shit, she was a babe in the woods when it came to sex. "I didn't expect you too. I'm sorry. It was my fault. I got a little carried away."

"Will you please stop apologizing, I was here too!" Now she was just humiliated and she turned her back on him, facing the sliders and wishing she could hide under her covers. "Maybe we should both just go to bed." Huh! Poor choice of words, she thought and rolled her eyes.

Mike walked over to her and placed his hands on her shoulders, feeling them stiffen under his touch. He wished liked hell he could start all over again and he bent to kiss her on the cheek. "Good night, kid."

Jenna felt a wealth of sensitivity in that one small kiss to the cheek and felt her eyes sting. "*Good night.*" She couldn't even get mad and yell that she wasn't a kid, because she was. He had just proven that she was indeed an *inexperienced* kid. She would have made a complete fool of herself if she had tried to do anything more with him. Jeez, just the way he'd kissed her was like having sex. With all his experience he'd probably be bored to death with her anyway. Oh, for the love of God why hadn't she just come to the island when she was supposed to?

CHAPTER THIRTEEN

"Ready to go up?"

"Sure." Paige took the hand Justin held out to her and felt her heart skip anticipating more great sex like they'd had in the wee hours of just that morning. But she couldn't help feeling a bit nervous too.

"There's a new toothbrush in the top drawer of the vanity, and towels and cloths are on the top shelf of the closet if you need them. I'm gonna go lock up. Just make yourself at home."

"Thanks." Paige gave Justin a little smile as he left the room then she went inside the bathroom to prepare for bed. She shut the door behind her and faced the mirror smiling, trying not to make too much of Justin's suggestion that she make herself at home. But she was happy, really happy.

She used the bathroom as intended, used the new toothbrush she found and finger combed her hair. She was about to leave the bathroom still dressed as she was when she spotted one of his T-shirts hanging on the back of the door. Well, she thought, he said she could sleep in one of his T-shirts so why not? She stripped and put his T-shirt on.

Paige felt ridiculously awkward once she re-entered Justin's room. She went over to his bed to wait feeling rather vulnerable and rethinking the T-shirt. Should she get under the covers? Or just sit on top? She chose to peruse his book shelf instead. There were lots of books about tattoos on the built-in bookcase as well as industry trade magazines for tattoo artists. There were several books on fixing up old homes and one about how to train your new Lab puppy. Paige smiled at that one. There were also a few nice oversized hardcovers on the history of Newport and lots of paperbacks that were either mysteries or crime related, some of which Paige had read too. She loved that he was a reader like herself.

"Hi."

Paige turned, startled when she heard Justin re-enter the room. She was momentarily speechless looking at him. He wore just his jeans unbuttoned at the waist and stood standing in his bare feet. She didn't think she could ever get sick of looking at his ink-covered body or the sexy muscles that showed them off so well. She couldn't stop staring. "You like to read."

"I do." *Wow!* His whole body pulsed to life and he smiled looking her over. "You look sexy as hell in my shirt. You take my breath away, Paige."

Paige felt her cheeks get hot and her pulse quicken. Breathing suddenly seemed harder. "Thanks, I hope you don't mind. You shirt's pretty comfy, I might have to steal it." Oh God, *he* took *her* breath away!

Mind? Hell no. Justin spoke softly. "C'mere."

Paige crossed the room and stood before him. "Hi." The buzz of the alcohol had completely worn off but she was buzzing with excitement and adrenaline now.

"Hi," he chuckled. "I had fun with you tonight."

"I had fun too, thank you for dinner."

"You're welcome." His fingers found the hem of the T-shirt as he bent to kiss her and they slowly moved up underneath the cotton. He felt the smooth skin of her hips under the shirt and continued to travel upward until his thumbs were on the underside of her large breasts. With his hands splayed across her back, he rubbed the pads of his thumbs across the thin material of her bra and felt her nipples turn to tight little points. His cock strained persistently against his jeans and Justin groaned in pleasure against Paige's mouth when she rubbed against him.

Paige molded her body into Justin's and deepened their kiss. His hands were manipulating her breasts and nipples expertly and she let out a breathy sigh. "You have really nice hands."

Justin laughed softly and slid them down further. "And you have an exquisite body that I can't keep my hands off of." He kissed her neck and bit an earlobe as he lifted his T-shirt off of her and stood back. She wore a black see-through bra and matching see through panties. *"Wow, Paige,"* he breathed. "You look good enough to eat. I really like these." He walked around her and ran a hand along her backside as he did. She had a great back side and Justin admired it before coming around to face her again. He stared down in front of her and admired that view too. The sweet smooth skin he saw through the material made him groan. "I *really* like these."

With his words Paige's face grew flush with desire and a little embarrassment. She felt like she was on display the way he was looking at her. *Good enough to eat? Oh boy!* "I bought them today to wear for you."

"You did?" Justin asked, surprised, looking at her.

"Well, yeah." Paige looked back at him now feeling presumptuous but the look in his eyes gave her quick relief.

"Thank you," he said genuinely. The fact that she'd been thinking of him and wanting to please him struck Justin right in the heart. He gripped the rounded globes of her ass and pulled her hard against him then bent his head to her breast and sucked a nipple right through her new purchase.

Paige groaned. His breath was warm and moist on the thin material and her nipple peaked responsively under his touch. Her hands went to his head automatically and she gripped his hair with her fingers, keeping his head in place and then guiding him to her other breast. Money well spent, she thought as her head fell back and she arched into him.

Justin held her around the waist and squeezed and played with her breasts with his free hand. She was so beautiful and he couldn't wait to have her naked in his bed. Not wanting to wait another second, he guided her backwards to it and climbed on top of it with her. He laid her head carefully down on his pillow and slowly, appreciatively peeled off her sexy bra and panties. He was as hard as steel as he revealed her fully and he could see she'd taken notice. Justin took her hand and placed it on the hard bulge in his jeans.

Paige gripped him obligingly, eliciting a tortured moan. "Take them off," she whispered.

Justin did so quickly and brought himself down carefully on top of her, placing himself right between her legs. "I want to dive right inside of you, Paige, but I want to devour every inch of you first. I'm going to go real slow and taste every inch of your body with my tongue."

"Oh God," Paige whispered, loving that he once again told her what he was going to do to her and trembling with the thought of it. She was already wet and ready for him as she watched him lower his head to her breasts. His lips and tongue were warm against her bare skin and seeing his hands touch and caress her had her squirming beneath him and trying to make contact with the exquisite erection between his legs. The tattoos across his knuckles and on the backs of his hands were visually stimulating her while his languid touch drove her crazy with need. Her own hands traced over his flexed shoulders and biceps and over the expanse of his taut back as his lips and tongue traversed their way even lower to her belly. Paige shivered under the tickling touch of his wet tongue and she arched shamelessly into him, inviting him to continue.

Her knee was bent to accommodate his large body between hers and when Paige felt his hand press firmly against that knee, dropping it to the bed, she gasped. He was opening her to him as he moved his body even lower still. Paige's hands gripped the soft material of the comforter tightly on either side in anticipation and then felt Justin's warm breath suddenly at her opening. *Oh God*, he would find out how wet she was now for sure! Paige had only been in one relationship that lasted three years and her ex had *never* once kissed her here, no one had! She nearly came knowing Justin was about to.

Justin couldn't believe Paige's body and how she was responding to just his touch. He just wanted to plunge deep inside of her but he needed to taste her first. He'd been dying to since the night before. He loved that she was silky smooth to the touch and that he could see so clearly everything he wanted to taste. She smelled so damn sweet, so edible and her warm pink opening was already so slick and ready for him; he was in heaven.

Using both hands he parted her plump folds with his thumbs and moaned in pleasure at the sight before he eagerly brought his lips there. She was so pink and pretty and he kissed her lightly, finding her hidden sweet spot and smiling against her when she responsively bucked her hips right up into his face. *Oh yeah*, let me please you, baby! Justin continued lightly kissing and licking the taut little nub, just teasingly at first with the tip of his tongue, playfully darting in and out around the sensitive flesh. He could feel Paige's body begin tensing beneath him in response and could hear her quiet moans of pleasure. She was close and sensing her need Justin pressed his lips more firmly against her so he could suck that tender, swollen piece of flesh between his lips and tongue. The tip of his tongue continued to make tiny circular motions over the small blood-engorged flesh over and over again as he kept a steady suction with his lips. His hands kneaded her heaving breasts greedily as he laved her and delighted in her soft sweet moans. *Oh fuck, yeah!*

He could do this all night, he thought, just tasting Paige and drinking her in. She was squirming fitfully beneath him and pulling on his hair which made him smile against her and only encouraged him more. He took turns alternately entering her hot wet opening with his tongue, drinking in what dripped there and then sucking on her swollen clit. He spread her legs further apart and kissed every blessed womanly part of her. He couldn't get enough of her and he slipped two exploring fingers deep inside her while he continued to suck and lick. Fueled by her body's reaction Justin now knew just where she was sensitive and how much pressure to apply, and he continued tasting her in a deliberate, steady rhythm until he was rewarded with her orgasm. He felt Paige's whole body stiffen before her release. She didn't just cry out, she screamed his name and when she did Justin yelled out loud with her, gripping her inner thighs, spreading them even wider still as he covered her ready entrance with his mouth, lapping up the warm sweet liquid that flowed generously there. His eyes were open, watching her in awe, his cock harder than he could physically stand as she continued to buck violently beneath his mouth and writhe crazily in his hands. *Holy shit!* She pulled the hair on his head hard and continued to buck sporadically until he'd licked all her juices away and finally he lowered her hips back to the bed.

"Ahhhhh!" Paige's eyes were sealed shut and she was breathing heavily, her body completely depleted. She felt Justin's sinful lips on her inner thighs, kissing her quivering muscles and feeling his large hands smooth over her taut skin, further electrifying every nerve ending in her body. She felt the weight of him suddenly on top of her and she dared to open her heavy-lidded eyes. What he had just done to her had stolen her mind, possibly her soul, she couldn't think, she could only try to catch her breath. She focused her eyes on his and could see the hunger and desire in them. "*Justin,*" she whispered hoarsely.

He looked down at her and laughed softly. "Are you okay there?"

Paige shook her head no and managed to smile. "I think I'm dead and you're my heaven." She laughed too, albeit a little embarrassed, then sighed. "Well, I can now check *that* off my list." She closed her eyes again, too embarrassed to see his reaction.

Justin chuckled but was taken aback. *What?* She had to be kidding. "Paige?" He touched her cheek softly, prompting her to open her eyes. "That wasn't already checked off?"

Paige shook her head. "Nope." She laughed quietly, feeling a bit vulnerable lying naked beneath him. He was poised to enter her, fully and probably painfully erect. He'd taken the time to please her first and my God had he succeeded.

What? Lucky him! "Wow, you didn't mention that your ex-boyfriend was actually gay," Justin said sarcastically with a frown, eliciting a burst of laughter from Paige. Justin could not comprehend at all that he'd been the first to orally please her! Her ex was clearly a schmuck.

"I'm a lucky guy, Paige," Justin said more seriously with a smile. "I feel honored that you let me be the first." He looked at her again in shock. "So *no one? Ever?*"

Paige's body still shook with laughter from his first comment and she shook her head no again and grinned. "Sad at twenty-nine, I know."

Justin sat up beside her, ignoring his aching cock, and started stroking her sensitive flesh again. "You liked it right?"

Paige gasped under his touch, her nerve endings still tingling. "Oh... yes." *Oh God!* Her body was still trying to recover.

"Well good, because I'll want to do that to you all the time if you'll let me."

Paige smiled up at him happily, "I think it's now my new favorite past time, so feel free." And knowing he wanted more thrilled her to no end.

Justin laughed and kept stroking her. He positioned himself beside her and rested his head in his hand. "I'm going to make you come again Paige. I have to taste you again, I'm addicted." He kissed her neck. "You taste so damn sweet, Paige; I can't get enough of you." And he was damn glad no one else had ever had a taste of her or she might not be in his bed right now.

His blunt words had her opening herself to him and her hand impatiently found his hard length. Paige held Justin's thickened cock and stroked him, softly at first, matching the rhythm with which he stroked her. His finger rubbed over her on just the right spot and with just the right pressure, and soon Paige felt her whole body tightening again. All her nerve endings danced beneath her skin, and her muscles contracted automatically, prolonging the pleasure that shot through her until she felt her explosive release. It came in electrified spasms, leaving her body weak and spent once more. My God he was good! Paige felt him come away from her side and then Justin's lips were on her once again just as he'd declared, his tongue lapping the warm liquid that spilled from her. She heard him moan as he drank her in and felt the after-shocks of her orgasm rock her, like fireworks bursting under her skin. She was gone.

Justin couldn't wait anymore and he positioned himself between Paige's thighs grasping her hands as he finally buried himself deep inside of her. Her blue eyes were on him, bright and wide as he moved inside of her methodically. Oh yes, this is what he'd been waiting for. Her heat sheathed him like a blanket and he never wanted to leave her warmth.

Paige intertwined her fingers with Justin's as he raised her hands above her head all the while moving in and out of her and watching her face. She had never wanted a man more and she was overwhelmed with her desire for him. The sex wasn't as frantic and wild as it had been the night before but it was just as good. Justin was definitely taking his time with her tonight. He seemed to be making it all about her pleasure and Paige couldn't remember feeling more desired. The way his eyes lingered over hers had her believing there was something much more than great sex happening between them and she hoped to her soul that there was.

Justin loved pleasuring Paige and watching the way she looked at him. He couldn't believe that after only two days he'd already been in her bed and now here she was in his and it felt so right, like they belonged together. As crazy as it seemed, she was already special to him and Justin wanted her to know it, to feel it.

He increased his momentum and felt Paige reciprocate. Her arms went around his back and pulled him down flush against her. She was so tight around his shaft and she felt so fucking great that it was taking all of his self-control to make it last.

Their bodies were in perfect sync, him thrusting inside her and her thrusting back at a pace that had them both panting heavily and sweat beading their skin. Paige was so glad that Justin was comfortable not wearing protection, he felt so good, bare as he was inside of her. She could see in his face as he hovered over her that he was about to come and when his body finally went rigid above her and he shouted her name, Paige clenched her inner muscles around him and felt his liquid heat invade her body and soul.

"Ahhhh!" Justin groaned out loud and collapsed against her, kissing her neck, her ears, and her lips. She was like no other woman he'd ever been with and his chest felt full as he held her to him.

Paige hugged Justin back and relished the feeling of him still inside of her. He was still hard and she could feel him throb every now and again as they lay there. "Thank you," she whispered into his ear. She'd been thoroughly pleasured, he'd spoiled her with orgasms and Paige knew he'd done it purposefully.

Justin kissed her and kept kissing her, he just wanted to keep them connected. He smoothed the hair back from her face and held her head in his hands while his lips memorized her own and his tongue claimed hers. The way she kissed him back and moved beneath him had him responding inside of her mere moments later, she turned him on so damn much.

Paige was surprised when Justin started to slowly pump inside her again, their kissing became more passionate as if they both knew this time around would be more like the previous night, hot and wild. Paige wrapped her legs around his hips again and pulled him in deeper with each thrust, hearing him groan in pleasure each time he entered her.

Justin couldn't believe he was hard again. When Paige wrapped herself around him and thrust back into him hard, he knew this time around she wanted it just like he did. He slid out of her fast, stood, and had her draped over the bed and on her stomach in two quick movements. He pushed himself back inside of her from behind and kept driving into her fast, his hands gripping her ass and pulling her back to slide over the length of him. Her hands gripped the bedspread and her toes pushed off the floor gaining the leverage she needed to push back against him. She was giving it back to him as good as she got and Justin loved it. "Oh Jesus, Paige, I'm going to come again." His hands gripped the sides of her hips and he held himself still as another hot blast shot right out of him and flowed deep up inside her yet again. *Oh fuck, yes!*

Paige felt herself finally go limp and she whimpered where she lay on the bed. Oh my God! Could it get any better? She felt Justin drape himself on top of her and she smiled as he breathed heavily against her back. She never knew sex could be this freaking great! "Oh my God, Justin," she breathed aloud from underneath him.

Justin left the warm cavern of Paige's body and turned her over; she sat up on her elbows and smiled at him. He was the happiest guy in the world right now just looking at her. "Stay right here." He went into the bathroom, cleaned himself off, and returned with a towel for her. He gently dried her then pulled her off the bed to hold her in his arms. He kissed her softly and ran his hands down the sides of her body. "This body is going to be the death of me. I can't remember the last time I came two times in a row."

Paige laughed. "Lucky me!" Her arms were around his neck and she looked up into his eyes. "Not to give you a big ego or anything"—she watched his eyebrows rise anticipating what she would say—"but sex with you is the greatest sex I've ever had in my life."

"Really?" Justin grinned happily. "I was about to say the same thing to you." He kissed the top of her head then bent to pick up the T-shirt he'd stripped her of earlier. He slipped it over her head and she put her arms through, wrapping them around his neck once again.

"Seriously, Paige, I don't know why you chose my shop, but I'm glad you did." Justin looked down and smoothed a hand over her tattoo under the hem of his T-shirt. "We're pretty good together for two people that just met, huh?"

Paige smiled and felt her heart swell; she nodded, not trusting herself to speak, and they stood like that for what seemed like a long time. He moved his hands slowly over her skin, just caressing her. Paige watched him do it and felt a swarm of butterflies in her stomach. She smiled to herself thinking she had them on the inside and on the outside. "I'm glad I came into the shop too," she whispered back. She didn't dare tell him she thought perhaps his shop sign was a sign of fate.

Justin kissed her on the lips, giving her a smile, then bent to put his jeans back on. "I'm hungry again, are you?"

Paige laughed at his relentless energy. "I guess I could eat something. What do you have?" He was fun too.

"Well, let's go see, gorgeous!" He grabbed her hand and pulled her along to the back stairs and down into the kitchen. Once there Sam perked right up and demanded to be set free. "We knew that was going to happen. Just a sec, buddy," Justin told him.

"I'll get him," Paige offered while Justin perused the inside of the refrigerator. She knelt to open Sam's crate and he bounded out in a playful jump right into her arms. "Oh!" she laughed, catching him. "He's excited!"

"Can you blame him?" Justin shot her a wicked grin. "I wanted to jump on you like that too when you opened the door for me tonight."

Paige laughed, loving that he was funny. She hugged Sam to her chest, feeling ridiculously happy.

"How about a turkey sandwich?" Justin suggested.

"Sure, I'll split one with you."

"You got it." Justin fixed them up a sandwich, piled some chips on the plate and grabbed two Sprites from the fridge. "This okay?" He gestured to the can of soda.

"Perfect." She smiled and let Sam down to scamper around her legs.

"You grab the food and drinks, I'll grab the pup." Justin picked up the crate and called to Sam who bounded after Justin's feet, nearly tripping on each step up to the bedroom.

Paige was cracking up watching the puppy try to conquer the stairs but unable to help with her hands full. "Oh, he's too cute! The stairs are too big for him."

"You should see him try to go down, it ain't pretty." Justin whistled and Sam finally made it to the landing, Paige right behind him. Justin set the crate by the bed and put the pup back inside. "Go to sleep."

Paige watched as the puppy plopped back on his blanket with a long sigh, his chin resting between his two front paws. "How pathetic," she laughed.

"Don't let him fool you." Justin threw back the covers and waggled his brows at Paige. "Get in and get comfy."

"We're seriously going to eat chips in bed?" She laughed.

"Yup." Justin stripped out of his jeans and hopped into the bed playfully smacking the mattress with his hand. "And a whole lot more."

Paige grinned and flushed. "You won't hear me arguing." She handed him the plate and a soda, placing her own on the nightstand then joined Justin in the bed. He brought the covers up over their legs and fed her a chip. Paige laughed as she crunched. "Chips before bed are probably not a good idea, we might have nightmares." But it was the best chip she ever tasted.

"Then we'll just have to stay awake all night," Justin teased, taking a bite of the sandwich with a big grin.

CHAPTER FOURTEEN

Mike woke up with a raging hard-on still fresh from the dream he'd been having. Shit, he was glad he would be staking out Scintillo's house on the beach all day, he couldn't be around Jenna. Kissing her last night had been unbelievable—but a big mistake. He had wanted her so badly and still did, which posed a problem. Like she said, she wasn't just going to jump into bed with him and he was only there for the week. While working on trying to apprehend Scintillo, he wouldn't exactly have time for courting Jenna. He would just have to stay the hell away from her and forget about her. It was probably better off for the both of them anyway.

After a cold shower and a quick bite to eat Mike was out the door and crossing the street with his beach and fishing gear, prepared to start his day of surveillance. The small cooler he carried contained his lunch, some sunscreen, and his HK 45; he'd always preferred his own Heckler and Koch to the FBI's standard issue nine-millimeter. He didn't anticipate using anything but the sunscreen.

As he walked toward the beach path he was still thinking of Jenna. Just as he'd feared she'd already become a distraction. Thankfully she hadn't been awake when he was getting ready. He had purposefully tried to be as quiet as he could in the kitchen and as he was leaving. He'd be gone for most of the day and hopefully their paths wouldn't cross when he returned either.

He took the foot path onto the beach and made his way down to the shore continuing to walk several yards until he reached the back of Scintillo's property. He gave it a passing glance as he continued by and noticed the man and very pregnant woman, Scintillo's son-in-law and daughter, drinking their morning coffee on the oversized deck. They all exchanged a polite nod in greeting and Mike kept moving, sighting his spot about thirty feet from their house. It was okay that they were aware of him; he wanted them to think he was just another friendly neighbor—actually their only neighbor. There were no other homes to the right of them beachside, just some gnarled brush and damaged trees from past hurricanes. And the only thing to the left was more beach, across from Tween Waters. The resort wasn't too far up the beach from where Mike planted himself and not too far from where he saw Simmons and

Bealls staked out.

He took the binoculars from around his neck and set them down on his chair. He then prepared his rod with a lure and walked into the water ankle deep to cast. When his line was out he walked back to the sand and inserted the end of the rod into the rod holder on the side of his chair. Rafe had told him where to help himself to all the gear in the garage and Mike had. He appeared to be a guy just about to relax in the sun and do some fishing.

Mike moved the binoculars aside, adjusted his sunglasses and sat back into the sun's rays. All in all this wasn't a bad gig; maybe they'd get lucky and Scintillo would show up today, Mike would have the rest of the week off to fuck around on the island and maybe do a little courting. The voice in his earpiece interrupted his nice thoughts.

"Well, good morning, sunshine, nice of you to join us."

"Fuck you, Simmons, I'm right on time." Mike's eyes darted to the little fishing boat resting off shore at two o'clock from Scintillo's property.

"Yeah well, while you were giving the shower tiles the old soft scrub this morning, a pristine navy and white Four Winns V458 made its grand entrance into the marina."

Nice! Junior had arrived right on schedule. "You know, I saw one of those at the Lauderdale show, that boat is nearly three quarters of a million dollars, fucking beautiful inside too." Mike shook his head continuing to stare out at the fishing boat. "Business must be jammin' in the clubs," he said sardonically.

Simmons gave a snort. "No shit. He and his friends haven't come off it yet though, but Reynolds has the bird's eye from his balcony."

"You think pops is on there?" Mike asked.

"Possible," Agent Reynolds chimed in, "but I don't see him walking off in broad day light do you?"

"Nah, he'll camp out until dark if he's aboard. Let's just hope it's that easy." Mike stood up surprised at a tug on his line so soon, and he reached for his rod. He felt the tension and walked into the water, slowly reeling in, then with a slight jerk he set the hook. Yeah! He could feel the heavy weight on the end of the rod. "Yeah, baby! Get your lenses out boys and see how it's done." Mike reeled the line in and heard the long drawn out whistle in his ear. "It's big whatever it is," he told them.

"No man, it's just right." Simmons whistled again. "Check it out, Bealls, wouldn't you say that's the perfect catch?"

Mike was still reeling in the line and cast a glance off their way. "I can't even see it yet, what the fuck?" Whatever it was; was fighting him. Shit, maybe he had a black tip on there; he'd have to cut the line if so. "I think I just caught us lunch, boys, whatever this is, it's friggin huge. Mike strained to reel it in closer.

"I'll eat that for lunch, dinner too, for that matter."

Mike listened to Simmons laugh and could hear Bealls laughing in the back-round as well. What the hell? Then he heard Simmons whistle again long and low and Mike knew they were not referring to Mike's fish. He chuckled, catching on, and turned to his right thinking he'd see some babe from Tween Waters on the sand nearby but there was no one there. He looked to his left and felt the rod slip from his hands as the large fish on the end got the best of him at the same time Mike spotted Jenna. She was walking toward him, dressed only in yet another skimpy bikini and a see-through skirt barely low enough to cover her. . . . shit! Mike turned and had to lunge for the rod before the fish swam away with it. He grabbed it and gave it a tug realizing the damn fish had got away. He was now wet to his chest as he made his way out of the water, checking his earpiece as he went. Unfortunately he could still hear Simmons and Bealls laughing in his ear, aware that he had lost the fish, and he muttered an expletive for their behalf. He exited the water with the rod; his T-shirt soaked through, and reached his chair just as Jenna approached. Putting the fishing rod down, he slipped his T-shirt over his head laid it over the back of his chair to dry and turned to face her. "Hi."

Jenna had seen Mike come out of the water and was surprised. She didn't expect to see him on the beach at all and had thought he'd be out spying or investigating or doing whatever he was on the island to do. She had almost laughed when she saw what had happened with his rod and wondered if she had distracted him. She hoped so. "Hi, having a little trouble there?" She grinned, looking down at the rod he had dropped on the sand beside his chair.

Mike took her in, the tanned, toned, just about naked whole of her. "Yeah, I had something huge on there, wrong test, the line wasn't strong enough." Her hair was down and hung like black silk down her back. His heart rate kicked up a notch or two.

Jenna stared as beads of salt water careened down, Mike's bare muscled chest, his body was ripped. Her breasts tingled, thinking of his touch the night before and she felt herself grow warm at the memory. "Probably a black tip." She dared to look up at his face and was grateful he was wearing sunglasses—until he took them off.

Mike watched Jenna take him in and felt his body respond yet again to her, seeing that look in her eyes. "Where are you going?" He took his sunglasses off and returned her heated gaze.

Jenna tried but failed to avoid his eyes. They captured and held her own. But it was the low deep undertone in his voice that made her shiver. "Walking up to the resort, what are you doing?" Her voice held its own husky tone.

Mike could hear Simmons in his ear running a steady commentary on Jenna's attributes and he swiftly disengaged his earpiece. "I'm just doing some fishing. What are you going to the resort for?" He for some reason didn't like that idea very much.

Jenna felt stark naked under his stare. "I have an appointment for a massage in half an hour."

"Like that?" Mike looked her up and down, not hiding his assessment.

Jenna smiled sweetly. "Actually no, I'll be nude for the massage." She watched in amusement as his brows rose.

"Who's massaging you?" Why did he care and why did he sound jealous even to his own ears? He had to send her on her way, she was driving him nuts. He saw the smirk on her face and knew he was busted.

"What's it to you?" Jenna felt a modicum of satisfaction at his possessive tone.

Mike wanted to kiss the smirk right off her mouth but sat down in his chair instead engaging his earpiece once again. "Nothing, kid, go have a nice massage." He slipped his sunglasses back on and turned his head up to the sun trying to focus on anything but someone else's hands all over Jenna's body.

Jenna stood there staring at Mike, not believing he'd just dismissed her. "Good luck fishing, looks like you'll need it." She walked past him in a huff and kept walking, fuming inside and feeling just a little hurt which made her even madder that she found herself caring at how he behaved. She knew one thing; if he called her "kid" one more time he was going to regret it!

Mike kept his eyes on her until he couldn't see her anymore all the while trying to ignore Simmons and Bealls throwing questions at him.

"Fine, I'll just have Reynolds or Murph try to get the 411 on her at the pool."

"On who?" Mike heard Reynolds ask.

"Like hell." Mike stood up, ignoring Reynolds and addressing Simmons from his chair and shooting daggers at the boat. "She's just someone I met, one of the neighbors." He didn't dare mention she was under the same roof as him; he'd never hear the end of it.

"There was so much heat between the two of you we thought the sand was going to catch fire. Are you sleeping with her already, Caplan? You've only been here two days, for Christ's sake."

"Negative, like I said just a neighbor." Mike swore under his breath.

"Uh-huh."

He heard them laughing again and told them where to go. Shit, Jenna had got him all riled up and he had to shake it off. He glanced back at Scintillo's only to find it quiet. "What's happening over there, Reynolds?"

"Junior and his crew left the boat a few minutes ago, looks like they were headed pool side."

A few minutes later Murph spoke up. "I'm here. Junior and friends are settling in by the bar. There are three other guys, and three women besides him, not hard to look at either." He laughed. "I'm at twelve o'clock from the bar. There's no shortage of beautiful women over here by the way, you should see the island girl that just walked by me, she's probably young enough to be my kid, but hot damn!"

Mike rolled his eyes, knowing it was an apt description for Jenna, Jesus, this was supposed to be an easy job this week.

"Long dark hair and wearing nothing but an itsy-bity bikini and tiny little sarong?" Simmons chuckled.

"Yeah, how did you know?" Murphy asked, sounding impressed.

"*Sarong,* Simmons? Really?" Mike shook his head in disgust, wishing like mad he could switch places with Murphy.

"Ask Cap, apparently that's his neighbor." Simmons laughed, ignoring Mike. "I'm suddenly reminded of another pretty boy agent and his friendly island neighbor. Does Daniels do this on purpose? Hey Bealls, you ought to get on Daniels good side, maybe he'll hook you up too."

"Shut up Simmons," Mike told him and took his sandwich from the cooler. It was way before lunch but he was starving besides he needed to sink his teeth into something!

"Is she really your neighbor, Cap?" Murphy asked. "What is she doing up here?"

"Getting a massage," Mike said around a mouthful. Why was Jenna now the topic of conversation? They should all be concentrating on Scintillo. Now she was distracting all of them!

"A massage?" Simmons asked and went on to tell them all in detail what he would do as her massage therapist.

Mike wanted to throttle Simmons and wished he had never agreed to this assignment. "What's Junior doing now?" he interrupted irritably.

"They're just hanging out, the bar just opened and they just ordered their first round." Murph had his heels up on the chair in front of him and he turned a page on the newspaper he pretended to be reading. He could go for a cold beer himself.

"Well, here's a surprise, fellas," Reynolds chimed in from his spot overlooking the marina. "I've got movement on the Four Winns." He took continuous digital shots with his camera from his balcony and e-mailed them to Daniels right away. Daniels would have someone put them in the database and make an ID. "Woman, blonde, Miami tan, fifty-something I'd say, and heading up on deck with a Bloody Mary."

"Sounds like my kind of woman," Simmons joked.

"This broad would chew you up and spit you out Simmons; she's definitely been around the block if you know what I'm saying." Reynolds kept taking pictures.

"All the better, my ex-wife never left our street never mind explored other neighborhoods if you know what I'm saying." Simmons laughed.

Mike shook his head; these old guys had no clue when it came to women. Rather than get sucked into the ridiculous conversation, he busied himself fixing his rod and remained patient on the beach. He was starting to cook though and wished he had remembered an umbrella. He slathered on more sunscreen.

"Okay, the blonde is driving the Four Winns out of the slip and heading north." Reynold's informed the team. "That's all you, Bealls, cover from the Gulf side and I'll head down to the Pursuit." Reynolds told them he'd follow the Four Winns on the bay side. He heard the fax warm up and spit out paper as he prepared to leave.

"Got a make and model yet?" Simmons asked Reynolds and Mike could hear Bealls start the engine and watched as they headed north.

"Technology at its best, Daniels just sent it over." Reynolds picked up the fax sheet and read. "Goes by the name Cherry Silver, ex-stripper from Scintillo's gentlemen's club on Ocean. Name on her driver's license, Cheryl Baroni, born September 1955."

"Interesting. All right, we're headed back that way," Simmons said. "Cap you're on your own."

"I'll be here, got me a black tip to catch." Mike would enjoy not having Simmons in his ear for the next hour or so. He settled back in his chair and finished the sandwich he had started, wondering what part of Jenna's body was getting massaged and about the hands that were doing it.

CHAPTER FIFTEEN

Jenna thanked her masseuse and left the spa, walking back out to the pool area on rubbery legs. She had paid for the massage and tip with her credit card over the phone and now wished she had remembered her wallet to buy herself a drink and maybe sit by the pool for a bit. She loved coming to Tween Waters with Nicki and Paige and hanging out by the pool. She laughed to herself thinking of the time the Hooter's girls were visiting the resort and one of the staff had thought Paige was one of them. She and Nicki had teased her relentlessly for a week, asking Paige to bring them hot wings and pitchers of beer every chance they got.

Jenna decided to just head back via the beach and make herself a drink and some lunch by Nan's pool. She could always come back to the resort later for a frozen drink. She wondered if Mike was still on the beach fishing and her heart did a little dance in her chest at the thought of running into him again. When she was halfway around the pool and nearing the bar she couldn't help but notice the group of guys and girls being somewhat loud and clearly having a good time ten feet in front of her. Their lounges and belongings were scattered about taking up a large area of the pool deck and causing Jenna to have to navigate through them.

"Hi there."

Jenna looked down to see a nice-looking guy about her age looking up at her from one of the lounge chairs. She slowed and smiled. "Hi."

He sat up and straddled the chair extending his hand. "My name's Jay, can I buy you a drink?"

Jenna looked at him and took in his handsome features. He had dark hair that was slicked back off his face as if he'd been swimming, and dark eyes framed by long dark lashes and dark brows. He was smiling at her, revealing a straight row of white teeth that contrasted nicely with his dark tanned skin. His angled jaw line and his defined cheek bones made Jenna think of a large Abercrombie poster she'd seen at the mall, especially when she looked down and saw the rest of his lean toned physique, he reminded her a little of Jake. She glanced at his friends who all seemed to be just as good looking, and she wondered if maybe they weren't all models; they all seemed to be a little on the skinny side, even the guys.

"C'mon, one drink, my friends here all brought their girlfriends and I feel like a fifth wheel. What's your name?"

Jenna took his hand and shook it, somewhat taken aback by his offer; she hadn't been expecting it. "I'm Jenna."

"Hi Jenna. This here is Rob and Becky, over there is James and Kendra and this is Damon and Georgie."

Jenna nodded hello to everyone and took the seat Jay offered her. What the hell? The waitress came by and Jay gave Jenna a coaxing look emitting a smile from her. "Okay sure, I'll have a frozen lemonade please." When the waitress walked away Jay gave her a big grin and she thought he was pretty cute. She imagined not many people turned him down, men or women; he had a charming way about him.

"So where you from, Jenna?"

"I'm from Boston, I'm here on vacation. My grandmother owns a house down the street," Jenna smiled and thanked the waitress when she returned with her drink moments later. "I just came here to get a massage today." She gave a little laugh when she saw his friends turn to look at her.

"Nice," Jay said. "This place is pretty cool. I bring my employees here once in a while for some R & R. These girls here all work in my clubs in Miami."

Jenna smiled politely. His clubs in Miami? He seemed pretty young to own one club, never mind clubs plural. She was starting to get why they all looked like models. "What kind of clubs?"

"You know, dance clubs, bars; that type of club."

"Cool." Jenna sipped her drink.

"I know you're on vacation but if you're interested in making any money I'm always looking for new girls. Matter of fact a girl just took some time off to go home a couple of days ago and I could use someone to replace her. Three nights this week and you'd probably make about seven to eight hundred dollars."

Jenna nearly choked on her drink. "That much? Doing what?"

"Serving, and it's easy, it's all booze, there's no food."

"You're kidding? In three nights?" She wouldn't mind making that kind of money, plus she'd still have all of next week to chill before the wedding. Miami was only two and a half hours from here and she'd always wanted to go. Wait, wait wait, what the hell was she thinking? She couldn't drive back here from Miami after a late-night shift; she'd fall asleep behind the wheel.

"I could set you up in one of the condos above the club, I'm sure the girls wouldn't mind one more roommate for a few nights. They're never all there at the same time anyway, right, girls?" Jay coaxed.

They all agreed, smiling, assuring Jenna in a most friendly way that there was plenty of room.

He'd put her up, why would he do that? "Wow, I appreciate the offer for sure, I'll definitely think about it." She wondered what the girls did for him to garner free room and board.

"If you liked it and wanted more shifts, I'm sure you could pick some up, you'd probably pull in over a grand. I'd love to have you on board, a beautiful woman like you would be an asset to any of my clubs." He gave her his best smile.

Jenna had to admit the idea was titillating. She thanked him, still surprised that someone that looked as young as he did owned nightclubs in Miami. When she pictured nightclub owners she pictured older men that looked like they belonged on *The Sopranos*. Her instincts told her there was much more to his story.

"Well, think about it please, but right now, I want you to enjoy yourself and hang out with us. In a little while we are all heading over to my sister's beach house for a barbeque. Would you like to come?"

"Oh thanks, but I don't think so, I don't even have any clothes with me, I walked here from the beach." Jenna looked down at her barely there attire then at Jay and shrugged.

"No worries, we'll be right on the beach out by the pool, we're all going just like this too and if you want I'll walk you back to your grandmother's house to get what you need to feel comfortable."

Jenna smiled, he was actually quite nice. This might be kind of exciting. "Well, sure then it sounds great." Paige would be proud of her getting right back out there and trying to have fun. Besides these might be the only young people she found to have any fun with. G. I. Joe certainly wasn't going to be a source of fun, he'd made that clear! Jenna put the hotter than hot kiss they'd shared out of her mind.

"Great, we'll finish our drinks and head over." Jay touched his plastic drink cup to hers and drank, smiling at her all the while.

Jenna smiled back and not long after they all left for Jay's sister's house, except Jay's friend Rob who said he'd meet up with them later. Jenna followed them out to the beach and was happy she seemed to have made some new friends.

* * * * *

Mike sat and alternated between watching dolphins meander by and having stare downs with the brazen white heron three feet to his right. The bird had balls, he'd give it that; it stood there waiting patiently just like Mike was, for something to bite on the line. "Doesn't look like it's gonna happen today, bud." Mike spoke to the bird and then shook his head realizing he had just spoken to the bird. He looked at his watch, one o'clock already and he was getting sun stroke. "Murph, Reynolds, give me something, will you."

Reynolds answered first from the Pursuit in the bay. "Simmons and Bealls are lingering around North Cap and Junior's boat is just anchored off the beach there at the pass. Cherry is sunning herself, topless, by the way, and Simmons is bitching to Bealls to take them in closer."

Mike smirked at the visual. "Whadda ya got, Murph?"

"Actually, Junior and friends are just getting up to leave and it seems they've made a new friend."

Mike took a sip of his water. "Yeah? Who's that?"

"It's the island girl, your neighbor."

Mike stood abruptly, spilling his water and nearly knocking his chair over. He looked up the beach toward the resort. He asked Murph calmly, "What is she doing with them?" but inside he was alarmed. Fuck! *What the hell was she doing with them?*

"Well, when she came out of the spa she sat down and had a drink with them, maybe she knows them." Murph reasoned. "She lives here, right?"

Mike ignored the question. "Are they headed back to the marina?"

"No, they're all heading out front toward the parking lot, all but one who's still lounging by the pool."

Mike wished he was up there, God, she better not get in a car with him. He swore under his breath, remembering how she was dressed.

Murph followed the group at a discreet distance and stepped onto the front porch of the resort, busying himself with some tourist guides. "Looks like they're crossing onto the beach and what do you know, they're headed your way, Cap, lucky me I can go back to my room and take a nap."

Mike waded back out to the water with his rod and through his sunglasses, looked for them up the beach. Moments later he saw the group walking toward him. Shit, Jenna couldn't possibly know who Scintillo was and probably thought she was hanging out with some normal people. He wondered what she would do when they came upon him.

As they got closer Mike looked straight ahead and concentrated on his line. When the group was nearly upon him he glanced in their direction.

"Catching anything, dude?" Junior called out to him.

Mike turned, still wearing his glasses, and looked directly at Jenna, who was watching him closely. "No, man, no bites yet, I had a big one on there this morning though." He continued to stare at her then made a spontaneous decision and addressed her. "Hey, Jenna." He saw Junior look between them.

"You know each other?" Junior looked confused.

Jenna grinned then laughed. "Actually I do, he's my..." She paused, thinking of what to say and "cousin" rolled off her tongue.

"No shit, your cousin? Nice to meet you, man, I'm Jay."

Mike gave him a nod.

Jay introduced the rest of the group.

Jenna was embarrassed looking at Mike, she didn't know why she'd said it. She just didn't want Jay to think it odd if he found out Mike was just a guy staying at her grandmother's house with her. Jay would think they were involved somehow and they clearly weren't, so saying Mike was her cousin was the first thing that came to mind.

They were all now stopped in front of Mike's chair so Mike came out of the water to greet them, never taking his eyes off Jenna. Her *cousin?* It was actually a good cover; if she hadn't said cousin then Mike was going to say *boyfriend*, but he supposed that would be less believable since right now Jenna was standing there with Junior and *not* him. She was actually looking at Mike as if she were worried he was going to blow *her* cover and he almost laughed seeing her discomfort. She clearly didn't want Junior to think there was anything going on between them, and that stung in a place that had been shut down for a long time. Mike tried to shake off the things this girl had started making him feel.

"Nice to meet you, I'm Mike." He held out his hand to each of the guys and gave the ladies his sexiest smile watching Jenna frown and roll her eyes as he did. This could be kind of fun playing her cousin, he thought, biting back a chuckle.

Although Mike should be the one frowning, he thought as he looked at her. He didn't know what to be more pissed about, Jenna hanging out with them, or Jenna hanging out with them practically naked. Jay Jr. was a good-looking kid and Jenna had no doubt noticed but it didn't change the fact that he was the son of a drug lord and was suspected of running his own illegal operations out of his daddy's Miami night clubs. Mike knew from being in some of those clubs that Junior probably had no shortage of women and Mike was going to make damn sure Jenna didn't become one of them. "So what are you all up too?"

"We're heading to my sister's house for a cookout, why don't you join us? It's right there."

Junior pointed to Scintillo's and Mike followed his gaze. "Wow, that's quite a place, I've been admiring it all morning. Thanks for the invite, I'd love too!" Mike smiled and winked at Jenna.

Jenna was seething. What did Mike think he was doing? He was deliberately going to hang out with them just to irk her and now she had to pretend that she liked him because he was her "cousin." She couldn't believe him! "Don't you have that thing you have to do?" she asked him. Why wasn't he out spying on someone?

Mike gave her a gregarious smile. "Actually, this is exactly what I'm supposed to be doing."

"Great!" Junior exclaimed. "Let's head up to the house and grab a drink!"

"Sounds good," Mike told him. "I'm just going to pack up my gear, I'll catch up." Mike waited until they were a few feet away then he slipped his now dry T-shirt back on and took his . 45 from the cooler, securing it in the special lining of his shorts.

I'm heading up to the house, let me know if any other visitors arrive."

"Will do," Murph replied. "Hey, why would the neighbor say you were her cousin?"

"Tell you later." Mike was glad he didn't have time to explain and caught up with the group in a few quick strides in the sand. He followed closely behind Jenna and discreetly gave her a little pat on the behind; he couldn't help himself.

Jenna felt Mike's light touch like a branding iron on her ass. She stifled the reflex to turn around and glare at him and kept walking beside Jay. Mike was infuriating and yet his touch had affected her once again. Wait until Paige heard about this!

CHAPTER SIXTEEN

Paige woke up to the sound of Sam whimpering and lifted her eyelids to become oriented. She was in Justin's bed. She turned her head gently and saw that he was sound asleep beside her, the covers hovering just above his narrow waist, revealing his naked torso. God, he was handsome, even while he slept. Paige wanted to reach out and smooth her hand over his chest but instead just watched the rise and fall of it as he breathed steadily in his sleep. Sam whimpered again and she quietly got out of the bed.

"C'mon, little guy," she whispered and opened the crate to pick him up. After going to the bathroom and brushing her teeth with him in her arms, she padded down the back stairs still holding him while he licked her face and made her laugh. "Hey, you big licker!" She unlocked the back kitchen door and let him out to do his thing. It was a gorgeous late spring morning, and Paige stood on the little back porch enjoying the warmth of the sun on her face while waiting for the puppy to finish. When Sam bounded back over to her, she coaxed him inside for breakfast.

"Now where does your daddy keep your food?" Paige went over to a cabinet by the refrigerator and opened it. "Not there." She looked at Sam and laughed as he stood up on his hind legs scratching his little paws at a nearby closet. She opened the door and saw the large plastic bin filled with dog food. "Smart boy, huh? Here's the mother lode!" She scooped some kibble from an enormous bag and placed it in Sam's bowl by the fireplace. "There you go, baby."

Paige sat down at the kitchen table while the pup ate and she studied the details of the finished kitchen. It was gorgeously modern and characteristically homey at the same time. It had all the modern conveniences combined with the architectural details that kept with the original character of the old house.

When Sam was done eating she let him back outside to play in the fenced-in yard then took her time touring through the first floor of the house again before finally making her way up the grand staircase where she stood looking out at the stained glass window. Sure enough it was spectacular with the morning sun shining through it. The window scene was of Newport harbor and the buildings that surrounding it from a long ago era. It depicted a typical summer weekend afternoon in Newport with people milling about or sitting on park benches. The colors were brilliant and cast a rainbow of prisms on the wooden planks beneath her feet as well as on the wood stained banister.

"Hey, down there."

Paige looked up from the landing surprised to see Justin at the top of the stairs smiling down at her, the shadow of a beard darkening his jaw line. He was shirtless again and wearing just his jeans unbuttoned at the top. Right below the tattoo on his muscled stomach was the sexiest line of hair leading into his unbuttoned jeans and she felt desire zing through her just looking at him. He was beyond sexy. Paige's heart soared and her stomach tightened at the sight of him.

"Hi."

"Did you sleep okay?" Man, his stomach did that damn flippy thing whenever he looked at her. He'd never had a woman in this house before and he liked that Paige was there.

Paige nodded feeling somewhat shy. She felt a little awkward to have woken up in Justin's house and wasn't sure how he was feeling about it. "I let Sam out and fed him, then let him back out to play."

"I saw that, thank you." Justin smiled and sat down on the top step. "How are you today?"

"I'm great." Paige smiled and walked over to the first step leading up. "What about you?"

"Never better." He'd woken up wanting her again.

His voice was rough in the morning and Paige felt that now familiar current flowing between them. She climbed the few steps it took to reach him and knelt between his legs. Placing her arms around his neck, she leaned in and kissed him.

Justin felt an overwhelming feeling of affection take over as he embraced her and received her kiss. The feeling scared the shit out of him. What was happening with him? He had just come out of a relationship that hadn't worked, mainly because of him and his lifestyle, so what was he doing with Paige? He pulled back gently and looked into her eyes. He saw something there that scared him even more: she was feeling it too.

Paige felt the unspoken feelings flowing between them and she bit her tongue. *Whoa!* They were staring into each other's eyes and she could see Justin wanted to say something.

"I think you're incredible, Paige." Justin kissed her lips softly, unable to help himself. Everything he'd been thinking he buried under his tongue.

Oh oh. Paige sensed a "but" in there somewhere. "I think you're pretty incredible too, Justin." She didn't know what else to say. She needed to think, things were moving so fast between them. Two days of mind-blowing sex was clouding her mind. Justin probably wasn't looking for a new relationship any more than she was. Right?

"C'mon, I'll make you breakfast and take you back so you can get ready for work."

"Okay, thanks." Paige moved away from him reluctantly. She couldn't help the disappointment that came over her at having to leave, she wanted to spend all day with him and Sam and help Justin around the house. She was already attached to that too. They both fell quiet and Paige wondered what he was thinking.

Justin wanted to take Paige in his arms again and just hold her, make love to her all day. He found himself nearly telling her that he had feelings that he couldn't even explain having so soon. He had to remember he had only known her for *two days* and that he needed to slow the fuck down. There was something at work between them and he needed to nurture it not steamroll over it. Paige entering his life was unexpected and he needed to think about how he was going to move forward with her. He didn't want to lose her just as soon as they'd begun, he needed to pull back here. Christ, he had already invited her to meet his parents! That wasn't cool. He really liked Paige but he didn't want her to think he was looking for a wife, for God's sake. He remembered the look of shock on her face at dinner when he had invited her to meet them, and she had thought he was joking. Man, he was an idiot! He had to take it down a notch.

"Why don't you get dressed and meet me in the kitchen, I'll go make breakfast." He smiled and kissed her cheek.

Paige returned the smile. "Okay, thanks." She followed him into his bedroom and watched as he used the back stairs to go down to the kitchen. She tried not to feel disappointed that he hadn't brought her back to bed and gathered her clothes from the top of his bureau. She brought them into the bathroom and leaned against the door once it was shut, wrapping her arms around herself. She couldn't believe she had such strong feelings for Justin already. There'd been a lightning fast connection with him she couldn't explain and she could hear Jenna in her mind calling it fate. Maybe it was fate but Paige wanted to be careful. She knew if she wanted something more to develop between them she would have to hold back her feelings for a while. The last thing she wanted was to scare Justin away, but it was going to be extremely hard to hide the way she felt.

She finished dressing and descended the stairs to meet him in the kitchen. He was just putting a big stack of pancakes on the table when she arrived and he turned and gave her a big smile.

"Good timing, I hope you like pancakes."

"Love 'em," Paige said and returned his smile feeling her heart burst wide open. Oh God, please don't let me screw this up, she begged.

They sat together and ate and it was comfortable. They exchanged a few family stories and Paige asked Justin more about his business. With each forkful and each swallow of the big glass of milk he had poured for her she found herself becoming more and more attracted to him, he was such a great guy. They lingered at the table after eating and he told her how he had come to purchase the old house and his love for them since he was a kid. His grandparents had owned an old colonial in Westin, Massachusetts, and he had loved running through all the old rooms, especially some of the upstairs rooms that he remembered having secret nooks and crawl spaces. Paige listened as he described it, completely enthralled.

"Do they still live there?" It sounded great to her and she would love to see it.

"No, unfortunately, they died four years ago and my dad and his brothers sold it—sucked. If I'd had the money then I would have bought it. I still wish that house was in the family though. You would have loved to photograph it."

They looked at each other and smiled. Paige felt a warm buzz run through her. He seemed to care about her passion for photography and that meant a lot. "Is the house still there?"

"Oh yeah. I have a few old pictures of it, want to see?" Justin stood.

"I'd love to." Paige was touched that he would be willing to share his childhood memories with her. She watched as he went around the island and pulled open a kitchen drawer nearby.

"Those were taken when I was about five." Justin came back around the island and handed her the old photos. He watched for her reaction.

"*Oh wow,* Justin. It's breathtaking!" Paige looked at him then back to the pictures. "It looks like something out of an old movie; I would have loved to see the inside of that!" Paige admired the photos of the house and one of a little boy who sat on the wide steps of the big old front porch. She couldn't help but wonder how it would be to have Justin's child and have it look just like the boy in the picture, only sitting on the front stairs of this house. She mentally slapped herself out of fantasy land, she was definitely losing it.

"It would be nice to think another couple or family is enjoying it like your grandparents did and like you did." She smiled looking up from the picture.

"Yeah, I hope so." Justin picked their plates up and brought them to the sink. Man, it would be so easy to tell her right now that he had feelings for her already. She was so easy to talk to and it was really nice sharing the photographs with her but Justin knew if he wanted whatever he had going on with Paige to last, then he had to slow the fuck down.

"I'm gonna go up and shower real fast then I'll take you back home, okay? What time is work?"

"Eleven," Paige answered him with a smile she had to force.

Justin moved to the stairs. "Okay, make yourself at home, I'll be right down."

Paige held her smile and the picture of him as a boy on his grandparent's steps as she watched Justin go upstairs. She felt that sting of disappointment again, this time that he hadn't asked her to come up to the shower, and then she chastised herself. She got up from the table mad at herself and let Sam back in, who promptly jumped against her legs playfully. Paige picked him up, putting Justin's picture in her back pocket so Sam wouldn't bite it or lick it and she hugged the puppy to her. He provided a moment of happiness but when Paige eventually heard the water running through the pipes, she found herself feeling more than just a little hurt. She tried to shake it off, but couldn't. Why wouldn't he have invited her up there after what they'd shared last night?

Paige put the puppy down with a sigh and wandered through the downstairs again. She inevitably found herself in the sun room looking up at the vast ceiling. She sat down on the small step separating the rooms and for what seemed like a good while, just thought. Her mind went back to the huge Christmas tree she could imagine in the room and she looked outside through the French doors to the early summer day beyond. She could see all the giant green leaves of the hydrangea bushes crowding along the rails of the front porch and she knew soon there would be giant, orb like blooms adorning them, making for a beautiful view from inside the sun room. She wondered what color they would be.

"Hey there, all set?"

Paige turned, startled from her daydreaming to see Justin freshly showered and looking crazy handsome in worn jeans and a black fitted T-shirt. She stood up and her insides fluttered. It still stung that she hadn't been invited back upstairs but she ignored the feeling. The way he looked now just standing there had her body responding and remembering the night before. The sex had been even more incredible than their first night and they'd had such a great time at dinner and again just at breakfast. Paige had felt so comfortable with him and she'd thought he had been with her too. So why did she feel like he was putting some distance between them this morning?

"I'm all set," she said, forcing another smile she didn't quite feel.

They left the house after putting Sam back in his crate and were on Justin's motorcycle driving through Newport's side streets on the way back to Paige's apartment. She held on to Justin and savored the feeling of him as they rode, knowing the ride would unfortunately end in a matter of minutes. When they arrived at her place, Paige reluctantly got off the bike and handed Justin back his helmet.

"Thank you so much, Justin, I had a really nice time," she told him with a genuine smile but already feeling a damn lump in her throat.

Justin sat straddling the bike and he held onto his helmet. "Hey *thank you* for coming out with me; I had a great time too." He wanted to say so much more but he found he didn't dare. He'd probably already scared her off asking her to meet his parents and showing her his old fucking pictures.

"Well, I guess I better get inside and get ready for work." Paige stood beside the motorcycle suddenly feeling completely awkward and embarrassed.

"Okay, sure, I guess I'll give you a call later then?" He tried to come off nonchalant instead of needy and possessive which was the way he was actually feeling. He didn't want her out of his sight, he wanted to go up into her apartment and make love to her again.

Paige immediately sensed the change in Justin's demeanor and tone. He *guessed* he'd call her later? What happened to meeting the parents? He didn't even have her number nor was he asking her for it! Paige's heart was sinking right into the sidewalk. She would wait until she was inside before she mentally beat herself up. She needed to talk to Jenna desperately.

"Yeah, sure." Paige let him off the hook, letting him think she'd be expecting his call. So much for meeting his parents, she thought bitterly. It would have been totally weird anyway. But deep down she'd really wanted to meet them.

Their eyes locked a final time and Paige felt confused about what she saw there; was that caring or regret in his eyes? She watched as he refastened his helmet and then departed with a simple wave, not a kiss, a wave, and then he was gone.

Paige took the stairs to her apartment two at a time. She was sick to her stomach and once inside she went right to the bathroom, ran the shower, and without waiting for it to warm she stripped and stepped under the spray and let her tears fall. What an idiot! How could she have possibly thought after two days there was something between them? How had she so easily given herself to him? Not only her body but her damn heart too!

Paige berated herself for a good ten minutes as the water got hot then decided she had to stop. The sex had been incredible and there was no changing that. She refused to regret it for even one second. She only regretted being naive enough to think that Justin could have developed feelings for her after only two days. Who did she think she was? She laughed regretfully as she started to wash and thanked God she hadn't said anything stupid or revealing to him. The thing was, she had seemed so sure that maybe he had some feelings for her. He had looked right into her eyes this morning and told her she was incredible and she had believed him. Even the way he had opened up to her at dinner had left her feeling that something could develop between them.

Was he put off because she'd slept with him so soon? She was nearly thirty for Christ's sake and could sleep with anyone she wanted to, whenever she wanted to! But her gut told her that wasn't it at all and she was just downright confused. She finished getting ready and was walking to Captain Jack's a half an hour later, texting Jenna.

Call me, super important

Losing it here

Need advice about Justin

luv P

Paige got to work on time and busied herself behind the bar, grateful when the lunch crowd finally came in to take her mind elsewhere. She took her own lunch break two hours later and was sitting at a table in the corner eating a salad when Jack told her she had a phone call. Her mind immediately went to Justin. Yes! He called her here! Of course! He knew she was at work and obviously knew this number, why hadn't she thought of that? She went back behind the bar and picked up the phone excitedly. "Hello?"

"Hi Paige; it's Justin."

She smiled with relief. "Hi."

"I'm sorry to call you at work but I realized I didn't have your number."

"No problem, I'm just on a break so it's fine. How's your day going?" Her heart expanded just hearing his voice and all her misgivings about him disappeared. She imagined him home working on the house and wished she were there.

"Well, actually that's why I'm calling. I have to cancel our plans for tonight; I've got someone coming in the shop for a sitting at six that's going to take me at least a couple of hours so I won't be going to my parents'." Justin felt like the worst piece of shit as soon as the lie was out of his mouth.

Paige nodded as she held the phone and the buoyancy she'd felt in her heart only a moment before now plummeted like a sinking ship right to her toes. She wouldn't let Justin hear the disappointment in her voice though and she wouldn't let Jack see it on her face, but she couldn't stop the swirling vortex of pain in her gut. Justin had told her when she met him that he didn't work on Sundays and now he was lying to her.

"Oh, no problem at all," she lied herself, "I'm not sure how busy we'll be here anyway, Jack might need me to stay late." She saw Jack raise a brow to her and she smiled sheepishly at him. "After last night I shouldn't be eating dessert anyway," she laughed sounding as carefree as she possibly could.

"Listen Paige. . ." Justin had thought it best to cancel so that she didn't think it was strange that he'd be taking her to his parents for their third date but now he just felt awful. He should have just asked her to do something else but he feared he'd have to explain why they weren't going to his parents and then what? How could he tell her his reasons this soon? And now he'd just fucking lied to her. "Can I call you tomorrow?"

"Sure." She wouldn't be working tomorrow but she'd let him think so. "My break is just about over so I better go finish lunch, good luck with the tattoo." Maybe he'd at least feel bad for lying to her if she mentioned it.

"Okay. See you, Paige." Justin was aware of her put on, overly friendly tone as he hung up the phone. "*Fuck!*" He yelled and put his head in his hands realizing he had just fucked up big time. He should have just made other plans with her. Why had he lied? They could have gone to a movie or just a walk on the beach; meeting his parents could wait, he just wanted to be with her. What was he so damn afraid of? He never lied to people and now he had, to someone he really cared about. Yeah, he thought, after two days he cared about her—a lot, and was scared shit to tell her.

Paige hung up the phone and gave Jack a forced smile, trying to hold back the tears that had welled in her eyes. Shit! She walked past Jack, feeling completely deflated, and back to her table where her salad sat half eaten. Her appetite gone, she took out her cell and tried to call Jenna but it went right to voice mail. Shit! Shit! Shit!

CHAPTER SEVENTEEN

"Are you expecting a call?" Jenna whispered to Mike haughtily from the side of her mouth staring at the pimped-up Bluetooth in his right ear. They stood, waiting on Jay who had just introduced them to his overly pregnant sister and her husband. He was now fixing both her and Mike a drink.

Mike looked down at Jenna and gave her a look pretty much like the one he had given her when they'd first met.

Jenna swallowed looking up at him but refused to be intimidated. He wasn't fooling her with that mean look again and she stuck her tongue out at him in response to it, noting the grin he was now trying hard to conceal. Why did he have to be so devastatingly good looking? She could see the way the girls were looking at him and she couldn't help but feel jealous but his Bluetooth was completely out of place and it made him look pompous. She supposed she should let him look that way, maybe the girls would be turned off. How could he even get a call anyway? Where was his phone? Back on his chair? He had to be out of range unless his earpiece truly was pimped out and had special capabilities. Given who he was she didn't doubt it. She threw him a sidelong glance and decided against saying anything.

Mike realized his earpiece probably did look out of place for someone who was supposedly relaxing on the beach so he took it out and held it in his hand. It wasn't like an ordinary Bluetooth, it was government issued with long range capability allowing him to be in direct contact with his team wherever they were on the island. He could control with a press of a tiny button on its side whether he talked to one man or all of them together. He could also take it out and be alerted to their calls by a slight vibration in his hand, so he opted to carry it. He looked down at Jenna as if to ask "satisfied?" and was surprised to see she was smiling and had her eyes on Junior, who was making his way over to them with their drinks. Mike didn't want her smiling at Junior, he wanted her smiling at him.

At six four Mike had about six inches and fifty pounds on the kid. He knew he presented an intimidating form and he was glad of it; he wanted this kid to be wary of him, he didn't want him near Jenna at all. He watched as she took a frozen drink from Junior's hand.

"And water for you my man, you sure I can't get you anything stronger?"

Mike took the plastic bottle of water. "No thanks, Jay, is it?" Junior nodded with a smile to him. "I'm good," Mike told him.

Jay shrugged and led them out to the deck where Jay's sister and his friends were hanging out. "I'll put the music on; let's take this down to the pool." He hit a few buttons on a nearby remote control and loud club music reverberated around the deck. Jay reached for Jenna's hand with a grin.

Jenna hesitated for only a split second before she accepted Jay's outstretched hand and followed him down the deck stairs leading to the pool. She could feel Mike's presence right on her heels and in fact bumped right up against him when Jay stopped short suddenly on the steps.

"Hey, I forgot; did you want me to take you to your grandmother's house to change or are you okay?" Jay asked her.

Jenna smiled, aware of her backside deliciously pressed up against Mike's hard muscular form on the stair behind her. She couldn't move forward without knocking Jay off his own tread so she was stuck against the solid unmoving mass of Mike and she felt heat swarm through her body.

Mike's stomach muscles contracted and his gut clenched at the contact with Jenna and he reached out automatically, placing his hands on her shoulders to steady her and maybe just to keep her pressed against him like that for a minute longer. "I can always run back if she needs something."

Jenna's felt her body actually shudder when Mike's hands rested on her bare skin and she turned her head back dazedly to look at him. The feel of his hands on her shoulders was almost electrifying. She couldn't help but notice that two of the girls behind Mike had come up short also and clearly didn't mind. They were giving each other a "Holy crap, he's hot" kind of look.

"Thanks, I'm fine," Jenna heard herself say to Jay with the corner of her eye focused on the girls past Mike's shoulder. Her stomach was doing somersaults due to the fact she was still pressed against Mike but she couldn't help the spike of jealousy that coursed through her. "It's so hot I'll be fine." She didn't know if she'd ever be fine again.

Mike followed Jenna's slight gaze and looked behind him. He gave the girls a sexy grin then turned back to Jenna giving her one as well. "It is pretty hot." He cocked a brow. "You're right about that."

Jenna rolled her eyes at him feeling that pang of jealousy like a spear and followed Jay the rest of the way down, the feel of Mike's hands on her shoulders still imprinted on her naked skin. What was wrong with her? She had a great-looking guy her own age right in front of her who was clearly interested and she was thinking about Mike and how his big strong body felt against hers; Mike who thought of her as an inexperienced kid. Why had he even accepted

Jay's invitation? Shouldn't he be working?

The music was much louder by the pool and the girls, Becky, Kendra, and Georgie, started dancing right away around the deck. They could move pretty well and Jenna wondered if they were trained like she was. She glanced over at Mike, who had taken a seat nearby, and she saw him watching the girls as well. It burned her, and she got mad that it did. Why should she care if he looked at them? She could out dance every girl there and teach them a thing or two while she was at it, but he'd never know it! Jenna wondered if they were turning him on, it didn't bother her one bit that Jay was watching them with a smile on his face, but the interested look Mike was watching them with made her want to go over to him and show him how it was done.

"So, have you thought any about coming to work for me?"

Jay was sitting on the edge of the lounge Jenna had taken and he moved closer causing their legs to touch. Jenna glanced over at Mike and was glad to see he had noticed; she leaned closer to Jay purposefully. "You know I have been thinking a little about it, I was thinking maybe I could come down and try it, see how it goes." It would also get her out of the house and away from Mike, which would probably make him happy.

"That's great, Jenna!" Jay put a hand on her knee. That's all he wanted was to get her down to the club and once there she'd get hooked just like the other girls. Once she got a taste of the money, he'd introduce her to some other things that would definitely keep her hooked and Jay knew just who she would be of interest to the most.

Jenna gestured to the girls dancing. "They're pretty good." The girls wore only their bikinis and she found herself glancing over at Mike again only to find he was still looking at her. Jenna quickly took a sip of her drink, embarrassed that he'd caught her looking.

"Yeah, they're awesome; they dance in the clubs too." Jay looked at her to gage her reaction.

"Oh, they come in when they're not working?"

"No, they actually dance *while* they're working." Jay smiled. "When they aren't serving drinks, they're up on stage, that's where they make most of their money."

Jenna felt like a complete idiot. *Ohhhh*, now she got it! "They're *strippers?*" she asked him out of the side of her mouth.

Jay chuckled. "Well, in my clubs they're called dancers, because they actually are," he explained. "They only take off their clothes if they want to. They obviously make more tips when they disrobe, but it isn't required. Some of them dance so well, the guys just want to see that, it's just as erotic. The clubs are all very laid back, all very cool, you know?" He winked at Georgie, who was watching their exchange carefully.

Jenna looked at Jay, rather surprised; he seemed like such a normal guy, not some sort of gigolo. He was typical of the kind of guys in Newport she'd gone to school with, only the type of business he was describing didn't seem to match up with the all-American boy next door type he projected. She could only imagine what Miami would be like.

"You of course wouldn't have to dance at all if you didn't want to; in fact, we have enough dancers. I'm just looking for a server." Jay casually took a sip of his beer.

Jenna didn't dare tell him of her dance history. "Yeah, I would definitely only be interested in serving." She wanted to make it clear that dancing was not going to happen.

"So you're interested then?"

Jenna glanced at Mike again and was shocked to see one of the girls, Georgie, had sidled up to him, dancing perilously close. Ugh! She was sure Mike knew all about Miami, being from there, and she could just picture him in a club like Jay's tipping some sexy chic because she danced naked for him. He'd probably even been to Jay's club! Jenna seethed and was completely jealous. "Yes, I am interested, when can I start?"

"We're headed back tomorrow. How about you come with us and we'll get you set up with the girls?"

Wow, this was unexpected but what was the worst that could happen? She would just try it out for a couple of nights, and see how it went; she'd probably have a blast in Miami. It would certainly be more exciting than staying on the island alone waiting for everyone to arrive for the wedding.

"That sounds like a plan. You'll just have to give me directions or I could just follow you down, I guess."

Jay laughed. "We actually arrived by boat. How would you like to motor back with us, I can drive you back by car in a few days." He laughed again and joked, "With my sister's baby coming any minute, I might be driving back sooner than I think anyway!"

Jenna laughed too. "Okay, it sounds like fun." She couldn't wait to text Jake and Paige. Jay would be right up Jake's alley, they'd be fighting over him for sure. She felt a pull in her gut at the thought of Jake; she missed him.

"It settled then, how about another drink?" Jay was psyched; Jenna might just get him out of a major jam.

"Sure, why not?" Jenna leaned back in the cushioned lounge chair when Jay got up and she snuck a glance over at Mike who seemed to be involved in an animated conversation with Georgie. Georgie had stopped dancing and was listening to him attentively and laughing every now and then. Jenna wondered if she were one of the girls who "danced" with her clothes off and cursed herself at her jealous feelings. She arranged herself on the lounge trying to look as sexy as possible, and checked every now and again to see if Mike had noticed. When she was getting nothing from him she stood up determinedly with a "hmph" and headed into the pool.

Mike knew Jenna didn't like the fact that he was talking to one of the girls. He was aware of her glances and he was getting off on the fact that she might be a little jealous but he wasn't sure if maybe she wasn't just mad because he was there in the first place, cramping her style. He watched her from the corner of his eye get up and remove her barely there cover-up then head into the pool. He noticed every guy there staring at her, too, including Junior, who had returned with what looked like another drink for her. Mike was seething inside.

"So Mike, are you into MMA?" Jay signaled to Jenna that he'd brought her another drink then put it down on a nearby table.

"I do some mixed martial arts training to keep in shape, yeah." Mike noticed the other guy's eyes were now on him, listening, and not focused on Jenna—good. He stole a glance to the upper deck trying to see if any new guests had arrived as his ear-piece vibrated in his hand. He itched to put it to his ear but instead just kept an eye out.

"Wow, impressive." I've taken a few Jujitsu classes, that shit is tough." This from one of the boyfriends.

Mike smiled politely and looked over toward Jenna in the pool. She was in up to her waist and she deliberately dunked down and swam to the deep end when she saw him looking at her. The ear-piece buzzed again and Mike again resisted the urge to put it in. He was fairly certain Scintillo wouldn't arrive in the light of day, but he stayed alert just in case, comforted by his gun pressing into his backside.

"It's pretty damn hot, huh?" Mike said to no one in particular. He wanted to go in the pool after Jenna but couldn't because of his gun and his earpiece. Instead he got off his chair and walked to the edge of the pool then sat with his back to the beach so he had a clear view of anyone new arriving to the house. He put his legs in the water submerging them from the knees down.

"So this is your sister's place, huh?" Little did Junior know Mike had been inside once before. It was Scintillo's house that had been used as a lookout when the Cuban refugees had smuggled drugs onto the island for Xavier D'nafrio just last summer. The house was impressive being that it was right on the beach and it was in a relatively private, prettily landscaped setting with only a few scattered homes to its left on the beach, but nowhere near as impressive as the home Rafe had stayed in two doors down.

"Yeah, she and her husband moved in last fall. She's about to have that baby any day so the family and some friends are all gathering around waiting. You know how that goes," Jay laughed, "it won't come until we all leave."

They all laughed and Mike agreed. "Yeah, that'll suck for anyone who traveled a long way." *Say from Mexico.*

"No shit, but it's not a bad place to sit and wait." Jay laughed and his entourage followed.

Mike gave a disingenuous smile and watched Jenna as she swam back toward them. She surfaced in front of him, her hair as dark as night and slicked back off her face. She looked up at him under long wet lashes and big dark eyes and Mike felt his balls tighten instantly. Then he watched Junior hand her her drink and his whole body went taut with anger. He just wanted to get her the fuck out of there. He didn't need Junior getting her drunk.

"Thank you." Jenna took her new drink from Jay with a smile and sat on the pool step beside him. She noticed the girls had gone back to dancing, and a couple of the guys danced with them as the Black Eyed Peas pounded through the outdoor speakers. Everyone else seemed to be eating and drinking on the upper deck and Jenna's stomach growled as the smell of grilled food wafted down. She hadn't eaten since breakfast and was on her third frozen drink; at this rate she'd be drunk real soon. She was already quite buzzed.

"So Mike, do you not drink at all?" Jay asked, curious about him. His sixth sense was in overdrive and he glanced up casually to his brother-in-law, who stood leaning forward against the top deck rail looking down on them.

"I do." Mike reluctantly turned from Jenna and gave his attention to Junior. He was aware of the watchful eyes from the top deck as well. "Just really hungover today." He grinned. "Gotta recoup."

Jenna shot Mike a glance. She'd seen him only have all of two beers the previous night.

"I hear you, man." Jay laughed. "Were you guys out partying last night?"

Jenna looked at Mike and felt herself blush remembering how he had kissed her like he was going to… She looked away quickly when he gave her that damn grin of his.

Mike chuckled. "Nah, this one wasn't into it." He nodded toward Jenna. "I ended up partying by myself."

Jenna's brows shot up and her mouth nearly fell open but she refrained from cracking up at Mike's revealing statement.

"Who says I wasn't into it?" She addressed him. "I just wasn't expecting to party so soon, I just got here, remember!" She gave him a little smirk and a tilt of her head. "But I didn't realize you ended up partying by yourself, that's too bad," she added with a helpless grin knowing damn well what he was implying and feeling completely turned on just picturing it, and knowing she was the cause of it.

Mike winked and gave her a crooked smile. "A man's gotta do what a man's gotta do. Maybe you'll be ready for me next time."

Jenna felt her whole body warm at the thought and her cheeks flushed again. *Next time?* She sipped her drink hoping Jay couldn't decipher their double entendres. Being that he was under the assumption Mike was her cousin, Jenna doubted he thought anything of their exchange.

"Smells like the food is ready," Jay announced seemingly oblivious.

He held a hand for Jenna again who took it and she glanced at Mike to make sure he saw. He winked at her and made a kissing motion with his lips throwing her off guard. What the hell? She scrunched up her face at him and shook her head, exasperated. Why did he insist on teasing her? She was going to let him have it when they got back to the house!

CHAPTER EIGHTEEN

Mike chuckled, enjoying the fact that he was getting to Jenna. He didn't want her feeling comfortable around Junior. He wanted to get her out of there as soon as possible. He discreetly put his earpiece back in as everyone headed for the upper deck, thankful for the opportunity. He hit the small button that would let the team know he was back on comm with them.

"We'll eat and then head back to the house," Mike said to Jenna. "I know Nan's expecting us to call." Immediately he heard Reynolds' voice in his ear.

"Finally! What the fuck, Caplan? And who's Nan? Cherry and two friends went diving off North Cap; they jumped right off the boat."

"They were in full gear, the men were unrecognizable but one was about the right size." Simmons laughed, "The other one is built like the Hulk."

Mike couldn't believe it; this could be over in a matter of hours.

Jenna nearly spit the sip of her drink out as she climbed the stairs. She didn't know whether to laugh out loud or yell at Mike for what he'd just said. He was really taking her fib a little too far. She would leave when she was ready; he could leave right now for all she cared. Who did he think he was? *Nan?* He was calling Nan Nan? He can't do that! It was pretty funny though. She turned around with her hand still in Jay's and she smiled, trying not to laugh, She noticed Mike had his earpiece in again and he seemed a little distracted. "I'm sure you can tell Nan I'm with new friends, she'll understand. Just tell her I'll call her tomorrow."

Mike narrowed his eyes at her as if to tell her not to challenge him but he was thinking of what Simmons had said. Scintillo obviously had some kind of bodyguard with him.

"In fact," Jenna continued pleased that she was now irking him, "maybe you should head back now and try to catch her before she takes her afternoon nap."

"Before who takes an afternoon nap?" Reynolds asked, confusion in his voice.

Mike gave her a "nice try" smirk ignoring Reynolds, and feigned like he was going to smack her on the ass.

Jenna quickly took the top step avoiding Mike's hand and nearly fell into

Jay. "Sorry," she laughed. "I tripped."

Jay laughed. "You can trip into me anytime; let's get you something to eat."

You can trip into me anytime; Mike mocked the words in his head. What a twerp.

They all ate hot dogs and burgers at a table on the upper deck and continued drinking. Mike passed on the food and kept with the bottled water, every once in a while getting another update from the guys. The Four Winns had made its way back to the marina and Cherry had come off. She was at the pool bar by herself now with Simmons and Bealls sitting nearby and Reynolds and Murph monitoring the marina. It would be another few hours before it was dark so they were all in stand-by mode.

Mike watched as Junior took a cell phone from his shorts pocket and he appeared to be reading a text. Mike was already plotting how he could get Junior's cell when the question Jenna asked next saved him the trouble.

"So are your parents arriving soon as well?"

Mike watched Junior carefully.

"My mom and dad are divorced and can't stand to be in the same state together, never mind the same house," he laughed, "but my mom is going to come next week, she's been traveling. My dad should actually be here some time tonight; his girlfriend just texted." He gestured to his phone.

Sometimes it was just that easy, Mike thought, grinning inwardly.

"Well shit, thanks for the heads-up, Junior," Mike heard Simmons say on comm. and Mike suppressed a laugh. The fact that Cherry was off the boat had Mike thinking and he excused himself to use the restroom. Once inside the room that was conveniently away from anyone's earshot he spoke.

"I want to take him on the boat. The girlfriend is off so it's just him and the bodyguard. There's a houseful of people here that could lead to a potentially dangerous scene if we wait to take him here." He also didn't want Jenna anywhere near the house if they took Scintillo down here; she made it clear she wouldn't leave until she was ready and he knew he couldn't drag her out. He'd rather a small scene at the marina then a potentially large one at the house. More than likely, Junior, the brother-in-law, and perhaps some of their extended family had firearms in the house; he did not want Jenna mixed up in that.

"It could work," Reynolds said, "but I'd like to get some of these people out of here if we can."

"You can't risk Scintillo seeing that," Mike told him. "If we converge on the boat, he's contained, if you start moving people out, he'll catch on and hightail it out of there, then we've got a chase on our hands and we'll be putting other boaters in harm's way."

"It could work," Murph agreed.

"It's the best scenario," Mike reasoned.

Simmons and Bealls concurred.

"I'm leaving here in five; let's meet in Reynolds' room in twenty. Bealls, stay on the girlfriend, if she looks like she's heading back, distract her." They discussed a few more details then Mike left the bathroom, his earpiece in hand. He took in the perimeters around him by habit and no one gave him a second look as he made his way back to the deck. He returned to the table and said his thanks and goodbyes to Junior and his friends.

"You're leaving?" Jenna asked, surprised, and couldn't help but feel a little disappointed.

He nodded. "Yup, gotta go call Nan, right, before she falls asleep?"

Jenna smiled but it was genuine. She was grateful Mike hadn't given her away and she wanted him to know it. "I'll walk with you to get your stuff." Jenna looked at Jay. "I'll be right back, okay?"

"Sure, gorgeous, we'll be right here."

Mike inwardly cringed.

Jenna smiled politely at the compliment and descended the stairs with Mike. He was walking pretty fast. "Hey!"

"Hurry up."

Jenna was surprised at his short tone. "Jeez, what's your problem?" She followed him all the way back to his beach stuff which he quickly gathered up. "Why are you in such a hurry all of a sudden? I just wanted to thank you for back there, you know?"

Mike stopped and looked at her. "Here take this towel and cover up, will you?" He tossed her his towel that had been folded in his chair and continued walking, this time heading back to the beach path that would lead him back to Jenna's grandmother's house.

"No," Jenna answered him like a petulant child. "It's friggin' ninety degrees and I'm hot!" She held his towel in her hand, surprised that she would feel happy to be holding something of his even though he was making her mad.

You have no idea, kid. He sighed in frustration. "Fine, but I want you to leave soon. Like real soon." Mike walked fast and he knew she was struggling to keep up on the shell-laden sand.

"Who do you think you are? I'll leave when I want to, I'll even spend the night if I want to!" she said defiantly, nearly tripping after him.

Mike stopped short and turned around this time as serious as he'd ever been. "Don't do that, Jenna."

Something in his eyes had Jenna momentarily alarmed as she neared him. "Well, I won't, of course, I'm just saying I could if I wanted to, it's not your business."

Mike took a deep breath and had the feeling of wanting to throw her over his shoulder and just drag her home with him, maybe with a good spanking thrown in. Knowing that wouldn't go over too well he just kept walking. "I know we don't know each other very well, Jenna, and you have every reason not to even like me, but I'm asking you as a personal favor to me to leave here very soon."

Jenna stopped walking and shook her head. "I don't get you!" she called after him. "You're the one who doesn't like *me,* remember? So what was with all the teasing back there? I'm just a kid, remember, an inexperienced kid at that, so what's it to you whether I stay or go?" Was he really jealous? Jenna wondered. But he just kept walking, ignoring her rant, and it made her furious. She resisted the temptation to run after him and continue arguing knowing that Jay would soon wonder what was taking her so long. So she simply watched Mike disappear up the beach path to Nan's then turned around disappointed and pissed off headed back to Jay and the party. She was fuming and inadvertently put Mike's towel up to her face. She bit into it and let out a muffled scream of frustration and when she stopped, the scent of him on the soft material had her closing her eyes in an altogether different kind of frustration.

* * * * *

Mike returned to the house, changed, and was bringing his gear to the Jeep in a matter of minutes. He was in Reynolds' room donning his Kevlar and weapons under his shirt five minutes before he said he would be. He wanted to get this done quickly and quietly so he could get his ass back to Scintillo's and get Jenna the hell out of there. Damn, that girl was stubborn. Who knew how Junior would react when he found out his father had been apprehended. Hopefully he could get Jenna out before word reached him. Mike would take her kicking and screaming if he had to. "Bealls?"

"Still here, Cherry's throwin' 'em back like a champ."

"Good, as soon as it's dark we're heading out." They had about a half hour to wait and coordinate their plan.

"What if she starts heading back?" Bealls asked nervously looking at the pool bar discreetly.

"Arrest her," Simmons said matter-of-factly.

"For what?" Bealls asked.

"Aiding and abetting a fugitive, we've got footage of her driving the boat," Simmons answered with satisfaction.

"Oh yeah!" Bealls remembered, causing the rest of the guys to roll their eyes and laugh.

"Bealls, please tell me your carrying your restraints," Simmons groaned, mouthing "newbie" to the guys in the room.

"Well, of course I do," he answered defensively.

"And confiscate her phone," Mike added. If Bealls had to arrest her Mike didn't want her sending a text alerting Junior or his sister to what was going down.

Simmons chuckled then turned to Mike. "So what are we going to do about Junior? How do you think he'll react when pops doesn't show up at the house tonight?"

"Well, he'll figure it out I'm sure but I'm hoping not until tomorrow. He'll be scared and won't want to stick around. My guess is he'll find a way back to Miami and we'll let him." Mike wanted him as far from Jenna as possible. Mike was sweating right now thinking of her still at the house, the Kevlar wasn't helping either.

"So how we gonna do this?"

The men formulated their plan and as soon as darkness fell headed out of the hotel room and down the cement staircase that led to the sand covered parking area and over to the marina. To any onlookers they appeared to be four men headed out for a night of fishing. Simmons and Murphy carried a large cooler between them and Reynolds a small bait bucket devoid of bait. Mike carried a couple of rods in one hand and they all donned fishing vests over their shirts that concealed the outline of their Kevlar vests perfectly. They reached the fishing boat Simmons and Bealls had been on earlier, now conveniently docked five boats away from the Four Winns and boarded the stern, Reynolds then scattered some empties around the deck that they'd stored in the cooler.

They put their gear down and proceeded to get boisterous as Simmons steered the boat away from the dock. There thankfully didn't seem to be any life aboard the vessels they passed and they could see the Four Winns looked desolate as well but they knew better. As they laughed and joked loudly portraying men who'd had too much to drink, Simmons deftly swerved their boat into the back of the Four Winns, causing the boats to jar together roughly, not enough for damage but enough to alarm the hell out of its occupants. Sure enough "The Hulk" emerged from the cabin seconds after the impact.

"Hey, what the fuck?" The big guy came out mad as hell.

Mike sized him up as the bodyguard swiftly made it to the stern looking for damage. Mike knew he would be the one taking the big dude down and he was planning his every move. The guy only had a few inches on him but he was definitely a card carrying member of the "roid" club.

Simmons held up his hands in a defeat like gesture. "Man, I'm sorry; I lost control there for a second." He added a hiccup and a stupid grin for effect.

"You shouldn't be behind that wheel drunk, asshole," the Hulk roared.

"Whoaaa," Reynolds slowly droned. "There's no need for name calling." His own lazy speech also let on that he may have had a few.

Mike stood up from where he'd been sitting on the cushioned bow. Simmons had the boat in neutral and it sat idling at the stern of the Four Winns. "I think we can straighten this out," Mike said, the voice of reason approaching Scintillo's bodyguard. "Let's just exchange information and if there's any damage at all we will certainly take care of it." He took the paperwork Simmons held ready in his outstretched hand and reached across to hand it to the bodyguard. As soon as the dude reached for it, Mike grabbed his forearm, used it to pull himself onto the larger boat and tackle the guy. He swung the man's arm up behind his back at the same time sweeping his legs out from under him and they fell in a loud heap with Mike on top, pinning him down.

Simmons, weapon drawn, yelled, "Freeze, FBI!"

Caught off guard, the dude had fallen easily but as soon as he was down he tried valiantly to roll over on Mike and Mike quickly went into wrestling mode, wrapping his arms and legs around the larger man's like a pretzel, squeezing them so he couldn't move. He heard Reynolds and Murphy jump on board and commandeer the cabin, and the sounds of scuffling ensued as they got hold of Scintillo inside and restrained him. Meanwhile, Mike kept the Hulk pinned while Simmons fastened the heavy duty plastic restraints around the guy's thick wrists and ankles.

It all happened in a matter of seconds and with very little fanfare; in fact, the only audience they had was the night dock-master of the marina who seemed to instinctively know to stay off to the side. Simmons had radioed in the bust and Mike could already see the dark sedans that had been lying in wait pull up on the sandy drive in back of the resort. They would take Scintillo right back to Miami where he'd be arraigned. His girlfriend and the bodyguard would receive a free escort as well.

Cherry had no idea of Scintillo's arrest until she'd been led by Bealls to a waiting sedan after the fact so there had been no danger that she'd tipped Junior off. Mike had personally checked her texts and call log and nothing had been placed after her one text to Junior about his father coming to the house at midnight. Mike had breathed a sigh of relief knowing they had bought some time before Junior would find out about the arrest. When his father didn't show up by the early morning hours, however, Junior would no doubt try to contact the girlfriend and when she didn't answer, he would get suspicious and Mike planned to have Jenna far away from him way before that happened.

* * * * *

Jenna couldn't believe she was packing her bags again so soon. Jay had changed his plans after his friend Rob had suddenly arrived at the party looking flustered and revved up about something. Jay had said he wanted to head back to Miami right away. Jenna was up for it, was excited, in fact, and had left the party just a little buzzed. She'd taken the beach path back by herself to get ready and Jay had promised to come for her in thirty minutes.

There certainly wasn't anything keeping her at Nan's, or *anyone,* she thought, brooding, as she packed a light bag. Miami would be a blast. Jay made it sound fantastic and she was excited to see how much money she could make. It was just for a few nights but she could use a fun adventure. She again wondered why Mike hadn't seemed to like the idea of her staying on at the party without him. Oh well, she wouldn't try and figure Mike out. She thought Jay was nice and as the night had worn on, she had even got to know the girls a little better, too, so she felt more comfortable with them as well. From what they described, the club was awesome and the money even better. Jenna knew a lot more was going on in Jay's clubs, she wasn't stupid, but if she just did her own thing and didn't get involved in what the other girls did, she'd be fine. She didn't care how they made their money that was their business. She had to admit the whole thing was a little exciting though.

Jenna put the essentials in her overnight bag and debated on whether to tell anyone where she was going and in the end just decided to call Paige. She would only be gone for a few days so not everybody needed to know her every move. She dialed Paige's number and took her bag out to the driveway to wait for Jay. He would be coming back soon to pick her up and she assumed take her to the marina where his boat must be. She had to admit she was kind of nervous. She had never been on a boat at night before and she had never gone as far a distance as Miami in one. She also hadn't expected to leave for Miami until tomorrow but she supposed it made no difference either way. Jenna couldn't help but think of Mike though and tried to put him out of her mind. He'd probably be glad to have her out of his hair so he could do his job without any "distractions," she thought. Paige's phone rang five times before she answered.

"Hi!" Paige shut her laptop to give Jenna her full attention.

"Hi!" Jenna smiled at the sound of her cousin's voice. "God, how are you? I haven't spoken to you since yesterday morning but it seems like a week ago!"

Paige laughed a little. "I know. How's everything there?"

"Oh Paige, you aren't going to believe it!" Jenna went on to tell her all about her encounter at the house with Mike, including her phone call to Rafe and the oh so hot impromptu kiss, then about meeting Jay. "And you aren't going to believe this but I'm in the driveway now waiting for him to pick me up to take me to Miami on his boat!" Her voice squealed with excitement.

"What?" Paige had just got through scanning some pictures into her computer. She'd taken a shower after her long head-clearing run on the beach and had been working on her laptop. Now she sat on the edge of her bed listening closely to Jenna. "What are you talking about?"

"This guy Jay, he owns all these nightclubs in Miami and he offered me a job while I'm here," Jenna told Paige excitedly. "I'm going there to try it out and see if I like it. They're going to put me up and everything; he says I can make over a few hundred a night just in tips."

Paige couldn't believe what she was hearing, Jenna was obviously excited and talking a mile a minute, "Tell me you're joking right now?"

Jenna heard the skepticism in Paige's voice. "I know it sounds crazy, but he's a really cool guy, he's not coming on to me or anything, he's just being friendly." Jenna told her how they'd had a drink at Tween Waters and about the party after that, not leaving out what had gone on between her and Mike there.

"This guy Mike sounds kind of fun and like he's definitely interested, why don't you stick around and see where that could go?" Paige suggested, praying Jenna wasn't serious about going to Miami with a stranger.

"Ha, he makes me think he's interested one second then he's calling me kid in the next. I'm done playing games with guys who think they're the shit." Jenna sighed. "Besides, I think this will be fun, I've always wanted to go to Miami, haven't you?"

"Well yeah, Jenna, but not alone with a stranger and by boat no less. You don't know anything about this guy." Paige couldn't hide the wariness in her voice.

Jenna rolled her eyes. "Paige, it's fine, he's nice, and his friends are nice. I met his pregnant sister for goodness' sake. He's a family guy, he's even driving me back in a couple of days, sooner if his sister has the baby," she laughed.

Paige was shocked. Jenna sounded awfully sure of this guy for some reason. How had this happened so quickly and what did this guy Mike think about it? "Where is your temporary roommate anyway? Does he know that you're leaving?"

Jenna scoffed, "I don't owe him an explanation! I barely know him either!"

"I'm a little worried, Jenna, I have to say. Have you told your parents or Nan or Nicki?"

Jenna gave an exasperated sigh. "No, I'm just telling *you*. It's just for a few days, Paige, then I'll be back, it's no big deal, Miami is only two and a half hours away by car."

Paige thought about it. Maybe she was overreacting, maybe it would be okay. She could see why Jenna would be excited, she just wished Jenna were driving. "Make sure you take your phone and your charger and call me when you arrive."

Jenna smiled, thankful Paige was coming around. "Of course I will." She leaned against the bumper of her rent-a-car. "So what was so important about Justin and why are you losing it? I'm sorry; that should have been the first thing I asked you."

Paige sighed as she lay back on her bed, telling Jenna everything that had happened in the past couple of days. "I'd be lying if I said it didn't hurt. I just don't know what to think."

"It's simple, he's scared," Jenna said matter of fact.

"Scared of what?" Paige asked with disbelief. "It's not like I've acted pushy or anything; in fact, he was the one who seemed to be moving things at a faster pace than me! I even wanted to ask him to the wedding but I didn't."

"Well maybe that's just it, maybe he realized he was moving too fast and rethought the whole dinner with the parents thing, maybe he decided to back off a bit." Jenna remembered the way Justin had followed Paige with his eyes in the bar. There was no way he wasn't interested. "And you should totally ask him to the wedding!"

"I don't know if I'll even have a chance to," Paige said softly fighting back emotion. "I'm quite sure I won't hear from him again." She sniffled. "Why did he think he had to lie to me?" Paige complained. "I think I need a dose of Nan."

"That's exactly what you need," Jenna agreed. "She'll tell you what to do but in my opinion, he's so into you, Paige, he doesn't know how to handle it. Seriously, Paige, imagine if you were in his shoes and went over to his house and found a picture of your house on his wall and then he tells you it's his dream house; you'd think that was pretty weird wouldn't you?"

"I'd think he was a stalker," Paige laughed. "Maybe that's why he didn't call, he's afraid of me." She laughed again, her spirits somewhat lifted talking with Jenna.

"Noooo," Jenna laughed too. "He can't believe he's found the woman of his dreams and he doesn't want to risk losing you by moving too fast."

Paige shook her head. "Yeah, right." If only that were true. "Let's hope you're clairvoyant."

Jenna laughed. "Hey, I may suck at knowing what the hell is going on in my own life but I'm an expert with everyone else's."

Paige laughed.

"Now I have to go, I have a date with a serial killer who's going to chop me up on his boat and feed me to the sharks." Jenna grinned, waiting for the inevitable.

"Jenna Grace Thompson, that is not even remotely fucking funny!" Paige sat up and yelled into the phone.

Jenna cracked up. "C'mon, it was a little funny."

"You're horrible and I'll never forgive you if you get chopped up, or myself for that matter for letting you go, text me every five minutes from that boat!" Paige was standing now, realizing just how dangerous it could be for Jenna and she knew just who she would call when she hung up whether it got her in trouble with Jenna or not.

"I love you, cuz," Jenna crooned, teasing her, then said more seriously, "Justin is going to come through, I can feel it."

Paige ignored her, not even thinking about Justin just then. "I love you too, Jenna, stay safe and call me!" Paige didn't feel right about what Jenna was doing at all!

Jenna said goodbye, her phone dying just as she went to send Paige a funny text about being chum for the sharks. Oh well, she knew Paige would worry but she felt better having spoken to her. She continued to lean on the car and remembered her phone charger was inside the house on the kitchen counter. She ran back inside to grab it and as she was leaving she saw the notepad and pen by the wall phone. She supposed a short courtesy note to Mike wouldn't hurt. She uncapped the pen and thought of several ways to start before settling on humor.

> ***Hey 'cousin',***
>
> ***Just wanted to let you know I'd be gone for a few days (going to Miami with Jay and friends). I know you're leaving Saturday so I just wanted to say I enjoyed meeting you and I guess I'll see you again at the wedding. (I'll be the kid dressed up like a grown woman, ha ha! And maybe I'll let you take me for a spin around the dance floor.) Anyway, good luck with your spying and enjoy the rest of the week without any distractions! -Jenna***

Jenna read it over three times, pleased that she managed to get a small jibe in anyway. She put the note on the fridge under the Island Pizza magnet and left through the front door once again. She couldn't help feeling a sense of disappointment that she wouldn't be seeing Mike again, not for a while anyway, and she wondered if anything would have developed between them if she had chosen to stay.

CHAPTER NINETEEN

Paige held the phone, contemplating her next call. If she called Rafe McDonough directly he might think she was overreacting and wasting his time; after all, she had no information she could give him other than to say Jenna was on a boat with a stranger headed for Miami. And although that sounded unsafe and potentially dangerous, there wasn't enough information for Rafe to do anything about it. She'd only known Rafe for about a year now and probably not well enough to make that phone call, so she decided to call Nicki.

"Hi Paigy, what's up?" Nicki rolled away from a smiling and sated Matt in their bed.

Paige knew she was about to change the jubilant tone in her cousin's voice.

"Well, I'm not sure, Nick, but I'm a little concerned about Jenna."

"What? Why?" Nicki sat up clutching the sheet to her chest.

Sure enough the sound of alarm was now in Nicki's voice and Paige reluctantly relayed the phone conversation to Nicki that she had had with Jenna.

"Paige, I have to hang up and call Rafe, I'll call you right back okay?" Nicki looked over at Matt, who was now standing next to their bed pulling his jeans back on knowing something was up, questions in his eyes.

"Nicki, we don't even know anything's wrong, what can Rafe do?" Paige was even more worried now that Nicki felt it necessary to call Rafe too. "Maybe we should just call the Coast Guard."

"There's things you don't know, okay, I'll call you back." Nicki hung up on Paige and turned to Matt. "Jenna's in trouble."

Paige stood staring at the phone in her hand and listening to the dial tone that replaced Nicki's panicked voice. Oh Jesus, what things didn't she know? Oh God! What was going on? Paige quickly called back Jenna and got sent right to voice mail. She sent her a text as well.

Don't go!
don't get on boat!
Call me asap!!!

Paige quickly got dressed and paced the floor frantically waiting for Jenna or Nicki to call back.

* * * * *

Nicki dialed Rafe's cell directly and breathed a sigh of relief when he answered. Matt stood beside her concerned.

"Hey Nick, is everything okay?" Rafe asked. Nicki had never called him on his cell before. He looked at the clock on the wall and at Ali's sleeping form beside him on the couch; she'd been painting at her shop all day.

"I don't know, but I just got a call from my cousin Paige who got a call from Jenna." Nicki gave him the little information Paige had given her. "I know your friend Mike is at Nan's house for a reason and I'm not asking you to tell me but apparently he was also at this guy Jay's house with Jenna today so I want to know, Rafe, is my sister in danger?"

Rafe stood up. Fuck! "Nicki, when did Jenna leave for the boat?"

Nicki heard the "agent voice." Oh shit! She heard her own voice falter as she answered and felt Matt's arms encompass her. "I'm not sure; Paige said she talked to her a few minutes ago." Nicki leaned into Matt, welcoming his strength and fighting the tears that welled up in her eyes.

"Okay, just relax." Rafe could hear the fear in Nicki's voice. "I'm sure we can reach her at the marina before she goes anywhere."

"Rafe, what's going on? Who is this kid Jay? Is Mike on the island to investigate him?"

Rafe took a deep breath. "I know I don't have to say 'off the record,' Nicki."

"She's my sister!" Nicki said, exasperated, she was presently low man on the totem pole at the *Boston Globe* but even if she were featured she would never use her sister as fodder for an article.

"I know, I know, I'm sorry." Rafe ran a hand through his hair. "You remember Jay Scintillo, D'nafrio's partner who fled the country?"

Nicki felt her stomach drop. "That's who she's with?" She envisioned an old man and didn't get it. Her sister was heading to Miami on a boat with a drug lord?

"No, Jay Junior is who Jenna is apparently with," Rafe clarified. "Mike is on the island to apprehend his father, Jay Senior, the fugitive. He's expected to arrive there for the birth of his first grandchild. I'm not sure of the circumstances that had Mike and Jenna at Scintillo's house together but let me make some calls to find out. In the meantime, call Jenna and text her, just try to get her to call you and tell her to stay put. There are agents all over Tween Waters. If you don't hear from her don't worry; I'll get someone on it."

"I can't believe this!" Nicki said a hasty goodbye and tried to call Jenna; when it went to voicemail she left a message and then texted her.

Jen, don't get on the boat!!!!!
Talked to Rafe- Jay is Scintillo's son
remember last summer's trouble?
Go back to Nan's!!!!
Call me asap!!!!
That's y Mike is at Nan's!!!

Nicki turned into Matt and buried her face against his bare chest. "She wasn't supposed to even go there until next week!"

* * * * *

Rafe was aware of Ali, now wide awake, staring at him as he dialed Mike's cell. "Everything's going to be fine, we'll find her."

Ali's heart sank as Rafe got off the couch to walk into their home office. She knew by the look on his face that he was worried. She got right up to call Nicki.

Rafe swore when he got Mike's voicemail and told him to call ASAP. He called Daniels next.

"You heard, huh?" Daniels asked, smiling. "Finally got the bastard, our assumptions were correct; he's been in Mexico, Cabo to be exact. Scintillo's got friends in high places."

Rafe would get the rest of the details later, for now Jenna was of the utmost importance. He interrupted Daniels. "Listen, I can't get ahold of Mike, I need you to make sure that Junior's boat doesn't leave the marina." Rafe quickly explained the mix-up with Jenna being at Nan's the same time as Mike and her subsequent meeting with Jay Junior. "She can't go anywhere with him, I need you to make sure it doesn't happen."

"Relax, they took Scintillo on the boat, our men are all over it right now, nobody's going anywhere on that boat."

Rafe breathed a sigh of relief but wondered what that meant for Jenna. Where the hell was she then? "Has anyone got a bead on Junior?"

"Give me a minute." Daniels left Rafe holding on the line while he got on comm and gathered all the information he could from the scene.

Rafe leaned against the edge of his desk watching Ali through the open doorway as she talked with Nicki. Their eyes met and held in a silent look of concern.

"Okay, Cap is already on route to Scintillo's house. If Jenna is still there he'll have her back to her grandmother's as quick as he can and will call you as soon as that happens."

"And if she isn't there?" Rafe questioned.

"Then Cap said, and this is a direct quote, 'I'll fucking get her home safe no matter what, tell McDonough I got this.'"

Rafe felt somewhat relieved but was anxious to hear from Mike directly that he had Jenna in his possession. "Thanks, Tom, keep me posted, okay?"

"Will do."

Rafe pressed end and hoped to hell Mike called him soon with good news; Cap had a lot of explaining to do.

* * * * *

Mike had jumped off the boat as soon as the arrests were made and the area secured leaving Simmons to deal with the search of the boat and any loose ends. Then Mike had run like hell to his Jeep. He'd just turned the key in the ignition when Daniels had called relaying his conversation with Rafe about Jenna. Mike had sworn a blue streak. Junior had obviously caught wind of the arrest; why else would he be trying to go back to Miami tonight? Mike remembered Murph saying earlier that one of Junior's friends had stayed behind at the pool; had he seen the arrest tonight and tipped Junior off? More than likely he'd been a lookout. Goddammit!

It was nearing eleven o'clock now and Mike could only hope Jenna was still at Junior's sister's house and she hadn't taken off with him yet. But she hadn't had her phone at Scintillo's so she must have gone back to her grandmother's at some point in order to have called her cousin. How Junior had convinced Jenna to go to Miami was beyond Mike but Daniels had relayed Rafe's information and it certainly sounded as if Jenna were going with him willingly. However, now that the Four Winns was not an option, that meant Junior would be driving. Still on comm. , Mike reached out to Reynolds.

"Reynolds, who's on the house?"

"Garrison. Why?"

"Junior's trying to head back to Miami, he knows about his father, I don't know how but he does and he's taking my um…" Mike paused. "Neighbor with him." Mike drove the short distance to Scintillo's in under two minutes.

"Against her will?"

"Well, no, it doesn't seem so, but either way, I've got to get her away from him. She's practically family with Rafe." The party seemed to have quieted Mike noticed as he exited the Jeep.

"Oh shit." Reynolds drew out a long whistle. "That's not good."

"Tell me about it." Mike had his own personal reasons for wanting Jenna away from Junior but he wasn't looking forward to hearing Rafe's anger over the situation either. "I've got to see if they're still here."

"I'll get on with Garrison and see if he saw anything, Murph and I will be right over to cover you."

"There's no time. I'm here now," Mike told him. He parked along the roadside and made tracks up the driveway that was camouflaged to the street by the dense landscape.

"We'll be outside in five anyway." Reynolds summoned Murph for back up and they headed toward the beach in their vehicle.

Mike's heart raced in his chest. Maybe there was a chance they hadn't left yet. He prayed silently. He was still dressed as he had been on the boat. He was going in on his own but he felt comforted knowing he'd have back-up shortly if needed. When he reached the front of the house he decided to head around to the pool deck rather than ring the front bell. By the number of cars left in the driveway it was clear the party had died down since he'd left. He walked right through the back gate and was making his way through the now small crowd when he spotted Junior's pregnant sister. He waved as she noticed him and he approached her with his best smile.

"Hey there, I was looking for my cousin."

"Oh, I'm sorry, Jay and his friends left a while ago. Jay said something about Tween Waters I think, right, hon?" Maria looked to her husband, who nodded yes.

Mike glanced at the husband and the man who'd come up to stand beside him. They were obviously related, brothers if Mike had to guess. They stood by Maria Scintillo's side and assessed Mike, not in a kind way either. Mike had no doubt they were well aware of Scintillo Senior's apprehension and he was quite sure his cover was blown but he didn't think they were stupid enough to fuck with a federal agent, especially when the island was swarming with them. "Okay, thanks, I'll see my way out and good luck to you both." He spoke to Jay's sister and her husband and ignored the other man, whoever the fuck he was.

"Hey."

Mike casually turned back around to the sound of the male voice beckoning him. He reached around to his back at the same time as if he needed to scratch an itch and heard Reynolds in his ear assuring him that he and Murphy had his back.

"What's up?" Mike nodded his head to the man he guessed was Maria Scintillo's husband and gave him a disarming smile, ready to unleash a hail of bullets if need be.

"Catch anything?"

Mike noted the Spanish accent and the slightly mocking tone. He looked down at the fishing vest he still wore over his shirt and Kevlar. "Caught me a big one as a matter of fact." Mike grinned, gave a friendly wave, and quickly left the same way he came in. Fuck that guy. The sister seemed innocent enough but Mike didn't like the way the husband and his sidekick had looked at him. And if Mike wasn't certain before that they knew what was up, he was now. But there wasn't a damn thing they could do about it.

He got back in the Jeep and back on comm filling in his fellow agents on the two Spanish males. Garrison planned to stay on the house and Reynolds and Murph went back to Tween Waters. All informed Mike they'd be in touch ASAP if they had any word on Junior or Jenna. Mike pulled into Jenna's grandmother's driveway moments later and quickly went inside. He searched the house pulling off his fishing vest while calling Jenna's name just in case, even though his instincts told him she was long gone; hell, if Junior had left right after the bust went down then they were practically to Miami. In Jenna's bathroom Mike noticed there wasn't a toothbrush on or near the sink. Her full size suitcase was open and filled with clothing by the closet in her room but he imagined she would have probably taken a smaller bag to Miami with just a few things. He left the room and searched the counter and then the fridge for a note feeling his gut clench when he actually saw one. Taking it from under the refrigerator magnet he held it. Even though he was worried sick Mike couldn't help feeling just a little bit happy that Jenna had written him a note and he swore at himself to focus while he read. The note confirmed that Jenna went willingly and he swore again, ignoring her wiseass remarks about seeing her at the wedding. He'd spin her around the dance floor, all right, right after he put her over his knee. He'd see her again in just a couple of hours if he had anything to do about it and he'd deal with her little wiseass then, gladly.

According to Jenna's cousin somehow Junior had convinced Jenna to work for him. Mike could only imagine how Jay had lured her with the excitement of Miami and probably the promise of a lot of money. He hadn't heard any of their conversation at the party over the loud music and he wondered in what capacity Junior had asked her to work. Jenna's cousin told Nicki something about waiting tables and Mike was curious to know if Jenna had any idea what Scintillo's clubs were like; probably not if he had to guess. He took the note and folded it up, putting it in the pocket of his pants. He was back out the door and in his Jeep disengaging his earpiece and dialing Rafe as he backed out of the drive and headed off the islands.

"Tell me something good." Rafe was sitting at the computer checking flight times.

"She wasn't at the house. I'm in the Jeep headed to Miami now. I'll get the list of clubs from Daniels and head straight to the closest one." Mike took a breath. "I'm sorry, man, I had no way of knowing she'd fucking make friends with him. She met him at the resort and walked right down the beach with him and his friends. What the fuck was I supposed to do? She introduced me as her cousin and they invited me to Scintillo's house for a barbeque. I went so I could keep an eye on her and when I had her alone I told her to leave but she got cranked up thinking I was telling her what to do. I didn't tell her who Junior was because at that point Senior was not in custody and I wasn't about to put her in danger by telling her what was about to go down." Mike took another deep breath. "I'll get her back and bring her home; I'm not going to let anything happen to her, Rafe."

Rafe could hear the stress in his friend's voice and the genuine concern. "I know it's not your fault, but I need you to find her, Cap. I got a lot of worried people up here."

"I will and that's a fucking promise."

"I'm flying in first thing in the morning," Rafe told him.

"You don't have to do that. I'll have found her by then, save your money."

Rafe hesitated but trusted Mike. "Call me as soon as you find her and God forbid. . . if you don't."

Mike gave Rafe his word and hung up. He pressed the gas pedal to the floor as soon as he hit I-75 and prayed he got to Miami before anything bad could happen.

CHAPTER TWENTY

Jenna smiled as they hit South Beach. They had parked and were now walking along the famed Ocean Avenue. It was pushing ninety degrees and the early summer night air was humid. Jenna marveled at the art deco buildings as she walked beside Jay. Each building had its own unique architecture and color scheme, their inviting entrances anchored with enormous potted palms and exotic flora, adding to the tropical flare around them. Techno-colored neon signs lit up the concrete structures and each structure they passed looked more inviting then the last. It was after midnight now and Miami Beach was in full swing. There were long lines at each club and outdoor bar they passed and Jenna found herself gawking blatantly at the scantily clad women she saw strolling on the sidewalk. She had to remember to keep her mouth closed each time a different one passed. Each group of women she walked by seemed to have less and less on and their heels kept getting higher and higher. Jenna felt completely overdressed in her cotton sundress that ended just above her knee, when just below the crotch seemed to be the style.

Jay began to notice that Jenna was a bit uncomfortable and he squeezed her arm. "Relax, you look fantastic."

Jenna smiled appreciatively at the compliment. "I feel a little overdressed." She watched another girl go by who may as well have been nude. *Damn!*

Jay laughed at her expression. "I like you, Jenna, you're funny; you're not like my other girls."

Jenna looked at him. "Your *other girls?*"

Jay grinned. "You know, the girls that work for me." He laughed, "I just sounded like a pimp, didn't I?"

"Li'l bit." Jenna eyed him again then looked around as they stopped at the crowded entrance to what was obviously Jay's club. She felt as though she were about to enter the rain forest with all the exotic plants surrounding the entrance and the large exotic birds that perched in vibrantly painted cages on either side of the doors. "Wow, this is beautiful!" she said, taking it all in.

Jay grinned, pleased that she thought so but anxious to get her inside. Miguel would be waiting for him in the upstairs lounge and Jay knew his father would want his oldest friend taken care of as soon as possible. Jay's father had been in exile at a penthouse suite in one of Miguel Soto's private resorts in Mexico for the last year. Last night, Soto on his way to Miami to oversee his newest resort being built, had taken a detour and personally escorted Jay Sr. to his son on the open Gulf. It had been nearly a year since Jay had seen his father and when he stepped off Soto's Italian yacht and onto Jay's new boat with his personal bodyguard and long-time girlfriend, Jay had been surprised at how drawn and tired his father had looked for a man that had been living luxuriously. Jay knew his father had wanted for nothing in his time under Soto's care.

Jay's father knew it was at great risk coming to see the birth of his first grandchild, but he had been adamant that he would make the effort for his only daughter. A part of Jay thought maybe his father had known what was going to go down. When Rob had come back to the house from Tween Waters, he'd told Jay that the FBI took his father fast and with little reluctance. Rob had watched it all from behind a small storage shed underneath the building that held rooms overlooking the marina. Rob had been paid to watch the dock all day and reported to Jay as soon as he'd seen the Feds crash into the Four Winns and arrest Jay's dad.

Jay wasn't surprised to hear his father had not put up much of a fight. He had expressed much regret in his last phone call, surprising Jay, and he had made his wishes clear, speaking as if he knew his time was up. He wanted Jay to take things over for him but to do it legit. Jay's father had been grooming Jay for years, teaching him the business and how to work a crowd and maintain solid business relationships with the men with deep pockets, but his father had never shown Jay anything illegal. Jay had watched and learned that end of the business all on his own, behind the scenes. Growing up he had seen firsthand where the real money was coming from and he wanted a taste of it.

When his father had disappeared last year, Jay had finally had his chance to start his own growing empire inside the clubs. His father's customer base had long since scattered when word came down that his partner Xavier D'nafrio had been busted and that D'nafrio was handing out names like Halloween candy, so Jay had slowly built up his own contacts and a new customer base. It had taken a few solid months but now he dealt with some of the wealthiest businessmen in the world including Soto, his father's oldest friend. Jay was making fistfuls of cash and spending arm loads, more money than even his father had been making nightly. But if his father knew that Miguel Soto had become Jay's biggest supplier he would find a way to slice the throat of his closest friend. Jay's father didn't want a life of crime for Jay, he wanted Jay to grow old with peace of mind, but Jay had his own plan; he would make his fortune in five years' time then sell everything. He'd be out neat and clean and his father would be proud of him.

Miguel had promised Jay a retreat of his own anywhere in Mexico and Jay planned to retire there at thirty and have everything he wanted. And he wanted what Miguel had; money to buy the finest of everything, and that included women. Jay looked at Jenna again; she had just the exotic look about her that he knew Miguel craved; his insatiable appetite for younger women was what had brought him to Jay in the first place. Jay had taken over the services that his father had discreetly provided to wealthy traveling businessmen for years, through the club, and had expanded upon it. Men now came from across the globe and paid extraordinary amounts of money to live out their erotic fantasies with Jay's girls. He called them "his girls" because he'd in fact sampled each and every one of them, so much so that the only thing that got him hard now was the money they made him. He beckoned Jenna to follow him.

Jenna watched two enormous bouncers dressed in black unhook a velvet rope to let her and Jay pass into the throngs of people inside and she lost count of the number of people who stopped to shake Jay's hand. They slowly made their way past an enormous dance floor where crowds of sexy people moved to a club beat Jenna was quite familiar with and over to a set of Lucite stairs which were illuminated from underneath with tiny blue lights that pulsed in time to the music.

Jay smiled at her and led the way up. Jenna followed and found herself about to enter a large open lounge area that appeared much more subdued than the hardcore party atmosphere coming from the main floor of the club. When they landed at the top Jenna immediately noticed the number of men in suits being catered to by girls who were all dressed the same, if you called "dressed" being practically nude. The girls wore a sheer gold slinky type halter dress that was more or less backless and looked to be held in place by a single thread around the neck. Much like the girls Jenna had passed outside on the sidewalk these dresses also ended just below the crotch line. Jenna wondered with amusement what the undergarment of choice was, thong or bikini brief. Her question was quickly answered as the girl closest to her reached across a table to pick up an empty glass. Jenna watched in awe as the girl's male customer slowly moved his hand across the girl's completely bare ass. *Okay then!* Jenna's brows rose. That answered that question. She continued to follow Jay through to the back of the lounge where he unlocked a solid steel door to what was obviously his office. Once inside Jenna admired the sleek ultra-modern furnishings and decor and was astounded by the number of celebrity pictures hanging on the wall. All the pictures were people with their arms either around Jay or an older gentleman she guessed was his dad.

"This your dad?"

"Yeah, pretty cool, huh?" Jay sat behind his desk and turned on the monitors that surveyed the club upstairs and down. He spotted Miguel right away in the back corner not twenty feet from Jay's office.

"Your dad's very handsome. I can see where you get your good looks." Jenna smiled over at Jay, just a little impressed with him and her surroundings. It was funny, there wasn't an ounce of chemistry between them and they both knew it. Somewhere along the drive to Miami Jenna had realized it would strictly be a working relationship and she was just fine with that and Jay seemed to be too.

He had been wearing dark pants and a long-sleeved dark shirt when he had arrived in Nan's driveway, surprising Jenna. He told her he had decided to drive to Miami instead of taking the boat back because it would be so much quicker and he was anxious to show her the club. The hitch was they needed to take her car because his friends had already gone ahead in another car and there hadn't been enough room for him and Jenna. Jenna briefly thought it was a little presumptuous but she didn't care, she was just relieved not to be going by boat. She had to admit the idea of being trapped on a boat all the way to Miami with people she barely knew had made her somewhat nervous. She had let Jay drive her car thinking it was perfectly logical that he wouldn't have his own; he had after all arrived to the island by boat.

"That's really nice of you to say." Jay accepted her compliment and was satisfied Jenna didn't seem to have a clue as to who his father was.

"I can't believe you've met all these people, what's that like?" Jenna perused the wall of photos.

"At first, just like you'd think, you're impressed and psyched that they're in the club, but then they get demanding and usually cause more havoc than anything. If they're cheap it sucks. I actually lose business because I usually have to close this upstairs lounge off for them and their entourage and I make less money than if I had it open to my big spenders and players."

"Players like gamblers?"

Jay laughed. "No, players that like to play with the girls."

"Oh." Jenna had had a suspicion when she'd stepped upstairs with him and seen all the male customers and the scantily clad girls. She had felt her first feeling of trepidation since meeting Jay. "Those girls out there are prostitutes?"

"God, no!" Jay laughed again. "We have private rooms past the bar where the guys can buy private dances, they can look but they can't touch," he lied.

Jenna had heard plenty of stories about the private rooms in Rhode Island clubs too and she was sure there was a lot more to what Jay was telling her.

"You look a little shocked." Jay smiled and motioned for her to sit down. "The girls downstairs try real hard to get shifts upstairs; it's double and sometimes triple the money for half the work."

Having sex with strangers was considered half the work? Jenna wondered if the girls would agree. She had to let him know right away she wasn't into that. "Jay, this isn't going to work out if you wanted me for the upstairs lounge."

Jay gave her a reassuring smile. "No, you'll be working downstairs and making the kind of money I mentioned, I promise. I really did have a girl leave unexpectedly so I could use your help, but you'll see, every girl downstairs is trying to get up here." He leaned back in his oversized leather chair and clasped his hands behind his head. She was going to take some work; she had a little more going on upstairs than most of his other girls, except Georgie, of course.

Jay looked to Jenna like a boy trying to fill his father's shoes as he sat behind the expensive desk in the large leather chair that seemed to swallow him up and she guessed that was pretty much the case. His father was probably grooming him to take over. The man in the photos looked old enough to retire if he wasn't already. He looked vaguely familiar too.

"Those men you saw out there are captains of their industry. They travel anywhere from New York to Tokyo to relax up here and be pampered by our girls. Some men and even some celebrities will come in and drop ten grand on a girl if they like her enough." He watched Jenna's eyes grow wide. "I've seen it happen."

Jenna gave him a look of disbelief. "For a dance where they can't touch? C'mon." Did he think she was an idiot? Actually, he just might, she thought, she did just jump into her car with him and drive to Miami after only having met him this morning. Shit. She had to let him know she wasn't as stupid as she'd behaved.

"I've been in clubs like this before you know," Jenna told him. It was a total lie, but she knew enough about these kind of clubs from guys at school to bluff her way through it.

Jay laughed, swiveling his chair around to look at the monitors. "Okay, so there might be some girls who are willing to do a little more to make a little extra, but nothing is required here, Jenna, and those arrangements are made strictly between the client and the girl. I have nothing to do with it and don't make any extra because of it," he lied again. Some girls were easy; the mere mention of the money and they were sold and would do anything for it. Jenna was obviously not one of those women and was going to require some influence.

"Good, because I'm here strictly to serve drinks." Jenna stood defensively with her arms crossed, and knew he was full of shit that he wasn't profiting from the "extra services" some of the girls provided. Maybe he was a pimp after all, a pimp who looked like he went to an ivy-league college and wintered in Aspen. Jenna realized for the first time that it quite possibly was a huge mistake coming here. What the hell had she been thinking? She wasn't scared—she could take care of herself—but she was feeling pretty stupid. She could be on the island right now, trading barbs with Mike and happily fighting the sexual tension between them. God, she was such an idiot!

"No worries, you would have to earn your way upstairs anyway, and you won't even be here long enough for that, right?" Jay grinned. "These men only want the best, Jenna, the best-looking girls and the best dancers. You don't dance by the way, do you?" he laughed testing her.

Jenna smirked; was he challenging her? *Earn* her way upstairs? Please! Was it that easy for him to con these girls, just prey upon their egos and promise them all cash?

"No, Jay, I don't dance," she lied, like he was. "Like I said I'll just be serving."

"You won't make this kind of money anywhere else, I promise you that." Jay grinned and kept his eye on Miguel, who ominously was looking right into the camera's lens. Jay felt himself squirm.

Jenna didn't doubt what Jay said about the money, she was just kicking herself for thinking he just wanted her here as a server. He clearly had brought her here to add to his harem. The thing of it was he seemed so normal, he was even likable. She supposed things were just different in Miami, who was she to judge? Hell, if they were in Vegas no one would blink an eye at this type of club she'd bet. At least downstairs seemed like a true nightclub, and Jenna could handle that, as long as no man tried to touch her; then the shit would fly.

"So what's the uniform like for downstairs? Do you think I could start tonight?" She'd just get this over with, work one shift and then get the hell out of there. Now she was utterly thankful she had her own car. She just had to get the keys back from Jay. God, if her parents knew where she was they'd kill her; this was not the kind of adventure she'd had in mind.

Jay gestured for her to come closer to the monitor that showed the first floor of the club.

Jenna spotted the servers wearing silver short shorts and silver sequined tank tops. They wore knee high white laced boots with a high platform heel. Okay so the boots weren't practical and she'd definitely pay the price later but the outfit was definitely better than the slinky gold dress. At least she'd be protected if she had to bend over. She nodded her approval.

"So you think you're ready to go on the floor tonight?"

"Yeah, why not?" Then she wouldn't have to spend the night; she could finish her shift, tell him it wasn't for her and head back to Nan's.

"Then let's get you to work. Jenna, you're gonna be smokin' in that uniform." Jay stood up to take her back downstairs. She was definitely going to be a tough one. She was tough like Georgie had been at first.

Jenna gave Jay a sideways glance as if to tell him he could dispense with the compliments, she wasn't buying the BS and he laughed knowingly. If nothing else, she thought, at least he was non-threatening.

She followed Jay and wondered if Mike had received her note. She wondered where he had gone in the first place and wished that she could have spoken to him face to face before she had left for Miami. She had really been attracted to him and she was sure by that kiss they'd shared that he had been attracted to her. Rafe had insisted Mike was just trying to put her off because she was a distraction and he needed to focus on the job he was there to do. Well, he'd managed to put her off alright, teasing her and trying to tell her what to do! Well maybe by the time the wedding rolled around he'd think again about calling her a kid. She only wished she didn't have to wait so long to prove herself. Mike had implied there'd be a "next time" and if there were Jenna would make sure things went down a little differently. Next time she wouldn't be so afraid to welcome him to her. Her body warmed just thinking about it.

"Whatever you were just thinking about, save it for the customers, that look in your eyes is sexy as hell and guys will pay to see it."

Jenna blinked, surprised to be caught off in fantasy land. She just laughed at Jay's comment, somewhat embarrassed.

"Let's go get you a uniform." Jay smiled and made his way to the stairs.

Jenna followed behind Jay, back down the stairs, unaware of the man in the dimly lit corner of the upstairs lounge watching her. Once down, they passed the dance floor and Jay took her into a back room lined with several lockers. They were anchored by men's and women's dressing rooms with bathroom facilities for both. The room was large and clean and seemed quite organized. There was a comfortable-looking lounge area in the middle of the open space scattered with tables and chairs and Jenna noticed a kitchenette area along one wall with all the essentials. "This place is pretty big," she commented more to herself. Jay was busy in a nearby closet.

"Try this, I think it'll be just right," he said, shutting the closet door and holding it out.

Jenna took the uniform and the new package of hose that he handed her and shook her head. Oh God, if they could see me now. She'd at least have an interesting story to tell back home. She could hear Jake now with the comments.

Jay watched Jenna disappear into the ladies room and smiled. Once she got a taste of the money she could make, she'd be hooked; they all got hooked—in more ways than one, he laughed to himself.

Jenna took off her dress and underwear and put on the nylons, uniform, he white boots and had to remind herself that it was just for one night, she have to do anything she didn't want to do and could leave at any time.

She shook her head, laughing at herself and the absurdity of the situation. If Nicki or Paige knew what she was about to do they'd have a fit! At the very least Jenna would make the best of it and try to leave with some cash. Hell, she wore much less at the public beach, so if it meant some good tips for the night she could stand the uniform. It's not like she could tell Jay she wanted to leave now anyway. He might get pissed. What if he did have a mean sadistic side and flipped out on her or something? She didn't honestly think that would happen but she thought it best to at least work this one night like she said she would. The fact that Jay had failed to leave out the whole sex thing going on upstairs was a little disturbing and Jenna felt somewhat naive for not considering it were a possibility, but she never would have guessed the kind of business he was running by looking at him. He looked like a walking cologne ad or like he could be cast in one of those new vampire movies.

When she came back out Jay was waiting for her and he whistled at the sight of her.

"Damn, that looks good on you! I knew when I saw you in your bikini this morning that you would look fantastic in it."

"It's not that bad, I guess." Jenna looked in the full-length mirror that covered one wall. She had to admit the outfit was pretty sexy and she couldn't help but wonder what Mike would think if he saw her in it; would he call her a kid now?

"C'mon, let's go make you some money." Jay had to play this just right, give her a taste of the money first then he'd put her right in with Georgie and get things rollin'.

CHAPTER TWENTY-ONE

Justin finished bandaging up his last tattoo before lunch and after some quick care instructions, he walked his customer to the door and said goodbye. Back in his workroom he cleaned, washed up, and hit the lights before heading out the door himself. He hoped Paige was on today so he could have lunch with her and apologize for the day before.

After telling Gwen and Stacy he'd be gone for the next two hours, he stepped out of the shop and into the warm air. It was another beautiful sunny day in Newport and he knew the shop would probably be busy with walk-ins.

The heavy door and all the windows of Captain Jack's were open to the street and Justin walked in from the bright sun to the natural lit interior. He spotted Jack right away behind the bar and took a seat. The Sox game had just started and all of the TVs around the bar were tuned to the game.

"How goes it?" Jack eyed him while he dried a glass beer mug with a hand towel.

"Pretty good, just you on today?" Justin asked nonchalantly, his eyes scanning the rest of the bar area.

Jack nodded. "She called in, family problem, doesn't work again until next week."

Justin looked at Jack, surprised and confused. Family problem? He felt his heart sink to his stomach and couldn't help but feel bad for himself that he didn't know about Paige's family problem, but why should he? Especially after the way he had treated her yesterday. "Did she say what it was about?"

"Why don't you give the girl a call?" Jack asked with narrowed eyes. His old eyes had seen the chemistry between his new employee and his neighborhood friend but Jack had also seen the hurt on the Paige's pretty face yesterday and that didn't sit well. But he was wise enough to keep his involvement to a minimum.

Justin got up to leave. "Yeah, I think I will." Pride and embarrassment kept him from letting Jack know that he didn't have Paige's phone number so he just waved and went out the door. Justin turned back toward the shop and contemplated heading back to work to brood but abruptly turned back around and decided to jog over to Paige's apartment. He hoped she was there, and he hoped everything was all right.

When he arrived fifteen minutes later he walked up the stairs and knocked on her door. He waited several minutes and started back down the steps in defeat. When he reached the bottom, the door to the first floor apartment opened and an old woman stepped out.

"Oh," she said, clearly startled by the looks of him. "You're Paige's friend?"

"Yes," Justin answered surprised the old woman knew that. "But she doesn't appear to be home. I guess I'll come back later."

"Oh, don't bother, she left for Boston this morning and isn't coming back until next week. She's visiting her grandmother, the sweet girl. Her grandmother lives on Beacon Hill, you know."

Justin took in the little old lady, who seemed rather impressed with the Boston address. "Do you happen to have a number I could reach her at?" Maybe Paige's grandmother was sick.

"Oh I don't know if that's something she would want me to give out," she told him warily.

Justin could see her reluctance and he smiled to put her at ease. "That's okay, I'll just see her when she returns, I guess, thank you for your time." He'd go back and beg Jack for her number if he had to, but he wasn't about to bother this old woman.

Agnes faltered; he seemed like a polite enough young man even though his skin was all covered in ink, making him appear a bit menacing, and he did seem crestfallen at not being able to contact Paige. Never one to stand in the way of a budding relationship Agnes reached for him before he could walk away. "Wait."

Justin turned to look at the old woman, who now held a slight smile and her hand on his arm. "Yes?"

"I don't think Paige will mind, I do have a number you can reach her at, just a minute."

Justin breathed a thankful sigh as the woman stepped back into her apartment and returned a minute later with a piece of paper. He grinned when he looked down. Written on the paper were not one, but three different phone numbers, two for Paige, one for her grandmother, and her grandmother's Beacon Hill address as well. "Thank you," he said, grinning at the old woman. "I think this will be helpful."

"You were the boy on the motorcycle yesterday morning?"

Justin smiled again. "Yes, how did you know?" Had Paige mentioned him to her? She was obviously the land lord and she seemed pretty nice.

"I saw you through the curtain, the noise startled me."

"Oh, I apologize," Justin said and meant it. She was a sweet old woman.

"Oh it's okay, once I realized you were with Paige I relaxed. However," she hesitated and frowned.

Justin waited. He was amused and wondered what she hesitated to say.

"Paige went inside and cried her heart out when you left."

That was not what he expected her to say. Shit. "What?"

"You know her bathroom sits right atop mine and noise travels right down those old pipes." Agnes gestured up with her eyes.

Justin couldn't imagine why Paige would have cried after he dropped her off yesterday. That was before he'd called her at the bar. But he did feel a slow burn creep up his neck as he remembered what had gone on in Paige's bathroom the first time he'd been here. He dared to look into the old woman's eyes and he blushed even further at the twinkle he saw there. Oh God.

"It seems you have some making up to do, young man, I don't like to see Paige upset, she's a good girl and I expect her to be treated with the utmost respect. That's why I gave you that information; I trust you will make it up to her, whatever you did to make her cry like that."

Justin was duly reprimanded and sick to his stomach to think Paige may have been crying over something he may have said or done. "Yes ma'am, I plan to and thank you for this." He held up the piece of paper and as an afterthought reached over and kissed her cheek.

"Oh my." Agnes touched her cheek and grinned. "You are a handsome bloke even with those colorful arms."

Justin laughed and thanked her again as he took off down the street, purpose in his step. He wasn't happy to hear Paige had been crying and he had to wonder what exactly that was about. She had seemed fine when he'd left; it had been he who had felt terrible leaving her at the curb when all he'd wanted to do was take her in his arms and tell her. . . . He hadn't known what he'd wanted to tell her and that was his problem yesterday, but not today. He was happy to now have a way to get in touch with her. He would make things right and tell Paige what he should have yesterday, that he wanted to start a relationship with her and that he felt like he'd been hit with a Mack truck upon meeting her and that after their first incredible night together he really cared about her. He thought there was definitely something between them and he knew he wanted to spend more time getting to know her and see where it would lead. He just hoped to God she would be receptive to the idea.

* * * * *

"Nan, I'm leaving," Paige called up the stairs from where she stood in the grand foyer of her grandmother's brownstone. She heard Nan's muffled reply as she grabbed her overnight bag, pocketbook, and keys from the antique hall table before stepping into the morning air; they had already said their goodbyes over breakfast.

Paige had driven to Boston the night before. She had been so upset about Justin that she and Nan had ended up having a long heart-to-heart and at Nan's suggestion, Paige was going to Captiva for a couple of days. Paige really wanted to go to Justin and tell her how she felt about him no matter the consequences but Nan had convinced her not to. She said that Justin had withdrawn for a reason and she should give him the time to figure it out but Paige couldn't help but wonder if he would figure it out, what if this was it for them? What if they were over before they'd even begun? What if he figured out that he didn't want a relationship right now? It would break her heart she knew but going to Captiva was a good idea on two counts, Paige thought. She could be there to help find Jenna if need be and she could get her mind off Justin, although something told her that wasn't going to be easy. Her heart had been aching something fierce since his phone call yesterday and her stomach was in knots wondering if she'd ever hear from him again.

Nan had tried to reach Jenna last night and failed and Paige didn't dare tell her what was going on; she just hoped Jenna would be home safe on the island before Nan ever found out that she'd left. Paige took her phone from her bag and was disappointed that *she* still hadn't heard from Jenna, but Nicki had at least left a message to call. Paige walked the short distance on the cobblestone sidewalk to her nearby parked car and threw her overnight bag in the back seat, dialing Nicki before driving off.

"Hey, Paige,"

"Hey, Nicki, have you heard anything?"

"Yeah, she's in Miami with that guy, but they drove down instead of taking the boat, thank God, and Mike is out looking for her. He didn't find her last night, but he didn't have much time either, Jenna had a head start so by the time Mike got to South Beach he had only made it to two clubs before closing time. He's going back tonight to the club he missed and he'll have help from some fellow agents who will go back to the clubs Mike was at last night just in case she shows up there."

Paige panicked at Nicki's words. Help from FBI agents? "Is that necessary? Is this guy, Jay, dangerous?"

Nicki explained to Paige who Jay was and the reasons everyone was so worried.

"Oh my God, Nicki! Mike has to find her, do your parents know?"

"No, Mike said he promises he'll have her home tonight. Rafe is ready to get on a plane but Mike told him to stay put, he's handling it. I'm not telling Mom and Dad just yet, you know they're in Vegas, right?" Nicki asked, not waiting for an answer. "There's no need to worry them if we don't have to. Jenna did go there willingly and this kid Jay has never been in trouble before, but I guess the FBI have been keeping an eye on his nightclubs ever since he's taken over for his father. Rafe didn't say why but I can only imagine," Nicki told Paige then added, "It's just not like her not to call us back so I'm worried about that."

"Yeah, I know," Paige said. "Her phone must be dead; you know how she is with remembering to charge it, that's the last thing I reminded her of, to bring her charger."

"So maybe we'll hear something from her soon then." Nicki prayed that they did.

"Nicki, do you trust this guy Mike? Why is he so involved?" Paige sat behind the wheel of her car and stared out at the Public Gardens and the summer crowd walking through them.

"I trust him completely, he's a really close friend of Rafe's, and according to Rafe and Ali he's already really attracted to Jenna."

Paige had a feeling it was something like that. She had also got the impression from Jenna that she was just as interested in Mike, too, even though she tried to play it off like she wasn't. "Well, I guess that's a good thing, he'll be motivated to find her for more than one reason."

"Yeah, it is," Nicki agreed, a smile in her voice. "Mike will keep her safe, Paige, let's just sit tight. You know, I tried to call your apartment, too, and it went to voice mail."

"Sorry, I'm at Nan's."

"Why are you in Boston? Didn't you just start a new job?" Nicki asked.

"I was able to get my shifts covered so I drove up last night." Paige paused. "I needed to talk to Nan."

Nicki could hear in her cousin's voice that something was wrong. "Anything I can do to help?"

Paige smiled. "Nah, I appreciate it though, I'll be fine."

"Well, if I know Nan, she had some good advice."

"She actually suggested I go to Captiva for a couple of days," Paige said. "It's a good idea, this way I can be there for Jenna if I have to."

Nicki sighed but was relieved. "I hope you won't have to." Nicki trusted Rafe and she trusted Mike, too, even though she, herself, didn't know Mike all that well, but she knew he was a good person. She had to trust him; if anything happened to her sister she wouldn't be able to bear it.

Paige brooded. "I should have tried harder to talk her out of going."

"Don't do that to yourself, Paige. You know Jenna, she's always looking for fun; she would have gone anyway. The thought of going to Miami must have been so exciting to her; she always wants to go when we're on the island." Nicki reminded her cousin.

"I know, she said that." Paige knew she wouldn't have changed Jenna's mind but she still felt horrible.

"Well listen, make sure you call when you get to Captiva and I'll call you if I get any new information," Nicki promised.

"I will and thanks, talk to you soon." Paige hung up with Nicki and read her texts, disappointed there wasn't one from Jenna but relieved to see Jake had responded to the text she had sent him earlier updating him and inquiring if he'd heard from Jenna.

Negative, haven't heard a thing!
WTF! Wut's wrong w/ that girl?
Does she know wut goes on
on S. Beach?
Wut happened to GI Joe?
Should I be worried here?
what can I do?

Paige texted him back.

I'm leaving this afternoon
GI Joe is looking 4 her
nothing you could do
until we know something

She texted Jake the new information Nicki had given her and Nicki's number as well, in case Jake couldn't reach Paige.

everyone seems to think he'll
have her back tonight, i hope so
i'll keep u updated

Paige started the car praying Jenna was alright and headed off toward the pike. She answered a call from the photo lab she dealt with and they let her know the print of the picture she e-mailed them was ready. Paige hesitated for a minute but told them to go ahead and mat and frame it with the combination she'd picked out online then told them she'd be in in a few days to pick it up. She thanked them before hanging up then reached in her bag and pulled out the picture she had accidently taken from Justin's just the day before. The little boy she saw sitting on the porch steps tugged at her heart, and she wished things hadn't taken such a bad turn between her and Justin.

Maybe while she was away he would think about her and figure things out like Nan said. Maybe he was a little scared of what had happened with them so quickly but it wasn't like Paige was looking to marry him, for God's sake. She hadn't said or done anything to him to indicate she wanted to jump right into a relationship! She'd thought she behaved pretty cool. Sure they'd had incredible sex, and a great night out, but big deal, right?

But it was a big deal to Paige and she had thought Justin had thought so to. And yes, she had to admit she had some inexplicably strong feelings for him right off the bat but it's not like she'd told him so. She knew enough not to do that. Her problem was she had convinced herself he felt it too. She'd cried like a baby to Nan that she had actually bought into Jenna and Nan's whole theory about fate and the signs fate was giving her and how ridiculous and embarrassed she felt now for even thinking that way. Nan had just smiled and said fate was a funny thing and reminded Paige that it was what two people did with the signs fate handed them that counted. Paige had only cried more, feeling like a fool.

It would be good to put some distance from Justin like Nan said. Whatever had spooked him was something he had to deal with on his own she said, and she'd promised Paige things would work out the way they were meant to. Paige wondered how Nan could possibly know that but prayed she was right anyway. Paige also prayed that Jenna would be back on Captiva safe and sound by the time she arrived there. Jenna would cheer Paige up and make her forget Justin, temporarily anyway. But Paige didn't know what she was going to do once she returned to Newport.

CHAPTER TWENTY-TWO

Jenna woke up disoriented and with a pounding headache. She could hear a shower running nearby and she slowly sat up to take in her surroundings. She was in a large comfortable bed, but she didn't know how she'd got there. She noticed a clock at the bedside table and it read three p. m. Oh my God! She sat up even further, feeling a wave of dizziness threaten to drop her right back to the pillows but she managed to settle herself by taking a moment to be still and take a deep breath. She looked around once again and saw her overnight bag on the floor with the uniform Jay had given her draped over a nearby chair. Jenna then looked down to see she was wearing a nightshirt she had packed but couldn't remember changing into it. She did remember working, though, and sitting down at the bar at closing with Georgie for a drink. She had told Georgie she was heading back to Captiva and had asked Jay for the keys to her car, and that's all Jenna remembered. If her headache was any indication, she'd had more than one drink and Jay had obviously known enough not to let her drive, thank God. She tried to remember what the hell she'd been drinking. She'd never blacked out before and it didn't sit too well with her that she had.

The room was dark and Jenna slowly got out of the bed to open the blinds. Miles of palms trees, and the sand and ocean that made up South Beach greeted her in either direction. With an intake of breath Jenna squinted her eyes trying to adjust to the brilliant sun shining high in the clear blue sky. Wow, it was an awesome view but where the hell was she? She glanced around the poshly decorated bedroom then reached for her bag. She took out the wad of cash she'd secured with a hair elastic and counted it. Five hundred dollars. She remembered that! Men had tipped her generously and she hadn't even danced for them. Apparently a smile went a long way with the men of Miami; no wonder the girls upstairs were making a fortune. If a smile made Jenna that much money then she couldn't imagine the tips the girls were getting in the upstairs lounge for "half the work." Ha! No thanks.

Jenna put the cash back in a small zipper compartment in her bag and unplugged her phone from its charger. She couldn't recall charging her phone either, but was grateful she had. She turned it on and was surprised to see six missed calls and four texts. Jeez. Nicki and Paige were anxious to talk to her apparently and Nan had called, too, surprised that Jenna was on Captiva a week early.

Jenna read her first missed text and smirked. Man, Paige had really been worried about that boat ride. At least she'd be happy to hear Jenna had come to Miami by car instead. Jenna went to Nicki's text next and felt her stomach drop to her feet as she read it. *Oh shit!* Jenna looked around the room, suddenly wary, and listened for the shower she'd heard earlier. The sound of running water had now been replaced with the sound of a blow dryer. Jenna didn't even know who was here with her. She must be in one of Jay's condos above the nightclub she figured.

She read Nicki's text again then quickly listened to her voicemail. Nicki went on so long that she got cut off. Jenna listened to the first part again. Oh God, that's why Mike had gone to the barbeque with her and had tried to get her to leave, not because he had been jealous, but because Jay's fugitive dad could have shown up there at any time. Jenna felt like such an ass. She had to think. Did Jay bring her up here last night? Had he been the one to change her into her night shirt? Oh God, she hoped not.

She had seen pictures of Jay's father last night and thought he looked familiar but she hadn't remembered the Scintillo name so she hadn't put it together. Of course it all made sense now, someone as young as Jay running all of this and having his own boat, and his sister who wasn't much older living in a beach house on Captiva? Jenna had drawn her own conclusions that they were obviously a wealthy family but she hadn't really cared enough to think about it much further than that. She'd just been excited at the thought of coming to Miami and making a bit of cash and maybe having a little fun while she was here. Jay and his friends had seemed harmless, spoiled maybe, but harmless.

According to Nicki's first message, Mike had helped capture Jay's father after he'd left the party. Jenna realized now that Jay's friend Rob who had stayed behind at the pool must have seen the whole thing and that's why Jay wanted to leave the island so quickly and why he didn't want to take the boat. Holy shit, were the Feds looking for Jay now too? Jenna supposed if they were after him, the nightclubs would be the first place they looked and they would have grabbed him already; besides Nicki had only mentioned trouble with the dad and not Jay, but then why had Jay wanted to leave Captiva so quickly?

Jenna dialed her voicemail again and listened to Nicki's continued message. It just said Mike was on his way to Miami to find her. *He was?* Jenna felt both a surge of excitement and annoyance at the same time. Was he coming because he was concerned himself or because Nicki had called Rafe? Unfortunately, Jenna suspected it was the latter. Did Mike think he could just pick her up and take her back to the island like an unruly teenager? It made Jenna look and feel like a child that Nicki was sending Mike here after her!

She looked at her comfortable surroundings and again at the view. She didn't feel like she was in any danger but she planned to leave anyway as soon as she gathered her things and found her car keys. She didn't want to get caught up in any of this bullshit. At least nobody was holding her hostage though; at least she didn't think so. Jenna went to the bedroom door and tried the knob breathing a sigh of relief when it turned in her hand. She tried calling Paige and then Nan but neither answered so she left quick messages for them both then she dialed Nicki's cell.

"*Oh Jenna, thank God! Where are you?*" Nicki asked in a frantic voice.

"God, Nick, I'm in Miami safe and sound, what is all the drama about?"

"You're kidding me, right? You have no sense of alarm being in the company of the son of a drug lord? Have you heard the expression 'like father, like son'?"

Jenna rolled her eyes. "Actually, believe it or not, I don't feel a sense of alarm, besides I'm leaving today anyway. I just woke up and I'm going to get my things together."

Thank God, Nicki thought. "Woke up where? Where are you?"

"I'm in a condo above the club, I think."

"You think?" Nicki asked incredulous. "You don't know?"

"I think I had too much to drink last night, I don't remember how I got here. I was going to leave last night after I worked, but I sat down for a drink with this girl Georgie and next thing I remember, I was waking up."

"Oh - my - God Jenna! That's not like you!" Nicki couldn't believe this. "What were you drinking? And you say you were *working* there?"

"I don't know what I was drinking, whatever she was drinking, and yeah, I made five hundred bucks too." Jenna scanned the room while she listened to Nicki rant.

"Doing what exactly? Did you also swallow your brain and crap it out? What the hell is wrong with you?" Nicki was pissed. Her sister had never acted like this before.

"Nice, Nicki." Jenna rolled her eyes at the visual. "I was serving drinks all night." Jenna rubbed her head and almost wished she could do what Nicki had suggested; maybe then her headache would disappear.

"Jenna, I don't like this one bit, Rafe was going to fly down there and bring you back himself, you know!"

"You've got to be kidding! I hope you put a stop to that!" Jenna rolled her eyes, not believing what a huge deal they were all making. The last thing she wanted was to have Rafe involved when she knew he was gearing up for his wedding. Given the current information, Jenna knew the situation wouldn't look so good if she were on the outside looking in but she truly didn't feel in any danger. Jay was like a spoiled frat boy, for God's sake. She wasn't afraid of him besides, and their cousins Ryan and John had shown her how to take care of guys like him.

"No, as a matter of fact Mike called Rafe off saying he would take care of it himself."

Jenna paced the room, suddenly infuriated but also feeling a little thrill shoot through her at the mere mention of Mike's name.

"Oh really, he did, huh? What the hell business is it of his?" Why would he do that? Jenna felt her heart trip.

Nicki sighed, exasperated. "Mike feels responsible, I think, for not telling you who Jay was in the first place but he couldn't say anything until Jay's father was apprehended. He was afraid your knowing would have put you in danger at the party."

Jenna rolled her eyes. "Jeez, Nick, I think I would know if I was in any danger. I would feel it in my gut."

It was Nicki's turn to roll her eyes. "Jenna, no offense, but do I need to remind you that you dated that D. J. for a year and never knew that he cheated on you until a week before you broke it off?"

"That's a little different, Nicki, and just plain low. Thanks for the reminder." Jenna smirked and sat down again on the bed, deflated.

"I'm not saying it to be mean; I'm trying to tell you that you are far too trusting of the wrong people."

"Well, you don't know Jay, Nicki, and besides like I said I'm leaving today, on my own, not because G. I. Joe is being sent to rescue me." Although a part of Jenna found the thought quite appealing, maybe she would hang out for a bit.

Nicki was relieved that Jenna was leaving and she couldn't help but grin even though she was still worried for her sister. "I happen to know you'd love to be rescued by GI Joe," Nicki teased, trying to ease the tension between them.

"Ugh!" Jenna almost hung up, exasperated. "Nicki, if I thought for one minute he was coming here because he genuinely liked me and not because he's doing an errand for Rafe on account of you being worried; then you know what? You're right, I'd be over the top excited, but I happen to know he just looks at me as a kid, so screw it! I'll decide whether I stay or go! I made a lot of money last night and I might decide to do it again tonight!" Suddenly the idea of staying didn't seem so bad, not if she knew Mike would be around.

So much for the tension breaker, Nicki thought. "You know I'd call Mom and Dad on this but I'm not going to ruin their vacation. I'm going to see how grown up you can be and let you get out of this yourself." Nicki was pissed again and terrified Jenna would stay. Her only salvation was that she knew Mike would be there soon and he would keep Jenna safe.

"Thank you! That's the best thing you've said since you picked up the phone," Jenna said loudly, just as pissed. "I'm going to hang up now."

"Will you at least tell me what club you're at?"

"Why, and make it that much easier for him to find me? Mike's a player down here, I'm sure he'll figure it out eventually." Jenna thought about it and changed her mind. What if she *were* in some kind of danger? "I'm on the beach okay? That narrows it down."

"Oh, thanks so much Jenna, that's a huge help," Nicki said sarcastically. "I'm still going to worry, you know, until I hear you're safely back at Nan's. Paige is on her way there, by the way."

"What! You got her involved too? She's supposed to be at her new job!" Jenna couldn't believe this.

"Nooo," Nicki droned defensively, "I had nothing to do with it, Nan told her to go, and not because of you," Nicki quickly added. "Nan doesn't know you're not at the house. She just thought Paige needed to get away."

That didn't sound good. Paige had really been affected by this thing with Justin apparently. Jenna shook her head. "Listen, Nick, I realize from Rafe and Mike's point of view this probably doesn't look good, but I'm telling you, I'm fine, I'm not in any danger." Jenna paced the room. Her head killed and she was tired of arguing and she felt herself relenting. They all just cared about her and were worried, she got it; she just didn't think there was any reason to be worried. "I'll be fine, Nicki. I'll call you when I get back on island, okay? I'll probably see Paige tonight."

"Okay, good." Nicki started to feel a little more at ease. "But I want you to call Mike first."

Jenna listened to Nicki rattle off his number but she had no intention of writing it down. "Fine, but will you promise to have Rafe call him off? I don't want him coming here making some kind of scene."

Nicki sighed. "I can't promise that, Jenna."

Ugh! Jenna said goodbye to Nicki and went to see where the hell she was and who was there with her.

* * * * *

Nicki called Rafe to update him so he could relay with Mike and then she called Paige and could only leave a message knowing she was airborne. Nicki didn't care if Jenna got mad at her; she needed to get her ass out of Miami and the more people to tell her that the better!

* * * * *

When Paige arrived at Southwest International later that evening she checked her messages and felt immediate relief at the sound of Jenna's voice, however, the message was disturbing. She sounded like hell, and said she was going to work one more night before heading back to Nan's. She joked telling Paige not to worry, that G. I. Joe was coming to rescue her.

Paige was glad of that but she didn't like the sounds of Jenna working in that club. Hopefully Mike would cut her evening short and bring her back home to the island.

CHAPTER TWENTY-THREE

Justin had left work early and after a shower and a quick bite to eat for him and Sam, he was behind the wheel of his Jeep with Sam resting comfortably in the back. He had Googled directions for Paige's grandmother's townhouse and he was on 24 North heading to Boston. His decision not to call first was probably not that smart but he was hoping the element of surprise would work in his favor.

He got off the exit an hour later and found himself circling around The Public Gardens. Every metered spot was taken and Justin realized finding a public garage was his only option. After pulling into a garage that was buried under ground, he parked and put Sam on his leash. They walked back up to street level and Justin let Sam relieve himself before they forged on. Justin had driven past the townhouse twice and knew just where he was headed but now that he was actually this close he felt a little unsure about his plan. What if he interrupted whatever "family problem" Paige was having? What if she was pissed at him? What if she rejected him? He strolled through the gated park giving himself a few more minutes to think it through. He really liked Paige—a lot and he knew he wanted to keep seeing her. If he was absolutely honest with himself, he was falling for her and even though it sounded crazy, he had to tell her, he'd come here just to do so. Yeah, she might think he was crazy after just having met him four days ago but stranger things had happened and he just had to go for it.

Bolstered now by his own mental pep talk, Justin came out of the park and crossed the street to Paige's grandmother's place. He had to admit it was pretty impressive. He climbed the granite stairs and stared at the ornate brass knocker on the large front door and hesitated before using it. He chose the doorbell instead. He then waited nervously with Sam on the front steps and took in the groups of people that steadily walked by. It was nearing eight o'clock on the summer night, still quite warm out, and the foot traffic was ample. Justin contemplated ringing the doorbell again and was glad he hadn't when he heard a click and the oversized, polished, wooden door opened.

He was immediately taken aback by the woman standing before him. She was not what he had been expected at all. Paige's grandmother was absolutely stunning. She reminded him of a glamorous old movie star. She was tall, nearly as tall as him, and blonde, her hair falling just above her shoulders in a current style, and she wore very little make-up. She was dressed casually in navy blue pants and a white top with a matching white lightweight sweater draped around her shoulders with a pair of black framed reading glasses perched on her nose. Her clothes looked expensive and perfectly put together. Justin's first impression by the way she held herself was that she was extremely classy. When she reached up to take her glasses off Justin then met her eyes, they were as blue as Paige's or rather Paige's were as blue as her grandmother's. She was a beautiful older woman.

"Hello, can I help you?"

Justin cleared his throat. "Hi, I'm looking for Paige."

Grace stared at the young man and took him in. He was just as Paige described and Grace found herself grinning. Her granddaughters sure knew how to pick them. She herself had the knack once upon a time, but that was too long ago to even think about. The activity by the young man's feet diverted her attention. "Is this little guy looking for Paige as well?" Grace bent down to pat the pup.

"Yes, ma'am." Justin pulled back on the leash to stop Sam from jumping on the elegant woman.

Grace laughed. "Oh, he's all right." She stood back up. "Why don't the both of you come in and have a seat."

Justin exhaled gratefully and he and Sam followed inside. Paige's grandmother led them to a large sitting room off the foyer and gestured for Justin to take a seat on a an oversized comfortable-looking sofa, which he did with Sam plopping down by his feet on what looked to be a very expensive oriental carpet.

"So you are here to see Paige?" Grace studied him. The boy had deep brown, soulful eyes.

Justin swallowed feeling extremely nervous all of a sudden. "Yes, ma'am. I'm Justin Reid, and this is Sam."

"Hello Justin, I'm Grace Thompson, Paige's grandmother. I'm pleased to meet you, and you too, Sam." Grace smiled down to the pup, who jumped back up excitedly at the sound of his name, emitting a laugh from Grace. "It doesn't take much at that stage, does it?"

Justin smiled. "No, it sure doesn't." Was Paige somewhere upstairs?

"Well, Justin, I have to tell you that Paige is not here." Grace watched for his reaction.

Justin took a deep breath knowing that this would be a possibility. She was probably out somewhere in the city and he had to admit the thought of that made him a little jealous. Was she with someone? He'd try and find her if he could. "Could you tell me when she'll be back or perhaps where she's at?"

Grace sat down on the settee across from him. "I'm afraid she's gone to Captiva Island."

"Oh." Justin stared at Grace and felt his heart sink. Okay, so he hadn't been expecting her to say that, and that's why he should have called first. He looked away from her and down at Sam, crestfallen and mentally kicking himself.

Grace watched the disappointment cross Justin's face and she felt for the boy, just as she had felt for Paige when Paige had cried and told Grace all about this young man between hiccups and sniffles. Paige had told her everything, from their first meeting up until yesterday's phone call. Grace had suggested to Paige that she give Justin some space. It sounded to Grace as if the boy needed some time to realize just what he felt for Paige. They'd apparently got off with a lightning fast start and Grace knew the pain Paige was feeling, she knew it first-hand, but she had assured Paige Justin would come to her when he was ready. Grace smiled inwardly—he'd come even sooner than she'd expected. Lust could turn to love overnight and it could be overwhelming when one realized the shift. It seemed Justin just may have.

"I can see you're disappointed with that news."

Justin looked back up at Grace and saw only kindness in her eyes. "You could say that, I was hoping to speak with her. It was important." Man, he really screwed this one up.

Hmmm, it seems she was right, the young man was just as affected as Paige. Grace smiled. "Can I fix you a drink, Justin?"

He hesitated but realized she wanted him to accept. "Sure, thanks."

Grace stood up and walked to the side bar next to the fireplace. She poured them both a scotch and walked back over to him handing him the short glass. "I hope you like it neat."

Justin grinned; she really was like an old-fashioned movie star. He wasn't about to tell her a beer would have done the trick, he just accepted the glass with thanks and took a healthy sip. "Whew," he shook his head in surprise.

Grace chuckled. "I like you, Justin, there's only been one other young man brave enough to accept my forty-year-old scotch without complaint and he'll be marrying another one of my granddaughters this fall." She laughed again. "But I can get you a beer if you'd rather."

Justin grinned, liking her too and thanking God he hadn't asked for the beer. "Are you kidding? Not after that testimonial." They both stared at each other knowingly and he was thankful for the appraising look she gave him.

Well then, he was truly serious about Paige. He had made light of it but Grace heard him loud and clear. "Justin, why are you here?"

Justin could tell Paige's grandmother was a tough woman and he could see that she cared deeply about her family. There were pictures of them all around the room. He stared at a large silver framed photo on the marble fireplace mantel just behind Grace. It was of Paige, Jenna, and another attractive girl he assumed was Jenna's sister, all with their arms around each other and smiling widely as if they'd been laughing. It couldn't have been that long ago either; Paige didn't look much different and was absolutely gorgeous in it. He turned back to Paige's grandmother. Grace wasn't the kind of woman to beat around the bush, so he wouldn't either.

"I owe your granddaughter an apology and I wanted to say it in person. I went to her apartment and her landlord told me she was here." Justin answered the pointed question and waited for the next, hoping she wouldn't ask it, but she did.

"And why would you need to apologize?" Grace knew he was uncomfortable but she needed to test the boy's salt if he was going to be with Paige.

Justin felt himself tense at the intrusion and then just as quickly he relaxed. This was Paige's grandmother and she obviously cared a great deal for Paige. "I broke a date and lied to Paige and I'd like to tell her how sorry I am and why I did it."

Grace nodded and after talking with Paige the night before Grace thought she had a pretty good idea of why he'd done it. "Can I tell you a story, Justin?"

Justin was grateful he didn't have to elaborate any further and he nodded yes. He wanted nothing more right now than to get back in the car and try to call Paige but he would never be rude especially to Paige's grandmother. She was definitely a woman he would like to get to know better.

"When I was just about twenty years old, years before I became a real estate agent, I was working as a chamber maid just across the street at what was then the Ritz Carlton hotel. It was fairly new and the most luxurious hotel in Boston at the time, as you can imagine. I suppose it still is, although they've changed the name and there are so many others now just as posh. Anyway, back then I saw so many glamorous people come and go while I worked there, even some movie stars." Grace smiled and paused, remembering. "It was great fun." She took a breath and went on. "Well, one day, I offered to cover for one of my girlfriends, so I had a few extra rooms to clean. I knocked on one particular door, as maids will do," she said and smiled, "And waited for an answer. When none came I used the pass key we maids carried and I entered the darkened room. I could see straight away that the bed was a mess; its pillows and blankets were all strewn about in a heap so I left my cart in the hall and took in only what I needed to start with. I emptied the trash then dusted the mahogany desk and gilt framed mirror against the wall. The rooms were furnished so beautifully back then," Grace told him, remembering.

"When I finished with the small things I proceeded to open the heavy brocade drapes before going over to strip the bedding. This particular room had a lovely view of the Public Gardens," she told Justin and he smiled politely. "Well," Grace continued, "as soon as the first sliver of sun hit the room I heard this God-awful moan and all this rustling about that nearly had me jumping out of my skin."

Justin grinned in anticipation.

"Well, I whipped around to the startling sound with my stomach in knots, and my jaw just about fell open; all this time I thought I'd been in the room alone!" Grace laughed and went on. "But I hadn't been. Lying there on the bed, beneath all those messy covers now completely thrown to the floor, was a stark, naked man."

Justin let out a soft chuckle grinning and listening.

"Well, I don't have to tell you how shocked I was." Grace put a hand to her chest. "But I must admit the man was so incredibly good looking in all of his glory that I couldn't bring myself to look away. He was all skin and muscles and. . . well, I don't need to go on."

Justin was amused as Paige's grandmother blushed, he felt himself blush too.

"We just stared at each other for what seemed like an eternity before he said to me in a low smoky voice, "Am I dreaming you or are you real?"

Justin laughed picturing the scene. He imagined Paige's grandmother as a young woman and thought he knew why the man thought he had been dreaming. "What did you say?"

"Why, I couldn't say anything!" Grace brought a hand to her chest again. "It was my first time seeing a naked man and I was completely mesmerized," she laughed. "I did however slowly approach the bed and gingerly pick up the covers and put them back over his body all the while with him staring at me as if I truly were an apparition." Grace laughed. "I was so darn nervous and thinking I was going to lose my job that I whispered to him just as I let the sheet go." Grace mimicked the scene and whispered for effect, "*This isn't real, you are dreaming.*"

Justin cracked up. "You didn't!"

Grace laughed, too. "I most certainly did and then I ran like hell out of the room."

"What happened?" Justin asked, chuckling.

"Well," Grace laughed, "the problem with dreams is that the people in them usually don't leave their belongings behind, like their cleaning supplies."

"Oh no." Justin continued to laugh.

"Oh yes! The man called down to the front desk and told them I had left my supplies in the room and my cart outside in the hall and could I please return to his room at once. And much to my mortification one of the staff found me in the break room, hiding there, and I was quickly sent back to the man's room to retrieve them."

Justin nodded with amused sympathy. "That couldn't have been easy." But if he had to guess the man was probably quite eager to see her again.

"Oh, until this day I remember the horror of going back up there." Grace's grimace was quickly followed by a smile as she thought back. "But when I knocked on the door again and he opened it, fully clothed this time mind you," she grinned, "it was like a punch straight to the gut." Grace put a hand to her stomach as if she could still feel it.

Justin looked at her in disbelief and realized he knew that very same feeling. It had happened to him with Paige. "What happened?"

"Well, to make a long story short, we became inseparable for the rest of his time in Boston which sadly was only a few short days. He was from New York and staying at the Ritz while he conducted some business here in the city. He took me to the finest restaurants and to the theater each night and each day we would walk up and down Newbury and Boylston streets and all the streets in between, talking and getting to know each other. I fell in love with him in a matter of days, probably the first time I laid eyes on him if I'm being honest." Grace's laugh held a note of wistfulness, but she smiled at Justin who seemed to be getting antsy sitting on the edge of her sofa.

"So what happened next?"

"We said a heartfelt goodbye and he went back to New York City."

"What? *That's it?*" Justin asked not even trying to hide his disappointment. "Why did he go back? Didn't you tell him how you felt?"

"Do you think I should have?" Grace asked with narrowed eyes. "After all, I'd only known him for such a short time; I was embarrassed of my strong feelings. I didn't want him to think I was a nut job!"

"But what if he had been feeling the same way?" Justin asked, completely absorbed in Grace's story. "That's pretty sad to think he never knew how you felt." Justin sat there disappointed at the sad ending and staring at Grace. He felt bad for her. She should have told the guy. So what that she'd only known him a few days, the guy probably would have loved to know how she'd felt about him, Justin knew how he would have felt. Jeez, he had been expecting a happy ending.

Justin and Grace stared at one another for a long moment and Justin studied the wisdom he saw behind Grace's brilliant blue eyes. A whole minute seemed to have passed as he processed her story and then he let out a small chuckle shaking his head in acknowledgment. He put his empty scotch glass down and stood up. "Grace, I think I need to go home and pack a bag."

"I know, dear." She gave him a satisfied smile.

Justin took the liberty of kissing Grace on the cheek. "Thank you." As he was leaving Justin stopped in the foyer and turned back to her. "Just out of curiosity, what made you tell me that story?"

Grace gave him another knowing smile. "Because of why you came."

Justin returned her smile, somewhat embarrassed. "Is it that obvious?"

"Gloriously so, my dear, gloriously so." Grace took her calling card from the hall desk and handed it to him telling him to call when he landed and she would give him directions and particulars on the house. "It was a pleasure, Justin, and I hope I'll see you again real soon." Grace walked him and Sam to the front door and bid them farewell. She shut the door after him and whistled a happy tune as she made her way to her kitchen for some tea. Two down, one to go!

Justin made it back to his house in Newport a little after ten. He let Sam out then ran upstairs to get on the computer and check flight times. There was nothing leaving tonight from either Green or Logan. The first flight left Boston at seven forty a. m. the next morning. He sat for a minute weighing his options then called his sister's cell.

"Hey bro, I talked to Mom tonight, you left work early, huh?"

Sara had answered right away thankfully. How did his mother know he'd left work early? Jesus. "Yeah, I had something I had to take care of. Listen, I need a big favor."

"Shoot."

"Can you take Sam for a couple of days? I have to fly to Florida tomorrow morning and I don't want to take him on the plane. I can't leave him at Mom and Dad's; they're having their floors redone this week."

"Oh Justin, I'm sorry I can't. I'm staying with Paul for a few days in Providence. He can't have pets here."

Shit, it figured. He couldn't stand his sister's boyfriend and wouldn't trust him around Sam anyway.

"I'm sorry; you know I'd do it in a second if I were there. How is the little stinker anyway?"

"I know you would, thanks anyway. And he's fine, about to take his first plane ride, I guess." Justin wanted to ask her why the hell she was still with that thug boyfriend of hers but he kept it nice. They caught up for a few minutes then said goodbye. He made a call to Stacy and then to Gwen and told them he'd be gone for a couple of days. It wasn't the best time to be leaving the shop but Stacy assured him she'd be fine by herself and Gwen would reschedule whatever appointments he had. Having that squared away he booked the flight for him and Sam and packed a bag. He thought again about Grace's story and smiled; he couldn't wait to see Paige.

CHAPTER TWENTY-FOUR

Mike had been watching her for three hours now, and each hour seemed to get worse. The first hour had been pretty uneventful; Jenna hadn't even noticed him. He had stayed along the perimeters of the overcrowded night club and watched her serve drinks to guy after guy. She was walking around in some killer boots and some damn little outfit that naturally she looked hot as sin in, making it even harder for Mike not to just pick her up and haul her out of there but Rafe had cautioned him that Jenna might not go with him willingly; apparently she was a little peeved people were looking out for her. Well, too bad, he thought.

Jenna had told her sister that working for Junior was harmless but she had also told Nicki she was leaving that afternoon, so why she was still here was beyond Mike. Rafe was still concerned and Mike had assured him that he had Jenna covered. He planned to sit in this club until she was done with her shift and personally escort her back to Captiva, making sure she arrived safely.

His patience was wearing thin though. A short time ago he had seen one of her customers run a hand up and down her near naked thigh and Mike had nearly lost it but Jenna had put the guy right in his place. She'd had a death grip on the guy's wrist and a tight smile on her face that read "fuck off." Mike had laughed to himself, enjoying the scene. She didn't put up with any bullshit and he liked that about her. Mike had also used the moment to make his presence known. He'd taken the empty table right behind the guy to let Jenna know he was there if she needed him. He would have laughed at the look of shock and surprise on her face when she noticed him but when she met his eyes his stomach flipped around instead, like a goddamn fish out of water and all he could do was hold her stare, feeling a little surprised himself.

When Rafe had informed Mike today that Jenna was at Junior's club on the beach Mike had cursed and found her easily enough. He'd started inland the previous night searching Scintillo's other establishments hoping he'd find her at either of them and not here, where he sat now, knowing what went on in this particular club. Mike had spotted her almost immediately when he'd arrived. A surprising jolt had shot right through him at the sight of her and he'd written it off as just relief that he had indeed found her, but the skimpy little outfit she had on may have prompted the feeling too. She looked as hot and sexy as they came. He was reminded instantly that he wanted her something fierce, but seeing her face again made him also realize he'd actually missed being around the pint-sized spitfire, and that got to him too.

Now that Jenna's initial shock at seeing him had passed, she'd taken to glowering at him. She was cute as hell when she was mad, especially when Mike's waitress had offered to dance for him. Jenna had actually looked jealous and Mike had been pleasantly surprised. He had declined the dance but sort of wished afterwards that he hadn't, if only to see how Jenna would have responded.

Now he was in hour three and hanging back in the shadows again; he didn't want her scowling at him anymore. He'd much rather see her smile, although not for a bunch of dudes like she was now. She was laughing and smiling as she waited on a group of ten guys who were young and full of piss. They were seated at a large table that surrounded a small stage in the center of it and Mike knew just what the stage was for; he'd sat at that very same table a time or two, long ago. He wondered which of Junior's girls would get up there and hoped like hell the guys behaved themselves with Jenna serving them. It was going to be difficult to stay in the shadows if Mike saw something he didn't like.

Sure enough moments later Georgie, the girl who had danced around him at the pool the day before, made her way up on the small stage and Mike kept his eyes on Jenna, who was delivering drinks and taking empties off the table below. The guys all seemed to have their attention focused on Georgie and Mike was glad for it.

The club music was loud and as Mike looked around he noticed several other girls dancing at similar tables. There were individual stages set up in the center of some of the larger tables that held big groups and Mike wasn't surprised to see most of the girls were up there topless. When he looked back at Georgie she too was well under way of becoming so. His eyes went to Jenna and he could see she was watching Georgie's half naked form every now and then as she made her way around the table and damn if watching Jenna watch Georgie didn't turn him on. He had to remind himself that he was there to protect Jenna and keep her safe, not lust after her.

The guys at the table were doing their requisite cheering and hollering and Mike could see Georgie now reaching an arm out to one of them, only it was *Jenna's* arm that suddenly appeared with the rest of her scantily clad body up on the small stage with Georgie. Oh shit!

Mike moved from the shadows and stood on alert as he watched Jenna get up on the small platform and move along with Georgie to the club's pounding beat. What the hell was she doing? His heart slammed in his chest and he felt the blood rush at the sight of her dancing up there. Shit, she moved like a dream. She was an incredible dancer and she now had the attention of every guy at the table. Mike watched as the two women swayed and danced seductively with one another causing the men to get very loud—some were now standing trying to get closer and Mike panicked when he lost sight of Jenna for a second. He maneuvered his way closer to the table until he could see her again and was relieved to see she was still covered in the clothing she wore.

Mike continued to watch Jenna move seductively to the beat and he couldn't help but be turned on, her legs, hell, her whole body was incredible. Thankfully the damn song finally ended and he watched painfully as one of the guys took Jenna by the waist to help her down. Mike's teeth clenched tightly as he saw the dude's hands slip under the hem of Jenna's top and he knew the dude was touching the skin of Jenna's midriff.

When her boots finally hit the floor her eyes came up directly and met and held Mike's. This time there was no surprise or scowl on her face and Mike was motionless. Her dark exotic eyes were locked with his and what he saw in them made his heart pound faster and his blood flow south. He wanted to go to her and carry her beautiful little body right out of there, preferably to his condo right around the corner, but instead he found himself giving her "the look" and was amused to see it still didn't scare her. She discreetly stuck her tongue out at him and moved away, heading back toward the bar.

Oh God. Mike put a hand to his chest as if he could actually quell the pounding that was happening beneath it by doing so. What the fuck was she doing to him? He moved back to the shadows and continued watching her in agony. He wasn't sure how much more he could take and what this would mean for him.

* * * * *

Jay had watched Jenna on the monitor in his office. For a girl who said she didn't dance, she was incredible, more than incredible; she looked as if she'd been dancing her whole life. Miguel had watched her too; he was in Jay's office sitting right beside him.

"Don't make me wait any longer. I want her up here now."

Soto had seen Jay bring Jenna through the previous night and Jay had been right, Soto wanted her right away, but Jay had to warm her up. Jay just hoped Jenna's cousin wasn't going to be an obstacle; he was counting on Jenna to use as a bargaining chip with Miguel. She could be the one thing that saved him. He owed Miguel two hundred thousand dollars and Jenna just might be the girl to help cut that balance in half. Miguel's obsession with young women had been the only thing keeping Jay alive. Jay provided Soto with the finest pieces of ass in Miami to do anything he wanted with and Jay had heard from the girls that Soto was into some weird and wild shit. The promise of someone new had bought Jay a little time and now after seeing Jenna, Miguel just might be willing to do a little bargaining as well. Jay wondered why her cousin had followed her here though. Jay had seen him watching Jenna closely and the cousin hadn't looked too happy. Jay would have to have one of the girls distract the cousin while he brought Jenna upstairs.

He picked up the house phone. "Get Georgie on the line."

She was there seconds later.

"I want her upstairs tonight, start feeding her drinks."

Georgie rolled her eyes. "Sure thing, boss, how would you like her, conscious, semi-conscious or oblivious?"

"Don't be a wiseass, Georgie, I need her upstairs, so whatever you think will make that happen get it done. There'll be a little extra something in it for you."

No thanks. She'd had that little extra something, been there done that. "I was hoping for something more in the monetary form this time."

"Georgie, are you not living in one of the finest penthouses on South Beach with your own personal driver and a job any girl in Miami would kill for?"

Huh, the friggin' least he could provide, Georgie thought but answered sweetly, "Yes, Jay, you're right, I'm sorry, I'll get to mixing my famous potion now."

Jay ignored her sarcastic tone. "I want her feeling good when she gets up here, but not legless, that will come later, she's got to be able to dance."

"Got it." Georgie rolled her eyes. She knew just how to get the girl going. Ha, another one bites the dust. She glanced toward Jenna out on the floor. The girl had no idea her world was about to change. Georgie hung up the phone behind the bar and got the blender out.

CHAPTER TWENTY-FIVE

Mike had been in the club watching her for a few hours now, and apparently he wasn't leaving anytime soon. When Nicki had said he was on his way to find her, Jenna had made the decision not to leave. She really wanted to see Mike again but first she'd made sure she wasn't actually in any danger, so she'd headed out of the bedroom she'd slept in to see where she even was.

Thankfully it was Georgie waiting in the kitchen for her and she had filled Jenna in on the previous night. They had been drinking rum runners and Jenna had passed out at the bar, Jay had helped carry her up to the condo above the club but Georgie had been the one to undress her and put her in her nightshirt. It was no wonder Jenna had passed out, she never drank rum, let alone a drink with three different kinds in it. She had thanked Georgie repeatedly and told her she'd changed her mind about leaving, she wanted to work one more shift and Georgie was glad and said they'd have fun. Jenna felt even more comfortable with her knowing Georgie had helped her out and any suspicious thoughts she may have had about Jay disappeared as well. Surely if he was going to harm her in any way, last night would have been the night to do it, but instead he had made sure she hadn't driven drunk and had given her a warm bed to sleep in. If nothing else, Jenna was grateful.

She was also secretly thrilled Mike was here. It didn't make a difference to her whether he was there out of obligation to Rafe or because he wanted to be, Jenna just wanted to be near him again. Although it was nicer to dream he was there of his own accord.

Just seeing Mike again got her blood pumping. He was dressed for the club and he looked devastatingly handsome, too handsome. Jenna had watched with dismay as his waitress had flirted shamelessly with him. Thankfully the girl had left her top on and Mike had turned her down for a dance. Jenna did not want to watch him enjoying another woman, so much so that she had dared to get up and dance with Georgie for the bachelor party. Jenna wanted Mike's eyes on *her* and not on any other woman! And it had worked because as soon as he realized she was up there dancing he had come out of the shadows to watch.

Jenna had let herself go and danced enticingly to the beat knowing Mike's eyes were on her and hoping he would no longer think of her as an inexperienced "kid." She knew when she'd finished that he had thought it was hot because she had locked eyes with him and just for a moment she had seen his raw desire. But then he'd spoiled it by giving her that menacing look of his. She'd simply smirked back and stuck her tongue out at him letting him know it just wouldn't work on her again, but the punishing look had deflated her. Jenna had fantasized about him coming over to her and taking her in his arms, telling her how much he wanted her. Ha! Fat chance of that! He was obviously there to keep an eye on her and nothing else and it had probably been Georgie's naked breasts that had brought the look of desire to his eyes, not Jenna's seductive dance.

She was due for a break and she made her way to the back room, aware of Mike discreetly heading in the same direction. Well, he wouldn't be allowed back there with her but she liked knowing he'd be waiting just outside. Georgie had said she'd fix them both a snack and Jenna sat down at one of the tables in the employee lounge to wait for her. Georgie entered moments later and Jenna wondered if she'd seen Mike on her way in. She also wondered how she would explain him if Georgie had noticed.

"Hey girl, you were looking good out there, nice moves. If I didn't know any better, I'd say you've done this sort of thing before." Georgie placed a tray of pinwheel sandwiches and two tall frozen drinks on the table.

Jenna ignored her compliment. "Oh my God, Georgie, I can not drink again, I thought you'd come back here with water or soda." Jenna laughed.

Georgie laughed too. "No worries, it's an energy smoothie, all good stuff, no alcohol. It will help get rid of all the poisons." She waggled her brows.

"Oh good, because I felt like I'd been poisoned when I woke up this afternoon." Jenna took a bite of a sandwich and a generous sip of the drink. "Ummm, that's yummy. What's in it, all kinds of caffeine and sugar?" She laughed.

"There's a little pick-me-up for sure." Georgie laughed too. "But I promise, you won't feel a thing tomorrow when you wake up." Not a blessed thing! She bit back a lascivious grin.

"Good, because today was brutal, I think this is the first time I've felt good all day. Thank you. This is really good." Jenna drank half the drink and felt the effects almost immediately. "I actually feel like I just got re-energized, you might have to keep these flowing for the rest of the night." Jenna picked up her glass and drained the rest of it, it was that good.

"Just ask and you shall receive, I have to get back on the floor, but I'll make another one for you." Georgie smiled.

"Thanks a lot. I'm having another great tip night too by the way." Jenna had already made three hundred and the night was still young.

"Awesome, it's only going to get better." Georgie winked and left the room.

Jenna was thankful Georgie hadn't seen Mike; he had probably done his secret agent thing and made himself scarce. She got up to freshen up before she went back to work and felt a sudden tingling in her arms and legs. That's weird, she thought, it must be the effects of the caffeine; she wasn't a coffee or tea drinker and rarely drank soda. Jenna shivered and felt the adrenaline rush wash over her body. *Damn*, that drink was powerful! She felt an overpowering excitement all of a sudden at going back out and seeing Mike. She was suddenly feeling quite flirtatious and decided maybe she'd even dare talk to him.

Jenna fluffed up her hair in the mirror and used some mouthwash by the sink in the bathroom. Her mouth was so dry suddenly and she went to the refrigerator in the lounge in search of some water. She had downed nearly half the bottle when Georgie came running back in with another smoothie.

"Here, I didn't want to leave it behind the bar, Alison had her eye on it and I didn't trust her not to drink it on you." Georgie laughed and ran back out with a wave.

"I don't even want to know how many calories are in this thing!" Jenna called out after her. She hesitated before she took another sip. Maybe now she'd be able to handle more tables. She laughed to herself; she'd be like the Energizer bunny out there. She'd have to have Georgie make her another before she drove back to the island tonight, too; this would totally keep her awake for the long ride. She wondered if Mike would follow her or stay here in Miami where he lived. That would suck! Had he taken all his things from Nan's house? She sure hoped not.

Jenna drank a few more sips, left the rest of the drink on a nearby table, then left the employee lounge looking for Mike as she felt the beat of the music invade her body. Her wondering eyes found him sitting two tables away from her section and she danced her way back there to relieve the girl who'd been covering her break.

Jenna was aware of Mike watching her every move. He was sitting with his knees apart and his elbows resting casually over the rolled arms of his chair and he looked damn hot. He appeared relaxed for the first time all night and Jenna smiled at him, feeling a sense of relief wash over her that he hadn't left. The intent gaze he returned to her made her whole body instantly tingle and warm and she continued to serve drinks with some difficulty. She couldn't even think straight knowing he was so close.

Every time she stole a glance at him she wished her shift would end quickly. She wondered why he hadn't just sat at one of her tables but she supposed he thought Jay or Georgie might realize he wasn't in fact her cousin, and his cover would be blown, especially if she were to act on the overpowering urges she now had. She wanted to dance for him—badly. She wanted to move right up against him and let him feel what she was feeling. It was a little overwhelming, in fact, her body was inexplicably on fire with desire and she had such an uncontrollable urge to dance.

"Hey, baby, let's see you move like that up here."

Jenna looked down, startled from her thoughts, and looked at her customer who was slapping the raised stage above his table with the palm of his hand. She had been unaware that she'd been moving at all, but as she contemplated his words and followed his eyes, she saw her hips gently swaying from side to side. Why couldn't she feel that? What the hell? She took the hand the man offered and in a dream-like state, let him help her up onto the small platform where she automatically began to move to the music again. It was like having an out-of-body experience as she felt her body sway to the beat. Jenna knew she was doing it but all she felt was a riotous tingling and a burning heat under her skin. It felt both good and bad at the same time and somewhere in her mind Jenna knew she shouldn't be dancing like this but she couldn't stop, she didn't want to stop! It felt too good.

She turned to Mike and felt herself grow wet as he watched her. *Oh God*, if she could only feel his touch, she'd come on the spot. Why was she so hyped up and turned on? Jenna had a fleeting thought about the energy drinks she had just consumed but the thought quickly escaped her. Her attention was directed at Mike, whose sky-blue eyes were piercing hers.

Jenna kept moving, the beat was slow and sexy, the lyrics explicit. She continued to watch Mike as her hands careened up the sides of her torso, and over the shiny material covering her bare breasts underneath. He was leaning forward now, his hands on his knees as if he were about to rise. Jenna's skin was so sensitive to her own touch that she heard herself moan as she moved her hands up and into her hair. She held the sides of her head while she danced then glided her hands all the way back down to her hips and over the tops of her thighs. The unexpected look of concern on Mike's face brought her momentarily back to earth. What was happening to her? She was feeling really strange suddenly.

"Jenna!"

She looked down to see Georgie smiling. "Hot stuff, babe, really, but Jay wants to see you upstairs."

Jenna took Georgie's outstretched arm, grateful to have a reason to stop dancing; she needed to get out of there. When her feet hit the floor she felt a little dizzy and caught herself before she bumped into the table. She looked at the hundred-dollar bill her customer was trying to tuck into the pocket of her little black apron and she felt sick. She moved away and let it fall to the floor, afraid to look back over to Mike. Oh God, what had she just done?

CHAPTER TWENTY-SIX

Mike had watched Jenna come out of the back room and he'd been relieved. He didn't like the fact that she'd been out of his sight for a period of time and he'd noticed her looking around for him, too. He was rewarded with her smile when she finally spotted him and he hadn't expected that; she hadn't smiled once or even spoken to him since he'd arrived and he wondered what had changed. He'd noticed, too, that she seemed a lot more relaxed. She was moving her body along with the music even while she traversed back and forth to the bar. He had wondered what had made her demeanor change. His own waitress, on the other hand, kept giving him the stink eye. He'd been drinking bottled water all night and she wasn't too happy with him, between the zero amount of alcohol he'd ordered and the refusal of her offered dances she was pissed. He knew he'd have to give her something soon or he'd probably be asked to leave. Jenna was definitely been behaving a lot friendlier though, shooting him smiles and heated looks and in a weird way it actually made him uncomfortable; something didn't seem quite right.

When Mike saw Jenna's customer touch her he began to rise up from his seat to clock the guy, but Jenna's eyes kept Mike rooted. Her eyes were locked on him as the man helped her up on the small platform that was a would-be stage. Jenna started moving to the slow beat all the while staring intently at Mike and he couldn't take his eyes off her, she didn't want him to either, but he knew it wasn't right letting her go on. Mike knew he should stop her, but he couldn't. He was mesmerized by her movements, entranced as she touched herself and looked at him like she wanted to do things with him he had only dreamt of doing with her. Oh fuck. His body responded to it all.

Mike had no choice but to keep watching Jenna. Her eyes were locked on him and because they were he was able to see into them. He studied hers carefully. When he realized she wasn't all with it his gut wrenched in two. Jenna's eyes were glassy and Mike could see that her pupils were dilated. She was on something! He recognized it and swore to himself. He should have known right away by her movements; she danced like pure sex! Mike had only just met her, but he knew this couldn't be normal behavior for Jenna. He had to admit though; it had caught him off guard.

Now Mike turned his attention away from Jenna and looked around for Junior. He wanted to strangle him with his bare hands. It hadn't taken him long to get his hooks into Jenna and Mike wondered if Jenna willingly took something or if it was slipped to her, the latter if he had to guess. He had to get her the fuck out of there now.

He was about to stand when his waitress suddenly returned placing an uncapped bottle of water on the table in front of him, Mike looked at it suddenly not so thirsty; all the other bottles she'd brought earlier had been capped. He wouldn't be surprised if his own drink had been drugged. While keeping an eye on Jenna, Mike had seen a handful of deals go down with patrons in just the short time he'd been there; at first he assumed it was just coke but then he'd seen vials of clear liquid being passed as well. The waitresses were taking money and exchanging it for the vials they kept hidden inside the black aprons they wore around their waists Mike knew the drug inside the vial had virtually no taste, no odor and no color, making anyone in the club an easy target.

Mike had been working the senior Scintillo case for a year and had not been involved in the recent investigation into Junior except on the periphery, but Daniels had brought him up to speed just yesterday when Mike had told him where he was headed and why. According to Daniels, the FBI had recently been alerted to the fact that Junior was possibly dealing GHB aka Liquid Ecstasy. One of the undercover agents had seen first-hand an employee spike her own water bottle and by the way she'd behaved after drinking it, the agent was quite sure he knew it was GHB, also known as the date rape drug. After being in the club for just a few hours Mike understood what was going on. If Junior could get these girls high on small doses of GHB, they'd do anything asked of them, dancing topless would not be a big deal, and if Jay could get them to go to the upstairs lounge, have another dose of GHB, the leap to sex wouldn't be such a big deal either. The girls would be willing participants and not even remember most, if anything, of what they'd done. And the types of men who frequented the upstairs lounge were probably banking on that and paying big sums of cash especially for it.

The FBI was well aware of the prostitution going on in the upstairs gentleman's lounge but they weren't looking to bust Junior on that alone; they wanted him for the drugs. They suspected he was filtering large amounts of coke through the club as his father had done before him, but the GHB was something new, and if Junior had indeed expanded his product line then they could get him on rape charges too, him and any of the sleeze-ball clients who paid for those particular services.

It made perfect sense to Mike as he'd watched Jenna; she'd had no inhibitions dancing and probably would do anything asked of her in the state she was in and that had to be Junior's plan. If he could get Jenna to perform like that for one of his big spenders upstairs, Junior stood to make a lot of money, especially if he could get Jenna to do even more, like head into one of his famous back rooms up there. Looking around at some of the other girls Mike wondered how many of them were high right now. The worst part was Daniels had said that one particular employee had taken the drug of her own accord, so how many others were doing that too?

Mike wanted Junior taken down then and there. Seeing Jenna this way infuriated him and he wanted to make Junior pay. Mike knew there were four undercover agents inside the club right at that moment and he wished he was on comm with Daniels to initiate a bust, but he was there on a personal mission, not as part of this team's surveillance. What the fuck were they waiting for? Mike could arrest three waitresses right off the bat and a search of the club would most likely turn up a stash of the GHB and probably enough coke too to put Junior away for a long-ass time. Unfortunately, Mike knew Daniels was waiting to find out who Junior's supplier was, and until they got a definite on that intel, Junior was free to go about his business.

"Thanks," Mike told the waitress and gave her a fifty, telling her to keep the change in hopes she'd walk away, but unfortunately she didn't. She started moving to the music right in front of him. He wondered if she was on the drug too but when he looked into her eyes to check he didn't see any telltale signs.

"That's a nice tip you gave me." She smiled seductively, taking his eye contact the wrong way. "This is the least I can do."

Mike sat stoned-faced as the girl deftly took her top off and moved like a pro in front of him. Great, he thought, just what he needed. He looked over at Jenna, but now she was gone. His eyes scanned the room and he found her talking with Jay at the bottom of the stairs. Mike stood to get a better view and make his way over there but his waitress aggressively put both hands on his shoulders and stuffed him back in his seat, wedging her way between his legs and placing her enormous breasts inches away from his face.

Jesus Christ. He looked toward Jenna again and was surprised to see both her and Junior watching the scene between him and the waitress. For a brief moment he could see the hurt look come across Jenna's face and he immediately stood up again this time forcing the waitress to back up. "Listen, thanks anyway, but I told you I wasn't interested in a dance." Mike moved her aside and walked away hearing the girl swear a blue streak behind him. He moved quickly to the stairs and watched with alarm as Jenna followed Jay almost to the top; instinctively Mike called out her name. "Jenna!"

Jay turned around as Jenna stopped behind him on the stairs. She was drinking the water he'd given her and he knew she was good and high now.

Between Georgie's smoothie and the water he'd just given her, Jenna wouldn't be coming down for a long time. He did not need her clingy brute of a cousin fucking things up though. "Tell him you have to work, Jenna; you can speak to him tomorrow."

Jenna was still in shock at seeing Mike's waitress with her bare tits in his face. Jay had pointed it out after handing her a bottle of flavored water she so desperately needed. He had laughed at the scene telling her he was glad her cousin was having a good time. He also said he could tell she didn't feel so good and he wanted her to take a break. When she was through taking a rest Jay said he had someone upstairs who wanted to meet her who was willing to pay a lot of money to see her dance. Jenna had refused, but Jay had just told her to drink her water to feel better and think about it. She was so thirsty and couldn't really think straight at all but she just did what he asked.

Jenna felt really strange, the water seemed to quench her thirst but did nothing to subside the tingling sensation all over her body and now she felt like crying on top of it all. She was angry too and she wanted to throw something. The light headedness she'd felt before Jay had given her the water had been replaced with a sudden surge of adrenaline.

"Oh, I don't have much to say to my cousin," Jenna told Jay. "I'll just be a sec. Will you hold this?" Jenna managed a smile for Jay but he took her water bottle with a frown. She knew he was upset. He had just promised her more money than she'd made all of last summer and she had told him she wasn't interested. He wanted her to wait on some rich dude in the upstairs lounge who liked the way she danced. She told Jay again she wouldn't dance for money but he wasn't really listening. He kept coaxing her to drink her water and relax, telling her he was just going to introduce her to the man and maybe she'd even like him, but Jenna's head was spinning and she'd barely listened to him; all she could focus on was Mike.

She couldn't believe he had bought a dance from his waitress. God, she had been such an idiot thinking there could be something between them; he really was there just to babysit her. She obviously didn't do it for him so he'd paid someone else. She had been in such a great mood too and starting to feel like having fun, admittedly feeling a little strange too, but in a good way, she'd been—turned on, *really turned on*, but Mike had given her nothing in return; in fact, he'd watched her as if he were completely unaffected. Well, screw him! She'd tell him goodbye and lie to him, saying she was going upstairs to make lots of money and that maybe she would just stay here all week! Maybe that would elicit a reaction from him. God, minutes ago her body had burned with desire for him, now she just felt hurt and angry, and *sick*. Tears were seconds from falling and she tried to get them in check before she turned to him.

Jenna told Jay she'd be right with him and on unsteady legs she walked down the few stairs to talk to Mike. It seemed funny to her that he'd been there all night and that this would be the first time they spoke.

Mike saw her coming toward him and he approached her cautiously. Now that he was this close to her he could see in her eyes that she was definitely on something. "Jenna. . ."

Jenna interrupted. "You can leave now, Mike, I'll be working the rest of the night upstairs and you aren't allowed to go up unless you want to pay lots and lots of money to have me dance for you," she laughed, sarcasm oozing. "Oh, that's right, you've seen that already and it's no big deal. So now you can go, you don't have to babysit me anymore. I'll be sure to tell Nicki, Matt, Rafe, and Ali that you did a good job. You were completely professional." She gave him a fake smile and leaned toward him, nearly falling into him in the process. He reached out but she pulled back quickly causing her head to swim. "And I'll keep that little dance between us." She gestured with her hand to where he'd been sitting with his waitress. "I hope you liked it, by the way." She raised a brow. "Would you like me to get her number for you?" Jenna laughed and it came out strained. "Oh look who I'm talking to, you probably gave her yours!"

Jenna couldn't seem to stop talking and the stone-cold look on Mike's face only encouraged her. "She had some pretty good moves. She's got a lot more going on than me so I'm at a bit of a disadvantage, but apparently there's a gentleman upstairs who seemed to enjoy watching my moves and is willing to pay me some big cash to see them up close, my moves, that is," she emphasized and laughed at her own joke then, suddenly felt nauseous and hated all the things that were coming out of her mouth but she couldn't seem to stop. She saw the look of pity cross Mike's face and she wanted to die on the spot.

"Jenna, you're not yourself." Mike reached for her hand. "Come with me and I'll take you home."

Jenna's head was reeling; all she wanted to do was go home with him. She briefly touched his outstretched hand and their fingertips grazed, she felt the immediate surge of heat race through her and she pulled back again quickly. It was as if all her senses were heightened. The music pounded in her ears and her heartbeat seemed to be keeping time with it. She could feel the blood coursing through her veins and the short contact with Mike had only made it worse, she wanted him more than anything and it killed her that he didn't feel the same. She took a deep breath and it was hard to do. Oh god, now breathing seemed difficult. What was happening to her?

"I have to get back to work. It was nice knowing you, Mike." Jenna faltered and felt the lump in her throat. "I guess I'll see you at the wedding."

"Jenna!"

Mike looked up at the sound of Jay's voice bellowing down the stairs. He gave Mike a curt nod and waited for Jenna to acknowledge him.

"I have to go back to work," Jenna repeated and started up the stairs, nearly tripping as she went. She was dizzy all of a sudden and she grasped for the railing to regain her balance. She was going to throw up.

Mike grunted angrily, gritted his teeth, and swore through them as he deliberately climbed the steps toward Junior after making sure Jenna had a good grip on the railing and demanding of her in a low growl that she stay put. When he reached the top of the stairs he got right up in Junior's face and spoke quickly and quietly into his right ear, aware of the overstuffed suits moving in. Mike's piece was tucked safely in its holster under his shirt and he just waited for an excuse to use it, although taking Junior out with his bare hands held much more appeal.

"I'm taking her out of here. If you or anyone else tries to stop me you'll regret it."

"Jenna's not leaving . . . *cousin* Mike, is it?" If he was her cousin, then Jay was a rock star. "She's not done with her shift." The guy's size and overall commando look would normally have Jay avoiding him at all costs but he spoke to him now without fear comforted by the fact that his two armed bodyguards were right behind him.

Mike had all he could do not to throw Junior headfirst over the railing and down to the crowded dance floor below. "I'm taking her out of here right now, then I'll decide in the car based on how she feels, whether she goes to the hospital first or the police station to press charges." Mike could see the flash of panic, then anger, come across Junior's eyes. "She won't be back again, so don't try to contact her, and if you do, you won't like the consequences."

The searing anger in his own eyes had Junior looking away. Mike turned back to Jenna, his blood boiling. Junior would have to wait. Jenna needed him. She was staring up at him, dazedly so, holding onto the railing as if she might pass out at any second. Mike reached her in two steps then scooped her up in his arms, carrying her down the rest of the stairs and ignoring her incoherent words and the curious looks from the thick crowd. Four men in particular had taken a keen interest to the scene but Mike gave them a little shake of the head. As much as he'd love to see Junior and his goons go down right now, he knew he'd be released and back in the club by tomorrow night. Mike wouldn't fuck up Daniels' game plan.

Jenna had her arms around his neck and was nuzzling him there as he carried her right out the front door. Mike had the valet bring his Jeep around, holding onto her while he waited, still ignoring the way she clung to him and doing his best to ignore her soft lips against the side of his neck and the feel of her silken hair against his cheek. She was under the influence, most definitely the liquid ecstasy, and he knew what she was doing wasn't real even if it was driving him fucking crazy.

The Jeep rolled up and Mike buckled Jenna into the passenger seat. He came around and got in behind the wheel and looked over at her. The drug had hit her hard and she was succumbing to it. Her head was back against the head rest angled toward him and she was smiling but she wasn't falling asleep, thank God. He'd have to hurry, he needed to get the drugs out of her system. He was taking her straight to the hospital. Mike drove without speaking because Jenna was doing all the talking. She wouldn't shut up. She was mumbling and every now and then something coherent would escape her lips but he had to ignore that too. Nothing she did or said mattered because it was all compliments of the drug. When she told him she thought she was in love with him and that she wanted him desperately, Mike had whipped his head around in shock, dangerously taking his eyes off the road to look at her. When he'd returned his eyes to the road he'd had to swerve to avoid hitting a curb. It would have been pretty comical if she had just had too much to drink; Mike could have teased her relentlessly about it tomorrow knowing it had just been drunken talk, but he knew she had been drugged and anything she did or said tonight, Mike would never dare embarrass her with by mentioning. He just kept driving, also paying no mind to the way her words had made him feel.

CHAPTER TWENTY-SEVEN

It was the early morning hours of the next day when they were leaving the crowded emergency room. Mike had used his credentials to bypass any paperwork when they'd arrived and he was grateful to the doctor and nurses who had treated Jenna right away.

"Just keep a close eye on her. We pumped her with fluids and she threw up quite a bit but unfortunately many of these club drugs get right into the bloodstream and have to run their course. She may have some residual effects throughout the day but her blood pressure is back to normal and her vitals are good." The doctor looked around and gestured toward the waiting room. "As you can see we have a full house here and not enough staff. I trust she's in good hands?" The doctor cocked a brow, looking the FBI agent over, and went on when Mike nodded affirmatively. "Watch her carefully and bring her right back in if she has any adverse reactions." He said this as he looked at his patient.

Mike let out a big sigh of relief and noticed the doctor regard Jenna. She sat in a wheelchair with her face buried in her hands, clearly embarrassed, and her shoulders shook as she cried. Mike's heart broke and he wanted to take her in his arms but that would have to wait.

"She found herself in the wrong place with the wrong people, Doc. She's not from around here." Mike felt the need to defend Jenna as he took the paperwork the doctor handed him.

"You know," the doctor replied, "most people don't know they've been drugged and it stays in their system for quite some time doing all types of damage. The fact that you recognized the symptoms saved her some definite withdrawal time and quite possibly her life. She's a lucky woman tonight."

Jenna dropped her hands from her face and looked up at the doctor, teary-eyed. "Thank you for helping me," she whispered then turned to Mike. "And thank you." She barely got it out before a sob escaped and she covered her face again. Thank God Mike had been there. She felt like such a fool! She really had needed a babysitter. She had never felt so rotten in her life. Her stomach felt like a bulldozer had run through it and her throat was as dry and scratchy as a piece of sandpaper despite the mouthwash and water the nurses had furnished her with.

Oh, what had she done? She needed to go back to the island. She wanted her clothes and her bed at Nan's. But her rent-a-car was in some unknown parking garage and she had only her tips from tonight; the rest of her money and things were inside Jay's condo and she couldn't go back. Oh God, a fresh wave of tears arose. She wiped her eyes and looked at Mike gratefully as he shook the doctor's hand and got behind the wheelchair to push. And when they reached the exit she couldn't ignore the curious glances of the people in the waiting room when Mike lifted her out of the chair and into his arms to carry her outside. Jenna could only imagine what it looked like to them, the way she was still scantily dressed and her tear-streaked face. She was ashamed.

"I can walk," she said softly, humiliated, but at the same time comforted that she was in his strong arms. She'd wanted to touch and be touched by him all night but this was not how she had envisioned it.

"I don't want you to walk." Mike's voice was gravelly and his heart was hammering. He never wanted to let her go—never wanted to let her out of his sight again, and his heart was breaking knowing that was going to be impossible.

Jenna wondered if Mike was angry with her; he looked straight ahead as he brought her to his Jeep and even when he set her down inside of it he still wouldn't meet her gaze.

"I'm sorry," she whispered hoarsely up at him then leaned her head against the headrest and looked out the window when he didn't respond. It would be dawn soon but the sky was still dark and star filled, giving the sky over Miami an ethereal glow. Under different circumstances it would have been quite romantic, Jenna thought regrettably, turning to look at Mike as he got behind the wheel.

Mike started the Jeep, feeling Jenna's eyes on him and he dared to look at her then. He was doing everything in his power not to reach out and take her in his arms again because he feared he'd never be able to let go. "We'll go to my place so you can sleep for a while, then I'll drive you back to the islands later today."

Jenna stared at him and saw the disappointment on his face. She wished she could change what had happened. She wished she had never come here with Jay. She wished she had stayed on Captiva and tried to win Mike over, prove to him she was no kid, but instead she had done the complete opposite. She could only imagine what he thought of her now. She turned back toward the window so she wouldn't have to see the way he looked at her. "Thank you," was all she said.

Mike drove in silence. He knew she was hurting and probably feeling foolish but it wasn't her fault. Sure she made a bad call coming down here in the first place but nobody deserved to be drugged like that. Junior had taken advantage of her and he was going to pay royally. Mike knew what Junior's game plan had been and if Mike hadn't been in the club who knows what Jenna would have done in that upstairs lounge while under the influence of the drug. He needed to call Daniels. He had living proof and a tox report to prove Junior was up to no good. In the meantime he just wanted to make Jenna feel better.

"Do you want me to stop for anything?"

The sound of Mike's deep voice in the stark silence that surrounded them startled Jenna and she turned to look at him meekly. "No thanks, you've done more than enough," she managed to say, her voice low and scratchy. She would kill for something cold to soothe her throat but she wouldn't dare mention it.

Mike pulled up to an all-night convenience store anyway. "I'll be right out, keep the doors locked."

Jenna watched him go inside the store and felt the irrepressible longing she'd been feeling since earlier in the night. She wanted him, but much more than sexually. Mike had kept a protective eye on her all night, and Jenna had watched him too, only finding herself falling for him. And now she'd gone and blown any chance in hell she had of ever being with him. Her heart ached fiercely with the thought.

Mike was paying at the counter now but Jenna couldn't see what he'd purchased. He left the store holding a brown paper bag and walked back toward, the Jeep meeting and holding her gaze through the windshield. The corners of his mouth turned up in the slightest of smiles when he got closer and Jenna felt her stomach automatically flutter in response. He was something else to look at and Jenna knew that *she* looked as bad as she felt and what she *felt* was disgusting still clothed in her stupid cheap uniform. She felt completely unworthy of his smile.

Mike got back in the Jeep and sat behind the wheel, handing Jenna the bag from the store. "I thought you might like this, it will make your throat feel better."

Jenna stared at him and then at the small brown bag he offered. He knew her throat was sore? She felt a twinge of hope that he wasn't too mad at her. He was still looking out for her. Humbled, Jenna opened up the bag and pulled out a freezing cold container of pineapple sherbet. Her throat constricted at once and she turned blurry-eyed in her seat to look at him. She sought his eyes and when he gave her that slight smile again she started to bawl.

Shit! Why was she crying? "What's the matter?" Mike took the cold container and bag from her hands and placed them on the back seat. "Jenna?"

He took her free hand from her lap and squeezed questioningly while she used the other to unbuckle her seat belt. Next thing he knew her arms were around his neck, surprising the hell out of him, but he couldn't have been happier that she'd done it. Mike held her tight, welcoming her to him, and felt her racking sobs against his chest. She felt so damn good in his arms, his heart swelled; he'd been dying to hold her like this all night. "Shh, it's all right now." He comforted her, not wanting to let her go.

"Pineapple sherbet… is my favorite," Jenna cried into his chest, sniffling. It was a sign straight from God! She just knew it; if Nan were here she'd say the same thing!

Mike chuckled in relief and smiled into her hair, thinking whatever was left of the drug must be making her emotional. "Mine too, who doesn't like pineapple sherbet?" He stroked her hair and her back while he held her, closing his eyes at the pure pleasure of it. Why was this happening to him now? How could fate be so cruel?

Jenna pulled back a little and was thankful Mike didn't let her go. "Lots of people," she sniffled. "Most people like lemon or lime or even orange, but not pineapple." She couldn't believe that's what he had picked out for her. "You can't even find pineapple by itself," she was still crying. "It's always mixed with two other flavors and there's never enough," she told him, taking a deep breath and wiping her tears. She found herself getting lost in his blue eyes. She wanted to kiss him so badly.

Mike gave her a crooked smile. "Jenna, it's just sherbet, it's really no big deal." They were close enough that he could kiss her but he didn't dare; even with the earnest way she was looking at him, he knew she wanted him to kiss her. And it took every ounce of resolve he had not to.

"Why are you crying?" His voice was nearly a whisper.

"Because I ruined a potentially good thing." Jenna cried again and dropped her head back to his chest. His strong arms around her felt so good and so right, she hoped he never let go.

Mike sighed, stroking the back of her head, thinking he understood. "Did you honestly think you were going to have a career at that place? Did you want one?" He couldn't imagine what Junior had promised her.

Jenna lifted her head and looked at him, half laughing, half sniffling. "Not the stupid job! *Me and you!*" She hit his chest and pulled back in frustration, feeling his arms suddenly drop from her and missing their comfort instantly. Jenna sat back in her seat, her head down, defeated and depressed.

"Maybe if I had stayed in Captiva I could have proven to you that I'm not a kid and you maybe could have fallen for me a little and I would have been so happy because—" a sob escaped and she hiccupped—"because I found someone who likes pineapple sherbet, too." Jenna leaned back and stared out her window again, her shoulders bouncing as she sobbed. She cried at what she had lost tonight, besides her dignity, pride, rent-a-car, belongings, and hard-earned money, she had lost the chance to prove to Mike that she was a grown woman worthy of being with him.

Mike swallowed and could only stare at Jenna, speechless. He couldn't believe what she was saying. He didn't want to blame it on the drugs and he didn't think he had to, even though the doctor said they might stay in her system for a while. She seemed cognizant. She was actually saying she would have liked to have started something with him. Mike felt elated suddenly, truly happy for the first time since he could remember. It had been torture watching her in that club and wanting to be with her and now Jenna was essentially saying she wanted that too. She wanted him to fall for her a little? Ha! Way too late, he thought to himself, he'd fallen a lot—much to his own surprise and heartbreak. As soon as he'd met Jenna Mike knew he was in trouble and then with every move she had made since then and every smile she had given, he had fallen for her. He'd wanted to kiss her again so badly from the moment he'd seen her in the club, and he ached to do so much more. How could he feel this way and not act on it? But how could he act on it and be fair to Jenna? Mike had never been more mixed up in his whole life. He had a plan, his life was already mapped out, and his plan was getting shot to hell by this beautiful little creature sitting beside him.

Mike restarted the Jeep and drove the short distance to his condo in silence. He parked in the garage and took the best purchase he'd ever made from the back seat along with a sweatshirt he had back there, then came around to Jenna's side of the Jeep to open her door. He took her hand to help her out and handed her the sweatshirt, noting her slumped shoulders and beaten expression that he fully intended to change. The early Miami morning air was cool. It was hours away from being warmed by the sun and Mike was glad she'd accepted his sweatshirt. He smiled as he guided her forward, loving how it swallowed her up.

Jenna was beyond embarrassed and just downright humiliated. Not only had Mike seen her drugged and vulnerable and had taken good care of her while in that state; now after being completely honest with him in the car, he was getting to see her *rejected* and vulnerable. And he was *still* taking care of her. Jenna wanted to curl up in a ball and die. She needed Paige. She needed Jake. She *wanted* Mike and he clearly wasn't interested. His silence spoke volumes. She would have liked it better if he'd have said, "Hey kid, I'm sorry but I'm just not interested." His blatant silence was far worse; Jenna took it as disgust and pity and after what he'd seen of her tonight, he was probably light years from interested.

Jenna followed him to the elevators and up to the fifth floor where they got off and walked a short distance down the dimly lit hallway to his door. He unlocked it and politely held it open for her. When she stepped inside, the room was mostly dark, all the blinds were drawn, and Jenna had to adjust her eyes to see her surroundings as Mike closed the door behind them. She expected him to walk past her into the room, flip some lights on so they could see but he didn't, and when Jenna turned to face him, he was staring down at her, all large and imposing like. Mike was nearly a whole foot taller than her and Jenna had to crane her neck just to look up at him. She found his blue eyes piercing her own and she was shocked at what she saw in them. "Mike. . ." Oh God!

Mike dropped the bag from the convenience store and indulgently pulled Jenna into his arms. He felt her breath hitch in surprise and felt her body tremble against him. He pulled back to look at her and slowly bent to kiss the remnants of tears on her cheeks. "Relax, Jenna," he said softly, "I've been waiting for days to do this."

Mike moved his lips over hers and felt Jenna respond the way he'd only been dreaming about. Her whole body went from rigid to pliable in a matter of seconds against him. Her lips were soft but firm and she kissed him back with equal vigor. Mike ran his hands up under the hoodie he'd given her and let them rest on the small of her back pulling her tighter against him. When he felt her body arch into him in response, he lifted her up in one swift move then groaned in pure pleasure against her lips as her long, taut legs came up to encircle his hips. She still wore her uniform beneath his sweatshirt and his hands smoothed over the silky material of the stockings she wore. He gripped her tighter and invitingly pressed her against the bulging swell under his pants.

Jenna moaned against his lips, her self-pity party completely forgotten. She'd had him all wrong; he did want her! She could feel it, she could *really* feel it! She found herself smiling beneath his lips and her heart beat wildly at his touch, and his hands on her stockinged legs and bottom were sending chills all over her body.

"Have you really wanted to kiss me for days?" she asked against his mouth.

Mike chuckled, happy that she was no longer crying and feeling down. He pulled back to look at her. "Are you really going to talk while I'm kissing you?"

Jenna grinned and nodded. "Yes, I want to know."

Mike looked at her and spoke seriously. "Not only have I wanted to kiss you again Jenna, I've wanted to do a whole hell of a lot more." There was no look of nervousness this time, just a seductive smile. He recognized that smile from the club and briefly wondered if the drugs were still alive in her system.

"Tonight I'm just going to kiss you though. You've had a rough night and when I make love to you I want you in tip-top shape." He grinned and kissed her again, wishing to God she hadn't had a rough night.

Jenna kissed Mike back and felt excitement and emotion course through her. *When he made love to her?* His words ignited the heat that had been simmering all night just beneath the surface. All her senses were on overdrive and her nerve endings twitched like live wires. Jenna adjusted her body against him, trying to position herself a little lower to feel his arousal. "My night wasn't so bad," she said softly, feeling brave.

Mike threw his head back and laughed out loud at the obvious understatement and loved that she seemed to be feeling better. "Be careful, kid," he warned, meeting her beautiful dark eyes, "it won't take much to change my mind."

"You know, that was the first time you called me kid that I didn't want to slug you." Jenna grinned and maneuvered herself again, moving just so, teasing him.

Mike grunted and gave her a look that said, "You asked for it!" He turned quickly and pressed her back against the door with a thud, guiding her hips even lower so that the length of his straining erection could press between her legs. He pressed himself against her and she squeezed her legs tight around him, holding on.

Jenna's breath hitched—she had been right, Mike was going to be a whole new ball game from what she had experienced before. Holy God!

The assessing look she gave him made Mike laugh. "Don't be scared," he joked quietly with her.

"I'm kinda scared," she admitted, looking down, only half joking.

Mike kissed her and whispered softly in her ear, "Jenna, when the time comes, I'll have you so wet and ready for me that I'm going to slip right inside of you, like I was meant to be there."

His soft intimate words sent chills running up and down Jenna's spine and a soft moan escaped her. She brought her lips to his and kissed him with everything she had then pulled back breathless. "I don't want to wait."

Mike eyeballed her. "*Jenna*, you have no idea how much I don't want to wait either," he stressed and then laughed as if the thought hurt. "But we're gonna." He put her down, feeling her legs slide down the length of his, and picked her sherbet up off the floor.

CHAPTER TWENTY-EIGHT

"You can sleep in my room and I'll sleep out here on the couch." This wasn't going to be easy, Mike knew—not the sleeping in separate rooms, not when they actually had sex and especially not when it was time to explain that that's all they could ever have together. Hell, maybe she'd be fine with it, Mike thought, she was only in Florida for a couple of weeks, maybe she needed this as much as he did and then they could go back to their lives. He was a fool to even imagine otherwise.

Jenna followed Mike to the kitchen, her body still humming, and watched him take down two bowls and get out two spoons from a drawer. He turned to her.

"Do me a favor?"

She nodded. Anything, she thought.

"Go around the corner into my room and take that outfit off, there's a million T-shirts in the top drawer of my bureau. When you come back out you can have this." He pointed to the sherbet with the spoons and smiled at her.

"Okay, deal." Jenna left him, his gorgeous smile making her wish once again that she'd never left with Jay. She could have been getting to know Mike for days if she had stayed on Captiva at Nan's. She cursed herself as she entered the bedroom and closed the door halfway behind her taking in the king-sized bed. It was neatly covered with a puffy white down comforter that looked thoroughly inviting. She yawned just looking at it. Heavy wooden blinds were drawn leaving this room, too, sufficiently dark even though Jenna knew the light of dawn was just beyond them. The furniture around the room was dark as well, rustic looking, and devoid of clutter. The room felt nice and cozy but masculine at the same time. It suited Mike, she thought.

Jenna removed the boots she'd been wearing all night and crossed to the side of the room on plush grey carpeting. She stepped into the attached bathroom discovering that it too was clean and neat and put her boots down on the white tiled floor. Then she peeked at herself in the mirror above the vanity and groaned out loud at her reflection. Her eyes were bloodshot from throwing up and crying and her hair was a mess. She opened a drawer to the sink vanity and luckily found a comb which she used to try to make a difference.

She wished for an elastic but made do holding her hair back with one hand while she splashed cold water on her face with the other then used a nearby towel to dry off. Feeling a little more presentable, she stepped back in the bedroom and opened the top drawer of Mike's bureau. She found it laden with T-shirts like he promised and chose a navy blue one that said FBI in big white letters on the back. Jenna smiled excitedly; she couldn't help but be impressed by him.

She threw the T-shirt on the bed and lifted off her uniform top, letting it fall to the floor, then shimmied out of the form-fitting short shorts and nylons, remembering with regret that she was without undies as she undressed. Jenna turned back to the bureau in hopes of finding a suitable undergarment and was rifling in the third drawer when she jumped in surprise. Mike had entered the room. She was completely naked and momentarily embarrassed to turn around. "Uh… hi." She laughed nervously, meeting his gaze in the small mirror that hung above the bureau.

Mike stood frozen in place. He had wondered what was taking her so long; he'd already dished out the sherbet and had come in to find her. He took her in, her backside anyway, and tried to remember to breathe. She was a goddess. He cleared his throat. "I came to get you. Your ice cream is melting." His voice sounded strained even to his own ears.

Jenna just stared at him in the mirror. "I have no underwear, I was just gonna borrow some."

"Turn around, Jenna."

Jenna swallowed her nerves and did it. She turned to face him fully naked.

Ohhh sweet Jesus. Mike's eyes drank her in slowly, from glorious top to heavenly bottom. She had a little tattoo low on her hip that was sexy as all hell and Mike's already semi-aroused state went from halfway there to hell fucking yeah I'm there, in a nano second. His eyes flashed back to hers.

Jenna had never felt so, so… desired. She felt an adrenaline rush and a crazy sense of empowerment from the way Mike was looking at her. The tension between them was much the same as it had been the first night they had met, when he had kissed her at Nan's and feeling emboldened, Jenna slowly started toward him.

"Don't!" he warned, his voice gruff, and Jenna stopped abruptly, her eyes widening and a slow burn creeping up her face. *Oh God*, she was *way* out of her league with him, she didn't even know what to do. She laughed nervously and reached to grab the T-shirt from his bed attempting to cover herself up in complete embarrassment.

Mike was at her side in a flash taking the T-shirt from her hands and throwing it back on the bed. He'd seen the look that had come across her face;

she'd misunderstood him. "Jenna." Mike lifted her chin so she would look at him. "I want you to stay right where you are so I could keep looking at you; you are so—damn—beautiful." He bent to kiss her and moved his hands down over her arms, from her shoulders to her wrists, loving the feel of her silky skin. She pressed herself against him and laughed against his big chest.

"I'm so nervous with you; I don't know what I'm doing. I really don't have much experience, you know, I mean I've got the basics down but I'm not going to be anything like you're probably used to, I've only been with that one guy I told you about, and that wasn't very often, so..." she rambled and took a breath, "I've got nothing." She lifted up her hands in defeat, causing Mike to laugh.

"Oh Jenna." He kissed the top of her head. "You've got everything," he spoke softly. "You're so incredibly sexy and beautiful, and *funny*," he added, smiling. "The fact that you aren't going to be anything like what I'm used to is what I can't wait for. I'm glad for your inexperience, I'm dying to be the one to show you *everything*," he stressed. "Just not tonight," he quickly added, trying to convince himself as well as her. "You need to rest."

Mike reached for his T-shirt and reluctantly placed it over her head, trying to ignore the sight of her pert breasts and bare mound. She wasn't stacked by any means but he knew those breasts would fit perfectly in the palms of his hands and they'd feel full and just right. Jenna's body was proportioned like a man only dreamed about. She was petite but everything was sized just right, and she was firm, lean, and toned. And for damn sure that bare skin of hers would haunt him, he knew.

When she put her arms through the T-shirt it fell to her knees and Mike laughed, hugging her to him and feeling that tug in his chest that was becoming all too familiar around her. "Let's go eat, before it turns to soup." Restraint was definitely not his strong suit and Mike had to take several deep breaths as he left the room. God give me strength, he prayed.

"Okay." Jenna laughed, feeling better and turned on by his words. She followed him and he led her out to the couch where she sat and he covered her with a lightweight blanket.

"That's as much for me as it is for you." Mike smirked and went to the kitchen to dish her out a fresh bowl of sherbet.

Jenna gave a little laugh and thought again how generous he was; he'd done nothing but take care of her. When he handed her the bowl of sherbet she smiled warmly at him and laughed when he just grunted. She knew he was frustrated, she just wished he knew it was unnecessary. "Oh God, this is like heaven," she said, eating a spoonful and feeling the instant relief on her sore throat.

Mike smiled and sat at the opposite end of the couch; being too close was dangerous. He could swallow this girl up and still want more. He watched her eat and felt himself relax for the first time in many hours. Jenna was here in his condo with him, safe. He'd called Rafe when she'd gone in to change and although Rafe was grateful Mike had got her to the hospital in time and she was now safe, Rafe wanted to kill Junior, too. Mike promised him that he would take care of Junior very shortly.

"I'm sorry about tonight and all the trouble I put you through." Jenna put down her half-empty bowl on the coffee table and pulled her legs up to her chest facing Mike. "I never would have come here had I known what was going on. I never would have spoken to him at Tween Waters if I had known who he was."

"That's my fault, you don't need to apologize," Mike said and found himself moving a little closer to her, like a moth to a flame.

"You could have just told me what was going on, you could have trusted me." Jenna studied the features of Mike's face and wondered who had given him those vibrant, blue eyes. There was so much she wondered about him.

"I did trust you, right off the bat, I liked you right off the bat, too." Mike smiled. "But I never imagined in a million years you would run into Junior and hook up with him." Mike liked her looking at him like that, studying him, and he wanted desperately to take her in his arms again. Shit, he couldn't not touch her. He put one arm under her knees, blanket and all and with his other arm lifted her onto his lap.

"Yeah, I guess you couldn't have seen that coming." Jenna's heart soared feeling Mike's arm cradle her against him and she leaned into his solid chest, placing her hand on it, tracing over the hard planes of muscle through his shirt. "I could have helped you get information, you know, he liked me." She couldn't believe she was here snuggled up against him, that this fine specimen of a man was interested in her.

Mike leaned back into the sofa enjoying Jenna's touch, giving in to the endorphins it released in his brain among other parts. "Yeah, he liked you enough to drug you and try to pimp you out." Mike would make sure the little bastard paid, too.

Jenna knew Mike was right and she was ashamed of herself. She pulled back abruptly and laid her head on the end of the couch to stare up at the ceiling; her legs were still on his lap and the blanket still covered them. "I feel like such a fool that I didn't see that coming."

She felt the tears burn behind her lids and draped her arm across her face to cover her eyes. Jenna couldn't imagine what Mike thought of her because of what she'd done. "I think it was Georgie, though, that drugged me and not Jay," she said softly, trying not to cry. "I'm normally not as stupid as I've been in the last two days; I think I was trying to rebel coming here—against everything. I don't know," she took a breath. "I was hurt coming to Florida, already feeling like a fool from that jerk." She wiped her eyes and looked at Mike, "You know the one I told you about?" She watched him nod. "And I just wanted a little adventure. I've always wanted to come here. I thought it would be so much fun." She laughed, irony seeping through. "Earlier tonight, before I was drugged..." she smirked, "When Georgie pulled me up on that platform? I thought if you saw me dance, you'd stop thinking of me as a kid. I wanted you to look at me and..." Jenna paused, her voice softening, her eyes cast to her lap, "want me."

"Jenna..." Mike said, touched by her honesty. "I did want you. I've never wanted anyone more." He squeezed her leg through the blanket for emphasis and watched her take a deep breath and look up at him. "I wanted to take you out of the club right then and there, but Rafe told me to take it easy, that you might be mad I was there at all."

"You're the reason I *was* still there," she admitted.

"What?" Mike drew his head back, not comprehending. "What are you talking about?"

"Nicki told me you were coming for me and I was secretly glad. I decided to stay," she admitted. "Even if Rafe and Nicki had sent you, I thought maybe I'd have another chance to prove to you I wasn't," Jenna paused, "*inexperienced.* I thought maybe you would wait for me after work and follow me back to the island and then..." She shrugged. "Who knows? I liked you." She gave him a candid smile. "I *like* you."

Mike leaned his back on the sofa and ran his hands over his face, taking a deep, frustrated breath, then turned his head to look at her. He couldn't be happier that she liked him and that she wanted him to want her but now he felt even more responsible for this whole mess. "Jenna, trust me, I know you're not a kid, all right?" he looked in her eyes and told her firmly. "It's just a term of affection. I know you're a woman, Jesus Christ, do I know you're a woman!" He half laughed. "There's nothing you have to do to prove it to me." He couldn't believe she thought she'd had to.

Jenna looked at Mike and realized how wrong she'd been about him. She had been so self-conscious about their age difference since he'd mentioned it at Nan's but he'd really thought nothing of it. "I'm sorry Mike. I guess I was a little sensitive because I am a bit younger than you. I guess I thought you wouldn't really be interested in me because of it." She looked down at her lap again. "I mean look at you; you probably have tons of woman falling at your feet." She was so jealous just thinking about it!

"C'mere," Mike smiled, amused by Jenna's jealousy and he opened his arms.

Jenna knew she had a little bit of a pout on her face and she felt silly as she sat up and leaned into him adjusting the blanket over their laps.

Mike wrapped his arms around her, and instantly warmed. Hell, she *was* young and relatively innocent, but not too young to love, just too young to hurt. He wouldn't be the next guy to hurt her. He refused. He already cared too much. He had to be honest with her.

"I haven't been with another woman in a good two months Jenna. I do not have women falling at my feet." He took a breath. "I work, Jenna; my job is my life. Once in awhile I get some time off, and I satisfy my needs." He shrugged when she looked up at him with a disapproving smirk. "I'm just being honest. There's never been anyone special. Having someone special in my life has never been an option, I've always been about the job and I don't know of any woman who would want to be in a relationship like that." There, he said it, explained the way it was. His job was his life. But saying it out loud sounded pretty sad even to him.

Jenna's face fell. She was crushed. Sure, she wanted to sleep with Mike, but a part of her, a *big* part of her, had envisioned a whole lot more than just hot sex and he had just snuffed that vision out in a few sentences.

Mike felt Jenna's disappointed sigh right against him and his heart fell. He felt disappointed too somehow. "That's not to say I don't want anyone special in my life," he found himself saying quietly. Jesus, where the hell did that come from? Sure it was true, but he had no business actually voicing the thought.

Jenna dared to look up at him and searched his eyes expectantly.

Mike's smile was a sad one as he returned her questioning gaze. Shit, she'd already become so special to him in such a short amount of time. "You know, Jenna, I wanted you at your grandmother's house as soon as I saw you standing there by the pool, but I was there to do a job so I thought it would be best to keep my distance." He laughed softly and tucked a strand of hair behind her ear. "But I haven't slept a peaceful night since then because of you." She looked at him in surprise and he went on.

"When I found out you had left with Junior I knew I had to find you, not because Rafe or your sister wanted me to, because I wanted to." He placed a hand on her chin to look at her. "I wanted to finish what I never got started," he spoke softly, interlocking his free hand with hers. "I just wished this had never happened to you tonight. I feel completely responsible. I should have dragged you with me out of that beach house."

"I would have fought you," Jenna told him seriously while his admittance to wanting her swirled pleasantly around her brain. "I didn't know what was going on remember? I would have thought you were being a Neanderthal." She laughed.

Mike laughed, too, and nodded his agreement. "You would have fought me like a wildcat. I saw you put that guy in check tonight in the club, you had quite a grip on him, what did you say to him?"

Jenna took a second to recall the incident then laughed. "I told him if he ever wanted to rub one off again, he'd better get his hand off my thigh. That I was trained in martial arts and could break every bone in his filthy hand if he touched me again."

Mike laughed out loud. "Could you have?" Man, he liked her more and more he thought with regret, she was made for him.

Jenna nodded confidently. "My cousins Ryan and John are trained in mixed martial arts, they taught me and my cousin Paige a few necessary moves a long time ago."

Mike looked at her and whistled, shaking his head in admiration. "Remind me not to mess with you, or your cousins," he joked.

Jenna smiled and laughed, knowing he was joking. She was quite sure Mike would be a challenge even for her cousins.

"You know, I couldn't help but be turned on watching you tonight," Mike admitted.

Jenna turned her body towards his. "You were?" She had been embarrassed to remember the way she'd been dancing so erotically.

Mike stared down at her in his shirt, the way her perfect breasts looked under it and the slightest points of her nipples protruding against it. "You're incredible, Jenna, how could I not be turned on?" He bent to kiss her and she tilted her head to accommodate his lips. Before he knew it she was straddling him and the blanket had fallen away. Mike was all too aware of her bare bottom pressed against the crotch of his jeans and her slowly grinding him there as they kissed. Ohhhh—man, the scent of her reached him instantaneously and drove him over the edge. With all his restraint shot to hell, Mike picked Jenna up, with her bare ass in his hands. Her slim, strong legs wound around his waist and the feel of them made his already hard cock strain further against his pants.

Jenna kissed him in a desperate way as he carried her to his bed. She kissed his lips, his neck and even his ears lobes, sending blasts of electric currents straight to his dick. Mike ripped the covers back roughly, but laid Jenna's body down ever so gently. His T-shirt was now up around her waist leaving her lower half fully exposed, and his whole body ached torturously at the sight of her. He actually felt a physical pain looking at her like that.

"Jenna." He closed his eyes and sat down on the edge of the bed. He wasn't going to do this right now, it just wouldn't be right. He was suffering on so many levels; she had turned his world upside down.

Jenna ached for Mike to touch her, she wanted him so badly but she could tell he was struggling with the idea. "What's wrong?" she asked, almost afraid to hear the answer.

Mike opened his eyes and looked into hers; she looked insatiable against his sheets with her long, dark hair fanned out underneath her, her dark features against all that white. He reached over and touched the hem of his T-shirt where it rested at her waist and started to pull it down, albeit slowly. He could do this, he told himself; he could wait. He breathed in as she lifted her hips so that he could pull the shirt past her bottom and he thought he felt his eyes water. This was absolute fucking torture, but he was in no way going to be with her like he wanted to right now, not after what she'd been through.

"You're killing me." he groaned, the sound coming out low and guttural. He rested a heavy hand on her naked hip and tried not to look at the bare mound between her beautiful, lean, toned legs, but it was impossible, especially when she looked at him and drew a knee up. Oh fuck. She was so smooth there and sweet Jesus she glistened. "Jenna," and his voice was rough with regret, "you have no idea how much I want you right now." He found himself tracing his fingers over her tattoo and watching the desire spark through her eyes, he felt his restraint slipping even faster.

Mike's voice was low and gruff and Jenna's heart raced frantically in her chest as she boldly placed her hand over his, ceasing his movement on her hip only to lift his hand and place it between her legs, pressing his long fingers against her.

Dammit to hell, she wasn't making this easy. Mike's fingers instinctively sought her warm opening and he became even more aroused at how wet she was.

Jenna watched Mike's eyes become two dark orbs and she felt his hand move oh so deliberately beneath hers, touching her expertly. She closed her eyes and let herself drown in his sensual exploration. "Well now you have some idea of how much I want you." It came out half whisper half gasp as Jenna felt his finger slide inside of her. Her head was spinning as if she stood up too quickly and her eyes were still closed when she felt his lips touch her own. She felt his tongue enter her mouth, his finger, first one and then another, move slowly in and out between her legs.

Mike's blood raced through his veins. She wanted him and my God he wanted her too. He covered her slick opening and his fingers explored her thoroughly, he wanted to feel her come. He rested his thumb between her folds and found the little pink treasure that pulsed there. Oh she was beautiful, pink and wet and swollen for him. He leaned over to kiss her lips, whispering to her how beautiful she looked down there.

Jenna breathed deeply as Mike kissed her lips and touched her expertly at the same time, his intimate whisper giving her goose bumps. She could feel how wet she was, his fingers entwined with hers as he pleasured her. When his thumb came to rest on her clit she gasped and kissed him even harder, her lips and tongue in a desperate wrestling match with his own. He applied more pressure and rubbed her just a little bit faster and her hand flew away from his to grip his sheets tightly. Jenna felt herself explode in pleasure, wave after wave of glorious pleasure rolled through her. It was so intense that she broke their kiss and heard herself cry out. "Oh God, oh God!" She'd always been quite adept at bringing herself to orgasm, but never as intense as what Mike had just done for her. His fingers were pure magic! She didn't dare open her eyes for fear he would stop, and she moved beneath his fingers again hoping he'd get the hint not to.

Mike laughed with pure joy and watched Jenna's Cheshire grin, her eyes still closed; her hips rising and beckoning him to continue. The woman knew what she wanted. *Oh yeah!* There was no stopping him now, not after that reaction. He wondered if there were any drugs left in her system and if they had intensified her orgasm. He'd like to think it was all him but ego aside he supposed she deserved to derive a little pleasure after her ordeal. He smiled looking down at her. Her little grin of satisfaction kept him laughing softly as he felt her wriggle beneath his hand. This girl was someone he could have a lot of fun with, he thought regretfully. His fingers were covered in her juices and he had all he could do not to climb on top of her and bury himself deep, deep inside.

Instead, he started up again, his touch soft and light, teasing her, watching her body writhe in response. He used a couple of fingers to massage her, applying just a little more pressure as he did and whoa, yeah! He watched excitedly as her whole body tightened, handfuls of sheets in her fisted palms, her breasts rising, her nipples erect beneath his shirt, and then he felt her spill onto his hand again. Oh, sweet mercy, if ever she were going to be ready to accept the size of him, now was the time.

"And I," Jenna panted breathlessly, "thought I," she inhaled, "was good at that," she let out a soft moan and covered his hand tightly stopping him from doing it again.

Mike laughed out loud and continued chuckling for a good minute, relieved that she was okay and happy as hell she was in his bed joking around. "Oh, you make me laugh, Jenna," he said still doing so. He pressed a kiss to her lips and came down beside her, his erection nearly tenting his pants.

Jenna smiled unable to open her eyes; her whole body still hummed and ached for him, oh how it ached. "Mike." She turned her body lazily to look into his eyes and plead with him, her hand coming to rest on his upper thigh. "Please don't stop, I don't need to rest, my body is wired, I need you, I want you." She wanted to touch him but didn't dare; it scared her and excited her at the same time.

Mike's laughter came to an end and he sighed at her words. He wanted nothing more than to be buried inside of her, so deep inside of her. "Jenna, I don't want you to regret anything, you probably still have some of the drug left in your system," he tried to reason with her. "Tomorrow you'll be so much stronger." They were the hardest words he'd had to say in a long time, he just wanted to cover her body with his own and devour her.

Jenna sat up, opening her eyes and gripping his arm, "*It is tomorrow* and even if I do have some left in me, I don't care. I need you, I want you, so, so—badly," she emphasized and lifted his T-shirt from her body. She saw his eyes go to her bare breasts. "This isn't about the drugs, this is about me wanting you since I first met you, but I was too nervous that night, I'm not now." She cautiously covered his body with her own, pressing herself to him, and kissed him hard, showing him she was strong and willing and aware of what she was doing.

Mike kissed her back and ran his hands all over her beautiful bare skin. Her hair blanketed his face and he grabbed a fistful of it and gently pulled her head back. "I've wanted you too since that night and I'm dying to show you how much, Jenna." He gently lifted her off of him and rolled her onto her back. "But I'm not going to show you tonight. I want to wait." Had those words really just come from his mouth?

Jenna felt her desire quickly turn to hurt. *Wait for what?* He wanted her! She could see it in his eyes, why was he turning her away? He had just sent her to the moon and back with two unbelievable orgasms and now she was supposed to what, turn over and go to sleep?

Mike could see Jenna was hurt and he sat up on an elbow beside her.

"Jenna, please don't be angry or hurt, this is for the best, trust me. I'd be a complete jerk if I did what I wanted to do to you right now."

Jenna rolled toward him and maneuvered a knee between his. "Why? I want you to, I feel fine, honest."

He gave her a half smile. "I know you think you do, and I'm glad you feel like you are, but I wouldn't feel good about it. I want to know you're completely drug free when I make love to you for the first time." And that's exactly what he wanted to do with her, make love, not just have sex. He had such strong feelings for this girl that it scared him.

Oh wow, he said make love again. Jenna studied Mike to see if he meant it *that* way or if he just used that expression to be polite. Her heart tripped in the silence between them. Could he really mean it that way? The way he was looking in her eyes certainly suggested so. She gave him a small smile. "Okay,

I get it, I understand."

Mike breathed a sigh of relief, glad she got it. "That doesn't mean I'm not in any physical pain right now," he laughed, lightening the moment.

Jenna laughed, too, and started to reach for him.

"Ohhhh no!" Mike grabbed her wrist. "As unbelievably good as that will feel," he half groaned, "I'm not going to let you do that either." He hopped out of the bed and pulled the comforter over her naked body. He laughed at the blatant look of disappointment on her face. "Baby, trust me when I tell you I'll make it worth the wait."

Jenna grinned and relaxed under the warmth of the comforter. "So sure of yourself," she said, suddenly sleepy, teasing him while she stretched out under the covers, her body sated from the pleasure he'd given her. She smiled when he arched a brow.

Mike came over to her side of the bed and sat on the edge. "I am sure of myself in that department," he said, looking at her intently. "I'm going to ruin you for any other man." Mike was only half joking, but it wasn't fair to her, he had no business thinking it, let alone saying it, but God help him he meant it. He didn't want her to be with anyone but him and what the hell was he going to do about that?

Jenna laughed and held her tongue. She didn't dare tell him it was too late, the only man she ever wanted again was him. "I like that you're so sure of yourself, and I do trust you." She sat up on her elbows, becoming serious. "Thank you for tonight, Mike, I owe you big. God knows what would have happened if you weren't there. I want to apologize again for the way I behaved, I hope you know that's not the real me. I want a chance to redeem myself, can you give me that?"

Mike looked at her with her hair falling around her naked shoulders, the covers just covering the tops of her breasts and her dark eyes searching his. She was so damn beautiful and he felt that twist in his gut again. He shook his head no. "There's no need to, I know you weren't yourself in that club. I met the real Jenna Thompson Saturday night and that's who I'm going to take out when she's rested and feeling herself again." He smoothed her hair back from her shoulder.

"You're going to take me out?" Jenna asked with a hopeful smile.

"Hell yes! I'm going to take you some place nice where we can talk and get to know each other better and then I'm going to take you someplace where I can rock your world, kid." He grinned. "Now get some sleep, I'll be in the living room if you need me."

Jenna was grinning as she lay back on the pillow, her body tingling with excitement just thinking about it. She felt her eyes growing heavy and she closed them. "I'm going to look forward to that." She turned over on her side settling in and said sleepily, "Your bed is super comfy by the way."

"You can sleep in it anytime you want," Mike told her, speaking softly. He watched her for a few minutes feeling a strange sense of peace come over him. He liked having her in his bed; it had been just him for so long. And now as Mike looked at Jenna under his covers, she looked at home there, like she belonged. He didn't want to think about the logistics of a relationship with her right now or the fact that she was from Boston or that in six months or less he could be halfway across the world. It was a bridge they could cross if it came to that and something inside of him hoped to hell it did.

Mike left the room reluctantly. He wanted nothing more than to fall asleep right beside Jenna with her in his arms, but he had some unfinished business and he wanted to get it over with so he could get back home, shower, and bring Jenna back to Captiva where she belonged. He shut the door behind him so the sound of his voice wouldn't wake her when he spoke to Daniels.

"Well, I hear you played the white night last night."

Mike smirked at the visual. "He drugged her. I have a tox report from the hospital and she'll press charges. Are you going to take him down or what? I saw about five deals go down right before my eyes, he's probably got a whole fucking pharmacy on premise."

Daniels sighed. "Cap, where's the proof that he personally drugged her? You know this shit takes time, we're close. What you have helps no doubt about it, but it's not enough."

"C'mon, Tom, you know we have enough between the prostitution and the drugs, you could get a warrant right now and you'd probably find a whole closet full of the shit." Mike was frustrated beyond belief. "And that's just one club; you know that shit's happening in the others as well."

"Mike, you know Junior is small potatoes, We want his supplier, because his supplier was probably his daddy's supplier."

"Soto." Mike sighed.

"It sure looks that way but until we find out for sure, we leave them both alone."

"Fuck!" Mike said in a loud whisper.

"Are you driving her back to Captiva today?" Daniels knew Cap was frustrated but they had to play it this way.

"Yeah, she just fell asleep. I'm going to get her belongings first though."

"Do you think that's a good idea?"

"Yes, I do, Junior's already on to me so fuck it. He knows I'm not her cousin. What he really thinks I don't know and I don't give a fuck but he has her car keys, phone, and other shit and I don't want her stressing over it."

"Well, I'll send Collins over to watch your back."

"Thanks, but I'm not expecting any trouble."

Daniels laughed. "You never are, Cap; you never are."

Mike shook his head and ended the call. He checked on Jenna one more time then grabbed his keys and left.

CHAPTER TWENTY-NINE

Paige woke up alarmed to the sound of her cell phone ringing beside her on the nightstand. She glanced at the bedside clock and was surprised to see it was only five a. m. She had only just gone to bed a few hours before. She had stayed up on the couch watching TV and waiting for Jenna. When she didn't show by two a. m. Paige had tried calling her again but it went straight to voice mail. Nicki had tried to reassure Paige on the phone that Jenna was in good hands with Mike watching over her, but Paige still worried because they had yet to hear from either of them. She went to bed but had barely slept.

"Hello?" Paige sat up against the headboard and pressed the phone to her ear, having not even looked at the caller ID.

"It's me," Nicki said. "She's safe. She's with Mike in Miami at his condo sleeping it off."

"Thank God!" Paige sighed in relief. "Sleeping what off?"

Nicki gave Paige the information Rafe had given her.

"Jesus Christ, she could have died!" Paige felt sick to her stomach. "Is she okay? Should she still be in the hospital?"

"Mike said she was doing great, and that he would drive her back to the island himself. When he finds out where her rental is he's going to make arrangements to have it picked up and brought to their Miami terminal."

"Well, thank God." Paige heaved a sigh of relief. "Did they arrest that sleezeball?" Her relief quickly turned to anger.

"I guess the shit's going to hit the fan today, probably as we speak." Nicki looked to Rafe, who was nodding affirmatively. She and Matt were sitting in Rafe and Ali's kitchen, having been there since the night before waiting anxiously to hear from Mike. Nobody had slept but a couple of hours and they were all looking forward to doing so now. "Go back to sleep, I just wanted to let you know she's safe."

"Thanks, Nick, I'll call you when I see her for myself and let you know how she is."

"Thanks Paige."

Paige hung up and slumped back down in bed. Thank God she didn't have to worry about Jenna. She pulled the covers up around her and turned on her side placing a bent arm under her pillow and trying to get comfortable again. Now that she knew Jenna was all right, her thoughts ran to Justin. She wondered if he were in bed sleeping right now. If so was he alone? Ugh! Don't go there, she admonished her conscience.

Paige missed his touch and would give anything to be curled up against him, only the thought of that made her heart ache unbearably. How was she going to get over him? Why hadn't he tried to get in touch with her yesterday? All he had to do was ask Jack for her number, but she'd never heard from him. He'd obviously had second thoughts about being with her and now Paige was just embarrassed and hurt and feeling like a fool. She fell back to sleep with tears coursing down her cheeks.

When Paige woke up again, it was an hour shy of noon and she was feeling less pitiful. She got up to start her day and looked forward to lying in the hot sun. A little color for the wedding would be nice, she thought and by noon, she had eaten and showered and was headed across the road with her beach gear. She followed the foot path to the beach enjoying the hot island sun permeating her skin and guessing it had to be close to ninety degrees but it felt great. When she reached the shore line she kicked off her flip flops and stood in the wet sand, letting the cool water lap over her feet. It was beautiful and inviting and she couldn't wait to get in. She went back to dry sand and slipped out of the shorts that covered her, adjusted her bathing suit bottoms and positioned her chair directly under the sun's rays. She draped her towel over the chair and put her sunglasses on top of her head before slathering sunscreen all over herself. Finally she sat down to relax back in the chair and soak up the heat. Taking a deep breath Paige realized Nan had had a great idea after all, she was completely relaxed. This was just what Paige needed, a little time away to gain some perspective.

CHAPTER THIRTY

Jay was in trouble. Soto was pissed, not only had Jay fucked up by not delivering Jenna to him last night, but he didn't have any money for the new shipment or the money he owed for the last. Jay had bought the Four Winns last month thinking the nightclubs would take in enough revenue while he floated the money, but business was off twenty-five percent and Jay had to cover the nut on all three clubs before anything else. He owed his liquor supplier fifty grand and another sixty-five to the Cadillac dealer; his special order Escalade was waiting for him over on Biscayne but it didn't look like it would be leaving the lot any time soon. Fuck!

When Jay had offered up Jenna in place of the money, Miguel had agreed to it but said she would only be worth half of the balance Jay owed. Jay would have to come up with the rest in cash. Miguel was going back to Cabo for a few days and he told Jay to have Jenna ready to go with him. Miguel gave Jay until he returned from Cabo to produce the balance of what Jay owed or Jay was a dead man. He also told Jay he was a disgrace to his father's good name and when Soto had left the club, Jay had cried like a baby.

And now that Jenna's "cousin" had thwarted Jay's plans, Jay was furious, and he wasn't about to let it slide either. No one took a girl from his club, "cousin" or not. Jay admittedly had been somewhat intimidated by the dude. Jay wouldn't fuck with him, but he had no problem siccing his father's goons on him. And Jay would definitely have a bodyguard with him later today when he tried to find Jenna. Hopefully she'd go back to the condo on her own. Jenna's money, car keys, cell phone, and clothes, Jay knew from Georgie, were all still there and she would surely have to come back for them at some point. Jay had no choice now but to produce Jenna and deliver her to Soto's yacht, no matter what it took. But there was no way he could come up with the rest of the money he owed.

* * * * *

Mike arrived at the building that was home to Junior's Ocean Drive nightclub and found it all locked up as he expected, but because Daniels had placed a call, Mike was now holding a key to the private entrance that led to the residences above the club. Their undercover door man, Agent Collins, had been working the club for the last twelve months and had access to not only the club but the residences as well. He met Mike around the corner to give him the key.

Mike got inside without incident and went straight to the bank of elevators on the right. Each floor consisted of three individual condos and Mike was informed that the girls resided on the top floor, which had recently been renovated, combining three units into one six-thousand-square-foot living space. Even the elevator was roomy and expensive with its chrome and floor-to-ceiling mirrors. Mike rode it impatiently until the doors opened at the top floor. According to Agent Collins it was home to two of Junior's top-producing girls. Mike knew Georgie was one of them and Collins named another as Michelle.

Mike quietly used the key card he'd been given and waited until he heard the tell-tale click before he opened the door. With his gun concealed at his side, he stepped inside to a sun-drenched living room with more floor-to-ceiling glass overlooking the famed South Beach. The one vast room was the size of Mike's whole condo. He looked around and found no one in sight then quickly deduced where the bedrooms were. He went through the large open kitchen first then down a spacious hallway where he saw an open doorway and he entered it. The room sat empty but there was a made bed and a bag on the floor. Mike picked it up and checked it. It definitely belonged to Jenna; there was an airport tag hanging from the handle bearing her name and address.

He looked on the nightstand and was surprised to see her cell phone and its charger running from the wall. Mike grabbed them both and threw them in her bag. Next, he checked out the bathroom and gathered the items he found there that he thought might belong to Jenna and stuck those in the bag as well.

Before Mike made his way from the room, he opened the travel bag further and really looked through it. He took out Jenna's wallet and opened it and as he suspected, didn't find a single dollar but he had a pretty good idea of where he would find her money. He'd nearly closed the wallet when Jenna's picture caught his eye. It was her Mass driver's license and he pulled it from its sleeve to see all of her smiling face. He read her information because it was there in front of him and suddenly felt a strange tingling sensation under his skin. He quickly slipped her license back in place and closed the wallet, then put it back in her bag and left the room. He knew he shouldn't bother, but he wanted Jenna to have her money, she deserved it. If nothing else she had worked for it, and he didn't want her to feel even worse about what had happened to her.

Mike took the bag and cut his way across the vast living room to the other side of the condo. The first door he tried was a closet, when he moved to the second he found a bath. Door number three led him into Georgie's room, which he realized upon discovering her in bed sleeping. He quickly scanned the rest of the room. Her night stand held only a clock radio, and a folded newspaper but he found her purse on a nearby bureau and quickly did an inventory.

"Aren't you supposed to be dressed in black when you rob someone?"

Mike turned at the husky voice to see a topless Georgie sitting up in her bed. "Where's Jenna's money, keys, and car?" he asked, addressing her in the eye.

Georgie grinned, ignoring his questions. "You're not her cousin, are you? I saw you in the club watching her last night, she's a lucky girl."

Mike ignored her comment as well, keeping his eyes on hers. "So where is it?" She made no move to cover herself.

"You know I can have security up here in three seconds, don't you?"

"That would be a mistake." Mike didn't want to have to kill anyone this early in the morning.

Georgie smiled. "I like Jenna, I didn't steal her money." Georgie got out of bed naked, taking her time and making sure she gave the big guy an eyeful before she slipped into her robe. "I make enough of my own." She threw him a set of car keys from inside her night stand drawer. "It's in the garage next door."

Mike didn't doubt for a second that she made enough money of her own, but chose not to insult her. He caught the keys and pocketed them. "I'll ask again, so where's the money?"

"Relax, handsome. It's here."

Mike followed her out of her room and into the next bedroom where apparently the other girl, Michelle, slept. He watched Georgie open the girls top bureau drawer and pull out a wad of cash wrapped securely in a hair elastic. "This is Jenna's money."

"How do you know?"

"Because I saw Michelle take it from Jenna's room."

"And you let her?" Mike asked with disgust.

Georgie shrugged. "I figured if Jenna didn't come back, there's no harm. Mich's been gone the last few nights, she went home for a visit so she hasn't made any money this week." Georgie shrugged again. "That's who Jenna was covering for." She smiled at him and gave him an admiring once-over.

Mike ignored Georgie's roving eyes and took the cash from her hand. "Was it you who drugged her?" He watched her pale before she exited the room.

Georgie swallowed. How the fuck could he know that? "What are you talking about?"

"Cut the crap. I'd find a new employer if I were you, unless you want to be facing criminal charges." Mike followed closely behind her into the living room.

Georgie felt her heartbeat speed up. "I'm perfectly happy where I am, thank you, besides I don't know what you're talking about." Who the hell was this guy anyway? "What are you some kind of cop?"

Mike just smiled and turned to leave, shoving the cash in his front pocket as she followed him to the door.

"I'm going to tell Jay you were here. He won't like it."

"Please tell him." Mike faced her with a biting smile. "Tell him I'll be back too." He wanted Junior sweating it out. He took the elevator down and left the building with Jenna's money and her things, glad he hadn't had to pull his gun. He'd get with Daniels later and get himself buried knee deep in Junior's shit, he wanted to bust the little punk so bad he could taste it, but right now he just wanted to get back to Jenna and be there when she woke up to let her know he'd retrieved her belongings.

CHAPTER THIRTY-ONE

Jenna finished writing Mike a quick note and left the condo to hail a cab. She didn't know where Mike was but figured he wouldn't be too long, she didn't intend to be either. She put her uniform shorts back on and took a new T-shirt from Mike's bureau, not sure what the rules were on a civilian wearing FBI garb. She figured at the very least it might attract some unwanted attention especially where she didn't have any shoes. At least the cabby wouldn't notice her bare feet and she planned to have her sneakers for the return trip anyway.

Jenna knew Georgie would let her in to get her stuff, Jenna just hoped she didn't run into Jay, especially while she was laying in to Georgie. Jenna felt completely betrayed, not to mention embarrassed, but mostly she was pissed off. At the very least Jenna wanted her stuff back; her travel bag and cell were in her room and she could only imagine who had tried to reach her. She fully expected her money from the first night to be gone, and knew she deserved it if it was.

When she arrived to the club, Jenna asked the cabby to wait for her then went around to the resident entrance at the side of the building and buzzed the condo unit from the vestibule. Georgie answered right away and buzzed her up. When Jenna got off the elevator, Georgie was waiting in the open doorway.

"You're man was already here," she said smugly.

"What?" Jenna approached Georgie and felt her anger escalate at the mere sight of her, knowing that Georgie had been the one to drug her with that energy drink. Jenna remembered all the funny feelings that had overtaken her body and wished she had figured it out at the time.

"Your man, who is totally freaking hot by the way, was here. I gave him your stuff." Georgie smiled sweetly.

"Why did you do it?" Jenna asked, ignoring Georgie's comments about Mike but amazed he'd done something so nice for her yet again.

"He asked for it, and who am I to turn down a gorgeous stud?"

Jenna glared and leaned menacingly toward her, fists clenched and fury rising from within. "No, *you bitch,* why did you drug me?"

"Whoa!" Georgie backed against the door frame holding up her hands in defense of the clenched fist poised in her direction. "No need to be hostile,

I was doing you a favor. No one likes to go upstairs to dance without a little assistance."

"I had no intention of dancing upstairs, Georgie!"

"No one does at first." Georgie laughed without humor. "But Jay would have convinced you, and a little something helps when you get into those private rooms." She waggled her brows. "Makes it like it never happened." She laughed again maliciously just as the elevator sounded and opened behind them.

Jenna was about to lunge for Georgie and throttle her but the sound of the elevator opening had her following Georgie's gaze instead, Jenna saw Jay standing there with a rather large man she recognized to be a security guard at the club. Her anger dissipated quickly as dread instinctively took over. She turned back to Georgie accusingly.

Georgie grinned and raised her brows. "What, you didn't think I'd call him?" She gave a snort and stepped back into the condo, quickly shutting the door behind her, leaving Jenna alone in the hall to face Jay.

"Hi there, Jay, I was just coming to get my things and then I've got to get back to the island." Jenna tried to sound nonchalant and not let him see how nervous she was. Jenna was glad Georgie had gone back inside; she didn't want Jay to know she figured out she'd been drugged.

"Are you okay, Jenna?" Jay asked, stepping out of the elevator and approaching her. His bodyguard stayed inside holding the door. "I tried to stop your cousin last night but he seemed quite determined to take you out of the club so I thought it best to let him. He seemed pretty agitated, I was worried about you. I hoped I'd have a chance to talk with you today, I wanted to make sure you're feeling all right." Jay decided being genial and concerned was the best plan of action if he was going to get her to go along with him. If he were hostile and forced her, she could make a scene.

Jenna couldn't believe his balls but she played along; she wanted to get out of there without an incident. "Everything's fine, thanks, it was just a misunderstanding and I think I was just feeling a little sick from something I ate and the drinking the night before. I'm not quite used to that, and it turns out…" Jenna laughed then felt sick as she suddenly realized they had drugged her that first night too. "My sister thought I was working here as a stripper and sent Mike in to get me. I set them all straight last night though." She thought on her feet and confidently approached the elevator. "I'm sorry if I caused you any trouble. I know you had someone waiting on me in the upstairs lounge."

"Oh, no worries," Jay said stepping aside for her to enter the elevator. He followed closely behind. "The gentleman is still looking forward to meeting you though. I did tell him you were sick last night," Jay said in a disappointed tone. "Turns out you really were, but you'll be good to go tonight, right?"

Jenna's stomach tightened. "Tonight?"

"Sure, he's paid for you for the next few nights. I want to talk to you about your cut and how you prefer to be paid; I have a couple of options for you."

Oh my God, he couldn't be serious. "Oh, I'm really sorry, Jay. I won't be coming back tonight, like I said I have to get back, my family is waiting for me." Jenna felt an instinctive thread of fear weave its way in as she looked into his now deviant eyes. She rode the elevator down and felt her stomach lurch.

"Jenna, this man is a good friend of my father's as well as a business associate of mine and has paid a small fortune to see you dance. It's only three nights, you had said you'd work a few nights, remember? Why don't you try it out tonight? If you aren't into it, I'll let him know and you can leave tomorrow. Although I think after you see what your cut is you'll change your mind." She had no cut of course and once the yacht got underway she could change her mind anyway she wanted, it wouldn't make a difference.

"I'm sorry, Jay, I just can't." Jenna was starting to sweat. "I came here to wait tables and ended up dancing twice and that's as far as I'll take it. The upstairs lounge is not for me. Georgie told me what goes on up there."

The elevator door opened at the ground floor and they all stepped out of it. Her cab was gone and in its place, a black suburban idling at the curb. Jenna felt Jay take her elbow. "What are you doing?" She stared down at Jay's hands on her and then at the tinted windows of the Suburban.

"We're just going to go for a little ride." He firmly guided her toward the Suburban.

"I really can't, Jay, Mike's actually waiting for me; we're heading back to the islands." Jenna glared at him defiantly. Did he honestly think she would go with him?

Jay looked at her and bent to speak in her pretty little ear. "No, you're not, Jenna, you're taking a ride with me and you're going to fulfill your obligation."

Jenna felt the fear grip her at the menacing tone of his voice and she looked around frantically for help as she yanked her arm back from Jay. The sidewalk was amazingly and unfortunately deserted. Didn't anybody come out in the daylight around here? Jenna knew under any circumstances she couldn't get into the car. She struggled out of Jay's grip easily enough but immediately found herself face to face with the brick wall that was Jay's bodyguard. She punched the giant hard in the stomach and screamed as loud as she could only to feel her head snap back and her teeth rattle in her skull with one swift punch to the face. The last thing she saw was clear blue sky as she fell to the pavement and passed out.

CHAPTER THIRTY-TWO

Justin pulled into the driveway and admired the house. He had been in awe of his surroundings ever since he'd driven over the Sanibel causeway. He'd stopped there along the beach to let Sam out of his crate to relieve himself, and had admired the kite surfers doing their thing. Once on Periwinkle, the main road in, he'd been struck at the vibe of the island; he'd expected a more resort like place and was surprised at its quaintness instead. The island wasn't overly built with high-rise hotels or commercialized with malls and chain stores like one would expect from a vacation area, instead there were small colorful buildings hidden along the road, consisting of inviting little shops and interesting restaurants. He did see a DQ and a CVS but those were the only familiar sights.

The homes became larger and the landscape more lush as Justin had neared Captiva and when he'd crossed a small bridge along the way, he finally got a grand view of the Gulf and had admired the beautiful clear water out his window. It looked damn inviting as did the small inlet out his right side where he'd spotted some kayakers enjoying the afternoon. There'd been people spread out among the sand soaking in the hot sun and swimming on the beach side and even a handful of people fishing out there on a small jetty. The water had looked placid and a warm breeze had passed through the car windows, keeping Sam's nose pressed against the bars of his crate to take in all the scents. It was paradise for sure.

Justin smiled and now admired the wood carved house sign as he pulled in; "The Three Sunrises," it read. He remembered Paige's cousin Jenna telling him that the house was named after a U2 song. He parked beside a small sedan and turned off the car's engine, sitting for a second and thinking. How would Paige react to him showing up like this? Justin started to doubt himself as he slowly got out of the car. What if this wasn't the best idea? He now knew from talking with her grandmother that there was no family emergency but Paige might be completely turned off that he'd come here. Justin had only known her for a few days and here he was invading her space and he'd come all the way to Florida to do it. Oh man. He ran a hand over his chin and leaned against the car door looking around, thinking, and taking in his surroundings. He admired the shaded walkway leading to the front door of the sprawling home. The path was lined by intermittent slate slabs and framed by exotic flowering bushes but Justin wasn't quite ready to venture toward it just yet.

He turned sideways instead and took in the rest of the place. The landscape that surrounded the light grey house was tropical and lush and he wondered if Paige wasn't out back somewhere beyond it. There was a white picket fence coming off the back of the garage and Justin took in the view to the bay beyond. It truly was a beautiful location and he felt himself relaxing despite his nervousness. It was peaceful and quiet, save for Sam's anxious bark coming from inside the car. Justin went around the vehicle and let the pup out making sure his leash was on securely before Sam leaped from his crate. Sam immediately put his nose to the ground and went to work on the shelled driveway. Justin could only imagine the overload of scents to his little nose.

He took a deep breath, mustering up courage, and took the path to the front door with Sam leading the way. Justin looked down at the puppy as he rang the bell. "This is it, little guy, let's hope she's glad to see us." They waited in the heat of the sun that filtered through the thick palm fronds high over the front door and Justin became aware of the cars passing along the road in front of the house. He turned at the noise and could just make out another luxurious home across the street. It was heavily landscaped as well but he could see the white façade and clay tiled roof peeking through. It looked pretty private and exclusive.

He turned back to Grace's front door and stared, starting to realize nobody was home to answer it. His next attempt was a loud knock and produced the same results. The sedan in the driveway was probably a rental but Justin didn't know whether it belonged to Paige or her cousin. Maybe Jenna had picked Paige up at the airport he thought. Maybe they were both at the beach right now.

Justin led Sam away from the door and walked toward the picket fence at the back of the garage; he lifted the latch on the gate and walked around the back of the house where he was faced with a pool and deck area that looked out onto a pretty expanse of the bay. Wow, Grace had herself quite a spot here. He turned to face the back of the house which was pretty much all glass, providing an unbelievable view from inside he bet, but there was still no sign of Paige, or Jenna either. When he had called Grace from the airport she had told him to use the spare key if for some reason this happened, but Justin didn't feel quite comfortable with that idea; instead, he decided to walk across to the beach first and see if maybe Paige was there; if not he'd hang out a bit with Sam and try back later. Already wearing shorts, Justin kicked off his sneakers and left them on the pool deck then led Sam back out to the driveway.

"Aw shit!" What the fuck? Justin looked down and swore as the bottoms of his feet were assaulted by hundreds of tiny shell shards. "Jee-zus!" He was already halfway into the driveway so he suffered to the street rather than turn back for his sneakers. "That was a wake-up call," he muttered to Sam, brushing off the bottoms of his feet once he reached the asphalt and wondering why it hadn't seemed to affect the dog.

He crossed the road, devoid now of cars in either direction, and stood in front of the impressive house he'd seen a peek of. Okay, so how did you get on to the beach? Justin looked around and walked a few feet to his right and came upon an overgrown path with a stockade fence running alongside it, an abandoned home site sat inside its perimeters. Justin hugged the outside of the fence and swiped at the palm fronds and brush that blocked his way as Sam kept his nose to the ground in exploration. And every few feet Justin heard something scatter in the brush, causing Sam to pull on the leash excitedly, and prepare to give chase.

When they finally cleared the unruly path, Justin scoped out the beach. To his right there was an older couple walking with their backs to him and to his left was a lone empty chair with nobody in sight. Justin walked straight toward the water with Sam while he decided in which direction to go. The right seemed like the more logical choice. He could just make out crowds of people further beyond the couple walking, and saw many matching beach umbrellas dotted in the sand. He wondered if they belonged to the resort Jenna had mentioned. Maybe the girls were up there having a drink.

Justin headed in that direction by the water's edge, figuring it was worth a shot. It would kill some time if nothing else and hell, he could use a cold beer himself. He pulled his T-shirt off; rather hot now that he was in the direct sunlight, and tucked it into the back of his shorts then looked around to make sure it was safe to let Sam off the leash.

"Go ahead boy, check it out." Justin splashed at the shoreline with his feet and pretended to throw a ball for Sam who fell for it like always. Justin laughed as the pup ran into the water up to his shoulders and sneezed as the salt water hit his face. Sam shook his wet ears, but stayed with it and seemed to get the hang of the doggie paddle right away. The sun was hot on Justin's back but it felt great, prompting him to empty his pockets for a swim. He threw the contents along with his shirt on the sand then he ran and dove right in with the dog. He swam waist deep for a few minutes and watched Sam paddle back and forth enjoying his new found freedom of buoyancy.

When Justin thought Sam had had enough, he coaxed him out, picked up the leash and his belongings, and continued his walk toward the resort. Sam followed alongside happily, playing in the shallow surf that washed in and out over his paws, but when Justin looked down moments later to check on him he swore out loud as he saw Sam running like hell in the opposite direction. He was heading toward that lone beach chair. "Shit! Sam, come back here!" Justin yelled.

* * * * *

Paige came out of the water and returned to her chair, surprised and thankful to have the beach to herself. With her head back and her eyes closed she gave way to relaxation and soon found herself daydreaming of Justin. She pictured him at work. Was he tattooing someone right now? Was he thinking of her? Paige took a deep breath. She had to stop torturing herself. She was only making the situation harder to deal with. Christ, it had only been a couple of days. If she continued on like this she'd be in a full-blown depression by the weekend. She let her hands fall lazily over the sides of her chair and come to rest in the cool sand. She sifted blindly through a small pile of shells under her chair and tried to guess their name by what she felt. She thought maybe in a little while she'd take a walk in search of some coquinas.

After a few minutes of the shell game, Paige grew sleepy in the hot sun and was well on her way to a semi-conscious state when she was suddenly rocketed out of her chair by the feel of a cold, wet something! It touched her right hand and sent her flying. Her resting heart rate had gone from barely pulsing to outright pounding in a nano-second. But her squeal of fright died off instantly as her sun blurred eyes came into focus. Paige stood staring down at a little black lab puppy that was quite enamored by her if the feel of his tongue all over her ankles was any indication. *What the. . . ? How could. . . ?*

"*Sam?*" Paige whispered in shock. Adrenaline rapidly pumped through her veins and she immediately looked up, moisture filling her eyes at what she was seeing. Paige reached down and scooped Sam up, hugging his wet little body close. "Oh Sam, I'm sooo happy to see you," Paige whimpered, her eyes never leaving the shirtless, sexy, man approaching them. She quickly swiped at her eyes as he got closer, her heart expanding in her chest.

Justin's own heart was pounding from chasing Sam down the beach and from realizing it was Paige the pup had run to. She stood before him in just a barely there bikini with Sam squirming in her arms and licking her to death. Her blonde hair was wet and dark, slicked back from her face, and tiny rivulets of water dripped down her arms. With a touch of sun on her cheeks, Paige's eyes mimicked the color of the gulf. She looked stunning.

Justin's heart continued to hammer away and he was damn thankful for Sam. The pup must have seen Paige coming out of the water. How the hell had he known it was her? Justin smiled cautiously as he approached her, unsure if

Paige was happy to see him or not. She was unsmiling and simply stared at him in surprise, her blue eyes glistening. Uh oh, were those tears?

"Hi." Justin came to a stop about three feet from her, afraid to move any closer.

"Hi." Paige wasn't sure yet if she were dreaming or if Justin was in fact standing in front of her and she were actually holding his dog. She put Sam down and the pup immediately paced excitedly between her and Justin. Justin was barefoot and shirtless. His shirt hung haphazardly from his waistband and by the looks of his wet, low slung shorts he'd been swimming too. He looked quite at home on the beach Paige thought, feeling her heart swell as she looked him over. He was so devastatingly handsome it made her weak in the knees just to look at him.

Justin could see so many questions in her eyes and he wanted nothing more than to answer them but he was still taking her in. "You look incredible, Paige."

Paige felt her body warm all over, from not only his compliment but the desire-filled look in his eyes. "What are you doing here, Justin?"

Shit, still no smile. "I went looking for you yesterday, first at work then to your apartment. I met your landlord." Justin took a cautious step forward.

"You met Agnes?" Paige asked softly, her heart fluttering. He'd gone to her apartment?

Justin nodded. "She told me you were at your grandmother's in Boston and she gave me your grandmother's number and address."

Paige would be bringing a big box of chocolates to Agnes as soon as she got home. "You called my grandmother?" Her heart was lodged in her throat.

"No." Justin shook his head. "I drove to her house last night." He took another small step forward.

Paige stared at him. "You went to Boston?" Her heart pounded excitedly.

Justin nodded again. "I had a nice talk with Grace." He smiled hoping for one in return—nope, not there yet.

Paige was shocked. "You spoke with Nan? About what? Why did you go there?" And why hadn't Nan called to tell her?

"I did," Justin answered her first question. "She gave me a drink and told me a rather sad story," he answered her second question and moved closer still, he was now inches from her. "Because I wanted to find you, Paige." He reached a hand out, answering her third question, and moved aside a strand of hair that had dried and fallen across her eye.

Paige swallowed the monster lump in her throat and closed her eyes at his touch, feeling her skin tingle. "Why?" she asked again softly, opening her eyes.

The moment of truth. Justin thought of Grace and her story and he thought of Paige and their short time together. He laughed, shaking his head. Now that he faced Paige he wasn't ready to be quite as bold as Grace's man but he would be as honest as he could and hopefully even that much wouldn't scare her off.

"I came here to tell you..." Justin looked out at the Gulf and then back to Paige's expectant eyes, "That I'm really sorry, and that I want to be with you. Just you." Whew, he'd said it, now he watched and waited for her reaction, praying he would finally get a smile.

CHAPTER THIRTY-THREE

Paige just stared at him. He was nervous, she could see it. He was waiting to see how she would react. He was sorry? He wanted to be with her? *Just her? Oh my God!* He'd been trying to find her to tell her that? Paige felt the widest smile overtake her face and she stepped toward him this time, shyly at first, but when Justin held his arms open, she flung herself into them and hugged him tight.

"Well, that was worth the agony of not hearing from you," she said softly, tears finally escaping. "And here I was wondering how I was going to get over you!" She half laughed, half cried against his chest.

Holy shit. Justin breathed a sigh of relief and lifted her off the ground to hug her to him, chuckling in relief. "Aw man, you scared the hell out of me for a few seconds there." He put her down but still held her. "I thought you were going to send me packing." He laughed against her hair. "I'm so sorry, Paige." Justin pulled back just a little to see her face. "I screwed up royally Sunday. I was afraid of what you would think if I brought you to my parents. I thought I was moving way too fast for you and I thought bringing you to my parents would scare you away. I should have just asked you to go to a movie or something, but I found myself lying to you instead. The way we connected so soon took me by surprise and I didn't want to ruin it, we'd only just met." He ran a hand along the skin of her warm back.

Paige laughed. "I'll admit I was hurt when you called and cancelled. I was surprised because I was sure there was something there between us." She looked at him with a serious expression. "Like something out of the ordinary there." She knew he knew where she was coming from. The whole thing with his house was just too coincidental; never mind his sign at the shop and her photo which she'd yet to tell him about. It just had to be fate, there was no other explanation.

Justin nodded getting it. "I lied to you and I'm so sorry for that. This. . ." He squeezed her arms. "*You,*" he emphasized, "really took me by surprise and I didn't know how to deal with it for a day or two there. . ." He smiled. "Until I talked to your Grandmother."

Paige grinned and laughed incredulously, her heart swelling even more.

"What did she say to you?"

Justin laughed too. "Well, she told me a pretty sad story that made me think about how short life is and that we only get one chance at it."

Paige tilted her head, touched that anything her grandmother had said to him had affected him in such a way. "What was the story?" Paige thought she just might already know it.

"She told me when she was twenty she worked as a maid at the Ritz in Boston, and that she met this man one weekend and fell in love with him, but she never told him. I sat there listening to the story waiting for the happy ending, but none came. It was awful, I felt so bad for her even though it was so long ago. She said she thought he would think she was crazy if she told him how she felt, since they'd only known each other for a few days, so they said goodbye and the guy went back to New York." Justin took Paige's hand. "I sat there in her living room thinking, man, I would have wanted to know how she felt and then I realized I had to find you and tell you how *I* felt."

Paige smiled and said softly, "Thank you for finding me and telling me." She put her arms around his neck as he bent to kiss her. It was the sweetest kiss she'd ever received. "Justin?" she asked, pulling back.

"Yeah?" He was so happy to have Paige in his arms again.

"Did Nan actually say that she *never* told the man that she was in love with him?" Paige couldn't help but blush.

Justin nodded. "Yeah, she said she didn't tell him and he went back to New York. Justin looked at Paige, furrowing his brow. "Why?"

Paige sucked in her bottom lip, trying to hide her smile. "So she didn't tell you the end of the story?"

"I thought *that* was the end," Justin said suspiciously and looked at Paige and her cunning expression. He gave a slight tilt of his head. "Is there more?" He squeezed her arms playfully, coaxing her.

Paige nodded with a crooked grin. "He came back to Boston two days later to find her," she smiled, getting a chill. "He went to the hotel and she wasn't there so he paid a hotel employee for her home address and she wasn't there either, but her mom, my great-grandmother, told him he might find her in the park, now the Public Gardens. You probably saw them across from her brownstone."

Justin nodded impatiently. "I walked through there. So did he find her?" He chuckled, knowing he'd been duped by Paige's grandmother. Here he was coming to find Paige just like Grace's man had gone back to find her.

Paige grinned seeing him catch on. "He did find her. He surprised her on a park bench, she was feeding the ducks. The story goes that he took her right in his arms and kissed her and when they finally pulled apart..." Paige paused, smiling shyly and finished, "He told her he'd fallen in love with her."

Justin nodded his head meeting Paige's eyes. "Your grandmother's one sly lady," he said softly. And he was embarrassed that Paige now knew why he'd come and the unspoken words he'd left between them. Why didn't he have balls like Grace's man?

"My grandfather certainly thought so." Paige smiled and ran her top teeth over her bottom lip. Oh God, was Justin in love with her?

"Grandfather! What!" Justin laughed surprised. "She certainly left out a major part of the story!" But he was glad to know there had been a happy ending after all. Now he just hoped for another one.

"I think maybe she wanted me to tell you the rest," Paige said, smoothing a shaky hand across his scruffy chin. She took in his half naked body and shivered despite the heat.

"Oh yeah, and why's that?" Justin asked huskily catching her hand and kissing her palm. He wanted to lay her down right there on the sand.

"Probably because something very similar happened to me once." She hesitated meeting his eyes again. "I met this really cool guy, and after only being with him for a few days, well..." She shrugged helplessly, she was afraid to say it.

Justin's heart tripped clumsily then finally righted itself when realization set in. "Oh," he said with a happy smile then pointed to his chest and mouthed, "*Me?*"

Paige laughed, nodding her head. "Uh-huh." He kissed her hard then and she pressed herself against him, deliriously happy he'd come for her. She owed her grandmother big time!

Justin's kiss lingered and went on, quickly intensifying and causing Paige to press herself tighter to him when she felt him stir against her. Her body came alive and heated quickly with anticipation. She felt and heard Justin's guttural groan against her lips and returned one of her own.

But it was Sam's little yelp of a bark had them laughing and reluctantly pulling apart.

"I'm sorry I had to bring him, it was so last minute there was nowhere to leave him," Justin explained, still holding her in his arms and trying to restrain himself from devouring her right there.

"Are you kidding?" Paige grinned, aware of Justin's discomfort; she had her own going on. "I love that you brought him, I've kind of connected with the little guy." She looked down at the pup and teased his sandy, wet fur with her foot.

Justin kissed the top of her head. "I can see why your grandmother likes this place, it's pretty special."

Paige smiled. "It really is, wait until you see the sun set later." She panicked suddenly and hugged him tighter pressing her lips to his chest. "Please tell me you don't have to leave right away."

He laughed. "No, I actually have a couple of days; I managed to get coverage at the shop."

Paige squeezed him, thrilled that they would have time together here on the island. "Oh, that's so great! And Jenna is coming back tonight from Miami."

Justin was confused. "She's not here with you?"

Paige shook her head. "It's a long story. I'll explain everything, but first let's go back to the house, take a look at the sky now." She nodded her head toward it.

Justin followed her gaze over the Gulf. "Where'd that come from?" The sky had turned a deep dark blue over the water.

"On the Gulf, it comes out of nowhere," Paige laughed. "But it won't last long. Hey, were you already at the house?" It just dawned on her that Justin must have looked for her there first.

"Yeah, I rang the bell and knocked, checked out back, then came across to the beach, which wasn't easy," Justin added. "Did you use that overgrown path?"

She laughed. "No, I'll show you an easier way, follow me." Paige gathered her things and Justin put Sam back on his leash, taking the beach chair from Paige's hands and leaving her to happily take Sam. "There's a path up this way, did you come through there?" She pointed between the abandoned property and the judge's house directly across from Nan's.

"Yeah, what's with that place?"

"Wait until I tell you, let's go have a drink and I'll fill you in on everything. Are you hungry?"

"Yeah, actually, I haven't eaten since early this morning."

"Well good, there's plenty to eat at Nan's." Paige smiled happily. "I can't believe you're here." She looked at him seriously. "I'm over the top happy."

Justin took her free hand in his and brought it to his lips. "Me too."

His words played over and over in her head trying to sink in. He hadn't actually said he'd fallen in love with her but his actions and the retelling of Nan's story told Paige all she needed to know. She'd basically just told him herself.

When they were back at the house, Paige helped Justin bring in his overnight bag, while he grabbed Sam's crate from the car, and she cracked up laughing at him as he swore every time his bare feet crunched over the shelled drive. When they were finally inside they put the stuff down on the living room floor and Paige went to fill a bowl of fresh water for Sam in the kitchen.

"Thanks." Justin smiled as he watched Paige take care of Sam. "Did I tell you how great you look in that bathing suit?" He didn't take his eyes off her as she bent to put the bowl down for Sam or now as she leaned against the refrigerator. Her breasts were ample and spilled from the skimpy triangle top that he itched to peel away.

Paige grinned feeling herself grow quite warm in the air conditioned house. "You might have mentioned something at the beach."

Justin was half sitting on a kitchen counter stool. "How about a tour of the house?"

"Sure," Paige answered feeling her pulse quicken at his husky tone. She still couldn't believe he was here on Captiva.

"Let's start with your room." Justin stood up from the stool and waited for Paige to lead the way.

Paige came out of the kitchen and took his hand, excitement coursing through her as she led him down the hall. She had taken the room across from Jenna's and she led him inside.

Justin shut the bedroom door behind them, leaving Sam to fend for himself.

Paige turned to face him, her body already humming, and moved her hands cautiously over his bare chest. "I thought you were hungry."

"I am." Justin reached under Paige's damp hair and untied the strings at her neck. The feel of her soft hands on him tugged at his heart; he'd really missed her. He slowly lowered the two triangles of material that covered her and revealed two nipples, hardened and dark against the pale skin of her breasts. She had already got some sun and there were tan lines outlining where her top had just been. Justin caressed and held each full breast in his hands. "God, these are amazing." His body was taut and so ready to take her.

Paige swooned at Justin's touch and felt herself become wet as his hands got re-aquainted with her. Her body burned with desire being so close to him again and she gasped when he put his mouth to her breasts. He took turns pleasuring them as she held his head in her hands and massaged her fingers through his short hair. She couldn't believe only hours before she had been merely dreaming of his touch. A slow moan escaped her.

Justin's hands traveled down over Paige's slim hips and back up the feminine curves of her sides. Her breasts were big and beautiful, her whole damn body was beautiful and he wanted to see more of it. He came down on his knees in front of her and gently pulled the sides of her bathing suit bottoms down over her legs to reveal the rest of her, his cock throbbing painfully at the sight. "Oh God, I missed this." He kissed her where no one but him had ever had the pleasure and he kept his hands on her firm bare behind, kneading and squeezing the rounded flesh and drawing her closer to him. He felt her soft hands grip his shoulders, and her hips press toward his face eagerly. Justin smiled, feeling proprietary, reveling in the fact that he'd been the only one to do this for her and he kissed her again, softly. He looked up at her as he smoothed his hands over the tops of her thighs and he saw her head hung back and her eyes half closed. He used the pads of his thumbs to spread her bare, smooth folds and his tongue and lips sought the moist little nub between them, then he took the tender sweet morsel between his lips and sucked, his tongue lightly dancing over it, tasting her, loving her, hearing her moan in pleasure. Justin felt her buttocks tighten and her legs spread for him as he pleasured her. "Ummm," he moaned right against her mound and kept sucking that little piece of flesh between his lips steadily until he heard her whimper with need, he felt her tight grip on his shoulders, her nails dig into his skin and he felt her legs go rigid. He placed one arm around the backs of her thighs and one hand on the small of her back to support her trembling body as she came hard and fast. Warm, sweet liquid spilled from her and he drank greedily before placing his hand there, cupping her to feel it drip between his fingers. He dipped them inside of her feeling her clench around him and heard her moan then he quickly stood to remove his shorts. When he had them off he fisted his cock and rubbed her juices all over it.

"God, Paige, you taste so sweet. I want you so bad, baby."

If it weren't for his arm supporting her, she'd have collapsed. What he'd just done to her had rendered her weak in the knees, Paige was so hot for him she throbbed, she could feel the actual pulsing between her legs, waiting for him to fill her. "I want you too," she whispered, watching his hand glide over the length of his arousal. "So much, Justin."

Justin walked her backwards to the bed and gently laid her back, admiring her incredible body once more before he brought himself down on top of her and gradually entered her. "Ohhh, yeah." He slowly and deliberately buried himself deep inside and stayed there a moment relishing the feeling. He kissed her slowly and meaningfully as she contracted around him. "Oh Paige. . ." he whispered and began to thrust inside of her. It felt so right, being with her like this again, this was how it was supposed to be, she felt like an extension of him and he kicked himself for ever questioning it.

Paige looked up at him. He looked so strong. His arm muscles bunched and flexed as he held himself above her and she traced over them with her hands loving the bulging, solid feel of them under his smooth skin. "God, Justin. . ." She felt her heart fill and her stomach tighten with the feelings swirling inside of her. She tried to hold back the tears she felt welling. It meant so much to her that he'd come to find her. And as they came together Justin whispered to her, "There's no place else I'd rather be, Paige."

CHAPTER THIRTY-FOUR

Mike had stopped at the market for some breakfast materials and was back at the condo by ten. He opened and shut the door quietly in case Jenna was still sleeping. He hoped she'd had enough sleep; he wanted that drug completely out of her system. He set her bag down along with the groceries and walked into his bedroom only to find the bed empty and made, surprised, he looked inside the open doorway to the bathroom and didn't find her there either. He backtracked and made it to the kitchen only to find that empty as well. Where the heck was she? He glanced over to the balcony sliders but they remained shut with the blinds closed. Mike turned back to the kitchen and felt that unsettled feeling in his stomach again when he noticed the note stuck to the fridge. Remembering with dread the last note Jenna had left him on a refrigerator, he tore it away from the magnet and read.

Mike,

Couldn't sleep anymore, heading back to club to get my stuff, my bag and cell are still there (shoes, clothes etc.) and who knows who's tried to reach me and is probably worried. I'm taking a cab and will be back as soon as I get my stuff. I hope you're there when I get back, (otherwise you'll find me waiting outside your door—just realized I'll have no way of getting back in, not gonna leave an FBI agent's door unlocked lol, I feel good by the way, just a sore throat) I really want to talk to you about last night. I can't thank you enough or tell you how foolish I feel but I'm so glad you were there. I feel real bad you didn't get much sleep because of me and I hope you'll let me make it up to you. Love, Jenna

Love, Jenna. Mike felt his stomach drop as he stuck the note in his front pocket and ran out the front door, dialing Daniels as he went. When Daniels finally picked up, Mike hurriedly explained the situation and requested back-up. He made it back to Junior's club in under five minutes, throwing the Jeep in park and leaving it at the curb. He used the same key from earlier and rode the elevator up once he got inside. He got off and let himself into the condo.

Georgie sat smoking at the kitchen table and doing the *Herald's* crossword. She looked up, surprised at the sudden intrusion. "Hello again." She smiled, feigning calm while her pulse quickened at the sight of Jenna's large scowling man. "Something you forgot?"

"Where is she?"

"Who?"

"Don't fuck with me, tell me where she is or your next dance will be in a holding cell downtown."

Georgie's quick retort died on her tongue. "I don't know, Jay was here and she went with him."

"She went with him, or he took her?" Mike moved closer, giving Georgie the full on perp treatment.

Georgie tried to swallow and found her throat dry. "They got in the Suburban, that's all I know."

Mike was dialing Daniels when he heard Agent Collins enter the penthouse.

"Oh thank God," Georgie said, recognizing the doorman to the club. "This guy broke in here and is harassing me." She stood tightening her robe and gestured toward Mike.

Mike ignored her while holding the phone and said to Collins on his way out, "Stay here in case they come back, don't let her out of your sight and for God's sake don't let her make you any coffee. See what she knows." Mike shot one more intimidating look at Georgie before he left.

Georgie looked from one man to the other, her mouth agape, and slumped back into her seat. She was totally screwed.

Mike informed Daniels about the Suburban as he rode the elevator down and headed off to search the other clubs and condos. He couldn't do this alone; it was time to call in the troops.

* * * * *

Jenna opened her eyes and immediately felt sick; her cheek hurt like hell and upon physical inspection, was quite swollen. She sat up from where she'd been lying only to fall back quickly onto the cushioned seat. She was on a boat, and the seas were pretty rough if the nauseating rolling sensation under her was any indication. She sat up again and grabbed the edge of the cushion to balance herself trying to inhale deeply and quell the panic threatening to rise. Her mind finally started to clear and she remembered Jay trying to force her into his car outside his club. Was it still the same day? He'd obviously succeeded in kidnapping her, no doubt with the help of his gynormous bodyguard, she thought. She would have given Jay a good fight one on one, thanks to her self-defense training, but she'd been no match for Jay's oaf of a bodyguard that had hit her, the son of a bitch! She ran a hand over her cheek again and felt her teeth with her tongue which thankfully were all in place.

Jenna looked around. The boat was actually a yacht. She was on a moving hotel suite. What the hell? Whose yacht was it? She wondered and then felt the panic she had been trying to quell, surface. Oh God, Jay had delivered her to that rich guy from the club, he must have; she didn't think the yacht could have belonged to Jay. His boat was still at Tween Waters, she remembered. Was Jay even here or was she alone with some rich perv? Jenna stood up and grabbed a nearby table to steady herself. Her stomach threatened to empty and she kept with the deep breaths to calm it. She was a good swimmer, but how far from land were they? She was not in the best of shape after last night and her throat hurt like hell.

She parted a short curtain that covered a long narrow window above the couch where she'd been passed out and she peered out of it. She saw nothing but water; no land, no high rises, nothing, not even another boat. Shit. She crossed the room and went to the other side of the yacht and opened the matching curtain on that side as well. Her blood pumped at the sight of high rises in the distance and miles of beach. Could she make it that far? Were they still near Miami? The sun was still shining and she wondered how long they'd been at sea. Looking around for a clock and not finding one, she noticed the luxuriousness surrounding her. This guy must be a millionaire, she thought. She saw a set of stairs toward the front of the yacht next to the kitchen area that she assumed led up to the top deck. She moved toward them. Should she just make a run for it? Someone was obviously up there driving the boat and if she had to guess it wasn't the owner, he probably had someone to do that for him; that meant he was around here somewhere and possibly Jay and the bodyguard as well.

Jenna searched the cabin, which was in actuality more like the inside of a penthouse. She looked for a weapon or a CB or something to aid in her escape. The kitchen area held promise and she got excited as she went to it pulling open drawers and cabinets, thinking for sure there would be a knife, scissors, or anything sharp but there wasn't even a plastic fork.

Apparently, her captors had anticipated her search and removed anything of use. Feeling her heart sink she went to the small matching couches and pulled their cushions off, looking for storage compartments underneath. Every boat she'd ever been on had storage under the seats—except this one. These were actually expensive couches you'd find in someone's living room, the storage was most likely on deck, shit!

Jenna kept taking calming breaths, she knew panic would be detrimental and she needed to think clearly and focus. She put the cushions back and sat down on the couch to think. She heard footsteps on the stairs and looked toward them, feeling her stomach lurch with fear.

"Ah, chica you're awake."

Jenna watched the man approach her and was surprised. He was in his early to mid-fifties if she had to guess, on the short side and dark skinned with dark hair. By his accent she guessed Mexican or Brazilian, but he could be from anywhere for all she knew. He was well dressed, in the kind of clothing one pictured on a man on a yacht such as this; he was just missing the ascot and captain's hat. He didn't appear the kind of man she would think needed to pay for a woman, let alone kidnap one, until she dared to look him in the face and then she felt her skin crawl. He came to stand before her and Jenna was assaulted right away by his dark beady eyes. He reeked with too much pungent cologne and when he looked at her hungrily she thought she might heave on his expensive loafers. His beady eyes looked funny, like he was on something, and she wondered if it were the ecstasy like Jay had drugged her with, the way he was looking at her suggested as much and she felt the adrenaline surge through her, ready to fight him off if she had to.

"Where are we? I want to go back to Miami now!" Ha! Like he would oblige her, she thought.

Miguel laughed. "Impossible, chica, we are well away from Miami."

Jenna felt the fear seep through her pores. She thought of Mike, who was probably looking for her, and she prayed that he was. She felt the tears well up just thinking of him. Oh how she'd give anything to be back in his bed, safe in his arms. Once again she'd been stupid, going back for her things. Mike had gone there himself to retrieve them for her; she should have known that's where he was when she'd awaken to find him gone.

"What do you want with me? Why am I here?" Jenna heard the quiver in her voice and hated herself for it. She couldn't remember the last time she was truly fearful.

He reached out a hand and touched her swollen cheek gently, ignoring her questions. "The brute has been punished for this; I do not stand for brutality against women."

Jenna stared at him as if he had three heads. "Oh, I see, but kidnapping is okay?" She cringed at his chuckling. There was something off about the guy and that scared her more than if he had punched her himself. "Why am I here?" she asked again.

"Chica, you are here for my pleasure. Young Jay owes me and you are the payment."

His smile was meant to charm her, but managed to bring the bile from Jenna's gut right up to her throat.

"You will dance for me and entertain me." Miguel stroked her cheek again, ignoring her distasteful expression. "But not to worry, you are not a prisoner here, you may move about freely and you will see in time you will come to enjoy these surroundings." He spread his arm gesturing to the luxurious open space around him. "And in time you will even come to me of your own accord."

Jenna's mouth fell slack. Was he fucking kidding? "I don't think so, Mr.... ?

"I am Miguel Soto, you may call me Miguel."

"Mr. Soto, I'm not for sale or for barter, I never was, I explained that to Jay from the beginning so if I were you, I'd have a talk with *him,*" she emphasized. "I bet if you turn the boat around now, Jay can furnish you with a girl that will be only too happy to be on this yacht and entertain you, but as sure as you're looking at me," Jenna shook her head emphatically, "I'm not it. Not going to happen," she stressed. Her fear was quickly morphing into anger and she felt adrenaline quickly surge through her veins. She looked toward the stairs again, wondering who else was on deck. "Is Jay on board, by the way?" Saccharin dripped from her tone. She'd like to kick his ass.

Miguel laughed. "You American women are tough, yes?"

Jenna smirked. "Yes, most of us." But apparently there was a small population in Jay's clubs with no self-worth.

"I like you, chica. You will be amusing."

Disgusted, Jenna said, "Mr. Soto, I respectfully ask that you deliver me back to Miami. I understand you think you've paid for me," she laughed at the absurdity of that, "but there has been a huge misunderstanding, like I said, I was never for sale."

"Ah, chica, everything is for sale."

He gave her a sadistic smile and walked away, going back up the stairs and leaving Jenna shaking in anger and fear where she sat. Oh my God! This guy was fucking diabolical! She had to get off this boat! She stood on unsteady legs and made her way to follow him up the stairs but as she started to climb Jay appeared at the top and started his descent down.

Jenna snapped at the sight of him and shouted, "You fucking sleezeball!" She grabbed him by the shirt front, taking him by surprise and pulled him the rest of the way down the short staircase. They landed together with a thud on the hard wooden floor of the kitchen. Jay was taller than Jenna and had about fifty or so pounds on her but Jenna didn't notice and she didn't care. Her cousins Ryan and John had shown her and Paige just how to fight and now she had the strength of an ox as she rolled on top of Jay. "You bastard! What the hell have you done? Get me off this fucking boat now!" She was lashing out at him, punching his face and rib cage alternately. He clumsily covered his face to defend himself and that infuriated her. She found an opening and punched him hard in the face again and heard and felt a satisfying crack beneath her fist.

"Fuck, Jenna! You broke my nose!" Jay shouted through the hand that now covered his bleeding nose and mouth. He managed to push Jenna off of him and stand up.

Jenna bounced up too and used the opportunity to do more damage; she swung her leg around like a ninja and connected with the side of Jay's head, dropping him to the floor once again.

"Ugh! What the fuck?" Jay yelled and curled up to protect himself as best he could. She was like a fucking pitbull attacking him.

Jenna heard Jay yell, and heard the heavy footsteps on the stairs behind her. She was still kicking Jay, this time in the balls. She wasn't wearing any shoes but she could see she was inflicting pain with the heel of her foot. She'd gone wild and wanted to kill him. She felt a pair of large hands grab her around her waist, bodily picking her up and away from Jay, and she turned to see the big bodyguard who had punched her in the face. A renewed anger rose within her as the oaf carried her out of the kitchen area and toward the couches. She spit in his ugly face and grabbed his beefy arm, trying to pry his fat hand off her waist to get to his pudgy fingers. She got hold of a couple on his left hand and bent them back as far as she could; she heard the telltale crack and knew she had broken at least one.

"Fucking bitch!"

She felt her feet hit the ground and saw the backhand coming, she tried to duck but he was too fast. She felt her head snap back and she fell, hitting the edge of the glass coffee table in front of the couch. Everything went black.

* * * * *

"We located the Suburban down at the Miami Beach Marina. Miguel Soto's yacht left here around ten forty-five this morning." Strong wind and a steady drizzle whipped around Mike as he updated Rafe on his cell phone. Several boats knocked against the pilings from the chop. There was a storm coming and Mike prayed they could get to Jenna quickly.

"What does Soto have to do with this?" Rafe asked, alarmed.

Mike took a deep breath; he did not want to deliver this news. "Junior couldn't afford his product this month so Soto agreed to cut the shipment and payment in half in exchange for Jenna." Mike felt sick even saying the words and listened to the dead silence on the other end of the phone. "Rafe, I left her in my bed sleeping, I never thought in a million years she'd go back to that condo." Mike would kill Soto with his bare hands if he found out Soto had touched her.

Rafe could hear the remorse and fury in Mike's voice. He knew his friend was blaming himself and feeling awful. The fact that Jenna had been in Mike's bed made Rafe wonder what else Mike was feeling. "How do you know this?" He didn't ask exactly what the exchange entailed, and Mike didn't have to say; it was understood.

"Collins called me ten minutes after I left Junior's condo and told me the girl Georgie was freaking out and gave up the information trying to save her own ass. She's Jay's partner in crime." Mike ran a hand over his face and exhaled. "Coast Guard's in the air as we speak, as soon as they spot them, I'm out." Mike stood in front of the fifty-foot Outerlimits Cat that was gassed up and ready to take him to the yacht. One of the benefits of living in Miami was having wealthy friends and the equipment you needed right at your fingertips. People liked their toys expensive and fast in Miami and Mike had known just who to call to help him out. Now he was just waiting impatiently on word from Daniels, who was in direct contact with the Coast Guard. Mike hated standing there feeling helpless, he just wanted to jump in the boat and go, but without any idea the direction Soto took he would be wasting valuable time and fuel.

"What's the plan?" Rafe was on line checking flights. His office was aware of the situation in Miami and knew Rafe had a vested interest in the case.

Mike looked at the twin Merc 1200s idling at the dock and smirked. "The plan is to overtake the mother fucker and get Jenna off his boat."

Rafe shook his head, "Let me guess, Tommy Sands." Sand's was a long-time friend of Mike's with a passion for power boats; his newest one was his pride and joy.

"He's at the helm now just waitin' on me." Mike looked over at his childhood friend and thanked God he was at the marina. It would have been unusual if Tommy hadn't been, he could usually be found there on any given day babying his new toy. The new catamaran was pristine and the love of Tommy Sands' life.

Rafe exhaled, feeling a modicum of relief. Soto could be halfway to Mexico and Sands' Cat would catch him in no time.

"I'll call you back," Mike said anxiously, "Daniels is beeping in." Mike jumped on the Cat and gave Tommy the hold sign while he listened to Daniels.

"Coast Guard's got them in the Ditch, heading north, they're going to make an attempt to get a guy on board but it's pretty rough out there."

"Okay, got it!" Mike hung up with Daniels, thankful they wouldn't be heading to Mexico, and he yelled, motioning to Tommy with his hand, "Go, go, go, Intercoastal North!" Ignoring the "no wake zone" sign, Tommy nodded and opened her up, and they were off.

* * * * *

Jenna was awake again, this time sporting a throbbing headache and what felt like a gash above her right eye. She touched it cautiously and winced at the sticky feel of blood. At least she could see, she thought, and touched her still swollen cheek. This was just great, she was still on the yacht and now her ass had been kicked. Where the hell was Mr. "I don't believe in brutality against women"? She hoped he'd seen her face and "punished" Brutus again, although his idea of punishment was probably not quite the same as Jenna's. The bodyguard was probably being deprived of a steak dinner or something equally as trivial rather than having his balls squeezed in a vice like Jenna had envisioned.

If Mike ever found her, and dear God she prayed he did, all these assholes were going to pay. It bolstered her just picturing it and just as quickly brought tears to her eyes again thinking of him. She thought of Nicki and Paige, too, and what they must be thinking. Did they even know she was missing? And if they did would they have told her parents, Nan, or Jake? She cried for a few minutes feeling sorry for herself and utterly defenseless. How was she going to get out of this mess? How the hell had she gotten herself into it in the first place? Paige and Nicki were right; she was too trusting of people. Jay made her cheating ex-boyfriend look like a saint.

She stood up and looked out through the big glass doors that led to the outside deck. She could barely see anything now; it was raining hard and she could feel the steady rock of the yacht under her feet. Jenna didn't know too much about boats but she was pretty sure it had to be pretty rough out there to make something this big rock and roll like it was doing. She breathed through the nausea and took in her surroundings once again looking for anything to use as a weapon. She thought she'd heard the sound of a helicopter overhead when she'd come to, but realized it was just her imagination when the wind had howled loudly soon after. Surely they would have to stop moving in this, right? Maybe if they anchored she'd be able to jump, but the thought of jumping into cold, stormy seas was far less appealing than staying on board perhaps for another beating. She just needed something to defend herself against the big guy and she had to have faith Mike was coming for her. He was the FBI, for God's sake; of course he would find her! She just had to hold these guys off while she waited.

Jenna felt better already thinking positively and she reached up to lift the curtain rod off the wall above the couch. It was wrought iron, about an inch thick and four feet long. She had to unscrew the decorative finial at one end in order to get it through the anchors but it came off easily enough and she pulled the curtain off with it, shoving both under the sofa cushion. It was not exactly something she could hide behind her back, but it would be easy to reach for just under the edge of the cushion, if she had to.

She looked around for something smaller to use as a weapon as well and headed again toward the small kitchen area, keeping a wary eye on the stairs. She noticed a small door to the left that she hadn't seen before and she opened it, surprised and thankful to see a bathroom and a luxurious bathroom at that. She used it quickly and took a look at herself in the mirror over the marble sink. She almost started crying again at her bruised and battered appearance but she held back, channeling her angst for anger. She searched the vanity drawers and cabinets and miraculously found a pair of sharp tweezers that she quickly hid on the waistband of her shorts like a clothespin, if she had to poke someone's eye out she would. She'd put on the stupid short shorts from her uniform again and Mike's oversized T-shirt which she was grateful for, but she had no underwear on to conceal anything, and she prayed the tweezers stayed in place.

She next found and used some hydrogen peroxide on her cut then patted it dry with some gauze she found in a first-aid kit under the sink. She then inspected the back of her head with her fingers and was happy to find she wasn't bleeding, but there was definitely a small egg there that had formed. She rifled through the rest of the first-aid kit and found nothing of use that could inflict harm but was slightly comforted by the tweezers and curtain rod she had hidden. She left the bathroom fully alert and went back to sit on the couch and wait for the bastards to come down the stairs again or for Mike to rescue her, whichever came first.

CHAPTER THIRTY-FIVE

"So, your cousin's best friend's fiancé is an FBI agent too?" Justin lay back against the headboard with Paige's head against his chest trying to follow along. It was late afternoon and pouring outside and they had made no move to leave the bed.

Paige nodded against him. "He and this guy Mike are good friends, I guess, they worked together in Miami last year, and they were on the island together last summer working that case I told you about."

"Jesus, I still can't believe your cousin's friend got nicked by a bullet."

"I know, that's why everyone was kind of freaking out about Jenna getting mixed up with Scintillo's son. I think they all started having flashbacks." Paige sighed. "Thank God she's all right and on her way home." She came up on her elbow and lifted her head, shaking it in disbelief. "And we had just been joking about this kind of thing in your shop when she mentioned how bored she'd probably be on the island."

"I'm happy for you that she's okay." Justin stroked Paige's naked back, looking at her now. "That club scene could have been really bad." He had known some friends who had been drugged unknowingly before and it hadn't been a pleasant experience. "I won't mind seeing her again either." Justin smiled. "I like your cousin. She's funny. I am a little surprised, though, that she got mixed up in all this, she didn't seem the type to just take off with strangers."

Paige nodded, sliding her leg over Justin's, getting comfortable. "She's just too trusting of people. She just wants to have fun, she's always had that 'to each his own mentality'." Paige shook her head again. "Even after she found out who Jay's father was she still didn't think she was in any harm. She told Nicki that Jay was a nice guy."

"She's accepting to her own detriment," Justin observed.

"Yeah, like the guy she recently broke up with, he was her first, you know?" Paige looked at Justin scrunching her face in sympathy. "And he was cheating on her probably for the last six months they were together."

"That sucks, she had no idea?" He knew first-hand how that felt.

"Not until she caught him herself. She felt pretty foolish, that was really the reason she came here. She was embarrassed and mad at herself. She said she was through with relationships." Paige sighed and stroked a hand along Justin's abdomen. "I think going off with this guy Jay was a little retribution on her part, plus the idea of going to Miami was probably exciting. We'd always talked about going and hitting the clubs, and then along comes this guy who owns them, for God's sake, and offers her a job. It probably never crossed her mind that he would harm her in any way." Paige smirked. "Plus she's ridiculously tough and I think that gives her a false sense of security that she can take care of herself."

"How do you mean?" Justin narrowed his brows.

"She knows how to defend herself pretty well," Paige told him. "My brother Ryan fights, you know... MMA. My brother John is his training partner. They taught the both of us a long time ago how to defend ourselves." Paige watched Justin's brows lift. "Jenna's more into it than me, I prefer to run mostly," she laughed as Justin teasingly squeezed her bicep. "But Jenna still works out with them when she can and she isn't afraid of anything or anybody for that matter. Not to mention she's been dancing her whole life. I feel sorry for anyone that ever tries to hurt her, but it's not like she's a six foot tall, two hundred pound man, she's a tiny little thing, you've seen her."

Justin nodded. He couldn't picture Paige's petite cousin hurting a fly "So do you two actually spar with your brothers?" he asked impressed.

"No!" Paige laughed. "They just give us a tough workout, show us self-defense moves. My brothers aren't beating on us or anything." She laughed at the image. "They're pretty cool guys." Paige told Justin about their previous back-round and small claim to fame before they'd become more heavily involved in the fighting.

Justin was surprised to hear about Paige's brothers; he was impressed and had of course heard of their Internet search engine *AX-S*. They sounded real interesting. "Well, one good thing will come of all this, I guess. Jenna will probably be a lot more selective when it comes to choosing her friends."

"I have a feeling she's chosen a new one already." Paige smiled at him. "I hope you don't have the wrong idea about Jenna, aside from her bad judgment these past few days. She is really very smart and so much fun to be around. I can't wait for you to get to know her better. I'm also looking forward to meeting this guy Mike, myself. He sounds good for her."

"I don't have the wrong idea," Justin assured Paige. "I met Jenna and I liked her right away, she does seem like she'd be a lot of fun to be around. Didn't you say this FBI agent is from Miami though?"

"Well yeah, but that doesn't matter, Rafe was living in Miami and look where he is now," Paige laughed.

Justin smiled. "So you're saying we men will go anywhere for a good woman?"

Paige laughed and tickled his stomach, "If you're smart. Hey!" she yelled, laughing harder as he rolled her over and pinned her to the mattress.

"Just making sure I can take you after what I just learned." He grinned and placed his lips to her neck.

Paige's legs wrapped around his like a snake and she squeezed tight.

"I should probably be alarmed right now at your freakish strength but I have to admit I kind of like it," Justin grinned, teasing her.

Paige giggled and proceeded to show him a few of her other moves.

* * * * *

Mike's stomach was in his throat and he felt his body compacting with each wave they landed. Tommy was on full throttle and they were literally flying through the air. When the hull came down to meet the water it was with such force, Mike's teeth would slam together and he thought he could feel each of his vertebrae crunch together with the impact. They were going at top speed, one hundred sixty miles an hour, and despite the whipping rain, Mike could actually see the outline of the yacht in front of them thanks to the goggles Tommy had thrown him. They were almost upon the yacht and Mike looked to the storm-ridden sky for his back up but saw nothing.

He had no idea how many people were on the yacht with Jenna. He was assuming four, Soto, Jay, whoever was at the helm, and possibly a bodyguard. Georgie had told Collins that Jay had been with a bodyguard. Tommy, thankfully, was armed like Mike. He carried a license due to the fact that he worried about someone stealing one of his precious toys, and Mike knew he was a good shot, they were at the range frequently together. Mike knew he could count on Tommy if he needed help, and hell, he'd take all he could get, he was going to have to handle at least four men and get Jenna to safety in the process. He hoped to accomplish all that without any gun fire.

They took another jarring jolt to the system as the Cat bounced off the water but thankfully Tommy was throttling back now, and the impact was starting to lessen as they got closer to the yacht. The problem with the Cat was that it was not inconspicuous, just the opposite, and Mike knew their arrival would set things in motion fast; he had to be ready for anything. Right now though the storm was working in their favor and it appeared that no one was top side.

Mike leaned into Tommy's ear. "Starboard side as close as you can, I'm just going to jump on."

Tommy nodded his head and cut their speed. Mike took off the goggles and checked the clip on his HK. He pulled Tommy's Glock from the back of

Tommy's waistband and checked his clip too before replacing it. Tommy, still with both hands occupied at the helm, furnished him with a sidelong, what am I fucking stupid look and Mike shrugged. Hey, he wasn't taking any chances.

Mike's shirt was completely soaked through and his jeans and shoes were too. It would make mobility that much harder but there was nothing short of getting naked that he could do. They were fifty or more feet from the yacht and Tommy had down shifted. The turbulent waves and raucous wind were making it hell to come up neat beside the yacht and Mike knew it was going to be a bumpy pairing. Tommy gestured under the seat cushions and Mike lifted them, finding a couple of bumpers. He tied them off quickly and threw them over the side, keeping his eyes on the yacht and wiping away the rain that dripped from his hair onto his face. Thankfully there wasn't anybody in sight, nobody standing with an AK waiting to mow him down, not yet anyway. He couldn't see into the fly bridge but he knew someone had to be manning it.

As they grew nearer, Mike could see his original plan of jumping onto the yacht starboard side was going to be shot to hell. The Cat sat much lower than the yacht and even if Mike timed it right with the swell, minimizing their distance, he'd be hard pressed to reach the side rails. He was going to have to jump from the Cat to the yacht's transom. He motioned to Tommy the change in plan and Tommy tried to maneuver as best he could.

Tommy was in neutral now and signaling Mike to get ready. The waves were fucking huge and Mike suppressed the nausea that churned in his stomach. He had one thing to focus on and that was making it on the transom without falling or slipping, otherwise he'd be chum in no time, his body churning between the inboards of the yacht like fruit in a blender. He took several deep breaths waiting for Tommy to bring the bow up as close as he could. The plan was for Mike to get on board and Tommy to take off and circle back; they couldn't chance someone on board disabling Tommy or the Cat. The plan was also to have the Coast Guard hovering over their heads right now but they were fucking nowhere in sight. As it stood now, Mike still couldn't believe there wasn't a welcoming committee waiting for him. The best he could guess was that the noise of the wind and rain were masking Tommy's idling Mercs. Either that or whoever was on board was waiting to give Mike a warm welcome once he made it on board and into the cabin.

Mike made sure his gun was holstered tight and he looked at Tommy and nodded. Fuck it. As soon as the next swell lifted the Cat, Mike dove for the transom of the yacht, he landed on his feet and grabbed for the jet-ski secured to the back of it and held on tight. He immediately lost balance as the yacht rode the next swell and he felt his soaking wet sneakers slide out from under him. Water washed over the transom with force and Mike held onto the jet-ski for dear life trying to get his footing back. When he was finally able to stand, he climbed over the hinge on the transom and got a leg up on the port side staircase and a hand on the railing. He half expected to be knocked back down once he started to climb, but still the yacht remained desolate, which was almost as disconcerting as the image of Soto's henchmen waiting for him with an AK. Where the fuck was everybody?

He made it to the top of the stairs and stood dripping on the aft deck, his gun at the ready, and was now somewhat protected from the pelting rain as he stood under the hard shell canopy that covered the main deck. He moved forward on the deck cautiously but quickly, making his way over to the double wide glass doors that led to the main cabin. He passed a fixed, gleaming teak table with seating for eight as he went and thought under better circumstances he could probably appreciate the impressive vessel he'd just boarded. But as it stood the roller coaster ride under his feet and the wind and sideways rain obscuring his vision made him want to appreciate good old solid ground again real soon.

Mike noticed the spiral staircase to his right that led to the fly bridge and he hesitated. At this stage the captain of the yacht was not a threat, unless it was Soto himself, but Mike highly doubted it, so he continued forward instead and opened the glass doors. He saw Jenna right away and a mixture of fury and relief twisted in his gut like a tornado.

CHAPTER THIRTY-SIX

Jenna had been waiting too long; where was everybody? She was afraid to leave her spot on the couch. No one was making any moves to come in and harm her but she didn't know what awaited her above or below deck, she did know the longer she sat there doing nothing the faster they were reaching their destination. She only wished she knew where that was. She had no idea how long she'd been on the boat. She'd been unconscious twice so far today with no inkling of how long. At least if they hit land, she'd have a chance to run, she only hoped where they were going there'd be police nearby.

She stood up fast when she thought she heard a boat engine close by. Whatever it was it had been loud and had just as quickly died away as though she'd imagined it. She couldn't see a thing when she looked out the windows and she didn't dare open the large glass doors to the storm. All Jenna saw when she looked passed the glass were high seas and white caps, she could go out there but what if she fell off the boat? She'd never stand a chance.

Her stomach was roiling even though it was completely empty. The last thing she'd eaten had been the pineapple sherbet and remembering this brought on fresh tears. Damn it! She hated feeling trapped. Where were they going and how would she get away? Was anyone even looking for her? *Yes*, she had to be positive, she knew Mike was looking for her, he had to be. She had left a note and not returned. He would definitely be looking. But he would most likely be looking on land, she thought with crushing realization. How in God's name would he ever find her here, out in the middle of the ocean? And was she even on the ocean or were they in the Gulf?

The horror of what was happening finally sank in and Jenna gave in to it. She sat back on the couch and pulled her knees into her chest, wrapping her arms around them, and she bawled like a baby. Why weren't they coming to check on her? It was almost worse feeling abandoned. What if they'd somehow left the yacht and she were the only one on it and it crashed and started to sink? She started to shake and think of everyone she loved, her parents who were probably having a grand time in Vegas and had no idea their little girl was on a death voyage to God knows where, Nicki who had tried to warn her, out of love and concern, Paige, who she knew was on Captiva expecting her, and probably worried sick, and Nan, who was in the dark like her parents. And just the thought of Nan made Jenna cry even harder. If Nan were here she'd know just what to do. Then Jenna thought of Jake. She missed him so much and she could just picture him reaming her out for getting herself mixed up in all this shit. And then she thought of Ali and Rafe's wedding which her whole family was supposed to attend in less than two weeks. She would ruin their wedding if she didn't get out of this!

She needed them all and if she lived through this she would spend the rest of her life telling them how much they all meant to her but the one she wanted to tell most of all was Mike. She sobbed thinking of him, remembering how she felt in his arms. She'd always thought of herself as a warrior. She was petite, but she was strong, she'd danced all her life and spent hours in the studio and gym every week, but in Mike's strong arms she felt like a delicate little flower. She felt feminine, like a damsel in distress and she loved that, he was so gentle and kind and he'd most definitely saved her life last night. She rested her head on her knees and sighed heavily through her tears, she had to get it together. Nobody was coming, she had to save herself; she had to live to see him again, to tell him how she felt.

The sound of the glass doors opening and then the screaming wind blowing into the cabin had Jenna raising her head fearfully. She was afraid to look but when she did, she gasped and great big sobs of relief escaped her mouth. The wind entered the cabin, forcefully whipping her hair around but there was no mistaking Mike standing there, framed by the open glass doors, his soaked T-shirt pasted to his wide muscular shoulders and chest, dripping wet from his head to his feet and pointing a mean-looking gun. Jenna had never seen a more intimidating, impressive, or welcome sight.

Mike approached Jenna, but his eyes were scanning the room. "Are you alone in here?"

Jenna nodded and stood with tears streaming down her face. She wanted to throw her arms around him and never let go but his tone and the expression on his face told her the action probably wouldn't be reciprocated. This was Mike the FBI agent who'd entered the cabin, the unsmiling man she'd first met by her grandmother's pool, not the man who had made her body putty in his hands in the wee hours of the morning. He was clearly angry but Jenna shook with relief anyway that he was standing in front of her.

"I haven't seen anyone in a while, I don't even know if there is anybody on board anymore." She cried and her breath hitched as she spoke. She watched him traverse the cabin determinedly. He then looked in the bathroom and glanced up the stairs, his gun pointed toward the ceiling, his body taut and his demeanor tense. He looked like he wanted to kill somebody, and Jenna sat back on the couch instinctively.

"That's where they always come from." Her heart was in her throat as he studied the stairs. Oh God, why wouldn't he look at her? Was he so furious at her he couldn't even meet her eyes? He'd barely glanced at her since he'd entered the room.

"They kidnapped me," Jenna cried defensively. "I didn't want to go, I tried to fight." She heard her voice cracking. "I could have taken Jay but he had his bodyguard and he was too big for me, he knocked me out before I could do anything but scream." Mike did look at her then and she saw the blind rage in his eyes. She cried even more and looked away ashamed. He'd had to come to her rescue once again and now she'd put him in danger. "I'm so sorry," she cried, covering her face with her hands.

Mike covered the short distance between them in two strides and his arms were around her instantly. Jenna grabbed onto them like a life preserver burying her head against his chest and the soaking shirt that covered it. "I'm sorry, I'm so sorry."

Mike's heart was breaking. "Jenna baby, shh, don't you dare apologize. I'm going to get you out of here, but first I need to find these guys and I have to keep you safe while I do it, do you understand?" He wanted nothing more than to comfort her right then but there wasn't time, he had to get her off the yacht.

Jenna looked at him and was grateful for the softened look on his face and behind his eyes. She nodded, wiping her tears and flinching at the pain from her cheek as she wiped. He was saving her again, he'd found her and he wasn't angry with her. She felt an on rush of love for him.

"Come with me."

Mike held out his free hand as he stood and Jenna placed hers inside of it, his was big and cold and wet and it warmed her heart. She followed him to the glass doors and he stopped and turned to her. He let go of her hand and brought it up to her face, lightly touching her swollen cheek and then the cut above her eye. His gun was at the ready in his other hand and it felt surreal to Jenna to be standing there with one of his hands touching her so gently while the other brandished a weapon that could kill. She looked into his eyes and felt his thumb wipe away a tear.

"Who did this?" Mike asked, barely containing his fury.

His voice was tight and held the anger that she had seen on his face when he'd first entered the cabin. "Jay's bodyguard, this morning outside the club when I was trying to get away then I woke up here. The second time, he did this." Jenna touched her cut. "He backhanded me and I fell and bumped my head on that coffee table." She gestured toward it. "I was out for a bit again, so I couldn't retaliate, he was gone when I came to."

The *second* time? Backhanded? Bumped her head? Retaliate? He put his hand through her hair and felt the back of her head while he fumed. Sure enough there was a small egg. Mike was going to kill this guy whoever he was. He took a deep steadying breath. "We're going outside on deck, my friend Tommy is out there and you're going to get on his boat. You're going to have to jump, Jenna, can you do it?"

She nodded, scared to death. The yacht was still rolling from side to side beneath her feet, but she would do anything he asked, she'd jump directly into the scary, turbulent water if he wanted her to, Mike had found her and was touching her, making sure she was okay and that was all that mattered.

He gave her the briefest, lightest kiss and Jenna felt it like an imprint, heard it loudly in her ears even though it didn't make a sound. She tasted the salt from his lips and savored it like it was her last meal. She was in love with him and she was so thankful he wasn't angry at her. She should have known he was angry at her captors, at the person who had left his mark on her face, twice. Mike would make them pay just like she'd thought, only now she was realizing that because of that he wasn't coming with her, he wanted her and her alone to jump onto his friend's boat.

"You're not coming with me?" They were on deck and he was lifting off seat cushions trying to find something.

Mike pulled out a life vest from a bench seat and helped her put it on. He stayed alert for company but still no one appeared. Tommy was coming up on them fast, and Mike waved letting him know they were ready. The rain seemed to be letting up somewhat but the Gulf was still rough and Mike worried about Jenna getting on the Cat safely. "I'll see you soon, okay?" He guided her down the port side stairs that led to the transom and told her to hold on, which she did with a death grip. "I know you're scared, baby," he said and kissed the top of her head, "but you can do this. Tommy will keep you safe until I can join you." Jenna looked up at him and he felt his heart break again, she was killing him. "When he comes up real close you're going to wait for the swell, then jump, okay?"

Jenna was nodding and watching the waves, the life vest felt heavy around her neck as she tightened the straps. She could do this no problem, she knew she could, she wasn't afraid of jumping; she just didn't want to leave Mike on the yacht alone. What if the rich guy or Jay had a gun? The bodyguard probably had one and Mike would be outnumbered. She spoke quickly as Mike's friend approached in a boat the likes of which she'd ever only seen on TV.

"Jay's on board, his bodyguard and the rich dude, I don't know who's driving, and I don't know if there's anybody else, and there's just one of you, let me stay and help."

Mike gave her a crooked smile and felt a surge of pride for her. "You would too, wouldn't you?"

"Damn right," she said, smiling through her tears.

"I got this one." He smiled back at her. "I'll be with you soon, okay?"

Jenna took a deep breath and nodded. Mike's friend was right up alongside them now and it was time to go. Jenna held on to the railing at the bottom of the steps waiting for the swell like Mike told her and when it came she didn't hesitate. Her feet left the platform and she was in the air. It seemed as though she were in the air for a long time before the speedboat finally rode the swell back up and the deck of the boat came up to meet her bare feet. She slipped on impact and came down hard on her butt and Mike's friend was immediately there helping her up. When she looked back, Mike waved them off and then he disappeared inside the yacht's main cabin. Jenna's heart fell and her stomach knotted in fear as she watched him disappear. She turned to Mike's friend to thank him and he smiled and winked at her, bringing on yet another burst of tears. Even Mike's friends were nice.

Tommy laughed. "We'll see him in ten minutes gorgeous, no worries." When Mike had called Tommy for his help, he had given him the short version on Jenna, and Tommy had been only too happy to help, but seeing her in person he now understood why his childhood friend had been so worried. She was a stunner even with the cuts and bruises, and Tommy knew whatever bastard had done that to her would be getting his balls handed to him at any moment.

Tommy kept right alongside the yacht this time. There was no way he was going to leave Mikey out here without any back-up, the damn Coast Guard had bailed, and Tommy couldn't blame them, nobody should be out in these conditions. But the rain did seem to be letting up, so maybe they'd be back around. He gestured for Jenna to go below deck. "There's dry sweats down there, get comfortable, I'll keep an eye on your man."

Jenna went below deck and saw a canvas bag on one of the seats. She felt like she'd stepped inside a virtual roller coaster ride, the bucket seats were lined up in a row and the harness style seat belts promised a thrilling ride, but surprisingly she felt less motion below the deck of this boat then she did on the yacht and she hoped the storm was coming to an end. She pulled out the sweats Mike's friend spoke of and took off the heavy life vest and Mike's wet T-shirt to put the warm sweat shirt on. The pants were ridiculously big so she just kept her uniform shorts on, the Dolphins sweatshirt fell to her knees anyway. She took the no longer needed tweezers from her waistband and put them along with the pants on one of the bucket seats and she held Mike's T-shirt securely in her hands and prayed. His friend had said ten minutes, and seemed pretty confident; Jenna hoped to God he was right.

CHAPTER THIRTY-SEVEN

Mike heard the chopper as he was climbing the stairs. He'd cleared the lower deck, and then the main deck again before heading to the fly bridge, and now he would see what awaited him up top. The barrel of his gun leading the way, he made it to the landing only to see a man in dress whites at the helm and Junior and his bodyguard passed out on the floor beside him. What the fuck? The man at the helm turned around and automatically put his hands up. Mike ordered him to cut the engines and he did so at once. Mike frisked him and found him unarmed.

"I no want trouble, sir, my orders are to drop men off on Captiva then bring yacht back to Mexico." The man motioned to Junior and his overgrown pal slumped behind a cushioned bench.

Mike looked at the men. Junior looked like hell and the big one even worse. "Where's Soto?"

"He take helicopter back to Mexico."

Helicopter? The canopy over the main deck must be a landing pad, Mike realized, and coincidently he could now see and hear through the fly bridge window the Coast Guard chopper in the sky. They were approaching with a sniper perched at the open door ready and waiting.

"Soto left in a helicopter?"

"Sí, yes, he fly. I take men to Captiva."

"He left alone? Just Soto?"

"Sí."

Well shit, where was the fun in this? Mike turned his attention to the floor. "What happened to these two?" Junior's nose was definitely busted and he had two black eyes as the result. The big guy's hand lay haphazardly across his own chest and it was swollen with a couple of meaty digits looking disfigured. Had Junior's bodyguard slugged him?

"They got shot."

"Shot?" Mike got down on one knee and inspected them both; there was no blood and no bullet wounds, "What kind of shot?" he asked looking up at the man.

"I not know, sir."

"A needle?" Mike pressed.

"Sí."

Okay so Soto drugged these two, but why? Something had obviously gone down between the three men.

Using a bull horn to announce their presence, the Coast Guard helo landed on the yacht's landing pad and moments later the sniper entered the fly bridge in full tactical gear, Mike felt a little underdressed in his soggy T-shirt, jeans and handgun.

"Special Agent Tom Daniels for you, Agent Caplan," the sniper addressed Mike and held out a sat phone.

Mike took the satellite phone from the officer nodding thanks and put it to his ear. "Tom?"

"Soto's helo left an hour ago, that's why your CG bird bailed. If you'd had the sat phone I could have told you, your cell went right to voice mail, no reception obviously. The Coast Guard followed him, he almost made it back to Mexico, but they forced his bird down on a cutter out in the Gulf, he's on his way back to Miami."

"He's in custody?" Mike asked, incredulous.

"You got it, what's the sit there?"

"Secure, Junior and his bodyguard thug are doped up and passed out, looks like they were injected with something." Mike looked down at Junior and his friend and prayed they woke up soon just so he could knock them out again.

"We've got more men on the way to search and retrieve the yacht. How's the girl?"

"Safe, with Tommy on the Cat." Mike paused. "She's got a swollen cheek and a cut above her eye and a small egg on the back of her head." He glanced at the bodyguard as he informed Daniels and prayed for the slug to come to.

Shit! Daniels was thankful the two men were already passed out. "Let the men do their thing when they arrive, Cap, I know how you're feeling right now, but take a deep breath, get out of there and take her home, a response boat is headed your way. Simmons and Reynolds, and two agents from DEA are on board, they'll take over."

"Tom, Soto wanted these two dropped off in Captiva for a reason. Why would he need to drug them? And why didn't he try to take Jenna with him to Mexico?" Mike wondered aloud, thanking Christ Soto hadn't taken her.

"That's what Simmons and Reynolds will find out." Daniels hoped they got there soon, too.

Mike was silent as he thought. "Why don't we deliver them as planned, and see who's waiting at the other end?" he suggested. He wanted to get Jenna back there anyway.

Daniels thought about it. "You are closer to the island than Miami, just a couple of hours out now, I'd say, and Garrison is still there so I guess I could just have Bealls and Murph meet you all at Tween Waters." At least Simmons and Reynolds would be on board to keep Mike from doing anything stupid.

"Good, I'm going to bring Jenna back on board then I'll call Rafe and update him."

"Already have, about Soto, just let him know how Jenna is," Daniels told him.

"I will, and thanks, I know this didn't go down like you thought it was going to."

"Hey we can hold Soto on kidnapping charges until we get information from Junior. It's not over yet Cap, keep me posted, I'll do the same."

Mike hung up with Daniels and spoke to the Coast Guard officer, leaving him to watch over Junior and his sidekick and Mike kept the sat phone with him. He left the fly bridge and went back down to the main deck to signal Tommy who was drifting beside the yacht. The water had calmed considerably along with the wind and only a fine sprinkle remained, the sun's rays could be seen trying to penetrate the thick clouds and it already felt warmer. He shouted down to Tommy.

"Bring her up I'm taking her back on board. Our man took off, there's just a couple of loose ends we're going to take back to Captiva. You up for a cruise?" Mike asked with a grin. "Dinner's on me!"

"Thanks anyway man, got a date!" Tommy grinned and bounced his brows up and down. "But you will owe me a dinner when you get back home!"

Jenna came up on deck at the sound of Tommy yelling to Mike and relief washed over her as she looked up and saw him standing on the yacht safe and sound. He gave her a wink when he saw her and her swoon had nothing to do with the rise and fall of the boat.

"You got it man, I owe you big." Mike made his way to the transom and balanced himself as Tommy maneuvered the Cat closer. Mike looked at Jenna and gave her a big grin. "I didn't think I'd be asking you to do this twice."

Jenna's heart was pounding but not because she was afraid. "That's okay, it was so much fun the first time I hoped I'd get another go at it." She yelled up and grinned back at him garnering a laugh from both men. She climbed up on the side of the boat with Tommy's assistance and turned to him. "Thank you," she said seriously.

"You got it, beautiful, keep that boy out of trouble will you?"

Jenna laughed. "Unfortunately, since I've met him, I've only kept him in it."

Tommy laughed. "Then you were made for each other!"

She gave Tommy a wide smile at that and jumped right onto the transom of the yacht, her landing much more graceful this time. She landed on her feet and right into Mike's waiting arms. She held onto him tightly as he moved them to the stairs and up to the main deck. They waved back to Tommy and watched as he gunned the engines and sped away.

Mike held Jenna tight for a moment then pulled back to look at her. "You okay?"

She nodded yes, not trusting herself to speak. He brought her up to speed and she was relieved to know the perv, Soto, was gone and had been captured. She was also quite happy to hear they were headed back to Captiva.

"We're going to have more company, but you'll be able to rest, okay?"

She nodded again and turned at the sound of another boat approaching. It was the Coast Guard in a boat almost as long as the yacht and there were about six men aboard, two of which wore FBI windbreakers. When they came up alongside, she could see two more wore jackets that read DEA. Seeing the agents laden with weapons solidified the dangerous situation she'd been in and Jenna felt herself start to lose it. The whole ordeal was catching up with her.

She tried to hold it together bravely as four men got on board and introductions were made. Jenna felt rather small amidst them and embarrassed as well. She took notice of how they all stared at her bruised face with looks of sympathy and anger not unlike Mike's reaction, just not as fierce. Jenna could only imagine what they thought.

With a reassuring squeeze to her shoulder, Mike left her side for a minute and Jenna watched him talk to his fellow agents. He was impressive when he was working and she felt a swell of pride just watching him. His gun was tucked into the back of his waistband and it actually turned her on to see it, making her forget temporarily what had nearly happened to her. When Mike finally turned back to her he was smiling.

"Let's go inside." He reached for her hand. "They're going to handle things for a while; I want to get you comfortable."

Jenna let him lead the way back inside the main cabin where she had been earlier and then down a set of stairs she hadn't even known were there; they led to the lower deck where the sleeping quarters were. They passed two staterooms and continued to what Jenna guessed was the master suite. It was just as luxurious as the rest of the yacht and once inside Mike shut the door behind them and took her right in his arms.

Jenna hugged him back and felt every emotion that had been hovering just beneath the surface spill forth. She started to cry again, actually bawled like a baby while he held her. After a few minutes she stopped and laughed softly. "I'm sorry, I just can't seem to stop crying around you, I'm normally a lot tougher than this."

Mike chuckled while his chest tightened with emotion. "Ssh, you've been through hell and back in the last twenty-four hours, it's understandable." He wiped the tears from her cheeks and saw her wince. "Ooh, I'm sorry," he said, lightening his touch. "And I'm sorry I didn't take you right into my arms when I first came aboard, I had to make sure the room was clear." He looked at her bruised face and quelled the instant surge of fury but didn't hide what he was thinking. "When they wake up, I'm going to kill them."

Jenna laughed, knowing he was speaking of Jay and his bodyguard. She was so relieved to be in Mike's arms again. "Please don't, I don't want to have to get to know you in prison."

Mike grinned. "Well, by the looks of it they already beat the shit out of each other."

"What do you mean?" Jenna looked up at him.

"Junior's got a broken nose, two black eyes and a welt on his forehead and his bodyguard has a broken hand or fingers I'm not sure which. Junior must have a hard skull," Mike laughed.

Jenna smile was one of satisfaction. "Fingers."

"What?"

"Fingers. I broke them and Jay's nose. The welt is probably from the roundhouse kick I gave him." She laughed at Mike's wide-mouthed look of shock.

"*What?*" He'd seen how she could handle herself at Junior's nightclub but this kind of defense was on a whole different level.

Jenna told him what had transpired and felt proud of herself at his look of admiration.

"Damn, baby, I'm really turned on right now. C'mere." Mike pulled her into him and kissed the laughter away from her lips, and kept kissing her until they were both falling back on the bed. They were all at once frantic, Mike pulling at the sweatshirt that swallowed her and Jenna tugging at his damp T-shirt. He quickly removed his gun from the back of his waistband and placed it on the bed stand, then sat up to peel his T-shirt off and help her with the sweat shirt. When they were skin to skin they held each other even tighter and kissed each other harder.

Mike reached for her bare breasts, one at a time and felt one slim leg wrap around his. He ground against her center and she writhed right back underneath him. He heard her say his name and it sounded desperate, he knew just what she was feeling; he wanted her more than he'd ever wanted anyone or anything in his life. Mike kissed her neck and shoulder and ran his hands through her hair. He kissed her swollen cheek and her cut and her bruised head and felt so damn happy and grateful she was alive and here safe with him.

When he moved his mouth to her breasts, she arched into him and held onto his head guiding him—and then the fucking sat phone rang.

"Oh no," Jenna moaned.

"Ignore it." Mike knew better but he continued kissing Jenna's soft skin and hard nipples, caught up in the essence of her, he was rock hard for her. The phone kept ringing.

"You have to get it or they'll know what we're doing, and I'll be mortified."

She laughed, but Mike definitely didn't want Jenna to feel any embarrassment, so he reluctantly stopped. Throwing her a "to be continued" look, he pulled the phone from the pocket of his damp jeans. "Yeah?" he answered gruffly.

Jenna lay back, looking up at him and grinning.

"I'll be right there." He ended the call. "They're awake in the main cabin, I gotta go up for a bit, okay?"

"Okay, but try and hurry back," she smiled seductively.

"Jesus, don't look at me like that, I have to get rid of this."

He looked down to the erection she could so clearly make out under his damp jeans. "I know how to get rid of it," Jenna teased.

"You," he pointed at her, "are nothing but trouble!" And Mike loved it, he loved her! He traced a hand over each of her arms and squeezed her muscles. "Why didn't I notice these before? You're like a little GI Jane with a beautiful mane of hair." He smiled to himself suddenly realizing the coincidence. He had heard her call him GI Joe, when he'd eavesdropped on her conversation with Nicki. He grinned thinking they were made for each other just like Tommy joked, then he felt sick just the same. The news about HRT would be coming soon.

Jenna sat up and stared at him wide eyed, "What did you just call me?"

Mike laughed and held his hands up. "Easy, don't break my nose, it was a compliment!"

Jenna laughed out loud, another sign! GI Joe and GI Jane! Another sign from fate! She couldn't wait to tell Nan. "I wholeheartedly accept it as a compliment; in fact I like it!" She was smiling like a fool.

"Well good," Mike laughed, shaking his head, happy he'd made her laugh and smile. He stood up to put his damp shirt back on. "I'll be back as soon as I can and I'll try to find you some food."

"Okay, I'll be here." She plopped back on the bed and smiled up at the ceiling, she couldn't wait to get back to Captiva with him.

CHAPTER THIRTY-EIGHT

"Didn't I tell you?" Paige leaned back into Justin's chest. They sat on the sand watching the last of the sunset over the Gulf. They had eaten, showered, and dressed and walked back over to the beach. The afternoon storm had given way to clear sunny skies so they had left Sam sleeping on the kitchen tiles and walked the beach to Tween Waters. They'd bought drinks at the pool bar and crossed back over to the sand to watch the sun go down.

Justin sipped his beer. He'd only been there for less than eight hours yet he felt as relaxed as if he'd been vacationing all week. "That was incredible." He kissed the back of her head. "I think you're incredible, thanks for bringing me here to see that, I'll never forget it."

Paige smiled looking out at the water still in disbelief that he was here with her at all. She squeezed his arms that held her. "Justin. . ."

Justin was pretty sure he knew what Paige was feeling, he felt it every time he kissed her or held her and it floored him. He knew how he felt about her, he'd just about told her, but truly saying the words still seemed so crazy. Feeling it and saying it were somehow so different. At this stage of their relationship saying I love you seemed preposterous just like her grandmother had felt, but damn if he didn't feel it, and he could feel that Paige did too. He hugged her to him. "It's crazy, isn't it?"

Paige laughed in relief, knowing what he meant and feeling so connected to him. "Yes!" she answered emphatically, touching his legs on either side of her own. "I feel ridiculous."

He laughed too. "Well then we can feel ridiculous together."

She turned her head to look up at him, "Yeah?" She's was bursting inside.

"Hell yeah!" Justin laughed. "Look where I am in the middle of the work week, this isn't normal," he laughed and kissed her. He hadn't taken any time off in the five years he'd owned the shop, but he'd do anything or go anywhere now just to be with Paige.

"Well I know, and I wanted to ask you about something along the same lines." God, she was nervous.

"Anything." He squeezed her.

"I was wondering if you would consider coming back in two weeks to be my date for Ali and Rafe's wedding. The wedding is actually on a Saturday, but there'll be parties the night before, I promise it'll be fun."

Justin was happy, real happy she'd asked and it meant a lot. "I'd really like that Paige."

"You would?" She breathed a sigh of relief. "You can get the weekend off?"

"Yeah, of course I would, and of course I can, I'm the boss, remember?" He laughed.

"We'll put you up of course and I'll take care of your plane ticket. I know this trip was unexpected so I'd like to pay when you come for the wedding."

"Completely unnecessary, Paige, it would be my pleasure. This trip may have been unexpected but I would have flown to Egypt if your grandmother had told me you were there." Paige meant the world to him and if he'd had to traipse it to find her he would have.

Wow. Paige turned in his arms to look at him and she'd never felt happier. "It means more than you'll ever know that you came here after me." She picked up her empty drink cup and stood. "C'mon." She held her hand out, smiling.

Justin took her hand and let her pull him up. "Where we going?" He downed the rest of his beer and took her empty cup. "Someplace where you can get naked again I hope." He grinned wickedly and threw their trash in a nearby bin.

"It's scary how in tune we are." Paige grinned back. "But you have to catch me first!" She took off down the beach with him right at her heels, when they were close to the beach path he scooped her up from behind and she screamed.

"You do not want to throw me in the water," she warned, laughing.

"I kind of do." He grinned and kissed her.

She kissed him back and pressed herself to him as he gently put her back down. "Don't you wish we could make love right here on the beach under the stars?"

Just the mere mention of the word love from her lips had his heart beat quickening like a teenagers; man, he had it bad. He looked her in the eyes. "Yeah, I do wish that, but I can make love to you anywhere and be happy."

She smiled at his words and looked into his eyes. "I can see everything in these eyes of yours, it's kind of intense."

"Then you must know what I want to do with you right now." he said gruffly.

Paige grinned and took his hand. Justin led them back up the beach path and across the street to Nan's house. They went back into the cool air inside and he opened the glass sliders to the pool and Sam scampered out.

"Have you got any music?" Justin asked. He watched the pup do his thing, thankful he hadn't had an accident in Paige's grandmother's house and thankful that her yard was fenced in.

"I have my iPod." Paige watched Justin take off his T-shirt and throw it on a nearby chair. Damn, he had a great body; he had his back to her and was looking out over the deck and to the bay beyond.

"Get it," he commanded, turning to her with a crooked smile when he saw her watching him.

Paige went to the counter with a grin and rifled through her pocket book. She found the iPod and put it in the dock at the sound system. "Any requests?" She realized she didn't even know what kind of music he liked.

"Surprise me."

"I'm afraid to," Paige laughed, "I was just thinking how we don't even know what each other's taste in music is, you might think I'm a total weirdo if the wrong song comes on."

Justin chuckled. "This is true."

"Hey!" she laughed and scrolled to her favorite. She turned on the outside speakers.

He turned to her and smiled as the music came on. He liked her music just fine. He motioned for her to come outside.

Paige went to him and stood facing him beside the pool. The stars hung low and bright in the sky and the full moon reflected on the bay illuminating the water like a spot light, a boat went by and sent the glowing water rippling against the wooden dock. Justin reached for Paige and her thoughts briefly went to Jenna and Mike, wondering if they'd be arriving soon, but she didn't want to ruin the moment by mentioning it. She'd just have to keep an ear out for tires pulling onto the shelled driveway. She let Justin undress her slowly and watched her clothes fall to her feet. Paige shivered in the warm night air and under his heated gaze; her head fell back as his lips touched the sensitive skin at the side of her neck, leaving a trail of warm tender kisses across her collarbone and back up to her lips. They kissed for a good long time under the summer night sky just holding each other and swaying against one another while the music played in the back ground.

"I know we won't be alone for long, I just wanted you naked under the stars, I wanted to look at you in the moonlight; you're so damn beautiful Paige." He kissed her again while his hands explored her. "I want to remember you just like this."

"Are you going somewhere?" she asked softly, teasing him.

"Not without you," Justin said seriously. "I just mean when I'm at work, or at home, I'll remember this day and this night and think of how lucky I am."

Paige melted in his arms. How did *she* get so lucky? She had goose bumps all over as they kissed and his hands gently explored her body, the words *I think I love you* were begging to escape but she kept quiet. Instead she tried to convey how she felt through her kiss and her touch on his own bare skin. "Want to go back inside?" she asked softly, then laughed as Sam gave a short bark and trotted by them on gangly legs into the house probably after a gecko. They hadn't put any lights on inside so Paige couldn't see where he'd run off to.

"Uh huh." Justin smiled and put his hand in hers following Paige inside but he came up short behind her when she stopped suddenly. She let out a loud scream just as the whole inside of the house lit up.

Paige put one hand over her crotch and her other arm over her bare breasts. "What are you doing here?" She cried, staring horrified at Nicki, Matt, Ali, and Rafe all carrying luggage, pizza boxes, and grocery bags. They were standing in the small foyer area off the kitchen with Sam running around their feet excitedly looking just as shocked as Paige. Paige quickly dove behind Justin who she thanked God was still halfway dressed.

"It's nice to see you too, Paigy!" Nicki laughed out loud, putting her bags down and averting her eyes from her cousin's naked body. She bent to pat the puppy instead as she stifled more laughter. Holy shit, Paige's man was so hot and covered in tattoos!

"God, I love this place!" Matt grinned making his way inside. "Hi Paigy!" He laughed, shooting wide eyes and raised brows to Nicki then putting the Island Pizza boxes down on the counter. He came into the living room and plopped down on the big couch, but not before Nicki smacked him on the ass and reprimanded him.

"Hi Paige!" Ali grinned, biting back her own laughter and turning to Rafe to reach up and playfully cover his eyes.

"I'm with Matt," Rafe joked, dropping his bags and bending to pat the puppy as well. "I always loved this place!"

"*Oh my God*, you guys!" Paige was mortified, "What are you doing here?" She hugged Justin's stomach from behind and pressed herself against his back.

"I'm Justin, by the way," Justin grinned and gave a wave. He was doing his best to cover Paige but couldn't help but see the humor in the situation.

"I'm sorry," Paige murmured against him.

They all greeted him with a little chuckle.

"Well, it's not every day my little sister, and your cousin gets kidnapped by a drug lord on his yacht and then gets saved, once again I might add, by a handsome FBI agent who we are all pretty sure has fallen in love with her." Nicki laughed along with her cohorts.

"Up until now those things only happened to me," Ali said, placing the liquor store bag beside the pizza and taking a counter stool. She grinned at Rafe, who just shook his head and winked at her.

"What are you *talking* about?" Paige nearly shrieked poking her head around Justin. "I thought Jenna was with Mike on her way back here! *Kidnapped?*" Paige was shocked, but still completely conscious of her nudity. Jenna was obviously now all right since they were all here laughing and making jokes but she couldn't believe what she was hearing.

"Hey man, would you mind tossing a towel from the bathroom right there?" Justin asked Rafe who stood behind the large sectional couch nearest the guest bath.

Rafe almost felt foolish for not having thought of it. "Sure." He grabbed one off the towel bar and threw it over Matt's head to Justin.

"Thanks," Justin smiled. He handed it back to Paige who thanked him and quickly wrapped it around herself then ran down the hall.

"I'll be right back!" she called out, miffed.

Justin looked back over Rafe's shoulder and now that the lights were on he couldn't help notice the large framed photograph hanging on the wall in the hallway. He hadn't noticed it before. Then he remembered he hadn't actually seen the rest of the house yet either. He looked away when Nicki noticed he was staring.

"Paige took that," she told him with a smile. "Right after Charlie." She poked her head out from the kitchen. "The Blue Wave it's called. Made the local paper too. It's so cool, isn't it?"

"What is it called?" Justin half laughed thinking he'd heard her wrong and he felt an electric charge go up his spine.

"The Blue Wave. She had to name it for the paper and that's what she called it." Nicki smiled then furrowed her brows. "You should see your face right now. You look like you've seen a ghost. What's wrong?"

Matt studied Justin and Ali did too, Rafe looked at Nicki and shrugged.

Justin laughed, incredulous. What the fuck? "That's the name of my shop."

"What shop?" Nicki asked, looking confused.

"I own a tattoo shop in Newport, it's called The Blue Wave and the sign I made that hangs outside looks pretty much exactly like that photo." He stepped more into the room, getting a little closer to it. Maybe he was in the fucking Twilight Zone. He wondered why Paige hadn't mentioned it or pointed it out.

Nicki looked at Ali wide-eyed and Ali looked at Matt who rolled his eyes and tilted his head back on the couch to see Rafe.

"You know where this is headed, right?" Matt asked.

"Of course." Rafe laughed at Ali and Nicki's awestruck faces.

Justin cleared his throat, feeling a little uncomfortable and called off Sam who was sniffing at Matt's feet.

"He's all right, man, he's awesome, how old?" Matt scratched the dog behind the ears and Sam fell to the floor for a belly rub. Matt laughed obliging him.

"He's about three and a half months."

"I'm Matt by the way," Matt stood up to shake Justin's hand taking in all the ink. The dude had two sleeves down to his hands, ink on his neck, one on his chest and one across his lower stomach, which now made sense knowing what he did for a living. He was pretty friggin' ripped too, Matt couldn't help notice.

"I'm Nicki, Paige's cousin." Nicki walked over to shake Justin's hand as well then gave Ali the wide eyes again in silent communication as she turned back to the kitchen. Paige's man was HOT! And how about this whole Blue Wave thing?

"I've heard a lot about you, all of you." Justin smiled politely, making eye contact with everybody and wishing he could reach his T-shirt, he felt a little like he was on display.

"Rafe McDonough." Rafe came around to shake Justin's hand. "Nice to meet you, this is Ali." Rafe gestured to Ali who got off the stool to shake Justin's hand, too.

"Hi Justin, we didn't realize Paige had company, we're sorry we barged in like we did." Ali sat back down and caught Nicki's eye. Holy crap!

"No apology necessary, I just arrived today, I was a surprise too."

"I personally find it's the best way to arrive." Matt grinned at Nicki and got a chuckle out of Rafe.

"Ignore him, that's a story for another time," Nicki told Justin. "We all came down just to see for ourselves that Jenna was okay, and it was a good reason to start the weekend early too," she laughed.

"And for us to go over some last-minute wedding arrangements." Ali grinned at Rafe.

"So what, are you two going to jump out of an airplane or parasail into the ceremony?" Matt turned to Rafe, grinning and seeing him shake his head.

"Shut up." Ali threw her brother a look. "We're gonna have a cool surprise for everyone, that's all."

"Who needs a drink?" Paige came back into the room in shorts and a tank and shrugged, smiling apologetically at Justin, who just grinned at her. She tossed him a new T-shirt that had been in his bag and he gave her a wide grin in appreciation.

"Thanks," he said gratefully.

Paige smiled. "You're welcome." She walked into the kitchen blushing as both Ali and Nicki mouthed the word "wow" to her conspicuously.

"Everyone could use a drink I would say," Nicki said and came over to hug

Paige. "You look great, by the way."

Paige gave her cousin a sarcastic grin.

Nicki laughed. "I don't mean naked," she laughed again, "I mean you looked great naked too, sexy tattoo by the way," she corrected herself and cracked up as Paige's cheeks flamed and her jaw fell. "I meant you just look great in general, jeez, a little help here, guys." Nicki turned to Ali, Rafe, and Matt.

The guys nodded their heads emphatically in agreement and shrugged a "sorry, man" look to Justin, who laughed looking at Paige.

"She does look great and I'd have to agree about the tattoo," Matt said grinning from ear to ear.

"Again I'm with Matt." Rafe grinned and Ali laughed pretending she was going to hit him.

Justin continued to laugh knowing they were all playfully teasing Paige and realizing how close they all were, he felt a little out of place.

"You do look great, Paige, you look really happy." Ali looked at Justin and then smiled. "Those are some really cool tattoos." She saw Rafe grin and shake his head at her. "What?" she mouthed.

"Thanks," Justin answered, chuckling at her and Rafe. Both couples seemed really into each other and it was cool to see. He took a seat on the couch across from Matt and Sam immediately came over to sit by his feet.

"Wow, look at that, he knows who his master is huh?" Matt admired the scene.

Justin laughed and petted Sam. "He knows who feeds him."

"Nick, we gotta get a dog," Matt said, watching Sam curl at Justin's feet.

"Yeah?" Nicki looked at him and smiled. A dog would be fun at home and fun to bring to the Cape house in the summer, she thought.

Matt nodded and smiled at her. "C'mon let's go claim a room."

"Ugh! C'mon you guys!" Ali yelled at them. "We just got here!"

Paige looked at Justin from the kitchen, grinning. He returned her smile and remembered she had told him Ali and Matt were brother and sister.

Rafe took Ali's hand and brought her over to sit with him on the couch. "You know he's just trying to rile you, when are you ever going to learn."

"Never," Ali laughed. "So Paige, when did you get here?"

"Only yesterday," Paige said, coming out of the kitchen with two bottles of Corona with limes. She handed them to Justin and Rafe, who thanked her. "Do you want me to make frozens or vodka and lemonade?" she asked Ali.

"Either would be great, surprise me!"

Paige smiled and went back to the kitchen. "We can take the pizza out back if you all want, it's beautiful out now, but you missed quite a storm this afternoon."

"Fuck no we didn't," Matt swore coming back down the hall from the bedroom.

They had just commandeered Jenna's room and Nicki followed Matt from the hall transferring Jenna's things across the house, laughing when Paige took notice and shook her head at her. "We flew through it, it sucked!" Nicki added.

"Ooohh," Paige winced at them. "That must have been scary."

"Yeah!" Matt complained. "I definitely need that beer." He took the Corona Paige had left on the counter for him and the pizza boxes and carried them out back, stopping to find some U2 on the iPod. Paige had the Joshua Tree and he selected it and turned up the volume on his way out. "C'mon out, Justin, come and eat."

Justin followed Matt out and everyone else joined them at the patio table pulling up chairs and getting comfortable. Paige brought drinks to the girls and came to sit on Justin's lap. He felt better having her so near and he instantly felt like part of their circle. They were all pretty cool and really funny. The guys were interested in what he did and they talked a lot about tattoos and he was asked to stand up and show all of his again. He laughed when the girls whistled as he took off his T-shirt and felt himself blush when Paige looked at him seductively in front of them all.

"We have to get some ink, dude, we're like two blank canvases crying out," Matt said to Rafe and winking at Ali and Nicki who rolled their eyes at him.

"I know," Rafe laughed, "I always liked Cap's, he's got some."

"Mike's got some?" all three women asked together like it was a huge deal.

"Jesus," Matt said looking at them and smirking at Rafe. *See?* his eyes said.

Rafe laughed and turned to the women. "Yeah, why?"

The girls laughed knowingly with each other and Paige smirked at Justin. "I told you," she whispered, "sooo sexy."

Justin shook his head embarrassed in front of the guys. He squeezed Paige's ass in a playful reprimand.

"That's it, we're getting some." Matt grinned at Nicki then turned to Justin. "Did you do Paige's?"

Justin grinned and laughed and Paige groaned, burying her head against his chest. "Yeah, that's how I met her."

"Don't be embarrassed," Matt teased, "I couldn't help but notice; it is sexy. He felt Nicki slug him in the arm. "What? You'd look great with some ink; I know just where I'd want it, too."

"Anytime you guys are in Newport come into the shop I'll tattoo all of you," Justin offered.

Nicki looked at Ali and they both looked at Paige and grinned. "Okay," they both said in unison.

"Oh God," Paige groaned, taking a sip of her drink. She knew the girls thought Justin was hot and she shook her head, laughing at them.

"Thanks for the offer," Rafe said, pulling Ali's hair playfully. "We'll definitely come in to see you if we decide to get some."

"I'm definitely getting some." Matt flexed his bicep, "Nick, what do you think?"

Nicki laughed and rolled her eyes playfully in answer then got up to get the guys more beer. "What time are we expecting Mike and Jenna?" she asked Rafe.

Rafe looked at his watch. "They should be pulling into the marina anytime."

"I just can't believe what has happened in the past few days. Tell me everything you know." Paige looked to Rafe.

Rafe filled Paige and Justin in and they all speculated about Scintillo and his son and Miguel Soto and what would happen to them.

"Why is Mike bringing Scintillo's son here and not back to Miami?" Paige asked and saw Rafe exchange a look with Matt and Ali.

"What?" Paige asked.

"Someone on this end is waiting for him and the FBI want to know who and why."

"Oh my God, so Jenna could still be in danger?" Paige pictured a big shootout on the dock.

"No, don't worry, Mike won't let anything happen to her," Rafe assured her.

"This is crazy, we should be there when she arrives." Paige looked at them all.

"I'm going to head up there soon," Rafe told her. "And between Mike and I will bring her back here safe."

Paige relented with a sigh and took comfort in Justin's encouraging embrace.

CHAPTER THIRTY-NINE

When Mike entered the main cabin he walked right over to the bodyguard who sat next to Junior on one of the couches. "Stand up," Mike ordered. He stood and Mike reached for the bodyguard's injured hand, taking it and squeezing it in a vise-like handshake. He watched the guy wince and Mike grinned maliciously when the large man grunted in pain. "How you doin'? I'm Special Agent Mike Caplan with the FBI."

"Fuck, man!"

"What's that?" Mike squeezed harder and the bodyguard put his uninjured hand over Mike's to try and stop him. "See that, Reynolds? Assaulting an officer of the law." Mike let go of the bodyguard's hand and brought his elbow up forcefully smashing it into the guy's face with a resounding crunch and breaking his nose. The bodyguard cried out in pain again and Mike gave him a fast punch to the gut that had the man collapsing back on the couch and wheezing. Blood flowed freely through the guy's hands as he held them over his face, doubled over.

"Now you two assholes are twins, it's a nice look." Mike sat on the opposite couch and laughed without a hint of humor as he looked at Junior's bruised face. "I love that girl, you know, and if I weren't with the FBI, I'd be spilling so much of your blood all over this boat that the sharks would be jumping on board to get to you, but as it stands, I enjoy looking at your ugly mug and knowing she did that to you. I won't mess with her good work though, she fucking kicked your ass," Mike said proudly and went on.

"You're nothing but a fucking worm, Scintillo, and I'm going to take pleasure knowing you're in prison getting man handled just like you let the men in your clubs do to those girls, only you'll be stone-cold sober when you have to take a hard fat one down the back of your throat and one up your ass. That goes for you, too, dick wad." Mike looked over at the bodyguard and shook his head. He was still doubled over.

Agent Reynolds stood by stunned, the blatant words Mike had just spoken shocking him. Cap *loved* that girl? Holy shit!

Mike and Reynolds took turns questioning Junior and the bodyguard while Simmons and the DEA agents from the response boat searched the yacht. The sniper was still up on the fly bridge with the Captain keeping them on course for Captiva and now that the storm had long since passed, the Gulf was calm in the night and the skies were clear and star filled.

Junior had confessed everything, crying like the spoiled son of a bastard he was. He was indeed dealing liquid ecstasy, GBH, and cocaine at his clubs, drugging the girls at the gentleman's club specifically so that they would willingly have sex with Jay's high-paying customers. He'd had Georgie drug Jenna thinking if she were high enough he could hand her over to Soto in exchange for the some of the money he owed him. He was in debt to Soto for two hundred large and Soto said he would have him killed if he didn't pay. Miguel Soto had been supplying Jay for the last six months and yes, Jay admitted, Soto had been his father's coke supplier as well.

"So tell me, Junior, why did Soto drug you then leave the yacht?" Mike asked continuing with the questions.

Jay shook his head, tears coming down his face. "He said he was going to drug me so I couldn't go anywhere and when I woke up," he sobbed. "he said I would meet my death."

"I guess it's lucky you woke up to find me then, huh?" Mike grinned malevolently.

Jay hung his head.

"Why?" Mike prodded.

I don't know," Jay whined. "We were arguing about the money. He was pissed I didn't have it and he was pissed about Jenna."

"What about Jenna?" Mike asked.

"He was pissed that Rocko messed up her face, he injected him with something because of it; I thought he killed him."

Mike looked over at the bodyguard who still held onto his face, the blood still flowing. "Rocko, huh? Seems Soto and I have something in common then."

"The little whore broke my fingers." Rocko spoke through the blood in the back of his throat.

Reynolds dove between them before Mike could get to Rocko then quickly secured Rocko's wrists with a plastic restraint and pulled him to his feet. "Let's go," Reynolds said gruffly and somehow his feet got in the way of Rocko's as the bodyguard tried to walk. He tripped over Reynolds' shoes and went down like a sack of potatoes instinctively putting his restrained hands out to break the fall and he cried out as his broken fingers took the weight.

"Now why can't you watch where you're going?" Reynolds asked, winking at Mike and leading Rocko up the stairs to hang with the Coast Guard sharp shooter for a while.

Mike grinned; he loved that old bastard Reynolds. He was still standing from when he'd been about to pummel Rocco and he now stood looming over Jay with his gun prominently displayed in his hand.

"So who's waiting for us in Captiva, Junior?"

Jay took note of the gun in Agent Caplan's hands. "My sister's husband Manuel. He's Soto's nephew."

Mike took this in with dead eyes, not letting on that this was news to him, but it made sense.

"I heard Soto call him and order him to kill me once we've reached Captiva," Jay continued. "Then Soto ordered him to take the yacht and Jenna back to Mexico right away." Jay looked at Mike with beseeching eyes. "You're not going to let that happen, right?"

Mike laughed. "Of course not!" He slapped Jay on the shoulder amiably. "Jenna stays with me." Mike glanced at Reynolds, who was coming back down the stairs and Mike's intuition kicked in. There was definitely something Junior was leaving out.

Reynold's descended the stairs while talking on the sattelite phone. He finished speaking to Daniels and held the phone out to Mike, who turned and glared at Scintillo's son.

"Hold your thoughts, Junior." Mike smirked and took the phone from Reynolds.

"Hey Cap," Daniels started right in. "I just got a call from Miami/Dade PD. Marine patrol stopped Tommy for speeding in Biscayne Bay. They boarded and found two kilos of coke."

"No way. Not his." Mike said unequivocally. Shit! What the fuck? He hoped Tommy wasn't locked up in Miami-Dade right now. "Where is he?"

"Relax, he's probably hosing down his boat right now; he's been cleared. He gave them your name and explained the situation. I got the call and straightened it out. The coke was in the life vest Jenna was wearing from the yacht."

Mike nodded with realization as light dawned. Looking to Reynolds, he pointed through the glass doors. He remembered putting the vest on Jenna thinking it odd that it felt heavy. He'd figured it had just been wet from the storm.

Reynolds followed his gaze and shrugged.

"Open the bench seats, grab all the life vests and bring 'em here," Mike told him and watched Junior visibly pale.

Reynolds went on deck and lifted the seat cushions; one side held five, and the other six. It took him two trips, due to their weight and bulk. He got Simmons on comm and told him to get to the main cabin along with the DEA agents.

"Hold on," Mike told Daniels, and watched as Reynolds took out his pocket knife and sliced a life vest open at the seam. "Jee-zus I'm glad this isn't the *Titanic*," he said, thinking how the life vest would have actually been a hindrance if Jenna had fallen in the water. He watched Reynolds open each one up. "They're all jacked," Mike told Daniels.

"Nice, now you see *this* is the way I wanted it to go down." Daniels said and Mike could just picture the satisfied grin on the SAC's face.

Mike relayed the new information about Jay's brother-in-law and his relation to Soto and they discussed a game plan. Daniels said he'd have everyone in place when they arrived at the marina. Mike hung up and turned on Junior with a growl.

"This shit the reason you're in debt to Soto?" Mike slapped a bag of cocaine on the coffee table. "This the shit you were willing to trade my girl for?"

Reynolds turned to look at Mike again in surprise. Cap was really throwing him for a loop with this girl stuff; he'd never expected it—Cap the consummate ladies' man, the workaholic, in love? Wait until the guys found out.

Mike watched Junior bow his head in shame and felt utter disgust for him. He started to cry again as Simmons and DEA Special Agents Burke and Marshall entered the cabin.

Ignoring Junior, they organized the bags of coke on the dining table and heaped the now flattened life vests in a pile. Reynolds had left and came back down with two more life vests from the fly bridge and added the stash to the table.

"I'm going to check on Jenna," Mike told them. He rifled through the refrigerator in the kitchen first and took out something for her to drink and turned as Reynolds approached him.

"Hey Cap, I just wanted to say. . ." Reynolds looked down suddenly embarrassed, "well, she seems like a nice girl."

Mike grinned and slapped him on the shoulder. "Thanks, Reynolds." He chuckled to himself as he went below deck. When he opened the door he found the room in darkness and Jenna sleeping under the covers. He tried to ignore the twist in his gut as he put the drink down and slid under the sheets beside her. She curled right up against him and his arm went right around her and he stroked her hair. "We're almost there, baby." Mike leaned against the padded headboard and let his body relax for ten minutes. He knew he'd have to be up again as soon as they got closer, but if he could have ten minutes alone with Jenna he'd take it.

"Did you kill anyone?" she whispered against him.

He laughed softly at her deadpan tone. "No, there won't be any conjugal visits for you."

"Good," she whispered.

"I thought you were asleep."

"Just resting my eyes. You know what I was thinking?"

"Tell me." Mike put his hand under the sweatshirt she'd put back on and rubbed her back. He was content around her and it was such a new feeling, one he was beginning to rely on.

"That when all this is over, you're going to take me somewhere nice and then rock my world."

He laughed huskily taking a deep breath. "I said that, didn't I?"

"Yes, and you can't take it back."

"I wouldn't think of it." He kissed her forehead. There was so much he wanted to do with her.

"Even though I'm a little banged up?"

"Especially because you're a little banged up."

"Ah, a sympathy date?"

He could hear the smile in her question. "No sympathy here. You forget I've seen the other guys." Mike had never been so proud of someone; she had defended herself pretty damn well for a little thing.

Jenna laughed. "That's right you have, so you're going out of fear and intimidation then."

Mike was laughing now too, loving that she could have a sense of humor after all she'd been through. "That's right, GI Jane; I don't want to end up on the wrong side of those guns. He squeezed the sinewy muscle of her arm causing her to giggle.

"Want to hear something funny?" she asked him.

"I thought I just did."

Jenna slapped his stomach playfully. "I called you GI Joe when I told Nicki about meeting you."

Mike pressed his lips together smiling and didn't say a word.

Jenna felt the bouncing in his chest. "Are you laughing?" She sat up to look at him in the darkness.

"No, of course not, GI Joe is cool, I guess. I know Barbie thinks so."

Jenna shot up and gasped. "Oh my God! You heard me talking to Nicki?"

Mike was cracking up and loving how her cheeks had reddened. He pulled her back against him. "You really think I look like him?" He conjured up his best GI Joe look.

"Don't make fun of me!" Jenna laughed too. "I meant it as a compliment, you remind me of a soldier and you're so intense with those brilliant blue eyes of yours." She touched the side of his head. "And your military cut." She ran a hand through his short hair. "This unbelievably hard, sculpted body," she said and smoothed a hand over his chest, feeling him grab her wrist and hold it against him. Her fingers naturally splayed over his skin. "The way you carry yourself," she went on looking at him, "you're so strong and confident. You're impressive, Mike, and even better than what I see on the outside is the incredible person I've realized you are on the inside. I've never met someone as kind and caring as you. I owe you for everything you've done for me." She smiled at him. "You're funny too and I like that I can laugh with you, even though there hasn't been all that much to laugh about." She gave another slight smile. "Anyway, I just thought it kind of a coincidence that you would call me GI Jane when I called you GI Joe." She shrugged. "Kind of funny, you know, I loved my GI Joe doll, he was my favorite," she said seriously, lowering her voice. She looked at him feeling her heart pound as he placed her hand over his heart.

Mike stared at her in the darkness. Oh man, everything she just said to him. Was she saying what he thought she was saying? "Jenna..." The sat phone interrupted them again and he swore out loud. Jenna laid her head back down on his chest, her hand still over his heart, and Mike held it there hoping she couldn't feel it breaking. When he hung up he lifted her chin.

"We're pulling in. This is going to be over real quick, okay, so just stay here until I come for you. Don't leave this room," Mike ordered with narrowed eyes.

Jenna nodded and smiled. "You sure you don't need me up there?"

Mike's facial expression relaxed and he couldn't help but laugh. "No, bruiser, we're good, just stay put." He laughed again getting out of bed and shook his head. She was something else. "I know I want to continue this conversation though." He looked at her seriously. What he would tell her he had no idea but things had definitely changed between them.

"Okay, but not until I've showered and am wearing something pretty."

"Deal." He kissed her and left the room.

CHAPTER FORTY

"That was Daniels, they're coming in, I'm heading up there." Rafe got up from the table slipping his cell back in his pocket and kissed Ali goodbye.

She got up to walk him to the back gate. "Be careful."

"Always, babe, I'll see you in a few." He waved to everyone then left the backyard and got in the rent a car to drive the short distance to Tween Waters. He pulled into the parking lot in front of the resort and checked his gun. He put on his Kevlar vest, a nylon jacket over it and a baseball hat. He left the car to walk around back to the marina and saw Agents Murphy and Bealls right away. Murph stood at the helm of a Pursuit tucked into a slip on the right side of the marina and Bealls stood on a second floor balcony over-looking the bay, binoculars in hand.

Rafe made his way to the end of the dock and gave a passing glance to Murph. He pulled up a green plastic chair on the edge of the dock and took a seat by the fuel pump under the overhead lamp. The running lights on the yacht could be seen a hundred yards out and to anyone approaching on land or on water Rafe appeared to be working the dock. Garrison who Rafe had worked with a few times in Miami served as the Dockmaster while the real dude Rafe knew had been given a couple of hours off with the assurance that the FBI would take good care of things in his absence. The marina was relatively quiet, Garrison, explaining the yacht's imminent arrival, had directed the few boat owners docked on the outside slips, to the opposite side of the marina, temporarily. Rafe could only see a few people across the way relaxing on their boats with an undercover agent nearby to keep them out of harm's way. Rafe's phone vibrated in his pocket. He took it out and put it to his ear.

"McD, glad to have you back, subject is parked in a silver town car right underneath Bealls. Assume he's armed, he's here to eliminate Junior in case you haven't heard, so we'll take him as he boards."

"Roger that, good to be back, Murph." Rafe hung up and watched as the yacht neared. Daniels had briefed him on Manuel Santiago when Rafe called to ask to be part of the action. His adrenaline was pumping and he was happy to be back with his old team. The yacht got closer and he waved to the fly bridge indicating the empty slips in front of him for the yacht to dock.

* * * * *

Manuel Santiago had kissed his pregnant wife Maria goodbye and told her he'd be back soon. He'd left her in the capable hands of his younger brother and driven the short ride to the marina and parked. He'd been waiting for his uncle's yacht to arrive, and was still waiting. He knew his uncle would not be aboard, his uncle would be in Mexico by now. When his uncle had called from the yacht this afternoon he had told Manuel of the change of plans. Jay Jr. did not have the money he owed them so Manuel would have to take care of things on his end. It would be up to Manuel to take care of Jay and his bodyguard, then to deliver the girl, the drugs, and the yacht back to Mexico to his uncle and cousin. The coke his brother-in-law was supposed to buy would now be cut and bagged and distributed throughout Soto's territories in Mexico, Manuel's brother Mateo would take a share as well for his own territories along the East coast. They wouldn't lose a dime.

Manuel sat in the car in a solemn mood. He didn't want to kill Jay. Manuel was married to Jay's sister, and Manuel was about to be a father. Jay was to be his child's uncle and godfather, but Jay had fucked up and Miguel Soto didn't allow anyone to fuck up, not even Manuel or Mateo, whom he'd taken in after their parents were killed fifteen years ago. He'd raised them alongside his own children and they had been raised no differently than Soto's own son. And now because of this obligation, Manuel wouldn't get to see his child's birthday, nor would he see his wife for a good long while but he would do what his uncle asked because that was his duty.

* * * * *

Mike opened the glass doors from the main deck. He'd been on the fly bridge checking their approach. He faced Jay as he entered the main cabin.

"We're going to take him as soon as he steps on board. He won't get near you so quit crying, you'll live, but where you're going you'll wish to God we let him kill you." Mike walked away from Junior and went to take up positions with Simmons, and Reynolds. They were in the kitchen in the main cabin while the two DEA agents were up on the fly bridge with the sniper guarding the captain and Rocko. Their backup was in place at the marina and they just waited for the yacht to come to a stop.

* * * * *

Manuel got out of the car and grabbed his suitcase. His gun was in his waistband and he felt the butt of it with his hand through his shirt. He was already feeling remorse but he knew what had to be done. It was business and it had been part of the business for as long as Manuel could remember, and it was the part he hated most. He took a deep breath and with a heavy heart started toward the docks. He walked up the short set of stairs and followed the wooden planks down to his right where the yacht had just pulled up. There was a man working the pumps and Manuel watched him get up from his chair to tie off the stern and then the bow of his uncle's Ferreti.

Manuel looked up at the fly bridge and waved to Carlos, his uncle's long-time captain. Manuel would kill Jay and his bodyguard in the main cabin once they were back underway and dump their bodies in the Gulf. Carlos would not have to know.

Rafe saw Santiago approach. "How's it going?" He smiled. "This your ride?" Rafe took in the suitcase.

"Yes, fuel her up please; we'll be leaving right away."

"Sure thing." Rafe turned to the pump and busied himself and watched as Murph drifted by in the Pursuit, nearing position behind the yacht while Garrison and Bealls on foot closed in under the thatched roof of the dock.

Manuel hopped onto the yacht's transom and climbed the stairs to the main deck. He placed his suitcase on a bench seat and immediately sensed something was not right. He automatically withdrew his gun. Carlos should have been right down to greet him already.

"Freeze, FBI!" Rafe yelled along with Murph when they saw Manuel draw his gun; they pointed their own at him. Rafe saw Mike, Simmons, Reynolds, and two DEA agents approach from inside the cabin, all with guns drawn as well.

There was a Coast Guard sniper on the winding stairs coming from the fly bridge and he held a rifle on Manuel Santiago. "Put the gun down!" he commanded.

Manuel looked all around him and saw the guns aimed at him. He looked inside the cabin at Jay and felt a great sense of relief that he did not have to kill his wife's brother, but Manuel would not go to jail, he could not live knowing he had failed his uncle and his unborn child, the shame would be far worse than dying. He put his gun under his chin and fired; his last thought was of Maria.

"Ugh! Christ Almighty," Simmons swore.

"Jesus." Reynolds shook his head and looked away.

Mike watched as the sniper jumped from the stairs and approached Soto's nephew. He felt for a pulse out of protocol and looked up, making eye contact with Mike, then cut a taut hand across his own throat. Manuel Santiago was dead.

"Guess he had a soft spot for you after all, Scintillo." Mike turned to look at Junior, who sat glassy-eyed looking out at the deck, from shock or relief that it wasn't him lying there, Mike didn't know and he didn't much care. "Look at the bright side; you'll get to see Daddy again." Mike walked out on the deck, being careful to avoid the blood that was pooling around Santiago's head, and he looked out at the dock below. He gave a wide grin when he saw Rafe standing there. "I knew you couldn't resist."

"And let you have all the fun, no way." Rafe gave him a grin of his own and hopped onto the transom. "Good to see you, man, now where the hell is Jenna?" he asked coming aboard and clasping Mike's outstretched hand; he gave him a shoulder to chest hug. "I promised a house full of people I'd bring her home safe."

Mike immediately bristled, feeling possessive. He didn't want to share Jenna with anyone right now, he wanted to take care of her himself. He didn't know how long he had left with her.

"Whoa," Rafe hit him in the arm. "You should see your face right now. You look like I just told you I was going to cut off your left nut, something you want to tell me?"

Mike looked at the crowd near them on the outside deck and walked back inside the cabin with Rafe following, they walked by Reynolds leading Junior out in cuffs.

Rafe gave Reynolds a slap on the back and they exchanged familiar smiles as Reynolds left to escort Junior off the yacht. DEA Agent Burke followed closely behind with Rocko the bodyguard. Reynolds called out, "Great to see you, McD! Looking forward to that wedding!" Then he disappeared down the dock where a car was waiting to take Junior and friend back to Miami.

"I can take Jenna back to the house as soon as I finish here," Mike told Rafe.

Rafe grinned. "What? You don't trust me all of a sudden?" He knew it! Mike had fallen for Jenna, they'd all predicted it. He looked around the swanky yacht and back at Mike. "Well?"

Mike shot him a look. "C'mon, you know how it is." Rafe was totally busting his balls.

Rafe chuckled. "Yeah, I sure do. So where is she? At least let me go back and let them know she's fine."

Mike nodded. "Yeah, of course, hang here a second, I'll be right back." Mike went below deck and into the stateroom Jenna sat waiting in. She was sitting cross-legged on the bed looking young and vulnerable and Mike's chest tightened yet again.

"Did I hear a shot?" Jenna asked wide-eyed and getting off the bed to go to him and thanking God he was all right.

"Jay's brother-in-law just offed himself on deck." Mike stood looking down at her and brushed the hair back off her face.

Jenna covered her mouth in shock. "Why?"

Mike explained briefly what had happened and Manuel Santiago's involvement.

"Wow, that guy we met at the party was the perv's nephew? I guess it all makes sense." She looked at him. "Does Jay's sister know? Oh God, was she out there when he did it?" Jenna thought of their unborn baby and felt sick.

"No, she isn't here, she'll know soon enough though. C'mon, Rafe is upstairs and wants to see that you're okay."

Jenna smiled. "So it's over?"

Mike smiled in return, feeling his chest squeeze tighter around his heart. "Yeah, it's over, you're home, well, the place you're calling home for a while anyway." He didn't want to think of her in Newport or Boston, or away from him. He didn't want to be reminded that time was no doubt running out for them.

Jenna looked at Mike; he sounded odd. "I guess you'll have some stuff to wrap up, huh?"

Mike nodded. "It could take a while, maybe you should head back to your grandmother's house with Rafe."

Jenna felt panicked. She didn't want to do that, she didn't want to leave him. "Won't I need to be questioned and give a statement and all of that?"

Mike heard the panic in her voice and misread it. She'd been through enough and probably couldn't wait to see her family. "I can arrange it so you can do it in the morning. You can see your family now and get some rest if you want." Mike put his hands in his pockets, feeling bad. He didn't want her to go. His fingers came in contact with the dampened piece of paper that she had written her note to him on this morning and he held it between his fingers, remembering how she'd signed it, Love, Jenna.

"I don't want to leave you." Jenna looked up and whispered, being honest.

Mike swept her into his arms, relief washing over him like one of the huge waves he'd been bouncing on only hours before. She'd just made his night. He knew he never wanted to leave her, but it would be inevitable.

"Good, then you don't have to. I want you here with me." He held her and kissed her forehead.

"Why didn't you just say so?" Jenna asked, a tear slipping down her face. She was so glad it was over but the thought of being apart from him again was awful.

"I know your family is worried, I know I can't keep you to myself," Mike told her, looking into her sad eyes. They were filled with tears and it made him want to cry too, for all he was going to lose.

Jenna searched his eyes. "But you want to?"

Mike touched a hand to her bruised cheek, his face and tone serious. "I don't want you out of my sight."

Jenna smiled and felt a million electrical charges dance under her skin. She stood on her bare toes and kissed him. "Then I'm not going anywhere."

Jenna followed Mike upstairs and saw Rafe as soon as she entered the cabin. He was just as crazy handsome as ever and he held his arms out to her, smiling. She went to him and hugged him tight.

"Hey Jenna, are you okay?" He looked at Mike over Jenna's head and held a mixed look of anger and sympathy. It must have killed Mike to see her banged up like she was. Rafe pulled back and took a good look at her.

"You should see the other guys," Jenna said proudly.

Mike grinned at Rafe, just as proud of her. "She aint kiddin'."

Rafe laughed, too. "Do you mean the two guys I saw being led out in cuffs? You did that?"

Jenna laughed narrowing her eyes at Mike. "Well, I don't know what they looked like leaving here, but I got some licks in."

Mike grinned. "Damn right you did."

Rafe nodded, impressed and happy for Mike. He could see the admiration and love Mike held for Jenna quite plainly. "What do you say I get you out of here and bring you to Nan's; Mike might be a while."

Mike bristled at the suggestion and glared at Rafe, who winked infuriatingly back at him. The bastard was really bustin' 'em tonight.

"No thanks, Rafe." Jenna went to stand in front of Mike.

He pulled her back against his chest, wrapping his arms around her protectively, and winked right back at Rafe with a grin.

"I want to stay, but tell everyone—wait a minute, who's everyone?" Jenna laughed.

"Ali, your sister, Matt, Paige and Justin and a cute little puppy named Sam." Rafe smiled.

"Oh my God! Justin is here with Paige?"

"Yeah, we all just met him and he's seems pretty cool, he brought the puppy so of course the girls like him automatically," Rafe laughed.

Jenna was so happy for Paige. "Tell them all I'll see them soon, okay, as soon as Mike's done, and Rafe?"

"Yeah?"

"Thank you for caring enough to come. I know you and Ali have a ton of other things you'd much rather be doing." Jenna smiled, feeling weepy again.

"I really appreciate everything you guys did to find me." She leaned into Mike and held his arms around her.

Rafe returned the smile." Hey, how many couples can say one of their bridesmaids was kidnapped two weeks before their wedding and was rescued by their best man? I wouldn't have missed this for the world." Rafe chuckled and grinned at them both.

Jenna laughed and Mike rolled his eyes with a smirk.

"Are you sure you don't want to go with him now?" Mike asked her, making sure.

Jenna turned in his arms. "I'm staying," she said firmly.

"Okay then!" Rafe grinned at the exchange. He was happy for Mike, real happy, and Jenna would never meet a better guy. "I'm off then; we're all staying at the house so we'll see you later, I guess."

"Thanks for everything, Rafe." Jenna walked over and hugged him again, kissing him on the cheek.

Rafe bent to hug her and said softly in her ear, "I hoped it would play out like this, you guys were made for each other."

Jenna smiled up at Rafe, touched by his sincerity and taking note that he was the second of Mike's friends to say so.

"Back off, Romeo," Mike told him gruffly and Jenna laughed.

Rafe laughed, too, remembering his own similar reaction when Mike had met Ali. "I'm going, I'm going, see you guys later."

They waved him off and Jenna smiled coming back to Mike. "Did that make you jealous?"

Mike smirked. "C'mere." Simmons and DEA agent Burke had entered the cabin but Mike didn't care. He took Jenna in his arms and kissed the hell out of her. "Yeah, it made me jealous, I want to be the only one to whisper in your ear," he whispered.

Heat washed over her. "Let's get all this stuff over with so we can get out of here."

"You got it," Mike agreed.

CHAPTER FORTY-ONE

Three hours later, Jenna and Mike were back at the Three Sunrises, having hitched a ride with Agent Garrison who was headed back to Miami, and now they stood in the driveway, hesitant to go in. It was nearing midnight and the island temperature was still warm, brilliant stars and a half moon lit the sky and a light breeze ruffled the palm fronds overhead. They could hear voices and laughter coming from out back and knew everyone was still awake.

"It's so beautiful here; I never thought I'd be so happy to be standing in this driveway again. Thanks for getting me here." Jenna looked up at him with sincerity.

"My pleasure." Mike chuckled at her doubting look. "Well, pleasure is a strong word, how about I wouldn't hesitate to do it all over again?"

"I don't know how to thank you, Mike." Jenna felt the sting of tears again and a lump in her throat. "God, I'm finding it real hard to want to walk inside right now." She needed him and just wanted to be alone with him.

"Why?" he asked her quietly, taking her small hands in his and giving them a gentle squeeze. "I thought you'd be excited to see your family and your friends."

"I don't want to share you, I guess," she answered honestly while looking up at him. She could see the caring look in his eyes and it melted her. "I want to run off somewhere and get to know everything about you before anyone else can. I feel this urgency, like we don't have a lot of time together for some reason." She looked up at him. "And I think I'm a little jealous that Nicki and Ali met you before I did." Jenna shrugged. "I can't explain it and I know it doesn't sound very mature. In fact I'm probably scaring you right now." She let out a little laugh. "I don't know why, I'm just a little insecure when it comes to you." Jenna looked down at the shelled drive and leaned against somebody's rental.

Mike stepped closer to her. "Hey." His heart was pounding with her admission. He didn't want her to feel insecure and it was strange that she felt their time together was limited. Was she picking up on something from him? When she looked up at him Mike felt his heart break looking down at her bruised face. If only he'd woken her up this morning and told her where he was going, this would never have happened. He felt terrible as he reached out and lightly touched her swollen cheek.

"No one has ever been as open and honest with me about their feelings like you have, Jenna. You've said some really incredible things to me tonight and none of it has scared me. You know what scared me?"

She shook her head.

"It scared me when I came back home this morning and found your note and I realized you were gone. When I found out where you were I was petrified that someone would hurt you." He paused running his hands over his face. "Jenna, I was so happy leaving you in my bed this morning and I couldn't wait to get back to you, I looked at you sleeping there and thought I could get used to this. I've never felt that way before about anyone, you got to me, kid, and it started right here at this house." He was saying things he shouldn't. He was making the situation worse but goddamn it he couldn't help it, he'd never felt this way before. He loved her.

Jenna's heart was pounding in her ears. Mike kissed her then and she held on to him like a life line. When he finally came away she took a deep breath.

"The things I really want you to know?" he continued softly. "I'm saving for when we are alone. Nobody inside is going to learn anything about me you don't already know, and I'm flattered and honored you feel the way you do." He smiled. "And I feel a little insecure too; it's not going to be easy for me either to watch you with people that already know you and love you, and I'll admit I feel a little territorial toward you after these last couple of days."

"Oh Mike, I'm glad that you feel that way." Jenna smiled teary-eyed.

He laughed. "You are?"

"Hell yes, you care and that means everything to me. You're my hero, Special Agent Mike Caplan." She smiled up at him. "I love that you protected me and kept me safe." And she wished he could do it always. "Now let's go inside, I feel much better and I'm dying to introduce you to my cousin Paige."

"I'm looking forward to it." Mike wished he had the guts to tell her just how much he cared. As for being her hero, how would she feel when he told her he was most probably leaving? He felt confident he'd be selected for HRT and it was just a matter of time before he heard something.

Jenna took Mike's hand and led him through the front door. She could see them all out back drinking and listening to music as they approached the kitchen. "How about a beer?"

"Sure, but I can get it." Mike smiled, seeing her light up at the sight of her family and friends. "You want something?"

"I'd love some plain old lemonade." She smiled.

"You got it, head on out and I'll bring it to you." And it would give him time to compose himself. Between yesterday and today he felt like he'd just completed an emotional triathlon.

She smiled at him and squeezed his arm. "Thanks."

Jenna stepped over the threshold of the sliders and everyone whooped and hollered. Matt stood up and swung her around and Nicki hugged them both, crying when she saw Jenna's bruised face. There was a little black puppy yelping and running all around them too and by the time Matt put her down Jenna was laughing so hard she was in tears and Paige waited for her with open arms.

"Hey cuz, you scared me half to death." Paige felt her stomach knot thinking of Jenna getting hit hard enough to bruise and swell.

"I'm sorry," she said, hugging Paige tight and turning to everybody. "I'm sorry I didn't listen to you guys, I was an idiot and I know how lucky I am to be here right now and how lucky I am to have all of you."

"Aww." Nicki hugged her again. "We love you, Jen, and are so glad you're back safe."

"Thanks, Nick, and thanks for not worrying Mom and Dad or Nan."

"You can tell them yourself when you're ready."

"Why did I know you were going to say that?" Jenna huffed jokingly. "My sister wouldn't be happy unless she had something on me," she joked with them all.

Ali laughed. "I got the same thing from this one, last summer." She kicked Matt's leg and he grabbed it, pretending he was going to tip her over in her chair. "Matt!" Ali yelled and Rafe grabbed her chair steadying her and laughing too.

Jenna smiled happily, loving that everyone was together. She turned to Justin and he gave her a welcoming grin and winked at her. Her eyes held an amused twinkle as she held out a fist, he reciprocated with a knuckle-bump and Jenna laughed. "Hey Justin, I'm quite happy to see you again and here on Captiva of all places." Jenna bent down to pat the puppy. "I gather this is Sam?"

"Hey Jenna." Justin chuckled at her greeting. "That's Sam, all right, and I'm happy to see you again too. It's quite a place."

"It sure is." Jenna smiled at him and then at Paige knowingly. They would have a long talk tomorrow for sure. She saw Paige's eyes shift to the sliders and by the look on her face Jenna knew just who was standing there. "Paige, Justin, this is Special Agent Mike Caplan." Jenna turned to introduce him proudly.

Paige took in the tall muscular man leaning against the door jamb. Jesus, Jenna wasn't kidding; the man looked like he'd grown up on the beach but just got back from his special ops mission in the desert. He was just missing the dog tags and the camo. Damn! Paige looked at Jenna and bit her bottom lip holding back the giggles. He was coming toward them. When he was next to

Jenna he handed her a glass of lemonade and Paige smiled at their obvious size difference, Jenna was a peanut next to him but somehow they looked so comfortable together, like they belonged together. Paige couldn't be happier for her cousin.

"Hi, how are you?" Mike held a hand out to Justin and couldn't help notice all the ink.

"Great, man, how are *you?*" Justin could only imagine what the guy had been doing in the last twenty-four hours to help Jenna.

"Glad to be back on land." Mike laughed.

"I'll bet." Justin half laughed, still incredulous over their ordeal.

Mike turned to everyone else and said hello. He gave Ali and Nicki both hugs and kisses and Matt stood as well to shake his hand.

"Thanks for watching out for this one." Matt nodded to Jenna. "She's been nothing but trouble since I've known her." He winked at her.

"Tell me about it!" Mike teased her playfully.

"Hey!" Jenna laughed and so did everyone else.

"Mike's nothin' but trouble, too, what a coincidence," Rafe said, laughing and taking a sip of his beer.

Mike mouthed a "fuck you" and smiled at Rafe, sipping from his own beer, happy to be amongst friends.

"Are you guys hungry?" Nicki asked. "There's tons of pizza left over."

"I'm starrrving," Jenna laughed and turned to Mike. "You must be too."

"I could definitely be talked into eating." He nodded.

"You guys sit, I'll heat it up." Nicki got up to go.

"Cold is fine!" Jenna and Mike called out at the same time then looked at each other and laughed.

Ali, Nicki, and Paige all looked at each other and grinned, the guys of course thought nothing of it.

Justin smiled at Paige. He could see how happy she was for her cousin and he hoped she knew how happy she was making him. It was really something being around her friends and family, they were a great group of people and he was having a blast here with them but he was dying to get her alone and ask her about the photo hanging in the living room.

"Okay, cold it is!" Nicki laughed, too, and went inside.

Mike took an empty chair next to Justin and pulled Jenna onto his lap. "How are you holding up?" He spoke softly against her cheek.

"I'm great." She smiled, tilting her head back against his shoulder. "I've never been better."

"Good." Mike kissed the top of her head then drank from his beer and looked over at Rafe, who was watching him. Mike grinned and shrugged his shoulders, Rafe got the message, Mike was toast. Man, if Rafe only knew how bad the sit really was.

Jenna felt her whole body relax for the first time in days as she leaned against Mike's warm, strong body. She thought nothing of snuggling up with him in front of her family and friends after having only known him for just a matter of days. They all seemed to know how she felt about him already, as if it had been a foregone conclusion. Maybe it had been.

Nicki came out with a box of Island Pizza and Jenna and Mike leaned forward to dig in.

"Ummm, sooo good," Jenna said around a mouthful. They each had a few slices before sitting back to answer the barrage of questions hurled at them. Jenna told them about her experience in the club and Mike told them how he knew to find her on the yacht and about getting to her in the storm. It was the first time Jenna was hearing it too and she was impressed all over again. Mike proudly described the damage Jenna had inflicted on Jay and his bodyguard and had the women hooting and hollering for Jenna. Matt and Rafe teased her pretending they were afraid of her and Justin told her how absolutely impressed he was. It was finally about two in the morning when Rafe told Ali he was tired and wanted to go to bed, creating a domino effect. Justin and Paige went next and then Matt and Nicki.

"I took my room back by the way," Nicki told her with narrowed eyes.

"You mean *my* room," Jenna droned.

"My room. I put your bag with Mike's in his room, along with a few things I thought you might need. I hope that's okay." Nicki grinned at her sister and squealed as Matt picked her up and put her over his shoulder. She dangled from the back of him as he walked her into the house.

"Stop tormenting your sister." Matt smacked Nicki on the ass.

"*Or* there's fresh sheets in the linen closet if you need to make up the couch!" Nicki yelled out, still trying to tease Jenna as Matt took her laughing down the hall.

"Sorry about that it's her mission in life to torment me." Jenna was leaning into Mike smiling and staring up at the stars. She was so content wrapped in his arms that she could fall asleep just where she sat.

Mike laughed. "You must be exhausted too." His pulse quickened at the thought of putting her to bed, unfortunately not another good night to be feeling what he was feeling. She may not be drugged up tonight but she'd been through hell and back and that would take a toll on anyone.

"I'm not really tired, still kind of wound up, I guess; I could use a hot shower though." Jenna felt him shift beneath her.

"C'mon, let's get you set up then."

Mike led the way inside, locking up the sliders behind him, and they both laughed and said goodnight to the sleepy-eyed puppy now in his crate.

When they got inside the bedroom, Mike went into the bathroom and started the shower for her and when the water was to temp he called her in.

Jenna had taken off Mike's friend's sweatshirt she'd worn all day and night and thrown away the stupid shorts from the club uniform she'd still been wearing. She had a towel draped around her and thanks to Nicki, a new toothbrush in her hand when she came into the bathroom.

"I'll give you some privacy." Mike kissed her forehead before she could protest and walked out of the room, shutting the door behind him. He quickly stripped down out of his still damp jeans and T-shirt and pulled on a bathing suit. He opened the bedroom sliders and took a running dive right into the pool.

CHAPTER FORTY-TWO

Jenna stood under the hot spray of the shower and closed her eyes. She felt such an overwhelming sense of relief that she was back here safe at The Three Sunrises. She felt like she'd been given a second chance and as she washed her hair she began to feel more invigorated and happy to be alive. She knew her feelings for Mike had developed at warp speed and even though they had only met days ago, what she'd been through with him made it seem as if she'd known him forever and she knew for certain that she was head over heels in love with him.

Smiling, she reached outside the shower curtain and took his razor from the sink. She shaved everything that needed shaving and washed the remains of the day off with his soap. She inhaled the fresh clean scent and finished rinsing the shampoo from her head. When she stepped out of the shower, she took a big dry clean towel from a nearby shelf and wrapped a smaller one around her hair. When she opened the bathroom door the bedroom was empty, but the sliders were left open and Jenna could hear splashing in the pool. She quickly rifled through her suitcase and found just what she wanted then grabbed the bag Nicki had put together for her and brought it back into the bathroom.

She could have kissed Nicki for putting her favorite scented lotion in the bag and for the hair brush and deodorant. She applied both and brushed her hair, then put on the bra and panties she had packed herself for a "just in case" kind of night, knowing beyond a doubt that this qualified. She dug around some more in the bag and her mouth dropped open at the box of condoms she found. Jeez, what did Nicki think? Jenna grinned; she'd obviously anticipated something happening between them, and Jenna had to admit she was grateful for the foresight even though she was on the pill.

When she was finished getting ready she slowly opened the bathroom door and peeked out; the room was still empty. She walked over to the night stand and put the radio on smiling at the song that was playing, yeah, it sure did "feel like the first time." She shut the bedside lamp off before cautiously approaching the sliders and the only light then came from the half moon and the smattering of stars in the summer night sky. The natural light illuminated Mike as she watched his big arms cut a path toward the low end of the pool.

He turned there and swam toward the deep end, toward Jenna, and she leaned against the door frame of the bedroom just watching him.

Mike had turned at the low end, submerged himself, and started another lap to the deep end. He would swim until he thought she was out of the shower and in bed, he'd keep swimming until she was sound asleep, all night if he had to, he wouldn't go near her. It wouldn't be right after what she'd been through. He sure as shit wasn't going to let her disappear from his bed tomorrow morning though.

Mike finished the lap and came up for air in the deep end, nearly choking on a mouth full of water as he did so. Jenna stood in the doorway to their room, wearing nothing but a white lace bra and panties, white lace that did nothing to hide the two dark luscious erect nipples under it or the small tattoo just below her hip peeking above her panty line. Oh fuck. He was instantly hard; so much for his good intentions. Mike placed his hands on the deck and popped out of the pool in a shot, he stood dripping on the concrete five feet from her while his eyes swept over her body hungrily. He reached up with both hands and slicked the water back off his hair and face then reached for the towel he had draped across a nearby chair. Jenna stayed still, just watching his every move.

She stood there, chills racing along her skin and her heart beating wildly, Mike was incredible to look at. His blue eyes pierced through the dark at her and she saw the raw desire that filled them. She felt self-conscious suddenly of her face and nonchalantly brought her hair forward hoping to cover the damage. God, she'd wanted him from the start and there was no way she could wait another hour to be with him let alone another night and from the way he was gazing back at her; he knew it was on. She watched as he slowly toweled himself dry, scanning her body with his eyes the whole while, causing the heat to rise beneath her skin and her panties to become uncomfortably damp. She was thinking about how those big hands would touch her and she ached for it, remembering all too well how he'd brought her to an earth-shattering orgasm, twice, and she couldn't wait for him to do it again.

Jenna studied his body and watched as the muscles in his arms and shoulders flexed while he rubbed the towel over his skin. She loved the way his tattoo looked on his defined chest and disappeared over his shoulder. She loved his perfect six-pack and the tapering of his waist and the defined line of coarse hair that led into his shorts. It was so over-the-top sexy and it excited and empowered her to see that Mike was turned on too. She could see his arousal beneath his shorts. It was blatantly evident and Jenna shivered watching him dry his long muscular legs. When he slowly started toward her she forced herself to stand still. She was nervous as a cat and she didn't want to let it show.

"You're not giving me much of a choice here, are you?" Mike asked. His voice was low and husky and he stood looking down at her.

Jenna shook her head no as she looked up to him and she spoke softly, "I can't wait anymore, Mike, I want you so bad it hurts."

Mike touched her flushed face then, using one hand to brush back her hair and uncover her bruised cheek where he bent to place a gentle kiss and then there was no going back. He lifted Jenna effortlessly to him and kissed her. His lips met hers and their tongues sought one another's in desperate need. One hand held the back of her head and the other her bottom, her strong legs wrapped around his waist just where he liked them and her arms encircled his neck possessively. Mike moved with her into the bedroom and slid the glass doors and their blinds shut behind him. His heart was hammering away in his chest at what they were about to do, he felt like he'd been waiting forever for her and once he took her he knew there'd be no going back. He was about to cross a line that was sure to hurt them both and he wasn't strong enough to stop it.

"Do you know how badly I want you?" he asked gruffly, pulling back and looking into her sultry eyes.

Jenna felt herself grow weak at the searing look Mike gave her. "Show me." She was nervous and utterly turned on at the same time and with one gasp she was flat on her back and on the bed with Mike's large form looming above her. He bent to kiss her lips then quickly moved to her breasts, bra and all. He kissed her through the lace and his heated breath made her nipples peak and her stomach tighten. She arched into his mouth and cried out as he playfully bit her nipple; he slipped the bra from her shoulders and unfastened it, taking turns sucking and caressing each breast before making his way to her belly and smoothing his large hand over her skin. Jenna watched him touch her and kiss her and felt her heart pounding in anticipation. Her nerve endings tingled with the thought of where his mouth and tongue would go, and it made her wet again before he even touched her there. "Mike..." She placed her hands on his head and smoothed them over the light shadow of stubble on his face. She looked down and laughed softly at the crooked grin he gave her.

"I've been dreaming of this." He slipped her panties down and inhaled the heavenly scent of her then greedily put his mouth between her legs.

"Oh!" Jenna moaned out loud and jerked in response. The tip of his tongue touched her wet opening and it sent instant shock waves rippling through her body. When he took her clit between his lips, Jenna's body convulsed and she instantly cried out, "Ohhh Mike!"

Mike smiled against her moist warm skin, he had her tender little nub between his lips and he used his tongue to flick over it, feeling her body buck and quiver beneath him and tasting the sweet warm liquid that gushed from her. It drove him wild that she could come like that and he was going to enjoy making it happen over and over again. He drank all of her in and started again, placing his hands under her bottom and bringing her even closer to his face, he couldn't get enough of her. His tongue danced inside of her warm opening and he relished the taste and the scent of her as she came yet again right into his mouth. He couldn't wait to make love to her. His cock strained with the need and he pulled back, lowering her hips to the bed, his eyes roving over her body once again. He rubbed the tops of her thighs, kneading the taut muscles there and watching her breath expand in her flat stomach. Her breasts were pale but flushed against her olive-toned skin and her nipples pink, hard peaks, her eyes were open and locked on his, and Mike felt his heart burst right inside of his chest. Oh man. He got off the bed and stood before her, his damp bathing suit doing nothing to hide his blatant arousal. He knew she was nervous about seeing him and he wanted to make her comfortable.

Jenna swallowed looking at him. He was freaking huge, and he was still covered, how was *that* going to fit inside of her? She looked from him to it and back to him. "I changed my mind," she joked and grinned at him.

Mike laughed, loving her sense of humor. "C'mere." He held out his hand to her and Jenna sat up on her knees on the bed in front of him. He took her hand and put it over him, his breath catching when she gripped him through the nylon shorts.

Jenna laid her hand on him and stroked the length of him through the thin material and then she gripped him, testing his girth. "Wow," she breathed, impressed looking up at him again.

Mike grinned and slowly pushed his wet bathing suit down stepping out of it. His cock was so damn hard for her and his balls so fucking tight it hurt.

Jenna couldn't believe what she was looking at and she automatically encircled him with her hand. His skin was still cool from his swim but felt as smooth as a sheet of satin sewn over a hard length of steel and she slowly stroked him, getting familiar with him. He had a smattering of hair at the base of his penis that lightened as it rose above to his navel in that sexy line. She used her other hand to lightly trace the line and felt his stomach muscles contract beneath her touch. Jenna looked up and sought his eyes, aware of her heart pounding in her chest. It wouldn't be long before he'd be placing this inside of her, she thought. She used both hands to caress him, awed at how large and how hard he was. He was as long as he was thick and Jenna once again wondered how it was going to be, she prayed she could accept him and not disappoint him.

Her touch was both pleasure and pain and Mike needed to get inside of her fast. Watching her explore him and feeling her light touch, he nearly spilled in her hands. He abruptly pulled her chest to his and kissed her, halting her ministrations. He felt her arms encircle his neck and her breasts and nipples rub against him, his throbbing cock all the while probing between them with a mind of its own, seeking. He gently laid her back down on the bed and settled beside her running his fingertips from her thigh to her breast and holding the weight of one in his palm. "I'm going to make you good and wet again before I slip inside you, okay?" He could tell she was concerned about their joining and he wanted to make it as pleasurable as possible for her.

Jenna nodded with a smile, closing her eyes and liking the plan. Mike began stroking her and she relaxed. She wasn't nervous anymore; she trusted him and she was ready for him, she wanted this more than anything. As Mike lay alongside her, touching her, Jenna opened her eyes and met his, and she knew they were going to fit together like hand in glove. It was like his friends said; they were made for each other. She smiled at him then and he smiled back with such warmth in his eyes that her heart burst, he knew it too she thought, and once again she felt the waves of explosive pleasure roll through her as his touch annihilated her nerve endings, she arched up and cried out. Oh my God! He knew just how to touch her.

"That's it, baby," Mike whispered, "one more and then I'm going to ruin you for any other man." He only half joked. He knew she was it for him and he planned to make her feel the same way, damning the consequences.

Jenna's laugh was rolled around a soft whimper; her body had never felt so weak from passion. She loved that he had a sense of humor too, and that he was just a little bit cocky. Hell, with that equipment he deserved to be. She smiled. If he only knew he had already "ruined" her for any other man.

Mike went down on her again and took her over the edge, he wanted her so wet and slick that he could slide right in and she would feel nothing but pleasure. When he heard her cry out again and felt her body quiver around him, he reached for a condom in the nightstand, tore it open, and rolled it on. Jenna lifted herself up on her elbows and watched him with heavy-lidded eyes, her breathing short. She was sexy as all hell.

"I didn't know they made those in triple extra-large," she grinned, teasing him. She never imagined she'd be joking with a man during sex but it felt so natural. She was having fun with him.

"You really want to be teasing me right now?" Mike cocked a brow and grinned, loving her more than he had a right to. "This is some heavy duty equipment and it's going to take a lot of serious maneuvering; I'm going to need your full cooperation here."

His voice was low and sexy and Jenna laughed and bent her knees suggestively, propping her feet up on the bed, placing her hands on either side of her slick entrance, inviting him. "Like this?"

Oh fuck, yeah. "Ummm, just like that," Mike's laughter fell short as pure lust overtook him. Seeing her spread herself like that for him was too much. "Jesus, you're beautiful." God, he loved this girl so much and he felt his gut tighten with the urge to tell her. He brought himself down on top of her, hovering over her, and looked into her eyes. "Jenna. . ."

Jenna lay back, taking in the silent communication that was passing between them, and she smiled up at him as he brought himself between her legs. He held his weight up with his arms at her sides and the head of his penis sought her opening. Jenna lifted her hips to welcome him and felt like she'd waited a lifetime for this moment, it was finally happening.

Mike's heart was pounding as he slowly and gently as he could, pressed inside of her. He wanted to plow right in but he held back, going in slow, feeling her stretch and her muscles relax around him, gradually accepting him. Holy mother of God, she was so wet and tight around his cock, she was like a warm, wet, vise squeezing around him. Nothing had ever felt so good. Mike watched her carefully for her reaction as he kept going in.

Jenna smiled up at him. He was being so careful and so thoughtful, but she wasn't in any pain at all. He was stretching her, no doubt about it, but it felt so incredibly good, and she was so ready for him. She lifted her hips a little more and felt the rest of him slip right inside. Whoa! Her eyes went wide and she let out a combined moan and soft laugh.

"Ohhh man." Mike met Jenna's wide eyes and smiled and they stayed frozen, joined as they were, both indulging the way they were feeling right at that moment.

"Oh baby," he half groaned and smiled in unadulterated pleasure. It was all he could do not to pump hard into her.

"I know." Jenna grinned and squeezed her vaginal muscles around him, laughing as he groaned out loud again and gave her a warning look. She kept her eyes locked on his as she slowly started to move beneath him. Her hands went around his wide back and ran over the muscles that bunched and flexed there. He felt so good inside of her and with a groan of pleasure he began to match her motion, being careful to hold his weight off of her. But Jenna wanted his weight. She couldn't get close enough and she held him tighter to her, needing the contact, feeling like she might not have it again for some inexplicable reason.

Mike moved over her with slow, firm thrusts. She was like heaven surrounding him and he didn't want it to end but when she lifted her hips up to him, encouraging him, he couldn't help but oblige her by increasing his momentum, fucking her harder and faster. He couldn't believe how she was taking him, she was so wet and he wished to hell the latex wasn't there. Her body felt so soft and delicate beneath him but strong too as she held his body tightly to her. When her legs came up to wrap around him Mike slipped even deeper inside and he felt the tightening in his balls and the beginnings of his climax. Oh man, he wasn't going to last very long.

Jenna took all of him in, pushing him in deeper with her heels and digging her nails into the muscles of his back. He was so hard, everywhere. Everywhere she touched him her hands met smooth skin and rock-hard muscle, and it turned her on so damn much. Their bodies were slick and damp with sweat now as they began moving more urgently together, he was pounding into her and her hips slammed against his lower body as she rose to meet each thrust. Her head fell back, and her breasts arched toward him and she cried out in pleasure each time he entered her. He was filling her to her very core, stretching her wide and touching every womanly part of her. It overwhelmed her, he was absolutely rocking her world!

Jenna soon felt Mike's every muscle grow taut, felt his big strong arms scoop her up, hugging her tight to him, and she felt his lips pressed against the side of her neck as he gripped her around the back and plunged forcefully into her a final time. His grunt and then his guttural moan of pleasure were muffled against her skin as he buried his face in her hair and Jenna moaned deep in pleasure herself, savoring what he was giving. He was so deep inside of her and she tightened around him not wanting them to come apart, she enveloped him as he shuddered on top of her all the while kissing her neck, her shoulder and her mouth. She'd never in her life felt so much love and gratitude for someone. This incredible man had saved her life, *twice*. He had cared enough to come after her and watch over her, trying to keep her safe. He was her hero no doubt about it, and without any doubts the most incredible lover on the face of the earth.

Mike breathed her in and held onto Jenna just as tight as she held him, his body still reeling with the aftershocks of his climax. Their bodies were slick with sweat and joined together and he was overcome with feelings for her. He'd wanted her from the start but watching over her and chasing after her these past few days had made him realize that it was so much more than lust. She had got in his head and in his heart, two places he'd never let any other woman before, for good reason.

"I'm falling for you, Jenna," he said softly by her ear, his cheek pressed against hers. He smiled at how good it felt to say and he felt sorry for himself at the same time, sorry for them both. In all of his thirty-two years he'd never told a woman anything close to that. He'd never even felt it and now, when he finally found someone to love, someone he could see spending the rest of his life with, he'd be leaving. He tried to lift his weight off of her, knowing he was crushing her by her shallow breathing, but she wouldn't let him go.

Jenna squeezed Mike tight not letting him go anywhere. He was crushing her but she didn't care. He'd just told her he was falling for her! Her heart was filled and overflowing inside, rivulets of happiness coursing through her veins, tears coursing down her cheeks. She wanted to jump up and scream for joy but instead she pressed her mouth to his ear. "You just made me the happiest girl on the whole planet," she whispered to him, trying her best to hold back her tears, but his words resonated like every love song she'd ever heard, like every romantic movie she'd ever seen and wished she were a part of. This was what she'd always imagined being in love would feel like and the tears were automatic.

"I did?" Mike asked, pushing up on his elbows, breaking through her stronghold on him. He searched her eyes and found they were brimming with fresh tears. Her cheeks were wet and his stomach clenched at the sight.

Jenna nodded in affirmation, meeting his gaze. "Yeah, considering that I've already fallen for you." It came out in a hoarse whisper over the baseball-sized lump in her throat and she hastily wiped her tears before they could fall. "I think it was that mean look of yours when we first met." She gave him a sheepish grin, sucking in her bottom lip, realizing she had just proclaimed her feelings for him followed up by a joke but she was still astounded by what he'd said to her and just a little shy of how he'd react to her own declaration.

Mike chuckled at her joke and then stopped abruptly when the first thing she'd said sunk in. Oh. Wow. The words she had said in her drug-induced state in the Jeep came back to him. He had known then that he couldn't put any stock to them, but now she was sober and had tears in her eyes and was looking at him so expectantly it melted him. "Are you serious, Jenna?" He had to be sure. He looked down at her, their bodies still melded, and he knew he was where he belonged.

Jenna nodded, terrified of saying it again. What was going through his mind? He said he was falling for her, but just because he said he was didn't mean he had quite yet. Who falls in love in four days? Oh crap. She turned her head toward the wall and laughed, embarrassed while she wiped her eyes. "Forget it, I know it sounds crazy, we need more time. I. . ." Mike moved her face back to him with a gentle hand on her bruised cheek and he sought her eyes.

"Jenna, I don't want to forget it." Mike was still buried inside of her and made no move to leave. He supported his weight easily above her and his eyes locked with hers. He could feel her heart thumping against his chest. He was inches from her face.

Jenna took a deep breath, her chest rising into his as she did. She looked into his beautiful blue eyes. Okay, here goes everything. "I know it sounds ridiculous," she said, trying not to cry. "We just met and there's a lot I don't even know about you, but what I do know," she paused and sniffled, "I love so much." It came out on a little sob and she shrugged her shoulders beneath him feeling vulnerable with his large body looming over her. Her hands fell away from his back where they'd been holding on and she wiped her eyes. "It's how I feel and I can't help it," Jenna told him, unable to stop her tears. "I'm so in love with you, Special Agent Mike Caplan."

The use of his title slammed Mike good, a painful reminder of who he was and what was to come. His chest actually ached looking at her and hearing her words. Her tear-filled little smile twisted around Mike's heart like an elastic, expanded in his chest then flung around his insides like a boomerang. Toast, that's what he was. He pressed his lips to hers and kissed her, then wiped the tears that fell from her eyes being careful of her bruise. Every defense he'd ever put up around other women, and even those he'd tried to put up with Jenna, came crumbling down. He had no defense when it came to her and he decided to throw caution to the wind despite his better judgment.

"It's not ridiculous." Damn, he was so happy right now, stupid happy. "Jesus, Jenna," Mike laughed, hanging his head, "I love you too." He looked back in her eyes. "I was holding back a moment ago." He laughed again a little embarrassed himself. "I've already fallen for you too, I just wasn't sure how you'd react to me saying so this quickly." He laughed again, elated. "I'm so fucking head over heels in love with you I can't think straight, Jenna." He kissed her. "And I've wanted to tell you so many times since I pulled you out of that nightclub."

Jenna was elated and crying and laughing and hugging his big body to hers, Oh my God! He loved her too! How they would even make it work she had no idea and she didn't care right now, she was just so overwhelmed, but she didn't want to keep crying she wanted to make him laugh. "Wait." She sat up on her elbows and narrowed her eyes at him, sniffling. She felt him move inside of her and she raised a brow and grinned. "You don't have a wife or like ten girlfriends that I should know about, do you?" It was a funny reminder that although they had just proclaimed their love for one another they still didn't know much about each other.

He bit down on her nipple, playing with her, and she slapped his ass. "Ten wives and one girlfriend." And a fucking job in my near future that could take me halfway across the world. He had selfishly just revealed his feelings and Jenna would surely end up hating him for it.

Jenna started to move under him, laughing happily. "So you love me even though I'm trouble?"

"God help me, Jenna, because you are." Mike wanted to live in the moment; he didn't want to think about the future, just this unforgettable night with her. He laughed, trying to enjoy the present. He closed his eyes, drowning in the feel of her as she moved her hips beneath him. How could he live without this?

"Just wait till you really get to know me, you won't be able to live without me." Jenna thrust up into him, smiling seductively.

Jesus she'd read his mind. "Oh yeah?" He thrust back. "What if—oh yeah," he grinned down at her, "I said... oh God." He closed his eyes. "I . . . already . . . can't?" His second climax came even faster and Mike opened his eyes to watch the sweet smile spread across her face, and he felt that now familiar tightening around his heart.

CHAPTER FORTY-THREE

It was dawn and Jenna sat between Mike's bent knees on the cool sand. "This is nice," she murmured, leaning back into his solid chest and placing her hands on his strong thighs. He wore cargo shorts and she smoothed her hands over his revealed skin.

Mike wrapped his arms around her and kissed her neck. He felt like he'd known her all his life, not just since Saturday. It amazed him how his life had changed in a matter of days. Before it had been all about the job and now all he could think about was Jenna; Jenna as his girlfriend, someone he loved. He'd never been in love. His past relationships had lasted no more than a month at a time and had been all about sex and he'd never felt anything beyond that, like he did now. He been drawn to Jenna from the very first night he'd met her and yeah that had been about sex, but there had been something else too. They'd shared camaraderie at dinner and again at his condo after he'd taken her home from the hospital and she'd made an impact on him. She was so honest and easy to talk to. They were compatible, she was funny, and smart and loving, and as tough as she was he loved how vulnerable she could be too. He wanted to know everything about her, her favorite movie, her favorite song, her favorite everything. And he wanted to share everything about himself with her too. But he couldn't, he'd already gone too far by telling her that he loved her.

Jenna watched as the sky slowly brightened and she sighed feeling Mike's chest rise and fall, he was so much bigger than her that it was kind of funny. She wasn't tiny by any means. She thought of herself as average, although she didn't carry any extra weight, so she supposed people viewed her as small as a result, but next to Mike she really was small and she liked the way it felt. She liked that his arms could envelop her whole body, that he could pick her up effortlessly in those strong arms and make her feel so safe and protected. He was large and imposing but also so caring and thoughtful. He could sear her with the desire in his eyes or make her cry with a soft touch to her cheek. Her attraction to him had been instantaneous but now it ran soul deep. He was part of her in every way and to feel this way after just a matter of days was frightening. She knew now her feelings weren't just a result of all the drama that had occurred. She had met her soul mate. Mike had joked about it, but he *had* ruined her for any other man. He was her hero, the man she'd been waiting for all her life, and she wasn't willing to give him up for anything.

"So quiet there, kid." Mike kissed the top of her head.

Funny how she now loved when he called her that. "Just thinking." His fingers found hers and they intertwined.

"Me too."

Jenna felt her heart pound when she heard the forlorn tone in his voice. "About?"

"You, us."

She hugged his arms tighter to her. "Do I want to know?" Why did she have a sudden feeling of dread in the pit of her belly?

Mike smiled sadly against her, hearing a note of insecurity and she had every right to feel it. "Maybe not, but it's something I have to tell you." No time like the present, he thought.

"Okay." Jenna's heart had fallen to her stomach.

The sun had risen and Mike could feel the temperature rising with it. It promised to be another beautiful, hot day in paradise. "I'm off until the wedding but after that I have to go back to work."

Jenna knew he'd have to go back to work in Miami eventually. "I know," she said cautiously.

"I have to go back today at some point to file some reports and get your things, but I can be back by tomorrow."

She was glad of that but she knew there was more. She squeezed his hands, wanting him to just spill it. She was already worried about what would happen after the wedding; was that what he was about to tell her?

"You okay?" He knew she was upset. Hell, so was he.

Jenna nodded. She was happy she would have him for at least two weeks and then they could deal with whatever was going to happen then. She didn't want to think about it now.

"Jenna..." Mike turned her in his arms so that he cradled her back. "After the two weeks are over..."

Okay, so they were going to deal with it now. She took a deep breath. "Yeah..."

He took a deep breath. "Jenna, a few months ago I applied for a job with a special unit of the FBI and I'm going to find out very soon whether I've been selected for it. I'm pretty confident I will be."

"Oh." She sensed more was coming. He sounded pretty grim.

Mike explained about the HRT and felt Jenna physically shrink in his arms and he felt that unpleasant squeeze in his chest again.

"So it's kind of like being in the military?" Jenna asked quietly, feeling her heart slowly break into a million pieces.

"Yes. I'll go through months of training not only in Virginia but other facilities around the country, and then I could be deployed anywhere, at any time, including overseas."

"Wow." Jenna hadn't seen that bit of information coming and she turned away from him to stare out at the Gulf, watching a dolphin lazily swim by, usually a happy sight but she looked upon the creature now with tears in her eyes. Why was this happening? How could fate be so cruel? This wasn't how it was supposed to be. You don't find the love of your life only to find out it could never work between you. How do you have a relationship with someone you don't even know will be there in the morning or if and when they'll return? It wasn't fair and she wanted to sob in his arms but she knew that wouldn't be fair to him. She took a deep breath. "Is it a permanent position?"

"You serve four years minimum." Mike had intended to do the four years and come back to Miami. Daniels would be ready to retire and they'd talked about Mike applying for the position. Now the four years sounded like a jail sentence, what the fuck?

Four years? He might as well have said forever. The tears were careening down her face and Jenna couldn't even look at him. "This is something that means a lot to you, huh?"

"Jesus, Jenna, I thought it did." Mike turned her back around, forcing her to look at him, his own face clearly pained. "Until I met you, now you mean a lot to me, and I never expected that." Shit, he'd applied for HRT knowing he was a free man and always would be. Relationships weren't for him, work was his life and he'd never let anyone get close or let himself get close to anyone because of it. Jenna had changed everything.

What was she supposed to say to that? "I don't know what to say." Jenna looked into his eyes and was surprised to see moisture there. Oh God, why was this happening? "I don't want to lose you, Mike, I love you," she sobbed and buried her head against him.

Christ, he was afraid to speak for fear he might sob right along with her. This fucking sucked balls. He stroked her hair and held her tighter. "I love you too, Jenna," he whispered.

CHAPTER FORTY-FOUR

They'd said a teary goodbye later that morning and Mike had driven off with another agent who had stayed at Tween Waters the night before. Mike promised he'd be back the next day and they would have nearly two weeks together before he had to go back to Miami, and by that time he would have heard about his acceptance. Jenna couldn't have been more miserable watching him drive away and she retreated to the room they'd shared to slip under the covers and sleep, his scent still on the sheets, making her sob all over again.

When she woke up it was dark and she lie in bed listening for signs of life in the house but all was quiet and the bedside clock read eleven p.m. She'd slept the whole day away but she was glad; she was that much closer to seeing Mike again the following day. She got up out of bed with a heavy heart and slid open the sliders to the pool, the warm night air instantly filtering in, and she used the bathroom to change into her bathing suit. A swim would wake her up and then she'd eat something. Maybe Paige would be awake and they could talk, she hoped.

After she dressed she approached the sliders but came up short when she heard a splash in the water. Knowing with all the couples staying at the house there was a possibility of interrupting something she might not want to see, she hesitated before peeking out. It was Rafe and Ali and they were alone. So much for a swim, she thought, and turned to walk away but stopped when she heard her name.

"Jenna will be crushed, does she know?"

"I guess they talked about it this morning but she doesn't know for sure he's been accepted. Mike just got the call from Daniels this afternoon. I was just checking in and could hear it in his voice something was up. Jesus, I didn't even know he'd applied. The HRT is intense, Al; we're talking the best of the best. It's an elite group of men and Mike has been chosen to be one of them. That's pretty amazing, not that I'm surprised."

"Didn't Daniels recommend you for that before we met?" Ali hadn't put much thought to it only because Rafe had turned it down.

Rafe nodded.

"What does it mean though? What will he do? Where will he go?" All Ali could think of was Jenna and how she was going to feel.

"He'll go to Quantico to train, and then it could be anywhere. They're on call 24/7 and when they're not on assignment, they're training nonstop in all kinds of situations and conditions. He'll be traveling a lot, but after he puts in his four years, he'll have incredible opportunities within the bureau. He really wants to go back to Miami and take over for Daniels when he retires."

"Rafe." Ali looked at him. "What about Jenna?" Ali's heart was breaking. "She's in love with him and he loves her, it's written all over them both."

Rafe leaned back inside the pool, his arms draped over the edge. "I don't know, babe, this is tough no doubt about it, but Cap is one of the best if not *the* best marksman in the country and he's being recognized for it. They need men like him; he's worked his whole career for something like this. He's known Jenna for less than a week."

Ali stared at him in disbelief. "Rafe, we knew each other for less than a week too."

Rafe knew she was right but it was different. He would never consider the HRT even though Daniels had recommended him for it last year as well. But Rafe had thought of his family at the time. He liked working on the home front, he didn't want to be overseas at any given time worrying about them or them worrying about him. He had turned Daniels down flat, especially after being involved with two domestic hostage situations in the past that had taken a little piece of him. No, he was happy to stay where he was.

Mike didn't have family though, other than an uncle somewhere in Texas. The FBI was his family and as long as Rafe had known him Mike had lived for the excitement and the adrenaline rush of the job. The HRT would be perfect for him, but Rafe could hear it in Mike's voice tonight that things had changed.

"I don't know what's going to happen and I feel bad too, believe me, I do." Rafe knew it was the first time Mike had ever been serious about a woman and the fact that it was Jenna made it even harder to watch.

Jenna held her fist to her mouth and slumped down on the floor in front of the sliders, where she quietly cried. Mike would be part of an elite group of men. He was one of the best marksmen in the country. They needed men like him and then he'd be afforded great opportunities when he finished his term. How could she interfere with that? Rafe was right, it had stung to hear him say it, but it was true, Mike had known her for less than a week; it was ridiculous to think someone would throw their career away because of a few nights of drama and passion. What had she been thinking? Fairy tales, that's what she'd been thinking. There weren't any signs of fate. It was all just coincidence; nothing meant anything because if it did it wouldn't be about to be ripped right out from under her.

Jenna stood up and put some clothes on then went out to the kitchen. She opened the refrigerator and looked again at the groceries Mike had bought. Why she hadn't noticed the first time she had no idea, but as she looked now she saw that she had bought almost the exact same items. He'd even bought a key lime pie and both of them sat untouched. She took one out and grabbed a fork.

"Not even gonna get a plate?" Paige teased as she came down the hall from her room and saw Jenna. She frowned when she noticed her cousin's eyes were swollen and red-rimmed. "What happened, hon?"

Jenna tried to swallow the now permanent lump in her throat and couldn't. She burst into tears.

"Oh no Jen, what?" Paige came around the counter and hugged her.

Jenna could see Ali and Rafe still out by the pool and she quickly told Paige the situation with Mike and what she'd overheard Rafe say.

Paige's heart broke for her. "Have you heard from Mike yet?"

"No."

"Well, try not to jump to conclusions just yet until you talk to him. Maybe there's some way it can work out." Paige wished she could make Jenna feel better.

"Paige, I would never ask him to give up his career. Nothing can develop between us, I just have to deal with that and let him go. He deserves this, they need him, Rafe said so," Jenna cried.

"Oh Jenna, honey, I'm so sorry." Paige's heart was breaking for her.

"I want to go home. I can't stay here and spend two weeks with him; it'll be that much harder at the end, what's the point? Nothing is going to change in two weeks." Jenna put the pie back in the fridge untouched. "When are you guys leaving?"

"Tomorrow morning, we have a nine thirty on Jet Blue. Justin has to get back to work and so do I."

"Do you mind if I try to get on your flight?"

Paige made a sad face. "Of course not, but are you sure that's the right thing to do?"

"Two weeks with him will kill me. I will physically die of heartache at the end. If I leave now I can pretend this week didn't happen."

"Oh Jenna, I know you don't want to do that."

"What's my choice?" she sobbed and retreated down the hall to her room.

Paige's heart ripped in two for her cousin.

* * * * *

Jenna took a few sheets of stationery from the nightstand and sat down on the bed to write Mike a letter. She believed what she was doing was right. It hurt like hell but it was for the best. When she was done, she took out her laptop and went online to book a flight. She was able to get on Paige and Justin's flight so she prepared her bags for the morning and got back in bed. She knew she should tell Nicki but she didn't want her to tell Ali. Ali would tell Rafe and then Jenna might get a phone call from Mike and that would be torture. She'd try to sneak out with Paige and Justin in the morning and if anyone saw her, then she'd swear them to secrecy. She knew Mike would be returning here with her things, like her cell and her clothes, but she knew Nicki would bring them home to her.

It was a long time before she fell asleep and when she finally did it was restless. Jenna dreamt of Mike in foreign countries and rappelling out of helicopters and getting shot at. She'd woken up at dawn, sweating.

* * * * *

Mike had talked to Daniels at length on the phone and he sat on the couch now going over the conversation. He'd been accepted to the HRT and he would begin training in a month's time. He should have been ecstatic and feel honored to have been chosen, but he was sick to his stomach. He'd finally found someone to love and that loved him, she'd called him her hero, for Christ's sake, and now he would be giving it all up to become someone else's hero. He ran his hands over his face. He couldn't believe the timing of all this, it was fucking unbelievable. Mike had had no business falling in love with her, and when he did he should have kept his mouth shut; now Jenna was going to be hurt and that killed him more than anything.

He lay back on the couch, tired from trying to figure it out, and he closed his eyes. He hadn't prayed in a long time, not since the night his parents and little sister had died in a car wreck when he was twenty-one. He'd prayed that God would take him that night, too, but it hadn't worked. Now he prayed for divine intervention, guidance, something or someone to tell him what to do but he wasn't hopeful tonight either.

* * * * *

Jenna sat in her seat staring out the plane's window, she'd left her heart back in Captiva and she felt like an empty shell as she sat there on the plane. There were no more tears, at least not now; she knew when she walked into her old room at the Bellevue house though she'd break down again. She'd pack and go stay with Nan. her parents were still in Vegas and she didn't want them to know yet anyway. Jenna had called her grandmother this morning and cried her eyes out, giving her the condensed version of her week. Nan had been shocked and worried and told her to come straight to her townhouse.

Jenna wasn't even sure she would move into Nicki's apartment in Southie as planned, she didn't know where she wanted to be anymore or who she wanted to be. She was all mixed up, heartbroken beyond repair, and generally disillusioned. All her life she believed she'd grow up, go to school, do something she loved and fall in love. Never did the dream entail such devastating emotional trauma. What the hell?

She'd said goodbye to Nicki and Matt this morning. They had been awake and eating breakfast at the kitchen counter and she wondered looking at her sister how she had survived all those years loving Matt and never letting him know. Could she survive even four years without Mike? Would he even still love her when his four years were up?

Jenna had said goodbye to Rafe and Ali as well and had begged their forgiveness but she didn't think she could be a part of their wedding. It was two weeks away and it would be too painful to see Mike again. She had to make a clean break. Ali had cried with her and Rafe had understood but they both said they wanted her there and hoped she would change her mind. But Jenna knew she wouldn't, it would be too painful to see Mike for one night and then say goodbye again forever; she just couldn't do it. She had to make this break.

Paige reached over and grabbed her hand. "Jen, I know you're hurting but I have to believe this is going to be okay, you're going to be okay." Paige still couldn't believe all that Jenna had been through and now this.

Jenna looked at her and saw Justin trying to be discreet and give them space even in the small confines of their row of seats and she felt bad. She didn't want to bring either of them down. They were so obviously happy with each other and starting something great and it made Jenna hurt even more. "Paige, I feel like someone I loved just died, it's devastating. I seriously can't see beyond it right now. I know it will eventually get better with time, but right now it hurts, it really hurts."

Justin looked over at the pained words and the break in Jenna's voice. "I'm sorry you're hurting, kid, but I'm going with Paige on this one, I think it's all going to work itself out." He was actually now a believer in the whole fate thing and the power of the universe bringing two people together. Shit, he and Paige were a walking, talking example.

Jenna gave him a small smile hearing him call her kid and wished there actually were something to work out. It wasn't as if there were options, not options that made sense anyway. "I hope you're right, Justin." She was being polite but Jenna felt nothing but gloom. She just wanted to land so she could get home and crawl under the covers and sleep for four years.

* * * * *

Mike had prayed for divine intervention and guidance and had woken up to the telephone ringing; it was Daniels.

"Hey Cap, change of plans, your vacation is going to be put off for two weeks, they want you there this weekend at Quantico. The Unit Chief called and left you a message, he only called me when he couldn't reach you."

Mike swore under his breath and felt the last piece of the floor fall out from under him.

Daniels was well aware of the situation Mike was now in with Jenna, and it just figured that it would have worked out this way, but he knew Mike would be happy with the HRT especially when he heard what they had to say. What they were offering Mike was incredible and Daniels knew it was meant to be; it just wasn't his place to tell him. "This is a great opportunity, Cap."

Yeah, it was an opportunity he had been gung ho to take before meeting Jenna, now he felt it was a life sentence. "When?"

"Tomorrow, there's a flight leaving at ten."

Fuck, one day with Jenna, one fucking day? "So that's it, I start training now? Why is this happening so quick? Is there a situation?"

"No, no, expect to be there about two weeks, you'll be back in time for the wedding and then you'll have orders on when to return."

Jesus, he hadn't even been thinking about the wedding. He would see Jenna there, but then he'd have to leave her again for who knew how long. "Okay, thanks, Tom. I have some things to take care of before I go."

Daniels could hear the downtrodden tone in Mike's voice and he smiled. Things had a way of working out and he had no doubt being part of the HRT was going to be great for Mike and he would realize it soon enough. "No problem, Cap, I'll talk to you in the morning." Daniels hung up and called his wife, smiling.

Mike showered and packed and overnight bag. Hopefully he could spend one more night with Jenna; he would just leave the island for Miami at dawn to get ready for his flight to Virginia. He didn't look forward to telling her their two weeks together were shot; it would be the second hardest thing he'd ever told her.

Mike arrived before noon to The Three Sunrises. He parked his Jeep, took his and Jenna's bags out of the back seat and the large freezer bag he had filled. He knocked on the front door and Rafe answered, letting him in.

"Hey Cap, how are you?" Rafe knew when his friend was feeling like shit and he could see it in Mike's eyes that he was hurtin'. The very last thing Rafe wanted to tell him was that Jenna had left.

"I've been better, I'll tell you that much." Mike set the bags down in the foyer and walked to the kitchen to empty the freezer bag inside the freezer. He took in the luggage in a pile in the living room. "You guys out of here?"

"Yeah, we have a two o'clock flight home," Rafe told him. "Hey listen, Mike. . ."

Mike looked at Rafe as he came out of the kitchen.

"Jenna's gone. She left with Paige and Justin earlier this morning." Rafe's heart went out to his friend and the stricken look on his face.

Mike hung his head and shook it, an ironic laugh escaping him in a "humph." He felt sick and looked back up to Rafe.

"I'm sorry, man." Rafe pulled an envelope from his back pocket. "She left this for you." Oh man, Rafe's own heart was breaking for the guy as he handed over the letter.

Mike saw the envelope and immediately had a bad feeling. She'd written him two notes so far since he'd known her and neither of them had resulted in a happy ending. He took the envelope reluctantly and walked over to the couch. "Where is everybody?" Mike asked wearily.

"Matt took the girls up to Tween Waters, Ali is just checking to make sure rooms are booked and the dinner is set." Rafe even felt bad talking about the wedding. "I'll just be out back making some calls." He walked by, giving Mike an encouraging squeeze on the shoulder, and went outside to walk down to the dock, wishing the circumstances could be different.

Mike stared at the envelope as he sat there. When Rafe was gone he tore it open.

> ***Mike,***
>
> **I first want to say I'm sorry for leaving this way but I honestly thought it would be the best for both of us. This past week has been surreal. I'll never be able to thank you enough for what you did for me, you saved my life twice, plain and simple and I'll never forget you, obviously, because of it.**
>
> **I also will hold dear the love I have for you. I fell in love with you this week and yes the timing is crazy and the circumstances were crazy, and some might say my feelings are simply manifested because of what I went through, but I know how I feel! And when you told me you felt the same way, I knew it was true and it was right. I guess I'm just having a problem with fate's hand in all this, I always believed in it but how can fate bring two people together and then rip them apart? Why**

is this happening? I keep asking myself that but I can't come up with any good answers. I do know that I'm in love with you and have the utmost respect for who you are and what you do and therefore would never expect you to give up on a dream or an opportunity when it came to your career. I overheard Rafe and Ali talking last night and I'm so proud to know you, Mike. To be one of the best if not the best in the country at what you do, and to be recognized for it is quite an accomplishment. It means something. Rafe was right, the HRT needs you and it would be unfair for me to say that I do, too, after only having known you for less than a week.

I have to believe that everything happens for a reason and I will go on about my life and I will think of you every day. There is no doubt in my mind about that. And perhaps after four years you may still think of me, too, and who knows, we may have a second chance at this but until then, know that you are loved deeply and please, please keep safe.

I've respectfully backed out of Ali and Rafe's wedding and will not be attending. I hope you don't think me a coward, but I know I will not be able to handle seeing you again or touching you, knowing that I can't have you, this is heartbreaking enough.

One more thing, and I'm smiling through my tears when I write this, Special Agent Mike Caplan, your incredible sexy smile is what will keep me going. I said it before but you are the most magnificent man I've ever seen, when you smile you transform, I can see all the laughter and the kindness in your eyes. I'll miss those stunning blue eyes of yours looking at me and making me feel so desired, I'll miss your strong hands touching me and your lips kissing me. My body is already desperate for your touch again, but if I have to wait four years for it I will.

Mike, thank you for everything, and please forgive me for not being there to say any of this in person, I know you think of me as a strong woman but when it comes to you, I'm not strong at all, I'm weak. I don't want to be strong around you, I loved how I felt when you took care of me and protected me and I'm

not ashamed to admit it. You're my hero and I love you and will miss you more than you'll ever know.

Love, Jenna

Mike folded the letter and wiped a hand over his face, squeezing the moisture that burned beneath his eyes with his thumb and forefinger. The only time he had ever felt this heartbroken was when he'd lost his family. Reading Jenna's letter, he was devastated for the second time in his life. She loved him, she was proud of him, and she would wait for him? He felt like sobbing but he held it together. He put the letter in his own back pocket and walked outside to see Rafe. He was on the dock leaning against the railing and Mike walked down to stand beside him.

"You okay, man?" Rafe knew he was anything but.

Mike looked out at the bay; it was another stellar day and there were plenty of boats going by. "How did this happen to me?"

Rafe gave a little laugh. "It just fucking happens, like that." He snapped his fingers. "There's no explanation other than it was meant to be, I guess."

"How could it be meant to be though if I'm fucking leaving? I feel completely torn in half. If I leave I'm doing something that will help a lot of people and potentially further my career, but I'm also giving up on something I may never have again in this lifetime." Mike cleared his throat. "Do you know she actually said she'd wait four years if she had to?" Mike laughed, amazed.

"Mike, I wish I had some good advice. I'd say follow your heart, but I know exactly what your heart is telling you and that would mean giving up a lot. I guess you have to examine what that would mean to you. Do you have any time frame set?"

"I'm headed to Quantico tomorrow for two weeks, but I'll be back before the wedding."

"Why so soon?" Rafe looked at him, curious.

"Daniels didn't say, but it's probably for the best, I'd go crazy with two weeks off just thinking about her and not being able to see her."

"I'm just so sorry this is happening."

"Me too, but listen, man, don't let me bring you down, you've got happy times ahead, you don't need my troubles." Mike slapped him on the shoulder.

"Mike, you and Jenna are close friends, and we all care about what happens." Rafe wished he could help somehow.

"Thanks, but there's nothing anyone can do so there is no use dwelling on it. Gotta move on, right?" Mike stared out at the bay.

Rafe followed his gaze out over the water and didn't know how to answer him.

"Do you think Nicki would mind if I stayed the night?" Mike asked. "I'll clean up and lock up and all that in the morning. I think I might head out on the kayak and just chill here tonight."

"I know she wouldn't mind at all. I'll tell her, don't worry about it."

"I'm sorry Jenna backed out of the wedding because of me," Mike told him.

"Well, that I intend to change if it doesn't bother you." Rafe wasn't about to let that happen.

"I have to see her again, Rafe." Mike ran a hand over his face. He couldn't not see her again. "I need to."

"Well, plan on it." Rafe wasn't going to let it end like this. There had to be something he and Ali could do for them.

"Take her bag with you, okay?" Mike asked somberly. "Her cell, money, and some clothes are in it, oh and tell her I had her rental picked up. It wasn't due back until next week so she should get a credit."

Rafe put a hand on his friend's shoulder. "Something's gonna give, Cap, this isn't right."

Mike descended the rungs of the wooden slats against the dock and got in the kayak tied below. "I have a lot of thinking to do, I guess."

"Call me tomorrow, okay? Let me know what's up."

Mike gave him a salute and paddled off.

PART TWO

CHAPTER FORTY-FIVE

Jenna finished teaching her dance class and chatted with some of the girls before she headed back to Nan's to shower. They were heading to Newport together for a boiled lobster dinner at Justin's. Paige had invited everyone to see Justin's house and Jenna was looking forward to seeing it.

It had been nearly two weeks since she'd returned from Captiva. She'd packed her belongings in Newport and had gone directly to Nan's. She wasn't sure where she wanted to live yet but Nan's was close to the dance studio she'd been teaching at, filling in here and there when she was needed. She'd taken lessons at the same studio from the time she was two until she'd graduated high school and they'd welcomed her, to help teach, with open arms. The dancing was managing to keep her sane and Nan's unwavering support was getting Jenna through too.

Her parents were understandably worried for her. Jenna had reluctantly told them what had gone on in Florida, but she had assured them she wasn't experiencing post-traumatic stress like they'd suggested, she was just heartsick. Nan of course understood and was being extra supportive and caring; Jenna thanked God for her every day.

Besides seeing the renovations Justin had made to his old house, Paige wanted to have a celebration before everyone flew back to Captiva in the next couple of days for Ali and Rafe's wedding. It was Wednesday and they would all be flying out Thursday and Friday. Jenna still wasn't going to the wedding and had opted to watch Justin's puppy instead. Jake was flying in early tonight from New York for the weekend and they were going to stay at Justin's together to dog-sit and frequent their old haunts. Jenna was really looking forward to it; she'd missed her best friend.

By the time Jenna had showered and packed, Nan had returned from a real estate showing and was set to go. When they finally got on the highway, Nan brought up a sore subject.

"I want to talk about Mike."

"Oh Nan, why?" Jenna groaned keeping her eyes on the road. "It hurts to even say his name. I don't want to cry anymore." Jenna had managed to stifle the pain of the whole experience into a dull ache.

"Jenna, sweetheart, our tears cleanse our soul; holding them back squeezes on your heart and makes it difficult to breathe. I want you to breathe and be happy again."

"Nan, I don't know if I can be happy again, not like I was with Mike. I feel betrayed by life, like the worst trick was played on me. How could fate be so cruel?" Jenna had tried to make sense of it day after day and still she grieved.

"You know, Jenna, I don't see anything cruel here," Grace said, turning in her seat and giving her granddaughter a little tough love. "First off, you both have your health and thank God for that! I'm hearing of two people that were lucky enough to fall in love that have been met with a tough obstacle, a challenge for sure, but weaker people face much worse every day. I truly believe that everything that is set in our path is put there for a reason. I know you're feeling disheartened and that it's unfair for anything to get in the way of love but this is clearly a cross for Mike to bear. You were put on his path for a reason, Jenna, and he has to figure out now how he continues on that path."

"But that's not fair!" Jenna shouted in complaint, slamming the steering wheel. "He has to choose between me, a girl he met days ago? Or a career he's been building for eight years? It doesn't make any sense, Nan!"

"It might not make sense now, sweetheart, but in time it will, trust me and have faith." Nan patted her granddaughter's hand in assurance.

Jenna sulked the rest of the drive. She didn't want Mike to have to make a choice, she wanted him to do what made him happy and what he excelled at, otherwise he'd always wonder what could have been and possibly even resent her. Jenna appreciated Nan's wisdom but she knew that getting over Mike was the only option. In the span of four years he'd probably meet someone else anyway; a beautiful woman from some foreign country who he'd no doubt save from a horrible terrorist situation or some other God-awful scenario. His life would be filled with excitement and danger and keeping a simple girl from Boston on his mind in all that time would seem ridiculous in comparison. Jenna knew she was right, he hadn't even bothered to get in touch with her these past two weeks.

They arrived at Justin's an hour or so later and Jenna managed to buck up for her family's sake. She and Nan marveled at the outside of Justin's house when they pulled up and when Paige let them in they were just as in awe of the inside. Justin gave both Jenna and Nan a big hug and led them on a tour of the house with the puppy in tow and they finally settled in the kitchen where everybody seemed to have converged. Matt and Nicki were seated at a big round table with Rafe and Ali and a very attractive girl Jenna had never seen before.

"It's unbelievable," Jenna whispered to Paige, leaning against the large granite counter. "It's everything you've always dreamed about. Hey guys!" she called out in response to Nicki saying hello. Nan had approached the table and was giving everyone a hug and a kiss and accepting a glass of wine.

"I know," Paige said agreeably. "I don't mind getting to visit though." She laughed.

Justin came up beside them, "I don't mind you visiting either." He smiled and kissed Paige on the neck. "How are you, Jen?"

"I'm doing okay Justin, thanks," Jenna smiled. "This place is incredible, that staircase is absolutely gorgeous."

"Thanks, it's Paige's favorite too. What can I get you to drink?"

"I'll have vodka with anything," Jenna said. She was staying over so she looked forward to having a few drinks.

"What time is Jake getting here?" Paige asked.

"He should be here soon; I think he landed at Green an hour ago." Jenna looked forward to staying up late and talking with him like she used to.

"Good, when he gets here, we'll eat." Paige smiled and guided Jenna over to the table after Justin handed her a drink.

Jenna accepted a kiss and a hug from Matt and Rafe and tried not to get emotional when Rafe gave her an extra squeeze. She noted the looks of sympathy from her sister and Ali.

"Jenna, this is Justin's sister, Sara. Sara, this is my cousin and Nicki's sister, Jenna." Paige made the introductions then sat down next to Justin at the island counter.

"It's nice to meet you, Sara," Jenna said to the beautiful dark-haired woman. She looked like Justin minus the tattoos and had the same intense dark eyes.

"You too." Sara smiled. "I've heard a lot about you from Paige."

Jenna returned the smile, happy for Paige that she was getting to know Justin's sister.

"Paige tells me you and Nicki are dancers."

"Yes, we've been dancing since we could walk I think," Jenna laughed.

"She teaches," Nicki said proudly.

Jenna smiled at Nicki and then said to Sara, "To kids mostly, it's no big deal, I enjoy it."

"It sounds fun," Sara said, meaning it.

"What do you do, Sara?" Grace asked, sitting next to her.

"I just received my master's in architecture and am out of work currently," she laughed and shrugged.

Nicki reached for her drink. "I could be too very soon." Things at the *Globe* were tentative at best. She held up her glass in a cheers.

Sara laughed, holding up her own drink. "Should we be toasting unemployment?"

Matt grinned. "I told her anytime she wants to strap on a tool belt, I'll hire her."

"Yeah, but you also said I couldn't wear anything else with it," Nicki grinned.

Matt laughed along with Rafe and Justin. "It's true," he admitted with a shrug.

"Matthew!" Grace smirked in reprimand then suggested, "You should mention Sara to Jason."

"That's a great idea," Ali agreed.

Matt had already been planning on it but for a totally different reason. "It is a good idea, Grace, I'll mention something this weekend," he said, smiling.

"Who's Jason?" Sara asked, curious.

"Our older brother." Ali told her. "He's an architectural engineer. He has his own firm in Boston."

"Oh wow, I'd definitely appreciate a good word." Sara was happy for Justin; this was a great group of people.

"Done." Matt grinned and winked at Ali and Nicki, who rolled their eyes, knowing just what he planned to mention.

Paige caught the exchange and chuckled then watched Sam bolt out of the room.

"Speaking of this weekend," Rafe said and looked at Ali, who nodded.

"I think Jake is here," Paige whispered to Justin, not wanting to interrupt Rafe.

"I'll get it." He winked and got up to answer the front door.

Jenna sat down next to Matt and looked at Rafe, waiting for him to go on as she sipped her drink.

"We're actually all here tonight to talk to you, Jenna."

Jenna turned to Paige and nearly choked on the sip she'd taken from her drink. "Huh?" Talk to her about what? Was this some kind of intervention?

"We want you at the wedding, Jen," Nicki told her.

"Please, Jenna," Ali pleaded. "It would mean so much to us; it won't be the same without you."

"I know it won't be easy," Rafe put in, "but I think it will be good for you." He knew it would be good for her but he wasn't about to elaborate.

Jenna still hadn't said anything and she looked at Nan, who was nodding and smiling, then she looked at Justin's sister, embarrassed. The poor girl was probably as uncomfortable as Jenna.

"She's going; she has no choice; I've already booked us two seats on a ten o'clock Friday morning," Jake announced, entering the kitchen with Justin, and he held his arms out.

Jenna stood up and threw herself into them, crying. "I missed you," she whispered against his cheek.

"Honey, I missed you too." Jake hugged her and took in the small crowd in the kitchen. "Introduce me, for God's sake, you're being so rude."

Jenna laughed wiping her tears and turned from Jake's arms, introducing him to Matt, Rafe, Sara, and Nan. Nicki and Ali got up to hug and kiss him, having met him before at the Bellevue house.

"Paigy." Jake turned to take her in his arms. "Holy crap, Batman!" he whispered in her ear.

She laughed, knowing he was referring to Justin. "You look well, Jake, thank you so much for coming." Paige smiled wide, hugging him.

"Anything for our girl here." Justin smiled down at Jenna.

"I thought *I* invited you here this weekend." Jenna scowled at him and then at everybody else, realizing she'd been tricked.

"No, doll, this has been in the works since Sunday, I've packed my Speedo and my sunscreen and I'm finally getting to go to Nan's house!" He smiled and winked at Nan, who laughed in delight along with the rest of the table.

"Jake, what can I get you?" Justin asked.

Jake looked at Paige and grinned wickedly. "A beer would be great, thanks."

Paige laughed at him. "Sit down, we were just telling Jenna how we want her at the wedding and how it will be good for her to go."

"What about Sam, we're supposed to dog-sit." Jenna sat on Jake's lap, watching Rafe and Matt exchange narrow-eyed looks. She laughed to herself; apparently Nicki and Ali had never mentioned to them that Jake was gay.

Jake took the beer Justin brought to him and thanked him.

"That's actually why I'm here." Sara laughed. "I'm taking Sam home with me."

Jenna looked around the table surprised Justin's sister had been in on it too and now knowing she didn't stand a chance. "I know when I'm outnumbered, guys. I'll be honored to be at the wedding, but this isn't going to be easy." She choked up. "Saying goodbye to him, again, will be the hardest thing I ever do." She turned to Jake and cried into his shoulder. "I'm sorry, I need a minute." She got up and left the kitchen to go outside.

"Let me?" Rafe stood, asking Jake, Nicki, and Paige, who were all making a move to follow Jenna.

They nodded their agreement and Rafe went out back. Jenna was sitting on a double wooden swing in the yard, her head up to the sky. Rafe sat down next to her.

"Hey, are you feeling ambushed?"

"No," Jenna assured him. "I know you all care, I'm feeling foolish, this is your and Ali's wedding and I'm now the center of attention, it's pathetic. I'm so sorry."

"Don't be ridiculous, we know what it's like to be in love, Jenna, we're rooting for you guys."

"What's to root for, Rafe?" Jenna looked into his eyes in defeat. "Unless you have a magic pill that can make four years go by in a week then there's nothing to root for. I'll be a distant memory to him in four years." She shrugged. "Maybe we'll bump into each other down the road at some function like when your first kid is born, and maybe he'll be interested again but maybe he won't. And what am I supposed to do in the meantime? I know it will get easier over time, but I don't want to move on, Rafe. I don't want to meet someone else, I just want him." Jenna knew she sounded pathetic and she was ashamed, especially when this was the last thing she was sure Rafe wanted to be involved in. He was in love and getting married in a matter of days, for God's sake, and she was being such a downer.

Rafe pulled Jenna in against him and kissed the top of her head. He'd only known her for a year but she felt like family already. "Do you trust me, Jenna?"

"Of course," she sniffled. She did.

"Come to the wedding, you won't regret it, I promise."

Jenna nodded. "Okay, I will, and you're probably right, it will probably be better to have some definite closure. I shouldn't have said goodbye in a letter anyway; it was a chicken shit move." Jenna sat up and wiped her eyes. "Thank you. Thank you for not being mad that I had backed out, it was selfish of me."

"Don't even think twice about it, okay?" Rafe stood and held a hand out. "Now let's go eat that feast Justin cooked up."

Jenna laughed. "He's great, isn't he? I'm so happy for Paige."

"He's a great guy, we're happy for her too. I'm glad he can make it to the wedding, it's going to be a blast."

"It is, you're right," Jenna felt better and felt the first twinge of excitement at the thought of seeing Mike again. "Now I wish it were tomorrow." She laughed softly. Even if it was only for one day she'd take whatever time she could have with Mike.

Rafe laughed. "I know someone else who is counting the minutes too." He smiled to himself; Jenna had no idea.

Jenna didn't let his words excite her. She couldn't . "How is he, Rafe?" Not a minute went by that she didn't wonder.

"You'll see for yourself this weekend." Rafe gave her a warm smile.

Jenna smiled from ear to ear and followed Rafe back inside, where Jake was right at home with everybody, making them laugh.

Paige hugged her supportively as she came in. "Jake is regaling us with tales from his brother's restaurant."

Jenna joined right in with the laughter just hearing Jake's contagious laugh. She went to sit by him and picked up her drink. When he was done telling his story and the laughter had died down she stood and raised her glass. "I just want to tell you all how much I love and care about you. I thought about you all when I thought I was going to die on that yacht and I hoped I would have a chance to tell you this. It means so much to me, your friendship and your love and I just hope you know how much I appreciate it."

They all cheered and told her how much they loved her too.

Jenna looked at Sara. "I apologize for the drama tonight, but I'd like to thank you, too, for pitching in with Sam. I love the little guy and I'm always available to babysit." She looked at Paige and Justin and smiled, "But you guys are right, I think going this weekend is the right thing to do, I wouldn't miss it for anything." Jenna then looked to Ali and Rafe. "And I'm sorry again if I put you out for a while there." Ali was shaking her head as if it were nonsense. Jenna smiled thankfully.

"Justin." Jenna turned to face him in the kitchen. "Thank you for all this, I knew when I met you I liked you, and I couldn't be happier that you and Paige found each other."

"I'll drink to that," Grace said and held up her wine glass.

"You sure you don't want two fingers of scotch there, Grace?" Justin teased her and Matt turned to face him.

"How do you know Grace likes scotch?" he asked, grinning.

"She so generously shared some of her private stash with me before I went to Captiva." Justin smiled at Grace.

Paige and Nicki whipped their heads around to Nan and then each other. Paige blushed when Matt cocked a brow at her.

"That's right, I did," Grace said, "but not tonight, Justin." She winked. "I think I'll save my next scotch for the wedding this weekend." She drank from her wine and smiled coyly at Paige and Nicki, who studied her with narrowed knowing eyes.

"All right then, let's eat!" Justin called out and brought a huge platter of steamed lobsters and corn on the cob to the table.

They feasted on the meal and it wasn't until eleven o'clock that night that everyone said their goodbyes and said they'd either see each other at the airport or the wedding. Later that night Paige lay in Justin's arms feeling happy that they had talked Jenna into coming to the wedding again.

"Thanks for having everyone here tonight." It meant so much to her.

"Absolutely." Justin smiled. "I really like all those guys; I'm really looking forward to meeting your brothers too."

"I know, I can't wait for you to meet them. I wish they were coming to the wedding, but you'll meet them when we get back for sure. I'll set something up." Their relationship was moving forward effortlessly but Paige had yet to tell him how she really felt about him, although she suspected he knew.

"Paige?"

"Yeah?" She felt her chest thud at the simple question in his voice.

"When are you going to tell me about the picture?" He ran a hand up and down her arm slowly, smoothing away the goose bumps. They'd been home for nearly two weeks and she still hadn't mentioned it, nor had he.

Paige took a breath. "I don't know, it just seemed too damn weird after the whole thing with the picture of your house." She laughed.

"I saw it over Rafe's shoulder that night when you went to get dressed and I thought, huh, weird, kinda looks like my sign brought to life." He felt her nod. "Then Nicki told me what you'd named it and when you'd named it. Paige. . ." Justin leaned over her. "It's friggin' crazy enough that you named it The Blue Wave, but you also took that picture and named it the same year I named and opened the shop."

Paige hadn't realized that and a chill raced up her spine. She turned in his arms and just looked at him, wide-eyed.

"Yeah," he said in disbelief himself. "You know, my sister and my mother believe in all this kind of stuff, and I always laughed at them and teased them about it, you know. Women are natural romantics about that stuff, I guess, but Jesus, Paige, it's beyond coincidental."

"I know, it's a little spooky."

"That's what I'm saying, and how do you just ignore it?" Justin asked, smoothing back her hair.

"You don't, you have to believe in it," Paige said seriously, realizing that she did. "My grandmother says it all the time, there are signs of fate everywhere. Some are obvious and some are subtle, ours happen to be blatantly obvious." She laughed softly, looking at him and hoped she wasn't being presumptuous.

"So you believe in it?" Justin asked. "fate? the universe bringing two people together?" He half laughed and rolled over onto his back, looking up at the ceiling. He couldn't even believe he was talking this way.

Paige could see Justin was uncomfortable with the subject. "I do." She rolled toward him this time. "How can I not, especially now?"

Justin took a deep breath and held her tight. He spoke softly too. "Believe it or not, I kind of like thinking there's something to it."

Paige felt her heart skip and she dared to look at him.

"Paige, I'm not going to lie to you, I feel like I'm holding lightning in a bottle here." He squeezed her arms and let out a breath. "I'm doing my best to take this slow, I don't want to take it for granted just because it's seems so easy and meant to be, I want us to be together but I want to be able to earn your love and trust."

Paige knew he'd been hurt before and she knew he was afraid of it happening again. She took a deep breath so she could speak without getting emotional. "I want us to be together too, Justin, and I understand your need to go slow, but these past couple of weeks have been incredible," she sighed. "I don't need the signs, Justin, but I'm paying attention to them. I think whatever this is can only get bigger, better, and stronger."

Justin thought so too. He cared about her more than he was willing to admit. It just seemed so crazy that he could have feelings this strong in such a short time.

"So Jake seems like a nice guy, huh?" he asked nonchalantly.

Paige sat up on an elbow and grinned at his speculative tone and abrupt change of subject. She didn't blame him; the topic was rather intense. "Is that a note of jealousy I hear in your voice?"

Justin smirked. "Well, he is a good-looking guy and he did have you in his arms, calling you Paigy."

Paige laughed. "Did I forget to tell you he was gay?"

Justin looked at her in disbelief. "Uh... yes, you definitely left that part out." Justin had thought it a little strange that Jake and Jenna were so close with one another. Jake had in fact been pretty friendly with all the women.

Paige laughed. "I'm sorry, I never even think about it, and for some reason I thought I'd mentioned it to you."

"No, it's fine." Justin laughed. "I'm relieved now, for Mike actually."

"You think he'll be jealous when he sees Jake with Jenna?"

Justin laughed. "I met Mike once and can say the dude would be jealous of *Sam* with Jenna. He's very protective of her, not in a bad way, but you could see how much he loves her when he's with her." Justin knew just how the guy felt.

Paige sighed. "I wish things had turned out differently between them."

"I hear you; I can only imagine how much he's hurting right now." Justin pulled her naked body against his and held her tight, thankful nothing was keeping him from Paige.

CHAPTER FORTY-SIX

Jenna laughed into her pillow reading her text. She and Jake were each in a guest room and had decided to go right to bed when Paige and Justin had but neither one could sleep and they were texting back and forth.

Jake texted.

OMG! How fkg HOT is tattoo man?
Where the hell was he when we went for
ours?? so not right, where else
do u think he has ink?

Jenna laughed and typed.

He is super-hot, and don't be gross!
who would have their c--k tattooed?

Jake raised a brow.

R U kidding? I would, and you can't
even spell out cock? u prudish texter

Jenna felt so good to be laughing again. She responded.

I am not a prude! lol,
ty for taking me to the wedding btw
if u think Justin is hot wait til
u see Mike!
This whole thing is so unfair btw

Jake felt so bad for her. He wanted to cheer her up.

NP the wedding will be fun
I can't wait to see GI Joe.
Life is unfair btw, for example
Matt and Rafe and Justin are straight

Jenna cracked up.

lmao! I knew u'd be checking

them out u slut

Jake chuckled.

Well shit girl, how could i not?

btw, your grannie is smokin'

for an ol' girl

Jenna smiled.

lol, she is, don't u just love her?

Jake looked up, hearing a strange noise.

yes, she's real cool

hey, r there fkg ghosts in this house?

weird noise coming from closet

Jenna laughed and rolled her eyes.

lol, fk if i know, go get the puppy

he'll protect u

Jake laughed, but kept an eye on the closet just the same.

lol, if u hear me screaming like

a woman in the middle of the night

call 911

Jenna grinned.

no, if i hear u hollering like a man

i will. u always scream like a woman!

Jake laughed again.

touche lol

Jenna yawned.

time for sleep i think

Jake rolled over so he wouldn't have to think about the closet.

jen- i ever tell u i believe in

fairy tales?

She smiled.

no, should i be surprised?

He smirked.

fk u lol, not joking- i see a happy ending.

Jenna sighed.

ty jake, i'm praying for one

Jake rolled his eyes.

go ahead I know u can't resist

Jenna laughed, he knew her so well.

i know how much u love

happy endings!

Jake chuckled. It was true.

there u go!

might even have one now

Jenna groaned, disgusted.

eww!!!

goodnight!

Jake laughed out loud.

lmao

you're easy, gdnt

love u J

Jenna smiled texting her last message.

love u too J

Jenna placed her phone by the bed and stared up at the ceiling, wondering where Mike was now. She had heard through Ali that he'd had to leave for Virginia the day after Jenna had left the island and that he'd be away until the wedding, so Jenna never would have had these two weeks with him anyhow. It was a reminder of just how unpredictable his job was going to be.

She wondered if he was thinking about her at all and the too familiar ache she'd managed to suppress crept back into her heart. It would be so wonderful to see him again but it was going to be hell on earth saying goodbye.

CHAPTER FORTY-SEVEN

Mike opened the door to his condo and threw his bag on the couch. He took a beer from the fridge and opened the slider doors to the balcony. He'd had an incredible two weeks and he was physically and mentally exhausted from it. He'd been through a battery of tests both physical and mental and had aced each and every one. He was to report back for duty in one month and he couldn't wait to go back. He'd called Daniels on his ride home from the airport and couldn't thank him enough.

Mike sat back now and looked out at the beach in the distance and he wondered what a condo closer to the sand would cost and maybe something even a little bigger. His pay was about to go up in a major way and he wouldn't mind being closer to the ocean. Maybe he'd make a few phone calls today. He had to pick up his tux and pick up a gift anyway so maybe he could even look at a couple of places while he was out. He finished his beer and smiled for the first time in two weeks.

* * * * *

"I'm not buying that!" Jenna hissed. They were at Victoria's Secret and Jake was holding a bra that looked like it came with its own set of boobs.

"C'mon, you want to fill out that bridesmaid's dress, don't you?"

"I'll fill it out just fine on my own, thank you! I don't want to be spilling out of it; it's already pretty low cut."

"You're going to have this guy for one more weekend, if that, make it so that he won't want to leave—ever!" Jake waggled his brows.

"If it were only that easy." Jenna gave him a smirk. "This one is fine." She held up a simple nude satin bra.

"*Fine* is not sexy!" Jake pointed to another one that at least required real boobs to fill it and Jenna actually liked it.

"That is pretty sexy, huh?" She held the red satin bra in her hands; it was lined with a leopard print and had matching lace bikini panties to go with it.

"Yeah, doll, that'll work, now pay and let's get out of here, I'm starting to like this place." Jake shivered like he had a chill.

Jenna laughed. "Go wait outside, you ass, I'll be out in a minute." She paid for her things and met him out front. "Captain Jack's?"

"Duh."

They had a quick lunch with Paige, who took a short break in the busy bar and then left, making their way up the street to The Blue Wave.

"So they're expecting us?" Jake asked.

"Yeah, I spoke to Justin last night," Jenna assured Jake.

The bells on the door clanged loudly as they stepped inside. Gwen the receptionist saw them enter and smiled hello.

"Hi, we're here to see Justin and Stacy," Jenna informed her.

"Great, I'll tell them you're here."

"I'll have Stacy again," Jake said after Gwen left to announce their arrival. "Justin would just be a tease." He rolled his eyes to Jenna then proceeded to flip through the boards of tattoo designs.

Jenna laughed. "Do you know what you're getting?" Jenna knew just what she wanted. She had done her research on the internet the night before and had found the perfect thing.

"Yes, but let's just surprise each other."

"Okay," she laughed, agreeing, and smiled when Justin appeared.

"So, back for more, huh?" Justin came out and kissed Jenna on the cheek and shook Jake's hand. "Sorry I didn't see you guys before I left this morning, I left early to drop Sam's food off at my sister's house, forgot to give it to her last night."

"No problem, Paige cooked us breakfast and we toured the house for the fifth time before she left for work," Jenna laughed.

"Paige cooked breakfast?" Justin asked, narrowing his eyes.

Jake nodded knowingly. "Don't worry, the fire alarms didn't go off. She did good actually."

Justin chuckled. "Good to hear. So who's going first?"

"Me." Jenna stuck her tongue out at Jake. "Don't get it where we talked about last night." She winked at him and actually saw Jake blush as she left the room with Justin.

* * * * *

Later that night after a nice dinner together, they all went to bed early to be rested for their flights.

Jenna lay in bed and couldn't sleep. She was anxious at the thoughts of seeing Mike again. She knew all the men would be spending the following night celebrating at Tween Waters, drinking and listening to music in the bar, while the women would be together at Nan's having their own fun and preparing for the wedding the next day. Unfortunately, Jenna wouldn't see Mike until Saturday, the day of the wedding. She removed the bandage from her wrist and studied the tattoo Justin had given her. She loved it, it meant a lot to her. At the very least she would have something permanent to remind her of Mike and how proud she was to know him.

* * * * *

They pulled into The Three Sunrises just after noontime and had to park right at the end of the driveway due to all the cars. Paige looked over at Justin. "I'm so glad you could be here with me."

He grinned and leaned over to kiss her. "No place else I'd rather be, Paige." He got out of the car and came around to help Paige with her bags, leaving his bag and his supplies in the car since he would be staying at the resort with the rest of the guys.

"It was really nice of you to bring your equipment; Ali will be so surprised. I can't wait until she sees Rafe with ink."

Matt had called Justin yesterday and asked if Justin would tattoo Rafe before the wedding as a surprise and Justin had said of course. Rafe knew what he wanted and it shouldn't take Justin but an hour, he would head right up to Rafe's cottage to get started after he said hello to everyone and left Paige with the women.

They stepped inside the house and Justin immediately had eight pairs of feminine eyes on him. Paige introduced him to her aunt Jacqueline and to Tracy, Ali's mom. He said hello and greeted Ali, Nicki, and Grace again and he and Paige were both introduced to Rafe's mother and his older sister Marly. Jenna was the only one missing. She and Jake had been on a later flight and all the other guests were up at the resort.

Paige grinned at her aunt Jacqueline as she gave Paige an appraising glance and laughed at Ali's mother, who was blatantly staring at all of Justin's visible tattoos.

"Mom!" Ali led her down the hall and whispered, "Stop staring!"

Paige was laughing as she heard Tracy ask, "Where are you girls finding all these gorgeous men?"

"There's a special catalog we order them from, Trace," Nicki called out and winked at Justin.

"What else do they have in that catalog? I have my own man but I wouldn't mind a little distraction if you know what I mean." Nicki's mom laughed along with Rafe's, who nodded knowingly.

"Ewww, Mom!" Nicki laughed watching Rafe's sister wrinkle her nose too.

Grace just shook her head and smiled, pleased all the women were having fun. This was what it was all about for her, family and friends gathered around and enjoying each other. There was nothing like a wedding.

Justin felt completely uncomfortable and looked at Paige pleadingly.

"Justin just wanted to say hi, but I think we should let him go up to Tweenies to see the rest of the men, what do you think?"

Ali came back down the hall with her mom carrying a pile of dresses.

"Don't leave on our account," Tracy winked.

"Oh my God, I'm telling Dad you are such a flirt, no wonder Matt's the way he is!" Ali jokingly complained.

Nicki laughed along with Nan.

"Oh, I'm just teasing the poor guy." Tracy smiled. "Don't mind me, Justin; I'm on my third glass of wine. It's not every day your only daughter gets married."

Ali walked up to Justin and whispered, "She'll be in bed by five o'clock."

Justin laughed. "Well, you ladies take it easy, and have fun tonight." He waved and walked to the front door with Paige, who followed him outside to the car once again.

"Wow, I felt like one of those strippers who arrive to a bachelorette party," he laughed, causing Paige to crack up.

"Now that would have been something to see," she said, sidling up to him. "Maybe we could have our own private party later."

"Umm, I wish it were later." He kissed her and reluctantly got inside the car just as another car pulled in behind him. It was Jenna and Jake.

"Wow, you guys made good time, huh? We haven't even been here all that long," Paige called out to Jenna's open window as they parked.

Justin got back out of the car to greet them. "Hey, I'm heading up to the resort," he said to Jake, "if you want to hitch a ride."

"Love to! I need a drink." Jake groaned. "Me and turbulence don't mix."

"Who's here?" Jenna asked Paige.

"All the women." Paige laughed. "Tracy seemed to take a liking to Justin."

"Not surprised." Jenna poked Justin in the ribs playfully and Paige snagged her wrist to look at her tattoo.

"It's awesome!" Paige looked at Justin. "You do such good work." She smiled and kissed his cheek. Jenna had kept her bandage on the night before at dinner and it was the first time Paige was seeing the tattoo.

"Thanks, babe." He grinned and winked at Jenna. "You ready, Jake?" he asked, turning to him.

"Yes!" Jake threw his bag in with Justin's and kissed Jenna and Paige goodbye. "Have fun, ladies, I'll see you in a while! Call me if you need me!"

Jenna laughed. "Behave up there."

Jake grinned. "Me? Always."

The girls watched them drive off then went into the house to cheers and shouts that Jenna was there and had completed their gathering. She kissed and hugged everyone, met Rafe's mom and sister, and went to sit with her own mother, who embraced her. Ali was handing out bridesmaid dresses and Nicki and Rafe's sister got busy trying them on. Jenna held hers in her lap while her mother spoke to her.

"How are you holding up?"

"I'm okay, I guess. I'm kind of nervous to see Mike."

"I'm sure you are, but it will be okay. I'll be right here and Daddy too."

Jenna gave her mother a small smile. "Mom, this isn't something you and Dad can help me with but I appreciate it." Her mother didn't seem to be listening to a word she said but grabbed Jenna's wrist instead.

"What the hell is this?" Jacqueline asked, horrified.

Jenna reverted right back to childhood, feeling like she was in big trouble.

"It's clearly a tattoo, Jacqueline." Grace smiled and winked at Jenna.

"I can see that, Grace." Jacqueline shot her mother-in-law a look. "But why, Jenna? You have such beautiful skin."

Jenna looked at Paige and hoped she wasn't offended or taking her mom's comment as a slight toward Justin. "Because I like them and it means something to me. I have another one too," Jenna told her defiantly.

"What?" her mother asked, shocked.

"Paige does too." Jenna grinned, roping her cousin in.

Jacqueline turned on Paige, shaking her head in dismay. "Does your mother know that?"

"I'm sure she will by the day's end, Aunt Jacki. Thanks so much, Jenna!" Paige threw a pillow at Jenna.

Grace smiled at Nicki, who was laughing at her sister and cousin.

"You don't, Allison, do you?" Tracy asked her daughter, wide-eyed.

"Not yet," Ali answered her mom, waggling her brows.

"I guess we're behind the times, Trace," Jenna's mom told her friend, shaking her head.

Rafe's sister Marly ceremoniously lowered the strap on her top and stood to show off the small tattoo above her breast.

"Whoo hoo!" Nicki yelled, laughing, "I love it! Show us yours!" she said to Paige.

Paige blushed but lifted the hem of her shirt then unbuttoned her shorts to reveal her tattoo.

"Oh my!" Ali's mother blushed and took a sip of her wine. "That young man was right down there, huh?"

Jenna cracked up. "Which time?"

All the women hooted and hollered and Paige picked up another pillow and threw it at Jenna again, which caused more raucous laughter and a pillow fight all around. Grace then moved to the center of the room and slowly started to unbutton her own pants, declaring, "That's right where mine is too!" causing Ali's mom to gasp and Jacqueline to spit her wine clear across the room before Nan could button back up and assure everyone she was joking. Rafe's mother stared at Grace with her mouth agape and all the young women, at seeing the moms' reactions were all doubled over in riotous laughter.

"Oh my God, Nan!" Nicki was cracking up and couldn't stop as she saw Jenna with tears in her eyes from laughing so hard watching their mother trying to wipe up the wine she'd spat all over the floor.

Ali took out her camera and was taking pictures, laughing just as hard as the others. Paige sunk to the floor with Jenna and they were in hysterics, holding on to each other.

"I'm going to pee my pants!" Jenna cried.

"Oh my God, Nan!" Paige laughed, "That was so freakin' funny!"

Grace was chuckling and having a ball. "Okay, okay, gather yourselves, ladies, we have reservations tonight at Sweet Melissa's, so let's go have some pool time and massage time then meet back here to get ready."

Jenna sobered up fast from her hysterics and slumped against the couch, looking to Paige for support.

Paige took a deep calming breath, her laughter subsiding. "I don't think he's here yet, Jen, and if he is, I don't think he'll be by the pool. I know the guys had plans of their own."

"Are you sure?"

"Yeah, don't worry."

CHAPTER FORTY-EIGHT

Mike threw his bag on the bed and called over to Rafe's cottage. "Hey, I'm here."

"Great, get your ass over here, Justin's giving me some ink."

"You're shitting me." Mike laughed. "You're getting ink the day before your wedding, are you crazy?"

"Hell yeah, my honeymoon will be that much better for it."

"Yeah, like Ali needs any incentive." Mike knew damn well how the girl felt about his best friend.

"Well, it won't hurt," Rafe laughed. "So you coming or what? Fridge is stocked, there's plenty of food, and after, we've got a boat rented at the marina; we'll do a little fishing in the pass and come back here for dinner."

"Sounds good, I'll be right down."

Mike changed into a bathing suit and T-shirt, grabbed his wallet and sunglasses, and left the room. He had a suite overlooking the marina and he had to walk back toward the front of the resort to get to Rafe's cottage facing the beach. As he headed that way he noticed two very attractive older women walking toward him across the sanded parking lot, both wearing wide-brimmed sun hats, one older than the other but both pretty classy looking. Mike smiled politely as he walked by.

"Excuse me, young man." Grace stopped and turned to the man passing. She put a gentle hand on Jacqueline's arm to slow her.

Jacqueline stopped alongside Grace and studied the imposing young man Grace spoke to.

"Are you Michael by chance?" Grace asked him, removing her hat.

Nobody but his mom had ever called him Michael and Mike smiled warmly hearing her say it and at the older woman's nice smile. "Yes, I am, Mike Caplan. Hi." He cocked his head. Should he know her?

"I'm Jenna's grandmother, dear, and this is her mother, Jacqueline."

Mike swallowed nervously, feeling his stomach clench. Holy shit. He felt like he was sixteen all of a sudden and his palms started to sweat. "Hi!" he said enthusiastically and took his sunglasses off to greet them properly. "It's really nice to meet you both." He shaded his eyes from the afternoon sun and glanced around wondering if Jenna was close by. He was disappointed not to see her and then momentarily shocked as Jenna's mother removed her hat and came forward to embrace him. Mike at once got choked up, not remembering the last motherly hug he'd had, and he looked at Jenna's grandmother over Jenna's mom's shoulder, embarrassed. She just looked on, smiling. She reminded him of an old movie star.

Mike's arms automatically came around Jenna's mom affectionately and it felt surprisingly familiar. He'd seen when she'd taken her hat off that she was an older version of Jenna. She was a very beautiful woman and Mike felt his heart ache with longing for her daughter.

"Thank you." Jacqueline looked up to him with tears in her eyes. He was tall, handsome and muscular and Jacqueline could see by looking in his expressive blue eyes why Jenna was enamored with him. "You saved my daughter's life."

Mike looked down at the ground as she stepped back, her sincerity touching him. He hadn't realized the emotional brink he'd been on until she'd hugged him so comfortably and looked at him so endearingly. Shit.

"There's no need to thank me." He cleared his throat. "I'd do it all over again in a heartbeat." He looked up to see Jenna's grandmother smiling at him. "I've heard a lot about you both."

"And we you." Grace smiled, but she felt for him; she could see the pain in his eyes. "She's here, you know."

Mike nodded. Rafe had told him she would be coming to the wedding and Mike had thanked God she'd changed her mind. He was anxious to see her. "How is she?"

"Anxious about seeing you," Jacqueline replied with a hesitant smile.

Mike nodded again then gave her his own hesitant smile. "I am too." He took a deep breath and met Jenna's mother's eyes. "I'm in love with your daughter," he told her determinedly, "just so you know." It just seemed like the right thing to say and he felt good having it out there.

Jacqueline smiled wide, wiping her tears. As if she would oppose! She thought she loved him already.

Grace took one of Mike's large hands in her small one. "It's all going to work out, isn't it, Mike?" She asked in a knowing way.

Mike tilted his head and grinned like a fool. "How do you know?"

Grace chuckled. "How can it not?"

Mike laughed and put his sunglasses back on, hiding his moist eyes and shaking his head with a slight grin and not saying a word on the subject.

Grace laughed happily. "Are you on your way to join the boys?"

"Yes ma'am, I guess they're all at Rafe's cottage."

"Well then we won't keep you, we're off to get a massage before dinner tonight. You have fun and we'll look forward to seeing you tomorrow."

Mike hesitated then kissed them both on the cheek, telling them how happy he was to have met them. "I'll look forward to it and I hope you both save me a dance."

Jacqueline grinned, charmed by him. "Count on it!"

Mike turned and kept walking, feeling a lightness in his heart he hadn't felt in a while. Jenna had a great family and he felt honored to be accepted by them; now he just needed to see her.

He arrived at the cottage, knocked on the door, and was greeted by Rafe's younger brother Jake. "Hey man!" They clasped hands and bumped shoulders. "Good to see you, how's Gotham treating you?"

"I'm loving it, man, got my own place in the village. It's cool. Next time you're out there come visit."

"Will do." Mike slapped him on the shoulder and moved into the room. Justin was at the small kitchen table with his equipment set up and Rafe's shoulder under his needle.

"Oh man, what the fuck?" Mike laughed. "Are you in pain?" He took the beer and the hand clasp Matt offered and took a long drink. He was in a great mood now.

"Nah, I don't feel a thing." Rafe grimaced and rolled his eyes.

Mike laughed. "Justin, do me a favor and bear down a little harder, I don't think that blue is showing up all too well." He winked at Matt.

"Leave the man alone, he knows what he's doing," Rafe said through clenched teeth.

"You up next, Mike?" Justin grinned, pausing the needle.

Mike looked at him. "I don't know, I wasn't expecting this." He looked around, taking in the small cottage. The kitchen counter was filled with platters of food; sandwiches, fruits, cheese and crackers, and sweets too. Mike knew the fridge would be stocked with plenty of beer as well. He helped himself to a sandwich.

"C'mon," Matt coaxed. "I'm not doing it till I get back to Boston, Justin's gonna design something special for me," he told him, "and Jay's gonna pass so you should get something, the dude does incredible work." Matt nodded to Justin, who grinned appreciatively.

"You got me thinking about it," Mike replied, swallowing a mouthful of sandwich. "Where is that bastard brother of yours anyway?" Mike laughed. "I've got a bone to pick with him."

Matt grinned. "He's on the porch with Jake."

Mike looked at Rafe's brother Jake and arched a brow at Matt.

"Another Jake," Matt told him, smiling, and reached for his second sandwich.

Mike nodded, comprehending, and went out to the small attached porch to say hi to Ali's and Matt's older brother Jason.

"Guys, check it out." Justin winked and cocked his head toward the small screened porch.

"Hey man!" Jason stood up and shook Mike's hand as he came out on the porch, happy to see him again. "I thought I heard your voice. Last time I saw you. . ."

"Yeah, don't remind me," Mike said, grinning, and shaking Jason's hand warmly. "I still can't look at a bottle of tequila the same way thanks to you." Mike smiled taking in the Red Sox T-shirt and ball cap, pretty much the same thing Jason had been wearing when Mike first met him.

"That was bad, wasn't it?" Jason groaned with laughter. "What the hell were we thinking?"

"Well, I know what I was thinking but I'm pretty sure I passed out before I could do anything about it." Mike laughed. "How did you end up making out?"

"Let's just say that I have a new affinity for the ballet." Jason grinned and bounced his brows.

"Nice!" Mike chuckled and looked at the guy sitting next to Jason. He looked like a male model, for Christ's sake.

Jason looked between the two men. "I'm sorry, Mike, have you met Jake Larson? He's a friend of Jenna Thompson; you know Nicki's younger sister? They just arrived a couple of hours ago, right?" Jay turned to Jake.

Jake nodded in affirmation, amused at the big guy giving him the once-over. Jake watched as his eyes narrowed and he smiled inwardly as the dude's already wide shoulders become wider. Had he just puffed out his chest at the mere mention of Jenna's name? Umm, umm, umm, Jenna hadn't been kidding! GI Joe brought to life. Hello!

"Nice to meet you, Mike."

Mike immediately felt his back go up. Did Jenna actually bring a date? What the fuck! "Yeah, you too," he replied. The dude was almost as tall as him but lanky. He looked like some Hollywood actor. His jet black hair was short and slicked back and his dark tan showed off kind green eyes. Mike pictured Jenna on his arm and felt jealous immediately.

"Speaking of Jenna, I'm going to go check on her and all the rest of the girls, they're by the pool and I told them I'd stop by for a drink." Jake had actually just been waiting on Mike's arrival to check him out and hot damn, he was glad he'd waited!

"Hey, better you than us," Jason laughed. "We're afraid to get yelled at."

"That's okay," Jake laughed, "I'm neutral; I can be in both camps." Jake winked and laughed at Mike's puzzled look then said goodbye to the guys in the front room as he left.

"Something wrong?" Jason looked inquisitively at Mike. He seemed pissed off all of a sudden.

"What's his deal?" Mike asked, fuming inside. Who the fuck was he and why did he need to check on Jenna?

Jason looked at Mike oddly. "I don't know, I just met him, seems like an okay guy." Jason shrugged wondering why Mike seemed agitated. "Let's go see how Rafe's doin'."

Mike followed Jason back into the room and when Rafe saw Mike's face he cracked up laughing. He nudged Justin with his leg.

"You were right; I should have seen that coming." Rafe continued to laugh and Justin gave Mike a sidelong glance biting back his own grin. The man didn't look happy.

Mike narrowed his eyes and gave Rafe a head nod. "She brought a date?" His good mood had turned dark thinking of the movie star with Jenna. Rafe conveniently forgot to mention him.

Jason looked at Matt who was grinning along with Rafe and Justin. Rafe's brother Jake looked just as confused as Jason.

"What's wrong, Cap? You seemed happy when you went out on the porch, now you don't seem so happy." Rafe goaded him then gave him a break. "He's just her friend Cap, her *gay* friend. You can, relax." Rafe grinned at Mike.

Mike let out a breath he didn't know he'd been holding and swore. Right! Jake was the texter with the New York number. "Jesus, McDonough! You could have warned me! I'm standing here hating the poor bastard and wishing him all kinds of harm." Mike laughed along with everybody else. "Thanks for the heads up, assholes."

"I think I'm missing a part to this story," Jason said, confused but was laughing just the same.

"Yeah, what's going on?" Rafe's brother asked.

"Our good friend Mike here is in love," Rafe told the room.

"Okaay." Jason droned, "that's. . . great but. . ."

"With Jenna." Matt smiled at Jason.

Jason looked at Matt. "Nicki's sister?" he asked, surprised. Jason had heard from Rafe about the shit that went down a couple of weeks ago and now it made sense. Matt nodded and Jason laughed harder, now understanding Mike's change in mood; he'd just been jealous of Jake.

Justin just grinned while he finished up with Rafe. "I wasn't too fond of him either when I first met him and he came into my house hugging and kissing Paige right in front of me," He laughed finally able to stand up and shake Mike's hand and give him a slap to the shoulder.

"You all could have warned me. I almost gave him my best perp glare. If he had stayed any longer I would have started an interrogation." Mike grinned and took a swill of his beer, finishing it. He sat down where Rafe had sat and pulled off his shirt, having made up his mind.

"Jesus, Cap," Rafe said, glancing at him. "What were you in PT the whole two weeks?" he asked, staring at his now leaner, more muscular friend.

Mike laughed. "Basically. You know we have to compete with the marines down there, so yeah it was intense."

"You know what you want to do?" Justin raised a brow sitting back down at the table across from Mike. Mike was definitely not someone he would want to fuck with.

"Yeah, actually, something I've wanted for a while just never got around to it." Mike pointed to his chest and drew a circle with his finger explaining to Justin what he wanted.

Justin felt the hair on the back of his neck stand up and he drank from his beer to cover his surprise. What the fuck.

"Couple of the guys had them at base," Mike told Rafe, referring to Quantico. It was a trademark tattoo for a sniper and Mike had always liked it. "That should be your next one," he suggested. Rafe had always scored nearly as high as Mike when they competed on the range.

"Yeah, maybe." Rafe said, peeking beneath his bandage.

Justin laughed. "Why do I know the moms at this wedding are going to hate me? Do you think you can hide the ink until after the wedding?"

They all laughed.

"Dad will probably want one," Matt laughed, addressing Jason and Rafe.

Rafe grinned. He liked to be included in their family banter. "Well, I know my dad will think it's cool," he told Justin.

"He'll probably choke up," Jake told his older brother. Rafe had had Justin tattoo his father's retired NYPD badge and number on his right arm.

Rafe laughed, nodding in agreement.

Justin used the tools he had to make an exact circle, finished drawing the stencil, then placed the paper over the spot on Mike's chest where he wanted it and rubbed it on his skin.

"Nice." Mike nodded, looking in the small mirror Justin offered.

"You're gonna have to lie down for this," Justin told him, indicating the couch.

"That's it for me," Jason joked.

"Me too," Matt chuckled." I say we crash the girls' pool party."

"Go ahead, we'll only be like a half hour," Justin told them, preparing his equipment for Mike. The tattoo was more or less an outline without any color so he knew it wouldn't take him long. "We'll meet you at the boat."

Rafe looked at Mike. "You okay with that?"

"Yeah, of course." Mike wasn't ready to see Jenna yet. He wanted her alone not in a crowd of people.

Everyone left and Justin got right to work.

"So a lot of snipers have this, huh?" Justin had only ever done one before oddly enough, and that was just yesterday.

"Yeah, it's pretty common." Mike looked down at the stencil of the target he was having tattooed over his heart with the letter J placed in the crosshairs

"Did you tell anyone you were having this done?"

Mike folded his arms behind his head on the couch and looked up at Justin as he worked tracing over the stencil with his needle. "No, I never even thought about it until these past two weeks when I was with all the guys, why?" Weird question, Mike thought. He flinched at the pain; he had no fat on him to buffer it.

"Just wondered," Justin said. "You know sometimes people talk about what they're going to get for a while before they actually do it." Justin wondered if Jenna had known Mike wanted this.

"No," Mike half laughed. "Just kind of decided on the fly a few minutes ago. It felt right, especially with everything that's going on in my life."

Justin felt that weird sensation again. Man, what had Paige done to him? Now he was reading into everything, but even he had to admit this was no coincidence. "So how is everything going, if you don't mind me asking?"

Mike looked at Justin and grinned. He told him his latest news and Justin couldn't believe the turn of events.

Not long after he started, Justin had finished the tattoo, all but the letter. "You know before I finish, my dad always told me to never ink a woman's name on my body unless I intended to marry her." Justin held up his hands. "I'm not trying to talk you out of anything; I'm just reminding you that this is permanent." Justin gave Mike a knowing grin and held out his own arm.

"Put it smack dab in the middle, my friend." Mike grinned back.

Justin laughed, knowing Mike was going to say that.

CHAPTER FORTY-NINE

The women were still laughing from Jake's comment when he joined them all at the pool.

"You could have warned me before I got to the cottage that I'd be walking onto the set of *Top Gun*!" Jake had fanned himself with a magazine and sat down between Ali and Jenna on a lounge. They had all shrieked with laughter and then when Rafe and all the guys but Mike and Justin had arrived to the pool, Jake had turned to Ali and told her he would be her wing man anytime. He was making them all laugh and Jenna was grateful for his presence.

Rafe greeted his mom and everybody else's with hugs and posed for a picture with his brother Jake and sister Marly. He told Marly he was looking forward to seeing her husband the next day at the wedding and was sorry he wasn't flying in until later, they would miss him fishing. Paige was capturing all she could for Ali and Rafe's photo album.

Jenna looked around, her stomach in knots, and Paige asked the unspoken question for her. "Where's Justin and Mike?"

Rafe sat down next to Ali on a lounge chair and smiled after kissing her hello. "They're meeting us at the boat in a half hour, Mike's getting some ink."

Paige loved how everyone had accepted Justin; she'd known they would. She continued to mill around their large group and snap some more pictures.

Jenna felt a pang of excitement at the mere mention of Mike's name and pictured Justin tattooing him. She wondered what he was getting and hoped to God Justin didn't tell Mike that he'd given her another one just yesterday. She'd be so embarrassed if he knew what she'd chosen.

Matt came over with some beers and a waitress, mugging for Paige. "I don't know what all you women are drinking, so give this nice lady your order." He distributed the beers and smiled at Paige. "No worries, your man is okay, and so is yours." He winked at Jenna then took a running leap into the pool, splashing them all.

A collective "Ugh!" ran through their crowd, who were now wet from the splash and Matt came up grinning. Paige made sure to capture it.

Jenna smirked at Matt's comment. *Her man?* She wished, but she wasn't about to correct him or sulk, they were all here to be happy and celebrate and she was determined to be part of it.

"Mom is toast, huh?" Matt asked Ali, coming over to the edge of the pool and draping his arms over the side. Nicki sat down on the pool deck next to him and handed him his beer. Ali laughed as she watched Jason leading their mother away. He waved and motioned behind their mom's back, raising his hand with an invisible drink and tilting his head back to take an invisible sip. They all laughed.

"Dad's gonna be pissed." Ali chuckled.

"No, Dad's gonna be happy." Matt grinned taking a drink.

"Eww!" Ali shook her head. "Matt!"

Everyone laughed.

The waitress brought more drinks and mostly everyone went in the pool except for Rafe, and Ali finally got suspicious after trying so hard to get him in.

"Something's up." Ali frowned and got out of the pool to go over to Rafe's lounge. If Justin was giving Mike a tattoo then she thought she had a pretty good idea of what Rafe was hiding. "Can I have your T-shirt, babe? I'm chilly." It was close to ninety degrees and not like Rafe to not be in the pool.

Rafe snuck a glance at Matt. "There's a towel right on your chair." Rafe reached over and handed her the towel then turned at Paige's laughter.

"You are so busted, just take it off, Rafe." Paige grinned.

"Yes, we'd love to see." Jake Larson smiled, twirling the straw around his frozen drink. He winked at a laughing Jenna and laughed at the playful scowl Rafe gave him.

"Oh my God!" Ali lifted Rafe's shirt sleeve and peeked under his bandage. "Check please!" she yelled out jokingly and laughed as Rafe pulled her onto his lap. "I can't believe it, it's awesome!" She kissed him seductively, showing him how much she liked it.

"My mom is looking," he teased her.

Ali blushed sneaking a glance her way. "Oops!"

"Let me see it," Nicki smirked, "I don't believe you actually got one!" She admired Rafe's tattoo and raised her brows to Ali, grinning.

"When we get back I'm getting an even bigger one," Matt told Nicki and winked, laughing when she rolled her eyes. "What? I am!" He pouted.

When Justin showed up forty minutes later by himself, Jenna was crushed and excused herself promptly to go back to Nan's. She was hurt that Mike hadn't made a point to see her; it was a clear statement and she got it. Not wanting anyone to see how crushed she was, and not wanting to bring anyone down, she left having made the excuse that she wanted to go for a run before dinner. When she got back to Nan's house she actually did go for a run. She ran five miles before she came back and found everyone taking turns in the shower

Luckily not all of them were at the house; Ali's mom was staying at Tweenies in a room with her dad and would meet them at The Three Sunrises before dinner, and Jake had gone fishing with the guys, which made Jenna smile just picturing it. He was probably in his glory.

She poured herself a tall glass of tap water and opened the freezer for some ice and gasped when she saw all the tubs of pineapple sherbet stacked inside with bows wrapped around them. When could he have done this? She turned at the sound of Nan's voice.

"That was here when we arrived; he must have brought it two weeks ago, the day you left."

Jenna had tears in her eyes. "What I am I supposed to do, Nan?" Jenna cried, taking out a tub.

"I think he intended for you to eat it." Nan smiled.

"Nan!" Jenna looked at her shocked. "How can you joke?" But Jenna did grab a spoon, uncovered the container, and dipped in for a healthy spoonful. She felt her tears spill as she savored the flavor on her tongue, remembering all too well when Mike had bought it for her the first time.

Nan just smiled. "Go get ready for dinner, sweetheart."

"Get ready for dinner? That's it? No comforting words of wisdom?" Jenna asked, dumbfounded, with her mouthful of sherbet, watching Nan walk away to her room. Why was Nan being so nonchalant about this? She was probably sick of Jenna sulking, that's why. Jenna put the container away and sulked back to the room she was sharing with Paige, then she got in the shower. Paige wasn't around and Jenna assumed she was in with Ali and Nicki getting ready so Jenna had the room to herself. She let her tears fall and sobbed freely under the spray. Her wrist stung from the fresh tattoo and she welcomed the pain as she looked at it. It reminded her of who Mike was and why he couldn't be hers, but it also reminded her that she'd had him at all and that was what she would hold onto.

* * * * *

Mike stepped out of the shower and dried himself off. He flinched at the sting of the tattoo and put some ointment on it then covered it with a bandage, knowing it would bleed through to his shirt if he didn't. He got dressed and was still laughing to himself thinking about the fishing trip. Rafe's dad, Matt's dad, and Jenna's dad had made it back from golfing and had joined them on the boat. It had been rather crowded with ten guys on board and three coolers, but they had managed to all fit.

The actual fishing had been pretty tight though and had created a lot of chaos when Rafe, Matt's dad, and Jenna's friend Jake had all had something on their lines. Rafe and Jake had reeled theirs in to much applause and ribbing at the size of their small fish, but Matt's dad had had some trouble getting his off. When they had all gone over to inspect the fish he'd caught, dangling off the line, a friggin' huge dolphin had risen up beside the boat and swallowed the fish whole, right off the hook, scaring the shit out of all of them. Matt's dad had nearly had a heart attack thinking it was a shark and Mike laughed out loud now as he put on his shoes, remembering the high-pitched womanly scream Matt's dad had let out as he pulled his hand off the rod with lightning speed. They had all had tears running down their faces from laughing so hard at that scream.

When the dads had all first pulled up at the marina, Mike had been admittedly nervous to meet Jenna's father but he had come right up to Mike and shook his hand, thanking him for all he'd done for Jenna, and once on the boat he'd asked Mike all about his career with the FBI. They'd had a rather intimate chat on the way up to the pass and Mike had walked away pleased to have met him and feeling pretty welcome when the opposite could well have occurred. Mike was having such a great time with Rafe and his family and friends and it really felt good to be a part of it all. There was only one person that was going to make it even better and he couldn't wait until the next day to see her.

Dinner, when they returned from fishing and got presentable, was at the resort and lots of funny stories were exchanged and jokes made at Rafe's expense. The only man missing was Jenna's friend Jake, who had opted to dine with the ladies, and Mike couldn't help feeling a little jealous that Jake would be seeing and talking with Jenna all night. Mike did feel a lot more comfortable however having gotten to know Jake better on the boat. He was a funny shit and he really cared about Jenna. He had been respectful of Mike and not let on if he knew anything about their relationship and where it stood and Mike had given him credit for not prying. Mike did, however, ask about her before Jake left the marina.

"I've never seen her like this before." Jake had been honest.

"Like what?" Mike had asked almost afraid of the answer.

"In love, destroyed, scared, and unsure." Jake had looked into Mike's eyes searching for answers.

Mike had nodded, hurting to his core at Jake's description of Jenna. "I'm going to fix that," he assured him.

Jake had grinned. "Can I ask how?"

Mike had shaken his head. "No." He'd laughed at the pout Jake had given him and told him he'd see him at the wedding.

They were in the Crow's Nest now and it was getting late. Mike had had his fill and decided to call it a night. The rest of the men all sat glued to the TV watching the Yankees and the Sox. Mike laughed at the ribbing Rafe was taking from his brother and father now that he was a Boston boy.

"How 'bout you, Cap?" Rafe's dad called out from his seat at the bar. "Who do you like? Don't tell me you like the Marlins!"

Ali's dad snorted. "Are they even a real team?"

Mike laughed when Jenna's dad winked at him. "Oh no, you're not dragging me into this," Mike told them. He was actually a Red Sox fan through and through but he wasn't about to get into it with a Yankees fan. He threw some money on the bar and all three dads shoved it back at him. He shook his head laughing, and said goodnight to everyone, thanking them.

"Get some rest, son; we'll see you when the sun shines." Jenna's dad gave him a friendly slap to the back saying goodnight and Rafe walked Mike out front.

"Today was a fucking blast," Rafe said.

"Yeah, it was." They doubled over in laughter again making fun of Matt's dad screaming on the boat and when they'd finally caught their breath Mike put a hand on Rafe's shoulder. "I'm so proud of you, man, and I'm happy for you, Ali is so great and she's gorgeous and you two are great together." Mike sighed. "It seems like just yesterday we were right here, doesn't it?"

Rafe grinned. "Yeah, it does. Ali still feels bad about the night you spent in the beach chair." Rafe laughed picturing it then became serious. "And thanks for saying that, Cap, I've never been so happy."

Mike rubbed his back, grimacing, pretending he was still sore from the all-nighter he'd had outside of Ali and Nicki's cottage the previous summer. "I know you're happy, Rafe; you're like a little kid at Christmas every time you're around her, man." He chuckled.

"It's a good feeling, isn't it?" Rafe looked at him, knowing full well Mike now knew the feeling too.

Mike laughed. "Yeah, man, it is."

"Tomorrow will be here before you know it." Rafe smiled.

Mike looked at his watch and cocked a brow. "It's here now."

"Well, there you go." Rafe grinned. "Go get some beauty sleep, Cap, we gots to get our dancin' shoes on soon."

"Can't believe you're making me wear a tux in ninety-degree heat." Mike shook his head, giving him shit.

"C'mon, the ladies love it." Rafe nodded.

"Let's hope." Mike smiled and shook his friend's hand saying goodnight. When he was halfway to his room he turned back around, knowing he wouldn't be able to fall asleep just yet. He walked back toward the restaurant and crossed the road instead stepping onto the beach. Once there he lay back on one of the resort's wooden lounges to stare up at the stars hanging low in the clear night sky and thought about his future and the major turn of events that would now shape it.

* * * * *

Jenna stood in the parking lot of Sweet Melissa's and laughed with Ali and Marly. Rafe's sister was a hot shit and had kept them laughing with stories of her kids and stories of her and Rafe when they were little. Jake had been his hysterical self and had managed to get a phone number from one of the handsome waiters.

"What?" he had asked. "Can't a guy try and get laid on vacation?"

The moms and Nan had all cracked up and the younger women had been mortified that he'd said that in front of Nan and the moms.

"Okay, who's driving me home?" Jenna asked, ready to go back. The rest of them were talking about going to the Jac, and she had no interest in going to the nearby bar. "Just go to the Crow's Nest, you'll be nice and close to home," she tried to sway them.

"We can't," Ali complained, just a little buzzed. "The guys will be in there and it's after midnight. It's bad luck for the bride and the groom to see each other on their wedding day."

Jenna rolled her eyes. "Okay, okay, but someone has to take me back."

"I will, honey, I need to get back to your father anyway." Jacqueline told her.

"I thought you were staying with us," Nicki asked their mom.

"Well your dad has a nice little cottage; I don't want to see it go to waste."

"Girls, your mom wants to get laid, stop grilling her," Jake teased and he and Jacqueline cracked up at Jenna and Nicki's gaping mouths and onslaught of disgusted groans.

"Oh my God!" Nicki hit Jake on the arm.

"You are so gross." Jenna shook her head at him.

Jake waved and walked away laughing as he jumped in the car with everyone going to the Jacaranda.

Jenna was quiet when her mom pulled into Tween Waters a little while later. It was late and there weren't many people around. She could see the bar was still open and she wondered who was inside, specifically if Mike was still inside.

"Nan and I met Mike this afternoon." Jacqueline told her daughter cautiously.

Jenna stared at her mom in disbelief. "And you're just telling me now?

Where?" Her heart started racing. Jeez, Nan hadn't mentioned it either!

"I didn't want to make you sad earlier." Her mom smiled sympathetically. "He's wonderful, Jenna."

Jenna stared out the windshield and at the back of someone's cottage; she wondered where Mike was staying. "I know he is." Her heart was heavy and she was so tired of feeling sad, too tired to even ask what he'd said or done, it would hurt too much to hear about their conversation.

"You want to take the car back?" her mom asked, placing a hand over her daughter's.

"No really, I just want to walk home on the beach." It was why she hadn't had her mom drop her at the house.

"Okay, sweetie; be careful." Jacqueline kissed and hugged her daughter goodnight and got out of the car.

Jenna left the car too and took her heeled sandals off to walk across the parking lot. The moon above was nearly full and the stars, suspended low, shone like crystals in the sky. A lone car stopped for her to cross the road and when she reached the sand, she walked straight down to the softly lapping tide line, grateful for the solitude.

She just stood there for a minute staring out at the moon's reflection. It glistened over the darkness of the water making the surface glitter and sparkle and she thought how she'd love to dive right in and swim right through it. She wanted to submerge herself under the sparkles and drift out to sea; be swept away somewhere where she couldn't cry or hurt anymore. And she'd go for it, too, if she weren't so afraid of what might come up and bite her on the ass. She turned instead and started walking slowly toward Nan's, letting her bare toes sink into the coolness of the wet sand as she walked. She looked forward to climbing into bed; she just wanted the night to end and the next day to begin so she'd be that much closer to seeing Mike.

CHAPTER FIFTY

Mike sighed and sat up, he'd lain on the uncomfortable wooden slats of the lounge long enough; it was time for bed. He stood in the sand and stretched and as he was walking toward the road a flash of white caught the corner of his eye. Mike saw a woman walking alone down the beach and his heart leapt into his throat as he recognized her form right away. The sure sway of her hips and the dark silky hair that hung down her back let him know it was Jenna and he moved quickly, instinctively, his heart pounding. He slowed as he got closer. Her shoes dangled from the fingers of her hands and he could just make out the silhouette of her body beneath the light-colored sundress she wore. His heart expanded in his chest and his body responded just looking at her.

Jenna's heart was thumping double time. She sensed someone coming up behind her and she gripped her heels tightly keeping one in each hand. She would use them to gouge an eye if she had to. Perhaps because of what she'd been through she was a little on edge but she had good reason and wasn't about to be a victim again, she wouldn't go down without a fight. With her vicious "three and a half inch heel" plan of attack in check, she stopped suddenly in the sand and whirled around, her shoes at the ready. Jenna froze in place at the sight of Mike, who was a mere five feet from her and closing. He slowed to a stop, one half of his mouth turned up.

"Hey there, Jane," Mike greeted her quietly with his hands raised in submission, amused but not surprised that she'd been about to attack him and he was struck, right down to his weakened knees, by how beautiful she looked. Her bruises had heeled and had disappeared and he was reminded of the very first time he'd met her.

Jenna tried and failed to swallow the baseball-sized lump that had instantly risen from her chest to her throat. "Hi there, Joe." It came out half whisper, half whimper. She was not going to be able to hold it together. He looked devastatingly handsome in the moonlight. His long-sleeved white shirt was cuffed casually at the sleeves revealing lean muscular forearms and it hung loose over worn comfortable jeans that sheathed powerful legs she remembered all too well. Birds of flight were flapping their wings inside her belly with nowhere to go. His hair was a little shorter she noticed, his scruff a little scruffier, and his eyes a little brighter against a deeper tan she imagined he'd received from being out on the boat earlier that day.

He'd moved closer to her now, looking down upon her and smiling a sad sort of smile that coaxed the first crocodile tear from Jenna. It fell from her face but she did nothing to disguise it. She lowered her weapons and stood frozen, staring up at him, drinking him in with her eyes, the only movement coming from her heart pounding inside of her chest. His thumb was on her cheek wiping the moisture away and at his ever so gentle touch, more gargantuan tears inevitably fell and kept falling, and then she found herself enveloped in his big strong arms, and she was sobbing and dropping her sandals on the sand so she could hold him tight. Jenna was unable to speak; only great big sobs escaped her. It wasn't fair, it wasn't fair!

"Ssh," Mike whispered against her hair, his heart simply aching for her. "Everything's okay now."

She didn't hear anything but the beating of his heart against her cheek as her hands roamed over his back to feel every muscle she had memorized before, they were even harder if that were possible and then she remembered what he'd been doing the last two weeks.

Mike felt Jenna's hands exploring him and he heated instantly to her touch. God, he'd missed her something fierce. He used his hand to guide her chin up and he bent to kiss her, softly and slowly, tasting her lips and then parting them with his tongue. He felt her small body mold its way against his and he held her even tighter and applied more pressure to his kisses. He was so damn desperate for her but he would have to wait, there were important things that needed to be said. He pulled back to look at her. "Oh Jenna baby, I missed you." Mike sighed and kissed the top of her head, inhaling the flowery scent of her hair.

Jenna still couldn't speak and she felt her hands and body shaking. She didn't know if it was adrenaline or nerves or what but she couldn't stop them.

Mike looked down at Jenna realizing just how upset she truly was. The front of his shirt was soaked from her tears and he put an arm around her guiding her. "C'mere." He led her up to the dry sand and pulled her down to sit next to him. His arm went around her shoulders and he rubbed his hand over the bare skin of her arm. He felt her head rest against his chest and he sighed contently. This was all he needed forever. "I love you, you know that, right?"

Jenna nodded, she did know, she felt it right to her soul. "I love you too," she said softly, feeling her heart shattering inside her chest. This was worse than she'd imagined it would be. It was so unfair and her shoulders began to shake again with her sobs.

Mike needed to talk to her and quickly or he was going to lose it too; she was breaking his heart. "Jenna, you know where I was these past two weeks, right?"

She nodded against him, her shoulders still shaking; her breathing shallow bursts as she tried to calm herself.

"When I got down to Virginia I was summoned to the Unit chief's office and he had some interesting things to say to me. He told me out of all the recruits for HRT I finished at the very top for marksmanship. I didn't make one mistake, Jenna; I was precise on every mark."

"That's amazing, Mike," she managed to get out and dared to look up at him. She felt anything but amazing but tried to be happy for him.

"The amazing part, Jenna, is that the Unit Chief now wants me at Quantico as an instructor one weekend a month."

He seemed quite happy about that so Jenna conjured up a smile through her tears and racking sobs.

"No going away," Mike continued, shaking his head, meeting her tear-filled eyes and trying to make her understand. "No training twenty-four seven. Just one weekend a month, the rest of the time I'm working in Miami like always."

Jenna stared into Mike's eyes, trying to register what he was saying. "So you won't be. . ." She took a breath through her sobs. "g. . g. . going away for four years?"

Mike smiled, his heart breaking at hearing her cry, he loved her so damn much. "No, just one weekend a month in Virginia. Have you ever been to Virginia?" he asked, wiping her tears.

Jenna shook her head, confused and afraid to feel hope. Her heart was racing and she felt the broken pieces of it slowly trying to come back together.

"What do you think of Miami? Aside from the nightlife," he asked, injecting some humor and feeling relief wash over him as she started to smile real wide, registering his words.

"Mike, are you telling me. . ." Jenna cried and buried her head against him, overcome, "that you're not going away, that we have a chance? We can be together?"

"Oh, Jenna baby, yes, we have a chance, more than a chance I hope." Mike smiled. "I want us to be together more than I've ever wanted anything."

Jenna was taking in all he was saying. "Oh God, me too," she whispered, her tears really coming down now and she hugged him. "And I still do like Miami." She sniffled then looked up and gave him a crooked smile.

"Enough to move there and live with me?" It was a huge, life-changing thing to ask and he held his breath.

Jenna's heart exploded all over again but in a good way. "Hell yes!" She ushed him back on the sand and covered his body with her own. She was rying and laughing and kissing his face all over, happily. When their lips inally met their kiss grew deeper and more passionate and she felt him stir eneath her.

"These past two weeks have been absolute hell," she whispered, moving her ips over him strategically.

Mike groaned in pleasure, accommodating her. "Worst two weeks of my ife," he agreed.

"Except for the good news part," she said, grinning.

"Except for the good news part." He pushed up into her and watched her yes close. He rolled her over gently so that he was on top of her and he kissed er again. "I don't think you understand how much I love you, Jenna. I knew had to do my two weeks in Virginia but I was going to give it all up, I was oing to tell the Unit Chief I'd changed my mind, I came back to the island he day you left to tell you that. When I read your letter it just killed me and I ealized even more what I'd be giving up by leaving you, the things you wrote it me hard, Jenna." Mike looked down at her; he could see the tops of her reasts above the bodice of her dress and each time she breathed they strained gainst it, she was so damn beautiful. "I wanted to call you from there so many imes and tell you, but I couldn't. I'm sorry if you were in pain or feeling hurt, he only one I could tell when I got back was Rafe."

Jenna cried softly. He had changed his mind, for her? She smiled emembering Rafe in Justin's back yard asking her if she trusted him. It made ense now.

"I worked my ass off for two weeks thinking about your letter and how you aid you would wait for me. Would you really have done that?"

Jenna nodded her head in the sand, yes, sniffling. "Only I was terrified t would be for nothing. I had convinced myself you would fall in love with ome beautiful foreign woman who you would no doubt have saved from some errible plight."

Mike chuckled softly at her description. "You're the only one I want to ave." He kissed her and brought her wrists up over her head holding them in lace with his hands while he moved his lips to her neck and the tops of her reasts. He felt her trying to loosen his grip on her and he looked up. "I'm sorry, abe," he whispered. "Am I hurting you?"

Jenna shook her head but Mike let go of her wrists anyway and brought hem back down between them. She saw him looking at them in the darkness nd she was a little embarrassed. Jenna started rethinking what she'd done; he'd never meant for him to see it and in fact had planned to hide it with racelets for the wedding tomorrow.

Mike felt an inexplicable tingling sensation all over his body as he picked up Jenna's wrist and studied it. Her tattoo was a black outlined target with the crosshairs in it, just like you'd see looking through to the end of a rifle scope, nearly identical to his, only in the center of her tattoo, dead center in the crosshairs, was a tiny red heart. He swallowed feeling. . . what? He didn't know what to feel, fucking blown away? He just stared at her incredulous. "When did you get this?" He could tell it was pretty recent.

"Yesterday, at Justin's shop." Oh God, she was so embarrassed, she had never meant for him to see it, not for at least four years anyway. She couldn't tell what he thought about it, but he wasn't smiling.

"Justin do it?" Mike asked. Justin hadn't said a word to him and Mike was thinking he must have been pretty fucking freaked out tattooing Mike earlier that day. Mike knew *he* was freaked out right now.

Jenna nodded.

"Why, Jenna? Why that symbol?" He was impressed that she would know anything about it.

Jenna felt her face flush. "I was reading about snipers on the Internet." Mike's brows rose and she shrugged. "I wanted to learn more about what you do and what you're so good at. I came across an article about sniper's tattoos and I saw the design and thought it would be pretty cool to have. It would be something I could look at while you were gone, to remember why you were gone, to remind me that what you were doing was important." The tears were back. "The heart in the middle?" she shrugged again. "Well, that's pretty self-explanatory."

Mike shook his head, amazed and blown away by the gesture and the coincidence. He bent his head to hers and kissed her hard, the love he felt for her consuming him; this had to mean something. He pulled back and started to unbutton his shirt.

Jenna's heart pounded, oh God, he was going to take her right here on the beach; she reached up and put her hands on the bare skin of his chest which he revealed with every button he unfastened. She paused when she saw the bandage taped over his heart and he slipped his shirt from his shoulders.

"I heard you got a tattoo today," she said softly, remembering how desperately she'd wanted to see him earlier that day. "What did you get?" she asked. She was completely turned on seeing him without his shirt again. He was even more ripped then he'd been before and he looked incredible.

Mike laughed, shaking his head, "I think you're going to be surprised." He un-taped the bandage and slowly peeled it back to show her his tattoo.

Jenna came up on her elbows like a shot and stared at it, then at Mike, then back to the tattoo. The red letter 'J' in the middle was not lost on her either.

but she couldn't get over the shock she was in. "Wait a minute," she laughed, realizing. "Justin told you! Right?"

Mike shook his head no.

"Then how?" she whispered, her flesh breaking out in goose bumps.

"Shit, Jenna I don't know how, I'm still not over the chills I got at seeing yours." Mike sat down next to her and took her wrist, studying it.

Jenna couldn't believe it. If this wasn't a sign she didn't know what was. "You know what this means, right?" she said with determination, her eyes wide. There was no doubt in her mind now and she was once again a believer, she should have never ever doubted it!

Mike laughed. "Yeah I think I do." He kissed the inside of her wrist. "You're amazing, you know that? And I love you, thank you." It meant the world to him that she'd chosen to have that tattooed on her body.

Jenna came up on bended knees and sat on the sand in front of him, she placed a hand on his chest. "And the 'J' is for me?" she asked in a sheepish tone.

Mike laughed out loud. "Well, it sure isn't for Justin!"

Jenna laughed loudly, too, in the quiet night. "But that's permanent, you know."

"That's what Justin said." Mike grinned at her.

Jenna frowned and narrowed her eyes, putting her hands on her hips. "He try to talk you out of it?"

Mike chuckled. "Not at all, we were just having a conversation about some advice his father had once given him. Mike grinned; that conversation he would save, but he didn't know for how long, now more than ever he knew what he wanted.

"I love you so much." Jenna looked him in the eyes.

"Stay with me tonight?" He needed her right now more than he'd ever needed anything. He needed her body under his, to be inside of her, loving her.

Jenna nodded, smiling, feeling her nerve endings tingle with life. She stood up and grabbed his hands, pulling on him. He purposefully wouldn't budge and she laughed. "C'mon, do you know how long these past two weeks have been? Hurry up!"

He laughed, too, standing up, "No one knows better than me, trust me."

Jenna put her arms around his trim waist. "Did you think about me?" Her tone was teasing, but she wondered.

"Every goddamn minute, Jenna," Mike said seriously. Every mile I ran, every shot I took, every test I took, and every night I lay in bed. I thought about you and coming right back here to you or wherever you would be."

"Oh, Mike." She squeezed him. "I can't believe this. I feel as happy as Ali must feel."

And he hoped someday soon it was Jenna walking down the aisle to meet him. "I'm glad you feel that way, Jenna, I want you to be happy; I want to make you happy forever."

"You do?" she whispered feeling his words sink in.

"I do." He grinned, kissing her and sweeping her off her feet to carry her off the beach, stopping along the way for her shoes.

"I missed being in your arms and feeling weightless," she said, snuggling into his strong body.

"You are weightless." He laughed and she was right where she belonged. He held on tight.

"Your muscles got bigger and you got leaner," she told him, smoothing a hand over his chest and laughing apologetically when he flinched as she touched his fresh tattoo.

"I was basically in boot camp for two weeks." Mike laughed and crossed the road with her.

"It looks good on you, real good." Jenna could feel the hard flex of his biceps as he carried her and she couldn't wait to get to his room.

"Oh yeah?" He grinned, stopping in the parking lot to kiss her.

"Oh yeah," she said in a sexy voice.

"Hey! Look who found each other!"

Jenna and Mike looked up, surprised as Justin came off the porch from the Crow's Nest. Mike's shirt was still unbuttoned and he felt Jenna move it open to reveal his tattoo and he laughed as she lifted her wrist to Justin and gave him a "what the fuck?" kind of look.

Justin was feeling pretty good and he laughed out loud, shaking his head and coming over to them. "Okay, yeah, about that—you two have officially freaked me out. I thought there was some weird spooky stuff with me and Paige, but you two take the prize, all these signs your grandmother talks about?" he said to Jenna, holding up his hands in surrender. "I'm convinced, okay? I get it. Mike? You convinced?"

Mike laughed. "Have to admit, I was pretty freaked out myself, I can't believe you didn't say anything earlier!" Mike laughed. "But hell yeah I'm convinced." He kissed Jenna's cheek. She was laughing hysterically at Justin's rant; he was definitely feeling pretty good. "See you in the morning, buddy!" Mike called out and continued walking to his room with Jenna.

"You can put me down now," she said, still laughing. "I can walk up the stairs myself." They were at the bank of rooms that overlooked the marina.

"I'm never putting you down; this is how we're going to the chapel tomorrow too." He tickled her playfully, happier than he could ever remember being.

Jenna giggled and felt the excitement course through her with the anticipation of what was to come.

Mike made it to his door and opened it with the key. He shut it behind them and turned pressing Jenna up against it, letting her slowly slide down his body all the while kissing her.

Jenna felt Mike's hands on her and moaned out loud, she had ached for his touch for weeks and now that she had it again she didn't know how she'd survived without it.

Mike moved her bodily to the bedroom, holding her in his arms once again and lowering her to the big bed. He took his shirt off and kicked off his sand filled shoes. He throbbed for her and caught her wrist as she reached for him. "Not yet," he smiled. He went to the night stand and put his iPod on.

Jenna smiled as the song they'd first made love to came through the speakers. It was on her iPod as well and she'd cried a thousand tears to it ever since that night. "I missed you Mike."

"I missed you too, Jenna," he whispered, and pulled her up by her arms to slowly lift her dress over her shoulders. She wore nothing underneath but a tiny pair of panties and his breath caught in his chest looking at her nearly naked body, he wanted her so damn much, he'd dreamt about her for two long weeks and he was finally going to have her again. His hands let the dress fall and he filled them with her breasts, kneeling in front of her on the floor, bending to kiss and suck them, fondling each one and cupping them as he suckled her nipples to taut peaks and heard her moan in pleasure. He gently lowered her back on the bed and smoothed his hands over her flat stomach and protruding hip bones, then down over the curves of her slender thighs and back on up to where her thighs met. He rested a hand on the dampened material that covered her and felt the blood pump right to his cock.

He pulled her slim hips to the edge of the bed so he could press his lips to the thin material and inhale her. She radiated heat and her sweet scent swarmed his senses and had him growing even harder. He ever so slowly moved the silky material aside teasing her as well as himself, prolonging the sight of the beautiful treasure he knew lie beneath and when he finally revealed her Mike touched her softly and groaned at the feel of her. Her soft bare folds were damp and when he separated them with his fingers he groaned again at the milky liquid he saw glistening between them. "Oh Jenna, you are so beautiful." He lowered his head and pressed his lips to her and drank her in, laving the liquid, feeling her writhe between his lips then buck and squirm against his face, she pulled his hair, massaged, and scratched him as she pulsed beneath him. He felt her buttocks tighten and her legs come up to wrap around his neck, she pressed against him with abandon and came with such force it took him by surprise. Oh hell yeah! He took it all greedily and wanted more. He used his tongue, his fingers, his hands, and brought her to orgasm five more times before she was pleading with him, begging him to get inside of her and he obliged, ready to detonate himself.

Mike stepped out of his jeans quickly and went to reach for a condom, he felt Jenna grab his arm and he looked at her, she was shaking her head and the silent communication was enough, his heart swelled as he brought himself down on top of her and entered her fast, burrowing himself inside. She cried out as he filled her and he was home; this was where he belonged.

Jenna cried out as he thrust into her and she met his eyes. He was bare inside of her, she was protected just as she'd been the first time with him but she wanted this for both of them, needed this for both of them. She moved with him and felt the size of him stretching her once again; filling her like no other man had or ever would. "I love you."

"I love you too, baby, God, I love you," Mike groaned as he drove into her. He was trying to use control. Her soft warm heat encircled him, sheathed him tightly and pulsed around his cock nearly milking him, he knew he wouldn't last and he just wanted to enjoy it for as long as he could.

Her nails bit into his back and then he felt her slide out from under him, when he realized what she was doing he moaned in anticipation. She pushed him back and straddled him, her long lean legs squeezing against his hips as she used her hand to grip his cock and guide him to her slick entrance. The feel of her hand alone on him nearly spurned his release.

Jenna felt the tip of him go in and she slowly lowered herself down over him, watching the pleasure overtake his face and smiling as he shut his eyes and grabbed her hips. God, he was spectacular looking. She rode him slowly up again and back down trying to take all of him in, crying out in a mixture of pleasure and pain when she would completely cover his shaft, he was massive and rock hard inside of her and it was exquisite.

Mike held her hips and began to fuck her from underneath, she was driving him crazy, her breasts bouncing as she rode his cock with her hands splayed on his chest. Her hair would sway and cover a breast then sway again to reveal it, it was the ultimate tease watching her nipples disappear then reappear. He was moving fast inside of her when she reached up and grabbed her breasts, looking down at him, squeezing her nipples, her eyes hooded, her lips swollen, oh fuck! He exploded inside of her, gripping her hips tight, pushing hard up into her and letting every ounce of fiery liquid fill her until he was depleted. He breathed deeply and pulled her down on top of his chest, hugging her small frame to him while still buried inside of her and he felt the wetness from her tears and knew just how she felt, his own were pretty damn hard to contain.

Jenna sniffled. "That was so amazing, I love you, Mike, and I missed you so damn much, my heart feels like it's exploding in my chest," she cried softly.

"I love you too, Jenna, so much," he said hoarsely. "I hated being away from you." He put her hand over his heart, over his fresh tattoo, and held it there. "I still can't believe the way it worked out." He felt so grateful, it was overwhelming. He had prayed and his prayers had been answered. He had picked up the phone that Friday morning and listened to Daniels.

"Listen, Cap," he'd said, "I've been thinking, and I made a few calls, don't be mad but we really need you here, you know I've been grooming you for my job for a long time now and that'll come in time but in the meantime there's always guys transferring out, getting reassigned, hell, you'll probably be a field supervisor in the next year. HRT is great, Mike, and I know I recommended you for it but I've changed my mind, I need you in Miami and I think you'll be happy with what the Unit Chief is offering. Go there tomorrow and hear them out."

Daniels had been breathless and Mike couldn't help but laugh. "You told Patty about Jenna, didn't you?"

"Well, yeah," he admitted, "but I agree with her. Jesus, Cap, you need this girl, you can't give her up for anything. What you do here at home is no less important than what you'd do for HRT. You've been keeping people safe for eight years, you're still going to do that, only I think you should do it with the love of a good woman behind you, someone you can go home to at night and grow old with. This life is too short, Cap, I know four years isn't a long time, but hell, four years without the woman you love would be an eternity."

"Tom, I appreciate the call, but it was unnecessary," Mike had told him, "I've already made up my mind."

And he had. He had been prepared to go to Virginia and face the Unit Chief and tell him he'd changed his mind but as it turned out he didn't have to. Daniels had made his calls for nothing, HRT had had their own plans for Mike based on his performance during the selection process, and Mike had readily accepted their position with honor. It felt right, it felt more right than going off and risking the loss of Jenna's love over four years; he'd lost too much in his life already.

"What are you thinking about?" she whispered, still lying on top of him.

He rolled them to their sides and locked her to him with his leg pulling her in close and keeping their intimate connection. "How lucky I am to have you, you're all I've got, Jenna, and you mean everything to me."

Jenna looked at him, surprised. "What about your family, Mike?" She didn't know one thing about them but she wanted to, she couldn't wait to meet them.

She couldn't wait to be a part of his family.

Mike told Jenna all about his family, every great thing about them and what it had been like growing up and how much he loved them. And then he told her how he'd lost them all in one night. This time as he watched Jenna's tears fall he didn't try to hide his own. He missed his family and Jenna made him realize exactly how much. "They would have loved you," he said and smiled.

"I'm so sorry, Mike. I didn't know." Jenna could barely speak, she was heartbroken for him. "I can't even imagine how you feel." Her heart grieved for him.

"I'm okay." He smoothed her hair away from her face, lovingly. "It was a long time ago, and until I met you Jenna, I never thought I'd love anybody else ever again. You made me remember how good it feels." He kissed her lips softly. He had managed to cauterize himself since the death of his parents and sister and not open himself up for that kind of pain again until he'd met Jenna and staying frozen inside was no longer an option. His heart had instinctively opened for her, as if he'd had no say in the matter, as if there were something stronger than him making the decision for him, and he now believed there was.

"Thank you."

Jenna hugged his big body to her. "I'll take that thanks, it means more to me than anything in this whole world," she said softly. "But Mike?"

He looked at her, his palm resting on her now healed cheek.

"My family will be your family now; they're going to love you as much as I do."

Mike smiled appreciatively. "I met your grandmother and your mom today."

Jenna pulled back and smiled, nearly dislodging him, and laughed as he grabbed her butt and pulled her back firmly against him. He throbbed inside of her at the motion and she gave him a sexy smile. "Mom told me but didn't tell me what you guys talked about. She said you were wonderful, and I told her I knew that." She tilted her hips into him.

"I was on my way to Rafe's cottage and they were on their way to the spa. Your mother is beautiful, Jenna, and your grandmother looks like a movie star."

She smiled. "Lauren Bacall."

"That's it!" he said, agreeing. "It was driving me crazy trying to think of who she looked like." Mike laughed, staring up at the ceiling.

"I love Lauren Bacall." She laughed with him. "We tell Nan that all the time."

"They were very nice. Your grandmother stopped me and asked if I was Michael."

"She did?" Jenna asked, though not surprised. Mike was an impressive man and she was sure Nan noticed him right away. "It must have been my dreamy lescription of you." She laughed when he pinched her nipple teasingly. "She :alled you Michael?"

"Only my mother ever called me that," he said seriously.

"Oh Mike." Jenna's heart went out to him and she smiled at the pleased ook on his face and she felt a surge of love for her grandmother.

"And your mom hugged me and thanked me." He kissed Jenna again eeing new tears form in her eyes. "I was glad to have met them."

"And how did it go with Dad?" She heard her Dad had made the fishing rip from Jake but maddeningly Jake hadn't told her anything other than, "It vent fine," with a grin and a wink.

"Your dad is a great guy, Jenna, he thanked me too and we had a nice long hat on the way up to the pass."

"About?"

"About you, about us, I told him I'd be asking you to move to Miami to live vith me, if that was okay with him."

Jenna covered her mouth in shock. "What did he say?"

Mike laughed. "He said he thought it was a great idea, and now he'd sleep t night knowing you couldn't get into any trouble."

Jenna laughed then smirked. "Jeez, he's so quick to want to get rid of me, nuh?"

"He happened to mention he knows how much you love me and he even :alled me son a few times." Mike laughed at her expression. He was laughing s he told her about it but it had felt real good hearing her father say it.

"I knew they would all love you!" Jenna was on top of the world. "We are going to have so much fun tomorrow."

"Today."

"Right!" she laughed. "Today!"

CHAPTER FIFTY-ONE

Ali woke up and knocked on Paige's door.

"Come in."

Ali opened the door and saw Paige lacing up her sneakers. "Oh good, I was going to see if you guys wanted to go for a run with me."

Paige smiled. "Hey there, bride to be, I'd love to, but Jenna isn't here."

Ali widened her eyes. "Where is she?" she asked, coming into the room.

"I got a call last night around one from Justin; he was coming out of the bar and guess who was coming off the beach with Jenna in his arms?"

"Ohh!" Ali clapped excitedly. "I'm sooo happy for them! So she spent the night with him?" she asked wide-eyed and sitting down on the bed.

Nicki poked her head in, hearing the excitement. "Who? What?"

Paige laughed. "Jenna and Mike, Tweenies, last night. She's not here this morning!"

"Oh, I'm so glad!" Nicki said, clapping too and leaning against the door frame, smiling happily.

"That's not all," Paige said conspiratorially. She told them Mike's news that Justin had relayed to her and laughed as both women cried happy tears for Jenna.

"I knew it! I knew it would work out!" Nicki clapped her hands.

"I cannot believe Rafe kept that from me!" Ali sulked.

Paige laughed. "And wait until you see Mike's tattoo." She filled them in on what Justin had tattooed on both Mike and Jenna unbeknown to either of them until last night.

Ali and Nicki both were slack jawed and got the chills.

"Wait until Nan finds that out," Nicki said, still shaking her head in disbelief.

"I know," Paige laughed. "Hey are we going running or not?" she asked Ali.

Ali stood and motioned for Paige to lead the way. "Let's do it." She turned to Nicki and grinned, waggling her brows. "You up?"

"Uh, no thanks!" Nicki put her hands up. "Me, Jake, and Nan are going to do yoga by the pool."

Paige and Ali cracked up just picturing it.

"Be careful with Nan for the love of God," Paige laughed.

"I'd be more worried about Jake if I were you," Nicki laughed. "He's about as flexible as Matt. I don't think they teach these boys how to stretch at the gym."

"I can hear you!" Jake groaned from down the hall on the couch where he'd slept.

The three girls walked down the hall and laughed at his mussed hair, a far cry from the usual perfect coif he liked to sport.

"Nan and I are as limber as kittens, don't you worry about us!" Jake said, yawning and sitting up. "Did you see her dancing last night? She's a wild thing."

They all laughed remembering.

"Did I overhear GI Joe and Barbie found their way back to Malibu last night?" Jake asked stretching and getting up.

Paige cracked up. "I'm guessing more like Xanadu!"

"Ooh! Nice reference! And thank Christ, now we can just be bawling about this one and how gorgeous she looks in her dress." Jake came away from the couch and hugged Ali. "Congrats, doll, it's gonna be a stellar day!"

"Thanks Jake." Ali and Paige said goodbye and left him with Nicki to do their yoga thing then went on their run. It was another glorious day on the island and they had all afternoon to enjoy it before the wedding that evening.

* * * * *

Jenna woke up to the smell of coffee and bagels and turned to see a tray on the bed beside her. She didn't see Mike but from the sounds of things, she gathered he was on the balcony. She got out of bed and slipped into his white button-down shirt, grabbing the mug of coffee on the way, and went outside to join him. She noticed the marina was already busy in the early morning hour.

"Hey gorgeous," he said, smiling brightly as she came out to join him. "Have a seat." He pulled a chair out but she bypassed it and went right for his lap. Mike laughed and pulled her right into his arms.

"It's beautiful today." She looked out over the bay and the activity below at the marina.

"Now that you're out here." He kissed her, immediately becoming aroused at seeing her in just his shirt. His heart swelled thinking that soon he'd be waking up to her every morning.

"Sweet talker." She smiled and ran a hand over his shadowy beard. "Do you know how sexy you are?"

"Yup."

She laughed and hit him playfully, taking a sip of coffee and a bite of his bagel. He placed his hand between her legs and she nearly choked over the jolt that went through her. "Let a girl swallow, will you?" she laughed.

"You got it." He grinned wickedly and watched her blush. He lifted her up and brought her right back to the bedroom where he placed her on her feet in front of a round table that served as both desk and eating area.

"What are you going to do with me?" Jenna leaned her back against his chest and felt his abundant erection through the shorts he wore.

Mike bent to whisper in her ear and she nodded, giving him the okay. He stripped her of his shirt and smiled as goose bumps pricked her skin. The room was hot, he had shut the air off when he'd woken up and opened the sliders. He knew her goose bumps were from excitement and that got him rock solid. He pulled her back against him and reached around between her legs to stroke her. She raised up on her toes and pressed herself into him, wrapping one arm around the back of his neck and trying to release him from his shorts with her other hand. Mike stopped to help her out and groaned against her neck when her soft fingers gripped the width of him. He pressed his hard cock into her hand and against her ass and felt her stroking him at the same time. When he bent her over the table and spread her legs with his knee, he reaching up between them and felt how wet she was. Oh man, she was ready for him.

He stepped back and just looked at her positioned there. She watched him from over her bare shoulder, her exotic eyes smoky, her long dark hair falling seductively across her face and pooling on top of the table. He could see every blessed bit of her with her ass raised high, and her legs spread apart. He held himself in his hand and stroked, watching her watch him and getting off on it. He knew once he entered her it would be less than a minute before he came; he could come right now just looking at her like that. Her teeth held her bottom lip captive as he brought the head of his penis against her opening and he teased her with it, sliding it up and over, spreading her moisture up and down then bringing it just a bit higher than she expected and watching her eyes widen. He grinned teasingly then lowered his cock to plunge into her slick opening. She pulsed around him and sucked him into her, her hands gripping the edge of the table as he drove further in. He had one hand around her waist and the other wrapped in her silken hair as he bent over her, thrusting deep inside, loving her more than he'd ever loved anybody else. He released her hair and reached for her breasts, feeling their fullness weigh in his hand, pulling on her taut nipples, slamming himself into her and feeling the curves of her ass slammed against his stomach. There were so many sensations attacking his senses, the smell of her sex, the feel of her skin, the sexy tone of her soft moans. He was lost, buried inside her to the hilt, and he was in heaven, he could die right then a happy man.

Jenna gripped the table hard, taking him all the way, it was unlike anything she'd yet to feel with him and it was overwhelming. He had asked her permission in an intimate whisper, and she had said yes, yes to him taking her from behind, yes to him plunging so deep inside of her they would become one, of course she had said yes! His desire-filled voice had sent shivers of anticipation washing over her. She placed a hand over the one that gripped her waist and their fingers intertwined. She gripped the table with her free hand and pushed right back into him as he drove in and out of her repeatedly. His fingers stroked her matching the rhythm and the sensations were too much. Her body succumbed and quivered almost violently from the overload and Jenna cried out at the same time she felt Mike stiffen and release himself into her. She felt him shudder around her and squeeze her tight at the waist, he was pressed against her, holding her tightly to him and she felt the beads of sweat on them both. His lips were on her back and neck, then she felt him slide out from her and lift her bent form from the table turning her in his arms to hold her.

"You're amazing, Jenna," he said, his voice husky. "You turn me on so damn much," he whispered against her hair. There was so much he wanted to do with her and he was glad she was willing to explore with him.

"No," she chuckled softly. "You're amazing." Every nerve ending had been annihilated, she felt like a rubber band in his arms.

Mike grinned. "Was that okay for you?"

"Intense." Jenna hugged him. "And definitely okay." She knew she'd be learning a lot from him and she looked forward to each and every lesson. "I feel like a porn star." She ran a light hand over his tat.

Mike laughed out loud, squeezing her to him. "Oh baby, you ain't seen nothin' yet!" He grinned at the thought of all he would show her and rubbed his hands over her tight ass. He couldn't wait.

Jenna laughed against him. "I suppose we should have shut the sliders before that, huh?"

"Nah," he laughed. "Who doesn't like to wake up to the sounds of sex?"

* * * * *

Justin pressed down on the erection he'd woken up with and tried calling Paige. It wasn't helping any that Mike and Jenna were making a racket in the next room. He knew what they were doing and he wanted to be doing that too. He got out of bed about to jump in the shower when he heard a knock at the door. He looked down at himself and grabbed a nearby towel to wrap around him. When he opened the door, he laughed as Paige flung herself at him.

He kicked the door shut with his foot. "Oh baby, you couldn't have come at a better time." He dropped his towel and started taking her running clothes off. She was kicking off her sneakers and kissing him and he was pulling down her shorts and thong. "Oh man, you're all sweaty, I love it." He threw her on his bed and kissed her all over before burying himself deep inside of her. Their bodies molded together perfectly, "Oh good morning to me!" he sang and thrust into her hard.

Paige laughed, moving at a quickened pace beneath him; they were frantic and couldn't fuck fast enough. They were both laughing when he came, grunting loudly. "Oh yeah!"

"Shh!" she laughed. "The people next door will hear you!"

"The people next door have been tormenting me all night and morning!" Justin laughed complaining. "Your little cousin is a loud one!" He collapsed on the bed next to Paige and brought her right up against him.

Paige covered her mouth. "Oh my God!" She laughed. "Jenna and Mike are in the next room?"

Justin grinned, nodding and catching his breath. "I almost banged on the wall a few times, but after a while it became entertaining."

"Oh no, she'll die when I tell her!" Paige laughed in his arms, slinging a leg over him; she began tracing his tattoos, a habit now.

"Don't tell her, Jesus, I don't want to embarrass her," Justin laughed, caressing her firm leg. "You know, I almost snuck over to your grandmother's house last night and knocked on your window." He'd wanted her so badly.

"You should have!" Paige laughed, knowing he was feeling deprived. "I missed you last night."

"Tell me about it, I don't like when you aren't in my bed," Justin said seriously. "You're staying here tonight." He loved her hands on him and he watched her fingers, he'd become used to her tracing the lines of his ink and he knew where she'd eventually end up. He was a little nervous about it too.

Paige looked at him and felt her heart speed up at his serious tone; she didn't like being out of his bed either. "I'm definitely staying here tonight." She kissed him and went back to her ritual, moving her fingers to the inside of his arm, tracing over the blue wave and the surfer riding it and the little red heart below... it... She looked up at him then back down to the heart that had never been there before, it had her initials inside of it. Paige's eyes became moist and she stared at it, recalling the conversation they'd had on their first dinner date. She had joked, saying she'd expected him to have a little heart tattooed on him or somebody's initials, and he had told her what his father's advice had been—don't tattoo anything to do with a woman on himself unless he planned to marry her.

"What do you think?" He grinned sheepishly looking down at it.

"I'm honored," she said softly, searching his eyes. She was surprised and felt her heart stuck in her throat. "I love it. Who did it? Stacy?" Her mind was racing. What did this mean?

"Yeah. Yesterday morning." He wondered what she was thinking.

"Wow!" Paige traced over it again. "Now you can only date girls whose names start with P and end in T," she joked, not being very subtle. She wanted to know what this meant. "I remember what your dad told you, you know." She looked at him seriously.

Justin rolled over on top of her and looked into her unsure, pretty blue eyes; he intertwined his hands with hers over her head. "I'm glad you remember what my father told me; I think it was pretty sage advice, don't you?"

Paige nodded, swallowing back the tightness in her throat. Oh wow!

"When we go back, I want you to meet my dad, my mom, too. Would you like to?" He felt it was long overdue.

Paige nodded again, her voice barely audible. "I'd really like to but what if your father notices this?" Paige touched the tattoo, her initials standing out in black ink against the red of the heart.

"It's the first thing I'm going to show him," Justin answered honestly.

"Oh." She looked up at him and saw the smile on his face and the love in his eyes, but still didn't hear the words. She was too chicken to say them too.

CHAPTER FIFTY-TWO

"Please, Mom!" Ali sat on the edge of the bed letting her mother put yet another bobby pin in her already secured updo. "It's not going anywhere!"

Nan and Jacqueline laughed. "Trace, she's right, and the soft tendrils look beautiful falling by her face, it's natural," Jacqueline said.

"I just want to be doing something for her," Tracy nearly sobbed. "When is she going to need me again?"

"Mommm." Ali started to cry, too. "I'll always need you! Stop making me cry! Nan, Jacqueline help!" Ali pleaded.

"C'mon, ladies." Nan took over, there's some champagne with our names on it out on the pool deck. Besides, Paige wants pictures."

"I'll be right outside, honey," her mom assured her.

Ali smiled in exasperation. "I know; thanks." She stood up to shut the door behind them and stopped to let Nicki in. "Oh my God!" she groaned then laughed.

Nicki laughed, too. "You look amazing."

"Thanks, Nick, I just can't wait to get there and see him. I can't wait to be his wife."

Nicki smiled knowing just how her best friend felt. "Everything is just perfect in our lives right now, isn't it?" she asked sitting on the bed, becoming melancholy.

Ali sat beside her. "It really is. I love this place and will never be able to thank your grandmother enough for letting us stay here."

"Don't be ridiculous, you're family, and will always be welcome. I'm just in awe of all the love that surrounds this house, this island! It truly is magical."

Ali laughed. "You're sentimental today, huh?"

"Jenna's moving to Miami with Mike." Nicki delivered the news feeling a little sad about it.

Ali gasped. "You're kidding! That's wonderful, do your parents know?"

"Yeah, Dad gave his blessing and Mom hasn't seen her yet but she knows." Nicki pouted. "I'm going to miss her."

"Aw, I know but you'll see her a lot, she'll come here when you're visiting nd now we can finally visit Miami! How fun will that be?" Ali tried to cheer ıer.

"I know." Nicki sighed. "You're right." Nicki got up and went to the door. I'll stop being sad and bringing you down, otherwise you'll do it to me at my vedding and I'll have to kill you for making my eyes puffy."

"That's fair." Ali grinned and hugged her. "You know, Nick, if it weren't for ou inviting me here last summer I'd never have met Rafe."

"I'd like to take the credit, Al, but if you hadn't met Rafe here on Captiva, hen it would have been somewhere else in this world, you guys were meant o be. I believe that and everyone looking at you both today will be able to ee it too if they haven't already. You're electric together, the chemistry, the ompatibility, it radiates off both of you. You guys are inspiring to be around, ruly." Nicki smiled at her best friend. "We're both marrying the man of our lreams." She lifted her hands palms up and smiled. "What more could we ask or?"

Ali nodded, not trusting herself to speak.

Nicki laughed. "C'mon, Paigy's waiting to take some pics, push those oobies up and grab your lip gloss."

Ali laughed and followed her outside; it was truly the happiest day of her ife.

* * * * *

"You had to pick summer in Florida to be married," Jake said to his older rother. "I'm sweating like a pig."

Rafe laughed. "Relax, we're leaving in five minutes, it will be cooler in the hapel." He finished tying his tie and smiled at his father, who was staring at ıim.

"I'm a lucky guy."

"Why's that, Dad?" Rafe winked at his brother, they knew their tough old lad would go soft on them today.

"I have two great boys and I'm so proud of you both, and Rafe, I couldn't e happier for you today. Ali is the best thing that's ever happened to you, just ike your mom was for me."

"Thanks, Dad." Rafe grinned and gave him a hug. "She is the best thing hat ever happened to me, and it means the world how much you and the amily love her, thank you."

"Mom loves her more than you now," Jake joked.

"I think that's probably true." Rafe laughed and smiled as Mike walked nside the cottage.

"Hey you're too pretty in that monkey suit, McD. Jake mess up his hair or something, will you?" Mike joked coming in and shaking hands with Rafe's dad. Rafe looked great, he looked happy.

"Look who's talking, I'm starting to think I should have gone to Quantico with you for the last two weeks just for the PT."

"Next time bro, next time. Besides, you've got nothing to worry about, you're as lean and mean as ever."

Rafe grinned, straightening his tie. "Thanks, man, I've been doing this new workout. . ."

"Are you two frickin' kidding me right now?" Rafe's father interrupted in his thick New York accent, looking between them and then looking to Jake. "Is this the McDonough, Caplan wedding or McDonough, Fuller wedding? Jesus Christ, I ever talked to a guy like that down at the precinct I'd have had my ass handed to me."

Rafe and Mike cracked up and Jake tried to hide his amusement.

"Dad, you should be proud, I get my fantastic looks from you!" Rafe winked at Mike and Jake. "Look how good you look in that tux, wait until Mom sees you."

Rafe's dad snuck a glance at himself in the mirror and straightened his own tie. He did look pretty dapper. He turned when he heard their chuckling and he waved a dismissive hand at them. "Oh, for God's sake, I'm going to get your mother, quit your primping and let's get this show on the road. Your mother promised I could have some whiskey tonight, heck, boys, your old man might even get lucky." He grinned.

"Way to go, Dad!" Rafe laughed.

"Really, Dad!" Jake made a disgusted face and Mike just laughed, enjoying their banter.

"How the hell do you think you got here, you little shit?" Their dad smirked at Jake as he left the cottage leaving them still laughing.

"I'm going to go make sure the car is ready for us," Jake told them, shaking his head and leaving as well.

Mike took two beers from the fridge and handed one to Rafe. "Here's to you, buddy, this is it. I couldn't be happier for you, man."

Rafe clinked his bottle to Mike's. "Thanks, Cap, and I couldn't be happier for you." He smiled and they both drank. "She see the tat?"

Mike nodded, chuckling. "She got one too."

"Oh yeah, what she get?" Rafe handed Mike the wedding rings to put in his coat pocket.

Mike put the box in the inside pocket of his tux and laughed. "She got the same damn tattoo as me, on her wrist, Justin did it the day before, never said a vord to me." Mike watched the surprise come over Rafe's face and he laughed again. "Tell me about it."

Rafe shook his head. "You know that's fucked up right?"

Mike grinned happily. "Yeah, I know."

* * * * *

"Okay, on three, everybody say—nobody's hair would look good if it veren't for Jake!"

They all laughed their way through it as Jake took their picture. Paige had ıanded him the camera so all the women could be photographed and Jake was loing his best at playing photographer. He had, in fact, improved a lot of their ıair styles with his own hair products. When he'd seen the older women using :ans of aerosol hair spray he'd nearly had a heart attack, causing the younger vomen to crack up laughing. "O-M-G! I can actually hear the steady drip of he glaciers melting. If I go outside right now, I'll probably be sucked right up nto the hole you two just created in the ozone!" Jake had joked to Tracy and acqueline, who had yelled at him when he took their cans away. He showed hem the hair paste he used, and now of course they were hooked.

When the last picture was taken they'd all climbed onto the trolley that Nan had arranged as a surprise to take them to the Chapel by the Sea. They'd aughed the whole short ride there. When the trolley pulled up, there was a small crowd already gathered and Nicki snuck Ali off to the side while everyone else either milled around outside on the sand or took refuge inside rom the hot sun. The guest list was small so the usually overflowing chapel vould accommodate everyone. Ali just had a few extended family members in attendance and so did Rafe, along with some fellow agents from the Miami ield office, who had driven over for the wedding.

It was a small, intimate crowd and Paige started photographing them right away. She'd already got some great shots at the house that she knew Ali would ove and when she spotted Justin standing by the doors with Ali's brothers, Matt and Jason, she continued to snap away, her stomach fluttering at how ncredibly handsome Justin looked in his sport coat and tie. He spotted her before he went inside and stopped to give her a warm smile. Paige knew that hot would be hers and hers alone.

"Paige, do me a favor and take a whole bunch of Mike for me?" Jenna asked coming up beside her on the sand and checking her purse for tissue. "My shoes are sinking," she laughed looking down. "So much for trying to be as tall as Mike today."

Paige laughed. "I know mine are too. Just walk on your toes until you get nside. And of course I'll take a bunch, already had it in mind. You don't think

Ali and Rafe will mind a whole album of just Justin and Mike, do you?" she joked.

Jenna laughed. "Well, Rafe might."

Paige laughed, too. "Has he seen you yet?" Paige looked at her cousin, who looked gorgeous in a periwinkle blue cocktail dress. Ali had let each girl pick their own color dress keeping it casual but elegant. Jenna's was satin with a flirty skirt that fell just above the knee and clung to her petite frame perfectly accentuating her curves and complementing her dark skin and hair beautifully. Her silver open-toed heels were quite high and added length to her already long legs.

Jenna shook her head, "I haven't poked my head in yet."

"Well what are you waiting for, that's a face I want to catch on camera."

Jenna smiled. "Do you think he'll like the dress?"

Paige laughed. "That question doesn't actually require an answer, does it?"

Jenna smirked and stuck her tongue out and to her chagrin Paige captured that face too.

Paige turned as she heard Ali's mom approach and she snapped a few of Ali's brothers about to walk their mom down the aisle. Jenna went next, taking Rafe's brother's arm and allowed him to escort her down the aisle while Paige snuck inside behind them and aimed her camera at the altar, where Mike stood with Rafe. The light sounds of a violin played inside the chapel and Paige smiled as she took shot after shot of Mike seeing Jenna and watching her every step as she sat down. Paige's eyes found Justin's and he was watching *her* a contemplative look on his face, a look that had Paige lowering her camera to stare back at him.

Justin watched Paige work and was impressed at how into it she was, she looked natural behind the camera and he could see she loved what she was doing and that made him feel proud and happy for her. Just watching her made his chest tight and his adrenaline rush, his feelings for her were intense and he knew their relationship had escalated to a higher level. Neither one of them had yet to speak of it, but tonight he intended to change that.

Mike couldn't take his eyes off Jenna. She'd walked in and their eyes had immediately found one another's. He'd been waiting for her, watching each guest come in and wondering when she would appear. When she finally walked inside the chapel, he felt the jolt shoot right through his body. She looked as breathtaking as he'd imagined and he couldn't wait to hold her in his arms again and dance with her. Jesus, her damn legs in those shoes had nearly had him stumbling up at the altar. He watched her sit in the front pew and cross one over the other and if Rafe hadn't laid a hand on his arm to steady him, he might have embarrassed himself.

"Down, boy," Rafe had whispered, chuckling.

Mike watched her now whispering with Rafe's sister but her eyes were locked with his. He was in love for the first time and it felt like nothing else. He was on top of the world; he felt invincible. He felt like every goal and every dream he'd ever set or had was even more possible with Jenna by his side. Things had worked out with the HRT the way they had because of Jenna, and his career would mean so much more to him now knowing he had someone else to live and fight for. He had been missing so much in his life and he hadn't even realized it until he'd met her. His life was forever changed now in such a way that made it possible for him to relax and slow down. He wouldn't be a workaholic anymore. He would come home at a normal time and be with Jenna, they'd have dinner each night, walk on the beach, make love in their bed and have long discussions about life, about the family they could have, about growing old together. He couldn't wait for it, all of it.

Watching Rafe anxiously await Ali's entrance, Mike envied him. They would leave this chapel as husband and wife, two people who knew where they were headed, knew what they wanted and because they had each other nothing could stop them. Daniels knew what it was like, too. Mike sought him out in the small crowd and saw him sitting with his wife Patty. Daniels had once been like Mike, all about the job and working sixty-five, seventy hours a week, until he'd found Patty, and his world had changed. Daniels was happy now. He didn't let the job stress him out. He was healthy, he was happy, and it was all because he had someone who loved and cared about him, someone he himself was head over heels in love with. Now Mike was part of that fortunate club and he'd never felt luckier.

* * * * *

"I think everyone is here," Ali said nervously to her dad and Nicki just outside the chapel. The sun hung over the gulf in a fiery ball of reds and oranges. Ali and Rafe had tried to time it so that by the end of the ceremony all the guests could watch the sun set on the beach and it looked like it was going to happen just that way. She looked around at the verdant colors of the surrounding palms and flowering bushes that set a vista for the Gulf beyond and was so grateful her dream of marrying Rafe on Captiva was coming true.

"Ready when you are." Nicki smiled.

Ali nodded and Nicki slowly made her way to the altar, smiling at Rafe and Mike when she got there and then finding Matt's eyes which locked with hers from the front row. They shared an intimate smile and then suddenly the chapel was filled with Vangelis' "Hymn" and all eyes turned to the entrance. The music was beautiful and haunting and suited the serene setting. Views of the placid Gulf could be seen through the large open windows and it was just about that time of evening before the sun was about to set. A warm breeze filtered inside the small chapel and carried the beautiful sounds of the music back out with it. Each guest rose in anticipation and when the doors opened this time, Ali stood on the arm of her father looking like a princess.

Her dress was made of a beautiful white silk that hung elegantly from her neck, halter style, and molded to her slim, fit figure perfectly. It just barely swept the floor and had a small train in the back that moved elegantly when she walked revealing white satin platform pumps that would bring her very near to Rafe's height. Her long hair was pinned up off her neck and soft wisps that had escaped framed her cheeks, giving her a natural, breeze-kissed look. The fragrant lone white gardenia that adorned her hair above her right ear looked beautiful and sexy and lent to the whole island theme of the wedding.

She carried a fragrant bouquet of gardenias as well which were wrapped in thick, white satin ribbon and were fastened with a row of pearls that complemented the large pearl and diamond earrings her mom and dad had given her as a wedding gift. Ali looked stunning and everyone in the chapel gave a collective gasp at the sight of her. Her brilliant green eyes glistened taking it all in as her dad slowly escorted her to the altar passing each sea-colored pew and the family and friends that filled them. And then her eyes were focused on only one person. Everyone watched with happiness as Ali's dad kissed her cheek and then as Rafe took Ali's hand to have her stand beside him.

She was the most beautiful woman Rafe had ever seen, and his heart expanded in his chest watching her walk to him. How did he get so lucky? Rafe met her eyes and felt his own well up at the happiness and love he saw in hers. As long as he lived he would do everything in his power to protect her and keep that look there. He could get lost in those eyes, and in fact had, more than once. She had mesmerized him from day one, right here on this island and he loved her to his soul, becoming her husband was going to be an honor and a privilege he would cherish as long as he lived.

"I love you, green eyes," he whispered, taking her hand.

"I love you too," she whispered back, and by the sounds of the soft "awws" coming from behind them, their guests had also heard the soft exchange. Rafe and Ali smiled, unembarrassed.

Mike grinned and found Jenna looking at him. She was smiling the sweetest of smiles and he knew she was touched by the ceremony. He listened to the minister speak of love and commitment and the importance of faith in one another and he found himself wishing Jenna were standing next to him at the altar and the minister were speaking to them. Of all the places he'd found himself wishing to be over the years, this one had never crossed his mind and he laughed inwardly thinking how life could change on a dime. He'd seen it first-hand many years ago, change for the worst; and now here he was having had it change on him once again, only this time for the best.

"By the power vested in me, I now pronounce you husband and wife," the minister declared and smiled. "You may kiss your bride," he said to Rafe.

Rafe took Ali in his arms and kissed her, a gentle, meaningful kiss, conveying to her just how he felt at that moment, like they were the only two people on earth. When he finally pulled back to all the hoots and hollers there were tears in her eyes and he laughed softly. "I love you, wife."

Ali grinned happily wiping her eyes. "I love you too, husband."

The chapel erupted in cheers and applause as Rafe escorted Ali outside the chapel. They were onslaught with congratulations and barraged with guests taking their photos. The sun was starting its decent and Paige directed them over to the beach. All the guests followed to watch the sunset and Paige took shot after shot of the newly married couple. When she had taken enough, she let the moms and dads take over and went to find Justin. She saw him talking with Ali's older brother Jason.

"Hi," she smiled, coming over to them.

Justin smiled and put his arm around her. "Hi, you look amazing."

Jason greeted Paige and then politely excused himself.

"I hope I didn't interrupt," she said.

Justin pulled her into his chest. "Paige. . ." He laughed happily, shaking his head and he stared out at the setting sun. He couldn't wait another second, the feeling was too intense.

Paige tilted her head looking up at him, smiling, she had taken off her heels in the sand and they hung from her hand along with her camera.

"I love you." Justin ran a hand over his head looking at her through expectant eyes.

Paige's heart slammed inside of her chest, God she'd been waiting to hear him say that. She'd felt it and that in itself was wonderful, but she had longed to hear him say it. She smiled wide and was surprised when he seemed unsure of how she'd respond. "Oh Justin, I love you too."

He exhaled, relieved. "I've known I loved you since the morning I woke up to you on my stairs, staring at the stained glass window. I knew I was in love with you then."

So much for holding back her tears. "Oh Justin, I've been dying for you to tell me that you loved me."

"Didn't you know?" he asked, smiling and feeling a little overwhelmed himself that she'd said the same to him.

"I knew, but I didn't know if you would ever tell me. I know how cautious you were being and that you were afraid this was all happening too soon, but it's not." Paige smiled. "It's happening just as it's supposed to happen."

"I know it is." Justin looked down and laughed. He really believed that, too. "This is the one thing in my life that I know is supposed to happen." His arms folded around her, turning her and he pulled her back against his chest. "Watch," he said.

The last of the sun fell into the gulf in a deep orange blaze and everyone on the beach watching, clapped.

"Party time!" someone called out and people cheered and started filtering off the beach, getting in cars and piling onto the trolley that would take them to Tween Waters.

"Come with me while I sneak in a few more shots?" Paige asked. She almost regretted that she'd offered to take photos. She wanted to sneak off and be alone with Justin and let his words sink in and hear them all over again.

"You got it." Justin put a hand on the back of her neck before she turned to go and he bent his head to kiss her. His tongue parted her lips and he tasted her, kissing her and feeling her mold her body to his. "Thank God my room is close by, we might have to run up and get you a new memory card or something."

"Or something," Paige whispered, her knees weak. "Maybe I'll just let the parents get some candid shots."

Justin laughed. "But they won't come out like yours. C'mon," he coaxed and moved her in front of him.

"Sure, get me all hot and bothered, how am I supposed to function now?" she complained, smiling.

He laughed and looked down, "Never mind you, just walk in front of me until we get to the trolley will ya?"

Paige grinned slyly, following his glance. "Can I sit on your lap on the drive over?" She laughed at the groaned response.

* * * * *

Jenna remained in her seat while everyone left the chapel. She watched Mike slowly approach and sit down beside her.

"You're the most beautiful woman I've ever seen." Mike picked up a handful of her silken hair and let it fall through his fingers."The color of this dress looks amazing on you too." He bent to kiss the side of her neck and inhaled the flowery fragrance on her skin. "Ummm."

Jenna's heart beat double time as his lips made contact with her skin. The truth was she was in awe of how he looked. His tuxedo was tailored perfectly and he looked as at home in it as he did in his worn jeans and T-shirts. He could be in a magazine ad, he should in fact be Armani's poster boy for tuxedos, she thought. His golden tan set off his incredible blue eyes and white teeth. His hair was styled, probably with something like Jake had used on everybody at the house and Jenna couldn't stop looking at him. Mike was gorgeous. He could be with anyone in the world and not only for his looks, Jenna knew first-hand what an incredible man he was and she felt incredibly lucky he had chosen her.

Mike slid a hand up her shin and stopped at her knee. "I love you, you know."

The sun was setting out the window past his shoulder and Jenna watched it for a minute enjoying the quiet that had fallen over the small chapel. "I love you too," she replied, turning her eyes back to his.

"Jenna, I need you to know I realize what a sacrifice it is to move your whole life to another state. And I'm grateful and humbled that you are willing to do it. I'm just worried that being away from your family is going to be real hard." He'd been watching her interact with everyone all day. They were a close-knit bunch and he wondered how it would be for her not to be near them.

Jenna was once again touched at his thoughtfulness. She leaned over to kiss him. "You are such a special guy and I'm so in love with you it's stupid."

"Stupid?" He laughed.

"Yeah, stupid good." She smiled. "We'll see my family whenever they come here to Nan's and you'll come home to Boston with me to visit whenever we can, right?"

"I'm counting on it."

"Good, then please don't worry about me. I can't wait to move to Miami with you." She smiled. "I'll get to learn so much more about you and all your wicked ways," she teased."

He laughed. "Like if I put the cap on my toothpaste?"

Jenna laughed. "By the looks of your condo I'm pretty sure you do."

Mike shrugged, chuckling. "I like it clean, what can I say?"

"No, I was thinking more along the lines of, when your birthday is, what TV shows you like, what kind of music you listen to. Oh, and I'm hoping you'll teach me some new things," she whispered conspiringly, looking around the chapel with a sly grin.

Mike kissed her. "That last parts a given, sweetheart. And I'm not waiting until we get back to Miami either."

Jenna shivered with anticipation at the thought. He turned her on just by looking in her eyes and the way he spoke to her. God!

"Oh and it's the same as yours by the way." Mike stood up pulling her with him and laughed at her confused look. "My birthday. It's the same as yours, minus a few years of course but who's counting."

Jenna nearly stumbled following him out of the chapel and demanded his license at once. Her jaw fell open when she read it. She looked up at him in shock. "Mike..."

"I know, I know," he laughed and then stopped her in the doorway to the chapel.

"You need to know something." He took her hands in his facing her. "I've never felt so lucky in all my life, and I want you to know what I see when I look at you." He cupped her cheek. "You take my breath away, when I see you I actually have a physical reaction, Jenna, right in my gut." He placed a hand there. "Those exotic-looking eyes of yours pierce mine and I'm gone. I look at this perfect body move. . ." His hand slowly caressed the side of her body and came to rest on her hip. "And my own betrays me. I'm aroused instantly." Jenna's eyes held his and Mike nodded. "Yes, it's true."

"I have this barbaric, cave man like feeling of wanting to possess you," he nearly growled and shook his head as he admitted it. "You're mine, and I want everyone to know it." A little smile played at the corners of her lips and he laughed. "I know that sounds ancient but it's how I feel. I want to protect you even though I'm quite aware that you can take care of yourself." He grinned "But I want to make sure you're never again in a position where you have to."

"I'm so over the top in love with you, Jenna, and so utterly grateful that something brought us together." He watched her eyes grow wide. "Hell yeah I believe that, why not? Call it fate, the universe, whatever, you showing up to your grandmother's house a week early was no coincidence. Having the same birthday, weird yes, but I don't think coincidence. I'm going to selfishly believe you were born for me on my birthday as a gift. God, fate, the universe, hell, they all knew I would need you someday and here you are. This is it, Jenna." Mike looked around the chapel, nodding his head and smiled back down at her.

Jenna watched him look around the chapel and the insides of her stomach danced. *This is it, Jenna.*

"Oh Mike." She was weeping at his beautiful words.

He smiled and wiped her tears. "Now, are you ready to go dance with me? I've been dying to dance with you since I first saw you move."

Jenna nodded composing herself. "I can't wait to dance with you." She took his hand and stood up beside him.

CHAPTER FIFTY-THREE

Dinner was in the Old Captiva House, inside the private room, and had been elegant and delicious. Not soon after, the party started to get wild quickly and was moved to The Crow's Nest where the band had started playing. As soon as Ali and Rafe had had their first dance, the party had begun. All the women were dancing and had even coaxed some of their men to join them. Whoever wasn't on the dance floor could be found at the bar and that's where Jenna, from the dance floor, spotted Mike with Nan.

"What do you think they're talking about?" she asked Paige and Nicki, who were dancing alongside her. The band was covering all the latest dance hits and doing a pretty good job of it. Rafe and Ali were making their way around the room and thanking the guests who had come all the way for the wedding and Matt was at the bar with his and Ali's older brother Jason. Justin was with them but somehow Nan had got hold of Mike alone.

Paige and Nicki just smiled knowingly.

*****

"So Michael, you're in love with my granddaughter."

Mike smiled recalling Jenna saying that her grandmother looked like Lauren Bacall, and she did. Jenna's grandmother looked glamorous in the off-white pant suit she wore. The beads sewn into the jacket made the suit feminine as did her matching shirt, open at the collar, revealing a thick strand of pearls. She looked both elegant and formidable.

"I am at that." He smiled, taking a sip of his beer.

Grace liked him immensely. He was without a doubt strikingly handsome, but he also had a twinkle in his eye which she knew denoted a good sense of humor. "And you don't think it's merely because of the circumstances you were put in because of her?" She was testing him, but she tested them all, it was her job.

Mike smiled and loved her forthrightness. "No ma'am."

"Call me Grace," she interrupted.

"Grace," Mike said and smiled. "There's no question the trouble Jenna found herself in brought us together, but I fell in love with her, not the drama that surrounded her. Hell, I'm surrounded by enough drama every day at work," Mike laughed as he leaned forward on the bar and took another swill of beer from his bottle. "And I've never fallen in love with it."

He spoke to Grace seriously then. "I did, however, fall in love with a beautiful, honest, caring, funny as hell woman," he grinned, "who is stronger than any one person I know. There aren't many people who could have handled what Jenna went through so easily, she was incredible. The way she defended herself blew me away, and the way she kept her head about her. But at the same time she has this subtle vulnerability that kills me." Mike put a hand to his chest and grinned. "I get this overpowering urge to protect her and keep her safe." He looked down, a little embarrassed at having shared so much. "I know she can take care of herself and I probably sound old-fashioned talking this way but. . ." He looked up at Grace, "I've never been in love before and it's pretty overwhelming."

Grace nodded her head in approval. "Annie dear," she beckoned the bartender, whom everyone was friendly with. "Two fingers of your best Scotch please."

Mike accepted the glass Grace slid to him moments later and held it up as she did.

"Thank you for what you did for my granddaughter and welcome to the family, Michael."

They touched glasses and Mike drank the liquid down with relish, feeling it burn the whole way. Holy shit, welcome to the family? —This from Jenna's grandmother, the matriarch of the family? Damn, he was choked up as she walked away before he could even say thanks. He watched Jenna dancing with her sister and cousin on the dance floor and he felt a quick surge of pride. It was a family he couldn't wait to be a part of and he smiled thinking how Jenna's grandmother for the second time seemed to be one step ahead of him.

Matt had watched the whole scene from the end of the bar and he made his way over to Mike when Grace walked away. "She something, huh?"

Mike took a sip of his beer trying to cool the still burning sensation of the hard alcohol in his stomach. "What? The fact that she can belt back scotch or that she seems to know exactly what's going on with her granddaughters and the men that love them?" Mike laughed.

Matt laughed with him. "Definitely both." Matt watched Nicki on the dance floor and felt the familiar pang he always felt watching her. She was beautiful and the green strapless dress she wore looked amazing on her. She was hot as hell and he couldn't wait to get her alone. "We're pretty lucky, I'd say."

Mike watched Jenna as well, she moved just like he remembered. "You got that right."

"Did I see you throwing back a scotch with Grace?" Justin addressed Mike with a grin as he came over to stand with him and Matt. He leaned back gainst the bar with his beer, watching Paige with her cousins on the dance floor.

Mike nodded and narrowed his eyes. "Is it some sort of ritual or something?"

Matt laughed. "Not anymore, I would say you just ended it."

Justin laughed, too.

"Shit, what I do?" Mike asked confused.

"I was the first," Matt told him, "Justin here had the pleasure a few weeks go, and now you. Grace only has three granddaughters, dude."

Mike looked at Matt, getting it. Wow, so welcome to the family really meant welcome to the family. He smiled. "How did she know we'd all be worthy of the honor?"

"Because she's a wise, astute woman," Jacqueline said, coming up beside them. "And it's written all over each one of your faces," she laughed. "Mike, I believe you owe me a dance."

Oh man, Jenna's mom was asking him to dance, Mike was instantly nervous. He put down his beer and held out his hand, smiling when she accepted it, then he led her to the floor.

"I think he just broke into a cold sweat." Matt laughed out loud.

Justin drank his beer and laughed along with him. "I think you're right."

Jenna was now sitting with her dad, grandmother, and Matt and Ali's dad s they watched Mike lead her mom around the dance floor. Jenna beamed watching them.

"He's a good guy." Her dad patted her hand.

"I know, Dad, I love him so much." She looked at him and felt Nan grab her hand under the table giving it a squeeze. Nan was talking with Ali's dad bout Nicki and Matt's upcoming wedding.

Her dad chuckled. "I know you do, sweetheart, I think everyone in this oom knows."

Jenna laughed happily. "Yeah?"

"Jenna, the way you two look at each other from across the room reminds me of your mother and me not so long ago. You look just like her you know. When I first met your mother she took my breath away, she still does, just look t her out there. She's hot, as you young people like to say."

"Aw, Dad." Jenna stuck out her lower lip. "That's so nice."

"Well, it's the truth, I know you and Mike are just at the beginning of

something special, Jenna, but you two have a strong foundation to work wit
and I believe you'll be two of the lucky ones. I know you're going to leave u
and move to Miami, but you know you're always welcome at home, the bot
of you." He smiled. "Mom and I will miss you but we're also very happy to se
you finally happy, you and your sister."

Jenna swallowed the lump in her throat and hugged her dad. He hande
her his handkerchief and she dried her moist eyes. "Thanks, Dad."

He got up and gave her shoulder a squeeze. "Now I'm going to go sho
your boyfriend how it's done."

Jenna laughed with Nan. "Go get her, Dad!" She watched as her dad tappe
Mike on the shoulder and cut in and she smiled as Mike handed her mom ove
to her husband gracefully and then Mike walked over to Jenna and held out hi
hand. Jenna stood, taking it and laughed when he twirled her onto the danc
floor.

"Ooh! Saved the fancy moves for me, I see!" she laughed.

"Damn right!" Mike smiled pulling her close and breathing her in. "I'v
been waiting for this all night."

"I've been on the dance floor, you could have come out any time," Jenn
teased him.

"I had to get all the male bonding out of the way first," Mike laughed
"I've been invited to a Red Sox game by Ali's brother Jason. I've got a golf dat
with your father and Ali's father before they leave the island, and you and
are having lunch with Jake tomorrow before he goes back to New York. Jak
Larson," he clarified with a smile.

Jenna nodded. "He told me." She smiled as Mike held her and led the slo
dance perfectly. "I'm glad you like Jake."

"I do like him." Mike smiled. "Have to admit though when I first met hi
yesterday, I was pretty jealous."

Jenna laughed. "Until you found out he'd be more interested in you tha
me, you mean?"

"Well, yeah," Mike laughed, too, admittedly. "Seriously though, he's
great guy, I wish him a lot of luck; he's a funny bastard. I bet he becomes ver
successful."

"I think he will. He really wants it." Jenna looked over and saw Jake slo
dancing with Ali's mother. He winked at Jenna and dipped, Tracy causing he
and Mike to crack up.

"I know I keep saying this but you have a great family, Jenna, and grea
friends."

"Thank you," she replied smiling. "And now a great guy."

Mike kissed her as the song came to an end. "I don't want to let you go," h nurmured against her lips.

"Then you have to keep dancing," she laughed. "C'mon, let's see what you ;ot." The band kicked up the tempo and everyone filtered onto the dance floor.

"Whoa! A challenge? I can bring it, look out!" Mike danced for her and he gawked at him.

"You can dance?" Jenna was shocked. The man could move!

"Babe, I'm from Miami, of course I can dance." He winked and took her ıands, moving her with him. "Wait until you see me salsa!"

"Oh, I would love to salsa with you." Her tone was sexy and he gave her a ook to say it would definitely happen.

Jenna moved to the music noticing Mike's and Rafe's co-workers staring ›pen-mouthed at the two of them dancing. "I think you're surprising the hell ›ut of your friends," she laughed.

Mike glanced over to find Reynolds, Simmons, and Daniels with their vives, openly staring at him and Jenna. He laughed at them and nudged Rafe vho had been dragged by Ali out onto the floor. "Look." He gestured. "They lon't know what to think."

Rafe laughed. "At least I don't have to face them at work; you however will ıever hear the end of this!"

Mike chuckled and twirled Jenna then dipped her in their direction. I know and I love it." He waved to them all to join them and they all did, aughing, as Mike and Rafe ribbed them, especially Daniels who was doing his ›est to keep up with his wife Patty.

Everyone was having a great time, if they weren't dancing they were at the ›ar drinking and laughing or they were sitting at the surrounding tables doing nuch of the same. It was about midnight when the band came on and asked veryone to clear the dance floor for Ali and Rafe's last dance. The crowd faded ›ack and clapped as the couple made their way to the center of the dance floor.

Rafe took Ali in his arms as the music began and he hugged her tight, I love you, babe. This was such a great night. I'm glad we came back here to ;et married, and despite whatever bad things happened, we have such great nemories here."

"We do, don't we?" Ali smiled through teary eyes as they danced. "I'm glad ve came back here too. And I'm choosing to only remember the good things hat happened here."

Rafe smiled and wiped her tears with a knuckle. "And just think there's nore to come."

"I can't wait."

They kissed, surrounded by much applause, and embraced as their song nded.

"If I could have everyone's attention," the DJ asked, "The bride and groon have arranged for a big surprise over on the beach if you would all join then out there."

The whole room buzzed with chatter as they followed Ali and Rafe, whc were hand and hand leading everyone across the street. The resort had put th cushions out for the cabanas and had put out enough chairs, grouping them together so that the wedding guests could stay relatively close. Ali and Raf directed everyone to sit and they did, all wondering why they were there unti they heard the first boom in the night sky.

A collective "ahh!" resounded over the beach as a brilliant display o fireworks began.

* * * * *

"This is amazing!" Paige exclaimed, leaning back against Justin on one o the lounges. Jenna leaned back against Mike in the lounge right next to them

They all agreed and quieted as the sky erupted in a kaleidoscope of color.

Paige hugged Justin's arms to her body and felt the solidness of his ches behind her. Everything about him was strong and solid but when he told he he loved her tonight she'd seen such tenderness in his normally intense eye that had really touched her. She knew it had been a leap of faith for him to sa the words and she couldn't be more thankful that he had. She loved him mor than she thought possible to love anyone in such a short time.

"What do you say we sneak out of here?" he whispered.

Paige nodded and sat up, giving Jenna a knowing glance.

"Goodnight guys," Jenna whispered and smiled.

Mike gave a salute and a grin. "See you at breakfast."

Paige and Justin managed to make it off the beach without anyone stoppin them and were back in his room minutes later.

Justin opened the sliders letting in the warm night air and they could sti hear the fireworks coming from the beach. The marina and the bay beyon however were quiet. "Would you like a drink? I think there's something in th mini bar," he said.

Paige smiled. "No thanks, I've had my fill." She went over to her suitcas and unzipped it, her heart beating nervously. She heard Justin rustling in hi own bag and figured he was looking to change into more comfortable clothing When she found what she was looking for buried under her clothes she took i from her suitcase and turned around. Justin stood there staring at her, a sma box in his hand.

Paige's heart pounded as she glanced at the box he held and she offered he gift out to him. "I wanted to give you this."

Justin grinned. "I wanted to give you this." He held his gift out to her.

Paige was surprised. "Why are you giving me a present?"

He laughed. "Why are you giving me a present?"

They grinned at each other and exchanged gifts.

"You first," she said.

"Okay." Justin took the large package and set it on a nearby table to open. He could pretty much guess it was a picture by its weight and size and he hoped it was a print of The Blue Wave the picture she had given her grandmother. He would love to have that hanging in his shop. Pretty sure that's what he'd find under the wrapping, he opened the paper excitedly. When he got the wrapping off, there was a layer of bubble wrap surrounding it and he discarded that too to reveal the picture beneath. He stared at it in surprise and felt emotion consume him. He lifted the picture up with both hands to study it and cleared his throat as he felt moisture collect at the back of his eyes. Aw shit, he did not want Paige to see him with tears in his eyes, for God's sake. "When did you do this?" His voice was hoarse and he coughed trying to cover it. It wasn't The Blue Wave. It was the picture of him as a little boy sitting on his grandparents' porch steps at their big old house he used to visit as a kid. He'd shown it to her the morning after she'd shared his bed.

Paige's heart swelled watching Justin's reaction. "Before I left for Captiva a couple of weeks ago."

Justin gave her an apologetic smile remembering how he had treated her.

"I'd taken the picture from your house by accident," she explained. "I'd put it in my pocket when I went to pick up Sam, I didn't want him to chew it." Paige smiled when Justin did. "I scanned it into my computer and e-mailed it to the lab that does all my pictures." She'd had them mat it and mount it in a beautiful nickel finish frame.

Justin shook his head. Paige had left for Captiva a couple of weeks ago, with a broken heart, knowing Justin had lied to her and that he'd been a complete jerk, yet she'd taken the time to bring this old photograph back to life for him as a gift. He felt like an even bigger jerk, but he also felt an overwhelming surge of love for her. He put the picture down and took her in his arms trying to hide the fact that he was all choked up. "Thank you, Paige, this is the nicest thing anyone has ever done for me." He kissed her then and held her face in his hands, he felt her body conform to his and he groaned softly against her mouth. He wanted her more than he wanted anything, but he wanted her to open his gift before he made love to her. He pulled back reluctantly. "Your turn."

Paige was touched that he loved her present; she'd known he would and she was glad she'd followed through with printing it. Now being in his arms, her blood was pumping and she wanted him desperately, she had almost forgotten about his present to her. She looked down at the box and the fleeting thought of a ring came and went quickly, that would be crazy to expect, and way too soon, she thought. Besides, the box was bigger than a ring box. Oh God, stop thinking about a ring! she chastised herself. Just open it!

"Don't you want to open it?" Justin grinned, watching her stare at it.

Paige laughed, somewhat nervously. "Of course I do." She lifted a corner of the wrap with a manicured fingernail and set the paper free revealing a plain white box underneath, when she lifted the lid there was a layer of cotton batting on the inside. She looked at Justin and smiled curiously before peeling it back.

He held his breath waiting and watched her face carefully.

Paige lifted the cotton and saw a single key lying under it resting on another piece of cotton. She stared at it for a second before she realized what it was and then she looked up at him. "Is this a key to your house?" Her breath hitched.

"It's the key to our house if you'll move in there with me."

Paige burst into tears and jumped into his arms excitedly. "Oh my God, Justin! Really? Are you sure? You really want me to move in with you?"

Justin held her tight and swung her around the room laughing. "Yes! Of course I'm sure! I love you, I want to wake up to your beautiful face every morning and I want to make love to you every night, I want a life with you, Paige, and I thought this would be a fun way to start." He wanted to marry her but that would come in time, he didn't want to rush her and figured this would be a good first step.

"I would love to move in with you," Paige said, smiling and kissing him, her feet back on the ground. Oh that house! Her dream house!

"But just so you know. . ." Justin pulled back to look at her, ". . . it's not an arrangement I'll be happy with for long."

Paige looked away feeling a bit abraded. "Okay. . ."

Justin laughed a little at her misunderstanding. "What I mean is, Paige," he lifted her chin. "I'm not going to be happy with just living together; I'll want to marry you." He watched her eyes grow wide and fresh tears form. "I'm not going to rush you, I want to have fun living together and finishing the house with you first, and then one day I'll just surprise you and hope that you'll say yes."

Paige felt lightheaded and she dragged him over to the couch so she could sit.

"Are you okay?" Maybe he shouldn't have said that, he'd practically just proposed.

"Yeah, I'm more than okay," Paige said, incredulous. She put her arms around him. "Are you serious?"

"I've never been more serious in my life." Justin kissed her then and showed her long into the night just how serious he was.

CHAPTER FIFTY-FOUR

Jenna turned over on her stomach and tried to read her book but she kept looking up to find a strange man staring at her and it was freaking her out. She was on the famed South Beach and admittedly it was difficult not to stare and people watch, but this guy had taken his fill and was borderline creepy and inappropriate. Plus it wasn't so much that he was ogling her as he was trying to stare her down, in an intimidating way. If she didn't know any better she'd think he was trying to scare her. She thought about calling Mike at work but she knew he was busy getting ready for Miguel Soto's trial and she didn't want to bother him with such a small thing like a perv; she decided to just leave. She'd already been at the beach for a couple of hours anyway and she was pretty hungry so it worked out.

Jenna thought about the trial. She was going to have to testify soon and she was nervous. Mike had gone over everything with her and explained what it would be like but the thought of seeing that horrible man again creeped her out. She was also going to have to testify at Jay Scintillo Jr.'s trial just days after Soto's but that one she actually looked forward to.

The FBI had dozens of girls who were willing to come forward and tell the court how they'd been drugged unknowingly and put in situations where they were having sex for money. Many of the girls weren't claiming that they had been forced because some had actually gone along with it, but they knew they'd initially been taken advantage of and they wanted Jay to pay for that and make sure he could never exploit innocent women again.

Jenna headed to her car, which she was thankful to now have. It had finally arrived last week after they'd had it shipped. She and Mike had only gone up north for four days on his vacation and had managed to pack all of her things at her parents' house, visit with them and make it down to Newport and back to Boston again. She'd taken Mike to all her favorite spots and they'd stayed one night with Paige and Justin and Mike had absolutely loved Newport. Jenna had been so happy he loved it there because it was her favorite place and he promised he'd plan a few vacations there each summer. Paige and Justin told them they were always welcome to stay with them and Mike said he would definitely take them up on it; he'd fallen in love with their big old house.

They'd spent their last night back in Boston with Nan and she had thrown a nice going away dinner for them. Jenna's family, along with Paige's had come, and the newly-weds Rafe and Ali, too. Jenna was happy Mike got to meet her cousins Ryan and John and was also happy for Paige to see how well her brothers got on with Justin. They had all had a lot of laughs and had had a lot of fun talking about Nicki and Matt's upcoming wedding, which was now just weeks away and Jenna and Mike couldn't wait to return for it. Nan had invited them to stay with her again and Paige and Justin to spend the night as well since the wedding would be right in the city. Jenna was so excited for the wedding and had even been able to squeeze in a last dress fitting before her move to Miami, making Nicki happy that everything was on track.

Jenna reached her car and unlocked the driver's side door, throwing her beach bag on the passenger seat as she slid in. As she started the car she couldn't help but glance back over her shoulder. The creepy guy was nowhere in sight. Figures, she thought, she'd probably left for nothing.

It was noon when she walked into the condo. She still couldn't believe she was living there with Mike. They had come back a few days after the wedding and he'd taken her condo shopping. He had been scoping a few out before Ali and Rafe's wedding and had wanted to see what Jenna thought about them. They had all been nice, more than nice actually, but she told him she just wanted to live right there for now. It was small but Jenna liked it because it was him and it made her feel nice being there. She was comforted by the fact that it felt familiar even though she'd only been there once before, and it had a fantastic view. Mike was only a couple of blocks away from the beach. She could walk to it in fact. He had seemed disappointed at first until she explained her reasons for not wanting to move from his place. She wasn't saying she wouldn't want to up-size in the future; she just wanted some time with him there before they did that and he seemed to understand.

She opened the freezer and took out some pineapple sherbet, scooped some onto a sugar cone she'd taken from a package on the counter and took it out to the balcony to eat while she enjoyed the view. She thought about her future plans. She planned to start teaching dance again in the fall when the kid's programs started up again and she was excited that there was a studio very close by. She'd applied and auditioned the week before and had been hired the same day. By the time she started, the trials would be over and so would Nicki and Matt's wedding. Jenna had been so excited when she found out she'd got the job and was really looking forward to it.

So far she loved everything about Miami. Mike had shown her where to shop, they'd eaten in some great restaurants, they'd jogged along some prettily landscaped parks and they'd even gone out on his friend, Tommy's, boat again, only this time it was for fun and Jenna had got chance to get to know Mike's childhood friend and thank him properly. He was dating someone new and Mike and Jenna both liked her. They had a double date with them in a couple of weekends to do dinner and some salsa dancing. Mike had even taken her to some fun, safe nightclubs and her experience this time was a far cry from the last one she'd had.

Jenna turned, startled from her thoughts when she heard the lock on the front door engage and she stood up from her chair. Her heart raced a little thinking of the weird guy.

"Hey sweetness!" Mike laughed. She stood on the balcony holding an ice cream cone with her hair in a ponytail wearing a flimsy beach cover up over a barely there bikini. "I dream about walking in on you looking like this, you know."

Jenna laughed too, happy to see him, and licked her cone seductively. "You caught me."

"Get in here," he said huskily.

Jenna obliged smiling and laughed when he took a big bite of her cone. "Hey!" she yelled.

"I came home to have lunch with you, did you already eat?" He licked the cool sherbet from his lips and kissed her.

"Umm," she moaned against his kiss. "Nope, I was having dessert first. I just came in from the beach."

"Oh good, I'm glad you're feeling comfortable enough to go by yourself." He was so happy she was living with him, they'd been having nothing but fun every night when he got home from work and on the weekends. He'd shown her everything around Miami and she seemed to love it as much as him. He had been surprised and a little disappointed when she hadn't wanted to move from his condo but he'd also been touched by her reasons. He'd been afraid she would think it was too small, but she actually liked it just for that reason, she said it made her feel closer to him and who was he to try and change her mind. He could be happy anywhere as long as she was with him, he knew they'd eventually get a bigger place but he agreed there wasn't any rush.

"Do you want to go out or stay here?" he asked, stealing her cone and taking another bite while moving into the kitchen.

Jenna lifted the cover up over her head and let it fall to the floor, then worked the strings on her bikini. "Here."

Mike turned at the sound of her voice and dropped the cone on the kitchen tile. She was in his arms and in his bed in four strides.

* * * * *

"I have to go back to work," he groaned. He lay beside her, spent. They'd ad many afternoon quickies since she'd moved in with him and he never tired f it.

"But you haven't eaten," she complained.

"Oh yes I have and I told you I could survive on that alone. You filled me p."

Jenna giggled and kissed his chest where her head lay. "I'm going to feel uilty napping while you work."

"Don't, I want to picture you just like this while I'm there, don't move until get home, okay? I want you for dinner too." Mike kissed her and got up to et dressed.

Jenna smiled lazily. "No arguments here." She sat up on an elbow and vatched him button his shirt. "I'm going to miss you this weekend." It would e his first weekend at Quantico as an instructor and she was thrilled for him ut she would definitely miss him, the only time they'd spent apart since she'd noved in was when he was at work.

"You know you can come," Mike reminded her with a smile as he holstered is gun, although he would be working twelve hour days and wouldn't have nuch time with her.

"I know." She smiled. "But I want to stay, I'm still getting the lay of the and around here and there's stuff I want to do for you while you're gone." She narveled at how sexy he looked.

"Oh yeah, like what?" She'd piqued his interest. He was still a little wary of eaving her alone but he knew she'd be looked after while he was gone.

"Like shop. You have a birthday coming up, you know." Jenna grinned nischievously.

"I do?" He returned the grin. He'd already bought her gift. "Hmmm, if I o, that means you do too. Shit," he contemplated, teasing her, "I hope they ave some nice things at the PX on base." He laughed deflecting the pillow he threw at him.

"If you come home with a T-shirt that says 'I slept with an FBI agent and ll I got was this lousy T-shirt' I'll cry," she joked.

Mike laughed straddling her on the bed and tickling her, evoking a squeal. What if it says, I slept with the FBI's number one sniper and all I got was this ousy T-shirt?" he teased.

"Um, now that's hot, I'd wear that." Jenna lifted her brows and looked at he gun holstered at his side. "You know how hot I think you are, right?"

"Well, if what you just did to me was any indication then I think I know." Aike smiled and leaned down to kiss her, feeling himself become aroused all ver again. "Jesus, I gotta go." He got off her reluctantly; he'd never get enough of her.

Jenna grinned and threw back the sheet when he got up. "You sure?"

"Jenna..." He stared at her and that little tattoo just above her hip. Oh fuck it. What's a few more minutes?

CHAPTER FIFTY-FIVE

It was the last day of the weekend and Jenna had finished her shopping and was now busy baking their birthday cake. Mike would be home later that night and she hoped to have everything done before he came home. The tenth was the next day, their birthdays, and unfortunately also the day Jenna had to testify in court. There was no doubt Soto would be incarcerated and Mike expected a short time for her in the court room. Jenna just hoped Miguel Soto was going away for a long, long time. The following weekend they planned to go to the Keys to really celebrate their birthdays and to be able to finally put the whole nightmare behind them.

When she finished frosting the cake, she set it in the back of the fridge. Mike planned to take her out for a nice dinner the next night to celebrate the trial being over and of course their joint birthdays and the cake would be for when they returned home. It was presently only four o'clock in the afternoon and Mike wouldn't be home until around eleven that night, which gave her plenty of time to complete her last gift. She changed clothes and made her call. Tommy told her he'd pick her up in fifteen minutes.

When Tommy pulled up into the parking garage right on time, Jenna was already by her car waiting and she laughed, shaking her head.

"What? You don't like it?" he said coming around to help load her things.

"I like it fine, it's just funny to me that anyone else in your position would be pulling up in a Ferrari but you drive a beat up pick-up truck. I love it. It speaks volumes about you." Jenna laughed and helped him load her supplies from her car to the bed of his truck.

"I like to keep the ladies guessing, I want them to love me for me." Tommy winked and opened her door.

Jenna cracked up. "I have no doubt they do." She knew from Mike that Tommy Sands was very rich and came from a family even wealthier. Tommy was into the stock market and apparently knew what he was doing. He had several lucrative businesses as well but other than the huge speed boats and mansion on Biscayne Bay, Jenna would never have guessed he was rich. He was so down to earth and just a regular guy when engaged in conversation. He was also very generous with his time and money. Mike had told her of the several charities Tommy was involved with and how he had helped fund a new pediatric wing at the hospital. Jenna admired him and was grateful Mike had such a nice friend he could count on.

Mike had given Jenna Tommy's number before he left and told her to call him if she needed anything. She had known right away she would call when she had asked Mike what he usually did on his birthday. He had told her he always started out the day by visiting the graves of his parents and his sister; he usually brought a sandwich or something to eat and would have lunch there. Jenna's heart broke just picturing it. He said he only went on his birthday and at Christmas. They were the only days where their loss seemed to affect him the most.

Jenna just couldn't imagine how she would handle such a loss and she wanted to do something special for Mike. She'd shopped at the local garden center and hoped the small gesture she planned would make him happy. She'd then called Tommy and asked him to bring her to the cemetery today.

When they arrived Tommy led the way to the gravesite making a few trips with the heaviest of Jenna's purchases. Jenna told him where to place them and glanced at her surroundings noticing the cemetery was large and quite different from those at home in New England. Instead of rolling hills and rows of shade trees, this cemetery was flat with a vast expanse of green grass neatly mowed and growing between the headstones. The regal palms that were interspersed among the rows of graves didn't do much to block the strong sun but they looked pretty and very tropical. It looked more like the well-manicured grounds of a tropical resort, Jenna thought, minus the headstones of course.

"I'll leave you to it then, okay?" Tommy looked at Mike's girl and felt a surge of love for her, in a strictly friendly way. He was grateful Mike had finally found someone worthy of him and who obviously loved him so much. He'd been friends with Mike since they were in grade school and he had known and loved Mike's family like his own. When Mike had lost them, Tommy didn't think Mike would ever get over it, if it hadn't been for the FBI, Mike probably would have went in the opposite direction and found himself in trouble. He'd really been damaged. He'd changed after the deaths of his family and had submerged himself in the Bureau. Mike had worked his ass off, setting goals and achieving them one after the other but never getting involved with a woman for any length of time, never opening up to any of them and Tommy had always wondered if it would ever happen.

Looking at Jenna now, Tommy smiled. She was a little thing, but she was Mike's match in every other way. They were perfect together. Tommy could see the bond they'd created in such a short time and could actually see and feel the ove between them when they were together, it was immense and he couldn't e happier for Mike, he was actually envious.

"Thanks Tommy." Jenna smiled up at him from where she worked. "I got it rom here, I won't be long."

"Take your time, sweetie. I'm going to nap under this tree right here." He valked over to a nearby palm and sat, pulling his baseball hat down over his yes to shade them from the hot sun.

*****

Jenna worked and poured the fresh bags of soil into the four cement urns he'd bought. They were large and would hold all the beautiful flowers she'd icked out to plant in them. Two would flank the three graves of Mike's parents nd sister and two would sit in between them. Jenna didn't know why but it felt atural to find herself talking as she planted.

"Mike talks about you a lot. It was hard for him at first, but it seems to e getting easier." She pulled an impatiens from a flat and loosened the roots hat ran through the bottom of the rectangular block of soil, like veins. "I want ou to know how much my family loves him, how much I love him." Jenna topped and looked up at the sky; there were a couple of clouds overhead that ad temporarily blocked the penetrating rays of the sun. She continued potting he red impatiens, enjoying the brief respite. It was still quite hot in the late fternoon.

"I think your son is amazing. You must have been some pretty special eople because he is without a doubt the kindest, most generous, caring, and oving person I know. You'd be real proud of him. In fact you are proud I bet." enna looked over at Mike's sister's grave.

"Jaime, I bet we would have been good friends. Mike told me you used to lance too." Jenna got choked up thinking of what it would have been like to e friends with Mike's sister and she stayed silent a while. She'd finished two lanters and had moved onto the next two. She glanced back at Tommy but he ppeared to be napping just like he said.

"I'm sorry about what happened to you all," she went on. "I don't know why uch horrible things happen, it's simply not fair." Jenna's heart broke for Mike ll over again as she faced the reality of the grave stones in front of her, and he thought of how things could have been different for him. Tears streamed teadily down her face. "I just want you to know that I love him so much and 'm going to take care of him. I want you to know that he is loved not only by ne but by my whole family too. He's not alone anymore." Jenna sniffed and viped her running nose on the back of her garden glove.

"Someday I hope to marry him and have his babies and we're going to tell them all about you. Your memory will always be honored." Jenna wiped the extra dirt from her gloves and piled up the now empty plastic flats. The urns were full and as she stood up she swore in agitation, realizing she hadn't brought any water for them. Shit.

"Tommy?"

Tommy slowly lifted his hat off his face, quickly wiping his moist eyes before Jenna could see them. He'd heard everything she'd said. "Yeah?" he answered hoarsely.

"I forgot water."

"No problem, doll, let's go get some," Tommy gave her a smile. Anything she wanted. Mike was a lucky guy.

"Thanks." Jenna smiled gratefully. Tommy helped her carry the trash back to the truck and as they were getting into the cab, the skies suddenly opened up causing their mouths to gape and make them laugh pretty hard. "What the—?" Jenna looked out through the windshield, incredulous. The sun was still shining bright but it was suddenly pouring as if it were a cloudy, stormy day.

Tommy looked at Jenna and then up to the grave stones they'd just left. He got a chill from the top of his head right down to his toes and watched as Jenna just smiled sweetly.

"Guess that solves that problem," he said, looking to the sky dumbfounded.

Jenna was too choked with emotion to speak.

* * * * *

Mike got home late and the condo was dark save for a night light on over the stove. He put his bag down in the hallway and quietly entered the bedroom where he found Jenna sound asleep. His stomach tightened at the sight of her as it always did and he quickly used the bathroom to get ready for bed before he got in under the sheets with her. He groaned softly at finding her naked and pulled her right in up against him. He cupped a breast and kissed the top of her head and smiled when her ass wiggled against his already there erection.

"You're awake," he whispered kissing her shoulder.

"I heard you come in," she confessed but didn't turn. "How was it?"

"It was great, intense, long and tiring, but great." He laughed softly. "I loved it and the best part is I get to come home to you."

"I'm happy for you, for us." Jenna had been afraid Mike wouldn't be quite satisfied with only instructing and might have some regrets that he wasn't going off with the rest of the HRT guys on whatever mission they had been assigned to.

"In another ten minutes it's your birthday." He stroked her side and the curve of her hip then slipped his fingers between her legs to ready her.

"Yours, too." Jenna hooked her arm through his and held it to her chest.

"Are you nervous for tomorrow?" Mike asked as he played with her.

"A little, I just can't wait for it to be over." Her legs tightened and stretched against him as she came.

"I'll be right there, everything will be all right." He pressed into her a little closer. "I have big plans for us tomorrow night."

"Oh yeah?" She started to turn toward him and he stopped her.

"Stay like this," he whispered.

His warm breath in her ear sent shivers over her and she felt him guide himself inside of her from behind. A noise escaped her lips and she moved her leg to accommodate him. His hands held her breasts and she settled her head in the crook of his neck as he gently and ever so slowly pushed inside of her. Her eyes closed and she gave in to the sheer pleasure of him; his solid chest at her back and his strong arms that enveloped her, once again making her feel safe and protected and loved. She could feel his love flow right into her and she held his arms tighter and locked his bottom leg between hers. They were connected and moving together in a languid pace, just relishing in the pureness of it and the greatness of it. They were great together, made for each other, they fit just like a puzzle.

Jenna knew when he was going to come and as he stroked her softly she felt the rippling wave rush right through her as well. It came crashing right over and around Mike's own explosive release. "Happy birthday, Mike," she whispered.

"Happy birthday, Jenna."

CHAPTER FIFTY-SIX

Mike woke up the next morning to the mouth-watering smells of breakfast. He got up smiling and came out into the kitchen in his boxers and nothing else.

"Damn, boy!" Jenna said staring at him, "Happy birthday to me!" She walked over to kiss him and give his morning erection a teasing stroke.

"Hey!" He flinched and felt the jolt from her touch wake him up. "Leave me alone, you're going to wear me out. Besides it's not you, I always get a hard-on when I smell eggs and bacon." He grinned.

"Liar." Jenna laughed. "But that's okay, plenty of time tonight for me to attack you. Look what I bought you." She brought out a plate of buttery croissants and placed them on the table along with a plate of bacon and eggs for him.

"Umm, baby, you're the best." Mike sat down at the table and inhaled. "Best birthday I've had in forever."

Jenna looked at him and raised a brow. "It's just breakfast, there's more to come later."

"I don't need more," Mike said smiling, lifting his fork and taking a bite. He groaned in appreciation and swallowed the food down. "You, this, it's all I need, ever."

Jenna's heart warmed at his serious tone. "Me too."

He grinned and pulled her onto his lap. "We'll get court out of the way and go have some fun today, okay?"

She nodded. She wouldn't admit to him that she had a horrible feeling in the pit of her stomach. It was just nerves she knew and she didn't want him to think she couldn't handle it.

"My parents called to wish me luck, Nicki and Paige too and they wished us both a happy birthday."

Mike smiled and nodded appreciatively. "I must have been out cold. I didn't even hear the phone. This is delicious, by the way, thank you."

Jenna smiled and fed him a piece of bacon. "They all called my cell. My dad asked if you would call him later with an update. He wants to hear the outcome from *you*, the FBI agent." She rolled her eyes playfully and grinned. "He's very impressed by you."

Mike laughed. "Of course I'll call him." He took a sip from the coffee cup she'd had waiting at the table. "So, do you want your first present now?" He had planned to wait for dinner to give it to her, but he couldn't wait; he had an overwhelming urge to give it to her now.

Jenna's eyes lit up. "My first present? I have more than one?"

"Of course, I told you I have a whole night planned." He bounced her on his lap.

Jenna's heart thumped at that news. "Sure then." She wondered what it would be, and tried to get the ridiculous thoughts out of her head that were spinning around in there. *Way too soon!* He would never in a million years. She felt a twinge of disappointment and berated herself. "Let's have it." She grinned and hopped off his lap.

Mike lifted her off him and got up from the table then went to his bag where he took out a small wrapped package. His heart was beating frantically and he hesitated before handing it over, suddenly rethinking it. He should be dressed properly, he should have waited for dinner, but something had come over him at the table and he didn't want to wait. No, this felt right, he shouldn't second guess himself, even though it wasn't what he'd pictured, it did feel right. He put the gift in her outstretched hands.

Jenna moved to the couch checking out the weird shape of Mike's gift and smiled politely. Quit being a baby, she reprimanded herself. He loves you, he bought you a present, be grateful and open it. She sat down and opened the present slowly. Under the wrapping sat a silly plastic snow globe, the kind you'd see at any airport gift shop or she guessed, and grinned, the PX. The words *Washington D. C.* were printed on its base and a plastic White House replica sat in the middle of a pile of Styrofoam snow under the plexiglass dome. Jenna looked up at Mike knowing it was a joke and she gave him an amused grin. "They were all out of T-shirts, huh?"

Mike laughed and grinned too. "Shake it." He dropped to his knees in front of her.

Jenna smirked and shook the silly thing. She looked intently when she heard something banging against the inside and thought the White House had broken free, but what she saw instead was a glimmering diamond ring that had moved through the water with the fake snow and thunked against the plastic white house. The Styrofoam snow settled around it again hiding it as it had before.

Jenna's heart burst and she started to cry as she looked up at Mike. "How do I open it? How do I open It?" she yelled. She was shaking it again impatiently, trying to get a glimpse of it again. "Mike!" Jenna couldn't believe it! Her heart was in her throat and he was just laughing taking the snow globe from her and holding it upside down. He twisted the bottom and opened it up carefully. Jenna watched him with bated breath as he reached in and pulled the ring out. He blew on it and she caught the glimmer before he moved it to the hem of his boxers and dried it off. He was on his knees in front of her and he took her shaking hand.

"I want you to know I love you more than anything in this whole world, Jenna, you've changed my whole life and I'll always be grateful to you. All I want is to spend the rest of my life with you, loving you, and making you happy. Will you marry me?"

Jenna's throat was closed and her knees were bouncing excitedly as she nodded enthusiastically. She watched him slide the unbelievably gorgeous diamond ring over her finger and a huge sob escaped her mouth as she threw her arms around him, repeatedly sobbing "yes" into his shoulder.

Mike held her tight and just smiled feeling the moisture in his own eyes. When he pulled back to look at her she was trying to clean her sodden face. He laughed and quickly grabbed a napkin from the table for her. "I'm sorry, I was going to do this tonight but I couldn't wait. I wanted you to start your day with this on your finger."

"Yes," Jenna whispered. "Yes, yes, yes, a million times yes." She stared at the ring in awe. Not only was the center stone quite large but there were diamonds encrusted in the band on either side of it of substantial size as well.

Mike laughed. "I'm glad to hear that." He'd been pretty sure of her answer but there was a part of him that thought she might think it was way too soon. "So do you like it?"

"Mike. . ." Jenna looked at him and then at the ring, ". . . it's phenomenal. It's gorgeous. It must have cost a fortune!"

"Don't worry about any of that, Jenna. You never have to worry about that, okay?" He was well off and had been for years ever since he'd let Tommy do his investing for him. He just chose to live a simple life, but now that Jenna was in it he wanted to spoil her and give her the world.

Jenna looked at him through bashful eyes. "I secretly hoped it would be a ring, and I was feeling bad for myself thinking you would never do it this soon. I had to try hard not to pout when I saw the funny shape of the package." She laughed, a little embarrassed.

Mike laughed out loud. "Aw, I couldn't wait, Jenna. I was feeling bad for myself, too, thinking I had to wait. I wanted to ask you on the beach the night before Ali and Rafe's wedding, but I didn't have the ring yet and I wanted to do it right."

"Oh my God! You did? I would have said yes then too!" She smiled, unable o stop admiring the ring. "But I'm glad you waited, this is the best birthday 've ever had. Thank you!" She hugged him and he lifted her off the couch to .ug her back. "I can't believe this," she said as he spun her around slowly.

"Me either and I want to make love to you so badly right now but look at he time."

Jenna looked at the clock on the kitchen wall and sighed. "Think of how ood it will be tonight." She kissed him and he put her down. She'd get through ourt no problem now; nothing could ruin this day!

* * * * *

Jenna was sworn in before the judge and jury and gave her testimony vithout incident. There weren't any sudden "*Objection!"s* or *"Sustained!"s* called ut by either the lawyers or by the judge and there hadn't been any heated ross examination by the defense like she always saw on TV and had actually nagined happening. The process was quite subdued and relatively boring. She nswered the questions asked of her and when she was asked to point to and dentify Miguel Soto, she did so confidently and with a steady hand. She'd ought Mike's eyes in the back of the courtroom afterward and had felt a surge f pride when he nodded and gave her an encouraging wink.

The judge released her from the witness stand and Jenna gladly, and with a .eep, relieved breath, went back to sit with Mike until the trial was over. Miguel oto was sentenced with enough charges that would keep him in prison for fe. They included drug trafficking, abduction, and attempted murder. The jury .adn't even taken an hour to deliberate. Jenna and Mike left the courtroom nly a few hours after they had entered and once in the hallway Mike pulled .er in for a great big hug.

"You did great, babe, one down, one to go."

Jenna nodded taking another deep breath of relief. Today was the worst of : but she still had Junior's trial left.

"Would you mind waiting here while I speak with Daniels for a minute?" Mike looked to make sure she was okay. He was proud of how she'd handled .erself in the courtroom; he knew it couldn't have been easy facing Soto again.

"How about I go grab us some coffee across the street?" Jenna smiled ouching her ring.

"Perfect, I'll meet you right back here in ten." Mike kissed her and tried to ive her some money.

Jenna waved him away, "My treat, birthday boy." She grinned and stood on .er toes to kiss him and said quietly, "You're the best gift I've ever received in ny whole life."

She walked away before he could respond and Mike watched her go down the hall feeling his heart swell deep inside his chest and aching for her on every level. She had worn a modest short-sleeved dress that started at her collar bone and hung past her knees. She wanted to dress professionally and respectfully for court but Mike had groaned inwardly when she'd put the dress on. The dress had the complete opposite effect on him, she looked damn sexy in a hot librarian kind of way. She'd even tied her hair back at her neck and he had wanted to dismantle the whole outfit and throw her on his bed when she'd come out of the bathroom earlier that morning. He smiled, remembering, and turned away as she left through the doors of the courthouse. Daniels stood in the hall waiting for him.

"You look like the cat who swallowed the canary." Daniels eyed him knowingly.

Mike laughed at the old saying. "Or the cat who just got engaged."

Daniels mouth fell open. "Holy shit, Caplan!" Daniels took him into a bear hug and congratulated him. "That's great news, really great news!" He couldn't be happier.

"Thanks." Mike beamed. "Thanks for everything, Tom, I mean that." Daniels had always been someone Mike could count on for advice, for friendship and just support in general, he was the closest person to a father figure Mike had.

Daniels was actually choked up. "Hey, kid, don't sweat it, I'm just happy everything worked out with HRT and today." He nodded toward the court room. "It went well and Jenna did great."

"Yeah, she did, one down, one to go. Everything all set for Thursday?" Mike asked.

"Yes, Junior will have his day in court." Daniels paused. "But Mike there's something you should know. . ."

Mike felt his stomach drop at the tone of Daniels' voice and at the same time he heard a loud screech of tires outside the courthouse followed by an even louder collision of metal. He looked at Daniels at first perplexed, and then raced for the courthouse doors when gut instinct kicked in. Mike flung the doors wide open and saw the scene play out like a movie in his head. On the street directly below him, two cars had collided and sat mangled with air bags spilling from their windows and smoke billowing from the wreck. A large crowd had already gathered on the busy street and people were screaming for an ambulance and to call 911. Mike managed to look back at Daniels, who appeared to already be making the call.

He then ran down the courthouse steps two at a time but it felt like he was running through mud or that invisible thickness that never let him move forward in his nightmares. He finally found himself on the outskirts of the crowd and he hastily pushed and shoved his way through them. He could hear omeone's voice yelling FBI! FBI! And only when he'd broken through the ight circle of onlookers did he realize it had been his own voice yelling because is throat suddenly went dry and his stomach threatened to empty itself when e tried to yell again.

The sight of Jenna lying in a dark pool of blood, coffee cups splattered on he street around her, had him falling abruptly to his knees and all of a sudden e could hear and see everything with a sharp clarity; the sirens wailing and etting closer and the people around him asking, "Is she dead?" And "What appened?"

Mike fell to his knees and scrambled to Jenna's side, feeling for a pulse. he blood was coming from her head and he felt himself start to panic until he elt a dull pulse at the side of her neck and a sob of relief caught in his throat. Ie thankfully heard the EMTs yelling for people to clear the way and they vere on Jenna immediately carefully putting her on a flat board and lifting er onto a gurney. Mike watched it all happen, her sensible dress was torn and er hands, her precious hands, were scraped and bleeding, her hair had come ndone from her barrette and a huge bruise was already covering her right high. Mike followed her to the ambulance and dazedly showed his ID. He opped in the back and then they were speeding downtown to the emergency oom. He knew they didn't have far to go but he yelled for the EMTs to hurry nyway. Mike held Jenna's limp and bleeding hand the whole way and was nindless of the tears that fell from his face.

They arrived at the emergency entrance no less than ten minutes later and Aike followed inside quickly beside the gurney as Jenna was pushed down he hall, only he was stopped and turned away at a double set of doors where he doctors and nurses took over and told him to wait. He was helpless now nd turned to find he was all alone. What the fuck had happened? She hadn't ven been away from him for five minutes! Something nagged at the back of is mind but he couldn't focus on it. He paced back and forth and went to the ront desk to ask questions he knew wouldn't be able to be answered.

Daniels found Mike minutes later sitting in a row of plastic chairs, his houlders slumped, his head in his hands. Tom approached quietly and placed hand to Mike's shoulder. Mike looked up at him a broken man, his face tear-tained and his eyes red raw.

"Any news?" Tom asked him.

Mike shook his head. "Not one word, no one has even come out, and *she*," Aike pointed frustratingly to the nurse at the desk, "won't or can't tell me nything. She says when she hears something she'll tell me." His voice broke nd he put his head back down. The nagging thought he'd had, surfaced again nd he turned his head in his hands to look at Daniels. "What were you going to say?"

Daniels looked at him, confused momentarily.

"At the courthouse," Mike prompted.

Daniels nodded reluctantly. It was too late now but he'd been about to warn Mike at the courthouse. "Maria Scintillo. She visited Jay this morning at county and told him she was going to seek revenge on you, for their father and for her husband's death. Junior said she blames you for everything that happened."

"After her husband's suicide, Maria went back to Mexico to be with his family and had the baby almost immediately. She came back to Miami this morning, alone, to see her brother. He said she wasn't herself; that she told Junior to tell their father that she loved him and Junior got nervous thinking Maria was going to kill herself. I think he thought by informing us, he could possibly help his sister and at the same time help himself, maybe make his trial go a little smoother because he'd cooperated."

Mike had felt in his gut that it was something like that— revenge. And Jenna had been caught smack dab in the middle of it. It was all Mike's fault. He'd told her it was over and that everything was going to be okay. How would he be able to tell her family what had happened? "Where is Maria now?"

"Dead."

Mike looked up, brows raised, but not all that surprised given the condition of the vehicles at the scene.

"We know she watched Jenna go into the courthouse with you this morning," We've got a beat cop who recognized her car in the accident. Said it must have driven by him five times before the accident occurred. Maria must have been waiting for court to let out and when she saw Jenna come out alone she probably figured hurting Jenna would hurt you more. Witnesses say she barreled straight for Jenna and Jenna actually managed to jump out of the way." Daniels watched Mike carefully. "It was the oncoming car that hit Jenna. According to witnesses, the car hit Jenna below the waist, knocking her down and out of the way before it smashed into Maria's car. Apparently Jenna hit the pavement pretty good when she landed on the street."

Oh God, he remembered the blood around her head and her bruised leg. Mike felt sick picturing it and shook his head in disbelief. He couldn't even imagine what had gone through Jenna's mind at seeing that speeding car coming at her on purpose.

"Maria and the driver of the other car died instantly with the collision. Maria from head trauma, the other driver from a heart attack. He was apparently an elderly man." Daniels believed Maria had wanted to die. She had left her newborn baby in Mexico with her husband's family, Soto's family and come back here to seek her revenge.

"It's her birthday, for Christ's sake." Mike shook his head feeling devastated.

Daniels heart went out to him; it was Mike's birthday too, he knew. Funny how much Mike and Jenna had in common, he prayed to God she would be all right. "Anyone you want me to call?"

Mike looked up and laughed without any humor, dreading any phone calls. "Call Rafe, will you? I've got to call Jenna's parents."

"You got it." Daniels headed outside to make the call.

Mike stood and took a deep breath. He didn't want to call without any information, but if he didn't call and... oh God, if something happened, they'd never forgive him. He dug in Jenna's bag; one of the EMTs had picked it up off the street and taken it with them. She'd handed it to Mike before she and her partner had left the waiting room. Grateful for that, Mike took out Jenna's phone, and flipped it open, scrolling through it. He used his own phone to dial the number since her father was expecting him to call anyway. Mike didn't want the poor guy to see his daughter's number and think she'd be on the other end.

Jenna's dad answered on the third ring and Mike took a deep breath before greeting him and telling him what had happened. When he hung up minutes later he cried again. Jenna's parents were taking the next flight out and before hanging up, her father had tried to comfort him! Telling Mike not to worry, that his daughter was a tough cookie and she would hang on. The guy should hate him right now. Shit, Mike hated himself! Why hadn't he just told Jenna he'd go with her? Why hadn't he just said stay and wait for him? He ran his hands over his head and dialed Paige next. He knew Jenna's parents would tell Nicki and her grandmother. Oh God, her grandmother, what if she couldn't handle this news?

CHAPTER FIFTY-SEVEN

Paige turned the blow dryer off when she thought she heard her phone. She answered it and wondered how long it had been ringing. Justin was downstairs making them a sandwich and she knew he hadn't heard it.

"Hello?" She didn't recognize the number.

"Paige? It's Mike Caplan."

Paige leaned against the bureau. Something was wrong she could hear it in his voice. "What is it?" Her voice cracked and she saw Justin walk into the room. Tears filled her eyes as she listened to Mike's words. When she hung up Justin took her in his arms. She recounted what happened and he moved quickly to his computer looking for flights.

Paige called Justin's sister Sara to watch Sam and they were out the door and headed to the airport an hour later. Paige had never been so worried in her life.

*****

Mike sprung up out of his chair when he heard and then saw the doctor come through the double swinging doors. It was the same doc who had been on duty the first time Mike had brought Jenna in nearly two months ago. The doctor scrutinized him at first then nodded in recognition.

"I thought our patient looked familiar." The doctor gave Mike a tired smile and Mike's heart sank.

"How is she?" Three little words and his whole damn world revolved around the answer to them.

"She's stable, for now." The doctor looked at Mike grimly, "But she's heavily sedated."

Mike looked at the doctor and sank back into his seat.

"There was some trauma to the back of her head, she lost a lot of blood and she needs to be sedated until the swelling goes down. There appears to be some pressure from the swelling but it's not as bad as we originally thought. Jenna is breathing on her own and we expect she will wake up soon, however we plan to keep her sedated until all the swelling has disappeared, but not to worry, the drugs we've given her will not be harmful to the baby."

Expect her to wake up soon. She's breathing on her own. Mike's head lifted slowly. *Whoa*, what the fuck did the doc just say? *The baby?* Mike stood back up like a shot, and the blood rushed right to his head. He dropped right back down to his seat again. "The baby?" he asked in a tortured tone.

The doctor laid a hand on Mike's shoulder. "You didn't know she was pregnant?"

Mike shook his head, staring at the doc through blurry eyes. The baby?

"She's newly pregnant, I'd say about six weeks tops."

Disbelieving laughter escaped Mike's lips and abruptly turned into a sob. He put a fist to his mouth quickly.

"They're prepping her for ICU now. Her right leg suffered a serious contusion but it's not broken. It will be sore and bruised for some time but will heal just fine. I'll send someone down to get you when she's been moved." The doctor gave Mike an encouraging look. The poor guy was obviously surprised.

Mike nodded. Jenna was alive and was going to stay that way and holy shit! Jenna was pregnant! Jenna was pregnant! With his kid! Mike was ecstatic, but he was also scared shitless. She wasn't out of the woods yet, and the baby, my God, how would this affect the baby? He couldn't think about it, he had to concentrate on Jenna. She had to come out of this okay, they both did.

* * * * *

Jenna's dad found Mike in the hospital's chapel hours later.

"How you holding up, son?"

Mike lifted his head in surprise and lent a grim smile to Jenna's dad. "I'm so sorry." It came out choked.

Jenna's father slid into the pew beside Mike and put a supportive arm around his large shoulder. "This is not your fault."

Mike looked at him. How could the guy be so kind? "I should have considered Maria to be a threat." He said it more to himself than to her father who he was sure had no clue who Maria even was.

"I've spoken to Rafe and Tom Daniels, they told me what happened. You can't blame yourself, Michael, the woman was crazy. You couldn't have known she'd go after Jenna."

Jenna's dad didn't understand. Mike should have considered the possibility. He just shook his head and slumped lower in the bench. "Have you seen her?" Mike had sat in ICU for three hours until they'd kicked him out. He'd cried all over again when he saw her lying in the bed. Her head was all wrapped up in bandages and she looked so small and helpless lying under the blankets with all the tubes and monitors hooked up to her. He'd held her hand the whole time and talked to her even though the nurse said she probably couldn't hear him. He didn't care.

He did care that they had taken off her ring and other jewelry and he had asked for it back, but they wouldn't give it to him because he wasn't "next of kin." Apparently the doctor hadn't disclosed that he was the father of Jenna's baby and the nursing staff didn't give a rat's ass that he was Jenna's fiancé. He was only in fact allowed in the room because of his FBI credentials and the ongoing investigation. He'd nearly exploded at that fact but Daniels had calmed him down and reassured him that when Jenna's parents arrived they'd get the ring back. It wasn't how Mike wanted her parents to find out. Their engagement should be a happy announcement.

"We did see her." Her father bent and rested his elbows on his knees. "It's not easy seeing your baby like that, I'll tell you that much."

Mike's heart broke as he looked at the man. Jenna's father was of average height and a good-looking guy, his hair was a dark silvery grey and he had bright blue eyes. He was distinguished looking if Mike had to describe him much like Grace, his mother, Jenna's grandmother. He'd also looked healthy and tan last time Mike saw him, but tonight he looked tired and had a pale pallor Mike imagined was put there from the news and the shock of seeing Jenna.

"The doctor said she's going to be all right." Mike had been saying it over and over to himself and it felt good to say it out loud.

"Yes, he did."

They were both silent for a few minutes, no doubt saying a silent prayer of thanks. Then Jenna's father stood and gestured for Mike to come with him.

"Why don't you come back down the hall, everyone's here and they want to see you."

Mike nodded and was grateful Jenna's family had come. He stood and followed Jenna's dad out to the hall and they walked back to the waiting room near ICU. When they approached, Jenna's mom started crying immediately and so did Nicki and Paige and Mike's heart quickly fell to his feet. "What?" he asked a little too loudly in the room. "*What?*" Oh dear God. Ali was crying too, next to Rafe.

Jenna's dad put his arm around him with an encouraging squeeze and led Mike into the room. Mike noted all the familiar faces, even Paige's immediate family had flown in. But it was Jenna's mother, Jacqueline, who came right over to him and threw her arms around him, hugging him tight. "Congratulations!" she cried and Mike felt the huge knot in his stomach untie. He'd thought there had been some bad news about Jenna. Instead he looked down at Jacqueline who held Jenna's engagement ring out to him. Mike took it from her gently and looked at everyone in the room who were smiling at him through their tears. He wiped his own away. Christ, he'd only cried like this once before in his life and he hadn't enjoyed it then either. Rafe stood up to take him into a bear hug, Matt and Justin followed then Ali, Nicki and Paige were bawling in his arms one by one.

"Guys, you're killing me," he said softly.

Grace was last and she squeezed him tight. "Our girl is going to be just fine, just fine."

Mike nodded because he was too overwhelmed to speak, he was amazed at their strength and outpouring of love, their support was humbling. Each one of them offered to get him something to eat or to get him some coffee but he declined both and was just glad he had them all there. It was strange to have a family around him. He looked at Justin, talking quietly with Paige's brothers who had also offered their sentiments. Justin was new to the family, too, but he seemed to fit right in, he was used to the dynamic of a family. Mike was only just remembering what it felt like.

The doctor came out again around midnight and politely reminded everyone that the best thing for Jenna was rest and that they could all come back the following day. Mike panicked at the thought of being kicked out and took the doctor aside. He was thankfully allowed to stay and he said goodnight to everyone assuring he would call if there was any change. They were all still unaware that Jenna was pregnant and Mike wanted it kept that way. He was quite sure Jenna didn't even know she was pregnant.

When Mike woke up the following morning it was to the sound of Jenna crying and he jumped out of the chair he'd slept in all night and quickly went to her side. Her eyes were closed but tears fell from her eyes and she made a small whimpering sound. He called for the nurse right away.

"That's normal," the nurse said, checking Jenna's vital signs and chart.

Mike looked at the nurse with agitation; nothing about this was normal! He was frustrated and even more worried; he thought for sure the new day would bring better results. He washed up in the bathroom and checked his phone. Tommy had left him a voice mail the day before wishing him a happy birthday and wondering how he'd liked Jenna's gift. He told Mike he was a lucky guy and that Jenna was one in a million, he'd better hold on to her. Mike swallowed back the ever present lump in his throat and after a long look at Jenna left the room to call Tommy back.

He told him what happened and Tommy said he would be there in less than an hour. When Tommy arrived at the hospital, Jenna's whole family was back and taking turns sitting with her so Tommy offered to take Mike for a quick lunch and with everyone's urging Mike reluctantly went.

"I'm so sorry man, I had no idea," Tommy said driving away from the city.

"Where we headed, man, I don't want to be too far away." Mike looked out the closed window, Tommy had the AC going in the truck, it was hovering around ninety-eight degrees outside and humid to boot.

"Don't worry I'll have you back in an hour, I packed us a lunch, figured with yesterday you didn't get a chance to do your regular birthday thing."

Mike looked at him, Tommy knew Mike visited the cemetery every year on his birthday and he was touched that Tommy thought to bring him there now. Mike had thought about his parents and sister only about a thousand times since he'd been in the ambulance with Jenna. "Thanks, man, I was planning on taking Jenna there before court but we were running a little late." He looked beside him to his friend and smiled sadly. "I asked her to marry me yesterday morning."

Tommy looked at Mike, remembering what Jenna had said at the gravestone, and he smiled in return. "I think that's fantastic man, I really do. Congratulations!" He slapped Mike on the shoulder and pulled into the cemetery. They parked and walked the familiar path to Mike's family's plot. He slowed and let Mike walk ahead of him watching him discover and take in all that Jenna had done.

Mike approached the head stones and turned sharply to look at Tommy who was looking on with pride.

"Jenna's birthday gift to you."

Mike sank to his knees and bawled like a baby right there in front of his childhood friend. Tommy had enough respect to stay back and give Mike his space and Mike was grateful. God, he'd almost lost her, she had to wake up and be okay, she just had to; he couldn't lose everything he'd ever loved in this world especially now that he was going to be a father. Jenna was going to be the mother of his child! What would she think about that? Man, they hadn't even had a chance yet to talk about when they'd get married. He didn't want her to feel rushed about anything.

Mike wiped his eyes and took in the pretty flowers and the large stone urn that held them. He glanced back at Tommy again. "You help her with this?"

"I helped carry them up, that's it, she did the rest; it was all her idea, she just asked me to take her because she didn't know how to get here."

"Thank you." Mike ran a hand over his face, overwhelmed.

"You're welcome." Tommy unpacked their sandwiches and handed Mike a cold drink when he came over to sit under the palm with him. "You know I sat here just the other day and watched her work." He looked at Mike. "She thought I was napping."

Mike searched his friend's eyes, waiting for him to continue.

"She talked to them, Cap."

Mike took a bite of his sandwich, feeling it lodge in his already constricted hroat and he tried to quell the emotion he felt surface. He put up a hand etting Tommy know it would be too difficult to hear then stared at the eadstones. Mike didn't want to know what Jenna said to them; it would feel ke an invasion of her privacy.

"I wasn't trying to eavesdrop; she just thought I was asleep, my hat was ver my face," Tommy explained apologetically. "I'm only telling you because was the sweetest damn thing I'd ever seen or heard. She had me crying, for God's sake."

Mike laughed softly. "She can do that to you." He ached deep inside that is family wasn't alive to meet her.

"It was the damnedest thing, Mike, the sun was shining just as hot and right as it is now. We forgot to bring water for the flowers, so we got in the ruck to leave and go get some and the damn skies opened up before we could ull away, like somebody up there knew it or something."

Mike laughed at that too. He wasn't surprised and he smiled a genuine mile for the first time since the day before and bowed his head in a silent rayer. It was as if they had rained down their approval of Jenna and Mike rayed now that they were looking out for her and the baby that grew inside f her.

It was the stealth approach of swift sounding wings above that had Mike oking up to the bright sky where wondrously a great white heron circled bove the grave stones. It was his mom's favorite Florida bird and Mike bowed is head again and chuckled softly. They'd given Jenna rain and now this was sign of his own.

"Everything's going to be okay, Tommy, she's awake now. We gotta get ack."

"What do mean, she's awake?" Tommy grabbed their trash and scrambled his feet to follow Mike to the truck. "Did you get a text or something?"

Mike just laughed. "Something like that."

CHAPTER FIFTY-EIGHT

Jenna had the mother of all headaches and she could barely open her eyes but when she did she was surprised to see her parents and Nicki and Mat staring at her.

They had called the nurse in and the nurse had poked and prodded alon with the doctor and had declared Jenna officially awake. She hadn't realize people had been waiting for her to wake up and she panicked wondering jus how long she'd been asleep. Her mother did all the talking which was a blessin because Jenna found she couldn't speak herself just yet. She heard the docto say her fine motor skills might take a few minutes to kick in and apparently he tongue had yet to catch up. She just wanted to know where Mike was. She wa happy to hear she'd only been asleep since yesterday, that was good news an she did unfortunately remember getting hit by the car. What she remembere most was recognizing Jay's sister behind the wheel at the last minute before sh managed to jump out of the way of the four-thousand-pound vehicle that wa clearly on a mission to mow her down. Unfortunately or fortunately as it ma be, she had jumped into the way of an oncoming car. If Maria had hit her firs Jenna probably would have been severed in half by both vehicles but Jenna ha jumped in front of the other car and been hit and thrown back to the stree then everything had gone black. Jenna listened to them all talking and felt th tears stream down her face. She wanted to yell for Mike and she actually trie

"Ssh, sweetheart," her father crooned.

"I want Mike," she cried, but all she could hear was a scratchy sound. O my God what if she couldn't speak anymore? She heard someone say, "He here!" and Jenna tried to turn her head to see him but that brought on a who new wave of pain, nausea, and tears and then miraculously Mike was in th room. She knew it by the way everyone scattered from her bedside to give hi space. He was smiling and tears filled his eyes when he took her hand an kissed her dry lips. Jenna cried at the sight of him and she heard his name pas her lips. Had it worked? Was that her voice?

"I'm right here, baby, I'm right here." Mike held her hand and touched he cheek with the other one. "I'm sorry I wasn't here when you woke up, I wa looking at your birthday present." He smiled and felt her hand reach up an ouch his face. She wiped his tears away and he melted. Oh thank you, God, hank you, God!

"Where's my ring?" she whispered, her tongue finally having caught up vith her brain.

"Sure, she can say that!" Nicki laughed through her own tears and so did everyone else.

"Let's give them some time," their mom said, warmed by the sight of her laughter with the man she loved, and everyone filtered out leaving Jenna and Mike alone.

Mike was still laughing happily and he took the ring from his pocket and lipped it back on her finger, kissing it. "Back where it belongs."

"If anyone tries to take it off again, I'll kick their ass," Jenna told him, her oice gritty and her eyes momentarily angry.

Mike smiled believing her. "How do you feel?" He was still so worried .bout her and he thought about the baby growing inside of her too.

"Like I got hit by 2005 Ford Taurus."

He laughed. "That's about right."

"She's dead, isn't she?" Jenna's eyes turned somber.

"Yeah, the other driver who hit you is too." Mike didn't want to upset her out he knew she'd ask and want the truth. She was a tough cookie after all, like er dad said.

Jenna's heart sank and she grieved for the families that would be affected. God, that's horrible." She cried looking at him. "How are you? You know this sn't your fault, right?"

Mike smiled and bowed his head. "So everyone keeps telling me." Like her lad, she was actually trying to comfort him—amazing.

"It's not, and I won't even let you think it for a second, the whole family is razy, they just aren't normal, I mean I feel bad she's dead and now her child loesn't have any parents but my God who does something like that?"

"You're right she wasn't very stable, in fact Daniels found out there's a istory of drug abuse there." It wasn't surprising given the environment she'd rown up in.

"Not surprising then," Jenna said, voicing his thought. She went to shake er head and stopped herself in time at the first twinge of pain. "What will appen to the baby?" She felt horrible for the innocent newborn.

"He's in Mexico with extended family." She said the word baby and Mike ooked at her stomach. She still didn't know yet.

"What is it?" Jenna asked.

Man, she could read him so well already. "I'm just happy you're awake."

Mike brought her hand to his lips and kissed her palm, pausing before he spoke. "I went to the cemetery, Jenna," he looked at her. "I've gotta tell you you're the most incredible person I've ever met, thank you for what you did."

Jenna smiled sadly. "I wanted to be with you when you saw it."

"I know you did and we'll go as soon as you're better," he told her. "Tommy told me what happened. . ." Mike smiled, "about the rain."

Jenna smiled, too, and laughed a little. "I took it personally, as a sign of approval."

"Oh, Jenna." Mike bowed his head again feeling emotion sweep through him. "They would have loved you, it was a sure sign and I knew you were awake as soon as Tommy told me what happened."

"How?"

"A little bird told me," Mike laughed looking back up at her. He'd tell her about the heron some other time. "I made Tommy drive that old truck like he drives the Cat to get here."

"You didn't miss much, I couldn't talk for a few minutes and that was scary." Jenna swallowed and felt the impact of it all. "I just wanted you and couldn't say so." She felt the tears burn beneath her lids again and her head hurt. "Right now I just need you to hold me, but my head hurts so damn much I can't move."

"Aw, babe." Mike bent down to her and put his head on her chest wrapping his arms around her as best he could and feeling hers wrap tightly around him. "Don't cry, hon, it'll make the pain worse."

"It already kills, what's the difference?" Jenna sniffed.

Mike moved his hand to her stomach and kissed her there on impulse. He wondered if it would be a girl or a boy. He didn't care either way.

"Hey?" Jenna looked down at him. He was awfully quiet.

Mike sat up and took the seat beside the bed taking her hand again. "I love you, Jenna."

"I love you too." She stared at him. "Are you sure everything is all right?"

Mike nodded. "I'm just relieved, that's all." He didn't want to tell her about the baby. Well he did, but he didn't want to put her in an awkward position in case she wasn't happy about it. He decided he'd let the doctor tell her and then she could decide what she wanted to do. He didn't want to influence her feelings. Jesus, what *would* she want to do? He knew she had choices but there was only one choice for him and what if that wasn't her choice? He had to stop panicking about it; he had to go find the doctor so the doc could tell Jenna.

"Do you need anything? Are you hungry?"

"I'm starving actually," she realized. She hadn't eaten since breakfast the day before and the IV drip just wasn't cutting it. "I actually have a weird craving for a cheeseburger and fries." Strange, she thought, she never ate like that.

Mike laughed happily and wondered if it was too soon to have cravings. "I'll ask the doc if you can have that." He stood up to go and she squeezed his hand.

"Come right back?"

"Absolutely," Mike assured her. "I'll send someone else out for food and I'll be right back." Suddenly he was anxious as all hell to find the doctor; he was dying to know how Jenna would react. She was considerably younger than him; would she think it was too soon to have a baby? Her dancing career would no doubt be affected, would that weigh on her decision? Plus the fact that they weren't even married yet. Would she be afraid of what her family thought? He reached the nurse's station and was thankful to see the doctor standing there reading a chart. Mike asked for a word with him and explained why he didn't want to tell Jenna about the baby himself. The doctor seemed to understand and he left Mike to go talk to Jenna.

Mike had also got the go ahead for food so he went into the waiting room and asked Rafe and Ali to make the run since Rafe was familiar with the area. He chatted with everyone for a little while and stood nervously when the doctor came back to find him. Mike excused himself right away and went back to see Jenna.

"Jeez," Nicki laughed, "you'd think he was an expecting father."

Everyone chuckled except for Grace, who looked up from the hospital literature she'd been reading. She looked thoughtfully at the swinging double doors Mike had just passed through. The doctor had told everyone that Jenna was going to be all right but Mike did seem to have a nervous energy about him.

Mike came back in Jenna's room and his stomach was in knots, her head was turned toward the window and the doctor had removed her bandages. There was a bald patch on the back of her head just above her neck where they had had to shave and stitch her up, but the rest of her hair hung long around the pillow. She'd probably be able to cover the spot easily if she wore her hair to the side or in a low ponytail. He didn't care if they'd shaved her bald completely, she was alive and laying there in front of him.

Jenna didn't move when Mike entered the room until he came to sit at the side of her bed to face her, and with tears in her eyes she reached out a hand to him. He felt his gut tighten. Were those tears of joy? He noticed her diamond ring shone bright with the sunlight streaming in from the window and hitting it just right, casting tiny prisms on the wall behind her head.

"I have to tell you something," Jenna sniffled looking at him, shocked beyond belief.

Mike sought her eyes expectantly. He had asked the doctor not to mention that Mike knew about the baby. The poor guy probably felt like he was in the middle of a soap opera but he seemed to understand Mike's reasons. Mike nodded for her to go on.

"I don't want you to say anything until I'm done, okay?"

Her tears were killing him and his stomach churned in fear for what she would say. He nodded again.

"I love you more than anything, you know that." Jenna gave him a small smile. "And I secretly hoped and prayed you would ask me to marry you, and you did." She smiled bigger this time. "And when I thought about the future and us getting married, I had envisioned having a lot of time together, having lots of fun together and then maybe starting a family someday. . ."

Mike listened and waited anxiously as she paused.

He was listening and smiling slightly, so far so good, Jenna thought, but she dreaded the punch line. What would he think? He'd probably run from the room. To go from being engaged one day and about to be a father the next huh! He was a flight risk for sure. She took a deep breath. "Do you even like kids?" She didn't wait for an answer. "Because we've never discussed it."

"Jenna. . ." Mike tried to interrupt.

"Wait," she went on. "I just want you to know I would never trap you or anything like that, if you didn't want children and I found out I was pregnant well I wouldn't expect you to still want to get married or anything." Maybe she just wouldn't tell him yet. She could find out what he actually thought about kids before she sprung it upon him that he was about to have one of his own in just nine short months. Only he was probably wondering right now, why she was even talking about it so much, and crying while she was doing it, no less!

"I guess this whole thing just got me thinking about that kind of stuff," she lied. "You know, another near death experience will do that to you." She laughed nervously trying to break the tension. Oh God, this was just not working out like she planned.

Mike tried to hold back his joyous laughter. She was afraid to tell him, she thought he wouldn't be happy!

"Jenna, hear me out now." His tone was serious and she looked him in the eyes and listened. "If you were ever to tell me that you were pregnant, say *now*. . ." he raised a brow and the corners of his lips went up. "Two months from now, or even two years from now, my reaction would be the same," he said with a full-blown smile and then laughed. "I'd jump for joy, I'd lift you up and swing you around the room, I'd tell you how much I love you and how I couldn't wait for you to have my child, *our* child. I'd be so overwhelmed with happiness because the woman I love most on this earth was going to be the mother of my

:hild." He wiped his eyes with the pad of his thumb. "Jenna," Mike laughed, ooking in her widened eyes. "I know you're pregnant."

Jenna squeezed her eyes and she sobbed with relief.

Mike nodded. "The doctor mentioned it when he told me that you were ;edated last night, he was assuring me the drugs they'd given you wouldn't be ıarmful to the baby; he thought I knew." Mike laughed again. "I was shocked! 3ut happily so and then I just prayed you would be okay, both of you."

Jenna was crying so much she had trouble talking again. "It must have ıappened the night before the wedding."

Mike nodded and grinned happily. "I figured that out too." It had been the irst time they'd made love without a condom. "So much for the pill huh?" he oked.

Jenna grimaced, feeling bad. "I didn't have my pills. My bag was at Nan's." Ie nodded and she went on. "I didn't even think about it. It didn't even cross ny mind. When I got back to Boston, I noticed how behind I was, so I just loubled up on them for a couple of nights, I've done that before if I missed a lay or two, I guess that doesn't work, huh?" She shrugged through her tears.

"I'm glad it didn't work, I'm really glad, Jenna." Mike was being truthful vith her.

"Are you sure?" God she didn't want this to ruin anything between them ut she could already picture holding their baby in her arms. "They cry you now, and they don't sleep."

"Then we'll have a lot in common," Mike laughed. "I've been doing nothing ut crying lately and you and I haven't slept since we've known each other."

"I guess this whole accident was the other shoe dropping, huh?" Jenna had elt something wasn't right yesterday morning and had even had the feeling for he past couple of weeks, things had been so perfect and she had been afraid here would be something to ruin it.

"Yeah well, now we are on solid ground for sure, you're alive, we're together nd there's nothing else to get in our way." Mike laughed. "I sure as hell could ıave thought of a better way to find out that you were pregnant though!"

"You know me I'm all about the drama." She grinned.

Nothing but trouble!" He leaned over to kiss her sexy grinning mouth.

CHAPTER FIFTY-NINE

Jenna stood at the alter nervously awaiting her Dad and Nicki's grand entrance. The walk down the aisle had been long and her cousin Ryan, a groomsman, hadn't made it easy, making her laugh the whole way down. They started down the aisle to Vivaldi's "Concerto for Two Trumpets" and he'd leaned over and whispered, "I feel like I'm about to joust for the king and the queen, what the hell is this music?" She had put a death grip on his muscular arm indicating he be nice and keep quiet, and not to say 'hell' while they were in church, but he couldn't resist once he'd felt the first shake of laughter in her shoulders.

"Look, Great-aunt Helen is already doing the bob and nod, I give her until the time we reach the altar before she's out cold and snoring on the poor guy next to her."

Jenna was going to kill him, her cousin Ryan was so funny and she'd had to squelch the giggles and try to look serious as she'd walked, she promised him major retaliation at the reception. Mike had been watching her from where he sat in the pews and she knew by the grin he'd had on his face that he'd noticed she was trying to keep her composure, it had only made her want to laugh more.

Their baby news was still a secret; they'd decided to wait until Nicki and Matt came back from their honeymoon to share it with everyone. They had skipped their own getaway trip to the Keys for their birthdays so Jenna could spend a couple of weeks recovering at home and be well enough to attend her sister's wedding. Mike had worked shorter days and had come home to wait on her hand and foot making sure she had everything she needed.

It had upset Jenna that she wasn't able to testify at Jay's trial; she'd been excused due to her attempted murder, which was still too surreal to even think about, but she was happy at the outcome. So many women had stepped up and with their confessions and testimonies, had put Jay Scintillo Jr. away. He was going to be spending the next fifty years in Miami's Federal Detention Center, and not coincidentally, he'd be living under the same roof as his father again, and the man who'd sold his father out, Xavier D'nafrio. Miguel Soto was already making a home for himself at the FDC amongst a few of his own friends and enemies, as well. Georgie, Jay's accomplice, who had been the one to drug Jenna in the first place, had also been arrested soon after Jay was brought in and she now resided at the Miami-Dade County Corrections and Rehabilitation Department. She'd be out in three years, and hopefully, Jenna thought, actually be rehabilitated.

Scintillo's nightclubs had all been shut down as a result of the bust and all of his and Junior's assets including his new Four Winns boat were now property of the United States government. Jenna still couldn't believe she had ever thought well of Jay and she admitted to Mike how it worried her that she had completely let her guard down and been swept up in the excitement of meeting him and going to Miami. She blamed the mental place she was at when she'd arrived on Captiva. She'd been hurt by her cheating ex and had wanted to seek some sort of revenge, a few nights in Miami had seemed like the answer, but she had only been hurt again in the process.

Jenna was so grateful she had Mike to lean on; he always set her straight and reminded her that she was not that person who'd been duped. She was human and had made a mistake but she had to get over it and get back to the strong independent woman she was used to being, although not too independent, he'd joked, he liked her relying on him too, especially now that she was pregnant. And she loved that she could rely on him. He was more attentive than ever and it made her smile thinking what a good daddy he was going to be.

He was watching her now, she could feel his eyes on her and she loved it. The hairdresser from Newbury Street that Nan had hired to come to her townhouse before the wedding and fix all the women's hair had pulled Jenna's hair to the side with a rhinestone clip and it now hung in soft curls over her collarbone. Nobody was the wiser to the large chunk of hair that was missing from her head or the stitches that resided there in its place. She'd joked with Mike saying that probably by the time the baby grew some hair; she'd have hers back too.

Jenna glanced at Paige, who looked beautiful as always, the cream-colored gowns they all wore, were flattering on all the girls as were the matching colored shoes and rose flowered bouquets. The whole wedding was done in shades of white and it was just as elegant as they had all known it would be with Nan at the helm.

When the bride's music started, all eyes were on the Cathedral doors and then Nicki appeared with their Dad, Jenna teared up immediately. She saw her teary-eyed mom watching proudly and Nan, too, from the front pew. They'd have to enjoy this thoroughly. Jenna smiled and snuck a peek to Mike; she wouldn't be doing this. She and Mike had already talked about eloping and Jenna was more than happy about it. Nan wanted to throw a big wedding for each of her granddaughters but Jenna had never dreamed of a big wedding. A tiny romantic ceremony with just her and Mike was all she wanted. She did however, want a big kick ass party sometime afterward. They planned to wait until the baby was born for that though so Jenna could celebrate properly.

Her dad walked Nicki down the aisle to Bach's "Air on a G string" and Jenna grinned now thinking of how she and Nicki had laughed relentlessly when Nan had suggested it, giggling like school girls at the name of the piece Nan had left her sitting room frustrated with them both but they had caught the upturn of her lips as she'd walked away. Jenna caught Nicki's eye now as she got closer and they shared a sisterly moment before their dad kissed the bride on the cheek and handed her off to her stunningly gorgeous husband to be. Matt had these killer eyes, they were as green as grass like Mike's were as blue as the sky, with long, thick dark lashes emphasizing them to boot Jenna smiled at the two of them, they were stunning together and as the priest delivered their vows and they in turn recited them, Jenna looked over at Mike and smiled; soon they would do the same and she couldn't wait.

At the pronouncement of man and wife, two hundred guests erupted in applause and followed the couple out of the church. Stretch limos awaited the bridal party and Jenna was once again separated from Mike. They stopped in the public gardens for pictures with the photographer Nan had hired since Paige was a bridesmaid. Nan said she did not want Paige working at her cousin's wedding; she wanted the whole family relaxed and having fun.

And by the time they finally got to the reception at the Seaport Hotel cocktail hour was in full swing. More pictures were taken amidst the heavily landscaped grounds and again inside with extended family and friends. When Jenna, Paige, and Ali were finally free from their bridal party obligations, they found their men, eagerly awaiting them at the open bar.

"The three of you are giving the bride a run for her money today," Jason Ali's oldest brother, told them as he stood with the guys and smiled as the women approached.

"Thanks, Jay, that was sweet," Ali kissed her brother on the cheek and then went right into Rafe's awaiting arms. "Matt looks spectacular, doesn't he?" Sh and Jason both looked at Matt and laughed together.

"And he knows it too," Jay said, agreeing with his sister and making everyone laugh.

Mike pulled Jenna alongside him and kissed her on the lips. He'd been hanging out with Justin all night and they'd both been impatient to get their women back, but they had also done a little confiding in one another and Mike was glad to now be able to consider Justin a friend. He handed Jenna sparkling cider that appeared to be champagne for anyone wondering and sh ipped from it gratefully.

"Thank you, it's almost as good," she said for his ears only.

"Think of how much better you'll feel in the morning." He grinned. "You ook absolutely gorgeous, by the way."

"Thank you." She smiled up at him. "These shoes make me almost as tall as ou again, not quite but almost."

He winked at her. "And like the last time, they'll be your only pajamas."

She hit him playfully and kidded, "At my grandmother's?"

"We're on a whole separate floor; do you think that's by accident?" Mike ughed.

"No," Jenna laughed, too. "Probably not." She looked around the grand allroom at all the guests and spotted Nan with her parents and some old riends of theirs. "This is some party, huh? It's a shame Jake couldn't make it ut I'm so excited for him." Jenna had spoken to her friend after the 'accident' s she preferred to refer to it, and Jake had told her of the soap opera role he'd nded.

"Most impressive wedding I've ever been too," Mike agreed. "And Jake vill be on the big screen before you know it. You'll see him real soon." Mike queezed her shoulder reassuringly.

Jenna smiled up at him and straightened his tie. "Nan would do this for us oo, you know, even under the circumstances." She didn't want Mike to think hey had to elope and hide the fact that she was pregnant. Jenna knew her amily would be happy when they finally told them the news. They would never ass judgment. It might not be how they'd envisioned things playing out for er but they knew how Jenna and Mike felt about one another and that was ll that mattered.

"Is this what you would like Jenna, because whatever you want, I'm down or," Mike told her honestly.

Jenna shook her head. "I want the Chapel by the Sea, just the two of us and week alone with you somewhere hot where the windows stay open and warm reezes filter in and gauzy curtains billow into the room and there's a view of he ocean from the big comfy bed that we just stay naked in all day."

Mike chuckled and looked at her, putting a hand to her cheek. "I love you o much, you know that?"

Jenna nodded as she met his eyes. "I do." She gave him a grin after saying he words.

"Practicing huh?" He pulled her against him. "I like that."

"Yup, don't want to mess that up." She hugged him. "I'm so happy." She aid contentedly.

He hugged her back. "I'm glad, because that's all I want is for you to be happy, it makes me happy." He kissed her forehead. "What do you say we go dance, sexy mama."

"Shh!" she giggled and looked around, taking his hand happily.

* * * * *

The reception went on well past midnight and by then everyone had waved Nicki and Matt off to the bridal suite. They would leave for Hawaii the next morning for ten days. Matt's parents had been disappointed he hadn't performed with the band at the reception, they'd wanted to show him off to family and friends who had yet to hear him sing and play guitar but Matt had claimed it would be a little self-indulgent and wasn't something he'd planned to do.

It had been a great night and Nicki and Matt had thanked Nan profusely and then had quickly escaped to the bridal suite that overlooked Boston Harbor. The lights from the city looked impressive on the crisp, early fall night and Matt opened up the balcony sliders once they were inside.

"I can't believe you danced so much!" Nicki laughed. "You were good too. Have you and Rafe been practicing?" she teased.

Matt came in the room and took her in his arms, dipping her back. "It's just one of my many hidden talents."

"Really?" she asked seductively. "What else have you been hiding?"

"This." He kissed her and kept kissing her until both of them were heated and breathing hard. "How difficult is this dress going to be?" Matt ran his hands up the back of it and felt a gazillion silk-covered buttons. He looked at Nicki and groaned.

Nicki laughed. "This is the ultimate challenge for you, but I'll give you some incentive, hold on." She went over to a side table that held her small purse with her cell phone inside. She scrolled through her pictures and came to the one she wanted. "This is what I have on underneath." She grinned and showed him a picture of sexy, white see through lingerie.

Matt raised his brows and looked at her then quickly set to work on the buttons. "Two down." He worked the tiny, slippery silk covered buttons and smiled at her as she laughed. "My underwear is see-through too, you know." Matt grinned, teasing and hinting around that he wanted her to start working on his buttons.

"Is that right?" Nicki laughed. "That I'd like to see." She reached for his jacket and slipped it off, followed by his bow tie and cummerbund. She worked his tuxedo shirt buttons effortlessly and slipped the crisp material over his shoulders.

"Not fair," he breathed as her hands touched his bare chest, "I'm only o umber fifty-three with seven hundred and eighty left to go."

Nicki was laughing happily as she undid his pant button. "Then I'm glad I lon't have anywhere to be," she teased and put her lips to his chest. "Lucky for ou I'm a patient girl."

"No one knows that better than me." Matt looked at her, taking on a erious tone, his fingers still working.

Nicki looked up and smiled gently at his words. She had loved him all her fe it seemed without him knowing and now she stood before him, as his wife. Ie was her dream come true. "Great things come to those who wait."

"Ah, so these buttons are a payback, is that what you're telling me?"

Nicki laughed again and worked his zipper.

He teased her playfully but only because he was about to make mad, crazy ove to her and he didn't want her crying. It was an emotional night and he oved this woman with his heart and soul, he wanted to give her all the love she eserved. She had loved him for years without him having even known and if took him the rest of his life he would make all that time up to her. "I love ou, Nicki."

"I love you, Matt, I always have and I always will."

CHAPTER SIXTY

"Where are we going?" Paige asked as the limo got on the highway. Somehov
Justin had finagled the limo driver to take just the two of them for a ride
They had dropped off Jenna, Mike, and Jenna's parents at Nan's and Justin ha
told Nan he'd have Paige back for brunch the next day.

"We're going home," he grinned and put the partition up that separate
them from the driver. "And it's a long ride."

Paige felt her body warm. "Did you commandeer the limo just so you coul
fuck me in it?"

Justin's brows shot up from where he sat casually in the back of the lim
"Did you just say *fuck me?*"

"Uh huh, you want me to say it again?" Her tone was seductive an
challenging. She'd maybe had a few too many drinks but she was feeling jus
fine!

Justin pulled her against him. "Uh no, I got it the first time." He pulle
her head back by her hair and kissed her neck, taking charge, working his wa
down to her collar bone. "I've been waiting to do this all night." He stoppe
to unzip the back of her dress and found her breasts covered in a strapless br
which he quickly rid her of. His mouth found first one breast and then th
other and he devoured both with his lips and tongue. "Your body drives m
wild, Paige, I've wanted you all night, I knew what was under this dress and
wanted it bad."

Paige's head hung back against the seat and she soaked up his words tha
sent shivers down her spine; he could make her so hot just talking to her. She'
wanted to do the same for him and the drinks she'd consumed during the nigh
had given her an extra bit of courage to be blunt. And apparently her word
had been effective.

Justin took his suit coat off and laid it on the wide floor of the limo the
he picked Paige up at the waist and brought her down on top of it, pulling he
dress down the rest of the way and sitting back in awe to stare at her long lea
legs sheathed in sheer thigh high stockings. Oh wow! "Jesus, Paige, you are s
damn hot."

She smiled looking up at him, loving his reaction.

"These are staying on." He smoothed his hands over the silky material, letting his eyes soak her in. His hands traveled downward along her skin to the sides of her panties and he slowly hooked his thumbs under and peeled them back. The butterflies he tattooed on her stood out against her golden tan and he feathered his fingers over them remembering the not so long ago day when she'd come in for the tattoo. He'd ached to touch her like this then. He traced her ink like she did to him nearly every night at bed and felt her quiver under his touch.

"This is what I wanted to do to you Paige when I put this here." He heard her intake of breath as he placed a soft kiss to her hip and the start of her tattoo. His hands caressed her curves; they glided up over her stomach to the swell of her breasts and came back down to the sides of her waist and hips. He continued to kiss her skin and then he lowered his cheek to her stomach and just held her to him. She was his whole world now; he couldn't imagine being without her.

Paige looked down at the way Justin held her and she felt so much love for him. "Justin?"

He came back up and lay on top of her. He kissed her gently and told her how much he loved her and then their kisses took on a familiar urgency and he was shedding the rest of his suit. Music had been playing softly but Paige had found the volume and now Nickelback pounded through the speakers. They both grinned at the lyrics as she sat up and pushed him back on the seat, taking him in her mouth. She moved over him with the beat and Justin laughed and groaned at the same time, she was wild tonight, more so than usual. They had both been drinking but he knew it was more than just that. They were just explosive together period, had been since day one, and it just kept getting better. He lifted her off him and threw her back on one of the long bench seats along the side of the car. Her hands went up over her head in abandon and she arched up into him. Her golden hair fanned around her and she closed her eyes, she looked so damn sexy and Justin took her hard just like that, he gripped her ass and pushed into her, hearing her cry out and nearly growling with pleasure himself when her thigh high covered legs wrapped around him and he felt himself sink deeper inside. That was it, she had him; they both cried out as his last hard thrusts took them over the edge. He came into her fast and collapsed across her chest feeling her shallow breathing under him.

Paige's head was spinning, from the sex, from the drinking, the music, and the ride. They'd just had sex going seventy miles an hour down the highway and it had been freaking fantastic. "Wow."

Justin chuckled, lifting himself off of her and pulling her to his lap. "We need to travel like this more often."

"I agree." She put her head to his chest. "I hope to God that guy can't see through that glass," she laughed.

"Nah, we would have crashed a long time ago." He grinned.

Paige laughed picking up her dress. "That's probably true." She turned down the music and started getting dressed as he did the same. "It'll be nice to sleep in our own bed."

"Yeah, it will." Justin looked at the time on his phone and it was just about two a. m. His dad would have been long gone by now and things would hopefully be as Justin had asked them to be. He was anxious as they pulled off the exit and got closer to the house.

"Why so quiet all of a sudden?" Paige snuggled up beside him on the seat.

Justin draped his jacket over her and pulled her in close. "Just thinking."

"About. . ." she coaxed.

"About how it feels like we've known each other forever and that we've loved each other that long too."

"Sick of me already, huh?" she joked.

"The complete opposite." Justin looked down at her. "I just can't get enough, Paige; you're everything that's important to me. I just can't imagine a life without you in it."

"Oh Justin," Paige said softly. "I couldn't imagine mine without you in it either. You're everything that's important to me too. I'm so happy that you asked me to move in, and I'm really getting comfortable calling our house home. I'm looking forward to contributing." She put a finger to his lips when he tried to protest, he still wouldn't take any money from her. "I'm looking forward to the rest of the renovations and furnishing the rooms. Ali's shop is open now and I told her we might come in next week when the sitting room was done. What do you think?"

"Absolutely." He smiled and kissed her, loving her enthusiasm.

"I'm really looking forward to Christmas too," Paige went on excitedly. "I cannot wait to decorate and put a tree up in the sun room. It's going to be just as high as the ceiling with room for an angel." Paige looked at him. "Unless you like a star better, I don't care either way, but it should have white lights because I think that will look stunning from the street, all the glass and the lights reflect. . ." Paige's ramble of words fell off when they pulled up to the curb in front of the house and she actually saw the lights. She looked at Justin and didn't wait for the chauffeur, she pushed her way out of the car and stood on the sidewalk looking at their house, she was aware of Justin settling up with the driver and then waving him off. They were alone on the street now and she stood looking at the white Christmas tree lights that reflected from inside the glass windows of their sun porch.

"When did you? How did you. . . . ?" Paige turned to him and her lower lip quivered as she tried to hold back the emotion that threatened to spill from her. It was the most romantic thing she'd ever seen.

Justin smiled taking her hand. "C'mon, I'll tell you inside." He swallowed back his nerves and unlocked the door letting her in ahead of him. When they walked into the sitting room that led to the sun porch, she saw it and he heard her gasp. He came up behind her and put his arms around her waist. "This is your house, Paige, it's where you belong, where we belong, will you marry me and stay here with me in it forever?"

Paige was shocked and unable to speak but she found herself nodding as she cried taking his hand and walking slowly around the twelve foot pre-lit Christmas tree, the exact tree she'd planned to order from Frontgate next month. She walked passed it and over to yet another surprise. He had hung the picture of their house, the one she'd taken before she'd met him, the picture he'd seen in her apartment. It hung perfectly between two windows in the sun room but it wasn't just the picture or the exquisite tree that had her bawling, it was his words and his question which were now sinking in.

She turned to face him. "Yes," she whispered hoarsely. "I will marry you and stay here with you in this house forever." She shook her head. "How did you do this? When?"

Justin led her back to the entry step that ran the length of the room so she could sit and admire the tree. "I saw the catalog in the kitchen one morning and what you had circled, I wanted to surprise you and then my plan kind of took off and I went a little further with it." He laughed still a bit nervous.

Paige laughed too. "But this wasn't here this morning; who did this?" She eyed it from top to bottom, it was gorgeous and filled the center of the room; it looked completely real right down to the scent.

Justin laughed. "My dad brought the tree over. I had it delivered to my parents' house, and my dad brought it over after we left this morning. He put it together. I swore him to secrecy, my mom just thinks I'm surprising you with the tree; I wanted you to be able to tell her about the rest."

The rest, as in—he'd just proposed. Paige laughed happily and leaned into him staring at the tree, and then she saw it. Her heart stopped and she sprung to her feet. How had she missed it? She went to the tree and lifted the thick white satin ribbon off one of the middle branches, dangling from it like an ornament was an exquisite diamond engagement ring. Paige turned to Justin and saw him looking up at her from the step where he sat with a shy smile on his face.

Tears once again sprang to her eyes. "Oh Justin," she breathed. "It's beautiful." Oh my God! Paige stared at the ring. They'd never even talked about rings or shopped for jewelry yet somehow he'd picked out a ring she'd have picked out herself. It was a round diamond in an antique platinum setting with diamond baguettes surrounding it. It shone like a star and had blended right in with the tree lights.

"It looked like you." He smiled, so relieved she liked it.

Paige sat back down next to him leaning into him again. "I just can't believe this." She held the ring in her palm and he took it from her, untying the ribbon and sliding the diamond off so that it rested in his palm. He took her hand and glided it over her ring finger.

"Does it make you happy?"

"More than you'll ever know." She kissed him and he put an arm around her. "I knew this old house was calling out to me." She smiled and hugged him tight. "I knew there'd be good things waiting inside."

"Now that you're in it, it's all good. I love you, Paige."

"I love you too, Justin."

CHAPTER SIXTY-ONE

Jenna lay in Mike's arms naked. Just like she'd asked for, they'd been married at The Chapel By The Sea in a sunset ceremony with just the minister and his assistant serving as witnesses and from there they had hopped on a sea plane that Mike had chartered from Tween Waters to take them to the Keys. They had a small one-bedroom cottage that looked out at the ocean, with white gauzy curtain panels that billowed into the room every time the warm breezes blew. It was picture perfect. It was late September and the weather was beautiful. It was still quite hot and every now and again they'd get out of bed to swim in the small private plunge pool attached to the cottage. The cottage as well as the pool were surrounded by bright red hibiscus and lush white gardenias whose heady scent wafted into the room every so often making Jenna sigh contentedly each time.

Mike held Jenna against him and rested a hand on her lower belly. She showed little indication that she was pregnant, it was still so soon into the pregnancy, but Mike knew that their baby was growing healthfully inside of her. She was two and a half months along and the doctor said Jenna was healthy as could be and the baby was growing perfectly. Mike couldn't be happier or more excited and when they got back from their honeymoon they planned to look for a bigger place to live.

"This is heaven, isn't it?" Jenna asked, turning to him.

He smiled. "Whenever you are naked beside me, it's heaven, yes."

Jenna grinned. "Do you think you'll think that when my big belly keeps me from doing this?" She pressed herself tight against him, her leg coming between his and locking them together. She felt his instant arousal and laughed. "This is going to be a lot harder to accomplish soon."

"First of all I'm going to love your big belly and second of all, I've already been dreaming of creative ways to make love to you while you're pregnant, so don't worry about me." He grinned, kissing her.

"I should have known." Jenna smiled and sighed. "I can't believe I'm your wife now." She looked at her hand and admired her diamond ring and new matching wedding band.

"Believe it, woman!" Mike kissed her neck and touched her breasts, he had noticed the change in those, they were slightly fuller and her nipples had become a little darker. "Your body is amazing, Jenna, our baby is lucky to be inside there."

She laughed. "I hope he looks just like you."

"I hope *she* looks just like you." He gave her a crooked smile. "If you weren't pregnant already I'd ask to make you that way now."

Jenna beamed happily. "I'd say yes, and given that we haven't really left the bed for any length of time since we've been here I'd say our chances would have been pretty good."

"Ummm," he moaned in agreement and let his hands travel between their bodies. If he could only keep her in his bed all the time and keep her safe from the world, he'd be even happier. He couldn't imagine the worry he'd have soon as a father.

"Nan knows." Jenna looked at him and grinned.

Mike stopped what he'd been doing. "She knows we got married?"

"She knows I'm pregnant." Jenna laughed. "The morning after the wedding she caught me throwing up in the guest bathroom."

"Oh." Mike grimaced. "What did she say?" He found himself worried about what Grace would think. He definitely didn't want to disappoint her or have her be disappointed with Jenna.

"She laughed at me!" Jenna complained. "Then fed me saltines. She said congratulations and that she couldn't be happier for us. She said when two people share a love like we do, it doesn't matter the order of things, she said it's already been mapped out for us and we just have to go with the flow."

"Wow!" Mike nodded, smiling. "I like that."

"I did too," Jenna laughed. "She said our secret was safe with her. I didn't tell her about our trip though. I thought she might be disappointed she wouldn't get to throw another big wedding. At least she has Paige and Justin as her next project."

Mike laughed, "Yeah, she has a whole year to dream up another gala event right up her alley."

"I'm thinking a nice summer party for us, what do you think?"

"Sounds great, but right now I'm thinking a pool party for two."

"Hmmm, I would like to attend that party."

He scooped her up and she squealed. "Let's go then, Mrs. Caplan."

"I prefer Mrs. Special Agent," she teased. "Or Mrs. Number One Sniper for the FBI."

Mike rolled his eyes and took the short walk through the sliders and out to the small pool walking right into the water with Jenna in his arms. The water vas heated and he sank them right down and under.

Jenna laughed when she came up. "What, you don't like those titles?"

"I like Mrs. Jenna Caplan."

Her arms hung from his neck and she kissed him. "I've been thinking of baby names, too."

"Oh yeah?"

Jenna nodded seeking his eyes "I was thinking if the baby is a girl we could name her Jamie." She watched for Mike's reaction and hoped he wouldn't think it was a bad idea; she didn't want to upset him with painful memories.

Mike swallowed the sudden lump in his throat and cleared it. "That would be really nice, Jenna, are you sure that's something you'd want to do?"

"If it wouldn't be too painful for you I would love to name her that." She kissed the moisture from his eyes. She knew it wasn't just pool water she saw there.

"It wouldn't be painful, it would be great." Mike smiled, loving her more than life. "What if the baby's a boy?" He grinned and leaned her against the pool's edge.

"Thomas."

His father's name and his middle name. "You're killing me, you know," he said quietly. Jesus, he laughed to himself, she could stir up emotions in him at the drop of a hat, emotions he'd always kept under control until she'd entered his life.

Jenna smiled gently and pressed herself against him. "We are going to have a nice life together."

Mike kissed her softly. "You can count on it."

THE END

COMING SOON

THE ONLY EXCEPTION

Third in the Island Series

Fall 2013

visit
www.kristenhartmanbooks.com